Everyone's
Meera Lester's F

THE MURDER

"A beekeeper gets a
solving murder . . . Lo
and honey recipes.
—*Kirkus Reviews*

"Framed with details of beekeeping, herb growing, and
living and working on a small farm in California, this
charming cozy also includes well-drawn, engaging
characters and a promising new romance for Abby."
—*Booklist*

"Lester ticks all the boxes . . . This one is for lovers
of cozy mysteries that are heavy on the cozy."
—*Publishers Weekly*

A BEELINE TO MURDER

"A mystery featuring a lady cop turned farmer
who can't help digging up clues? What fun!"
—**Joanne Fluke**, *New York Times* bestselling author
of the Hannah Swensen Mysteries

"Lester's novel is a fun read with some eccentric and
intriguing characters who all seem equally as likely to
be capable of committing a gruesome murder."
—*RT Book Reviews*

"Farming tips and murder vie for the reader's
attention in Lester's appealing debut cozy, set in
the California wine country . . . Recipes, including
one for doggy treats, appear throughout."
—*Publishers Weekly*

"Meera Lester's engaging debut, *A Beeline to Murder*,
offers beekeeping, organic gardening, pastry baking—
and an engaging mystery. Crammed full of homey

farming advice, beekeeping tips, and recipes, this debut cozy will be popular with readers who love G.A. McKevett or Joanne Fluke."
—*Library Journal*

"Abby's a fun character—thanks for giving me the chance to meet her! Ex-cop Abby Mackenzie may have traded her badge for a garden hoe and a beekeeper's hood in Meera Lester's first Henny Penny Farmette Mystery, but danger and crime won't leave her alone. Beekeeping and garden tips, yummy recipes, and a darling dog named Sugar give this honey of a debut a special flavor that will leave readers buzzing happily."
—**Leslie Budewitz,** Agatha Award winning author of the Seattle Spice Shop Mysteries

"This fun cozy mystery brings a triple treat: a California wine country setting, a touch of romance with a handsome Frenchman and country hints and recipes from the writer's own farmette."
—**Rhys Bowen**, *New York Times* bestselling author of the Molly Murphy and Royal Spyness mysteries

"*A Beeline to Murder* is a must-read for anyone who loves animals, loves helping them, and enjoys a crime-fighting romp that blends rescue and romance with the irresistible woman-plus-pooch sleuth duo leading the way."
—**Katerina Lorenzatos Makris,** author of *The Island Secrets Mysteries*

"If you love mysteries, and dogs, and food, this one's for you. We learn about bees and how and why they swarm, and enjoy delightful farming tips and recipes. And, of course, there's a dog—the wonderful Sugar. If you're a mystery buff, don't miss this charming, cozy series. A treat!"
—**Hudson Valley News**

Also by Meera Lester

The Henny Penny Farmette Mystery Series

A Beeline to Murder

The MURDER
of a Queen Bee

Meera
Lester

KENSINGTON BOOKS
www.kensingtonbooks.com

KENSINGTON BOOKS are published by

Kensington Publishing Corp.
119 West 40th Street
New York, NY 10018

Copyright © 2016 by Meera Lester

All rights reserved. No part of this book may be reproduced in any form or by any means without the prior written consent of the Publisher, excepting brief quotes used in reviews.

If you purchased this book without a cover, you should be aware that this book is stolen property. It was reported as "unsold and destroyed" to the Publisher and neither the Author nor the Publisher has received any payment for this "stripped book."

All Kensington titles, imprints and distributed lines are available at special quantity discounts for bulk purchases for sales promotion, premiums, fund-raising, educational or institutional use.

Special book excerpts or customized printings can also be created to fit specific needs. For details, write or phone the office of the Kensington Special Sales Manager. Kensington Publishing Corp., 119 West 40th Street, New York, NY 10018. Attn. Special Sales Department. Phone: 1-800-221-2647.

Kensington and the K logo Reg. U.S. Pat. & TM Off.

ISBN-13: 978-1-61773-915-6
ISBN-10: 1-61773-915-4
First Kensington Hardcover Edition: October 2016
First Kensington Mass Market Edition: September 2017

eISBN-13: 978-1-61773-914-9
eISBN-10: 1-61773-914-6
Kensington Electronic Edition: October 2016

10 9 8 7 6 5 4 3 2 1

Printed in the United States of America

For my Scribe Tribe,
my readers,
and all the mystery writers—past and present—whose
books have inspired me.

Chapter 1

Speaking of flowers, behold the deadly
beauties that hide in plain sight.

—*Henny Penny Farmette Almanac*

Abigail Mackenzie reached across the lace cloth
covering her patio table, lifted a corner of the
bread from a bite-size tea sandwich, and grimaced.
The bread had dried out, and the lettuce clinging
to the mayonnaise had gone as limp as a rag in a
wash bucket. If the egg salad filling had gone bad,
it would be the final straw. Pretty much everything
that could go wrong on this day had.

Heaving a sigh, Abby let go of the bread and
sank back into the patio chair. She locked eyes
with Katerina Petrovsky, her former partner with
the Las Flores Police Department. When Abby left
the force to buy and renovate the old farmette,
they'd stayed best buddies, and when the situation
warranted it, they still had each other's backs.

"Don't say it, Kat."

Ignoring the peeved expression on the face of
her blond, blue-eyed friend, Abby stewed in si-

lence. It was the hottest day in April, but for Abby, it had been raining cow patties from heaven. The intimate luncheon for Fiona Mary Ryan, who had wanted to talk to Abby as soon as possible without saying why, had seemed in jeopardy when Abby discovered dead bees at the base of her hives. Worker bees were a tidy bunch; they kept the hives clean and clear of bee corpses. Large numbers of dead bees at the hive entrances had meant Abby would have to open the hives and check them. Several neighbors in rural Las Flores kept bees. It wasn't unheard of for marauding bees to take over a hive, often fighting it out at the entrance. It was something Abby hadn't personally witnessed, but that didn't mean it hadn't happened.

Flinging open the door to the garden shed to retrieve her beekeeper basket containing her suit and smoker, Abby had recoiled at the stench of a dead rodent. Forgoing the rodent problem to assuage her concern about the honeybees, she had spent the next couple of hours smoking the bees and examining the ten frames in each hive. Relieved that there hadn't been a rogue bee invasion, Abby had searched for an increase in mites or anything else that might explain the die-off. Finally, it had dawned on her that farmers within a five-mile radius might have applied insecticide on their fields or chemicals harmful to bees on their garden plants. *And folks wonder why the honeybee population has been diminishing. When food prices hit sky high, maybe then everyone will take the issue more seriously and realize how much we need our pollinators.*

After disrobing from the beekeeper's suit and pulling off her jeans and T-shirt, Abby had showered the smoke scent from her body and hair. She negotiated a quick wardrobe change into sandals and a seventies-inspired peasant dress. Although she wasn't too crazy for the dress, with its embroidered detail on the bodice, she knew Fiona would love it. She wove her reddish-gold hair into a shoulder-length braid and secured the end with an elastic band. After sliding a chocolate sheet cake into the oven, Abby was setting about making the tea sandwiches when she heard Kat calling from the farmette driveway.

Finally, it seemed that the negative energy of the day had shifted into positive territory. Grateful for an extra pair of hands, Abby tossed a pinafore apron to Kat and put her to work dressing the table with a cloth of ivory lace and matching napkins. They laid out silver serving pieces and arranged the food—egg salad tea sandwiches, bowls of freshly picked strawberries, a rich chocolate sheet cake, and an antique sugar bowl filled with crispy gingersnaps. The tea in the vermeil pot smelled fragrant with leaves of spearmint and lemon balm, lavender buds, calendula flowers, and chamomile—Fiona's favorite. All that remained was for her to show.

Abby chitchatted with Kat—first about the flapper-girl haircut Kat now sported and then about the upcoming county fair and whether or not Abby should enter her honey and jams—and the time passed quickly. But all that talking made Abby thirsty, and she soon realized she'd forgotten to set out the water pitcher and glasses. After hustling back to the kitchen, she rinsed and cut a lemon into thin slices before dropping the slices into the clear glass pitcher and adding water. Glancing at the wall clock on the way back outside with the pitcher and glasses, Abby frowned, pursed her lips, and blew a puff of air. Fiona was over an hour late.

"What do you think's keeping her?" Kat asked.

"Darn if I know." Abby set the pitcher and glasses on the table. She dropped onto a patio chair, leaned back, and surveyed the surroundings.

The backyard ambiance of her farmette created the perfect setting for a tea party. Blossoms and birdsong in the apricot and cherry trees seemed to proliferate. The tall tea roses held aloft large peppermint-striped blooms. The verdant lawn appeared as green as a hay field in spring. Cream-colored flowers dotted the blood orange, tangerine, and lime trees, their scent permeating the backyard with sweet, citrusy fragrance. Quite possibly, her garden had reached its zenith on this very day. Abby secretly smiled at the notion that despite a shaky start, the day had turned so lovely. The garden seemed as pretty as a Monet painting, and the luncheon would be something that she and Fiona and Kat would talk about for a very long time— whenever Fiona managed to show up.

While Kat rambled on about the handsome new hire at the fire station, Abby strained to hear the sound of a car approaching on Farm Hill Road. As it sped past her farmette, Abby's thoughts ticked through plausible reasons for her friend's tardiness. If there had been an accident, surely someone would have called, since Kat routinely chatted up the police dispatcher ladies, and they always seemed to know how to reach her. And if Fiona had fallen ill, she would have answered when Abby phoned the cottage and the botanical shop Fiona owned. Abby quickly abandoned the idea that Fiona had suffered an accident while out searching for herbs, since she no longer hiked much in the mountains after being assaulted by a stranger. And if she did go out alone looking for wild herbs, she always took her cell phone. She hadn't answered that, either. So one glaring possibility remained— Fiona had bailed on their luncheon.

As her concern shifted to irritation, Abby grasped the stand of the patio umbrella and gave it an aggressive twist. With the shade now covering the food and Kat's side of the table, Abby moved over next to her former partner, leaving the spot in the sun for Fiona. Good thing Fiona loved the heat. Eyeing the herb garden from a new vantage point did little to assuage Abby's frustration. And her frustration level was rising by degrees, like the heat of the day. As if mirroring her mood, the drifts of lemon balm, elderflower, skullcap, sage, oregano, motherwort, and other herbs seemed to struggle to stay upright in the partial shade under the late April sun.

Kat finally spoke. "She might be helping somebody. You know what a sucker she is for every Tom, Dick, and Harriet with a sob story."

"True," Abby conceded. "She helped me a lot when I dawdled over whether or not to plant the herb garden—you know herbs can take over a place. I do appreciate how she spent hours with me discussing the culinary and medical uses of them. And it was her idea to put in a miniature medieval garden in raised beds, laid out with a Latin cross design. She was the one who found the illustration in an old gardening book." Abby waved her hand toward a cluster of raised beds on the east side of her property. "The garden was pretty this morning. Now it looks wilted."

"Oh well." Kat crossed her legs, repositioning the napkin over her lap.

Abby heaved a sigh. *Okay. Not interested. So luncheon tea parties are about delicious food, polite manners, and convivial conversation. Move on.* Abby changed the subject. "Fiona told me she'd recommended my honey and herbs to some of the local businesses," said Abby. "Already, Ananda Bhojana, that new vegetarian eatery, and Smooth Your Groove, the smoothie shop run by those commune people, have placed orders. And Fiona is stocking my honey in her Ancient Wisdom Botanicals store on Main. I mean, she gets a lot of traffic from Cineflicks, Twice Around Markdowns, and even the Black Witch."

"You don't say. The Black Witch, the only bar in town and a biker bar, to boot. Bet they don't buy much honey. I mean, how many mixed drinks use honey as an ingredient?" Kat asked. She seemed unimpressed.

"Well, there's the Bee's Knees. It uses gin, lemon juice, and honey syrup." Abby struggled to think of others.

Kat rolled her eyes. "Seriously, Abby. Can you see a biker strutting up to the bar and ordering a Bee's Knees?"

"Point taken," said Abby.

In silence, the two sat staring up into the towering peppertree at the center back of Abby's property line. The tree's lacy green fronds and bracts of newly formed red berries hung in perfect stillness. Now and then a berry dropped into the chicken run.

"You ever grind those peppercorns?" Kat asked.

Abby nodded. "Once. Too much work. You have

to clean, toast, and roast them first." Her stomach growled, long and loud.

"Sounds like you're as hungry as I am," said Kat.

Abby pushed a springy forelock of her reddish-gold hair away from her face and cupped a hand over her light eyes to gauge the position of the sun. "Where on God's earth can Fiona be? We could get sunburned out here without hats. Maybe we should move the food inside. Darn it all! Everything was perfect an hour ago."

Kat leaned forward. "My advice, girlfriend, call or text one more time, and if she doesn't answer, we will eat without her."

"If she didn't answer the six previous calls, what makes you think she'll pick up on the seventh?" Abby snapped, even as she tapped Fiona's number on her cell again and listened for one, two . . . five rings, with no answer.

"The tea is tepid," Kat said, touching the pot next to the perfusion of orange nasturtiums in a widemouthed jar. "Dried bread, soggy sandwiches, and tea that probably should have been iced to begin with—"

"Oh, Kat, for goodness' sake, please stop grousing."

"Guess the heat and hunger are making a beast of me. I'm losing all sense of civility," said Kat.

"Well, you're not alone. My feathers couldn't be any more ruffled than if I were a hen with an egg stuck in her butt," said Abby.

Kat flicked at a small insect moving on the strap of her blue cotton sundress. The tiny creature spread its wings and flew away.

Abby blew air in exasperation. "It won't hurt you."

"How would I know?" Kat snapped. "There have been two cases of West Nile virus already reported in the county."

"Mosquitoes," scoffed Abby. "West Nile is carried by mosquitoes, not ladybugs."

"Whatever," said Kat. "I don't rehabilitate bugs, like some people." She rolled her eyes at Abby.

They sat in tense silence. Kat shooed the flies.

Abby fumed. After a couple of minutes, she reminded herself that there might be a good reason for Fiona being late. It served no good purpose for her to be locking horns with Kat.

"Sorry to be so testy, Kat," said Abby. "I'm worried and annoyed at the same time. I was in Fiona's shop yesterday and reminded her of our tea luncheon. I can't believe that in only twenty-four hours, she could forget. And . . . it's not like her to bail."

"I hear you, girlfriend." Kat used her napkin to wick away the moisture collecting on either side of her nose. "Okay, so here's an earthshaking idea—maybe she's in a funk. You did say she had hit the big four-o, right?"

"Yeah, but that was a week ago, and, anyhow, the forties are the best years of a woman's life."

"According to?"

Abby gave her a quizzical look. "Lidia."

"Vittorio?" Kat asked incredulously. "The old lady on Main, with the jewelry store?"

"The same."

"Yeah, well, Lidia should know. From the looks of her, she's hit the big four-o twice already. Maybe three times."

"Oh, please. Even if she is retirement age, she's still working. And Main Street hasn't exactly attracted a Ralph Lauren Home store, an upscale art gallery, or an artisan chocolate shop. Lidia and her handcrafted jewelry shop are our town's best hope for a bit of class now that the patisserie is gone."

"Suppose you're right about that."

Abby decided to wait five more minutes. Then she and Kat would devour the food and enjoy the rest of the day. Maybe they'd go antiquing. It would be Fiona's loss, and she'd have some explaining to do when they next saw each other.

"Fiona's store is nice in a hippie, Zen kind of way," said Kat. "But it bothers me that it occupies the same space as where the pastry shop used to be. I can't go in there without thinking about Chef Jean-Louis. Her herb-inspired, nutrient-dense, gluten-free, low-salt, low-taste bars made of who knows what can't compare to our late chef's exquisite madeleines." Kat reached for a tea sandwich. She parted the bread and tossed the lettuce onto her plate before taking a bite. Chewing, she said, "I think Fiona's a hippie, living in the wrong era."

Abby stared incredulously at her friend for throwing aside the lettuce. "Seriously, Kat?"

"What?" Kat asked. "Your chickens will eat this, won't they? Even if there's mayo on it?"

Abby shook her head. "Whatever." She reached for the pot and poured herself a cupful of tea. "Fiona sells good stuff. Almost everything is eco-friendly. And she isn't a hippie."

"Well, she dresses like one."

"In fairness, she wears those bohemian circular skirts, because that's the way the other women in the commune dress. You must have seen them. Some work here in town."

"Yeah, I know. I've been up to their compound, if you can call it that. We've had a lot of complaints. The families in those mountains do not like the drumming, chanting, and clapping. They complain of harmoniums droning on endlessly. And they don't like the weekly bonfires. They're afraid that one of these days a spark will ignite the mountain. It's a tinderbox up there, Abby. You know that."

"Maybe in summer . . . not right now," Abby said. "I was just up there last week with Fiona, checking on the progress of the commune gardens. From bio-intensive double digging to planting heirloom seeds, she's taught those devotees everything she knows. The gardens are lush and green and thriving. But don't take my word for it. You should go see them. The gate to their property is always open."

Kat stopped chewing long enough to say, "Nah." She wrapped a blond lock of hair behind her ear and pushed back her bangs, as if preparing to lean forward and do some serious damage to the pile of sandwiches. "And you couldn't pay me to live there. As far as I can tell, the place looks like a dumping ground of old buses, RVs, and shacks."

Abby corrected her. "The guru has a nice house."

"Well, he would, wouldn't he?" Kat said.

Abby shrugged. "The gardens produce an abundance of organic vegetables. The commune residents have opened their facility to people who want to view and purchase the produce. They're also selling it along the roadside up there. Fiona told me the gardens are what she loves most about the place."

"If she loves them so much, why isn't she still living there?" Kat poured herself some tea and stirred in some milk.

"She moved into the cottage on Dr. Danbury's estate because she can't stand that guy in charge at the commune." Abby finished drinking her tea. She placed a silver tea strainer over her porcelain teacup, reached for the pot, and poured its luke-warm tea through the strainer into her cup.

"You mean Hayden Marks?" asked Kat.

"He's the one." Stirring a spoonful of rose-infused sugar into her tea, Abby said, "Got himself appointed the successor when the old guru left for India. But according to Fiona, Marks modified his predecessor's teaching to make it more under-standable to Westerners, and then he changed how the commune worked, establishing a hierarchy of power, with himself as the supreme authority."

"Yeah, well, we know Mr. Marks," said Kat. "He's the charismatic son of an ex-con, who supposedly found solace in the Good Book and became a preacher."

"Really?" Abby arched a brow. "Fiona never said anything about that. Maybe she didn't know. But she sure couldn't abide that Marks insisted all the devotees call him Baba. It means 'wise old man' or 'father' or something like that. She found him to be the antithesis of a father figure, more like a dic-tator. For refusing to show proper reverence, she was asked to leave. Imagine that . . . for not calling him Baba."

"Baba-shmaba. A pig doesn't change its trot-ters." Kat's hand formed the shape of an *L*, for *loser*. She pushed back from the table and wiped her mouth with the napkin. "We've been watching that commune bunch for a while."

Abby swallowed another sip of tea and looked at Kat over her teacup. "I'm all ears."

"You hear the talk. Let me put it this way. Why would a peaceful sect of New Agers need fire-arms?" asked Kat.

"I don't know, but it's not illegal if they have permits."

"Yeah, well, according to the gossip along Main Street, they're stockpiling up there, and not only firearms. Do you want to know what Willard down at the hardware store says?"

"What?" Abby slid her cup back into its saucer and set both on the table.

"They've emptied his place of axes, freeze-dried food, and bottled water. He says he can't keep canning supplies or even basic tools like shovels in stock."

"Why?"

Kat devoured two sandwiches in quick succession and then wiped her fingers with the napkin. "Who knows? But you can't blame the locals for getting paranoid." She reached for the antique silver serving knife, slashed off a slice of the sheet cake, and dropped the slice onto a dessert plate, licking the excess buttercream frosting from her fingers.

Abby raised a brow. "You're like the sister I never had, Kat, so I hope you don't take this the wrong way. You're eating like a cop who doesn't care anymore whether or not she can make it over the training wall."

"Yeah, well, I missed breakfast, and I'm starving."

Abby brushed a crumb that had fallen from the silver serving knife. "I can see that. So eat, already.

Getting back to the subject of the commune, I'm not taking sides, but we do live in the land of earthquakes, mudslides, and seasonal wildfires. Maybe Baba thinks a natural disaster is in the offing."

"Or the end is near, and they want to be ready, like that Heaven's Gate cult, who waited on a spacecraft following the Hale-Bopp comet," Kat said. "We can only hope the shovels aren't for burying the dead."

"Now, that's just too far-fetched," Abby chided.

Kat smiled and began nibbling the cake. She licked her lips. Holding the empty fork aloft, she looked at Abby. "Lord, have mercy, girlfriend! You nailed the cake." She took a bigger bite and writhed in pleasure. Swallowing, she reached for her cup of tea to wash it down and then did a little shoulder dance. "Um, um, um!"

"Glad it meets with your approval." Abby grinned. "I added last summer's raspberry jam to the buttercream."

Kat used the silver serving knife to coax a chunk of buttercream from the chocolate cake. After dropping the buttercream onto her plate, she scooped it into her mouth with her fork and licked her lips. "Don't know about it being an end-time cult, but it's a cult. Of that, I'm sure. But like I said, my peeps are watching. When Baba's gang breaks the law, we'll make the arrests."

Laying aside the fork, Kat poured herself a glass of water. "For the life of me, I can't imagine why anyone would join a commune or a cult. You have to give up your personal ambitions in life, sell your possessions, and donate all your money to the group. Fiona doesn't seem the type, although I can't say I know her that well." She pushed down the lemon slice and sipped some water from the glass.

Reaching again for the teapot to refill both empty cups, Abby felt as though Kat didn't understand Fiona's quirkiness. "She's just searching for deeper meaning, and perhaps joining that commune and dressing in that folk-boho style are an extension of that."

"Someone should buy her a watch and suggest she check the time once in a while," Kat said. "I'm not saying it to be mean-spirited, but it's thoughtless of her not to call and let you know she's been delayed."

Abby popped a piece of a sandwich into her mouth and nearly choked when the sound of gunfire rang out. After swallowing, she exclaimed, "Darn it, Kat! That ringtone is just plain annoying."

"Tells me it's Otto calling," Kat said, then licked her fingers and fished her cell from her pocket. After sliding a dry knuckle across the screen, Kat answered, "Hello, big daddy. What's up?"

Abby knew Sergeant Otto Nowicki wouldn't be calling Kat on her day off without good reason.

"Don't tell me. He's calling you in?" Abby whispered.

Kat nodded. "He's up at Kilbride Lake."

"What's going on?" Abby asked softly.

Kat shook her head and listened intently. She then whispered, "Canal patrol found a body in a burning car."

Abby stiffened. "A body?"

Kat listened, locked eyes with Abby. Her expression darkened. "It's Fiona's car."

Abby's stomach tightened. Her heart pounded. *Oh, good Lord.*

"So, it *is* a woman's body. Okay. See you in a few," Kat said. After thrusting the phone into her pocket, she grabbed a couple of sandwiches in a napkin and slipped them into her other pocket. "Could be a long night. I'm hoping it's not Fiona."

"Who else could it be?" Abby said, pushing away from the table. "I'm coming, too."

Tips for Making Rose-Scented Sugar

Rose-scented sugar is easy to make. All you need is a screw-top mason jar, granulated sugar, and scented roses that are fresh, fragrant, and pesticide-free.

1. Gather one to two cups of heavily scented rose petals that are free of blemishes and tiny insects.

2. Wash the petals, pat them dry with paper towels, and snip off the white part (which can have a bitter taste).

3. Alternate layers of sugar and rose petals in the jar until it is filled, leaving half an inch of space at the top.

4. Screw on the lid and set the jar in a cool, dark place for at least two weeks.

5. Sift out the petals before using the sugar.

Chapter 2

To repel moths in the garden, plant
rosemary and lavender; to keep them
out of your closet, hang the herbs in
sachets.

—*Henny Penny Farmette Almanac*

Guiding her Jeep out of Las Flores and along
the blacktop roads that twisted through the
foothills, Abby managed to keep Kat's vintage silver roadster in sight all the way to the summit.
However, after the cutoff, which was only about
eight minutes from downtown Las Flores, Abby
lost sight of her former partner. After the cutoff,
Abby negotiated the steep switchbacks of the narrow two-lane road until it dipped into a heavily
forested area of pine, oaks, and redwood trees.
Through the open Jeep windows, the mountain
air smelled of sun-drenched earth and dried plant
matter. Soon she turned off onto a link road leading to Kilbride Lake. The mountain lake supplied
drinking water through a series of canals and
reservoirs to Las Flores residents, as well as to the

mountain people who lived on the western side of town.

Pulling off the road behind police cruisers and a fire truck, Abby guided the Jeep beneath a towering sequoia with a trunk nearly as wide as the fire truck Kat had parked behind. Abby jumped from the Jeep and slammed the door. The stench of burnt plastic, rubber, and human flesh turned her back. She opened the door and searched the vehicle for something to use as a mask. Behind the driver's seat, she found a package of work gloves. After ripping open the plastic bag, she removed a pair, then held them against her nose and mouth as she strode toward the coterie of first responders.

Firefighters from Cal Fire had already extinguished the blaze and were mopping up. Las Flores police chief Bob Allen and Sergeant Otto Nowicki assessed the scene. Kat, in her sundress, looked totally out of place as she stood next to a uniformed officer. Sheriff's deputies, a canal patrol agent, and the local forest ranger huddled together a few feet away, chatting, apparently awaiting the arrival of the coroner.

Abby's heart pounded as she spotted Fiona's car. She took in as many details of the scene as possible as she made her way over. A booming voice called out her name.

"What the devil are you doing here, Mackenzie?"

"Hello, Chief," Abby said. She lowered the gloves from her nose and stared at him. "I wanted to see for myself why my guest of honor didn't show up for our garden party today."

The police chief fixed one of his famous steely-eyed stares on her. "You know the vic?"

"I know Fiona Mary Ryan. Until I get a look at who is in that car, I won't be able to tell you if the woman is Fiona or not." Abby scrutinized the car. It had not been wrecked. There were no signs of any exterior damage beyond what the fire had done. So, there had been no roadway accident.

"Petrovsky says it's her," the chief said. "But another ID couldn't hurt, since we found no purse or documents in the glove compartment. Get over here, Mackenzie."

Abby walked toward Otto, who was ogling Kat in her short sundress. Abby picked her way through the grass and weeds until Chief Bob Allen's voice boomed again.

"Watch out there!"

Abby halted. *You always could bark like a rabid dog, Chief,* she thought.

"Back up and go around," the chief snapped, as if addressing a rookie. "Can't you see the tire impression?"

Abby had indeed noticed the partial tire print and had sidestepped it by more than a foot.

"Get the crime-scene tape over there." Chief Bob Allen bellowed the order at the uniformed officer behind him.

Abby wanted to bark back, "Should have been taped long before now."

"If you'll recall from your academy training, Mackenzie," Chief Bob Allen continued, "that tire track could be a clue. It might belong to the killer's vehicle."

Whatever. Don't talk down to me. Abby knew only too well Chief Bob Allen's passive-aggressive personality after working for him for seven years. She took his barked comments in stride, because she felt pretty certain that the police chief had a deep-seated inferiority complex and felt his confidence elevated only when he was demeaning someone else. Abby returned the gloves to her nose. The stench of Fiona's body and the burnt car was over-powering. She peered inside the driver's side door.

Fiona's pale complexion was black and red in areas, but the bone structure was still intact. Her shoulder-length dark hair clung to her scalp in clumps, like tufts of wild weeds dotting an arid field. Abby looked at Fiona's neck. She took a sharp breath and peered more closely. Where was the necklace with the Celtic cross that Fiona always wore, believing as she did that it held a link be-tween her and her pre-Irish ancestors, the Celts?

Abby fought back a wave of nausea. Oh, Fiona, what happened to you?

Fiona's attire suggested to Abby that she'd dressed especially nice for the luncheon—a gauzy white blouse, a chiffon gypsy skirt, lace leggings, and flats. The smoke and the agony of seeing her friend's body in such a senseless and sickening state caused her eyes to sting. But this was neither the time nor the place for an emotional display. Abby muffled a sob and wiped the gloves across her cheeks to erase any evidence of tears. Her throat tightened. *Do not cry. Not here. Not now.* She gulped hard and fought for composure. She would have only these moments to study the car and her friend's body. She sniffed hard, as if doing so might help her dis-associate from her emotion and instead focus on the car interior.

The fire had claimed the front end and most of

the dash. The driver's and the front passenger's windows were down, and the doors unlocked. The backseat was devoid of baskets and books, which seemed to accompany Fiona wherever she went. There were no signs of a struggle, no purse, no pills, or flammable liquids that might have started a fire. Nothing. *Weird.* Fiona seemed to have been sitting peacefully behind the steering wheel, waiting to burn up. Why hadn't she tried to escape?

Stepping back, Abby turned to face Chief Bob Allen. After sighing heavily and clearing her throat, Abby said. "It's her, Fiona Mary Ryan."

"What was your relationship with her?" Chief Bob Allen asked pointedly. He scrutinized Abby's face like he would that of a perp who might be hiding something. If he felt any sympathy for Abby's loss of her friend, he didn't show it.

"We shared a love of gardening." Abby swallowed hard against the lump that had formed in her throat. *Hold it together. Stand strong, straight-faced.* "Fiona owns the botanical shop on Main—Ancient Wisdom Botanicals. She was supposed to join us for lunch today but was a no-show." Abby swallowed hard. "Now we know why."

"What time was that lunch to be held?"

"Noon."

"Does she have family in Las Flores?" Chief Bob Allen asked.

"I don't think so. She lost her parents several years ago in a car crash. She has a brother. I've heard a lot about him, but I've never met him. Does a lot of international travel, I gather. When he's on the West Coast, he stays with her." Abby sniffed again and then waved the smoke away with her gloves.

"What about a husband, children?"

"Children, no. Husband, yes. She's married to Tom Davidson Dodge. Separated now. She goes by the name of Ryan. Divorce isn't final. He lives down the road, in that mountain commune, when he isn't staying with her, which he occasionally does. Or did. Their relationship was a little strange, but you had to know Fiona. There's a boyfriend, too, recently estranged. Laurent Duplessis."

"Duplessis. Unusual name," remarked the chief. He looked over at Otto, who was jotting down Abby's comments in a notebook, as if wanting to make sure Otto had duly noted that name.

"He's Haitian, I believe. I only met him once," said Abby. "Seems all right."

"Any idea where we can find this boyfriend?"

"Last I heard, he had rented a room over Twice Around Markdowns."

"All right, Mackenzie. Good information. Stick around. We're going to need your statement."

"Yeah, I know the drill, but thanks for reminding me."

"Coroner's van is here," said the chief, looking over the latest vehicle to arrive.

Millie Jamison stepped from the van, setting one black flat on the ground and then the other. A black dress with red piping showed her curves as she quickly slipped on a disposable gown, pulled booties over her shoes, and threaded her fingers into latex gloves.

"Oh, my, my," said Otto. "You'd never know she had a baby a few months ago. She's looking pretty hot."

Abby and Kat shared an eye roll.

"Really, Otto. Get over your bad self," said Kat.

Abby watched Millie make her way over to the body. "Glad she's here. She's good, no question. But when is the county going to hire a permanent chief medical examiner? Didn't the grand jury's report make that recommendation? Bringing a chief medical examiner on board makes more sense than having the two assistant medical examiners working cases with the coroner, don't you think?"

Kat shrugged. "It's all about funding. There isn't any. The system's working, so I guess the consensus is, if it isn't broken, don't try to fix it."

Otto strutted to the crime-scene tape and, lifting it, said, "We believe our vic is Fiona Mary Ryan."

"Noted. Thanks," said Millie, darting under the tape. She was clearly all business.

The local TV station van pulled in behind the coroner's vehicle, diverting Abby's attention from Millie to the crew. In a heartbeat, they were setting up for a live shot from the scene.

Abby shook her head and said to no one in particular, "Boy, they got here fast." She knew the news reporters listened to the same scanners as the emergency responders, fire, and police. Fat chance of keeping the lid on the murder investigation, if that was what the chief wanted—and that was what he always wanted on any investigation. He hated bad publicity for the town and always tried to put a positive spin on negative news. But it was difficult to spin a murder, especially when the victim was a local businesswoman.

Abby watched Chief Bob Allen straighten his jacket, walk over to meet the news crew, and point them to a spot farther away from the body in the car. He probably offered to step in front of the camera, with the proviso that they wait for a shot of the car until the body was in the coroner's van.

"Well, here we are again, just like the old days," Otto said. "You still shucking corn and shelling peas, Abby?"

Abby smiled and nodded. She liked Otto. His wife, the West Coast regional director of an ambulance company, was gone a lot. Back in the day, when she was still on the force, Otto often offered to buy Abby and Kat dinner or drinks at the Black Witch, just to have a little company. But Otto could be annoyingly blunt.

"If you're asking if I'm still farming, the answer is yes," replied Abby. "Corn in the fall, peas in the spring." She smiled sweetly at Otto, then added, "Listen, guys, I've got a few of Fiona's things at my place."

"Oh, yeah?" replied Otto. "Like what?"

"Nothing special. A trowel, a scarf, and an armful of old books. She tended to write notes on scraps of paper and stuff them inside books. I doubt you'll find anything in them relevant to her death, but just the same . . ." Abby swallowed and took a deep breath. "I'll hand them over so you can give them to her next of kin."

Otto nodded. Kat stared expectantly at the coroner, who was approaching them.

It was the first time Abby had seen Millie in over a year, and Millie's countenance reflected a new mother's glow.

Stepping carefully, she ducked under the crime-scene tape to approach Abby, Kat, and Otto. Peeling off her gloves, Millie said, "Been a while since I've seen the three of you on scene together."

"Yeah, well, it looks like we pulled you away from something pretty special," said Otto.

"You look stunning," Abby chimed in.

"Hope it wasn't the christening," added Kat.

Millie smiled. "No. My hubby and I were at the symphony, on a rare date. I got the call in the middle of the 'Méditation' from *Thaïs*." Met with a blank stare from Otto and Kat, Millie looked at Abby. "You know that piece, don't you, Abby?"

"One of my favorites," Abby replied.

"Still pick up your violin once in a while?" Millie asked.

"Not really." Abby tried to sound indifferent, as if it didn't matter anymore. Millie sounded sympathetic, as if she knew that the thumb injury that had sidelined Abby's law enforcement career had also deprived her of one of her personal, secret pleasures, playing the violin. Her gun hand was also her bowing hand. It required a stable thumb. And hers wasn't. Safely locked in its case, the violin that Abby couldn't play but couldn't part with gathered dust on the top shelf of her closet.

Glancing at her watch, Millie asked, "So which one of you is in charge?"

Otto replied, "Technically, that would be me, although Chief Bob Allen is over there, doing the live interview, and you might want to talk with him, as well." Otto ran a hand over his crew cut and hitched his duty belt a little higher, as if doing so somehow elevated his stature.

"So, my best guess is the death occurred sometime between seven o'clock this morning and noon," Millie said.

"Ah, jeez, Doc. Could you be a little more specific?" asked Otto.

"Hard to say exactly. You know how this works. We might be able to get a little closer after the autopsy."

Otto nodded. "Cause and manner?"

"That, too, is hard to pinpoint in the absence of obvious signs of trauma, wounds, ligature, punctures, and cuts. We got severe thermal burns. Carbon monoxide poisoning is the most frequent cause of death in burn victims. But there's no cherry-pink and apple blossom–white skin mottling. That tells me she wasn't breathing during the fire. As I said, the autopsy will tell us more."

Millie's driver approached with a collapsible transport gurney, a body bag, and a form, which he handed to Millie. Otto presented a pen to Millie, and she filled out the form.

"So, here's the release number. I've put my contact info on there, as well," Millie said, handing back the paperwork.

Abby's thoughts raced. She had a zillion questions she wanted to ask, but this wasn't her investigation, and this wasn't the right time. Otto scanned the form and then looked over at the burned car. Kat's expression mirrored the solemnity of the moment. Abby felt her stomach tighten, knowing how they all had to compartmentalize emotions when dealing with cases like this one. Millie seemed to do it best. She respected the bodies and had deep empathy and compassion for their families. In that way, too, Millie and Abby shared a similarity.

Millie turned to leave, and Kat called out, "Before you go, Dr. Jamison, can you tell us with any certainty that Fiona did not just sit there and died of smoke inhalation? That's kind of hard to think that might have happened."

"Indeed," said Millie. "I'd think if she were still alive, she would have tried to escape, unless she was incapacitated, of course. But to answer your question, if she was in the car, breathing in smoke, we will undoubtedly see evidence of soot in her lungs during the autopsy." Millie flashed a sympathetic smile. "We'll get to the bottom of this. Unfortunately, we'll just have to wait and see what secrets her body gives up."

After Millie left, with Fiona's body bagged and tagged in the back of the coroner's van, Abby spotted Chief Bob Allen walking toward her, Otto, and Kat. Abby groaned. "Okay, guys. This is where I say, 'See you later.' " She knew that Kat and Otto would understand the strained relationship between their boss and her. The tension between them was old history.

"Understood. Go," Kat urged.

Otto nodded.

Abby gave them both quick hugs before hurrying back to her car. Otto and Kat were smart, diligent cops. Abby knew they would draw up a time line for the last twenty-four hours of Fiona's life. They would make a list of the people with whom she'd had contact and would make note of the reasons Fiona had associated with them. A person of interest would soon emerge. Abby knew that killers always had a relationship with their victims—however fleeting.

Passing through town, Abby stopped by the doggy spa to pick up Sugar.

"Zowie! Somebody looks better for an overnight stay at the Diggity Do," she said, hugging Sugar, who seemed just as eager to see her. After taking the leash from the worker at the spa for pets, Abby walked an excited Sugar to the Jeep. She patted the car seat, and Sugar hopped in. Her tail wagged almost as hard as she panted.

Fifteen minutes later, back on the farmette, Abby poured herself a cup of cold tea from the pot she and Kat had abandoned. She strolled with Sugar from the patio to the backyard and sank onto the seat of the free-standing porch swing that she'd placed between two apricot trees. The cloying, sweet fragrance of citrus blooms permeated the air. A family of twenty crows that had taken up residence in the tall eucalyptus tree on the vacant wooded acre behind her property cawed in a raucous chorus. Abby rocked on the swing, hoping to push out the images stuck in her mind, images that sickened her as she thought about how Fiona might have died at the hands of her killer. What had been troubling Fiona? Why had she wanted advice from someone who had worked in law enforcement? Abby knew she might never get the answers to those questions, but she was sure going to try.

Dusk descended like a diaphanous veil over the farmette. Its hues of silvery violet and pale lavender reframed the landscape. A barn owl winged its way overhead, then disappeared into the dark canopy of trees. Abby struggled to fight back tears, which finally overtook her, hot and salty, spilling down her cheeks, wetting the fabric of the retro-hippie-chic peasant dress that Fiona would never see.

Abby rocked until the moon rose. Until her stomach was no longer knotted. Until her heart hammered no more. Her thoughts turned to the usual suspects: husband, boyfriend, known associates, and people harboring grudges.

Ancient Wisdom Botanicals had opened less than a year ago—a year after Fiona and her husband, Tom Davidson Dodge, had separated. He lived most of the time at the commune, in an old VW bus that bore the rainbow colors and peace symbols of a bygone era and rested on railroad ties and concrete blocks. Tom had gotten a good deal on the van from a mountain mechanic who'd kept it over a dispute about payment for repairs the mechanic had done. But why, after separating, had Fiona and Tom occasionally still shared a bed at her cottage on Dr. Danbury's property? People in town knew that Fiona had wanted a child with Tom before her biological clock made it impossible. They also knew that even when she'd dated others during their separation, Tom remained her one true love.

Fiona's most recent boyfriend, Laurent Duplessis, could drum, sing, and attract more girlfriends than a Haitian masked booby could find fish in the sea. But his relationship with Fiona hadn't endured. She had liked that he seemed to know more about herbs than most people in town, particularly how to use them in Haitian food. His voodoo religion was, according to Fiona, mind-blowing, and they'd shared an interest in learning about various spiritual paths and practices. She had allowed herself to be comforted by him as her relationship with the commune people became increasingly strained. She'd let him work in her store for a while. But in a reversal of roles, she'd ended up as the caretaker of Laurent, who became increasingly irresponsible. When their relationship grew toxic, she had moved on. He hadn't. Abby recalled that Fiona had confided in her that she believed Laurent had been following her around. He had seemed to be stalking her. Just three days before the luncheon, she'd asked Abby for a meeting. Now Abby wondered if the purpose of the meeting was to find out about how to get a restraining order. Or was it something else?

She owed Fiona a debt of gratitude for all the help with the farmette herb garden. Abby vowed to repay the debt by finding out how Fiona had ended up alone and dead in a burning car, instead of dining on egg salad sandwiches in Abby's lovely garden, in the company of friends.

Egg Salad Tea Sandwiches

Ingredients:
6 hard-boiled eggs (chilled or at room temperature)
½ cup mayonnaise
¼ cup finely minced red onion
2 tablespoons minced sweet gherkin pickles
2 tablespoons coarse-ground mustard
1 teaspoon organic honey
½ teaspoon finely minced fresh dill
Kosher salt, to taste
Freshly cracked black pepper, to taste
12 slices white or whole-wheat bread
6 chilled, crisp lettuce leaves or 24 thin slices Armenian cucumber

Directions:

Peel and chop the hard-boiled eggs and place the chopped eggs in a medium bowl. Add the mayonnaise, onion, pickles, mustard, honey, dill, salt, and pepper to the eggs and mix thoroughly. Set the egg salad aside.

Stack 2 slices of bread on a cutting board so that they are completely aligned and cut off the crusts with a sharp knife. Repeat this process until all the slices of bread have been trimmed.

Spread a thin layer of the reserved egg salad on 6 bread slices. Top each with a lettuce leaf or 4 cucumber slices and then a plain bread slice to make 6 sandwiches.

Cut each sandwich into 4 squares or, if you prefer, 4 triangles with a sharp knife. Arrange the tea sandwiches on a large plate and serve at once.

Serves 4 to 6 (4 to 6 tea sandwiches per person)

Chapter 3

Don't get sidetracked by the hens' antics if the rooster is in a foul mood.

—*Henny Penny Farmette Almanac*

Houdini, the rust-colored bantam rooster with weapon-like spurs, eyed Abby, as if ready for attack. She saw him.

"Did somebody get up on the wrong side of the roost?" she asked.

She stepped up the tempo of her chores in the poultry area, collecting eggs and hosing down the water dispenser before refilling it. Keeping Houdini in her line of sight, she plucked the aluminum feeder from its suspension hook and added crumbles. Sooner or later, he was going to make his move. Out of the corner of her eye, she saw Houdini begin to pace. Hurriedly, she rehung the feeder. Sidestepping the hens, Abby fetched the bag of wilted spinach and lettuce leaves from the wheelbarrow next to the gate and dumped the entire mound into the large cracked platter on the ground. "Here you go, my darlings."

So Houdini had gotten his hackles up. Abby wondered what had triggered his agitation this time. She was almost finished with the chores when Houdini flew at her, screeching a shrill warning and flapping his wings as though his tail feathers had caught fire.

"Oh, cool your spurs, big boy," Abby said, dodging the assault and grabbing the garden hoe. She held the hoe handle in a defensive position and eased out of the gate, stepping backward.

Like an opposing warlord, Abby locked eyes with Houdini. The rooster blinked first. Apparently satisfied that he had sufficiently established dominance over his domain, the rooster promptly herded Henrietta, Heloise, Tighty Whitey, Red, Orpy, and the wyandotte sisters with aggressive pecks. He stopped when finally they stood bunched together in a huddle under the henhouse. The bantam rooster began macho prancing. Abby had seen it before . . . and so had the hens. The girls watched in seeming boredom as Houdini executed the moves of his scratch dance, trying to entice them into exploring what his sharp toenails might have unearthed. On the off chance that he had uncovered a worm, two of the hens wandered over. No worms. Not so much as a grub or a speck of birdseed. They ambled off to a sunny spot for a dirt bath.

"Listen up, ladies, and you, too, Mr. Fancy Pants," said Abby. "Keep an eye peeled for hawks circling. I've spotted three already this morning. One is sitting sentry up there in that pine tree. I don't want to come home to a pile of plucked feathers and no chickens, and trust me, you don't want that, either."

After latching the gate, Abby picked up the basket of eggs, most in hues of brown, white, and tan, with a blue-green one from the Ameraucana. She walked to the water spigot in the middle of the yard. Sugar bounded over.

"You've been chasing my songbirds, haven't you?"

Abby leaned down and turned off the water to the hose. She would have filled the second water dispenser, as she usually did on hot days, but the rubber ring inside the screw-top lid on the older dispenser had snapped, making the dispenser unusable. Knowing that if a chicken went without water, it could stop laying eggs for up to three weeks, Abby made a mental note to keep a close watch on the water level in the sole dispenser. The temperature was expected to climb into the triple digits by late afternoon. On her way back to the kitchen, she plucked a stick from the grass and flung it into the air. Sugar bounded after it and trotted back, leaving the stick where it had landed under the white tea roses.

"Would it be asking too much to bring the stick back?" Abby knelt and massaged the dog's neck. "If you weren't such a cutie-pie, with a personality to match, I would have found you a new home long ago. But when the vet said your genes showed English pointer, beagle, and whippet, I got the idea that you might have a talent for tracking. That talent is useful in investigative work. Can you see where I'm going with this?"

Sugar pushed back and gave an impatient, high-pitched *yip, yip*. She might not be the world's greatest interpreter of dog speak yet, but Abby felt pretty sure that Sugar wanted a treat or a walk. But conversation . . . not so much.

"Okay, already. Let's find you a treat and get the leash."

In the kitchen, Abby searched for the bag of doggy treats. There were only three places in her unfinished kitchen where the bag could be hiding: on top of the double ovens, which had been installed without an upper cabinet; in the pantry of dry goods, next to the fridge; and in the drawer under the counter where she kept potatoes and onions.

"Shoot. Did you eat them all already?" Abby avoided eye contact with Sugar. Without looking, she knew that Sugar was gazing up at her with expectant eyes, making her guilt even harder to bear. How could she not remember having thrown out the empty treat bag? And, worse, why hadn't she ensured an adequate supply in the first place?

After grabbing her purse, the leash, and the car key, Abby slid open the screen door. "Come on, big girl. We'd better go get that gasket for the chicken water dispenser and more doggy . . ." She stopped short of saying the word. No point in getting the dog super excited all over again.

Twenty minutes later, Abby navigated the Jeep into the parking lot behind Crawford's Feed and Farm Supplies. She liked going in through the back door since there was always plenty of parking behind the building. Regular customers parked on the street out front. The store's employees parked at the rear, where truck deliveries were handled, where the bales of hay and straw were stacked, and where owner Lucas Crawford had a designated place for his pickup. Lucas had been widowed for almost two years now. His wife had died early in her pregnancy from virulent pneumonia. After the funeral for his wife and unborn child, Lucas had thrown himself into running the store, continuing to make deliveries around the county, and working on his cattle ranch near Abby's small farm. Up there, away from the town and the eager advances of women who wanted to console him, Lucas found solace in raising his grass-fed beef and riding his horses, keeping to himself.

When he had learned that Abby had bought the farmette downhill from his place, Lucas had made a special point of giving her permission to use his old truck if the need ever arose. He'd held on to his late wife's car, he'd told her, so there was no inconvenience. Abby smiled as she stared at his red truck. She'd borrowed it only twice—once to haul compost from the recycling plant to her gardens and another time to transport some lumber to repair the farmhouse kitchen. Each time she had washed the vehicle and had hung the extra key back on its nail on the wall inside the old gray barn where Lucas kept it.

The ringtone of her cell sounded, jarring her from her thoughts.

"Just a reminder. The estate sale is Saturday." Kat's voice practically trilled the words.

"What happened to hello?" asked Abby.

"You have caller ID, girlfriend. Just making sure you remember *not* to do the farmers' market. I thought we could take your car to the estate sale since your Jeep has more room than my roadster," said Kat.

"I've circled the date on my calendar, Kat. And yes, we'll take my Jeep. No problem."

Abby was more concerned about what the cops had discovered in their investigation of Fiona's death. With a killer on the loose in Las Flores, Abby could hardly think of bargain hunting. "What's new with the murder investigation?" she asked, tapping the speaker mode of her cell and setting the phone on the dashboard. She needed both hands to snap the leash onto Sugar's collar. The dog had already started barking her impatience.

"Lot of info, but few leads."

Sighing, Abby said, "So no one heard or saw anything?"

"More like no one is saying if they did. We're ruling out those closest to her and moving out from there. Checking alibis. Working the angles."

"Gotcha. So exactly where is the estate sale?" Abby asked, still struggling with the leash. Sugar wiggled worse than a bowl of gelatin on a picnic table during an earthquake. Abby had tried three times to connect the leash latch to the ring on her harness and finally gave up.

"Vineyard Lane . . . at the Richardson estate. Two doors down from where Fiona lives."

"Lived," Abby said, correcting her. Sugar whined. "Oh, hold on, Kat, while I deal with this dog."

"Where are you?"

"We're at the feed store, on a run for chow and treats. Parked around back."

"And I'm right around the corner. Be there in five. It'll give me a chance to check out Mr. Action Hero with the washboard abs. I can't for the life of me figure out why a man that good-looking hasn't remarried. He can't still be in mourning."

"If you mean Lucas Crawford, I'm watching him walk out the door right now. You better hurry, or you'll miss him," Abby said, instantly wishing she could call back her words. Kat was her dearest friend, but until Abby figured out why she felt those butterflies in her tummy whenever Lucas met up with her, she didn't want anyone—including Kat—complicating the situation. Not that there was a *situation*. And Abby could certainly understand why the single women in town might fantasize about the quiet rancher who lived a stone's throw up the hill from her farmette.

"Stay put, Abby. I'll be right there," Kat said and clicked off.

Abby laid the cell on the console. No point in taking Sugar inside until Kat had come and gone. Through the windshield, Abby watched Lucas check his phone before sliding it into his jeans pocket. Man, did he ever look good in slim-legged, boot-cut dungarees and a cotton flannel shirt. She hadn't seen him since those heavy winter rains, when he'd dressed in a knee-length slicker. Drought-stricken California always needed rain, but twenty-one straight days of it had worn heavily on the people who had to work in it, like farmers and ranchers. But her misery over the incessant rain and mud had had a bright spot when, at the end of that rainy period in March, Lucas had dropped by unannounced. He'd come to ask about the aged French drain around Abby's farmhouse. Was it still holding strong and redirecting the rising water?

He'd offered to bring her some sandbags if flooding seemed imminent. Abby smiled as she recalled how surprised she'd been to see him and also at the excuse he used to explain the visit. The French drain? Seriously?

She'd offered him coffee, a freshly baked cinnamon roll, and a towel to dry his face and his wet hair. His eyes, the color of creek water, gazed at her with such intensity that it seemed almost as if he could see into the depths of her heart. It was then that Abby felt the first flutter of attraction. That day in March, he stood facing her, dripping with rainwater like a drowned kitten, and gave her a rare smile. He took the towel she'd offered, shoved it through his curly, brown locks, and swallowed several sips of the steaming black brew. Under the intensity of his gaze, the butterflies in Abby's tummy took flight. She wondered then if he felt them, too. But she guessed not, since he suddenly said thanks, handed her the cup, gave Sugar a pat on the head, and left. That was the way of enigmatic Lucas, a man of few words, but full of surprises.

Now, as Abby watched Lucas climb onto the seat of his truck and slam the door behind him, she had to wonder why he hadn't been around of late. His red truck disappeared around the side of the feed store where an alley turned into the street. Most likely, he was taking off for a new delivery. Nobody provided that kind of customer service anymore. It endeared Lucas all the more to the people of Las Flores and his customers countywide. And today Abby was grateful that she'd parked under the dense walnut tree, next to a pallet of starter feed for laying hens, where she could secretly watch Lucas.

Kat eased her vintage roadster into a parking space just as Abby slid out of the driver's side of the Jeep. She held Sugar on the leash as Kat exited her sports car and threw her arms around Abby in a demonstrative hug. Kat wore a navy pantsuit with a crisp white shirt, and a vintage brooch pinned to her lapel. Kat loved anything Victorian, from her cottage behind a large Victorian-style home in Las Flores to her collection of sterling silver thimbles and decorative combs, which she sometimes wore, although not today. Her blond tresses sported an expensive-looking cut and, with mousse, had been coaxed into an edgy style. Kat rarely wore makeup, although Abby could tell that today was one of those days when she did—mascara on her lashes and a sheer pink gloss on her lips.

"You get dressed up to come to the feed store? Impressive," Abby said, amused.

Kat grinned. "Don't be silly. I'm testifying in court today. But you, girlfriend, look like you're taking Fiona's death hard. You've got badger eyes."

Abby heaved a sigh. "It was a long night. Couldn't sleep thinking about the case. Anything you can share?"

"Not really. The people closest to her all have alibis, so we're going a little further out in her orbit, interviewing friends, customers, vendors, even the commune residents."

Before Abby could ask more questions about the investigation, she noticed Kat jerk her head toward the feed-store door.

"Did Prince Charming go back inside?"

"Nope. He hoisted some hay onto his truck and hightailed it out of here."

Was Lucas the reason Kat had gotten so dressed up? She could have just worn her police uniform to court. Abby felt her stomach lurch.

"Your dance card is usually full, Kat. Are you saving a tango for Lucas?"

"Maybe."

Concealing her surprise, Abby asked, "What happened to the security guard?"

"Oh, that's so five minutes ago. But I recently had drinks again with the chef at Zazi's."

Abby brightened. "Oh really? So how did that go?"

"Oh, you know, he's nice enough. . . ."

"But?"

"I don't know. I prefer my tomatoes and onions on a plate, not tattooed on the forearms of the guy handing me the plate. Always . . . with the sleeves up. I've got nothing against ink, but I'm not feeling the sparks. Wishing I could find a nice Silicon Valley engineer type to hook up with. The trouble is, most around Las Flores moved here with a wife and kids."

"I'm not making the connection here between your chef, the engineer you want, and Lucas Crawford. Can you clue me in?"

"Well, Lucas, now, he's a looker. He's also eligible, available, and as you told me, he can cook."

Abby felt taken aback. Kat had remembered that detail. Momentarily caught off guard, Abby sputtered, "Yes, so I've heard. But he isn't really your type, is he?"

Kat's brow shot up. "And what type would that be?"

Abby fumbled for words, waved her hand, as if to dismiss the notion. "I . . . ." She blew air between her lips. "I don't know. Polar opposite, maybe?" She wished now that she'd said something long ago to Kat about how she felt around Lucas.

"Polar opposite? Really?" Kat looked surprised. "Well, opposites attract, or so they say. Lest you forget, it was you, Abby, who suggested I be more choosy, set my sights higher. Lucas Crawford would be a great catch. Maybe I could get him off that ranch. He might enjoy dating a fun-loving cop."

Abby leaned against the Jeep, nodding her head. *He might indeed.* She'd said enough. She had trusted Kat with her life when they were partners on the force. Life had taught Abby a hard lesson about trust and betrayal. When Abby was in her midtwenties, her best friend, Josephine, had seduced Abby's then boyfriend behind her back. He had left Abby for Jo, then had ditched Jo to romance a female recruiter for the military and had soon joined up. Kat wasn't Jo. Abby knew that. If Kat only knew how a mere look from Lucas could stir Abby's emotions. But Kat didn't know. *And whose fault is that?*

Sugar wanted her treat. She clearly didn't like being tethered while Abby chitchatted with Kat. The medium-sized dog had lunged at a passerby and now had grown bored barking at a gray squirrel in the tree. Abby applied a reassuring pat on Sugar's head to calm her.

"Well, who knows?" Abby said to Kat with a smile. "Maybe Lucas will rock your world."

"The way I see it, Abby, Lucas needs a good woman in his life. The whole town felt bad when his wife passed away so young, being pregnant and all. I'd just like to be there for him."

Abby smiled. *You and every other single woman between twenty and sixty. But your heartfelt sentiment is sweet.* Kat was gorgeous, openly flirty, intensely funny, and had a heart of gold. If Kat wanted to start something with Lucas, Abby wouldn't stand in the way.

"Has he asked you out?" Abby asked, not sure she wanted to hear the answer.

"Not yet," Kat replied. "And I never seem to catch him here at the feed store."

Her spirits suddenly buoyed, Abby grinned. "So people don't usually dress up to buy feed. What were you going to tell him you were shopping for?"

"Dunno. Don't have any pets. There's a mouse in my house. Maybe a trap?"

"Seriously?" Abby snorted. "Wouldn't that be just the thing? A trap?"

Kat chuckled. "I see what you mean." She glanced at her watch. "Listen. I have to go in a minute, but about the estate sale . . . I've heard there will be lots of antiques and dishes and farm tools."

"Great," said Abby, relieved the conversation had taken a new direction.

"I happen to know that old lady Richardson collected gobs of fine china. I'll be looking for porcelain and pottery marks while you hunt for garden stuff and old books."

"You know I like good china, too," Abby replied. "But back to Fiona for a moment. I saw a box or two of old gardening books in her shop that she planned to donate. What do you suppose will happen to those volumes?"

Kat's brow puckered. "I couldn't say. At some point, there'll have to be a funeral. Might be a good time to ask her brother, who has to settle her affairs."

"To hear Fiona tell it, he was the only stable person in her crazy quilt of a life. How's he taking her death?" Abby asked.

"Like a man who has lost a loved one to a murderer. He's grieving. Wants her killer brought to justice."

Abby nodded. "We all want that. What did Fiona's autopsy reveal?"

Kat glanced at her watch again. "Cardiac arrest due to asphyxia was the cause of death. No trauma to the body. The coroner's report is inconclusive. And, as you know, the toxicology report takes as long as it takes. For now, that's about all we have."

"Asphyxia?" Abby blinked with bafflement. "Drowning causes asphyxia. Inhaling a toxic gas causes asphyxia. Choking . . ."

"Before you ask me if she was choked," Kat said, "the answer is no. There were no marks on her neck or the rest of her body."

"Well, that's just weird," Abby said. She recalled Fiona's body in the car, with the front windows down. Fiona was seated behind the wheel and was leaning back in the seat. But her feet, as far as Abby could tell, didn't quite reach the brake or the gas pedal.

"You and I were a great team, Abby. We still are. But Chief Bob Allen told me not to involve you in this case, so what I tell you can go no further. Abigail, I'm dead serious about the need for secrecy. Otherwise, I could lose my job." Kat's expression reflected the sober reality of what she apparently felt.

"I would never do or say anything to jeopardize your job, Kat. I hope you know that." Abby suddenly lurched as Sugar pulled against the leash with a high-pitched *yip, yip, yip,* apparently after spotting a pair of squirrels scrambling along a limb of the tree.

Kat nodded. "Of course, but I need assurances that we're on the same page. So, here's a scoop. Fire investigators say an accelerant was used, but the coroner says no smoke or soot in her lungs, meaning—"

"Fiona was dead when someone torched the car," said Abby. She leaned against the Jeep door, shaking her head, feeling sorrowful all over again.

"Oh, but there were traces of emesis in her mouth," said Kat. "What do you make of that?"

"She threw up?" Abby asked, frowning. "You know, I've been with Fiona when she's plucked a leaf from a plant and chomped down on it. I often wondered how she always seemed to know whether or not it was poisonous." Abby scratched her head. "Maybe she knew from the bitterness or chalkiness or acidity. I don't know. Regardless, it's possible that this time she ate something toxic, something that caused her to vomit."

"No evidence of it in the car or anywhere we searched . . ." Kat's sentence trailed off.

"So if she was poisoned and threw up, the killer cleaned her up. Don't you have any idea where the killer took her life?" Abby asked, trying to make a linkage without enough facts.

"No, we don't. It's possible she was at her cottage, or someone took her someplace else. What's certain is that the murderer wanted the body and the car burned."

"To cover his tracks." Abby tried to wrap her mind around the puzzle. "Any sign of a struggle at her cottage? Or even the foul scent of someone being sick?"

Kat shook her head. "Nope. And there were no

traces of botanical material on the car seats, floorboards, or in the trunk."

Abby scratched her head. "So here's a hypothesis. Fiona ingested or inhaled a lethal dose of something that caused her asphyxia. But it would have had to be quick acting, wouldn't it? She threw up before dying. Her killer cleaned her up and drove her to the site at Kilbride Lake. He staged her body behind the wheel, used an accelerant, and set the car afire to conceal his crime. Car torched, body burned, and the killer gets away." Abby waited for a response from Kat.

"It's plausible. The toxicology screen will tell us more," said Kat.

"But we both know forensic tests don't happen in the real world like they do on TV. A toxicology screen is going to take a while—two to three weeks or more. Right now, I think the murderer would have had someone to help with the move and the disposal, possibly a second person to drive a getaway car from Kilbride Lake."

"Makes perfect sense," Kat said. She glanced again at her watch. "Oh, my gosh, I've got to get to court."

Abby nodded. "Oh, before you leave . . . What about the tire print?"

"That piece of tire tread was awfully small. I don't think the lab will be able to use it," said Kat.

Abby nodded. "And Chief Bob Allen made such a big deal about it, as if I were a rookie whom he had just pinned. Whatever. I'll help the investigation any way I can, Kat, but for now I'd better hustle home before Sugar snaps this leash."

Kat was already climbing back into her roadster.

"Let's get an early start Saturday, say seven thirty. Don't be late, or we'll lose out on all the good stuff."

"You just worry about getting the coffee ready. I'll bake lemon scones and bring fresh strawberries and crème anglaise," Abby said. She waved as Kat pulled away.

Abby dashed inside the feed store, with Sugar behaving like a dog who knew good behavior would get her a reward, and she and the clerk located a rawhide bone, a chew toy, and some dry doggy biscuits, along with a bag of dog food.

"Check back with us about that water dispenser gasket," the clerk said. "I'll let Lucas know we need more."

"Sounds good," said Abby. She left with her purchases in one hand and Sugar's leash in the other.

Watching Sugar devour her treat, Abby decided to take another look at where Fiona had lived and died. *We're already in town. That puts us halfway there.*

"What do you say to a drive into the mountains, Sugar Pie? Would you like that?" Abby fastened her seat belt, shifted the gear into reverse, and backed up the Jeep. Sugar cocked her head to one side. Looking over at her, Abby could almost swear Sugar was smiling back.

Abby stuck to the back roads through Las Flores, then drove through the mountains until she reached the red barn signifying the turnoff to Fiona's cottage. After navigating up the short gravel road, she parked at the mailbox and read the sign on the front porch: WELCOME LITTLE PEOPLE, FAIRY FOLK, AND BEINGS OF LIGHT. Abby smiled and wondered how Fiona had managed to persuade Dr. Danbury to let her put that up. But then again, who would read it, except maybe the mail carrier and the two of them? Of course, there was also the occasional transient Fiona brought home when rain or freezing temperatures threatened. A couple of weeks ago, Fiona had told her about picking up an Iraqi war vet who was hitching his way through the mountains to the valley of towns on the other side. He had slept on her couch for two nights. Abby sighed at the realization that for all her compassion, Fiona's rescuing personality might have been her undoing.

Turning off the engine, Abby looked for signs of life. Perhaps the doc would peek out the window. Dr. David Danbury had been a successful surgeon at the local hospital. He'd purchased the property right after marrying a pretty psychiatrist from Stanford University who was doing the rotation part of her residency program at his hospital. When their growing family outgrew the cottage, the doc built a larger house right next door and connected the two homes with a breezeway. Later, when the marriage failed and his wife moved back east, taking their daughters with her, the doc gave up his lucrative practice to make wine. He rented out the little cottage and eventually became an alcoholic recluse.

Fiona had confided to Abby that she and the doc had initially got on just fine. But with booze on board, it was another story. The affable doctor turned into a pushy, mean drunk. He would talk about his life and insult each person as he remembered them. There was never a kind word for anyone. When Fiona didn't want to keep drinking with him, he insulted her, too, saying she was an emasculator, like his wife had been. After that,

Fiona had to tread upon the proverbial razor's edge between being friendly with the doc and spurning his advances, which put her chances of staying in the cottage in jeopardy.

She loved her small home, positioned as it was in the middle of Dr. Danbury's ten-acre vineyard. At the back, there was a Christmas tree farm that bordered another forty acres of wilderness. The latter provided refuge for wildlife, a small stand of old-growth redwoods, and many indigenous plants. When Fiona decided to leave the commune for good, it had been a stroke of good fortune to find Dr. Danbury's cottage. She'd tried to stay in the doc's good graces by offering to plant him a garden that included heirloom vegetables and herbs. One day, he'd pointed to a swath of land near a large olive tree, which he said he'd planted years ago for the wife who left him. The doc had plowed a section under the tree and had told Fiona, "Plant there." That was the extent of his interest in gardens with anything that wasn't a grapevine or a Christmas tree.

Abby held Sugar's leash securely. She'd brought along the scarf Fiona had left at her house. Now, with Fiona's scarf in hand, she approached the mailbox and looked around. Maybe if she stood there long enough, someone would notice. She didn't want to look like a trespasser, a prowler, or, God forbid, an identity thief. She was, in fact, standing next to the mailbox. Mountain people didn't take kindly to strangers walking about, so Abby hung back and held Sugar in check by her side.

After a few minutes, when nobody had acknowledged her presence, Abby embarked upon the path through the grassless yard—a patchwork of poppies and plants growing in wild abandon near square-shaped raised beds of herbs. Chaotic and ordered, wild and cultivated, the garden seemed an accurate reflection of Fiona.

Raising the knocker over the carved brass female image on the front door of the cottage, Abby felt a twinge of sadness. She tried to push from her mind the image of Fiona's engorged, partially burned, black and red blistered face. She rapped the knocker three times. Waited. Rapped again. The dark green patina gave dimension to the brass face, accentuating the creases in the laurel wreath surrounding the woman's head. The banshee of Irish folklore, Fiona had told her, was a potent image—the harbinger of death. When Abby had asked Fiona why she would dare hang a banshee door knocker, Fiona had replied, "I felt inexplicably drawn to her. She's the woman of fairies and has power and magic. She foretells death through her wailing. The death is often violent—that much is true. But, look, there are lots of square knots in her cloak. They provide protection."

Humph! Some protection.

When no one answered the door, Abby put her hand on the knob and slowly turned it. The door flew open. Abby stumbled down two steps into a bright interior. Surprise registered on the face of the man who had opened the door from the inside. Sugar barked without letup.

"Who are you?" the man asked. He stood maybe five feet, ten inches. He had striking pale blue eyes and curly, brown hair with silver threads running through it. His face looked gaunt, and his puffy eyes were ringed in red, as though he had gone days without sleep.

"Abigail Mackenzie, formerly with the Las Flores Police Department." Abby extended her hand. "Are you Jack Sullivan, Fiona's brother, the ethnobotanist she always talked so enthusiastically about?"

"You found me. What is it you want?"

Abby decided to be straight with him. He looked like he'd been through the ringer. "Sorry for your loss. To be honest, I'm looking for clues. Fiona and I were friends, and I made a promise to find the person who hurt her. I was hoping to take a quick look around, if that's okay with you."

If it was possible for his expression to harden, it did. "Excuse me," he said, "but the police have already been here. I've got funeral arrangements to make. I can't see any reason for them to send an ex-cop to poke around. So if you don't mind, please just leave. Take that dog with you."

Taken aback, Abby gave him a wide-eyed stare. "Your sister's passing has shaken me up, too. I didn't mean to be insensitive. Our whole community is worried that a killer is on the loose among us."

He glared at her.

Abby proffered the scarf. "It's Fiona's. She left it at my farmette the last time we were together. I meant to return it."

"Sure you did," he said, his tone conveying a biting sarcasm. "That scarf is your cover. You came up here to snoop," he said, warily eyeing her. "Did you think you'd unearth some salacious details about my sister's life? Juice up your copy? Hit on a provocative headline?" He tightened his hand around the doorknob, pulling the door open. "I'd really appreciate it if you would just go."

Abby's stomach clenched. "Look, Mr. Sullivan . . . you've made a mistake."

"I don't make mistakes about women like you. I can smell small-town reporter." His brows furrowed. "I've had to protect my sister from people like you in the past."

Her shock was met with a sobering stare.

"Ms. Mackenzie, do I have to ask you twice?"

"Of course not." Abby felt her throat closing up, her lips tightening. "My condolences." Tugging on Sugar's leash, she said softly, "Come on, sweetie."

Abby tramped from the foyer to the porch, then beyond the mailbox, and was at the end of the driveway, by the big red barn, before she realized she had walked clear past the Jeep. Turning around, Abby had one thought. What did he mean by having to defend his sister in the past? What did Fiona do?

Tips for Making Tea from Fresh Herbs

Homemade herb tea starts with fresh herbs picked at their peak around midmorning, after the dew has dried. If dust clings to the leaves, wash them and dry them with a paper towel. Drop two handfuls of the leaves into a one-gallon glass jar and fill the jar with water to within three inches of the rim. Add fresh organic orange slices or lemon slices or zest (wash the rinds before slicing) to the jar. Place in the refrigerator and let it stand for one to two hours. Strain the herb tea into tall glasses with ice. To sweeten the tea, add honey or rose-scented sugar. Some of the herbs that make delicious tea are the following:

- Mint—Choose from the estimated six hundred varieties of mint, including apple mint, chocolate mint, ginger mint, mojito mint, orange mint, peppermint, pineapple mint, and spearmint, to name a few.

- Lemon Balm—This is also known as balm mint, and it is a calming herb.

- Bee Balm—This herb is also known as wild bergamot. The red blooming variety, known as Oswego tea, was the tea of choice for the American colonists after the Boston Tea Party.

- Hyssop—This herb is used by herbalists to improve digestive issues. However, it contains a chemical that may affect the heart and lungs.

- Sage—This perennial mint has a long history as a medicinal and culinary herb. It was cultivated in medieval monastery gardens.

- Horsetail—Herbalists have noted that this herb's high silica content is beneficial for the hair, nails, and bones.

Note: Although humans have used herbs for thousands of years for culinary and medicinal purposes, it's always a good idea to check with your doctor before including herbs in your food and drink. Some herbs are more potent than others and may have unwanted side effects, and they can interact adversely with prescription drugs.

Chapter 4

An ant seeking a source of sweetness is
as persistent as an old boyfriend who is
trying to get back into your life.

—*Henny Penny Farmette Almanac*

The ants had found the honey buckets. Coagu-
lating into a black mass, thousands of them
marched in lines like an army on the move to
cover the shelf above the washer and dryer where
Abby kept the honey buckets. She'd wiped down
one of the buckets after refilling the large jar for
her daily use—honey for tea, yogurt, waffles, and
general good health and well-being. She'd even
gone so far as to swaddle the bucket in plastic
wrap, securing the wrap with duct tape. But a single drop of honey left unwiped had been enough
to attract a full-blown invasion. Cleaning the mess
took most of the morning.

It was close to noon before Abby finished. She
flipped on the local farmers' network news, intending to eat a quick snack before beginning the
apricot jam–making process, which would occupy

her for the next two hours. The cots were ripe, maybe too ripe to set up properly into jam without having to cook out all the nutrients or add pectin, and too much boiling or pectin would change the texture. She considered whether or not it might be better to dry them instead. The hour she saved washing the jars and stirring the jam could then be used for another project. Maybe she would add manure to the three raised beds where she would then plant heirloom blue tomatoes, smoking hot Caribbean habaneros, and some sweet bell peppers. Suddenly, her thoughts filled with images of the myriad projects needing to be done around the farmette.

Swallowing a sip of sweet tea and nibbling on a peanut butter toasted sandwich, Abby focused her attention on the radio announcer reading the news. First up was a piece about the latest developments in the grass fire on the south side of Las Flores Boulevard, which was now "eighty percent contained." The announcer continued, "Partying high school students lobbed eggs against two vehicles parked on Cottonwood Lane last night. They also made off with boxes of produce outside Smooth Your Groove shake shop on Chestnut. A block away on Olive, vandals draped a tree in toilet paper and broke into a pickup truck belonging to a local man, stealing his rifle. And finally, the murder of a local woman is no closer to resolution today, as investigators have yet to identify a person of interest in the case. Services for Fiona Mary Ryan will be held at the Church of the Holy Names."

Abby winced. A sudden onset of sorrow soured her stomach. Tears burned at the backs of her eyes. Fiona's passing had been such a horrible shock,

Abby had felt numb at first and later mercurial—normal one minute and tearing up the next. But what good were tears? They wouldn't bring Fiona back.

Dumping the remainder of the tea down the sink, Abby stared at the disappearing liquid and contemplated the case's complexities. After a few minutes, she washed and dried the cup and set it in the cupboard. Dabbing her eyes with a tea towel, she muttered, "I swear I'm going to find out who killed you, Fiona, if it's the last thing I do, though I doubt it will ease the guilt I feel. I should've demanded that you go to the police with whatever was bothering you. I didn't, and now . . . what a terrible outcome." For a fleeting moment, Kat's words of warning to stay out of the case intruded. But Kat needn't worry. Whatever information Abby might unearth from a few discreet inquiries, she would pass on to Kat and Otto. Studying the toast she no longer desired, Abby glanced up at the wall clock above the coffeemaker and noted the time—exactly twelve o'clock. Mountain traffic, she reasoned, would have thinned by now. She gave her last bite of toast to Sugar.

"Farmette work will wait for us, Sugar Pie. I'm going to help the good guys track down a bad guy who might still be in the mountains."

Sugar stretched her neck upward and let go a piteous howl, as if to protest being left behind while her owner tracked down a killer.

"Oh, don't worry," said Abby reassuringly. "You're coming with me."

*   *   *

The locals had superior knowledge. They knew what outsiders didn't about driving the mountain roads on the western side of Las Flores. They were familiar with the most treacherous stretches of the road, where it narrowed without shoulders or guardrails. A split second of inattention meant a car could drop a hundred feet. Hidden by dense brush and trees, a car and driver might never be found. The two most dangerous sections involved double S curves halfway between Fiona's cottage and Kilbride Lake. Previously, both had been the scene of traffic fatalities. Both accidents had involved people who didn't know the roads. Both had happened during bad weather. Today there wasn't a cloud in sight. Still, Abby wasn't about to tempt fate. She tapped the brakes as she entered the first of the curves.

Out of nowhere, a horn blared. A silver pickup screamed around the blind corner. It flew past Abby's Jeep, claiming the greater part of the twisting blacktop. Shoving the brake pedal to the floorboard, she felt the rear wheels slide. The Jeep fishtailed as she fought for control. Adrenaline raced through her body. Her heart slammed against her chest. Instinctively, she righted the wheel, and Sugar flew against her with a high-pitched yelp. The stench of locked brakes and burnt rubber permeated the Jeep. Coming out of the curve, Abby steered her car to the widest section of the shoulder and parked, set the hand brake, and cut off the engine.

Her hands shook. She leaned her head against the steering wheel and struggled for composure. Sugar pawed at the window, barking and whining without letup. Smelling pee, Abby lifted her head and realized the dog had peed on the seat. She ordered Sugar to stop barking, but she knew the dog was only feeling what she herself was experiencing—alarm and fear. Slowly and rhythmically, Abby began to stroke the dog's neck.

"There, there, girl," she cooed. "Scary, I know, but it's over." The dog yipped once, twice more, and then licked Abby's hand. "We're safe. That's what matters," Abby said. She hugged Sugar close.

Looking around for something to wick the urine—a napkin, a towel, or even an old shirt—and finding nothing, Abby remembered placing Fiona's scarf in the glove box before driving away from Fiona's cottage after her unsettling conversation with Jack Sullivan. This situation called for desperate measures. She pulled out the saffron-colored cotton scarf stamped in red with the symbol Aum scripted in Sanskrit, the trident of Shiva, and the Kalachakra, the wheel of time. Abby thought that it was odd that Fiona, raised Catholic, had lived in a commune that embraced Eastern traditions. And it was strange, too, that she had gotten involved with a boyfriend who practiced voodoo Haitian style. But Fiona was a woman of many contradictions and interests. The search for spiritual meaning in life, a stint at commune living, and growing and selling herbs were all expressions of her free spirit. *Wherever you are, Fiona Mary Ryan, I hope you know I admired you, and I mean no disrespect by using your scarf this way.*

Abby compressed the scarf into a wad and dabbed it repeatedly against the wet spot. She thought about the maniac in the silver truck, a danger to anyone on the road. After dropping the scarf on the floorboard, Abby turned the Jeep around, maneuvered it back onto the road, and headed in the direction the silver truck had gone.

Only after she had passed the big red barn at Doc Danbury's driveway could she see down the other side of the mountain, where the road stretched out in long undulations. The silver pickup was tailgating a slow-moving winery truck loaded with oak barrels. Passing was impossible because of the line of cars streaming from the other direction. Abby accelerated. When she'd closed the gap between the Jeep and the silver pickup, she jotted down the license plate number using the pencil and pad she kept in the console.

After the last oncoming car had passed, the pickup shot around the winery truck. Just when Abby lost sight of the pickup, the winery truck pulled off, giving her an open view of the road ahead and the silver truck as it turned right onto a compacted dirt road. Abby continued to follow, undaunted by a message scrawled in white paint on an old fence board nailed to a tree—NO TRESPASSING. VIOLATORS WILL BE SHOT.

Eventually, she arrived at a stand of oaks at the top of a high hill. Pulling over in the shade, Abby watched the silver truck park near a rustic cabin. *Who would want to live in such isolation?* The answer came as easily as a bloom on a mustard stalk in springtime—woodsmen, potheads, drug dealers, survivalists, anarchists, and people desiring to disappear for a while. Abby wondered whether the truck driver belonged to one of those groups. Parked at such a high elevation, she could easily

see the creek, the woods, and even the tall pole
with the Christmas star on it that marked Doc Danbury's tree farm and his vineyard.

When the man climbed out of the truck and disappeared into the cabin's dark interior, Abby
squinted against the sun. Difficult to tell, but she
estimated his height to be six feet. Grungy clothes,
a scraggly gray beard, and salt-and-pepper hair
pulled back into a ponytail added up to a shabby
appearance. Suddenly, it dawned on her who the
man might be. He fit the description Fiona had
given her of the man who'd assaulted her when
she'd been out looking for herbs.

Abby tapped the number on her cell to speed-
dial Kat. "I need a favor, Kat. Could you run the
plates on a silver pickup? The man driving it is the
same one, I believe, who accosted Fiona back in
February. And he just ran me off the road."

"Are you all right?"

"Yes, I am."

"How can you be sure it's the same guy?"

"I can't. Not positively. My gut tells me it is."

"So this is where I ask you if you recall our chat
outside the feed store about how I could lose my
job if Chief Bob Allen finds out I'm involving you
in this investigation."

"I wouldn't ask, but that idiot drives like he's
high on something. He's a danger on the road, and
he frightened the daylights out of Fiona."

"Did she call the cops?"

"Well . . . no."

"So, you know as well as I do that scaring someone isn't illegal. If Fiona had feared for life and
limb, she would have dialed nine-one-one. Any

sane person would. But, as you've pointed out, she didn't. So what are you not telling me?"

Abby hesitated, swallowed hard. Fiona had asked Abby not to reveal anything about her encounter with the man, for fear of being arrested herself. But what did it matter now? Fiona was gone. "Here's the deal, Kat. I kept quiet about it because Fiona asked me to. She was trespassing on the man's property when he attacked her. When she wrestled free of him, she used his pickax, hitting him hard, I guess. Fearing for her life, she ran away. He might have been lying on the ground, unconscious and bleeding, but she couldn't know whether he would die or get up and give chase. And she never went back there again."

"And how do you know she was telling the truth?"

"I can sense when someone is lying. Fiona trembled when she explained to me what had happened. The way she was shaking, it was like the cells of her body remembered."

A beat passed before Kat said, "You'd better tell me the full story, and don't leave out anything."

Abby inhaled a deep breath and let it go. "February is mustard season. In late winter, you see how the mountain meadows and vineyards turn bright yellow."

"Yeah, yeah. Hot-air balloon rides and all that . . . Tell me something I don't know."

"So . . . in late February, Fiona went exploring on Doc Danbury's property, looking for wild mustard. There's also a forty-acre parcel that shares a boundary with the doc's land at the back, right?"

"Uh-huh."

"So, the doc told Fiona about the caretaker's cabin but assured her that no one lived back there anymore, so she felt safe searching alone for wild herbs. She'd gone pretty far when she wandered upon the creek and figured she'd also look for mushrooms and native herbs along its shady banks. She heard a twig snap. She said she spun around and was shocked to see a man watching her. He stood about six feet tall, had salt-and-pepper hair and a scruffy beard, and was dressed in a blue flannel shirt and stained jeans. She noticed one of his work boots had been wrapped in duct tape. He carried a pickax."

"Hold on," Kat said. "Was he working back there? Clearing the creek, building something?"

"Fiona didn't say, but she told me she wasn't afraid, at least not at first," said Abby. "They talked a bit, and then he became aggressive. He dropped the ax, lunged at her, and tried to drag her toward his cabin. She screamed and fought, and they fell. She threw dirt in his eyes and wrenched herself free." Abby caught her breath and swallowed hard, realizing how far-fetched the story sounded.

"Was that when she hit him with the pickax?" Kat said.

"Yes. After she had wrestled free, she grabbed the ax, took a wild swing, and hit his head. She said blood gushed out. The man staggered and fell. She said she ran all the way home and pounded on the doc's door."

"What did Dr. Danbury do?"

"Nothing. He didn't answer the knock. Fiona said he often drank a lot. Maybe he'd passed out."

Kat cleared her throat. "And then what did Fiona do?"

"Retreated inside her cottage," said Abby. "After that, she added a couple of new slider locks on the inside of her cottage door, but she still didn't feel safe . . . so she moved into her store for a while and slept on a fold-up cot in her office."

Abby waited for Kat's next question, but Kat remained silent. She had to be pondering the merits of Fiona's story.

After a moment, Abby said, "You know, she felt guilty for leaving the man bleeding like that and not knowing how badly he might be wounded. But, Kat, she feared for her life. I think that same man just sideswiped me less than an hour ago. Clearly, Fiona didn't kill him."

Kat cleared her throat. "I'm not convinced the two incidents are linked. And given that Fiona is gone, the story you've just relayed is hearsay, as you well know."

"I believed her," said Abby. "If you could have seen her . . . hands shaking, her lip trembling. It was like she was living through it all again. But, listen, I need you to run that plate. My situation at the moment is dicey."

"Oh, for heaven's sake, Abby. Don't tell me you followed him home."

Abby chewed her bottom lip. "He might be squatting in that caretaker's cabin."

Kat maintained a calm tone but exhaled a heavy sigh. "You see, this is what Chief Bob Allen was talking about, for crying out loud."

Abby recited the license plate number for Kat. "Sorry. I wouldn't ask, but . . ." Abby tried to think of some humble pie thing to say or offer to do for Kat.

"Oh, just hang on a sec," Kat muttered.

Abby waited in silence.

Momentarily, Kat spoke again. "The registered owner is Timothy Joseph Kramer. It'll take me a few more minutes to cross-reference to see if he has any prior contact history with law enforcement."

"I'll wait." It was a relief to know that Kat still had her back.

Abby stared at the cabin door. For a split second, she thought she detected movement. Yes, the screen door inched open. The man stepped out. He held a rifle. Abby's heart pounded in double time as she watched the man lift the gun to his shoulder and take aim at the 3:00 position. Then, to her horror, the man swung the barrel around and pointed it straight at her.

Abby dropped the phone. She thrust the Jeep gear into reverse and backed up. Cranking the steering wheel to the right, she floored the gas pedal. The crack of a gunshot rang out. She instinctively dodged. Ignoring the dips in the road, which thrust her body and Sugar's upward with such intensity that her head banged on the car's ceiling, Abby pressed on. One thought occupied her mind: *Get away from that nutcase as fast as you can.*

She drove to the main road and steered in the direction of Fiona's cottage. Approaching a turnout, Abby pulled off the road, taking comfort in the line of cars now passing her. Sugar panted hard. Who could blame her? Poor thing had experienced nothing but pandemonium this morning. Abby gave her a vigorous rub on her neck and back.

"Whew! That was close, baby girl. Remind me

not to follow a rat into its hole when there is only one way out."

Kat came back on the line. "Abby? You there?"

Abby picked up the phone. "Yes."

"Sorry that took so long."

"Listen, Kat, he got a gun from inside that cabin."

"Gun? He's armed?"

"And dangerous. Took a shot at me."

"Abby, get out of there. Now. I'll send a couple of officers to pick him up. Says here Kramer has a warrant for assault and breaking and entering. I've already notified the county sheriff."

Abby breathed a sigh of relief. "Thank you. Listen, I can meet your officers if you like."

"Not necessary. What I want is for you to get off that mountain. There's no point in you staying in harm's way. We've got the doc's address, and one of the officers I'm sending grew up not far from there."

"Right. Listen . . . it's good to know you've still got my back," said Abby.

Now wouldn't be the time to tell Kat that Abby hadn't yet finished her business in the mountains. There was still the location of Fiona's car to check out. The police would have collected the car, of course, and taken it to the impound lot. But a visit to a crime scene could produce intangibles, such as a feeling, an intuitive insight, or a previously overlooked connection.

Sugar hunkered down on the seat; her large brown eyes focused on Abby. The dog whined.

"You put up with a lot today, sweetie pie. I promise I'm going to make it up to you."

After driving past the landmark red barn, Abby

took the next cutoff to Kilbride Lake. She knew Fiona hadn't filed a report against Timothy Kramer, but she wondered if the assault on Fiona had been the only contact between the two. Might Timothy Kramer have had the motive to kill Fiona? Had he been stalking her? Was that why Fiona had wanted to talk to Abby and Kat? Had Fiona believed that she needed police protection from Kramer?

Abby put Sugar on the leash, and they took a long walk along the old Indian trail still used by the canal patrol officers and forest rangers. When Sugar seemed sufficiently exhausted and had slurped her fill of water, Abby secured the leash with an extension that allowed Sugar to rest in the dappled sunlight. Ambling away from Sugar and the Jeep toward where Fiona's car had been found, Abby walked slowly, eyes on the ground. She had not gone far when her cell went off. She didn't recognize the number. But after the call clicked off, she listened to the message. The volume of the man's voice rose only slightly above the din in his background. "Hope you got my postcard, Abby. It's been a while . . . way too long. Can't wait to see you. You know who this is, right?"

She stiffened. Her heart galloped. Oh, she knew who it was, all right. Hearing Clay Calhoun's husky voice took her instantly back to Valentine's Day the year before, when he'd left her in shock because he'd accepted a job on the East Coast. After planting a perfunctory kiss on Abby's cheek—as though he'd be home by dinner—Clay had driven off into his new life. Around the edges of her heart for months afterward, Abby had felt an inner wound that no herbal poultice could heal.

Her thoughts raced. *What postcard?* There had been nothing from him since he left. And what did he mean by "Can't wait to see you"?

Abby shook her head in dismay. Who knows what he meant by that? She congratulated herself for not taking the call. Talking with Clay would only confound her; it would be too confusing, and it was a conversation she didn't want to have. Right now, she had murder on her mind.

By late afternoon, Abby arrived at her mailbox on Farm Hill Road. After pulling down the hatch of the metal box with the chicken on top, she reached in and retrieved the contents, then flipped through the bills and the assorted junk mail. Then she saw it—the postcard. Her stomach knotted. Inhaling and letting go a long exhale, she flipped over the picture of Seattle's Space Needle to read the sprawling handwriting on the reverse. Large-size letters, big ego—that was Clay.

The memory of her heart breaking flooded her thoughts. The back of her eyes burned with tears, as if Clay's good-bye were happening all over again in the present moment. A little voice inside her head whispered, *You don't have to read it now.* She tossed the mail onto the seat and drove forward, wheels crunching on the gravel. After rolling to a stop, Abby got out and let Sugar race to gulp from her water bowl just inside the gate. She followed Sugar through the gate to the patio table facing the back of the property and the acre behind. Tossing the mail onto the patio table, she sank into a chair. Sugar barked and pawed at the door.

"No, sweetie. We're not going inside just yet. Get down now. Down. Let me rest here for a few minutes."

Sugar was relentless with the barking and pawing, so Abby walked to the aluminum garbage can at the corner of the patio, removed the lid and a rawhide bone, and tossed the bone across the yard. With Sugar chasing after it, Abby tried once more to relax, sinking into the chair.

The breeze stirred the hollow copper rods of a wind chime that had been harmonically tuned to play an ecclesiastical-sounding melody. Clasping her hands behind her head, she leaned back, closed her eyes, and drank in the sounds of the farmette's healing presences. Contented chickens clucked as they scratched in the dirt. A blue jay screeched as it flitted from the firethorn bush to the olive tree. Squirrels chattered their *kuk-kuk-kuk* as they scampered along the roof. Sugar whined, apparently wanting Abby to get up and play. After such a harrowing day, here, at last, was bliss.

Abby's thoughts drifted, but soon something she had seen moments ago began to trouble her. Then a realization took hold. The vertical blinds at the sliding glass door were closed. She had left them pushed back when she and Sugar had departed for the feed store. But she remembered locking the door. Suddenly, alarm bells sounded. Eyes flew open. Panic ensued. To close those blinds, someone had to have gone inside. Maybe was still in there.

Adrenaline pumping, she sucked in a deep breath and let it go. Abby rose slowly and crept to the fence, where she'd left a steel flat-headed tamper used to flatten the earth when patching the lawn.

With the tamper raised in an assault position, she reached for the patio door handle, quietly pushed the door along the track, and stepped through the long blinds.

In the middle of the kitchen stood a hot pink six-drawer tool cabinet on locked wheels. A drill in a matching shade of pink and its charger rested on top of the open toolbox atop the cabinet. Frowning, Abby placed the flat-headed tamper on the floor next to the double ovens, took a step forward, and studied the toolbox. "What in the world? Who would . . . ?"

"Like it?" asked a familiar husky voice emerging from the bedroom hallway.

Abby looked up at her intruder, feeling her body shake against her will. "Darn it all, Clay! You're as crazy as ever. There's a law against breaking and entering. I could have killed you!" She knew deep down she would have let him in, had she been there, but it angered her that he was in her house without her permission.

She stared at him. Dressed in a white polo and jeans, he looked tan and fit, and taller somehow than his five feet, eleven inches, but he still exuded that rugged vitality and those good looks, which she'd always found irresistible. The smile had evaporated off his face, but as he strode into the kitchen, those dark eyes still beamed with excitement at seeing her.

Sugar came bounding in through the open door. In an unusually vocal defense of Abby, she sounded a high-pitched alarm. Now Abby understood why the dog had made such a ruckus before. Sugar had known someone had come onto the property and had entered the house.

"I see you got a new protector," Clay said, crouching and holding out his open palm for Sugar to smell.

The dog backed up and barked nonstop.

"I'm a friend, not a foe," Clay said in a tone that clearly conveyed a calm self-confidence. But Sugar was having none of his small talk.

"It's okay, Sugar Pie," Abby said. She wheeled the tool cabinet aside, and Clay stood up. In one swift movement, he reached out and tenderly touched the hair at Abby's temple, letting a finger pull forth a reddish-gold curl.

Abby froze.

He clasped a hand beneath her chin and tilted her face upward. "I've missed you, woman." He leaned in for a kiss, but a quick maneuver enabled Abby to avert it. She turned toward the slider.

"We can't do this, Clay," Abby said, unable to face him. "Over a year of not hearing from you." Her voice cracked. She busied her shaking hands with opening the blinds.

Sugar sniffed Clay's loafers, his socks, and pant legs before retreating backward a few steps. She gave another fierce *yip, yip, yip,* as if to say, "You don't get a pass yet, mister." After running past Clay to the bedroom, the dog quickly returned, then gave a final *yip* as she trotted outside.

Abby left the slider ajar but slid the screen door shut. She watched Sugar chase a butterfly to the back fence, where the ten-foot Sally Holmes spilled over in a perfusion of blooms. A memory came flooding back to Abby of her planting the rose from canes Clay had gotten from a neighbor after she first bought the farmette. She shook off the memory and wondered how Clay had managed to get himself and the tool cabinet to her place. Maybe by taxi, since his truck wasn't on the property? But the question remained, but how did he get in? The realization came suddenly. He must have used his old key. Abby mentally chastised herself for not changing the locks, but what was the point now? The more pressing question was, why had he come back?

"I always told you one day I'd have to go, Abby. I never lied about that. But, Abby . . . Abby, turn around. Look at me."

He stood near enough for Abby to smell the soft notes of his Armani cologne. Like it or not, her body had longed for his presence. His hand stroked her hair, pulled the elastic band from the ponytail, letting her curls tumble loose, and then taking hold of her shoulder, he spun her around to face him. With both of his hands on her shoulders, she had nowhere to run.

Galvanized by the intensity of his gaze, Abby struggled to quiet her heart—make it still and unfeeling.

"If I could ever promise anyone a lifetime, Abby, it would be you. You are like a root of one of your plants, deep and strong and stable."

Abby felt her cheeks color under his gaze and waited for the *but* . . . and the excuse that would surely follow.

"But my spirit is restless. It's a curse," he said. He released his grip on her shoulders and leaned back against the kitchen counter. "Abby, you awake each day with the certain knowledge that you are exactly where you belong. But for me it's the opposite. Four walls are thresholds I have to break through. I wish I could settle. Why do you think I choose work that takes me all over God's creation? I keep thinking I'll find that one place where I belong. Put down roots. But I don't. I can't. I guess I'm flawed that way."

Despite her best efforts at control, Abby's heart hammered. "But what you did, it . . . was unthinkable. We never talked about your leaving. I thought you were happy here. And I thought you'd at least write or call or stay in touch. At least that."

Rubbing a palm over his cleanly shaven cheek, he spoke in a tone tinged with emotion. "I'm here now."

The ache in her chest moved to her throat. Abby swallowed against the lump that had formed. She pushed back. "It's not that simple, Clay. We can't just pick up and carry on like nothing happened. Why did you even come back?"

His face took on a tortured look. He swallowed. "The truth?"

"Of course, the truth," she said, her tone rising. "Always the truth."

"It's pretty simple. I tried living without you. It turned out to be harder than I ever imagined. I hoped that you'd forgiven me, that maybe you'd give me another chance."

Abby felt a shudder pass through her. "Just like that? You didn't think to check with me before just showing up? Before breaking into my house?"

"I didn't break in. I used to live here, remember? And I could never part with the key. Call it fate or whatever, but my inability to give it back maybe suggests that deep down I wanted us to have another chance."

"And how do you know I haven't moved on, Clay? Found someone else who makes me happy?

You don't know, and yet you waltz in here like that could never happen."

His eyes registered hurt. "Is there someone else?"

Abby sighed. "That's not the point."

When he spoke next, his tone seemed tinged with regret and longing. "I kept thinking about the way we used to dance through this old house before we got the flooring in—from the front door right out the back and into the field. We danced under the moon and danced even when there was no moon. I thought a lot about our dreams of building that wine cave, planting wine grapes, laying a massive stone courtyard, and filling it with pots of lime trees. You know, like those trees that shade the gardens of that place you always talked about wanting to visit in France."

"The Midi," she said. "Where they filmed *Chocolat*."

A hint of a grin flashed across his face. "So they're still showing films like that at Cineflicks, are they? That place is probably the only theater in small-town America that still serves homemade treats at the concession stand."

It was a point of civic pride for Abby, but she said nothing, knowing that it was possible he was baiting her.

Clay's expression darkened. "Believe me, Abby, when I say that no matter what I did or where I went, I felt an aching. Couldn't get rid of it. I know this is probably hard for you to accept. I had a longing that kept turning my thoughts to you and this place." His eyes conveyed unmistakable sadness.

Her resolve weakened. "Oh, Lord, Clay. Why couldn't you have just let things be?" Frustrated, she reached past him for the bottle of Napa Valley cabernet she kept on the counter, pulled open a kitchen drawer, and handed him the opener and the bottle. She collected two wineglasses from a shelf and gave one to him. Holding the other glass for herself, she waited while he poured the garnet-colored liquid.

"Shall we drink to our reunion?" he asked. His eyes crinkled, as if he was smiling with renewed hope.

Abby felt momentarily baffled that his mood could switch so suddenly and now seem so buoyant under the circumstances. She considered her confused state. "How about we drink to clarity and trust? We'll need those for any salvage operation, if there's to be one."

She knew he understood that he might have ruined the relationship they had shared by his secrecy and the callous way he'd left. If they were to give love another go, it required a new paradigm.

Clay clinked his glass against hers. "Nice bouquet, lovely taste," he remarked. "Just like you."

Abby smiled in spite of herself and walked outside to check on Sugar. The dog bounded across the backyard, after a squirrel scampering on top of the fence, which Abby called the wildlife superhighway. The afternoon sun had disappeared behind the ancient towering pine. Its soft light, shining like a halo, splayed across the patch of green lawn, the raised beds of yellow and orange nasturtiums, and the bright green citrus trees interposed between the beds.

Sighing, Abby sat down in her grandmother's rocker and rhythmically rocked, staring at the fig, with its fruits beginning to swell. By late summer, they would become dark, aubergine globes, super-sweet, ready for the picking. She wondered if he would be gone by then.

Clay sank into a patio chair opposite her, long legs stretched out, wineglass balanced on his thigh.

"At first I could only dream that you'd come back," Abby said, tearing her gaze from the figs to look directly at Clay. "Back then, I was in a terrible state. Days and weeks passed with no word from you. Hope faded that you'd ever return. I threw myself into the farm-work. Lord knows, there was plenty of that." She sucked in a deep breath and exhaled.

Clay didn't flinch or break eye contact with her. He listened, jaw tensing and relaxing.

"The first winter was the hardest. Not a lot to do with the bees and the garden during the rainy season. But now it's a new spring. I'm back in my skin, feeling like my old self. And my heart . . . Well, I guess it's grown stronger."

Clay nodded. "I'm sorry I put you through all that."

"Yeah, me too," said Abby. "What we had, Clay, that was special. I've thought about what I might feel when you returned. Joy, certainly, but also a sense of dread."

"Dread?" His brow shot up in surprise; his expression darkened. He sipped his wine, swallowed, and leaned forward to place his hand on her knee. "Why dread, Abby?"

Her heart raced. Her breath quickened. There was nothing to lose by holding her feelings inside. "Because, Clay, I know what's coming."

Honey-Drizzled Grilled Figs

Ingredients:
Extra-virgin olive oil, for preparing the grill
⅓ cup plain goat cheese (or try herbed goat cheese as a variation)
8 ripe fresh figs (Brown Turkey figs work best)
8 slices prosciutto
⅓ cup raw honey (Henny Penny organic honey preferred)

Directions:
Prepare the grill by brushing the grill grates with extra-virgin olive oil.

Fit a pastry bag with a medium round tip, and fill the bag with the goat cheese. Puncture the bottom of each fig to permit the insertion of the pastry bag tip.

Insert the pastry bag tip in a fig and gently squeeze the bag, pushing about 2 teaspoons goat cheese into the center of the fig. Do not overstuff, as this will cause the fig to split. Arrange the stuffed fig on a plate and repeat this process until all the figs are stuffed.

Heat the grill to medium-hot. While the grill is heating, wrap a slice of prosciutto around each stuffed fig.

Grill the figs for 2 to 3 minutes, flipping them once. Remove the figs from the grill to a clean plate, drizzle them with honey, and serve at once.

Serves 4 (2 figs per person)

Chapter 5

The rooster may raise a ruckus, but it's
the hen that rules the roost.

—*Henny Penny Farmette Almanac*

Clay had flustered her, but Abby was deter-mined not to let that man confound her into losing the laser focus she needed to examine the place where canal patrol had found Fiona's body. Fiona Mary Ryan deserved better. Abby had asked Clay to stay in town until they'd sorted out their feelings. After much discussion, which hadn't ended until almost midnight, he'd agreed, but only if she promised to meet him for an early dinner the next day. He'd left her with the hot pink tool cabinet and a kiss before returning to Las Flores to book a room at the Lodge. Clay knew his way around town and her farmette. But she understood better than he that navigating the physical landscapes would prove far easier than the emotional terrain of her heart.

Abby pulled a hair clip from her blue-green work shirt pocket, and after flipping her head forward, she twisted her reddish-gold, shoulder-length mane out of her eyes. Bent over, hands on thighs clad in khaki-colored cargo shorts, she stared at the scorched earth littered with burnt wires and ash-covered shards of glass deposited by the towed car. Thank goodness she'd left Sugar at home, safely locked in the backyard, with plenty of water and food and access to the house. She hadn't planned to be long and wanted neither distractions nor the curious pooch pawing through the crime scene.

Fiona's body had been sitting upright behind the steering wheel, with her hands at her sides. Abby recalled that the seat hadn't appeared close enough to the pedals for Fiona's feet to touch them. Fiona was petite, about the same height as Abby's five feet, three inches. Someone taller must have driven Fiona's car to the site and erred by not returning the seat to the correct position for Fiona to drive. And if the killer had made that error, perhaps he or she had made others.

Abby stood and shielded her eyes to sweep the wilderness around her. Such a lovely, forlorn place—the type of place a hunter might enjoy, a bird-watcher would like, or lovers would meet for a private tryst. Her thoughts kept returning to the locals: they knew the terrain and the access roads. The killer might also be a woman in Fiona's orbit. Who stood taller than she had? Abby sighed in exasperation as she realized that almost everyone in town stood taller than Fiona had. Her thoughts went to the time line. Perhaps she would try persuading Kat to share the names of the people who saw Fiona in her last twenty-four hours.

As Abby thought about it, she realized she was

one of them. She'd last seen Fiona alive on Saturday, when she'd driven into Las Flores to drop off the ribbon-tied sample jars of honey that Fiona sold in her botanical shop. Besides delivering honey, Abby had reminded Fiona about their luncheon the next day. When Fiona had excused herself to prepare a bank deposit, Abby had drifted around the shop for a few minutes, looking at the sale items. She recalled looking up when the ribbon of bells had jangled as Premalatha Baxter, the commune manager, and Dak, the new guru's bodyguard, stepped through the large glass door. Premalatha had asked Fiona about some herbal smoking compound that was out of stock. It had seemed an innocuous request at the time, but the exchange was puzzling. The commune didn't allow smoking.

Noon approached. Under the heat of the midday sun, Abby continued walking a grid pattern, searching. The tall grass led her thoughts to weed control and herbicides. Fiona would never use anything toxic on her plants, but Abby knew mountain families might. They could be a stubborn lot—liked doing things their way. They didn't like being told about the dangers of misusing fungicides, herbicides, or pesticides, regardless of what modern science had revealed about human health risks. They also didn't much like having a commune in their midst. They had made no secret about that, either. The doc and others knew Fiona's past included time spent in the commune. The locals didn't mingle with the commune residents. What if the killer was a local, knew the mountains, knew Fiona, and had tampered with her garden or herb patch by using an herbicide?

Missing was a motive. Disliking someone because of where he or she used to live hardly qualified.

Meandering through stands of red-bark madrone, manzanita, and tan oak trees and finding little of interest, Abby was considering abandoning further searching when she noticed an old footpath overgrown with weeds that led up a slight incline. With dried leaves crunching under her hiking boots, she followed it. She soon realized that unless Fiona had been searching for trilliums, wild huckleberry, or poison oak, she wouldn't have found herbs here. The more Abby looked around, the more convinced she became that this was a place chosen by the killer to hide his crime and not one that Fiona would have visited by choice.

Peering into a growth of poison oak and California broom, Abby spotted a paper smaller than a business card caught at the base of some weeds. Peering intently at it, Abby soon realized it was a medicinal patch, like one that could deliver a dose of nicotine. It looked like it had been recently dropped or discarded. Abby covered her mouth with her hand, and she considered whether or not it might be evidence. Deciding to mark that site so she could find it later, Abby propped a stick against a bush near the patch.

After hurrying back to the Jeep, she retrieved her cell phone from the console, found Kat's contact stored in the phone, called, and waited. "It's me again, Kat," she said. "I'm at the Kilbride Lake site. Who's running the investigation into Fiona's death? The county sheriff or Las Flores Police?"

"We are. Naturally, our investigation is cooperating with the sheriff's office. Why?"

"I wanted to notify the correct authority," Abby

said. "I have a medicinal patch, like a smoker might wear."

"Really? Did you know Fiona to smoke?" Kat asked.

"No," Abby said. "But she told me once that Tom had tried to quit a few times."

"Did Fiona ever mention him using those patches?" Kat asked.

"No, but this patch might have relevance to the case. It's just a hunch."

"Yeah, well, let me get there and see for myself where you found it and what kind of shape it's in. Goes without saying . . . Don't touch it. Oh, and, Abby, be careful. We've issued a BOLO for Kramer. Our uniforms went to the area where the cabin is located, but he'd hightailed it out of there."

"I promise to keep looking over my shoulder until you get here," said Abby. "Let's hope your BOLO gets him found and into custody."

Abby knew that Kat would have to call county communications to get clearance to be dispatched to collect the evidence, and that this could take a minute or two. Time dragged. She took a picture of the evidence with her cell phone and waited some more. If Kat couldn't get away, Abby would send the photo by text or e-mail. But she didn't have to wait much longer. Eventually, Kat arrived. She wasn't alone in the cruiser. She'd brought with her Nettie Sherman, the Las Flores PD's only crime-scene technician. Abby had worked with Nettie, too, but hadn't seen her in a while. The last time was at police headquarters when Abby had been working a case, and Nettie had been hobbling around on crutches following knee surgery.

Now Nettie hopped out of the cruiser like a new cadet.

Abby smiled and walked over to the women. Nettie looked svelte, having shed some pounds from her five-foot-seven frame now that she could run again. She could almost pass as one of Kat's relatives, with her jade-green eyes and hair the color of pine nuts. She wore her longish bangs teased off her face today and sprayed in place.

"Hi, ladies," Abby called out. "Good to see you, Nettie. Knee all healed?"

"Just about." Nettie held a large manila-colored evidence envelope, its bottom flap already secured with red sealing tape printed with EVIDENCE, CITY OF LAS FLORES POLICE DEPARTMENT.

"So, Chief Bob Allen has reassigned you back to CSI now." Abby grinned broadly. She knew how Nettie had hated that temporary desk job. But after her knee injury, she had had to be reassigned somewhere.

"Yep. Finally. That so-called light-duty desk job he gave me until my leg healed turned out to be the longest six weeks of my life. He had me hobbling to that damn coffeepot and the records room all day long. I hate to say it, but there were times when I found him more noxious than the scent of skunk on my mailbox post. And he had the gall to suggest that now that I was working at a desk, I could assume some other tasks, like repositioning the speed-trap trailer to slow traffic along Main and doing some DUI checkpoints. If you ask me, his micromanaging is off the hook."

Abby laughed. "Oh, Nettie, I feel for you. Can't say I miss working for the chief. So am I right that you are now the community service liaison, the

CSI tech, and the property officer assisting Bernie down in the evidence room?"

Nettie shook her head, as if she couldn't believe it herself. "Complaining doesn't help," she said, adjusting the camera strap over her right shoulder. "Chief told me women multitask better than men. He said he meant it as a compliment, but we both know it was a lame excuse to give me more work."

"You just have to hang in there," Kat said with indifference. "He'll forget about you after a while, and it'll be someone else's turn to feel his wrath." Sniffing and gazing into the distant forest like a preservationist studying a stand of old-growth trees, Kat added, "It's what we all do."

Everyone fell silent. A beat passed.

Finally, Kat said to Abby, "Okay, eagle eyes. Let's get to it."

"This way." Abby walked toward her marking stick. Kat followed. Nettie brought up the rear.

After they'd covered a short distance, Kat said to Abby, "Thanks for that tip on Kramer. I'm curious to see what a search of his cabin turns up."

After handing Kat the evidence envelope, Nettie took camera shots of the patch at various angles and then realized she stood in a growth of poison oak. "Oh, my gosh. Is this what I think it is?" Her eyes widened in a fearful expression. "I'm allergic. Good Lord, it's everywhere. I know this is my job, but if I go into that area, I'll be out on sick leave, suffering for who knows how long."

Kat tucked the evidence envelope under her arm and stuck out her free hand to pull Nettie from the growth. "Come on out. I'll get it."

"I'm sorry," Nettie said, trudging a yard or two away.

"If I didn't trust your sixth sense, Abby, I'd be leaving this trash right where it lies."

Abby nodded. "We can only hope it has a fingerprint, some sweat for a DNA test, a strand of hair or fiber, something with a linkage to Fiona."

"But it wouldn't be the first time that trash found at a crime scene was just trash," said Nettie. "On the other hand, sometimes you think a thing isn't important, and it ends up breaking open the case."

Noticing Kat's short sleeves, Abby removed her work shirt and handed it to Kat. "Slip it on. It might be a tad short, but no need to expose your bare skin to the poison oak. If you brush against it and get some of the oil on you, I've got vinegar in my Jeep you can use to remove it. It's an old Girl Scout trick. I'm not immune, but I don't seem to get those itchy, weeping blisters. Apparently, Nettie does. Just avoid touching it."

Kat slipped her arms into the sleeves of the work shirt and then slid her fingers into the nitrile gloves she kept in a holder on her duty belt. Gingerly reaching into the poison oak, she retrieved the white patch and dropped it into the evidence envelope.

"I can't imagine any woman in her right mind traipsing around up here alone," Nettie said as the trio walked back to the cruiser.

"Who says she was alone?" Kat chewed her lower lip, as she did when she was trying to puzzle through something. "She might have arranged to meet someone."

"All we know is that somebody killed her," Abby said. "We don't know where, how, or who."

Kat said, "She had lots of friends, some, admittedly, rather strange."

"Yeah," said Nettie, slapping at the small flies lighting on her as she walked. "Like her current squeeze, Laurent Duplessis."

"They broke up a while ago," Abby said, correcting her.

"Whatever," said Nettie. "Strange coupling, if you ask me, but there's no rhyme or reason to why some people are attracted to each other."

"True," said Kat. "But you have to marvel that in the midst of building a botanical business, she still managed to have a social life." Kat opened the cruiser door and placed the evidence envelope inside the vehicle. She slammed the door and walked to the shade. There she sipped water from a bottle she'd retrieved from the car. Nettie got a bottle for herself and handed one to Abby.

Abby chafed at Kat's comment. The implication was that if Fiona could have a social life, why couldn't Abby? Kat was a study in contradictions—being a cop who tended to keep a low profile about her police work, she could also be a social butterfly. Abby wondered if Kat would ever understand why the farmette work offered a solitude that nurtured her, even if the work seemed never to end. Kat would probably never appreciate why Abby stuck with it when it generated so little money, and why Abby had so little time or energy to build social relationships or find romance. Only another person who loved living close to the earth, like a farmer or a rancher, could appreciate Abby's lifestyle. Not everyone needed or wanted the world's constant distractions and drama.

As the trio sipped in the shade, Nettie said, "Duplessis sings, as well as plays the drums. I heard him once, back when Zazi's tested out local musicians during the restaurant's early-bird dinners. Some were chosen to perform during evening meals, as well. I expected jazz, not Caribbean, with all that drumming." She rubbed her arm, as if already sensing the start of a poison-oak rash. "Lot of nervous energy. Oh, and he's a smoker. Saw him light up with the other musicians outside afterward. Just saying."

Abby shook her head. "According to Fiona, he liked smoking herbs through a hookah. Less harsh on his vocal cords. Apparently, among the young Haitians in North Miami, where Laurent grew up, the herb of choice is *Cannabis sativa*. From what Fiona said, he was always careful never to overdo, as he had a thing about alertness. Relaxed was okay, but losing control was not. And he was a controller."

"So he used marijuana. Did he also sell it?" Nettie asked.

"Possession with intent to sell is a felony under health and safety code one-one-three-five-nine," said Kat.

"Now I know this isn't my imagination. I feel itchy all over," Nettie said, running a finger around the neck of her uniform shirt.

Kat might have been looking at Nettie, but her thoughts were clearly somewhere else. "So, Abby," Kat finally asked, "are you trying to make some linkage here between Laurent's weed smoking, the nicotine patch, and Fiona's murder?"

"We're trained, are we not, to allow the evidence to lead us to a conclusion. Not sure yet," said Abby. "But if he smokes dope, you've got to wonder if he's got a criminal past. You know as well as I do that drugs and alcohol are often linked to violent crime."

"So true," Nettie said. "So maybe drugs played a role in her murder."

"And yet he's not the only person in Fiona's world who smokes." Abby dabbed the perspiration from the corners of her nose and her forehead with her shirttail.

"Yeah?" Kat's eyebrows shot up. "I'm listening."

"I heard Premalatha asking Fiona for a special blend of smoking herbs this past Saturday," Abby revealed.

"Oh." Kat's eyes grew wide. "And what time was that?"

"Two-ish."

"Did she walk in with anybody?"

"The guru's bodyguard Dakota, or Dak, as he calls himself, was with her," Abby said. "You know him. He's heavyset, with a stocky build. Tats all over. Never says anything, never smiles, and never looks you in the eye. But here's what's interesting. Why would Premalatha ask for smoking herbs when the commune doesn't permit smoking?"

Nettie stepped back and swatted at a cloud of gnats. "Maybe for the teacher, Baba. Unlimited power must be nice."

"So you think Baba sent his bodyguard and manager to buy herbs?" Kat asked.

"Maybe," replied Nettie. "And that's not a crime. But which herbs was Fiona blending for smokes?" asked Nettie, stepping back some more and waving away the gnats.

Abby said, "Skullcap, marshmallow, uva ursi . . . I think there might have been others. I never actually heard anyone ever asking for weed or cannabis. And I do not believe Fiona would get mixed up with anything like that. That would be so out of character."

Kat asked, "So Premalatha and Dak were asking Fiona for smoking herbs. Anything else you haven't shared?"

Abby thought for a moment. "Fiona said she was temporarily out of stock and offered to mix a version of the compound if they could wait a day. Premalatha didn't want to come back." Looking straight at Kat, Abby took a deep breath and asked, "What's Premalatha and Dak's alibi for the morning Fiona was murdered?"

Kat shot her a quick warning look but answered, "They vouched for each other."

Abby shook her head, inhaled deeply. "Well, that Premalatha is one cold fish, and I think there was no love lost between her and Fiona."

"Why do you say that?" Kat asked.

"On the way out of the store on Saturday, she paused at the door and asked Fiona, 'What did he ever see in you?' "

"He . . . ? Who was she referring to?" asked Nettie.

Abby shook her head. "Don't know."

Nettie mused, "But 'What did he ever see in you?' sounds like a jealous barb over a man."

Kat withdrew a notebook from her shirt pocket and flipped through the pages. "So, the men intersecting Fiona's life included Laurent, the ex-boyfriend, and Tom, the soon-to-be ex-husband. There's her brother, Jack, and her landlord, Dr. Danbury. The former teacher is out of the picture, but we still have Hayden Marks and Dak, the body-guard."

Abby looked out over the deep blue lake. "So if a man was the reason Fiona was killed, you'll have to find a linkage between the two women and the men they both knew. Just out of curiosity, what was Premalatha's alibi for the time Fiona died?" Abby asked.

"The guru vouches for Premalatha, and she alibis Dak," Kat replied.

Nettie chimed in. "They eat lunch together, but all the other stuff, like meditating, doing yoga, or reading, they do alone. But as commune manager, Premalatha always supervises the preparations of the guru's meals."

"They were all together in the dining hall at twelve thirty," Kat said, adding, "This business of meditating in your room leaves everyone essentially unaccounted for until those lunch preparations start. It's proving difficult to nail down the commune contingent, but we're working on it."

"And what about her husband, Tom Davidson Dodge?" Abby asked. "I'd be curious if he slept at Fiona's the night before her death."

"He did. He says he left her in bed at six forty-five Sunday morning for a job on the other side of the summit. The work involved renovation for a local winery. The thing is," Kat said, "that the winery has been closed for a few weeks. No one can vouch for him until around nine."

"So no other persons of interest, no promising leads?" Abby asked.

Kat sighed and shook her head. The chatter on Kat's radio had picked up. She frowned as she cocked her head toward the radio to zero in on dispatch's message. Looking intently at Abby, she said, "You must have spooked Timothy Kramer. He has evaded the BOLO, and now his cabin is on fire. Cal Fire's on the way, and Nettie and I have got to go."

Abby nodded, and her heart raced at the implications. Another fire perhaps deliberately set. Now, what exactly was Kramer trying to hide? Abby's thoughts ran rampant. There was no way to know for certain that he had set the fire. But if he had, why would he do that, unless he was attempting to cover up something? she mused as she watched Nettie and Kat get into the cruiser.

Kat started the engine and prepared to make a U-turn. She stopped for a moment, rolled down the window, called out, "No telling where Kramer is now, Abby. I can count on you, right? To go straight home?"

Smiling to reassure Kat, Abby replied, "That's a ten-four."

Twenty minutes later, Abby drove along Chestnut. She wheeled into the parking lot of Smooth Your Groove, where she bought a cup of green tea with blended mint and almond milk. Rather than nursing her tea in the smoothie shop, she opted to stroll four blocks down Chestnut to Main Street to take a look in the window of Fiona's shop. She had a lot to think about, and a walk would be just the thing to clear her head.

Passing Lidia Vittorio's jewelry store, Abby resisted the urge to check out the latest marcasite offerings. With no money to blow on earrings, she avoided looking at the window displays. Next, she strolled past Cineflicks and peeked at the latest consignment displays in the window of Twice Around Markdowns. Finally, standing in front of Ancient Wisdom Botanicals, she wondered how to gain access to Fiona's shop without breaking the law. But as she stood before the door with the CLOSED sign facing the street, she could see someone had turned on the interior lights.

After depositing her smoothie cup in the nearby trash receptacle and tightening her grip on the shoulder strap of her purse, Abby pushed against the door handle. To her surprise, the door creaked open. Tiny bells on a red ribbon announced her arrival. New Age instrumentals played softly in the background. Fiona had programmed the music to come on when she flipped on the shop lights.

Abby called out a greeting. "Hello. Anybody here?"

No answer.

Her senses went on high alert. She stepped across the welcome mat and ventured past a bamboo table display of soaps wrapped in paper and tied with twine. Well, this was odd. Who was in the store, and why weren't they answering her shout-out? Suddenly, Abby felt a little shiver. The soft lights and the soothing New Age music did little to calm her nerves. Inching forward, she eased past a large display of Ayate washcloths, loofahs, and aromatherapy massage oils. Instinctively, her right hand reached for a weapon on a duty belt she no longer wore. She heard a snap.

"Hello. Who's there?" Clearly, she was not alone. She quickly considered possible intruders. Fiona's husband, Tom, topped the list. Jack, Fiona's brother, surely had a key. What about Laurent? Fiona had said he'd come here whenever they fought. *Who else?*

She crept past a rounder of all-natural fabric clothing. She slipped past a bookcase tightly packed with new and used books on the culinary, medicinal, and apothecary uses of herbs. Rounding another glass display case, Abby saw bottles of essential oils, a selection of teas, and a basket of herbal smudge sticks tied with red cotton thread. She bumped the basket with her elbow and quickly righted the smudge sticks and the boxes of tea.

At the shop's rear on Lemon Lane, a dog sounded an alert, barking incessantly.

"Hello. Anybody back there?"

Abby stepped into the room at the rear of the shop that served as Fiona's office. File cabinet drawers stood open. Manila files and their contents lay strewn about on the black metal surface of the desk. Upon spotting the back door slightly ajar, Abby hurried over and yanked it wide open. She saw Laurent Duplessis dashing toward a green sedan with a dented front fender. He tossed a black briefcase across the driver's seat to the passenger side before jumping in and starting the engine. The car lurched forward, engine revving, tires squealing.

Abby raced into the cloud of exhaust. Wildly waving her hand in the air, she yelled, "Hey . . . stop. . . . Somebody stop him!"

She pulled up, breathless, retrieved the little spiral notebook she habitually kept in her shirt pocket, and jotted down the license plate number.

Turning back, she quickly returned to Ancient Wisdom Botanicals. As she stood in the middle of Fiona's office, staring at the mess, her imagination conjured a visual of what had just happened. Laurent Duplessis had been searching the small office, but for what? Had he found it?

The way Abby saw it, Laurent looked out for Laurent. With Fiona, he had had a free and easy lifestyle. He could wake up whenever he wanted. He could smoke dope as he liked, and he could hang out at the beach. He could party and play drums half the night and then waltz back into Fiona's cottage when he got hungry or needed sleep. What a deal. Maybe the best one Laurent had ever had. Most women would have kicked him out long before Fiona had. When she finally ended Laurent's free ride and broke things off between them, she still helped him find a place to live—the apartment above Twice Around Markdowns.

Walking to the front of the store, Abby took out her cell phone and tapped the number for the Las Flores PD. "Abigail Mackenzie here. I want to report a crime," she said. "Ancient Wisdom Botanicals on Main Street has just been burglarized."

Tips for Cleansing or Consecrating a Space with an Herbal Smudge Stick

The burning of herbs to release scented smoke in order to cleanse a space of negative energy or a negative presence or spirit, or to consecrate a garden or a

sacred space, is not a new practice. The ancient Greeks, the Egyptians, Romans, Babylonians, Hebrews, Tibetans, Chinese, and Native Americans all practiced smudging. You can easily make a smudge stick with herbs and flowers from your garden. You'll need the leaves of herbs and wildflowers (optional),
scissors, and cotton thread or string.

- Pick a bouquet of sage leaves and wildflowers. Trim the stems of the wildflowers so that they are three to four inches long.

- Use the thread or string to tie the flowers around the sage leaves.

- Lace the thread or string up and down the bouquet, tying it tightly.

- Hang the smudge stick to dry for several weeks before using it in a well-ventilated area.

Chapter 6

Honeybees have five eyes—compound
eyes on either side of the head and
three small ocelli on top—enabling
them to see ultraviolet light and detect
color.

—*Henny Penny Farmette Almanac*

Within minutes of Abby's call to the Las Flores
PD, two officers arrived on scene and secured Ancient Wisdom Botanicals.

"You are positive the man you saw was Laurent
Duplessis?" one uniformed officer asked.

"Yes," Abby answered.

"And he was definitely inside the shop?" the
other asked.

"Well, I can't say positively. I believe so," she
replied. "My friend Fiona never left drawers open
and file folders strewn all over the place. When I
spotted Duplessis, he was the only person I saw out
back, and was running like his tail feathers were
on fire."

Abby patiently answered every question put to

her until they got another call from dispatch. Watching the cops get into their cruiser, she considered briefly chatting up Laurent's landlady but just as quickly dismissed the notion. The cops would certainly do a knock and talk in their follow-up. If she preempted them, they'd surely see it as interference.

Standing in the sunshine on Main Street, Abby glanced up at the sign above the door of Ancient Wisdom Botanicals and wondered if someone new would buy the place. She couldn't imagine Fiona's brother hanging on to it. According to Fiona, he was more at home in rain forests and living amid primitive cultures than modern ones. Maybe that store space was jinxed. Previously, it was the site of the pastry chef's murder. With the chef's death, Las Flores had lost its innocence. Now, once again, a killer was on the loose in their lovely small town.

Abby felt hot. Her skin prickled. Was it the afternoon heat or a hormonal response to all the drama? *Whatever.* She slipped out of her long-sleeved shirt, exposing bare shoulders except for the straps of her turquoise tank top. She tied the shirt around the waistband of her jeans, pulled her thick hair into a more secure ponytail, and began walking back toward Lidia Vittorio's jewelry store, where Main intersected Chestnut. Maybe she'd get the Percy Sledge CD from the glove box and during the drive home listen to it to get into the mood for her date with Clay.

A smile slipped across her lips as she remembered how Clay had called her in the first weeks after she'd moved to the farmette. He'd dialed her on his way to buy lumber at the big-box DIY store. Wrist deep in the dirt where she had been harvesting garlic, Abby had shaken off the soil from her hands to take his call. He'd told her to tune in to the local radio station and then had hung up. Abandoning the bulbs on yellowed stalks, Abby had walked to the patio and turned on the radio in time to hear the refrain of "When a Man Loves a Woman." Even thinking about that moment brought a smile to her lips. It was the first time Clay had put words to his feelings for her, albeit through song lyrics belted out by another man. But that day her knees had gone weak as she listened.

As she approached the corner of Main and Chestnut, Abby felt a newfound sense of joy and hope bubbling through her being. How wonderful it would be if that old excitement she used to feel with him could be rekindled.

"Abby, wait up."

Turning, she saw Clay jaywalking across the street, dodging a car, to catch up with her. He wore a baby blue polo shirt, open at the neck, slim jeans, and loafers.

"Just thinking about you," she remarked with a smile. "What brings you to Main Street? Visiting old haunts? Renewing old friendships?"

Clay flashed a disarming smile. "And why not? I made a lot of friends here. I can't believe how many people missed me."

Her smile withered. *Does it always have to be about you?* "Look, I haven't forgotten our date tonight. You did say six o'clock, right?"

"Yeah, but seeing as how you are already here . . . got a minute? I've got something to show you."

Abby sighed. It was useless to protest once Clay set his mind on something. Best to just go along. She nodded. "I'm game."

He put his hand on her back at the waist and gently nudged her toward Lidia Vittorio's shop door. After pulling it open, he braced it with his foot while Abby walked through. In frosted diffusers with bamboo reeds on the countertops, the shop's signature scent of ginger and pear permeated the interior. Soft music and spotlighting that splayed off the highly polished surfaces created a welcoming ambiance for the handful of customers browsing the gem-studded offerings.

"My old eyes must be playing tricks on me," called out Lidia. "Abby, dear, it's been such a long while." Lidia wore a classic tailored black dress with a black lace Peter Pan collar. At the center of the collar, she'd pinned her favorite cameo. She wrapped her thin arms around Abby and hugged her tightly.

"What's kept you away, my dear?" Lidia asked, pulling back from the hug and holding Abby at arm's length to look at her. "Oh, to be young again . . . I dare say you don't need jewelry to enhance your beauty, like some do." Scooping threads of silvery hair away from her face, Lidia pinched the strands together and tucked them back into her coiled braid, held in place at the nape of her neck by hairpins. "Sorry you missed our big sale on marcasite on Valentine's Day." She smoothed her coif with her hands, blue veined, with tissue-thin skin, and nodded an acknowledgment to Clay.

At the mention of Valentine's Day, Abby flinched. "You couldn't feel any worse than I do about that, Lidia. I was elbow deep in bare-root season, and then in March I was spraying organic oil all over the fruit trees before they leafed out. And now that the weather has already turned warm, I'm expecting my bees to swarm."

"Well, dear, it sounds like you are working awfully hard." Lidia turned her attention to Clay. She smiled broadly, revealing the stains of habitual tea drinking on her uneven lower teeth. "Perhaps your friend Calhoun here could help you out." She smiled, as if she was conspiring with him in some grand scheme.

Abby looked at Clay. His face instantly wreathed in a boyish grin; his dark eyes gleamed due to his apparent happiness that Lidia had remembered at least part of his name.

"Oh, I'm itching to help her," Clay said.

Abby's brow arched upward.

Clay thumped the glass display and spoke in a voice tinged with excitement. "I've got plenty of ideas for fixing up the place," he said. "Starting with ripping out that master bath. From the looks of it, that bath was an afterthought to the old bunkhouse. I wouldn't be surprised if the back of the shower stall was breeding mold."

His remark seemed unduly critical, but Abby believed he meant to emphasize his vision for making the place pretty and more functional. She sighed. "What do you expect of a two-room farmhouse built in the late nineteen forties?"

Clay said, addressing Lidia, "What Abby needs is a bathroom with a marble floor, a couple of big view windows, and a spa tub with jets."

As much as Abby liked that idea, she wished Clay would use a little more restraint in his conversations with townspeople with whom she would have relationships long after he had taken off again. Lidia didn't need to know how dilapidated the farmhouse was. It would only give her reason to worry about Abby. Locals took a strong interest in the welfare of their own. That was just the way small towns were.

What was clearly apparent to Abby now was that the drill and the tool cabinet Clay had brought to the farmette had been part of his plan all along to ingratiate himself back into her life. So be it. If he insisted on building a new master bath, she'd be an idiot not to let him. And while he was at it, he could finish her kitchen, too. Then, immediately, Abby felt guilty for having such thoughts. The less emotional, more rational side of her mind took over. *Give him a break. Accept him for who he is. Or end it. But stop punishing him.*

"I saved it for Calhoun," Lidia said, winking at Clay and leading them to a glass display case. Lidia's bony fingers unlocked the case and pulled out a small box. She set it on the counter and opened it, exposing a pair of earrings. She picked up a hand mirror.

Abby's heart skipped. Her breath caught in her throat as she stared at the earrings. A chiming sounded as customers entered the shop, but nothing could draw Abby's attention from the gold earrings in the shape of honeybees before her. Each bee's eyes were small cabochons of aquamarine. Diamond chips formed the head. The thorax was embellished with citrines, while the embellishment for the wings and dark brown abdominal bands featured chocolate diamonds.

"Excuse me, will you?" Lidia said. "I'll just see what the other customer wants. Be right back, dear."

"Of course," said Abby, taking the hand mirror from Lidia. She held an earring against her left

ear. "Oh, my gosh," Abby remarked. "These are exquisite."

"The eyes there," Clay said, pointing to the bees,
"are roughly the same color as yours." He seemed
quite pleased with himself for noticing.

"Ha. I wish," Abby said. She peered at the shade
of blue green, but she secretly liked the red in the
citrine and its smoky-brown undertones, because
she could see them reflected in her hair where she
stood under one of the counter spotlights. "These
beauties do not go with my old shirt and faded
jeans." Abby lingered a moment longer in front of
the mirror, holding first one earring up to her ear
and then the other one to her opposite ear. Finally, she sighed. "I've never seen such lovely earrings."

"Let me buy them for you," Clay said.

A beat passed. Abby thought for a millisecond.
They were over-the-top beautiful, but with a
thousand-dollar price tag, they were also expensive. And where would she ever wear them? He
would spend his money, and the earrings would sit
in her jewelry box. "How sweet of you to offer,
Clay. I don't know what to say, except, well, I really
couldn't accept them. They're lovely but too pricey."

Abby placed the earrings back in the open box
and then reached for his hand and wrapped her
palm around it. Looking into his wide-set dark
brown eyes, she said softly, "You don't have to buy
me presents. People should be able to find their
way back. . . ." The words trailed off into a sigh.
"How can I say it?"

*I don't want to hurt you, but why rush us into begin-
ning again?* she thought.

"Time . . . I just need time, Clay. That's all I ask."

She squeezed his hand and found it eager, warm, and willing to hold hers. She searched his expression for signs he understood her confusion.

Although he nodded in acquiescence, his expression seemed to have darkened. He pulled his hand away and busied both hands with rearranging the earrings in the box. With resignation written all over his expression, Clay finally closed the lid.

Abby turned to see where Lidia had gone. And when had Tom Davidson Dodge entered the store? Abby watched Tom, thin-boned in a T-shirt and jeans, with a navy watch cap hiding a head of curls, take several items from his brightly striped Peruvian bag. He set them on the counter's glass surface. Lidia emerged from the back room with a vial of liquid and a scale in her hands. She faced Tom on the opposite side of the counter.

Tapping Clay on the arm, Abby placed a finger against her lips and cocked her head in Lidia and Tom's direction.

Tom held up a braided gold chain with a Celtic cross dangling from it.

Abby sucked in a deep breath. *Oh, my gosh. You can't be pawning Fiona's favorite necklace. If that isn't coldhearted, what is?*

Tom placed the necklace on the counter and reached into the bag again. He plunked a wedding ring set next to the necklace. Then he reached into the bag again and pulled out a silver cuff bracelet embedded with semiprecious stones. Abby watched Tom look for a reaction from Lidia.

"They belonged to my late wife," Tom said in a soft tone. "Heirlooms they were, she told me. The rings have to be worth a small fortune. She said they once belonged to her great-grandmother from County Kerry."

"Well, yes, that would make them estate pieces, wouldn't it?" Lidia smiled politely. "The necklace has a solid resale value. However, gold is not worth what it was a while back. How much do you want for everything?"

"I was thinking ten grand," Tom replied.

"Oh, dear, that would not be possible. Even if they were worth that—and I don't believe they are—I'd have to pass." Lidia laid aside the loupe she'd picked up, and stared frankly at him. "You do understand that I have to resell these items for a profit."

"Yeah. So then what could you give me?" Tom asked.

"Well, let me see." Lidia stroked her lower lip with a forefinger. "Gold is going for slightly more than a thousand per ounce, but a lot depends on the purity and the weight of your pieces, of course." She reached under the counter and pulled forth a scale, then set the rings on it and noted the weight. Then she pulled a vial of liquid from under the counter and placed a drop on the rings. She repeated the process for the gold necklace before returning the scale and the small vial to the shelf beneath the counter. Lidia picked up the loupe and used it to study the Celtic cross. "The craftsmanship is superb. Would you take six hundred for this?"

Tom seemed antsy, shifting his weight from side to side. "I guess so. What about the other stuff?"

Abby looked at Clay, shook her head slowly, and raised her hand, palm to the floor, to indicate that they should stand down and stay quiet.

Fiona had confided in Abby that the Celtic cross necklace was worth close to two grand. Lidia was driving a hard bargain. The fact that Tom would accept less than half of what the object was worth perplexed Abby. Did he not know the value, or was he just desperate for money? What alarmed Abby more was why Tom was hawking the jewelry in the first place. It was behavior that was unbecoming, to say the least, and highly suspicious, since those valuable pieces had belonged to his dead wife. That raised a whole bevy of questions about who would profit most from her death. Was he Fiona's designated heir? Who had her will?

Abby motioned for Clay to follow her. They left the bee earring box on the counter and quietly walked out of the jewelry shop into the sunlight. From down the street wafted the scent of red beans, rice, roasted jalapeños, and grilled sausages, reminding Abby that she had long ago digested the peanut butter toast she'd had for lunch. She disregarded her hunger and hastened toward the traffic light.

"Abby, hold up. Zazi's is open," said Clay, his voice tinged with hopefulness. "What say we grab a table and you tell me what's going on?"

"Later, later." Abby kept up her brisk walking pace. The traffic signal flashed the white pedestrian walk light and sounded the familiar *ding-dong, ding-dong, ding-dong*. Abby raced across the intersection. She gestured to Clay to catch up. After dashing inside the Dillingham Dairy building, the first floor of which was taken up by police headquarters, she headed straight for the window where a male police officer staffed a desk behind bulletproof glass.

"You might want to let the homicide team know that the husband of Fiona Ryan is pawning her jewelry at Village Rings & Things across the street!" Abby exclaimed, sucking in a deep breath. "It's just a hunch, but he could walk out of there with enough moola for a flight to Timbuktu. Just so you know."

Tips for Inspecting a Honeybee Hive

Make routine hive inspections. Conduct inspections every ten days. Changes in the apiary can happen quickly. When inspecting a hive, approach it from the rear or the side and do the following:

- Check for dead bees at the front of the hive. This is normally not a grave concern; however, a large pile of dead bees could indicate a recent pesticide poisoning.

- Look for spotting in the area at the front of the hive and also on the hive boxes. Spotting is an indication of illness in the colony.

- Ensure that the hive entrance is open to permit easy access for the bees during the honey flow, when pollen-laden bees fly fast toward the hive.

- Lift the hive up to assess its weight; a heavy hive indicates a hefty honey store.

- Check for overcrowding and, if necessary, add a second story to the hive to accommodate the increasing population, or the bees will swarm.

- Reduce the hive entrance to a small opening if you suspect that predators or bees from other hives are robbing the hive. This is often indicated by bees darting back and forth or fighting in front of the hive.

- Observe worker bees pushing out dead bees to clean the hive. This is normal.

Chapter 7

Thyme spices up vanilla cake. Lavender
glorifies pudding. Basil intensifies butter, and rosemary elevates potato. But
what herb knits a broken heart?

—*Henny Penny Farmette Almanac*

With Clay's hand on her elbow, Abby walked
out of the Las Flores Police Department and
reentered the late afternoon light filtered through
the crepe myrtle trees along Main Street. Friday afternoon pedestrian and street traffic had gotten
worse now that the days were growing longer and
the weather had turned warm. Summer hadn't officially arrived yet and wouldn't for a few weeks,
but people in the outlying valley towns had already
begun their summer caravans through Las Flores
and the mountains to the beach communities. Every
weekend, the traffic would back up for miles.

"How do you know the jewelry that guy was
pawning belonged to his dead wife? Did he kill
her?" Clay asked, releasing Abby's elbow to take
her hand. They strolled toward the crosswalk.

"What say you bring me up to speed while we eat?" he said. "I'm starving."

Abby pulled Clay to an abrupt stop. "Could you give me forty-five minutes? I'd like to run home, shower, and change first." She cocked her head slightly to one side. "It's been one thing after another, and I've been out in the heat all day. I'd like to clean up, slip into something a little more feminine."

He leaned down and kissed her neck. "Not necessary." He was smiling, but Abby could tell he didn't want her to go. "You look fine, and we're already here." He glanced at her sideways and thumped the pedestrian walk button on its metal pole with the side of his hand. "And regardless, Zazi's has a restroom. Can't you freshen up there?"

Abby flinched. He'd missed the point. She wanted to hear their song on the drive home. She wanted to wash and primp and feel pretty again. She wanted a sentimental and sexy reunion. It had been so long.

"Jeez, Clay, we weren't even supposed to meet for another hour." Abby flashed her sweetest smile. Noticing his jaw tensing, as if he was holding back his growing frustration with her, Abby let her smile fade. She tried another approach. "I have an idea," she said. "While I pretty myself up, you grab a stool at the bar at the Black Witch and have a glass of that Kentucky bourbon you like so much. I'm sure the boys around the dartboard will want to hear all about your travels."

"Probably," Clay said. "But I thought you would."

Ouch. His remark stung, but Abby wasn't about to let him see her react.

After a moment of tense silence, he said, "If it's

so important to look good while you eat, Abby, then, by all means, go on home. Don't worry about me. I can find some way to cool my heels." His eyes darkened. Abby recognized his shifting mood.

She stared at the concrete. The pedestrian walk light began flashing, accompanied by the *ding-dong* repeatedly sounding, but neither she nor Clay moved.

He let go a long, audible exhale. He stared at the tall building across the street. His lips tightened into a severe line, and then, after a beat, he said, "Go on home, Abby. I'll see if Zazi's can rustle up something to tide me over until you get back. I'm too eager, I guess. I just want to spend some time with you."

She knew this maneuver. He would tell her to do whatever she wanted, but if he didn't also want it, he would make her pay for her choice by closing down emotionally. She hated his silent treatment. It was the classic passive-aggressive ploy. Abby shifted her gaze toward the theater marquee. A little foreign film from Hong Kong, *In the Mood for Love*, was playing for another week. Maybe she would see it. Maybe they would see it together. Or not.

A struggle had begun between her heart and her mind. Clay had come back. He'd said he couldn't live without her. Maybe she was creating an unnecessary problem. Surely she could set aside her desire to be romanced and just muster more generosity of spirit. But then again, if she gave in, wouldn't they just revert to their old way of being together? Nothing would change. That wasn't what she wanted for her life. If they were going to have a real chance of starting over and building a relationship that would thrive, this moment might be pivotal. Her thoughts raced as she remembered something Fiona had said about how two people could believe they loved and needed each other, but that didn't necessarily mean that they should be together or that they would even find enduring happiness. Sometimes coming together was just to finish off karma. Fiona had pointed to her own failed relationship with her husband, Tom, as an example. An icy finger of fear suddenly twisted around Abby's heart.

"On second thought," said Abby, "just forget about me getting all gussied up. We'll just grab a seat at the picture window at Zazi's, have a glass of old-vine zinfandel, dine on the bistro special, and watch the sun set on the mountains. Just like back in the day." She'd gone an emotional distance with Clay. Her heart was stronger now. She could choose to appease him, but on her terms. She'd let him buy her dinner. But that was all.

Clay locked eyes with her. The tension in his face relaxed as a smile played at the corners of his mouth. "That's my girl. I don't like the idea of a killer on the loose and you out there on the edge of town by yourself. Guess I've come back just in time."

Oh, really? You have no idea how silly that sounds, do you? "My neighbors are great," Abby said, thinking of Lucas, who lived up the hill from her farmette. "And I've got Sugar and my gun."

"So you don't need me?" Clay said, as if she'd just rejected him.

"I didn't say that."

"You didn't have to."

Abby released his hand as they stepped into the crosswalk. She pulled the strap of her purse tighter against her shoulder as a sudden hot gust of wind kicked up. The trees planted along the sidewalk bent and swayed, strong yet pliant. *We need to be like those trees, Clay, able to withstand whatever comes at us and still grow. I'll have dinner with you, listen to your stories, and smile at your jokes. But when it's time to go home, I'm going home alone.*

Inside Zazi's, Abby settled into the four-poster chair Clay had pulled out for her. She gazed out the bistro's front window and decided to file their tension-filled exchange under "knee-jerk reactions" and let it go. The window afforded a view of Main Street and beyond to the south, where the blue-green mountains towered behind the red barrel-tiled roof of the centuries-old grain mill. The wealthiest Las Flores families chose the mountains' southern slopes to build their mansions, up high, where the view overlooked the downtown. They hid their estates—some with vineyards—behind tall stone walls with gates. But the downtown merchants had a daily reminder that the mountains hid the nouveau riche. During certain times of the day, the sun would strike the glass windows on those lofty ridges, transforming the mountainsides into a mosaic of shimmering light, just as it did now under Abby's pensive gaze.

Clay ordered a bottle of zinfandel, touted on the wine list as having been produced from locally grown grapes on vines planted around 1910. The dutiful, dark-haired, white-aproned waitress who had encouraged Clay's choice scurried away, then returned a moment later with the bottle and two glasses. She coupled the task of opening the bottle with a soliloquy on the importance of having the correct wineglass, because of how it directed the flow of the liquid so that it hit certain parts of the palate. In different ways, this enhanced an appreciation for the wine's aroma and flavor. But opening the bottle proved impossible when the corkscrew malfunctioned. Clay offered to have a look; it seemed as good a moment as any for Abby to freshen up. She excused herself and left for the powder room.

Abby splashed cool water on her cheeks and washed and dried her hands. After pulling a comb from her purse, she freed her reddish-gold locks from the elastic band and coaxed them into thick waves that graced her bare shoulders. She untied her pale green work shirt from around her waist, slipped her arms back into it, and fastened it, leaving the top button undone, so a sliver of her turquoise tank top peeked out. Clay would like that, although he surely would prefer that she left the shirt off. She tucked her shirt into her jeans; this showed off her figure, kept trim and muscular by all the farmette work. Even if it didn't matter to Clay, it mattered to her that she did not look as though she'd just finished cleaning the chicken house before taking a seat in Main Street's best restaurant. Just as Abby unfastened her belt buckle and unzipped her jeans to tuck in her shirttail, two ladies entered the powder room, in the middle of a conversation.

"Edna Mae should know. She's lived here all her life. If she says that the community up there has become a cult and the town would be better off without them, then there's got to be something dark going on up there. Edna Mae has never known a stranger. And there's not a bigoted bone in her body," said the woman with hazel eyes and short gray hair. The wrinkled lobes of her pierced ears supported shiny gold hoop earrings. She held open the powder room door for her companion, a tall, freckle-faced woman with glasses and wearing a cream-colored shirt over brown leggings.

"So why is there a commune up there?" the freckle-faced woman asked. She flashed a fleeting smile of acknowledgment at Abby before disappearing behind the toilet door adjacent to her friend's stall. "I thought it used to be a convent."

Abby had zipped her jeans and buckled her belt and was reaching for her purse to leave when she heard the woman with the hoop earrings, now in the first stall, answer, "The nuns sold it to a builder who defaulted. A real estate developer grabbed it, the one that Zora Richardson married, I think." The woman lowered her voice. "Rumor has it that he's in cahoots with the commune's new leader. That murdered Ryan woman and her husband, I heard, were mixed up somehow with that commune, too. That new leader has attracted the riff-raff that are coming into town. Don't know much else about the dead woman except that she had a husband *and* a boyfriend."

Abby's antennae went on high alert. While straining to hear the rest of the conversation, she rummaged for makeup in her purse.

"So who killed her?" asked the freckle-faced woman.

"I heard the husband did it."

Abby stared in the mirror at the reflection of the woman's spiky gray hair as it appeared and disappeared at the door's upper edge, looking like a rat bobbing along the top.

After unlatching the door, the woman stepped out and continued her conversation with her friend. "You and I can fly back to Milwaukee, but Edna Mae will never leave Las Flores." The woman looked at Abby with a forced smile and proceeded to wash her hands. "I just hope for her sake they make an arrest soon."

Abby returned the woman's smile. "The murder of Fiona Ryan is just awful, isn't it?" said Abby, jumping into their conversation. "Our police are a good lot, though. They'll find the killer," she said with confidence. She searched for items in her purse until she located red-tinted lip gloss. Using the lip brush, she swept a wide stroke across her bottom lip. "I couldn't help overhearing you mention Edna Mae, the owner of the antique store. Are you related?"

"I'm her cousin twice removed on her mama's side," the freckle-faced woman replied.

"Nice lady, that Edna Mae," Abby replied. She pulled a paper towel from the dispenser and dabbed at the corners of her mouth.

"Spirit as pure as bleached linen, and she's got the lowdown on those commune folks," Freckle Face said as she exited her stall and waited her turn at the sink. "Dark and unrighteous acts going on up there."

"That so?" Abby twisted the lid back on the gloss and dropped it into her purse. "Like what?" Abby tried to sound shocked.

Freckle Face heaved a long sigh. "What's that they say about idle hands doing the Devil's work?

That dead girl romancing two men? Could be that they're all into polygamy."

Abby winced. Her friend Fiona had been free as a feather, but polygamy? *No way. Absolutely not.* But before Abby could utter a word in Fiona's defense, the gray-haired woman corrected her friend.

"Polygamists are people with multiple spouses. The dead girl had only one husband . . . and they were separated." The gray-haired woman stepped to one side and pulled a paper towel from the dispenser. Wiping water from her hands, she spoke in a matter-of-fact tone. "Is there anyone in town who doesn't believe those people live out on the fringe?"

"What do you mean?" Abby asked.

"A cult of Satan," the freckle-faced woman stated decidedly. "Arcane arts."

"Arcane arts?" Abby asked, wondering if the woman was referring to telling fortunes, scrying, or conducting séances. "What exactly do you mean?" Abby hoped to find out what the women thought they knew about the inner workings of the commune.

Freckle Face chimed in. "They do séances to contact dead spirits. I heard that leader up there reads the Good Book differently than other men of the cloth."

The gray-haired woman pushed her fingers through her locks and said, "You hear talk around town. He's got a thing about the number eight, justifies some of his actions with Old Testament verses about the eight wives of King David. Maybe he thinks he's king, too, and requires eight women to dote on him."

"Oh, my goodness!" exclaimed Abby. "How narcissistic!"

Apparently encouraged by Abby's interest, Freckle Face added in a hushed tone, "Eight women sleep on the floor of his room every night. They call it energy balancing. The chosen ones wear a necklace—a black knotted cord with a figure eight symbol."

Abby shook her head, as if in complete disbelief. "You don't think someone in that commune might have had a reason to hurt that woman who is dead now, do you?"

The two women looked at each other.

The freckle-faced woman flicked water from her hands and spoke up. "Well, you've got to wonder what happens when a woman like that falls out of favor with the so-called prophet."

"Or if she incurs the jealousy of the other women," the gray-haired lady remarked thoughtfully. She quickly reapplied her lipstick and looked at Abby. "Several of those commune people work down at Smooth Your Groove. I'd be careful about eating anything there. Who knows what they're putting in those smoothies."

"Thank you. I will," Abby said, lifting her curly hair with the front of her hand and flicking it from her bodice over her shoulder. She plucked the reddish-gold strand clinging to her shirt and let it drop to the floor.

"Yes," chimed in Freckle Face. "You can't be too careful."

The gray-haired woman adjusted her scarf, tucked her purse strap over her shoulder, and waited for her friend. "We're here for a mini reunion," she said. "Edna Mae and the two of us went to nursing school together, but that was aeons ago."

"Really?" said Abby. "That's so nice."

"Edna Mae's retired now. That antique store is her second career."

"Lovely how you've remained friends for such a long time," said Abby, rolling the cuffs up on her shirt. She glanced at her watch. "Ooh, and speaking of time and friends, I've got to get back to my date, or he'll come looking for me." Abby opened the powder-room door and glanced back at the two women preening in the mirror. Their conversation had shifted from murder and the commune to the Amish quilts Edna Mae now carried in her shop.

On the return trip to her table, Abby thought about the "cheap trinket on a cord" remark and the symbolism of the number eight. What might seem like the mindless prattle of outsiders could have relevance. She made a mental note to look into it.

Clay whistled softly. "You had me worried, woman. I was beginning to think you'd slipped out the back door and left me for good." His dark eyes danced. "I would have come after you. We've got plans."

Abby arched a brow. "Oh, do we?" She plucked the white napkin from under her fork, shook the fabric loose, and laid it across her lap. Clay poured the wine and intercepted Abby's hand as she reached for her glass. He drew her fingers to his lips, kissed each with tenderness, as though reacquainting himself with the feel of her flesh.

"To a fresh start with the only woman I have ever truly loved. The one who has claimed my heart and soul. To you, Abby, my main squeeze."

Shouldn't that be "my only squeeze"? Her thought

remained unspoken as she lifted her glass and touched it to his. He probably hadn't even recognized his faux pas.

Clay took the lead in filling in the blanks of his life from their year apart. He had always enjoyed talking about himself, and this time was no exception. As Abby listened, she realized as perhaps never before how thickly Clay could lay on the Kentucky charm. He was as smooth as the old-vine zinfandel they were drinking. Eventually, he got around to a topic besides himself—the farmette—and inquired about her renovation projects for the summer.

Abby told him of her desire to rip out the aging shower-tub combo in the master bath. "There's mold growing behind that cheap vinyl enclosure. I just know it," she said. She sipped the red liquid, relaxing into the warm, contented mood it evoked.

"And I've got a plan to fix that," he said, with a grin that bared nearly all his pearly whites.

"Well, I like the plan you conjured up while we were inside Lidia Vittorio's jewelry store," Abby said. "I can't afford a marble floor or a fancy jetted tub, although I'd love them."

"We'll see," said Clay. "There are several architectural salvage yards in the county and at least three stone suppliers who fill their Dumpsters daily with castoffs from custom cuts. With permission, we might be able to find enough similar pieces of marble to lay a small floor."

Abby looked at him in surprise. "Do you know anything about cutting marble?" she asked. "It's stone. Thick stone. A slab of a mountain."

Clay smiled like a Cheshire cat. He devoured an appetizer-sized serving of bruschetta, mozzarella melted over chunks of heirloom tomatoes and fresh basil on a toasted crostini that had been generously brushed with olive oil. Wiping the corners of his mouth with his napkin, he leaned forward to gaze at her with smoldering intensity. In a tone of supreme confidence, Clay said, "All you need is the right tool for the job . . . and the knowledge of how to use that tool. And, thank the Lord, I've got both."

Abby's cheeks flamed at the double meaning. Her pulse quickened. "Oh, I'm sure you have. But if mold," she said, in a not too obvious shift in the conversation, "is in the drywall, that section will have to be removed." She guided her finger around the rim of her wineglass. *Sip the wine more slowly.* It wouldn't do to lose her objectivity, and he seemed intent on weakening all her defenses. "Is it so simple?"

"Oh, it is. Trust me," he replied.

Trust. Not so easy. Abby sank deeper into her chair, only faintly aware that she drew comfort from the solid support of the oak planks.

Leaning in, he put his hand over hers. "A tub for two is on my wish list."

"Flooring and kitchen shelves are on mine," Abby muttered hastily. "There is almost no storage space, and I'm tired of that plywood subfloor in the living area. It looks okay covered with an area rug, but how much nicer the space will be with warm hardwood floors. But that will be a big project." She didn't want to sound too depressing. But when everyone else talked renovation, they were dreaming of new doors, windows, crown molding, and countertops, but she wanted finished walls and floors.

"Everywhere you look, Clay, there's a project," Abby said. "Once upon a time, I was working from a master plan for the farmette. Now I tackle what needs fixing before the next rainy season sets in . . . and pray that the tap on the money trickle doesn't dry up. I've got honey, eggs, produce, and herbs to sell, but the real money comes from my part-time investigative work for the DA. And at present, there isn't any."

Clay leaned back in his chair, nodding, reassuring her that things would change now that he was back. "I'm home now, Abby."

The wine had lowered her emotional barriers. She leaned toward Clay, as if to share a secret. "You know," she said after polishing off the last sip in her glass, "I dream of buying that acre of land at the back of my property. The heirs who own it are lovely people, and right now they don't want to sell. But maybe they'll have a change of heart someday if I come up with the right amount of cash. Who knows?" Abby leaned back in her chair. "With the additional acre, I could get goats, make cheese to sell, and still have enough room to increase my hives and the number of chickens— which means more honey and eggs. If I could fix up that old house back there, I could rent the farmette house for yet another income stream." Suddenly, Abby's face flushed with warmth. With a sheepish grin, she quickly added, "A pipe dream, I know."

Clay rubbed his chin. "How much do you think you'd need?"

"Well, that's just it. It's not on the market."

He pointed to his watch. "We could always auction off this baby."

She knew how difficult it would be for him to part with the designer watch. He'd set the watch as a reward for achieving his dream of making a six-figure income. And he'd done that on his last job.

"A down payment, maybe," Abby said with a sigh. "But you know as well as I do, California land is like gold. That acre behind the farmette won't come cheap." She lifted her glass and waited for Clay to refill it. After taking a sip, Abby held the wine on the back of her tongue and then swallowed. She felt warm and inexplicably happy, reveling in the anticipation of good things to come. Maybe this was Clay's greatest gift to her—inspiring ideas, imparting hope, sending her spirits soaring with the belief that anything she truly wanted was possible if her belief, desire, and will to manifest it were strong enough.

Clay gazed at her with an expression that Abby interpreted as both soulful and contented.

She studied his youthful, tanned face, the faint frown lines threading across his forehead and around his eyes. He certainly didn't look forty-two. He exuded vitality from his rock-hard body. Abby doubted that any woman could remain immune to Clay's charm and intensity. And until she sensed a wind of change blowing again toward their relationship, she would enjoy the buoyancy of spirit his presence brought her. At that moment, Abby realized she would give him a second chance.

They agreed upon a dessert course of fresh ewe's cheese and honey, along with an espresso with a lemon twist for Abby, while Clay enjoyed most of the second bottle of zin. Abby offered to drive him back to the Las Flores Lodge.

With his arm draped over her shoulder, she

helped him as he stumbled to the door of his room. Clay leaned against the door frame and faced her. He pulled her close, as if with an awareness of cloth and skin separating their beating hearts, and he wanted more. He tugged on the elastic band holding Abby's hair and freed the mass of waves and curls, which came cascading down upon her shoulders.

"God, you're beautiful," he whispered. Leaning in, he grazed her mouth with his, caressed her lips in a series of tender, sweet kisses, murmuring how much he loved her between each. Then, in the next moment, he smothered her mouth with a commanding mastery. Finally pulling back, he smiled, as if with secret knowledge of the depths of her soul.

Even Abby felt surprised at her eager response to his sensual hunger. The emotion of the moment had rendered her pliant, even weak. She'd longed for that kiss, and yet now that it had come, it confused her. She didn't want to feel weak with Clay. Why did he still have the power to seduce her?

Suddenly, he reached for the doorknob. "Babe, the hallway is spinning," he said, slightly slurring his words.

"Uh-oh," said Abby, hesitant to point out the obvious. *You've had too much to drink.* She heaved a sigh. "Give me the key. Let's get you inside."

She waited while he fished inside his pants pocket and finally produced the key. After unlocking the door, she helped him to the bed, where he sprawled out. Abby tugged off his shoes and fetched him a glass of water. She'd heard somewhere that booze dehydrated the body and the brain. A glass of water for every glass of wine could help avert that morning-after headache. When she returned with the water, Clay lay quietly snoring. Abby kissed him on the forehead, set the glass of water and his key on the nightstand, and locked the door before pulling it shut behind her.

She decided to use the shortcut through town to the farmette. The road twisted back through a piece of the mountain and eventually dropped down onto Farm Hill Road. She'd be at her door long before midnight.

From Las Flores Boulevard, she turned onto Main Street and stopped at a red light. Enjoying the fresh night air wafting in through her open windows, Abby heard a familiar laugh and looked in the direction of the ice cream parlor. There she saw Kat giggling like a schoolgirl as she wiped drips off the bodice of her sundress and quickly licked a double-layer cone. Had the police made an arrest? Or did they have someone in their sights? Why else would Kat be out for ice cream when the cops were expected to work the case doggedly until it was solved? Abby had even thought that they might have to cancel their date for the upcoming estate sale. Then, seeing Lucas, Abby's heart lurched.

After strolling out of the ice cream parlor with a handful of napkins, Lucas Crawford smiled as he handed the napkins to Kat. Abby's stomach tightened. Lucas—that gorgeous man of few words, with soulful eyes the color of creek water—appeared to be sharing a sweet moment with her best friend. What was up with that?

Honey-Lavender Ice Cream

Ingredients:
2 cups whole milk
⅛ cup fresh lavender leaves
2 tablespoons honey, plus 2 teaspoons
¼ cup granulated sugar
2 large eggs
1 cup heavy cream

Directions:
Combine the milk, lavender, and honey in a medium saucepan and bring to a gentle boil over medium-low heat. Stir occasionally.

Remove the saucepan from the heat and let the milk mixture rest for 5 minutes. Next, strain out the lavender and return the milk mixture to the saucepan. Bring the milk mixture to a simmer over low heat and cook for 5 minutes. Stir often.

Beat the sugar and the eggs in a medium bowl with an electric mixer set to medium speed until the mixture is pale yellow, thick, and well blended, about 3 to 5 minutes.

Add half the milk mixture to the egg-sugar mixture and whisk together. Pour the egg mixture into the remaining milk mixture in the saucepan and cook over low heat until the mixture coats the back of a wooden spoon.

Remove the mixture from the heat. Stir in the heavy cream. Freeze the mixture in an ice cream maker, following the instructions provided by the manufacturer.

Serves 6 to 8

Chapter 8

Drink a tea of rose petals and rosemary
sprigs to heal the heart's conflicts.

—*Henny Penny Farmette Almanac*

Abby eyed a tight space behind the long line of
parked cars at the Richardson estate sale.
"Sheesh. Looks like the whole dang town is here."

Kat groaned. "I might have guessed. Flyers have
been plastered all over downtown. We should have
gotten an earlier start."

"Well, we're here now," Abby said with optimism. She maneuvered the Jeep behind a sleek
black Hummer with the license plate letters SVC-
WHIZ. Convinced that a fling between Kat and
Lucas wouldn't last even if they did get something
going, Abby entertained the hope that Kat would
soon find a new Mr. Right. Maybe a nudge in that
direction couldn't hurt. She pointed to the plate
and said, "Looks like he's here!"

"Who?"

"That new boyfriend you wanted—the Silicon
Valley engineer type. But finding him in the
throng . . . well, that might take a little sleuthing."

"My luck," Kat replied, "he'll drive a beater, his wife will be the whiz, and that Hummer will be her wheels." She swung her long legs from the Jeep to the ground as the wind tousled her short, blond locks. She slammed the Jeep door shut and walked around to Abby's side.

Abby suppressed her eagerness to ask Kat about Lucas and the ice cream moment and decided she'd wait for the right time. From her perspective as Lucas's neighbor and a frequent shopper at his feed store, Abby had some insight into the man. He wasn't the kind of guy who would jump into any relationship without giving it prudent thought. She doubted he could be hurried. Perhaps his meeting Kat had been a chance encounter. End of story. But there was no denying Kat's dark mood today. Abby was pretty sure her friend would get her groove back during the estate sale. She just needed to find some special item at a bargain-basement price. And Abby was going to help her find it.

Clicking the Jeep's lock button on her key and starting the short hike down the road, Abby glanced briefly past the red barn that led up to Fiona's cottage and Doc Danbury's house. Both the cottage and the main house had their doors closed and their blinds down. With the houses set back from the road, the residents could easily spot visitors or intruders. As she walked, Abby thought about what Kat had said on their drive up the mountain. Tom Davidson Dodge looked the most promising as a suspect, but the case was weak. The evidence was circumstantial, but he didn't have a verifiable alibi. Cops knew the killer was the last person to have seen Fiona alive. It was Tom's bad luck that he'd slept at his wife's cottage the night before she was found dead.

The fog was lifting, and the birds were singing. Abby's tummy was full of Kat's strong coffee, herb omelets, and a miniature lemon scone with chilled crème anglaise and fresh strawberries from her farmette garden. All seemed right in Abby's world, except for the niggling doubt that Tom Dodge is the actual killer.

As they walked, Abby's thoughts shifted to Clay. How bold Clay had been to invite himself along on her outing with Kat after Abby had briefly mentioned it. She'd talked him out of it that morning in a phone text, placating him with a promise of a home-cooked meal . . . soon. If Clay were to move back to the farmette and continue to be generous with his money, it would take the edge off her financial situation, at least for now. Still, Abby chafed at the idea of needing Clay's help. She wondered whether or not to broach the subject with Kat and finally decided to go for it.

"You'll never guess who has walked back into my life . . . Clay Calhoun. Can you believe it?"

Kat turned and looked at her, wide-eyed. "Oh, no. I thought you'd never see that man again. So what's his story?"

"Not clear."

"Never is with him. Surely he's told you where he's been and what he's been doing?"

"Nope."

"What do you want to bet that he's jobless now? Or he's had a breakup with whatever new woman he found after leaving you high and dry."

"I don't know," said Abby. "I'm just trying to be present with it."

"Take my advice. Don't let him get under your skin, girlfriend, unless you want to get hurt again."

"Yeah, yeah . . . I'm picking up what you're putting down, Kat." Abby believed Kat had her best interests at heart. If she didn't welcome Kat's input, she should have avoided bringing up the subject of Clay in the first place. "Look," said Abby, pointing into the yard where the estate sale was being held. "I see a gorgeous armoire."

Vintage furniture made up the bulk of the sale. Antique armoires, carved wooden headboards and footboards, along with cabinets, a chest of drawers, two desks, and assorted chairs, stood in one area. Banker boxes of books were lined up in neat rows on a threadbare Oriental carpet—a bargain at a dollar apiece. Bakeware, pans, lids, and assorted serving pieces were scattered about on several old tables. Lamps and other household bric-a-brac covered utility tables like the one Abby carted to the farmers' market on the first and third Saturdays during summer.

Kat made a beeline to a table that held old silver-plated serving pieces and post–World War II/midcentury curios, along with small collectibles, china, and sundry pottery pieces. Abby followed and asked the question that had been at the back of her mind on the ride up the mountain.

"You said the BOLO your peeps put out on Laurent netted him at SFO. So where was he going?" She picked up a deeply tarnished but otherwise lovely old pie server with a claw curve, decorative engraving, and a filigree handle.

"Where else? Port-au-Prince," Kat replied with a frown as she attempted to decipher a pitcher's pottery mark.

"Going home to Haiti. Figures." Abby laid aside the pie server and picked up a nineteenth-century opal-glass rolling pin imprinted with a poem. "You see this?" she asked Kat, who loved all things Victorian.

"Yeah. I'll pass. It's an old sailor's souvenir—a collectible for someone, but not me," said Kat. She spied a Devon cottage creamer. "Now, this is sweet. . . . Johnson Brothers. You got to wonder how Zora's mother came by it." A beat passed. "But I'd want it only if the sugar bowl came with it, and I don't see one."

Abby followed her to another table and watched as Kat plucked a bone china gravy boat with an ornate floral pattern to study. "This is nice, too." She turned the boat over in her hands. "Ha. I guessed it. Another Johnson Brothers. There is a crack in the handle and a chip in one of the blue flowers," she bemoaned, returning the item to its matching plate.

"So about Laurent . . ." Abby handed Kat a demitasse cup and saucer in the 1930s flow blue style. "Why hightail it out in such a hurry?"

Kat inverted the cup, as she had every other piece. "He said his mother had taken ill and the voodoo healing spells have not helped. But, of course, we know that he wanted to escape prosecution on a burglary charge." Kat pointed to a hairline crack through the center bottom of the cup. She set it back on the table, apparently not deterred from searching on.

"I'm insanely curious about what you found in his briefcase," Abby said.

Kat brushed a lock of her blond hair behind an ear and hoisted the straps of her empty cloth bag a little higher on her shoulder. "He didn't have a briefcase."

"But . . . ," Abby stammered. "I saw him toss a black briefcase into a green sedan before he drove off."

"No green sedan, either. We caught up with him. He was locking the doors of his old beater pickup and getting ready to board a bus from the long-term airport parking."

Abby frowned, confused. "So what happened to that green sedan?"

"He told us it belongs to a mountain mechanic friend, who loans him the car whenever Laurent schedules work on his truck. Apparently, he went to Fiona's store to retrieve his black zippered portfolio containing publicity photos of him and local bands. Thought her shop more secure than his apartment."

"Really?" Abby sighed heavily. "I *didn't* make a mistake, Kat. I know what I saw. And I think I know a briefcase from a portfolio."

"Of course you do. But we couldn't find the briefcase, and he's not admitting to even owning one."

Now thoroughly perplexed, Abby pointed to a framed tapestry. "Did you let him go?"

Kat looked over at the tapestry and made a distasteful face. "We couldn't hold him on burglary. He had a key to Fiona's shop and free access, he says. But he began to sweat when I asked him about his immigration status. So we've got him cooling his heels in a cell until ICE can interview him." Kat reached across a table of mismatched plates to retrieve a lavender-glazed teapot with a silver lid. Beaming, she handed it to Abby. "Speak to you?" Kat asked. "Fraunfelter with an Ohio stamp on the underside."

"It does," replied Abby as she pulled the round ball on the silver dome and the lid lifted, revealing a chain that held a four-cup tea-leaf strainer inside. "So cute. You seldom find these with the strainer and the round rubber ball that releases steam," observed Abby. "I'm sure it belongs to the twenties flapper era."

"So buy it," Kat said, apparently happy that at least one of them had found something.

"Well, I think I will . . . but it depends on the price Zora wants for it," Abby said. "You keep looking."

"I'll be over there." Kat pointed to the side of the house where stacks of framed art rested against an old wheelbarrow.

Weaving through the crowd with the teapot in her arms, Abby finally spotted Zora. The tall, thin woman in her late thirties wore gray slacks with a pale pink oxford shirt and a gray, hip-length vest. Over her outfit, she had put on a frilly strawberry-patterned apron with oversize pockets embellished with pink rickrack. She was counting out change for a woman who had just purchased a large chamber pot. Abby smiled, imagining how lovely a mass of purple petunias would look in that pot on a wide gray porch with white trim. Suddenly, a burly, balding man with a chair pushed in line in front of Abby.

Excuse you. *What is it about yard sales that bring out bad manners?* Rather than listen to him haggle over the price, she moseyed over to a bench that wrapped in a semicircle around the trunk of an ancient oak. Seated in the shade, she could avoid the pressing in on her by others and quietly browse the contents of a box that someone had placed on the bench. After setting the teapot down beside her, Abby picked up a book from the top of the stack in the box. She recognized it as a dust-covered volume of Culpeper's *Complete Herbal*. Absorbed in thumbing through the pages, she didn't see Jack Sullivan stroll up.

"Mackenzie, isn't it?" His tone conveyed no hint of the causticity that had characterized their last conversation.

"It is," Abby replied while assessing the handsome man with curly, brown hair streaked with threads of silver. She squinted up to see intense pale blue eyes gazing back at her. He wore tan cargo shorts with side pockets near the knees, a navy stretch polo, and running shoes with white ankle socks.

"Fiona's books," he said, looking at her intently.

"Seriously? You're selling them?"

He nodded and pointed toward Zora. "She dropped by yesterday. Said I could bring down to the sale whatever I was clearing out of the cottage. I'm afraid it all has to go." He paused for a beat and looked at her intently.

His warm, friendly demeanor perplexed Abby. It was certainly a different vibe from that of their last encounter.

"Listen, I know I made a mistake with you," he said. "Any chance we could put that behind us?"

Caught off guard by his sudden admission, Abby tilted her head quizzically, as though she hadn't heard him right.

"I'm not usually so high-handed," Jack said. He

gestured to the open space on the bench on the other side of the box. "May I?"

Abby nodded.

He sat down, chewed his lower lip, as if trying to figure out how to engage her. "My thoughts seem to be duller and more muddled than usual since I arrived in your charming hamlet," he said, looking over at her. "I'm obsessing and not sleeping."

"Try a spoonful of honey in chamomile tea." Abby had hardly spoken the words before she wished she could call them back. An ethnobotanist would know the herbs that could help with sleeplessness.

He nodded. "Tried it. Under normal circumstances, it works. But nothing is normal now, is it?"

Abby shook her head. She considered whether or not to ask if he knew anyone who'd want to harm his sister as she watched Zora listening politely as the bald man argued over a fair price for the tufted armchair. Zora shrugged, and the man stomped off, leaving the chair for Zora to put back. Instead, she sat down on it. With no one else in line, Abby realized it was now her chance to ask the price of her teapot. She laid aside the book to stand. Jack spoke.

"I treated you shabbily," he said in a voice tinged with humility.

Abby sat back down. "Oh, forget about that. Completely understandable," said Abby, her gaze darting between him and Zora.

"Accept my apology?"

Abby managed a feeble smile and nodded.

Jack continued, "You said you were Fiona's friend. Did you see each other a lot . . . ?" His words trailed off.

"Quite a bit. She was great fun. Always saw the bright side of things."

"That she did. I'll wager she set your ears afire with her stories." He blew a breath out through pursed lips. "Got that from our mother's brother . . . Quite the storyteller, he was." He looked as if he was weighing what more he could say. A beat passed, and sadness took over his features.

"Give yourself time, Jack. You've had a shock, and grief can be crazy messy and confusing. Even when you have prepared for a passing, it still leaves a hole in your heart."

His light eyes locked onto Abby's. He looked away toward the line of trees and wire fencing that hemmed the property. "You know what's bloody awful?"

Abby shook her head.

"I can't get a straight answer about how she died. They're saying maybe poison." His jaw tensed.

Abby spoke softly. "It takes some time to process the pain. Grief is like that. It's a sneaker wave that creeps in to wash over you. It takes you under. Then it brings you up again to an unknown place. All the while, you're gasping in despair." Abby swallowed. "But with time, the pain lessens, and your heart heals."

His eyes blinked as he stared at the ground. Finally, he looked at her with curious, questioning eyes. "You lost someone, too, didn't you? Whom did you lose, Abigail Mackenzie?"

She tensed. His question had triggered the old, familiar ache. Hoping to reclaim her equilibrium, she searched for light amid the negative spaces in the leafy oak canopy. The conversation was one she didn't want to have.

"Family member? Lover?" He continued to probe.

Abby's fingers tensed around the edge of the bench. She wasn't about to confess to a total stranger that the reason she'd entered law enforcement could be traced back to the death of her younger brother during her first year in junior college. He had been visiting her over the Christmas holiday and had asked her to run errands with him, including a trip to the bank. It had been a blustery, rainy day, and she'd been baking cookies and watching Jane Austen's *Pride and Prejudice* on cable. She couldn't miss the ending of her favorite movie, so she'd declined his offer. There had been a robbery at the bank just before closing. Her baby brother had been in the wrong place at the wrong time. Becoming a cop had been a way for Abby to deal with her anger.

She shrugged off Jack's question. "Cops see a lot of grief."

Jack's gaze seemed piercing now. "Fecking senseless loss. How do you come to terms with it?" His voice cracked.

"Counseling," said Abby. "It's a process. Acceptance is the last stage."

As the ensuing silence engulfed them, Abby pushed down her sadness. She felt terrible for him and for herself and for everyone who'd cared about Fiona. Her hands sought something to do, and she reached for the book again. She stared at its cover while spurning the tears stinging at the back of her eyes.

Jack sniffed. He reached over and pinched the book's cover between his forefinger and thumb and opened to the frontispiece. "Fiona was so excited when she found this at a yard sale back in

Holyoke. Mid-teens, junior year in high school, I think, and before the auto crash that turned our lives upside down. With our folks gone, we had to finish our growing up in the care of relatives in Boston." He turned the page. "She pinched the corners, wrote in the margins. If the book weren't in such terrible condition, it might be worth something. It's a first edition, nineteen forty-seven."

"Yeah?"

"Far older editions are still in circulation." He released the book into Abby's hands and leaned back against the tree trunk.

Abby thumbed through the pages, noting Fiona's underlining and pencil notations. Some seemed pointless, as if she'd been doodling in the margins, thinking about something else. The most common mark was a figure eight. Sometimes a cross or a *T*, and in other places the Aum symbol. There were astrological signs next to names. Abby searched for the photograph of a monastery garden laid out as a Latin cross. Not finding it, she stretched up and then relaxed her shoulders. What did it matter? She had the real thing, the herb garden that Fiona had created just for the farmette.

"Nicholas Culpeper," Jack said, "the author, was a physician and a botanist and also an astrologer. He wrote the first version of his *Complete Herbal* in sixteen fifty-three."

"Really?" exclaimed Abby. "Now, that would be quite the first edition to own, wouldn't it?"

He let go a mirthful laugh. "Culpeper's observations about the characteristics of herbs were extraordinary, but linking herbs to astrological signs and planets defies modern explanation. Of course, in his time, it was undoubtedly considered rigorous, muscular thinking, I suppose. I mean, the man searched for symbolism and linkage."

"May I ask you a question about that?" Abby turned to lock eyes with him.

"Certainly." He flashed a quick, mercurial smile.

"Do you know of any special meaning associated with the number eight?"

"Symbolism, you mean?" He thought for a moment. "Well, in the great religious traditions of the world, there's the eightfold path in Buddhism. Then there's the Jewish ceremony of the circumcision of a male child eight days after his birth. An eight-pointed star symbolizes Lakshmi, the goddess of wealth in Hinduism. And, incidentally, it is also the symbol of the ancient Babylonian goddess Ishtar." He paused to think. "In the early centuries of the Christian church, baptismal fonts were generally eight-sided. There's ample evidence of them in the walls of ruined churches throughout Ireland." Rubbing his chin, he added, "In botany, the genus *Coreopsis*, I recall, produces flower bracts divided into two series of eight."

Abby's eyes widened. A smile played at the corners of her lips. "And let's not forget there were eight maids a-milking in 'The Twelve Days of Christmas,'" she said.

"That too." He grinned. "And the eighth month in our calendar year is August, the month of the astrological sign Leo. In tarot, the Strength card."

Abby looked at him with wonder. "Holy moly!" He'd seen her innocent question as a challenge, and clearly, he didn't want to fail in meeting it.

"And in mathematics, an eight on its side symbolizes infinity, while in the Chinese culture, eight symbolizes prosperity. Shall I go on?" he asked.

"That's quite sufficient. How did you come up with all that right off the top of your head?"

Jack's grin grew deeper. "It is a little association game I play to remember things. Now I have a question for you."

"Shoot."

"Why are you intrigued by that number?"

"I see Fiona has drawn figure eights throughout the book."

"Is that so?" he said. "I hadn't noticed. Can't imagine why she would. But what say you keep this book? I'm pretty sure my sister would have wanted you to have something with which to remember her."

"Why, thanks," Abby said, cuddling the book against her bosom.

Jack rose and motioned toward Zora. "I've got to talk with her about handling these books and a bunch of other stuff. When I've completed the cleaning out of Fiona's cottage, I'll have to deal with the botanical shop."

"So you're going to sell the business?"

"Sadly, yes. I know how much she loved it." He took a step away before spinning around to face Abby. "There's no chance that you . . . well . . . Would you be interested in helping me go through all her stuff?"

"Sure, if you want me to." Abby wasn't about to pass up the opportunity to scrutinize Fiona's possessions for possible clues to her murder.

"She was a voracious reader," Jack said. "And a writer, too. I counted twenty-five journals, if you can call them that. People who keep journals mostly just jot down their thoughts. Not my sister.

She stuffed hers with scraps of paper, letters, notes, feathers, found objects, bits of glittery things, broken seashells, all kinds of stuff."

"Just another reflection of her free spirit, I suspect," Abby replied.

His rugged features lit up at her positive spin on his statement. "You clearly understood my sister as others haven't. So when would you like to start?"

"Well . . ." Abby thought about her farmette work, her farmers' market obligations, and the promises she'd made to Clay. How much longer could she reasonably expect him to wait before moving back in? And if Clay knew she was planning to spend time with another man—even if it was for a good cause—might it not provide him a reason to leave again? *Oh, but why am I even thinking about that now?* Abby felt her forehead creasing into a frown.

Jack's facial expression darkened. "Look, I don't want to make any demands on the rest of your weekend," he said, "but how about Monday morning, say, nine o'clock?"

His tone made it sound like an entreaty.

Mustering courage, Abby replied, "Okay. I'll bring breakfast." Had that sounded too eager or forward? she wondered. Breakfast meant conversation, and she had a lot of questions for him.

"You can bring your dog, if you don't think she'll get in the way. I like dogs. I do. Sugar. That's her name, isn't it?" His thick brows arched mischievously; his pale blues widened.

You like dogs. Could've fooled me. "Wow. That's quite a memory," Abby said.

The breeze tousled his curly, brown hair as he

leaned over to grip the box in his large hands and hoist it high into his arms.

"It's selective," he said with a wink and walked away.

Tips for Growing Kitchen Herbs in a Container

Plant seedlings of your favorite culinary herbs in a terra-cotta pot with a saucer, a wooden box filled with potting soil, or even a large bag of soil that you have made a rectangular opening in on one side. Maintain a regular watering schedule. Choose from any of the following culinary herbs: basil, chervil, chives, cilantro, dill, English thyme, French tarragon, lavender, lemon balm, lemongrass, oregano, rosemary, savory, and sorrel.

Chapter 9

Sweetened by sugar or salted by brine, a
pickle strikes a nice balance . . . unless
the pickle's a jam and you're caught in
the middle.

—*Henny Penny Farmette Almanac*

Leaving sleepy Las Flores for the mountains on
Monday, Abby looked forward to spending the
day in Fiona's cottage, helping her brother pack
her belongings. Last night, she'd told Clay she
needed another day or two to stow things away and
make room for his stuff. Surprisingly, he had ac-
commodated her without too much protest, but
he hadn't spared her his sad-faced Eeyore expression.

As for Jack, she sincerely wanted to lend a helping hand. Apparently, he didn't know a soul in
town other than his sister and her estranged husband. But as Abby thought about it, she realized
that sometimes in the most innocuous of settings
and situations, one learned things. One little detail, overlooked at first, could sometimes break a

case wide open. Abby took her time negotiating the Jeep around ever-higher curves until the fog abruptly yielded to sunlight. In the forest clearings, she observed the low ceiling of clouds still hanging over the valley floor. But once she'd pierced the gray shroud of fog, the sunlight of the mountains dazzled through canopies of towering blue-green redwood trees. The morning air carried the humid scent of pine sap, wild thyme, and decayed plant material.

At Dr. Danbury's big red barn, Abby turned onto the weedy gravel driveway and drove up to Fiona's cottage. She cut the engine and sat for a moment, wondering if she should have dressed more conservatively. It was going to be a hot day, and she'd chosen loose, cool clothes—a lacy black camisole and a see-through white cotton shirt with three-quarter sleeves. The shirt hung several inches over black cropped pants with side and rear pockets, in case she needed to stash a note or two for safekeeping. The only thing not color coordinated was the chartreuse bandanna around her shoulder-length red-gold curls. *But why am I thinking about clothing now, as if changing anything at this point is even an option?*

She glanced at the shed that served as Dr. Danbury's garage. The door had been thrust wide open. Inside, a partially covered, mud-splattered all-terrain vehicle, or ATV, had been parked at the rear, behind the spot where the doc customarily parked his Volvo. The Volvo was gone. Abby couldn't help wondering where the doc had gotten off to so early today. The other weather-beaten shed—the one closest to Fiona's cottage and where she kept extra stuff for her store—had a sturdy lock hanging from its latch. Abby grabbed the cloth bags of breakfast fixings from the passenger seat. She scooted out of her Jeep and strolled to the cottage door.

Surprised that the banshee door knocker was missing, Abby knocked three times before the door swung open. Jack, fresh faced, with his brown and silver curls bouncing in every direction, greeted her in bare feet. Wearing blue jeans and an unbuttoned white shirt with the cuffs turned up a couple of rolls, he seemed happy to see her and made a sweeping gesture for her to enter into the step-down living room. Light flooded the interior through the bank of windows offering a sweeping vista of green mountain ridges running north and south, parallel to the Pacific Ocean. Stacks of boxes awaiting assembly, bags of packing peanuts, and rolls of tape had been piled in a corner by the fireplace for the work ahead. The fragrance of freshly brewed coffee and the soft strains of Celtic music playing in the background created an ambiance that Abby liked. A lot.

"I've got eggs, herbs, an onion, a bell pepper, cheese, whole-grain muffins, and some andouille sausages," Abby said, hoisting the bags into his arms. "All I need is a frying pan, a bowl, and a wire whisk. In two shakes of a lamb's tail, I'll cook up breakfast."

"Sounds wonderful," he said, leading her to the kitchen and placing the bags on the rustic barn-plank table, which, with its ladder-back chairs, took up most of the room.

He finished buttoning the shirt over his exposed muscular chest and tucked the shirttails into his trousers. "What can I do to help?"

Everything about him seemed different—gone was the anger of their first encounter and the forlornness of their second. Today he exuded a quiet self-assurance. Abby could only speculate that the shock of his recent loss had morphed into acceptance of its undeniable reality.

In a voice exuding sweetness and warmth, she replied, "Could you empty the bags?"

"That, I can do," he said in a tone tinged with relief. "Holding my breath, I was, out of fear you'd ask me to cook something. I've eaten all the canned fish and devoured the box of crackers. Any more of that diet, and I'll be growing me feline fangs." His eyes shone with impish mirth.

Abby smiled back. "Someone's in rare form today."

"I finally got some sleep . . . and a hangover . . . to thank for it."

Abby reached for a spatula from a glazed crock of utensils on the counter and pulled opened a cabinet door. "Where can I find a bowl to scramble the eggs?"

"There." Jack pointed to the adjacent cabinet.

"So," Abby said, taking down a bowl, "what happened to the door knocker?" She gave him a sidelong glance. Faint laugh lines on either side of his blue eyes crinkled while he seemed to be thinking through a response.

"Just . . . well . . . gone." He reached into the bag nearest him and pulled out a carton of eggs and the hunk of cheese wrapped in plastic. After peeling away the plastic, he removed a knife from the set on the table, sliced off a sliver of cheese, and popped the piece into his mouth.

"Yeah? Where?" she asked, probing.

"Back there," he said, waving the knife toward the back of the house. "Or there." He pointed the knife in the opposite direction.

Abby set the bowl on the counter and gave him a bewildered look. "Well, which is it?"

"I suppose the landlord disposed of it when he cleaned up the broken glass." Jack chewed his lip like a small boy confronted over having been caught red-handed in some questionable act.

"Wait. What glass? I'm confused. The cottage door has no glass."

"Oh, right you are. So, it was the glass window at the back of the house."

Abby detected a bit of beating around the bush. "This sounds like a fishy story, which you need to start from the beginning, now that you've hooked me."

"Heaved it, I did," he admitted, feigning a thick Irish brogue, "toward the East Coast, and I might have uttered a curse as I sent it flying." His face bore a sheepish expression. "Aye, and nearly ripped my arm from its pit."

Abby sucked in a breath. "Ohhh, so you tossed that pretty little knocker away?"

"That I did. The winds were howling something fierce, and there was nothing to slow the wailing over the mountaintop. But the gusting was to my advantage, or so I thought. Once thrown, the object would be carried by the wind even farther from me. The problem, I soon discovered," he said before pausing to swallow, "was that the wind was blowing directly at me. But I, being a wee bit tipsy, hurled that banshee with all my might. I could have sworn it was gone for good."

"Was it?"

He exhaled heavily. "Nay. She landed a foot away. But the Irish have a saying. 'He who isn't strong must use cunning.' So, I summoned my strength and hurled it in the opposite direction."

Seriously? Not only did he look like a leprechaun with that wild hair, but now he sounded like he'd kissed the proverbial Blarney stone. She resisted the urge to laugh out loud.

"I suppose 'twas then I heard the window shatter."

"Oh, no . . . Don't tell me." Abby put her hand over her mouth to hold back the laughter. "That door knocker was an art object, Jack. Surely you didn't believe it had anything to do with Fiona's passing."

"No, of course not." He continued in his affected dialect. "But I had a deadly buzz on. Opened the door for a little night air, I did. Then I spied it hanging there. It ignited my anger something fierce. I ripped it off and sent it flying away from the cottage. And then I picked it up and turned to fling it again. That's when the glass shattered, and the landlord came staggering out to ask what the bleep I was doing."

"What did you tell him?"

"What could I say? Out chasing ghosts? I didn't mean to break his window."

Abby leaned over the bowl and howled with laughter. "Oh, Lord, have mercy," she said after regaining her composure.

His deadpan expression shifted to a sly smile. He did a shoulder roll before laying aside the knife to reach into the other bag. He pulled out the mushrooms. "Ah, fungi. These will add flavor without the hallucination that some find so annoying."

Her laughter erupted again.

"Ever been to a fungus fair or foray?" he asked. "I hear that in California, mushroom connoisseurs engage in those sorts of activities."

"Well, I don't." Abby took the button mushrooms from him. "My luck, I'd pluck a basket of deadly toadstools."

"Or a psychoactive *Psilocybe* species with hallucinogenic properties," he uttered in a flat monotone.

"That too." She had expected a somber mood from Jack, but she found the unexpected display of humor rather delightful. However, it did seem strangely juxtaposed against the deep sadness she'd witnessed in his eyes during their first encounter. Abby understood only too well how shock and mourning could take all kinds of expression. Just because someone felt grief deeply didn't necessarily mean he or she couldn't experience moments of lightness and humor. Laughter could serve as a counterbalance to the burdensome, at times unbearable, weight of sorrow. She liked this side of him—it was so very much like Fiona.

Jack took the bowl back, washed the mushrooms, and laid them on a cutting board for slicing. "These will taste great in the eggs," he said, dropping the accent.

"Absolutely," Abby said. "Especially with chives, parsley, and a teensy bit of English thyme. Just a little of each." She focused on chopping the herbs, along with the onion and bell pepper. Next, she grated a half cup of cheese. Removing the casings from the sausage took a minute more. She cut them into slices under his watchful gaze. "I'd ask you to beat the eggs, Jack, but with your sore shoulder from all that heaving . . . well, I'm happy to do it," she teased.

"I'll be in your debt for that," he said.

When the eggs were frothy, Abby made the omelet. "So, tell me, did Fiona always share your interest in plants?"

Jack set plates and silverware on the table. "Not in an academic way. Fiona loved edible garden plants and herbs she could grow and eat. I, on the other hand, harbored an interest in all kinds of plants in cultures, and how indigenous people use their plants throughout their lives in foods, medicine, and spirituality practices. That is the very definition of *ethnobotany*—my field of study." He tore two paper towels from a roll to use as napkins. "Fiona got serious about herbs after she suffered a bad reaction from taking milk thistle for a liver cleansing along with the allergy drug a doctor had prescribed for hay fever."

"Here in California, milk thistle grows wild like a common weed. So Fiona used it as a liver tonic?"

"Yes. She would often fast and cleanse. But after that adverse reaction, she was much more diligent, reading voraciously about herbs and never using them as tonics or medicine unless she understood their drawbacks, as well as benefits."

Abby turned off the burner. She cut the omelet in half with the metal spatula and slid the halves onto the plates.

Jack pulled a chair out for her and sank into the other one. "In fact," he said, "tradition holds you can use milk thistle in emergency situations involving poisoning by *Amanita phalloides*, the death cap mushroom. That's because milk thistle seeds have silymarin—a chemical that protects liver cells from toxins."

Abby held the whole-grain muffin in her hand

in midair. "So, if Fiona knew that she'd come in contact with some toxin or poison, she'd likely know the antidote to take, right?"

Between forkfuls of omelet, Jack said, "Oh, yes. I think so."

"Unless she couldn't," Abby said, speculating, before she pinched off a piece of the muffin and ate it.

"Wouldn't that beg the question of why she couldn't?" he asked.

Abby nodded. "When we know that, I think we'll have the key to solving her murder." Abby washed the bite down with a swig of coffee. "Tom spent the night with her and left here early in the morning on the day she died. Would she have gotten up and made breakfast for him?"

"Of course," said Jack. "For Fiona, making a meal was a means to demonstrate love." Jack leaned in, as though sensing Abby was about to make a point.

Abby set the muffin aside. "On the day the cops found Fiona's body, this kitchen—in fact, the whole house, according to my sources—looked like a cleaning crew had just serviced it. Two people for breakfast and showers meant a kitchen to clean, a bed to make, and bathroom laundry and towels to throw into a basket or the washer. Someone cleaned up."

"It had to be Fiona," Jack answered. "She kept a tidy house." He forked a sliver of green on the edge of his plate and stabbed a piece of omelet, then ate it with masculine gusto.

"Suppose that makes sense. Did you know she was coming to have lunch with me on my farmette?"

He shook his head. "If she told me, I didn't remember. So you see, my memory *is* selective."

"Talk to me about poisoning. What kinds of poisons might she have encountered around the environs up here?" Abby asked, using her fork to break apart the omelet. She took a small bite, savoring the taste as she chewed.

"Well, around the cottage, most likely, the doc keeps pesticides, herbicides, fungicides to deal with weeds and pest infestations. Could be that there are several species of spiders, insects, snakes, mold, mushrooms, and all manner of plants, perhaps even some that possess powerful neurotoxins. Certain plants can exert a paralytic action or adversely act upon the cardiopulmonary system, causing stoppage of the heart."

"For example?" Abby eyed him intently.

"The death cap, for starters. Some say it took the life of the Roman emperor Claudius, although it is possible that eating a mushroom painted with a poisonous toxin could have done him in. The death cap has taken more lives throughout history than any other mushroom, but it's not quick. After ingestion, it could take maybe fifteen to sixteen hours to kill."

"What might someone ingest that would have a shorter action time?"

"You mean fast-acting plants?" He pursed his lips and blew air through them. "You've got deadly nightshade, monkshood, and hemlock, which killed Socrates. Let's not forget *Digitalis purpurea*, also known as foxglove. For generations, it's been grown at the back of flower gardens, but every part of the plant is poisonous. Its leaves look like comfrey leaves, which also has toxic properties. People who are allergic to foxglove could experience fatal anaphylaxis. But I believe there would be signs of an allergic reaction to foxglove contact or ingestion."

"Like what?"

"Hives."

"I didn't see any hives on Fiona," Abby said, deciding to spare him the details about Fiona being clothed and burned, which had limited her view of Fiona's exposed skin. "If Fiona had ingested a plant poison, I think it would have had to be fast acting or at least have taken her life within the few hours given as the time frame for her death."

"Well," said Jack, "depending on the poison, the coroner or medical examiner might find traces of it in her body or possibly the by-products. Plant alkaloid poisoning, such as you might see in monkshood, could happen as quickly as within half an hour of ingestion."

"But wouldn't the medical examiner or coroner need to be looking for those alkaloids?"

Jack turned his gaze on her. "I couldn't say. Do you think someone used a poisonous agent to kill her?"

"My sources in the police department tell me they are taking a hard look at Tom as a person of interest," Abby said matter-of-factly. "Do you think Tom capable of hurting her?"

Jack trembled slightly and shook his head in an immediate denial. "Not the Tom I know."

Abby took a slow sip of coffee, giving him time and hoping he might elaborate.

"Fiona loved him, you know. Right up to the last. She believed their marriage would work if he could just break his ties with the cult. I guess she saw something in him that he couldn't see in himself."

"What was that?"

"Fatherhood. Fiona wanted to start a family. I'm not saying there weren't issues."

Abby brows shot up. "What kind of issues?"

"Fiona tried to wrest Tom free from the clutches of the commune, which she said of late had become a cult. She told me they blocked her at every turn. But she kept trying. She told me that she thought they had changed tactics and had someone keeping tabs on her."

"Like a stalker? Did she say who?"

He folded his arms across his chest and stared off into space. "I don't know. Maybe more than one person."

"Did she ever mention the name Laurent Duplessis?"

"To her," said Jack, sipping his coffee, "Duplessis was a dalliance, nothing more. But I gather, to him, she was everything good about America. He believed they had a future."

"I'm sure he did." Abby reached for the pot and refilled Jack's cup before pouring the last of the coffee into her own. "So why was it so hard for Tom to break free from the cult?"

"Brainwashing and rigid rules. You are required to relinquish all your possessions, money, and all links to the outside world, except if you are making money, which you must give to the compound. Fiona couldn't bring herself to return to such a tight structure and swore she'd never raise a child there. According to her, they were grooming Tom. They had convinced him that he had the potential to be the new leader when the time came for the current cult leader and the commune manager to start new branches throughout the world."

"Do you mean Hayden Marks and Premalatha Baxter?"

"Yes, those two." Jack finished the last bite on his plate, dabbed his mouth with the napkin, and nodded. "I can't imagine Tom hurting Fiona. Kill the goose who lays the golden egg? What would be his motive?"

"Yeah. My thought, too. But maybe it was someone else who had the motive and some way to stack the deck against Tom. In effect, forcing him to kill," said Abby.

Jack shook his head. "No. I can't see it."

Abby wondered if he knew about the jewelry incident. She took a deep breath and watched Jack's expression closely as she broached the subject. "Tom was caught pawning their wedding rings and jewelry."

The color blanched from Jack's face. His eyes locked onto hers.

"You didn't know?"

He shook his head in disbelief. "That makes me sick." He leaned forward, rested his elbows on the table, closed his eyes, and pinched the bridge of his nose.

Abby said, "Hard to believe, I know. But it's true. I was there." She rose and collected the dishes, placed them in the sink. "I wonder if you might show me Fiona's garden. I've seen what she grows in front of the house, but she has a patch on the north side, right?"

He ran his hands through his hair and looked up. "Yes. It's lovely." After pushing his chair back from the table, he rose and strolled from the kitchen to the back door. "Mind the hole there." He pointed to an opening in the floor large enough for a child to climb through to reach the crawl space beneath the house leading to the rear of the structure. It was partially covered with a rug.

Abby sidestepped the hole. "I've been up here to see Fiona a couple of times and never noticed that hole. Wonder why Dr. Danbury hasn't fixed it." Abby let the back door slam behind her.

"Because of Paws, Dr. Danbury's cat. The good doctor would forget to feed and water the cat when he was drunk. At least, that's what Fiona told me," he said, leading Abby to a large area uphill from the cottage, fenced to keep out the deer. "Paws liked hanging out with Fiona, and why wouldn't he? There was all the canned fish in the world in her cupboard." He chuckled, holding up a large tree branch for Abby to pass beneath.

"I've yet to see that cat," Abby said.

"The cat wasn't the only creature to enter through that hole, either." Jack leaned down to unwire the gate.

"As floor holes go, it's pretty large," Abby said.

Jack wrestled open the garden gate. "Finding a lizard in her shoe," he said, "freaked Fiona out. Another time, a chipmunk found its way in and raced around the house until Fiona got it to go back out through the hole."

Abby smiled. Leaning down near a row of parsley, she plucked a green leaf and chewed on it. "So Fiona took in strays of all kinds, not just humans?"

"That she did."

Fiona's garden had clearly reached it apogee, evidenced by the riotous color of both sun-drenched and shade-loving plants—the latter protected by two apple trees with thick, stubby trunks on the garden's southeastern axis. In the full sun, crimson climbing roses sprawled over the wire fencing, while sunflowers dazzled with their bright yellow blooms.

Pointing to a stand of colorful hollyhocks, Jack asked Abby, "Did you know that evidence of *Alcea rosea*, or the hollyhock, was found in the grave of an early human—a Neanderthal dating back some fifty thousand years?"

"No, I didn't know that." Abby enjoyed his ability to pull out—seeming out of the blue—facts about common plants, as it enriched her experience of being in the garden with him.

"Foxglove blooming right on schedule . . . late May," she said, pointing to the purple and white blooms atop four-foot spires along one side of the fence. "And just look at those delphiniums," said Abby, "just beginning to show color. They're gorgeous."

"And deadly," Jack said. "Seeds and very young plants, if ingested by cattle or other farm animals, are highly toxic."

"And over there, feverfew!" exclaimed Abby. "I love its daisy-like flowers, always so cheerful. And chives, bee balm, and lots of herbs I don't recognize are growing along that row there."

"Just point to them, and I'll tell you what they are," offered Jack. He stood near a narrow footpath. With green shoots poking up everywhere, it looked like the others Fiona must have tried to weed without success. As Jack strode the narrow paths, he began to point out to Abby various plants, calling out their Latin names, as well as their common ones. "Fiona favored the old heirloom perennials and open-pollinated plants," he said. "She liked seed saving, because plant diversity all over the planet is shrinking with every generation, and she wanted to do her part to save some of these old favorites, which soon will be gone forever."

"Well, I believe she was right about species loss," said Abby. "It also happens to be my philosophy."

He stopped and turned to look at her. "I see why my sister liked you so much. Fiona may have been, as you say, a free spirit, but I detect an independent spirit in you, as well. I like women who know their minds, blaze their own trails. I'd love to see your garden."

His proclamation had taken her by surprise. Abby hoped her expression revealed only her amusement and not her concern that it could be awkward for her if Clay was present. But despite her misgivings, she heard herself say, "Sure."

They returned to the house. Jack wrote out his cell phone number and, grinning, handed it to Abby.

Abby felt a subtle ripple of excitement. She plucked the paper from between his fingers and tucked it into her back pants pocket. "We'd better get to packing," she said.

The morning hours quickly passed, and by the time Abby glanced at the clock over the fireplace, her stomach was growling. It was nearly four o'clock. They hadn't eaten since breakfast, unless you counted the stale nuts, crackers, and cheese that had fortified them as they sorted, cleaned, wrapped, and packed each room in turn. Fiona's books had been carefully placed into boxes, and the boxes labeled with the word LIBRARY printed with a black felt-tip marking pen. These they had stacked behind the front door. She had counted out the items in Fiona's dish pattern and had noticed only one cup missing, while the remaining dishware and extra pots and pans had been wrapped and tucked into boxes for Jack to decide how to dispose of them. Fiona's clothing and shoes had gone into bags for the women's shelter and had been piled along the living-room window. Perishable food items and toiletries had gone into garbage bags. Jack would go through everything else when he had the time.

Abby stood and stretched as the CD of Portuguese fados finished. She had listened to the music of the world: country tunes, Peruvian pan flute, Urdu *ghazals*, folk music, Hindi devotional *bhajans*, movie scores, and Gregorian chants. Fiona's eclectic musical taste was nothing short of amazing. Who but such a free spirit could feel inspired by music spanning such diverse traditions and cultures? And Jack seemed to enjoy it, too. He had chosen to spend his life in a discipline that would take him to diverse cultures in the world as he studied plants and their uses. Had they both received some exotic gene in their makeup, or had they been influenced by someone in their formative years? Abby made a mental note to ask him.

Picking up a towel to fold, Abby gazed at Jack, who stood in the kitchen doorway with glasses of iced tea. She put down the towel and sank onto the couch. He handed her a glass and stretched out next to her to sip from his. After catching sight of a picture among family photos scattered about on the floor, he picked it up and stared at it. In a field, a boyish-looking man embraced a young, dark-haired woman who was attempting to tuck a dandelion flower in his hair. The sun seemed to be rising and casting its warmth and glow upon them.

"She met Tom," Jack said, his voice cracking, "at the Wash and Dry in Boulder Bluff. It's where she landed when she first came to California. She was in a group of women who shared a vision of living a more spiritual life apart from religious dogma. They learned to be midwives and herbalists and earth mothers in every way. It was her journey, and try as I might to dissuade her and point her toward a real education, she stayed with that group."

"Marching to her own drumbeat," Abby said after swallowing a sip of the tea. "You have to admire her for that."

"By their expressions, you can tell they are in love, can't you?" Jack asked.

Abby stared at the image and nodded. "Yes, seems so."

A moment of silence ensued. Jack swallowed several sips of tea and then announced, "I want to see Tom. Is he in jail or at the commune?"

"Easy enough to find out," Abby replied.

"I have to ask him," Jack said. "I have to know." His tone sounded resolute. He impaled her eyes with a soulful gaze. His expression appeared full of strength and determination.

She nodded in agreement.

"You take her journals. See if you can learn anything. Before we put Fiona in her eternal resting place, let's you and I face him. I will know if he's lying."

Abby looked up to meet his gaze. "I do hope so, Jack."

Tips for Creating Drama in a Garden of Flowers

- Color: Plant drifts of plants with blooms in the same color for maximum impact.

- Paths: Create paths from pea gravel, stones, packed earth, or another material that meander into secret sitting/viewing areas. Or use the paths as linear elements in formal gardens.

- Statuary and Garden Art: Choose garden art or statuary that finds resonance with the type of garden you are creating. For instance, use whimsical pieces in cottage gardens and regal pieces in parterres or other formal garden designs.

- Surprise: Tuck a tea table, a whimsical element, a stunning mosaic birdbath, or a fountain in a hidden place, to be discovered by visitors to the garden.

- Theme: Consider a theme-oriented garden. For example, include plants with red and orange blooms to symbolize seduction, plants with white blossoms to represent purity and peace, or plants with flowers in primary and secondary colors to symbolize impressionism.

- Tiers: Use the three-tier approach to plant height: place the tallest plants in a bed to the rear, those of medium height in the middle, and the smaller bedding plants at the front.

Chapter 10

Don't be tempted to put eggs in your
pocket if you're passing by the
henhouse in your bathrobe. Forgetting
about those eggs could add an hour of
cleanup to your workday.

—*Henny Penny Farmette Almanac*

Woman, get a move on!
Abby read Clay's text message twice. A sense
of indignation and fury brought a flush to her
cheeks. Clearly, Clay felt pissed. She should have
expected it. Their plan had been for her to take
him from the Lodge to the farmette at some point
in the late afternoon. She hadn't known that the
work of packing up Fiona's cottage would take so
long. When Abby had realized how tardy she
would be, she had done the decent thing and had
sent Clay a text with an apology and a new ETA of
6:30 or 7:00 p.m. at the latest. And that home-
cooked meal might have to be a midnight supper,
but what did it matter? He could just cool his jets.
Her day, however, would be exhausting and long.

Why was she welcoming Clay back into her life when he was already making demands on her? What was up with that?

After a deep breath, Abby put the phone down and tried to breathe away the tension she felt. Her being late was becoming a pattern when it involved Clay. Was it a message from her subconscious to face her fears about starting up again with him? She did love him, but they shared a painful history, and a lover once wounded was forever changed. He had scarred her heart. The way she saw it, his emotional interior remained impenetrable, in spite of what he'd said about being unable to live without her. Now he would be in one of his dark moods again.

As her damp palms clenched the steering wheel and adrenaline pumped through her body, a twinge of anger drove her foot against the gas pedal. She felt the Jeep respond as she navigated into the passing lane along the straight section of the road back to town. She wasn't speeding, but she'd been driving faster than usual after turning from the mountainous spur road onto the highway. She hoped that a deputy sheriff or one of Las Flores's finest wasn't hiding in the thick blooming acacia along the roadway. From writing tickets back in the day, she knew all the places where the cops could radar while remaining half hidden; accordingly, she braked before passing each one. The sunset was still a couple of hours off, but what did it matter now? Clay would still be hungry. And she would still be late.

Sorting through Fiona's personal items had proven to be a daunting task, more so than either she or Jack had anticipated. They'd lost track of time while organizing and packing up the cottage. When she had realized she'd be more than an hour late meeting Clay, Abby had sent the text. His terse reply had seemed irascibly impatient. But as she thought about the day she'd just spent with Jack Sullivan, the anger and frustration fell away. She couldn't recall the last time she had laughed as hard as she did, in fits and spurts, at his unstoppable witticisms and funny stories. Perhaps her company and his use of humor had somehow helped him get through the otherwise somber task of sorting through his dead sister's possessions.

The hours had passed quickly, and they'd tarried far too long as they examined the small treasures Fiona had collected: clipped articles, pictures, strange found objects, and religious paraphernalia. Abby glanced over at the box of journals now resting in the passenger seat. Jack didn't have time to go through them, but he thought someone should, instead of relegating them to a bonfire, lest they contain information helpful to the murder investigation. And Abby had been only too happy to take them.

She slowed the Jeep to the posted twenty-five miles per hour after taking the Main Street exit. From there, she drove straight to the shelter. Someone had hung the CLOSED sign on the front door, so Abby continued around back. After spotting a large empty bin, she came to a stop, climbed out, dumped the black plastic contractor bags of Fiona's clothing and household items, returned to the car, and headed straight to the Las Flores Lodge.

Eight minutes later, she pulled into the driveway and spotted Clay pacing the wide stone veranda.

His computer bag rested near the front steps. He trudged past a potted fuchsia on leaden feet, his hands thrust deep into his jeans pockets, a scowl creasing his forehead. When his expression brightened upon seeing her, Abby felt her tension evaporate.

"Hi, handsome," Abby called as he dashed toward the Jeep.

After hopping in, Clay tucked the computer bag behind the seat, buckled up, and heaved a long exhale. "Finally! I've got the appetite of a grizzly for that home-cooked meal you promised."

"I'll get right on that," Abby said, thrusting the gear into reverse and turning around the Jeep. "Just as soon as I feed the dog, check on my bees, and lock the chickens in for the night."

"I see how it is!" he exclaimed. "In order of importance, I'm dead last."

Abby shook her head. "Seriously? You didn't just say that."

"Well, I'm growing weary of no wheels, those four walls where I'm staying, and the air conditioner humming twenty-four/seven. If I turn it off, all I hear is traffic and the sounds of the town. I'm a country boy at heart, Abby. I'll be the first to tell you, I'm looking forward to shutting off the alarm and waking up beside you to the call of that rooster of yours. What's its name?"

"Houdini." Abby merged into the traffic on Las Flores Boulevard, heading northeast toward Farm Hill Road.

"So named because?"

"He was herding my hens through a hole in the fence, trying to make a run for the border."

Clay chuckled. "I see. Taking his women with

him. Smart guy." He adjusted the seat to accommodate his long legs and leaned back. When Abby braked for the red light at the intersection of Main, he unlatched his seat belt, leaned over, and planted a sloppy kiss off-kilter on her lips.

"Hey, that'll get you arrested, mister. I'm trying to drive here," she said.

"It's still there, woman. I can feel it," he declared in a jubilant voice while reattaching his seat belt.

"What's still there? What are you talking about?"

"Love. You still love me."

"Oh, *really?*" *You can't possibly know how I feel when I'm not even sure myself.* Although Abby wanted to call him on his tendency to jump to conclusions, she also realized this wasn't the time or place. She wrinkled her nose at him instead.

"I'll wager you've been thinking about me all day, haven't you?"

Abby recalled her day with Jack. *If only you knew! How is it I never noticed just how maddeningly full of yourself you can be, Clay Calhoun?*

He continued, "Because I've thought of nothing but you today. Ever since I woke up and remembered. Still can't figure out why you didn't stay awhile after that smooch."

She looked over at him momentarily, arching her brow with interest. "It was a good night kiss, Clay. You knew I had to get back. And besides, you didn't feel well." Admittedly, he looked kind of cute and sexy today. He'd gotten his dark brown locks shorn, probably that morning, while she'd been up at the cottage, helping Jack. With the cowlick and sideburns gone, Clay's equally dark brown eyes, lashes, and brows dominated his features.

He flashed a dimpled grin. Before she could say anything more, he added, "All I can say is that you're a good kisser, you little seductress."

"Yeah?" Abby tried not to show her surprise. She hadn't seduced him. He, however, seemed to be the one on a relentless pursuit. But it was nice he'd remembered their kiss even after drinking the better part of two bottles of wine. Had he also recalled how much of a struggle it had been to climb the front steps of the Lodge? Or to get through the lobby and to his room with her five-foot-three-inch frame as his only support? That hadn't been sexy. But in a moment of weakness at his door, she'd yielded to passion. To say she hadn't enjoyed it would be lying. But clearly, he'd read a lot into it.

After a pause, he said sheepishly, "You need me, Abby. Haven't I been punished enough? I want to leave the doghouse."

Abby chortled. "I wouldn't characterize the Las Flores Lodge that way. The facility has lovely rooms and all the amenities anyone could want."

"But it doesn't have you."

"True," Abby said. "I've just been busy, and I wasn't expecting you to visit. I have all the bed linens to wash and groceries to buy. That reminds me. I ought to make a stop at the feed store to get more crumbles and scratch grains for the chickens. Not only that, but also some ground corncob for the henhouse floor, which I first have to clean, and then there's—"

"Now you're just being silly." His tone grew soft

and serious. "We have done this before, Abby. I can lighten that load you're carrying all alone. I want to help. I want to be with you."

And how long would that be exactly? Abby thought about that line used by Bernie, who worked in the evidence room at the police station. *I'm here for a good time, not a long time.* Her stomach tightened. She hated having doubts about Clay. But always at the back of her mind, the same old question drummed on: how to fall back in love and trust again after a betrayal.

"I see I'm going to have to woo you again," he said. He leaned back and closed his eyes. "Well, that's okay, Miss Abby Mac."

A smile toyed at the corners of her lips. He'd used his pet name for her. In the early days of their love affair, he would come into the farmhouse at night from whatever project he had been working on and call out, "Miss Abby Mac, I'm home." Then he'd act like he'd been working at some forklift plant all day and missing her. He would take her into his arms, snuggle his face against her neck, and tell her how much he had missed her. Remembering those moments felt like a balm on an old wound. It put to rest, if only momentarily, Abby's self-torturing doubt.

She focused on driving the last stretch of Farm Hill Road, deep in thought about clearing space on her calendar to accompany Jack to a jailhouse interview with Tom. She was about to mention her busy schedule to Clay when he broke the silence with a declaration of his own.

"I've made arrangements to have my truck shipped from the East Coast. It arrives at the farmette next weekend."

Abby didn't try to hide the shock her expression surely must have registered. "You did what? Aren't you getting a little ahead of yourself?"

"Why put off the inevitable? I'm ready. You're ready."

"I haven't said that."

"You didn't have to. Your kiss last night said it all."

After they'd arrived at the farmette, Abby declined Clay's offer of help with the chickens. Still peeved, she pointed him to one of two lidded garbage cans on the patio, where he'd find Sugar's dry food. Her water and food bowls would need filling. Then he could help himself to some tea from the pitcher in the fridge and amuse himself while she dealt with the hens. Following that, she'd make dinner. And he'd just have to wait until she was good and ready!

As she walked toward the henhouse and the chicken run, a racket overhead impelled Abby to look up. Large black crows flew in an erratic back-and-forth, straight-line pattern, as if trying to drive away some threat hidden in the towering pine tree. She strained to see what had gotten the crows so riled. Then she spotted it—a hawk with a wingspan of maybe four feet and a seven- or eight-inch reddish tail lifted off a tree limb. It swooped straight across the farmhouse, rose up high above the chicken run, and alighted in the aged, gnarled oak that rose majestically on the vacant wooded property behind Abby's.

"Whew. That was close, ladies," Abby said, approaching the gate of the chicken run. "And thank you, Houdini, for rounding up the girls and bunching together like little frozen statues. I don't believe that a hawk can penetrate the hole in the poultry-wire ceiling of the run, but all the same, I'll put Clay to work on it tomorrow."

Suddenly, she didn't feel so miffed at Clay. If she played nice, he might prove useful in banging out some of the projects, like the chicken run and the bee house, which she longed to complete but never seemed to have enough time to do. She poured a helping of scratch grains from the twenty-five-pound bag into a large pottery saucer on the ground and checked the hanging canister of food. Still half full. After dumping the stale liquid from the water dispenser, she listened momentarily for its refilling with fresh water.

Clay met her as she crossed the lawn to the patio, where the strains of sultry jazz floated across the evening air. "We always had music playing, regardless of what we were doing. You remember, Abby?" He reached out to her and pulled her close, kissed her hair. "We are good together."

Abby's guard went up, although she wasn't entirely sure why. This was what she'd wanted, wasn't it?

Sugar left her bowl of nuggets and bounded across the yard, then jumped on Abby with a happy *yip, yip, yip*. Abby pulled back from the embrace and knelt to hug the dog. When she stood up, Clay had walked to the fence and was staring into the deserted wooded acre behind Abby's farmette. Although food preparation was the last thing on her mind, she walked to the kitchen and grabbed a pot from under the counter and started water boiling for pasta. After setting out the olive oil, pine nuts, and parmesan cheese, she inserted the blade in the food processor. She dashed outside to the patio herb pot to pluck a handful of fresh basil to add to the other ingredients. With the pesto made and the pasta still bubbling away, she washed some organic tomatoes and then sliced the tomatoes and fresh provolone for a Caprese salad. From the cupboard above the counter, she pulled half a loaf of sourdough bread, which would pair well with cultured butter flavored with fresh basil and garlic and made less than a week ago. It was simple fare, but just the kind of home-cooked meal Clay would enjoy.

Clay plugged in the twinkle lights that Abby had strung around the partially framed patio. Her dream was to one day turn it into a screened-in room that allowed light and air in, while keeping out flies, bees, and mosquitoes. But until then, it afforded a place away from the hot kitchen in the cool night air without having to flip on the outdoor lights mounted on the wall.

"I have a confession, Abby," Clay said in a serious tone. He twirled the pasta on his plate around his fork.

"Another one?" Abby asked, leaning back against the patio chair cushion. "So, go on. . . . I'm all ears."

"I've ordered lumber. The local DIY guys will drive it out in the morning."

"Here?"

He snorted, "Where else?"

"Lumber? For what?"

"The master bath."

"How could you know what to order when you haven't taken measurements?"

"Who says I haven't? That first day, when I brought the tools out here and waited for you in the house, I borrowed your new measuring tape."

"Oh . . . Will these surprises of yours never end?"

"It's part of my master plan," Clay said with a broad grin. "Get ready for this place to transform."

Transform, huh? Your master plan? What about mine? Abby mustered a polite grin and pushed back her plate. Leaning back against the chair cushion, she listened intently to the chorus of peepers and crickets. Perhaps their sound could drown out the voice inside her head that complained about him moving too fast. She searched the deepening violet sky for the early evening star as Clay began to spin a spell, talking through his ideas for the bath but never once asking for feedback or her opinion. She knew any plan he conceived would be an improvement on that nasty, cheap shower enclosure around the chipped tub, but why hadn't he asked her what *she* wanted?

Empowerment could take many paths, and maybe this was hers. Although it had been a long time coming, she was beginning to understand that passion could carry them only so far. Before their romantic love could become an enduring bond that could last a lifetime, there had been an abrupt rupture. And the great irony was that during Clay's absence, she had found stability from learning to trust the surest voice around her . . . and it had emerged from deep within her being. Now that selfsame voice sounded a niggling doubt that she could ever be a dutiful wife waiting for her man to come home after another of his far-flung trips.

When he got up and pulled her to a standing position to kiss her, Abby mustered a generosity of spirit, rationalizing that if she could allow herself to relax into his embrace, her misgivings might evaporate. The sweet moment ended almost as it began when Clay began swatting at the mosquitoes puncturing his bare forearms.

"Our cue to go inside, I guess," said Abby.

"You want help rinsing the dishes?" Clay picked up her plate and put it on top of his and then loaded the silverware and glasses.

"Nah. I'll do the dishes. You relax."

"Couch or bed?"

"Suit yourself."

By the time Abby had finished the dishes, made a cup of green tea with roasted brown rice, and locked the sliding glass door to the patio, Clay had fallen asleep on top of the coverlet. Clothed only in his underwear, he had stretched his tan body across the middle of the bed and was tangled in the sheet. Abby retrieved the laptop at his side and briefly noted the screen display of bathtubs. After turning off the laptop and placing it on the floor, she paused to look at how Clay's body curved against her bed pillows and sheets. Just like in the old days. All she could think about over the past year was his coming back to her. Here he was. But her desire to crawl in next to him was weaker than her desire to read Fiona's journals. She padded barefoot away from the bedroom, with Sugar trotting right behind her.

Abby sank onto the oversize leather couch with her cup of tea. She reached for the journals, an eclectic mishmash of styles, colors, and shapes. From the dates inside the journals, Abby soon figured out the chronological sequencing and put them in order. Some of the journals were plain composition books with lined pages, like those used by high school students. Other journal covers sported elaborate designs, perhaps appealing to Fiona's imagination. Scanning the first of them, Abby realized that the disparate artwork on the journal covers found resonance in Fiona's cursive ramblings. She had written some passages in a careful cursive, while scribbling others. In the earliest journals, Fiona had kept a record of her meditation practice. She wrote about how the teachings of different gurus jibed or conflicted with her Catholic upbringing. Through her inner spiritual experiences and analysis, Fiona had unwittingly charted the intellectual and spiritual contours of her mind.

I feel the surge of energy in my spine, at my heart. Then my throat. My body spins. Awareness expands. I'm on the ceiling, then turning, facing down to look upon my body. How strange that I am there, as a body, but also here, as the mind. Who is it that sees me?

Abby swallowed the last of her tea and set aside the cup. She grappled with Fiona's ideas of duality, not sure why it mattered so much. A gentle breeze stirred the long copper tubes of her harmonically tuned wind chime. The notes sounded peaceful, like a spiritual hymn. The breeze grew stronger, entered the open screened door to caress Abby's arms and legs. By lamplight, she read on.

Abby realized that Fiona's yearning to be fully present in her life as a spiritual being—equally at home in the invisible and the visible world—lay nakedly exposed across her handwritten pages. For a moment, she felt conflicted about continuing to read. Fiona would not have wanted her life dissected, as cops were obliged to do when working to solve a murder. And although exuberantly free-spirited, Fiona probably would have balked at having her sacrosanct journals combed for clues by others. Thinking about putting aside the journals, Abby reminded herself that the search had to be done by someone. That being the case, Fiona likely would have wanted the reader to be a friend.

Abby meticulously thumbed through the pages, then suddenly stopped. She ran a finger under sentences in a section about a seer who foretold a bright future for Fiona. Elsewhere, she read about Fiona's desire to make sense of her dreams. She read, too, about instances when Fiona's inner vision collided with physical reality.

> *I pray and meditate today, as usual, in the big blue paisley chair next to the window. I feel the bliss of the religious rainfall Samadhi. It feels strong. My resistance diminishes the bliss. It eventually subsides. Dr. Danbury's other cat, Clea, is pregnant. I've been feeding her, and now she climbs into my lap. She starts birthing her babies. I get up and put her on the towel in a box behind the couch. New life . . . a beautiful thing to witness.*

Abby lost herself in Fiona's world as page after page of entries revealed the restless spirit of a woman who refused to live her life on the train tracks of habitual routine and mindlessness. During the last three months of her life, Fiona had written about relief at ending the dalliance with Laurent Duplessis; her deepening love for her husband, Tom; and her fear that someone wanted to harm her. The anxiety showed up in entries posted at all hours of the night, some of them about nightmares with dark imagery. Fiona had clearly tried to extract meaning from them. Tucked into those pages, Abby found a brown wool scapular bearing the face of Jesus. Making a mental note to give it to Jack, she thumbed through the next few pages and found papers that had been shredded. She realized after reassembling them that they were the divorce papers Fiona had never signed. On the last page of that journal, Fiona had written the date of the Friday before the weekend she died. In the margin was the numeral eight and snake figures. *He's setting me up. I know what's going on now, and I have proof.*

Abby turned the final page and found a key taped to the inside back cover. She stared at it, speculating about what it might open. Seeking answers, she'd found more questions. Now she was stumped. Her neck ached. Eyes were tired. She laid aside the book and reached for the soft blanket draped over the couch. Pulling it over her, she turned off the table lamp.

Before her mind's eye, a bizarre gallery took form—images of Fiona's inner circle. The snake that Fiona had interpreted as a dream symbol of deceit and betrayal had figured prominently in more than one dream. Abby wondered what could link the partial tire track, the smoker's nicotine patch, Fiona's necklace, Laurent's missing briefcase, the journal notations of a snake, the number eight, and that key. She stifled a yawn, knowing that she needed to let her brain rest, if only for an hour. Perhaps things would become clearer after the sun came up.

Tips on Cleaning Eggs to Sell

Don't dunk dirty eggs in water and wash them. You'll remove the bloom, the natural coating that prevents bacteria from entering the eggs. Instead, do the following:

- Rub the shells with a dry cloth to remove poop and other debris.

- Use a pot scrubber, a loofah, or a sanding sponge to gently sand off dirt, debris, or poop.

- Or dip a clean cloth in warm water (20 degrees Fahrenheit warmer than the temperature of the eggs) and wipe the eggs clean.

- Avoid submerging the eggs in water or allowing them to stand in water. Instead, try briefly spraying the eggs with water and then wiping clean.

Note: Clean eggs that are commercially refrigerated at 45 degrees Fahrenheit and 70 percent humidity will keep for about three months. In a standard refrigerator with less humidity, the shelf life of an egg is about five weeks.

Chapter 11

Two roosters will not a harmonious
henhouse make.

—*Henny Penny Farmette Almanac*

The one-room post office adjacent to the police
station smelled of paper dust and a lemon-
scented disinfectant from a recent mopping of the
green tile floor. Abby wrinkled her nose and walked
straight to the wall of mailboxes to retrieve her
business mail, hoping that the stench wouldn't
hang on her white blouse and navy blue crop pants.
When her key failed to release the box-locking
mechanism, she soon realized why. She had taken
Fiona's journal key from her daypack's zippered
pocket instead of her mailbox key. Using the other
key, she removed the mail—most of it junk—from
the box before closing and locking it. Abby tossed
the circular ads and discount cards in the large
corner recycling bin but held on to the bee catalog she'd requested from a Sacramento-based
company.

Leaving the post office, she noticed the attention-grabbing catalog cover. It featured a completely assembled painted hive with ten top bar frames, metal frame rests, an inner cover, and a lid—all for the unbelievable sale price of eighty dollars. A completely assembled and painted hive box for under a hundred bucks? No way. Something must be missing! She glanced up at the pedestrian walk light, which gave her the go-ahead. Abby stepped into the crosswalk and stole glances at the catalog cover as she made her way to the other side of the intersection.

A car horn blared. Tires screeched. Abby's hand flew out for balance and hit the hot hood of an approaching car. Adrenaline rushed through her. Her heart pounded. In a single movement, she clutched the catalog to her chest and gripped the shoulder strap of her daypack in order to race across the intersection.

Only after the champagne-colored BMW Alpina B7 started to roll forward through the intersection and turn onto Chestnut, where Abby stood at the corner, did she see the driver. Premalatha Baxter and her passenger, Dak Harmon, glared at her, as if the incident had been Abby's fault. Had they been carelessly speeding? Or had they tried to scare the wits out of her? Abby took a deep breath and shrugged off the incident. With murder on her mind, as it had been of late, she could be overreacting.

Except for her friendship with Fiona, Abby's dealings with the commune people had been minimal. She'd just as soon keep it that way. But she couldn't help wondering how anyone in that commune could afford a car that cost in the neighborhood of over a hundred grand.

The BMW rolled along Chestnut, toward the commune-owned Smooth Your Groove, with Abby watching and trying to shake off the tension her body still registered. After sliding the catalog into her daypack and zipping the daypack shut, Abby hitched her pack over her shoulder and set off again. Her cell phone vibrated in her pants pocket. It had to be either Jack or Kat replying to Abby's earlier texts. From Kat, she wanted to find out if Tom Dodge had been arrested, as reported, or simply detained for questioning. And from Jack, she wanted to know if he could help her figure out what lock Fiona's journal key might turn.

Glancing at her cell phone's screen message, Abby felt the dark energy from the near accident lift as she read Jack's short text: **See you in a few**. Abby kept a watchful eye on the parked BMW until she approached Lemon Lane, where she turned right. No harm in taking a look at the shops facing Main Street whose back doors opened onto Lemon Lane. That was where the delivery truck, vendor, and hired help activity took place. Fiona's shop, now shuttered and locked against the likes of Laurent and anyone else, held the most interest for Abby. She saw no one around Fiona's shop. But at the rear of the other shops, the activity was as brisk as that at the entrance to a beehive illuminated by the first rays of morning sun.

On the approach to Tilly's Café, the seductive scents of pancakes, maple syrup, bacon, and fragrant coffee drew her inside. She waved to Pedro, the short-order cook, who was slaving away over an egg scramble on his commercial grill. He lifted his spatula in acknowledgment as she claimed a counter stool and dropped her pack onto the adjacent seat for Jack. She didn't have to wait long for him to show. Within five minutes, the bell on the front door jangled. Abby looked up and felt a lurch of excitement as Jack strolled toward her.

He seemed in a cheerful mood, calling out with an affected Irish accent, "Well, look at you there. How are ya?"

Abby smiled. He seemed to enjoy speaking with an Irish brogue when in a good mood. Or whenever it suited him.

The twentysomething waitress grabbed menus, sauntered over, and plunked them down on the gray Formica countertop. She turned over the coffee cups. Pushing back a tuft of pink hair that had slipped over her ear, she asked Abby, "Know what you want?"

"Just orange juice for me," Abby said.

"I heard that," Pedro called out. "No harvest pancakes and scrambled eggs? I know you love them."

Abby laughed and called back, "Oh, yes, I do, but I cooked eggs before I left the farmette this morning."

Jack stared at the menu. Damp and loose curls in a halo of light brown clung to the sides of his face and his forehead. His whisker stubble further accentuated his angular cheeks and nose, making him look like a rugged sailor.

Definitely eye candy, Abby thought. She tried to gauge the waitress's reaction to him, but the girl was all business.

"Your order, sir," the waitress said.

Jack laser focused his baby blues on the face of

the pink-haired waitress. "Something with a wee bit of elixir, if you'd be so kind. The stronger the kick, the better."

"Seriously," Abby said, shaking her head. "And what about breakfast?"

"Well, if you insist," he said with a sly grin. "A pint of plain will do. Rich in cereal, grain, yeast, and alcohol."

Abby arched a quizzical brow.

"What?" he asked with a broad grin. "It's got your four main food groups, plus some extra benefits!"

Tapping her notepad with a fake fingernail, the waitress seemed to lose patience. She raised a pencil-thin brow and said, "We don't serve alcohol here. You might try the Black Witch, a few doors down."

"He's teasing," said Abby.

Jack continued grinning. "Now, don't you be losing patience with me. I'll just be having what she's having," he said, with a nod to Abby.

"So . . . two glasses of orange juice?" A defiant brow arched as the waitress scribbled the order.

"Hang on." Jack winked at Abby. "Aye, and the breakfast special . . . a feller needs filling up after living on tins of salmon, sardines, and crackers for days." Winking at Abby again, he explained, "Getting sick of cat food."

The waitress cocked her head. "So you're changing your order from just juice to the special now?"

"Indeed." Jack seemed to enjoy annoying the young woman.

The waitress exhaled heavily and walked over to give Pedro the grill order.

Jack reached for Abby's pack with one hand and grasped her elbow with the other. A warm shiver from the touch of his hand on her arm sent Abby's thoughts spinning and her heart racing. *This is just silly. Stay focused, and get a grip.*

He guided her to the last table at the back of the room. "She'll find us," he said, cocking his head toward the waitress. "Here it's a little more private for us to talk," he said in a serious tone, devoid of the accent.

Abby laid aside her pack and took a seat.

When Jack pulled a chair out from the table, the chair legs screeched over the ceramic tile flooring, and Abby flinched. Her thoughts flashed back to the crosswalk incident. Her nerves jangled; her stomach churned.

"Can you believe those commune people nearly picked me off in the crosswalk?" Abby's face flushed with heat.

"What do you mean?" Jack's eyes expressed alarm as he dropped her pack on the floor next to her chair and took a seat. "When?"

"A few minutes ago. I had the green light to walk and was in the middle of the crosswalk. She had to see me."

"Hold on," said Jack. "You know the driver?"

"Yes. Premalatha Baxter, the commune manager. She was with that gorilla, Dak Harmon, the leader's bodyguard. The commune business must be turning a nice profit for her to be driving a brand-new BMW."

Jack leaned in, his expression dead serious. "Why would you be on their radar?"

Abby blew a puff of air between her lips. "I'm guilty of being friends with Fiona and with you. You are Tom's brother-in-law, and he's one of them. So as far as I can tell, that's it. Well, unless being inquisitive is an affront to them. I do ask a lot of questions."

"My advice, if you want it," said Jack, "is to cut that Premalatha a wide berth."

Abby nodded.

"So your text said you had found a key," he said, leaning back into the chair.

Abby nodded and reached in her watch pocket, then placed Fiona's key on the table. "Taped to the inside cover of one of Fiona's journals. Any idea what it unlocks?"

Jack turned it over. He stared at her, seeming baffled. He shook his head.

"At first I thought it might go to a post office box." Abby fished out her mailbox key and dropped it next to the journal key. "See what I mean?"

"Yes. They're quite similar." Jack's gaze was riveted on her face and then moved beyond the keys on the table to the open collar of her white eyelet-trimmed blouse.

Her fingers flew to the blouse's undone top button. Abby's cheeks burned. "What about a safety-deposit box, like at a bank or a credit union?" Abby asked, hoping she might shift his attention.

"It's possible, I suppose." His expression registered faint amusement, but he stayed on topic. "But which bank and which box number?" Raking his hands through his curly locks, he said, "Maybe Tom would know."

"That's what I thought. Next point . . . who gets access to a box in a financial institution? As Fiona's husband, Tom is her next of kin, barring a surviving parent, which doesn't apply, since your parents predeceased you both. And she bore no children, right?"

"Right."

Abby looked up as the waitress arrived with their glasses of orange juice. Before continuing, she waited until the young woman had departed for the area where Pedro plated the food. "Do you know if your sister made a will?"

"The police asked me about that," Jack said. His pale blue eyes locked onto hers, and for a millisecond, Abby felt a slight shiver of pleasure. "In her original will, Fiona left everything to that old teacher from India and his organization. But then, when the old man left and Hayden Marks took over, Fiona told me she was quitting the commune life. A year after starting her business, she told me she'd revised her will."

"Oh, I'll wager the homicide team would want to see that . . . find out who stands to gain financially from her death."

"They asked me for it."

"And . . . ?"

"I would have given it to them if I knew where to find it." His long, tapered fingers rubbed the stubble on his jaw. "We didn't find it in the cottage. We both know that. Was there no mention of it in her journals?"

"No." Abby leaned in, tilting her face slightly up toward his. "If we could locate the box this key fits . . ."

"Maybe we'd find the will." Jack's tone sounded conspiratorial.

"Except for one inherent problem." Abby sighed.

"What's that?"

"Let me lay it out. Let's say Fiona had a safety-deposit box where she banked. A bank employee could open the box and look for her will. That's good. The banker would try to determine whom she named as executor of her estate. That's good, too. If Fiona named you, you would get access to that box. But here's the bad news. If it's not your name, but someone else's, most likely, the bank would try to contact that person."

"What if they can't find that person or he's in jail?"

"You might need to consult an attorney. I'm not an expert, but I think the bank employee would most likely turn the contents of the box over to the county probate clerk."

"So, we need Tom's help?"

"Yes, I think we do." Despite her churning tummy, Abby finished her juice and leaned back in the wooden chair. "Jack, can you think of anything else about Fiona's life? During her last days, did she fall out with anyone, like an acquaintance or a business associate? Can you think of anything at all that might have bearing on the case?"

Jack chewed his lip in silence, apparently mentally parsing the details of his sister's last days and weeks of life. His pale blue eyes drilled into Abby, although he seemed unaware of it. Still, Abby felt energy, like a whisper, passing between them. Her grandmother Rose, who had had a rich and imaginative inner landscape, would have counseled Abby to notice it without naming it. Naming something would confine and narrow the scope of it. But even as Abby's thoughts whispered, *Fiona*, her hands grasped for the cool Formica tabletop. A beat passed. She reached for the keys.

Jack snapped out of his reverie, took the keys from her hands for a final comparison. Then, pressing both keys back into her palm and cradling her hand in his, he said, "You know, I talked with Tom by phone right after I learned of her passing." He choked up, hardly able to utter an intelligible word. "He asked if I could handle the burial if he chipped in some money. He said he just wasn't up to dealing with it. And one more thing . . . ," Jack said, with his eyes narrowing. "Tom told me he felt responsible, but wouldn't say why."

"Not exactly a confession," Abby said, only too aware that Jack was still holding her hand. She gently pulled away from his grasp and slipped the keys into her pants pocket.

He downed his juice and set the glass on the table. "I don't think Tom would hurt an ant, and certainly not Fiona. What I can't fathom is why he'd try to pawn her jewelry. Why can't the police eliminate him as a suspect? And why—if he knew anything at all about that key you found in her journal—did he not mention it to me during our phone call?"

Abby absentmindedly tapped a fingernail against the table surface. "Fiona pretty much penned the narrative of her life in those journals. Toward the end of the last journal, she wrote about her foreboding sense of doom, her nightmares, and moments of extreme anxiety. It appeared that she had panic attacks, without knowing why or seeking help. I suppose, put into perspective, all her observations could add up to a premonition of her death." Abby breathed in a shallow, quick breath to push away the raw emotion she felt.

Not a minute later, she remembered the scapular. "Oh, jeez, I almost forgot," she said. She unzipped her pack, fished out the religious item, and handed it to Jack. "I found it in the same journal as the key," Abby said, zipping the pack and dropping it onto the empty chair beside her.

After dabbing his mouth with his napkin and laying it aside, Jack took a close look at the scapular. He smoothed the strings connecting the two square pieces of brown wool and just stared at it.

Seeing his eyes fill with tears, Abby looked away. She watched as the pink-haired waitress across the room arranged plates of food on a tray, picked the tray up, and started walking toward their table. The young woman set before Jack a steaming plate of scrambled eggs, a bowl of fruit, a side of sausage, a platter of pancakes, and a serving of toast. Jack sniffed and cleared his throat. He slipped the scapular into his pocket.

"Enjoy your food," said the waitress, before sashaying away to grab the coffeepot and head to another table.

"I should have warned you that they serve large portions here." Abby chuckled.

He said, wiping his eyes with his napkin, "Good. All I need are some bangers and beans to make it a true Irish breakfast."

Watching him first devour the mixed fruit and then a slice of toast, Abby said, "You know, Fiona was never going to divorce Tom. I found the papers, which she'd torn up and tucked inside a journal. Do you suppose Tom knew?"

Jack nodded and helped himself to a forkful of sausage and egg. "Like I said, in the end, they may have chosen different paths for the life that each wanted to live, but they loved each other. Of that much, I'm sure."

The bell on the restaurant's front door jangled. Abby looked up to see Otto Nowicki, in his blue uniform and black boots, his shiny silver star on his chest, heading to the counter. After waving him over, Abby watched as he changed course, making a beeline to her.

"Gotta say, Abby . . . you must have a good reason to be hanging here at our café when you've got all that healthy food at your place," Otto remarked.

Abby smiled and presented an open palm toward Jack. "Otto, this is Jack Sullivan, Fiona's brother."

"I know," Otto replied. "Mr. Sullivan and I have already met." Otto extended a thick pale hand, which Jack shook vigorously.

"Of course you have," Abby said.

Pulling out a chair for Otto, Jack asked, "Have you arrested my brother-in-law, Tom Dodge?"

"*Detained* is the word. For questioning," Otto replied, eschewing the chair.

"But I heard on the radio that Tom has been arrested," said Abby.

"That's the local media for you. Rushing to a headline, they beat out the competition. We haven't charged anyone. Nor is an arrest imminent."

Abby looked at Jack, knowing how much he wanted his sister's killer to be found and locked up. The dejected look on Jack's face could have chilled the butter pats on the hot pancakes. Jack put down his fork and stared at Otto.

"What did he have to say," Abby asked, gently probing, "about pawning his dead wife's favorite necklace and jewelry? He had to know that would look suspicious."

"He did. And it was," Otto answered. "But not illegal. He said his wife had given them to him in case he ever needed money. He wanted money now for her funeral." Looking at Jack, Otto said, "I asked you, sir, if this was true. As I recall, you said it would not be unlike your sister to give him the jewelry. And you also said he'd told you he needed help with the funeral expenses."

"And both statements are still true," Jack said.

"So you detained Tom but didn't arrest him?" Abby asked.

Otto wrapped a thumb around his duty belt. "Yep. But we requested copies of those pawn receipts from the jewelry shop owner. As for Tom Davidson Dodge, we've cautioned him to stick around. I assume he's back home by now."

"You mean up at the commune?" Abby said in an attempt to clarify Otto's statement.

"Yes." Otto shifted his attention from Abby to Jack. "I want to let you know, Mr. Sullivan, that there'll be a couple of our guys in plainclothes keeping an eye on things at the funeral. Okay with you?"

Jack nodded.

Abby pushed back a lock of reddish-gold hair from her forehead and once again straightened the open collar and tugged down the eyelet-trimmed sleeves of her blouse. "A quick question before you go, Otto. I'm trying to reach Kat. Is she working today?"

"If you call patrolling the fairgrounds work."

Abby chuckled. "Of course. I forgot she was pulling that duty. I'll catch up with her there. It'll give me a chance to find out if any of my jams and honey did well in the competition."

"You do that, Abby." Otto turned away and ambled over to a table where he could sit facing the room.

"Doesn't he like our company?" Jack asked.

"He's not unsociable," said Abby. "If he eats here alone or with other cops, he'll get a free meal. The owner likes having cops around, and cops like to sit with their backs to the wall. Call it self-preservation. He's in uniform, a clear target for cop haters and killers on the loose, even in a small town."

Tips for Keeping Roosters and Hens Safe from Predators

- Bury the bottom of a poultry-wire fence around a chicken run about eight to twelve inches to deter foxes and raccoons.

- Weave a poultry-wire ceiling across the top of the chicken run to thwart attacks from above by hawks and eagles. A poultry-wire ceiling also keeps chickens from flying out of their protective zone.

- Running a double layer of poultry wire around the chicken-run fence can keep foxes and raccoons from tearing through the fence and attacking the chickens.

- Use a strong, heavy-duty poultry wire that is 2.0 to 2.5 mm thick for best results.

- Electric fencing works, too, as a deterrent to wild predators; however, it must be incorporated into the fence at the top and the bottom. This is not a good option if there are children and pets on the property.

- Always lock your chickens in the henhouse for the night.

Chapter 12

The sixteenth century had its own version of smoothies: smoldering passions were cooled by drinking water sweetened with honey, sprinkled with florets from lavender buds, and spiced with cinnamon, nutmeg, and cloves.

—*Henny Penny Farmette Almanac*

"Hold up there, daddy longlegs!" Abby exclaimed.

She and Jack were strolling along the sidewalk on Lemon Lane, the short paved street that ran between the fenced play yard of Holy Names parochial school and the rear entries of the shops that faced Main Street. The key she'd found in Fiona's journal had piqued her curiosity, prompting Abby to suggest that she and Jack visit his dead sister's shop. With his hemp-colored cargo shorts swinging around muscular legs and his moss-colored T-shirt proclaiming his activism with the slogan MY LIFE DEPENDS ON PLANTS, Jack, with his elongated strides, had Abby speed walking to keep up.

"Do you think you could slow the pace a bit?"

Jack turned to look at her, as if not fully registering what she'd just asked. Erasing the thoughtful, brooding expression that had claimed his unshaven face, a slight grin emerged at the corners of his mouth and widened into an impish smile.

"Where did you get those long legs?" asked Abby.

"Well . . . we can't all be little people," Jack jested in his affected Irish accent. "Blame it on my gene pool."

Abby smiled. "Was your father tall?"

"Ha! No taller than a rasher of pork-belly bacon stretched full out. But Uncle Seamus, my mother's brother, now he was the fir in our family of fruit trees. With uncut hair and his tweed cap on, he stood five feet, eight inches tall. And that was barefoot in his boots. He was fully an inch taller than the rest of our clan in Sneem."

"Sneem is a funny name. Is that near where you grew up?"

"No, but I have cousins there. A river splits the village into two parts, and relatives of mine live on both sides. One side sits nearest to the North Atlantic coast, and the other looks toward the Macgillicuddy's Reeks, Ireland's tallest mountains. Sneem is a pinprick of a place but, in my estimation, one of the loveliest in the world. We might come from what was once a village, but those of us in our tribe who are short—not me, of course, but the others here and afar—make up in attitude what we lack in height."

Sashaying sideways to avoid colliding with a wall planter, Abby lost her balance. Jack caught her and held her steady in an embrace until she pulled away. Her heart hammered erratically. *Thank you for blocking my fall. I'm not reading anything into it. Let's just keep moving.*

Even after they had resumed walking toward Fiona's shop, passing Cineflicks and Twice Around Markdowns, Abby still felt flustered. She pulled the shoulder strap of her daypack a little tighter and muttered, "Such a klutz. I can't believe I didn't see that. I could've smashed in my nose."

"And what a shame that would be," said Jack. "I rather like that nose, especially the freckled bridge, which looks as though the fairies have dusted it. And those eyes . . . the color of the sea along the Cliffs of Moher."

So, this silver-tongued devil is flirting with me. Best to ignore it. But Abby was beginning to think that his playful demeanor and overt flirtation could crumble the resolve of even the most stalwart woman intent on resisting him. His flattery made her nervous.

Abby mustered a feeble smile. There were a lot of things she wasn't sure about, but one thing she knew for certain: it would be a bad idea to flirt with Jack, even if he'd started it, because they soon would be alone inside the shop. One thing could lead to another, complicating and confusing the well-defined parameters of their current relationship. And she already had invited Clay back into her life. No, this was business, and they would keep to it. As they neared the shop's back door, she considered what she could say to tamp down any amorous intention he might harbor.

"You know, Jack, I mourn the loss of friendship with Fiona. Your sister was beautiful, smart, accomplished, and one of the funniest women I have ever met. She lifted self-deprecation to a high art, often remarking about how lightweight she was."

"Aye, lightweight and short, that Fiona. Served her right for refusing to hang with me from the backyard oak or drink water from the secret well in the woods."

And there's the accent again. Charming, to be sure. But do you not know I'm trying to be serious here? It occurred to Abby that Jack's remembering his and Fiona's youth helped him with his grief.

"And she refused to sample the ale Cousin Jimmy brewed in his basement." Jack's grin accentuated the deep dimple creasing the left side of his face.

Abby locked eyes with him. His look warmed her to her toes, weakened her knees. *Oh, good Lord. Seriously?* She reached out to the stucco wall, then ran her hands the six inches to the back door. Avoiding his gaze, Abby wondered if he felt it, too. She promptly changed the subject and injected a serious tone. "Speaking of secret places, I can think of only three things in Fiona's shop with keyed locks. Two of them are file cabinets, and the other is her desk drawer," Abby said. "I'm hopeful, though, that we might find something the key unlocks and, even more importantly, whatever she's hidden that Laurent Duplessis sought when he tossed the place."

Jack slipped the key into the back door keyhole and turned it until the mechanism released the lock. "You could just ask him."

"I'll get right on that," Abby replied. "Just as soon as we find him. Last I heard, he was being detained for a chat with immigration officers. They might have deported him, or if he managed to clear things up, he could be in Haiti or still around here. That said, I haven't seen him lately, but I'd sure like to know what he was looking for that he thought he could hide in that briefcase of his."

"I'll wager he was shoplifting while he was searching for whatever had gone missing."

Jack pulled open the door and motioned for Abby to pass. She flipped the light switch to the on position. The music started. Abby stared at the room's disarray. Files and papers littered the floor, the cabinets, and Fiona's desk. Jack swore under his breath. He picked up a book from the desk and returned it to an empty slot in the bookcase.

"I want to find that guy. All I need is about eight and a half minutes," he said.

"To do what?" asked Abby.

"Beat him into a brisket and whack his cabbage," said Jack.

"Seriously?" Abby tightly clamped her jaw and stared at him. If it weren't so funny, it would be sad. How could an otherwise intelligent man believe that a round of fisticuffs could fix anything?

Stepping from behind Fiona's Queen Anne desk, with its inlaid leather writing surface partially covered by files, Abby took note of the cut-glass bowl of peppermints wrapped in cellophane and the old-fashioned Rolodex. The latter seemed incongruous with the tech world of nearby Silicon Valley. She inserted the journal key partway into the lock of the desk drawer. When it didn't fit, she opened the drawer and searched it. Maybe there was a secret compartment, like the ones Kat would sometimes locate in period furniture whenever she and Abby went antiquing. After searching the drawer, Abby knelt and felt around underneath, but soon surmised that Fiona's desk had no such secret hiding place.

Jack walked around the small office, picking up folders from the floor and slapping them against the desktop. He fumed, "All heart, that Fiona. And just look at the jokers she attracted into her life— idiots, ne'er-do-wells, and Duplessis, who epitomized them all." He picked up another pile of folders from the floor and dropped it alongside the stack on the desk. Glancing at Abby, he quickly added, "But among her associates, you, Abby, were the exception."

"Duly noted," Abby said. Her attention flitted around the room, from pieces of furniture to a wall calendar hanging near a collection of nature photographs in cheap black frames. A dinner plate–size wall clock hung above a tall metal filing cabinet that stood between the wall and the doorway that opened into the showroom. She tried the file cabinet lock, but the key didn't fit in that lock, either.

Jack plucked a peppermint from the bowl on Fiona's desk, twisted and peeled off the wrapper. Popping the candy into his mouth, he pointed to a small credenza supporting a multifunction printer. "There's a keyhole we haven't tried." He held out an open palm, apparently indicating that he wanted Abby to give him the key, as though with a different hand, it might unlock something.

Abby walked away from the tall filing cabinet and handed him the key. After opening and closing each of the credenza drawers, Jack squinted at the lock and tried the key. It didn't fit. He then scanned the room for anything else with a lock.

"You've got to wonder why she had locking cabinets and drawers when she didn't lock any of them," said Abby, strolling to the credenza.

"Maybe she wasn't the only person with access." Jack passed the key back to her. He peeled away the cellophane from another mint.

After pocketing the key, Abby pulled open the credenza's top drawer and took note of its three separate compartments. She then thumbed through business payables, IRS documents, license renewals, liability insurance, employee records, tax returns, and a massive file of legal documents. Leafing through the legal material, Abby recalled a comment Jack had made to her when they first met. Maybe now was the right time to ask him about it. She glanced over at him. Apparently having decided to eat the whole bowl of mints, Jack had plopped down in Fiona's chair. He was hunched over the bowl.

"These candies are seriously addicting," he declared. His face remolded into a sheepish expression.

"Listen, Jack," said Abby. "I've been wondering about something. That day when Sugar and I showed up at Fiona's cottage, you accused me of being a reporter and said you'd had to protect your sister from small-town reporters in the past. Why? What had she done that required summoning her big brother from far-flung ports of call to protect her?"

His brows knit in a pained expression. "Accusations . . . mostly."

"Of what? Against whom?"

"A woman died," he said, crushing a mint between his teeth. "But it wasn't Fiona's fault. She was just . . . there."

Abby rolled her eyes. Clearly, she was going to have to wheedle the story out of him. "Jack, please."

He peeled away the wrapper from another mint as meticulously as if he was removing a floret from a lavender bud. Finally, he said, "Fiona was living in a community in the foothills of the Sierras, learning about herbs while serving as an apprentice to a local midwife. She worked there as a doula."

"A what?"

"Doula, a labor coach. No medical training, but in every other way assisting before, during, and after the delivery. She said the midwife used herbs in her practice to induce labor or ease the pain of labor, herbs that have been used and deemed safe for centuries."

"All very interesting," said Abby. It truly was, but how had the woman died? And what did that death have to do with Fiona? She glanced over at Jack just as he finished unwrapping yet another mint. He popped it into his mouth.

"So . . . what happened?"

"Well, that's about it."

"Well, a woman died, Jack, so there must be more to it," Abby said, no longer trying to hide her frustration. After stepping away from the credenza, she reached over to retrieve the bowl of mints.

Jack made a tsking sound. "The woman had the baby, but . . . then the trouble began."

"Tell me. I'm all ears."

Jack sighed. "It bothers me to talk about it."

"I can see that," Abby said, deciding to try a different approach. She flashed a disarming smile,

"Good Lord. That sounds like a fate worse than death," Abby said.

Jack nodded and grew quiet.

With their drama over and the tension finally leaving her body, Abby considered female rivalry as a motive for Fiona's murder. When she realized Fiona wasn't going to divorce Tom, Premalatha could have envisioned a more permanent solution to secure the man she wanted to marry. If that was the motive, did she also have the means and the opportunity? Kat had mentioned a phone call that Premalatha had made to Fiona at the time of her death. If she'd called her from the commune, that suggested that Premalatha could not have been with Fiona. What about Dak?

On the console, her phone rang, jangling her nerves and jarring her from her thoughts. Clay's image showed up on the screen. Abby slid her finger across the screen and tapped the green speaker icon.

"Is everything okay?" she asked.

"Why wouldn't it be?" Clay replied. "When are you coming home, woman?"

"Why? Is something wrong?" Abby exchanged glances with Jack, who now sported a bemused expression. Contrary to his usual politeness, he seemed all too ready to listen to her conversation with Clay. Abby could have removed the call from the speaker, but then she'd have to pull off the road. It was mid-afternoon, time marched on, and she still hadn't gotten through her to-do list.

"You've got to see how far along I got in the master bath today. I just had to pop out a small section to accommodate the jetted tub measurements. The framing is done, and I've got most of the copper piping done. Tomorrow I'll be ready to feed the electrical cabling through the studs. Shoot, at this rate, you could be soaking in your new tub by the weekend."

"Oh, that's lovely!" Abby exclaimed. "So . . . nothing wrong on the farmette?"

"No. Although, I can't hear a thing with that nail-gun compressor going. Or when I'm drilling, for that matter. But while I was eating a sandwich, I noticed your red-colored chicken limping around."

"Ruby? Did she pick up a piece of glass or a thorn during her dirt scratching?"

"I wouldn't know. Oh, and you might want to know that a bunch of your bees left their hive and are circling a limb of that huge peppertree out back."

"A low limb, I hope," said Abby.

"Not hardly. More like twenty feet up."

Abby groaned. "Dang it . . . Those limbs are rigid. And I'm going to need a spring action to shake the bees loose, so they fall into a hive box." She let a sigh escape through her teeth. "And how am I gonna get up there?"

"You'll be glad to know that I put a tall ladder on my purchase order for the materials delivered today. If you get home before dark, you can use it. I'll help. Otherwise, bee rescue will have to wait until tomorrow. I don't mess with bees after dark."

"So, I'm on my way. I haven't gotten your extra nails yet, but the DIY place stays open until nine o'clock. Be there as soon as I can."

Jack sneezed.

Out of habit, Abby said, "Bless you."

"You got somebody with you?" asked Clay.

Abby caught her breath. She looked in horror

at Jack, whose eyes expressed a wicked amusement.

"Wuh . . . I told you about my friend Fiona, who passed away." Abby tried to sound matter-of-fact to reassure him. "I'm driving her relative home."

"Just so long as it's not a hot hunk." Clay cleared his throat. "You've got one of those renovating your house, and tonight could be your lucky night."

Abby's cheeks grew hot. Was Clay trying to embarrass her? She wanted to hang up. If he felt uneasy over the possibility that she was with another man, just wait until he saw her shiner. How was she going to explain that? "Listen . . . let me call you back in a few. Okay?"

Silence ensued for a moment.

Clay's voice came through. "Whatever." His tone sounded like someone had just punctured his party balloon. Abby suspected that when she finally did get home, he would be in a mood and would be displaying that passive-aggressive behavior she hated.

"Later," Abby said, feigning cheerfulness. She tapped the phone to end the call.

Her heart galloped as she struggled against familiar hurt and lingering uncertainties about her relationship with Clay. She stole a look at Jack and wondered what kind of explanation she could give. To her surprise, no explanation was necessary. He had rested his head against the seat back and closed his eyes. Abby sighed in relief that she wasn't going to question her. But then again, why would he? Clay had made things pretty clear.

Abby drove to the turnoff at the big red barn and then navigated the Jeep up the bumpy driveway to Fiona's cottage. Once the car was parked and turned off, she sat gripping the steering wheel, in no hurry to move.

"Your hand still hurt?" she finally asked Jack, locking eyes with him.

He nodded. "Uh-huh. Your cheek?"

"Yes."

"Not life-threatening injuries," Jack said in good cheer. "And comforting to know that a doctor lives next door."

"Most likely blitzed out. In a stupor." Abby knew her words were unnecessarily negative, and that wasn't like her. Clay had put her in a dark mood. She inhaled deeply, let the breath go, and looked around. "But you know what . . . ? I don't see the doc's car. Oh . . . that's a scary thought."

Jack looked at her. "Just means we're alone up here on his ten acres. Why does that scare you? You think I'm going to take advantage of you?"

Abby laughed nervously. "Well . . . one can always hope," she said in a jesting tone. "No, it's just that Dr. Danbury shouldn't be drinking and driving." She tried to hide the fact that it did worry her to be alone on the mountain with Jack, because she could no longer deny her attraction, and it was getting harder not to show it. But Abby would not let herself go there, because doing so would just muddy up everything. They needed clear heads to solve this case.

The stifling heat inside the cottage took her breath away. "Sheesh, you could fry an egg on the floor in here."

"I should have left the windows open," Jack said. "But last night it was darn cold up here, and that wind off the Pacific comes through with a piercing howl. Keeps you awake at night." He began to open the windows one by one.

Abby hurried to the kitchen and filled two resealable sandwich bags with ice from the refrigerator's freezer. Then she pulled out a chair, sat down, and used her elbow on the tabletop to support her hand as she held one of the ice packs in place over her eye and cheek. She pointed out the other ice pack to Jack as he walked through the kitchen on his way to the bathroom. When he returned, she noticed he had cleaned up the dried blood on his face and had brought a damp washcloth and a tube of antibiotic ointment.

"Good on you, Abby, for insisting I not toss this tube during our purging of the place." He laid the ointment on the table. "Now, let me see that cut." After pulling up a chair to face her, he sank onto it and leaned forward to scrutinize her wound. "I'll have you right as ready in the blink of a crone's eye." He placed his hand around the back of her head. At his touch, Abby inhaled an abrupt breath and winced, not so much from pain as from the anticipation of it. With the damp cloth, Jack traced the edges of the laceration. His stroke was sure and steady. He paused to give Abby an arresting look.

Feeling a rush of adrenaline racing through her body, she closed her eyes, hoping she hadn't telegraphed anything.

"Now . . . just relax. I've got you. Tilt your head back a little more against my hand. That's my lass." The ointment smeared light as a butterfly wing fluttering along the length of the cut. The touch of the fingers soothed her. Then . . . there was no touch. No movement.

Abby opened her eyes to find Jack's eyes smoldering with intensity as he gazed at her, his lips so close they would have touched her if she'd nodded forward. He said nothing. She said nothing, but her cheeks flushed with warmth.

"You know, Abby," he said, his voice a husky whisper, "you smell awfully sweet for someone who's just been in a fight."

Abby's lips curved into a smile. "And here I thought I needed a shower."

He leaned back, pulled the neck of his T-shirt up to his nose, and sniffed. "No, if anyone needs a shower, it would be me." He rose and moved his chair back to its original position at the table.

Abby's thoughts raced back to when they first met. Having been interrupted during his shower, he'd answered the door annoyed. But then later on, when she had helped him sort through Fiona's things, he'd greeted her in an unbuttoned shirt, revealing a lean muscular torso. A shiver ran through her. *Oh, Lord. Don't think about that now.* Clearing her throat, she said, "Let me see your hands. You were shaking one of them pretty hard in the car."

"Aye. Jabbing that bollock brain was like a bare-fisted punch at a dicot angiosperm."

She looked at him, bemused. "Come again?"

"Hardwood tree."

"Yeah, well, your lightning jab broke his hold on me." Abby noted the impish grin that lit up his face, and turned her attention to his hands. "Bruising and swelling, but no cuts. Use that ice pack on them. Got any painkillers?"

"Oh, yes." He opened the fridge and took out two bottles of Guinness, popped off the caps, and handed her a bottle. "The liquid variety."

"I can see that," said Abby, suppressing a smile. She tapped her bottle against his.

Jack took a swig. "I'll just change my shirt," he said, then set the bottle on the table and hustled off to the bedroom.

When she could no longer tolerate the ice against her eye, Abby tossed the ice pack in the sink. She sipped from the beer and moseyed to the screen door at the back of the house, where an audible breeze rustled through the pines and redwoods. Looking out at the edge of the clearing between the house and the trees, Abby spotted the doc's cat stalking a bushtit. The bird flitted between a patch of sweet broom and a thicket, as if teasing the cat.

"Mind the hole," Jack called out from the bedroom doorway behind her.

Abby stopped short. She glanced down at the rug partially covering the hole. How could Fiona have allowed the hole to go unrepaired? With her landlord right next door, it could have so easily been fixed. As Abby thought about it, a realization began to emerge. *Hole! Oh, sweet Jesus.* She leaned down and pulled the rug back. "Jack, bring a flashlight, will you? And a cap or something for my hair."

"What? What's going on?" Jack asked.

"Just trust me."

A moment later, he handed her a blue plastic flashlight and an Andean-style woolen cap with earflaps, a braid down each side, and one garnishing the top.

"Seriously?" Abby handed him her bottle of beer, took the flashlight, and plucked the cap from his fingers.

He winked at her. "In case you haven't noticed, I've got a big head. It's not easy to find caps that fit."

"And it's only going to feel like a hundred degrees with all my hair under that hat, but never mind." She pulled on the hat, flicked on the flashlight, and looked at him with an expression of childish delight. "Spell *hole* backward."

Shaking his head, he stared at her like she'd lost her mind. "Okay. I can do that. . . . E-l-o-h."

"Precisely. Your sister's secret code. High time we found out what's in that hole."

Abby knelt and then lay flat on the floor, her face over the hole. She shined the light in. "Um . . . don't see anything. Maybe if I can squeeze my arm farther in and get my head down in there for a better look. Hang on." She moved into position. "Okay, let's see. Okay, okay. There it is."

"What? What do you see?" Jack asked.

Abby wiggled, willing her arm to reach farther, but soon realized her effort was futile. "Shoot. Can't reach it. And if I can't reach it, how in the heck did Fiona get it there?"

"What? How did she get what there?" Jack's tone sounded impatient.

Abby felt his body stretching out on the floor beside her. She wiggled and stretched some more.

"Pull your head out of that hole," he demanded. "Let me try."

"Would if I could," Abby called from under the floor. "How about a little help?"

Jack shifted his position. Abby figured he was up on his knees. She felt his hands around her hips, pulling her back until her head was out of the hole.

"There's a light-colored fire safe down there, and it's got a combination lock. I'm betting there are four numbers in the combination."

"The year Fiona was born." His eyes were shining when Jack took the flashlight from her. He wasted no time investigating the hole. "I see it."

Abby said, "Think you can reach it?"

"Doubt it." He tried. No success. "We need something with a hook. Let me think." He sat upright, with his back to the wall. "But what? We threw almost everything out."

Abby pulled on the side braids of the woolen cap. "There's a poker in the living room. And a three-prong trowel out by the garden fence. I remember seeing it when you showed me Fiona's garden. If you cut these hat braids off, we've got yarn to tie the trowel to the poker."

Jack uttered a long, low "Ohhh." After a moment, he said, "Genius. Going to the garden. Back in a minute."

Abby's phone buzzed with a text as she was pulling the poker from the tool stand next to the fireplace. Certain that it was Clay again, she figured it could wait. But curiosity got the better of her. She removed the phone from her pocket and glanced at the screen.

Just FYI, girlfriend. Health Dept. just closed down the smoothie shop.—Kat.

Abby texted back. **Holy chicken feathers. I want all the details, but busy right now. Will call you later.**

Sitting next to the hole, she looked out the back door at Jack hurrying toward her. She had the pole for the hole, and Jack had the hook. *Time to go fishing.*

Tips for Making Scented Dusting Powder

Scented oil derived from chamomile,
lavender, lemon balm, patchouli, peppermint, rosemary, or other herbs can be
used to create your own signature dusting
powder. To make six tablespoons (two
ounces) of scented dusting powder, thoroughly mix four to five drops of scented
herbal oil with one tablespoon of
cornstarch. Next, mix in five tablespoons
of unscented talcum powder. To retain the
fresh scent, the dusting powder is best
stored in a jar with a screw-top lid. Use a
powder puff, a cotton ball, or a brush to
apply it.

Chapter 14

A male hummingbird does not penetrate the female to mate—he presses his cloaca against hers in a cloacal kiss that lasts three to five seconds.

—*Henny Penny Farmette Almanac*

Abby lay stretched out on the floor, watching Jack maneuver the hooking tool they'd made by using the yarn from his cap braid to bind the fireplace poker to the garden trowel. After numerous unsuccessful attempts, he finally connected the trowel end of the tool to the handle of the fire safe beneath the floor. Concentration furrowed his brow as he inched the safe with precision toward the hole in the floor.

He stopped with a sudden gasp and drilled her with a blue-eyed stare. "I do believe it's within my reach. Take the tool," he said, handing her the makeshift rake. "Mind the yarn. I want you to rebraid it and stitch it back on my cap, where you cut it off."

"Seriously?" she asked.

"Oh, quite," he said with a straight face. He put his arm into the hole until his upper shoulder nearly disappeared.

What a picture this is. Abby thought about capturing it with her smartphone camera app but abandoned the idea when Jack, grunting, pulled the fire safe upward. He set it on the floor with a thud.

She reached up and removed his knitted cap from her head. Her reddish-gold locks tumbled in a loose mass over her shoulders. "Here you go," she said, tossing the hat to him. "You should have put it on before you put your head down there." She leaned over and plucked a cobweb from his hair. "Hope the spider wasn't still in it."

"Indeed," he said. "I should have thought of that. You know, it might be my favorite piece of clothing, that cap."

"You're kidding, right?"

"You've got to have your head covered if you are braving the cold wind in the high Andes."

"And when are you going there again?"

"Maybe never. But you never know."

"So . . . let me get right to work on that braid, then," Abby said in jest.

He smiled broadly, with amusement lighting his eyes. "You know I'm pulling your leg, right?"

Abby pursed her lips to keep from saying what she was thinking. *Oh, believe me, I know when you're pulling my leg.* She felt a little giddy.

Jack turned the safe upright and took a look at the numeric pins of the combination. "I'll punch in Fiona's birth date, but I'm going to need that key in your pocket," he said.

He spun through the numbers of the combination. Then he slid the key Abby handed him into the lock. It clicked and released. Jack let go a high-pitched squeal.

Abby jumped. "You scared me. What was that?"

"That, my girl, was the sound of happiness, the kind of joy that screams for a wee bit of bubbly."

"Shouldn't we see what's inside the safe first?"

"Right, you are. Come to think of it, I don't have anything with bubbly. Beer either. Rain check that idea," he said.

"Let's take the safe to the living room," Abby suggested. "We can examine the contents there without worrying about anything flying down that floor hole."

"Good on you, Abby. Always one step ahead."

After pulling Abby to her feet, Jack reached for the metal fire safe and carried it to the couch. He parked himself with the safe on his lap, then patted the couch seat beside him. "Come sit here."

Abby positioned herself right next to him. When he flipped open the safe's lid, she took note of a few papers, a framed picture, and a small ledger. The white envelope marked with the word WILL caught her eye. "You should open that," she said. To her surprise, he handed it to her.

"It saddens me to see it. I can't imagine she had much to leave anybody. And I would so much rather have her than a token of her life."

Abby lifted the flap of the unsealed envelope, pulled out the document, and read it. "I don't know if you'll welcome this news or not, but she left you the botanical shop. It says here that you can keep it or sell it to pay off the five-year loan she secured to start the business."

"Running a shop? I don't think I'm cut out for that sort of thing."

"Tom gets her jewelry," said Abby. "Well, I guess there's no surprise there. He already has it . . . or had it. I guess Lidia Vittorio at Village Rings & Things has it now."

Abby felt Jack push against her to look at the will. The warmth of his body was a tad unsettling, but she continued to read and share Fiona's bequests and instructions with Jack. "Says here there's a life insurance policy for fifty thousand, with Tom as the beneficiary. . . . Oh, but there's a proviso." Abby pointed to a line near the bottom of the page. "Tom gets the money only if he leaves the commune." Abby cocked her head to look at Jack. "Fiona seemed intent on Tom making a clean break with that cult. Perhaps she grasped better than anyone else what an isolated life he lived up there, with Hayden Marks and Premalatha Baxter dictating when and where he could go and taking his hard-earned wages."

Jack asked her in rapid-fire succession, "So how could the commune loan Fiona money? Do you think the leader wanted it paid back right away and knew about that policy? Do you think they could seize Fiona's insurance money from Tom to settle the debt?"

Abby looked astounded at Jack's insightful perceptions and chose her words carefully. "I think it's not only possible but also probable. And to answer your question about how Fiona could get a loan from the commune leader and his minions in the first place, I'd say they've got lots of money, unlike before. Fiona told me that before the previous leader returned to India, the community scraped to get by. Now the commune organization finances legitimate businesses, like Smooth Your Groove and

Ancient Wisdom Botanicals. As a nonprofit, they seek and get donations. Let's not forget the residents who work and contribute their wages, and their families who lend support."

Jack nodded. A muscle quivered in his jaw. He reached into the safe and took out a silver filigree frame that held a photograph of Fiona, bedecked in a red scarf and hat and throwing a snowball. Tom, bundled in a pea jacket, jeans, and muck boots, apparently had been hit by a snowball and stood sideways, with his hands in a defensive position. "Check out Red Riding Hood and her wolf having fun in the snow." He peered closely at the image. "Looks like the picture was taken up here, behind this house. See all those Christmas trees? A whole section of them."

Abby pulled the frame toward her to inspect the photo's background more closely. "You're right. I wonder who took this picture. Dr. Danbury?"

"But surely, it doesn't snow here in the mountains, with the ocean just over those ridges, about thirty minutes away?"

Abby released her grip on the picture frame. "Sometimes it does."

Jack thumbed through the ledger. When a folded sheet of paper fell out, he handed it to Abby and continued to examine the ledger entries. "These entries make no sense. Just numbers and notations, with no documentation key for deciphering anything," he said.

Abby unfolded the sheet of paper and quickly read it. "Well, this explains a lot. That ledger belongs to Laurent. Probably, it was what he was looking for when he burgled her shop."

Jack's brows shot up. "So that's why she went to all the trouble to hide it in the safe under the house."

Abby nodded. "I'm speculating about this, but perhaps Fiona wrote out this letter as a means of self-protection. If anything untoward were to happen to her, somebody at some point would discover this and learn the truth. She's telling us from the grave what she feared could happen. The letter explains that she knew what Laurent was doing and accuses him of stealing from her and selling illegal drugs. He packaged them in tins, otherwise used for mixtures of blended herbs and cut tobacco marinated in molasses, which are smoked in hookah pipes."

Jack laid the ledger in the safe and leaned over to scrutinize the paper with Fiona's handwriting that Abby held. "But how did he have access?"

"He worked there for a while. Could have made a key." Abby scooted to create a little space between herself and Jack and then twisted slightly so she could look directly at the handsome Irishman. "Don't you remember the HELP WANTED sign in the botanical shop's front window? Fiona was looking to hire a store clerk, but while she went through the interviewing process, she likely paid Laurent to help her." Abby gazed into his blue eyes. "Come to think of it," she said, "Fiona could not keep those smoking herbs in stock during his tenure, or at least that's what she told me."

She stared again at the note in Fiona's handwriting, with its explanation of the notations in the ledger. "Each type of drug had a code name, and the amount sold, the date, and the customer's name. Premalatha's name shows up a lot."

"I suppose she would have met Laurent at Ancient Wisdom Botanicals. Otherwise, how would their paths have crossed?"

Abby chuckled. "Las Flores is a small town with a small-town consciousness. People know who the residents are and who the outsiders are. Whom to trust, and whom not to trust. It wouldn't surprise me if the briefcase Laurent carried from Fiona's shop contained his drug stash. Probably already had another place lined up. Just so he could keep doing business as usual. Fiona trusted him, but he was just using her."

"My sister trusted everybody," Jack said with an exasperated sigh. "That was her undoing." He crooked an arm around the back of his head and stared out the bank of windows that looked out over the distant mountain ridges.

"The police will want to see this," said Abby. She carefully refolded the paper and placed it back inside the red ledger. As she did, a small object protruded from the bottom of the ledger—a necklace bearing a number eight charm. A cold shiver shot through Abby's body. After pushing the necklace back into the ledger, Abby closed the safe's lid and spun the tumblers. So . . . Fiona would have had insider knowledge about the significance of those necklaces. There was no need to burden Jack with an explanation about that now, she decided. That discussion could be put off awhile.

Abby considered the slow and methodical way the commune had evolved under the tutelage of Hayden Marks. He used isolation tactics. Moreover, he wielded a renegade authority to dominate the community, performing sham marriages and forcing wedges between legitimate husbands and wives. Wasn't that how many cult leaders gained control? Through dividing and conquering and also through isolating members from their families? Brainwashing certainly appeared to be the root of Tom's plight. He had seemed too scared to leave. Abby sighed heavily.

When she stirred to get up, Jack clamped his hand gently on her knee. "I know you need to go, but I don't want you to. I like your company."

Abby arched a brow and grinned. "And I like yours, too, but . . ."

"Well, there you go again with those buts."

"But, Jack, much as I'd love to hang out here, I've still got errands to run and dinner to cook and chores to do."

"Okay, then. Take me with you into town. I'll get my rental car tonight, so you won't have to deal with that tomorrow, before the funeral. But I'm going to ask for one more teensy favor. It's important to me, and not just because it means a little more time with you."

"And what would that be?"

"Fiona's body is at the church. I wonder, do you think you could spare the time to accompany me there?"

"Uh . . . um . . . I . . . uh—"

"Somebody ought to say the rosary for her. . . ."

How could they go into a church, the pair of them, looking like they'd just gotten the worst end of a street brawl? How could she possibly conceal her black eye and her cut face? In spite of those reservations, Abby couldn't bring herself to say no. Her intention to help Jack through the awful process of dealing with everything while his heart was raw meant doing this, too, barring incapacitation. She wasn't incapacitated. And Fiona wasn't just a victim; she was a good friend. But now, with stops at the police station and the church, how would she explain to Clay why she'd gotten home so late?

"I can't go to church looking like this. I don't suppose you have a shirt I could borrow? My blouse looks like I've been wallowing with a pig."

His expression brightened. "I've got shirts in the dirty, the dirty-dirty, and the dirty-dirty-dirty basket. From which basket do you want me to pull it?"

Abby laughed out loud. "Oh, good Lord. Seriously, Jack? You don't have a clean shirt?"

"To do laundry, I have to be in the mood," he replied with a boyish smile. "I've not been in the mood," he said, laughing.

"Oh, never mind." She brushed her hands over her blouse, as if by some miracle, the soil from her wrestling with Dak could be rubbed out. "Let's just go, but we have to drop that off at the police station first." She pointed at the fire safe. "And let me answer any questions, if they arise, about why we look the way we do. Let's just stick together. We don't want conflicting stories out there, and for all we know, Premalatha and Dak could come here complaining that we assaulted them."

He rose and helped her to her feet. Then, without warning, he pulled her into a tight embrace. "Yes, on all accounts, especially about sticking together."

Abby's legs felt like jelly. Her heart hammered. She closed her eyes for a brief moment and melted into the warmth spreading through her body in the embrace of his strong arms. *What am I doing?* She eased out of his arms and said, "What if the church is being used this evening? Sometimes the church allows a couple of other priests to hold charismatic Masses."

"Never been to one of those," said Jack.

"It's Mass, but more like those held during the first centuries of the Roman Catholic Church, with lots of music, praying in tongues, and anointing of the sick with holy oil."

"Well, we can't know until we get there," said Jack.

"You're right about that. The church secretary will have gone home for the day, and I don't think they put the dates for those special Masses in the church's regular recorded messages."

After explaining to the officer at the Las Flores Police Department how they came by the safe and how it was relevant to the open murder case, Abby drove Jack to Holy Names. The funeral home had delivered Fiona's casket, which rested on a stand in a private area to the side of the cavernous interior. Only two other parishioners, whom Abby didn't recognize, occupied the place. Jack and Abby lit candles and quietly said the prayers of the rosary. Afterward, Abby dropped Jack off where his car was parked near Tilly's Café, made a quick stop for the nails that Clay wanted at the DIY center, and headed out of town to her farmette. Hoping to make it before dark, she arrived just after sunset.

Sugar rushed toward Abby, and Clay called Abby's name, as she headed toward the side gate to the backyard with her daypack and the box of nails. She frantically brainstormed simple explanations for why she looked as though she'd been in a brawl, without admitting she had.

"Abby, the bees—" He stepped forward, looked her up and down. "My God, woman, what happened to you?"

"Obviously, I ran into something. I can be a klutz at times . . . but do you mind waiting until breakfast for the highlights? I know I'm late, and I'm sorry."

"Fine. Are you sure you're okay?"

"Perfectly." As much as she wanted to take a hot shower and to climb in bed, Abby knew Clay expected her to cook something. After all, he'd been working on her farmette all day. She'd have to praise him for whatever work he'd done in the master bathroom.

"I know what it is to be drop-dead tired," Clay said. He opened the gate, took the nail box from her, and set it on the ground. After drawing her into the yard and latching the gate, he embraced her tenderly, ignoring Sugar's incessant whining for attention. Abby pulled away long enough to kneel and hug Sugar.

"Good girl. I missed you, too. Settle down, now. Quiet."

Clay pulled her close again. "How about I tell you," he whispered in her ear, "that I've already eaten and so have Sugar and the hens? I refilled the chicken feeder with crumbles, checked the water level in the dispenser, and brought in the eggs. And the bed's already turned down."

"Music to my ears," Abby whispered back. Her eyelids felt heavy, but she dared not close them out of fear of falling asleep right then and there, on her feet, in his arms.

"Let's go inside," he murmured.

"Mmm . . . yes. If we don't, the mosquitoes will have us for dinner."

Abby awoke from sleep as a breeze gusted through the harmonic chimes beyond the bedroom window. Lying on her back, with her head resting on the cool cotton pillow, she breathed in the scent of night-blooming jasmine and tuberose mingled with Clay's citrusy aftershave. She could hear Sugar snoring like a big dog at the foot of the bed.

Turning her head slightly, she opened her eyes to narrow slits. Clay rested next to her in a semi-upright position against a pillow, scrolling through images on his laptop screen. Her eyelids fluttered closed, and she lay listening to his pattern of clicking and stopping before clicking again. It was kind of nice having his company, although it no longer felt as special as it once had. Still, he loved her and wanted to give her his life, or so he'd said. She would give their relationship a chance. *Scroll . . . stop . . . linger.* When Abby opened her eyes to see if he was shopping for building materials, her breath caught in her throat. He wasn't shopping for building materials; he was shopping for a woman. Abby's heart scudded against her chest wall. *Oh, no . . . no, no, no, Clay.*

Apparently unaware Abby was watching, Clay spent a minute more gazing at the woman with long raven-colored hair, who wore tight jeans and cowboy boots. The name Randi was printed in big sparkly letters on the paper fan she held, as if her very presence could turn up the heat. Clay clicked off Randi, only to pause again to view a woman with toffee-colored hair who wore red lipstick and a frilly knit shirt with an image of the state of Texas outlined on it. When he reached for his smartphone, Abby felt her anger rise like a simmering pot on the verge of a boilover. *The Lone Star State . . . Oh, really? His next port of call? A new location, a new woman?* She could hear him entering the woman's information, or at least she assumed that was what he was doing. Abby closed her eyes, feeling too tired and too angry to confront him. She lay still as a corpse, listening to her heart gallop like a stallion fleeing a wildfire.

As if mirroring her discord, the chimes clanged from a sudden wind gust. She rolled away from him to face the window, slowed her breath, and tried to center herself. Her mind struggled to process her discovery. What possible explanation could there be, except that he was surfing dating sites? *Why are you so surprised? Despite what he said when he showed up here, he just needs a place to land between jobs. He must have figured he could rekindle your feelings for him faster than a rooster could hop a hen.* Abby pulled the sheet over her eyes to blot her tears.

She lay there for a long time, so long it seemed like several hours had passed since Clay had turned off his laptop and fallen asleep. Even after she'd reasoned through her feelings of betrayal, she couldn't stop obsessing about exactly when he might leave her. He would have the electrical work on the master bath completed sometime tomorrow. The next day, most likely, he'd get the windows and insulation in place. Then the backer board would have to be installed before he could move in the jetted tub and the showerhead. He would need another day or so to hang Sheetrock.

Hopefully, he'd stay long enough to tape and plaster the walls. That would leave her with sanding, tiling, painting, wiring the lights, and laying the floor—jobs he knew she could handle. It would just take some time. Oh, how perfectly he had played his hand. She wanted to punch him.

After some deep breathing to calm down, Abby remembered that Clay had mentioned his truck would arrive on Saturday. By her rough calculations, he'd likely be free to leave on Tuesday or Wednesday. Clay must have had a pretty good idea of his exit date from the moment he waltzed into her house. Abby wished he could have just been straight about it, could have told her the truth. Why had he felt it necessary to give her the "I can't live without you" speech? And she'd bought his act, which lessened her guilt about spending so much time on Fiona's murder case and with Jack. Fuming inside, Abby decided to let the future unravel. Why confront Clay when she wasn't thrilled to be in this relationship, anyway? Maybe the wisest thing would be to remain civil and keep up appearances until he left. She hated dramatic scenes and honestly just didn't have the energy to "go there."

The next day, before sunup, Abby checked on Ruby after feeding and watering the chickens. The Rhode Island Red hen had no problem running to the feeder or following Abby around in the run. Perhaps Clay had misread Ruby's walk or imagined a problem when there wasn't one. However, the bee swarm was another story. Abby thought about not bothering to ask him to help her and trying to retrieve it herself. But it was too high. She needed a pair of helping hands. Luckily, he was nearby and eager to assist. Perhaps he felt guilty about surfing the Internet for a new paramour, she thought.

Abby donned her beekeeper's suit and positioned the empty hive box under the swarm. Without a second suit for Clay, she relegated him to remaining on the ground while she climbed the ladder and, on her cue, to pulling hard on the rope to dislodge the bees. Worried that the bees might also just fly off, Abby devised a means to try to capture the greatest number of them and, hopefully, the queen for her hive. In the garden shed, she located a five-gallon plastic bucket and cut away the bottom. Using duct tape, she attached a black plastic contractor's bag to the bottom opening, and using wire and a couple of screws, she connected an extendable painter's pole to the bucket's top rim.

Pulling her elbow-length goatskin gloves over her bee suit sleeves, she told Clay what he needed to do. "Stand to one side, and when I give you the signal to pull, give the rope a hard yank." Abby hustled up the ladder and positioned the plastic bucket on the pole directly beneath the swarm after extending the pole to reach the swarm. She made a motion like pulling on a bell and readied the makeshift swarm catcher.

Clay jerked so hard, he snapped off the end of the limb. Luckily, most of the swarm dropped into the bucket and right on down into the contractor's bag, just as Abby had envisioned. She descended the ladder, struggling not to drop the bag of bees, while Clay took off running. Thousands of bees, still sensing the queen's pheromones, which were telling them to swarm, encircled Abby.

"Get farther back," she called to Clay. She could see angry scout bees buzzing past him as he watched the spectacle.

Abby turned the makeshift swarm catcher upside down and shook the bees into the empty hive box. She adjusted the box's position so its opening faced the tree that had just held the swarm. That would make it easier for the bees still circling to find their way into their new home. After laying aside her makeshift swarm catcher, Abby walked over to the patio and retrieved ten wax frames, drained of honey and previously cleaned by the bees. These she inserted into the hive box. Slowly, she slid the lid along the box top, leaving a two-inch gap for any bee laggers to make their way in.

With the bees dealt with, Abby unzipped her suit and stepped out of it. She folded it and placed it in the large basket that held the smoker, pellet fuel, the powdered sugar medicine, the hive clamp, and the wax scraper. She took the basket of materials and the swarm catcher back to the apiary. Before returning to the patio, she dropped to her knees by a raised bed and picked some fresh strawberries for breakfast.

"So what's your plan today?" Clay asked after they'd dined on yogurt, fresh berries, and toast spread with homemade apricot jam. "I feel bad that we've hardly spent any time together." He handed Abby his empty yogurt bowl. She set it on hers, strolled to the sink, and placed the bowls alongside the mugs of coffee and glasses of juice they'd drained.

"'Fraid I'll be gone most of the day, dealing with things in town again," she said in a quiet tone. She avoided looking at him, hoping not to slide into the anger simmering under her calm exterior. "I've got to take care of some farmette business and attend Fiona's funeral." She changed the subject. "There are sandwich fixings and potato soup in the fridge . . . and don't go claiming that you can't cook, as it's something we used to do a lot together."

"I remember," he said, pinning her at the sink and slipping his arms around her. "When will you be home?"

Abby shrugged. "I'm not sure. Why?"

"Well, I thought that if I knocked off early, we could share a glass of wine and cook dinner together. After that, we could see what kind of trouble we could get into."

Perfectly understanding his intention, she nudged him back, reached for the tea towel, and began to wipe her hands. "I'll let you know if I'm going to be later than seven o'clock." She hung the towel over the oven door handle and leaned down to pat Sugar on the head.

"I hope you don't think I'm pushing you, Abby," said Clay. "I can't change what I did before, but I'm trying to make it up to you now." His tone became animated. "You just wait. Your master bath is going to be so dramatic, it'll stop traffic on Farm Hill Road."

"It's a little early for such hyperbole, isn't it?" She forced a smile. "But you must know that I appreciate your efforts, Clay. I am truly grateful."

Abby opened the patio slider and pulled back the screen door. Sugar bounded out, and Abby followed, then closed the door behind her, hoping Clay wouldn't follow. Walking the farmette with Sugar had become one of the most relaxing things she did. Today, more than ever, she wanted to stroll solo through the orchard, past the raised beds of strawberries, over to the herb garden and the vegetable patch, and then back to check on the chickens and bees. Luckily, Clay didn't follow, which, as she walked quietly with Sugar, soon brought Abby a measure of peace. She stopped to listen to a mockingbird sing its bright song— *thweeet-thweeet-thweet, right-here, right-here, worky-worky-worky.* A few minutes later, the nail-gun compressor started up, drowning out the bird's song.

Potato Soup with Fresh Herbs

Ingredients:

4 tablespoons unsalted butter
1½ pounds russet potatoes, peeled and cut into
    1-inch dice
1¼ cups chopped yellow onions
1 teaspoon salt
Freshly cracked black pepper, to taste
3½ cups chicken stock
1 tablespoon finely minced fresh herbs (equal
    parts parsley, English thyme, lemon balm,
    chives, and marjoram), plus a pinch for
    garnishing
½ cup half-and-half

Directions:

Melt the butter in a large heavy saucepan over medium-low heat. Add the potatoes, onions, salt, and pepper and gently stir to coat the potatoes with the butter. Cover and cook for 10 minutes.

Add the chicken stock and the herbs to the potatoes, cover, and cook over medium heat until the potatoes are soft, about 15 minutes.

Pour the potato mixture into a food processor or a blender and puree. Return the soup to the saucepan and stir in the half-and-half. Adjust the seasoning.

Pour the soup into a tureen or soup bowls, garnish with the remaining herbs, and serve at once.

Serves 4

Chapter 15

When the old honeybee queen dies, the
first new queen to emerge from her cell
will sting the other queens to death;
only one queen rules the hive.

—*Henny Penny Farmette Almanac*

Abby stood in the apiary, with her hands clutching the metal lid of the new hive box. Her psychic and emotional equilibrium had been knocked out of balance. Irrational as she knew it to be, she had somehow managed to turn the anger she felt toward Clay inward, blaming herself. Why had she let him convince her they could pick up the pieces and move forward? Why had she believed him, instead of trusting her own intuition? Why, when her heart had finally healed, had she set herself up for disappointment? She didn't need Clay, she didn't need any man, and the years he was gone had taught her that. Besides, there were other men around, like Jack or Lucas.

The sound of the bees, their vibration, and the smell of their honey comforted her so much, she'd lost track of how long she had remained near the hives. More than anything else, she wanted to avoid Clay. She would not literally or telegraphically communicate her disappointment. She refused to give him the satisfaction of knowing that he still had the ability to wound her.

Leaving the comforting presence of the hive, Abby returned to the house and gathered her clothes for the funeral. She carried them into the small bathroom. After showering and drying off, she slipped into a belted, knee-length black dress with cap sleeves and a wide cowl collar, and French heels with ankle straps. She twisted her reddish-gold mane into a French twist, anchoring it with pins and a hair clip embellished with roses worked in marcasite. She decided to keep her makeup understated. She applied an ivory foundation over her face and chose a lipstick and blush in a tangerine hue to complement the color of her blue-green eyes. A pair of silver and onyx drop earrings and dark sunglasses completed the solemn, respectful look she sought.

Driving the Jeep along the silent black ribbon of asphalt to Las Flores, Abby thought about Tom and Fiona. Their love might have seemed true and strong to Fiona, but if it were, indeed, so strong, why wouldn't Tom break his ties to the commune? Why had he sought a divorce instead? Abby could only imagine what their relationship might have been like as best friends, lovers, spouses . . . and now he was left to bury her. Tom probably felt guilty, as if his leaving had led to her death. *How do you go on after something as horrible as that?* She thought about two lines in a poem by Henry Scott Holland, long since dead himself: *There is unbroken continuity. Why should I be out of mind because I am out of sight?*

Abby hit the scan button on the radio until she found some agreeable music to keep her company on the way into town. After arriving at her destination, she dashed up the steps of the Church of the Holy Names and hurried into the narthex. Girding herself against the guilt she felt for lapsing in the religion dutifully instilled in her, she dipped her finger in the basin of holy water and made the sign of the cross. Her French heels clicked against the patterned marble floor as she approached the glass doors to enter the nave of the church. She strolled into the interior, now bathed with light streaming through old-world-style stained-glass windows depicting the Stations of the Cross. The doors creaked shut behind her.

Father Joseph had already led the procession of the flower-draped coffin and the congregation down the aisle and was sprinkling the holy water. The church smelled of lemon-scented wood polish, candle wax, camphor, and the scent of flowers— gardenias, lilies, lavender, and sweet peas. As she approached the altar, Abby spotted Jack, paused to make a slight bow before the altar, and then sidled over to the pew. She genuflected and trod softly over to where Jack sat with his hands in his lap.

"Hi," she whispered, scooting into the seat.

Attired in a white button-down dress shirt, a black suit, and a black-and-gray-striped tie, Jack looked up and acknowledged her with a smile. Despite the somber occasion, he exuded masculine vitality. Squeezing her hand, he whispered back, "Thanks for coming," and then, "Your cheek looks puffy. . . . How's the eye?"

Abby lifted her sunglasses so he could see the black and deep red circle surrounding it. She watched Jack's lips tighten into a thin line. He hung his head, as if he blamed himself for the whole affair. After the opening song, for which they stood, and the prayer that followed, Abby stole a glance at those gathered behind them. Tom sat two rows back, flanked by Premalatha Baxter and Dak Harmon. They stared at the coffin. Tom's puffy red eyes and grim expression seemed to reflect a man lacking a rudder and floating adrift in dangerous waters. He looked over at Abby. Apparently sensing her concern for him, he touched his heart with his hand and nodded.

A few townspeople and Main Street shop owners had come to pay their respects, but it still wasn't much of a crowd. Abby spotted Kat, dressed in a tailored suit, at the back of the nave and a man Abby didn't recognize but suspected was an undercover cop, across the aisle from Kat. Abby took comfort in the knowledge that cops often showed up at wakes, the funerals of homicide victims, and celebrations of life gatherings. They would come not only to observe the friends and family of the deceased, but also to notice if one or more of the individuals in attendance were suspects or persons of interest. No place was sacred if cops had sufficient reason to arrest someone.

The church secretary stepped before the podium situated on the right side of the church, in front of the baptismal font. Pushing back her short, gray hair to tuck the tips of her wire-rimmed glasses behind her smallish ears, she began her reading. The woman's monotone set Abby's thoughts adrift . . . back to happier times when she and Clay were both on the same page about their feelings for each other. But, like a meteor in the night sky, that love—if it truly ever was that for him—had flamed out. At least this time, Abby knew the way forward. This time, she would be the one to sever the fragile thread that held them together. She forced her thoughts back to the funeral.

After listening to the readings from the Old and New Testaments, Abby heard the double glass doors at the back of the nave creak open, and she turned to see Laurent Duplessis slide into a pew. Later, during Father Joseph's short homily about the gift of life and the inevitability of death, she heard the doors open again. Someone had either come in or gone out, but since the priest was looking right at her, Abby didn't turn around.

By the time the Mass had ended and they'd caravanned to the graveside at the Church of the Pines—roughly a mile from town and up a mile or so in the mountains—for the final Rite of Committal, Abby noticed Laurent Duplessis had not come to the site. Then Father Joseph spoke. "The earth is the Lord's and all it holds, the world and those who live there. . . . Who can stand in his holy place? The clean of hand and the pure of heart . . ." At one point, Tom cried out in aching agony, his lament sounding sorrowful enough to summon Fiona's spirit. Abby trembled and fought against the tears stinging the backs of her eyes. Despite her eyes brimming with tears, she saw Premalatha reach out for Tom's arm to steady him. He jerked from her touch.

After the recitation of a psalm, there were other prayers. Then a parishioner played a haunting rendition of "Amazing Grace" on the uilleann pipes. Six men lowered the casket into the ground. And then . . . it was over.

After the commune people had left and the few townsfolk had departed, Jack thanked Father Joseph and left the grave diggers to do their work. As he'd ridden with Abby and Kat to the cemetery, Jack remained only long enough to say a private good-bye and then rejoined the two women at the Jeep.

"So what now?" Jack asked. He rubbed the right jaw of his cleanly shaven face as his question was met with Abby's silence and Kat's blank stare. He sighed and said, "In our family's ancestral village generations upon generations ago, according to my grandparents, we'd lay out our deceased family member in nice clothes for the final viewing. The menfolk would arrive, their pockets bulging with bottles of spirits. The women would make food enough to feed half the county, and then we'd open a window for the spirit to depart. Of course, if the wind was wailing and the rain sheeting, we would crack that window a wee bit, but only for as long as we thought the spirit might be around. We'd eat and drink . . . mostly drink . . . and tell stories about the times we'd spent enjoying that person's company."

Jack paused to chuckle. "Mind you, sometimes this would take all night. Come morning, with our heads pounding from hangovers, we'd drag ourselves to the church for Mass and then follow the casket, the poor deceased's body bumping along the country road to the cemetery. We'd face that freshly dug hole and lay our loved one in it." He paused again, this time looking wistfully toward the sky. "Then we'd drink some more. At least, that's the way it used to be."

"Sounds like we should have a drink," Abby said.

"Couldn't hurt," Kat agreed.

"And what about your associate, Kat?" Abby asked.

"He's busy back at the church," Kat replied.

"Busy? Doing what?" Jack asked.

"Inviting Laurent Duplessis down to our police station for a little chat," said Kat. "Otto is probably having a go at Duplessis now."

"To discuss the robbery or the murder?" Abby asked.

"That too." Kat massaged the corner of her eye with her middle finger. "We had plenty of questions about that botanical shop burglary. Then Fiona's note that you brought to the station last night, thank you very much, raise more than a few questions, so we wanted to see what Duplessis had to say." Kat flicked a speck of an undetermined origin from the shoulder of her dark suit jacket. "My shift ended a half hour ago, so what about that drink . . . ? Black Witch okay?"

Abby shot a questioning look at Jack.

"Sure," he said.

Kat leaned closer to Abby and whispered. "The place has a new, superhot part-time bartender, who just might be working tonight."

Abby's brow shot up. "Yeah? I thought you and Lucas Crawford . . ."

"Yeah, well, let's not go there."

"Let's do," Abby protested.

"Can it wait until you and I are alone?"

"Sure," said Abby, all the more intrigued by Kat's reticence.

Twenty minutes later, Abby parked the Jeep on Main and led Kat and Jack into the Black Witch. She threaded her way through the crowded bar and climbed onto a tall wooden stool near the dartboard and the back bathrooms. Kat took the other stool, while Jack dragged over a third, wiping peanut shells from its seat.

Kat surveyed the room. "I can't believe this place is so packed. Happy hour is still forty-five minutes from now."

A bleach-blond waitress—one of the old-time workers at the bar—appeared. "What's your poison?"

Kat followed Abby's lead in ordering a glass of merlot.

"Make mine a Celtic Barrel Burner," Jack said.

Abby and Kat both snickered.

"What's so funny?" he asked.

"Sounds as dangerous as a Kamikaze," said Kat.

"Or a Revolver. We make those, too," the waitress said. Her wrinkled lips parted into a tired smile. She spun around and wove her way back to the bar with the drink orders.

Jack removed his tie, unbuttoned his shirt collar, shrugged off his jacket, and laid them on the stool. Rolling up his white shirtsleeves and exposing muscular arms covered in light hair, he leaned in and said, "If you ladies will excuse me, I'll make a quick trip to the men's room."

When he'd gone, Abby nudged Kat with her shoulder. "Okay, it's just the two of us. Now spill."

"What?" Kat's blond brow furrowed, as if she'd totally forgotten.

"You know what." Abby eyed her intently. "You and Lucas Crawford . . . details, please."

"Well, I'll be happy to provide the nonexistent details after you've told me the truth about that black eye."

Abby touched the tender cheekbone just under the edge of the afflicted eye. "I thought you knew. I explained last night at the police station. Dak Harmon and I had a misunderstanding while I was visiting the commune, and we got into a tussle."

"I just heard about the evidence you turned in, not the tussle."

"The long and short of it is that Harmon got into a tizzy when I didn't jump at his order to get off the commune property. We got into a little shoving match, my eye got hit by an elbow, and I left with Jack shortly afterward. End of story."

"No, not the end of story. I expect you to tell me what happened up there."

"Honestly, Kat, nothing worth mentioning happened, and you are stalling. Jack can verify my story when he returns from the bathroom."

Kat arched a brow and remained defiantly silent.

"I'm waiting," Abby said.

Kat let go an exasperated sigh. "Lucas and I never even got out of the starting gate. Turns out we're ill suited."

"But you liked him, set your sights on him."

"Oh, yeah, well . . . ," Kat said. She slipped off the dark gray suit jacket and laid it on her lap. She spent a few seconds fiddling with the Victorian floral pin at the throat of her crisp, buttoned-up white blouse. "It takes two, now doesn't it?" Her eyes swept the room and then went back to Abby. "You know me better than anyone else, so I'll use an analogy you'll instantly grasp. In Jane Austen's *Pride and Prejudice*, which guy would you fall for? Mr. Darcy, who has that quiet, smoldering intensity? Or the charming, seductive bad boy, Mr. Wickham?"

"Oh, you know who I'd choose. What's your point?" asked Abby.

"I don't have enough patience for a Darcy type—the handsome, secretive fellow who can't be pushed, the one who takes his own sweet time about everything."

"So your fling is over?"

"What fling? I would not describe what happened—or, more correctly, did not happen—as a fling. I don't think anyone has a fling with Lucas Crawford." After folding her napkin into what looked like a piece of bad origami, Kat fixed her attention on the waitress, who was approaching with their drinks.

The waitress slapped three more napkins down on the table and set the drinks on them. "Anything else?" she asked, taking the bills Abby had placed on the table and counting out the change.

Kat hesitated and then asked, "Will Santiago be tending bar tonight?"

The waitress shook her head. "Dunno. I just got here myself. I can check for you." She sauntered away.

As if preparing for an affirmative answer, Kat slid her hands over her new Roaring Twenties haircut. "Oh well."

Jack returned, swung a long leg over the bar stool, and slid onto it.

Kat lifted her glass. "Here's to the past remaining in the past. I, for one, am always ready for a new beginning."

Catching a glint of interest in Kat's eyes as she tapped her glass against Jack's, Abby lifted her glass and said, "New beginnings." Then she did something that surprised even her. She reached for Jack's hand and gave it a gentle squeeze.

The Celtic Barrel Burner

Ingredients:
½ shot Baileys Irish Cream
½ shot Jameson Irish Whiskey
¾ pint Guinness Stout

Directions:
Pour the Baileys Irish Cream into a shot glass. Next, pour the Jameson Irish Whiskey over the Baileys. Pour the Guinness Stout into a chilled pint-size beer mug or beer glass and let it settle. Add the contents of the shot glass to the stout. Drink at once, as the beverage tends to curdle and becomes less appetizing if it sits.

Serves 1

Chapter 16

Watch out if your rooster lowers his
head and struts around you—take it as
a sign of fowl aggression.

—*Henny Penny Farmette Almanac*

Tires crunching against gravel alerted Abby that
someone had rolled into her driveway. She
had been sorting snap peas on the patio but got
up to greet her visitor as Sugar bounded across the
yard with a *yip*. When the dog's tail began waving,
Abby knew it was a friend, not a foe, who'd come
calling at her farmette. Still, Houdini, who could
never be accused of shirking his duty as a rooster,
hustled the hens—whom Abby had let free range
in the yard—closer to the chicken coop.

"Hey, girlfriend," Kat called.

"Hey, yourself . . . What brings you all the way
out here?" Abby picked up another pea, ran her
nail along the ridge to open it, dropped the four
peas into a bowl, and discarded the shell in a basket on the ground.

"I had to take care of some business out this way,

and now I am on my way back to town. But I thought since I was so near, I'd quench my thirst and see that master bathroom Clay's been working on. Where is he, anyway?" Kat sank into a patio chair.

Abby arched a brow. "Why? Is there a problem?"

"No. Just curious," Kat said, stretching out her long legs.

"I suppose he's somewhere in Las Flores."

"How did he get there? Your Jeep is parked out front."

"His truck. Five minutes after the transporter arrived this morning and unloaded his pickup, Clay hopped into his truck and told me he was going to buy four recessed-light kits and a bathroom exhaust fan. And he suggested that when I'm done sorting the peas," she said, laying aside the basket of shells and the bowl of peas, "I could go ahead and finish hanging the drywall."

"How nice of him to give you something to do . . . because everyone knows you have way too much time on your hands," said Kat.

"Yeah, well, it was just the smaller pieces of drywall. It's done. He's gone. And, frankly, I hope he stays gone for a while. I could use some thinking time. Sweet tea?"

Kat smiled. "Oh, I thought you'd never ask. I'm wilting in this heat."

Abby traipsed into the kitchen. She took out a couple of tall glasses, filled them with tea from the fridge, and plopped in sprigs of mint from the plant in the garden window. After stepping back out through the open slider and screen door, she handed a glass of tea to Kat.

"You said you were around here on business. What kind of business?" asked Abby, sitting back down and touching the cool glass to her warm cheek.

Kat took a swig of sweet tea before answering. "A garbage truck nearly sideswiped a cow on Farm Hill Road."

"Sheesh, that could have been disastrous," said Abby before taking a sip. Using her forefinger, she pushed the mint sprig deeper into her glass.

"Turns out that heifer belongs to your handsome neighbor, Lucas Crawford. When I told him one of his cows had escaped from its pasture and a garbage truck had narrowly avoided hitting her, he showed more animation than when we shared ice cream in town. I watched him swing upon that horse of his faster than a felon on a jailbreak."

Abby smiled at Kat's analogy. "Oh yeah? Horse, huh?"

Kat looked off philosophically. "Damn fine man, that Lucas. Too bad we couldn't get a little something going."

"Yeah, too bad," Abby said in sympathy, feeling secretly delighted, but not wanting to telegraph it to Kat. She took another sip of tea and turned her gaze toward the hill and Lucas Crawford's old gray barn.

The chatter coming through Kat's radio drew Abby's attention back. The dispatcher was asking for Kat's location.

"Uh-oh," Abby said with a frown. "Our illustrious police chief checking up on you?"

Kat nodded while pushing the button on her two-way. She gave her location as Farm Hill Road, between the Henny Penny Farmette and the Crawford Ranch.

Abby listened intently. The dispatcher requested

that all available officers respond to a ten seventy-one near Ridge Top Road. Shock registered in Abby's body. Her pulse raced. That road intersected the main traffic artery near Dr. Danbury's cottage. Knowing that a ten seventy-one was Las Flores Police code for a shooting, Abby fought against mounting concern for Jack and the doc. She took a deep breath and reminded herself not to make assumptions or jump to conclusions.

"I've gotta go," Kat said. She chugged down the rest of her tea before setting the empty glass on the table, said, "Thanks," and sprinted back to her cruiser. Abby and Sugar followed.

"Kat," Abby called out, "that's near Dr. Danbury's place."

"Know it."

Abby called out again as Kat climbed into the cruiser. "Text me. I'll be worried sick until you do."

"Affirmative," Kat called out. She started the engine and flipped on the lights and the siren. The cruiser's tires spun against loose gravel as the car tore out of the driveway and sped off.

Covering her nose and mouth with her hand against the cloud of white dust and listening to the siren's wail grow fainter, Abby stood rooted on the spot and fretted. A drive-by shooting was an all-too-familiar occurrence in nearby Silicon Valley, but in the mountain foothills of Las Flores, it was unheard of. Abby's thoughts turned to her recent altercation with the commune people. She texted Jack, but with no reply, she stood rooted in her driveway, in the hot sun, with a cold chill descending upon her like a vapor.

* * *

By nightfall, Abby still had not heard from Kat. Jack hadn't replied to her text, either. To keep from obsessing about the shooting, she busied herself by working on organizing receipts and stapling them to sheets of paper marked HONEY/BEE EXPENSES, CHICKEN SUPPLIES, GARDEN EXPENDITURES, and RENOVATION/BUILDING MATERIALS. Around eight o'clock, Clay strolled into the house with a pepperoni pizza, a bottle of a red blend wine, and an apology for being gone so long. Sugar still barked at him as if he were a stranger, but eventually settled down next to Abby on the couch.

"I've got the light and fan kits in the truck. Put out the pizza with some napkins, and I'll be right back," Clay said, with a devilish grin.

Somebody's in a good mood. Abby tucked the pages of receipts inside four manila file folders and carried them back to the small credenza in her makeshift office at the end of the hallway.

"I don't feel much like eating," she said when Clay had finished lugging in the boxes from the supply store.

"Why's that?" he asked, putting the boxes on the floor next to the wall and proceeding to whip out his pocketknife to cut the foil from the wine bottle. He thrust the corkscrew into the bottle, twisted it a few times, and eased out the cork. After finding two wineglasses in the cupboard, he took them down and poured a splash of red into each.

"I guess you forgot that I'm not a fan of pizza," Abby said, sliding into a chair next to his at the dining table and taking from him the glass of jewel-colored wine. She hesitated in telling him what was really on her mind—that she was worried about the shooting, Jack's safety, and the reason why Kat hadn't yet texted or called.

He shot a peculiar look at her and then reached for a large gooey slice of pizza. "Suit yourself," he said and wolfed down the slice.

It had been four hours since Kat had been dispatched to the scene. Abby would never intrude when Kat was out on a call, but the waiting and not hearing from either Kat or Jack was crazy making. Now, after swallowing a small bite of pizza and telling Clay not to buy pizza again, because she could make a more wholesome version using garden herbs, homegrown veggies, and slices of fresh mozzarella and goat cheese, Abby felt the phone in her pocket vibrate. She dropped the pizza onto her plate, wiped her hands on the napkin, and plucked her phone from the appliquéd pocket of her yellow print sundress. Finally, the update she had been expecting had come as a text. But as she glanced at the screen, Abby saw it wasn't Kat's message, but rather Jack's. **Tom critically wounded. Meet me at Las Flores Community Hospital.**

Abby looked up at Clay, who seemed wholly occupied with pigging out on pizza and wine. He reached for the bottle and began to refill his glass. She put her hand over her glass, scooted her chair back from the table, and said, "None for me, Clay. Sorry, but I've got to go."

Training his dark brown eyes on hers, Clay frowned and opened his palms in a gesture that suggested he was waiting for her explanation.

"Fiona, the friend we buried yesterday . . . Well, now her husband has just been shot," Abby said. "He could die."

Clay's brow shot up, and then his expression

turned into a scowl. "Let me get this straight. Just why do you have to go?"

"Because Fiona's family has asked for me. Look, I'm sorry. But these things happen."

"Only to you, Abby. Only to you. You don't work for the police department anymore, and you're not a victims' advocate. I can't see any good reason why you have to go, unless it's to avoid being with me."

"Good grief, Clay. This is not about you. And now isn't the time to cop an attitude. Save it for later." Abby dumped her slice of pizza in the garbage and set her dish in the sink. She dashed to the bedroom for a summer sweater and her purse. Sugar, apparently picking up on Abby's anxiety, began to whine.

"You want me to drive?" Clay called out from the kitchen.

"No," Abby replied, kneeling to hug Sugar. She returned to the kitchen with the sweater, her purse, and the car keys. "Do you mind if I leave Sugar here? I don't think hospital security will let me take her inside, and I don't want to leave the poor baby in the Jeep for hours." Abby hurried back to the dining table to grab one of the six water bottles that she always kept in the bar area opposite the table. She resisted her natural inclination to tell him more about her plans; he hadn't exactly been forthcoming as to where he'd been all day.

Clay bit into another slice of pizza, took a moment to chew and swallow, and another few seconds to wash the bite down with wine. "You're planning to be gone for hours?"

Abby heaved an exasperated sigh. "I don't know. It could be a while."

Clay stared at his pizza. "Fine. Leave me. Leave your dog. We're getting used to your absences."

"That remark is so unnecessary, Clay. I'll be back as soon as I can. In any event, I'll text you."

"Whatever."

Clay's irritation riled her, propelling Abby out the door and to the Jeep. Inside it, she started the engine and reminded herself to breathe through her tension and to let it go. Clay had apparently forgotten that he was a guest in *her* house. Yes, she'd been away a lot, helping Jack clean out the cottage, attending Fiona's funeral, and now keeping a possible vigil at the hospital. Friends helped friends. And if Clay wanted to fault her for that, so be it. He was the darling boy child in his family, the bearer of the family's hopes and dreams, always getting his way. Abby reminded herself how self-focused he could be. *Well, the world doesn't spin around you, Clay. And I'm not thinking about you anymore . . . tonight.*

At the first traffic light in town, Abby braked for the long red light and glanced down at the message from Kat on her phone screen. **Vic is Tom Dodge. Transported. Finished working the scene. Need to interview him.**

The light changed to green, and Abby pushed hard on the gas pedal. The Jeep responded with a squeal of its tires. The hospital was still a half mile away. Abby wanted to get there as quickly as possible, but in one piece. Tom just had to pull through—the police would need to hear his version of the shooting. If he died, it would mean the already overtaxed LFPD would have two murders to investigate at the same time and Jack would have lost two family members. So occupied were her thoughts in making a linkage between Fiona's murder and the attempt on Tom's life that Abby nearly missed the turn into the hospital parking lot.

Not finding Jack in the waiting area of the emergency room, Abby approached the triage nurse, a perky young woman in green scrubs, and asked where she might find the patient with the gunshot wound who had been transported in earlier by paramedics.

The nurse trained her green eyes on Abby and asked, "Are you family?"

"I'm a friend meeting his family, who is already here," Abby told her.

"They took him to the OR, second floor. There's a waiting room up there near the surgical suites, but if you hit the surgical ICU or ward, you've gone too far." The nurse pointed to the gray door marked STAIRWELL. She then reached for a clipboard with paperwork for her next patient.

Abby hurried to the door, pushed it open, and entered the dank, cool stairwell, where she sprinted up the concrete steps. Pushing open the second-floor door and stepping out into a hallway, she saw a sign with an arrow indicating the direction to the waiting area. She spotted Jack pacing toward her. She dashed into his embrace.

He exhaled a long sigh. "Thank you for coming, my girl," he said, stroking her hair. "Can you believe this?"

"Thank God it wasn't you," Abby said, easing out of his embrace to glance toward the operating-room doors. The area smelled of air freshener, used to cover up the other disagreeable scents that permeated the environment, but Abby could still smell them—antiseptic mouthwash, hand sanitizer, iodine, alcohol, and stale coffee.

Jack led her to a dimly lit alcove with six identical chairs next to a small table, with a slew of magazines strewn about. He fixed his pale eyes on hers, as if anticipating a barrage of questions.

"What exactly happened?" Abby asked.

"The police say it was a drive-by. Tom was alone in his truck and, apparently, the target," Jack said. "An eyewitness in a Ford Escort had followed Tom for some distance when a motorcyclist cut in between the Escort and the truck. When the road straightened out of the switchbacks, the biker pulled even with Tom's truck and fired two shots into the cab."

"Oh, my gosh," Abby said. "Then what happened?"

Jack took a deep breath and exhaled. "The truck went into a skid. Tom—despite being seriously wounded—apparently fought for control of his pickup. You know, Abby, there are places up there where there are no guardrails. That was one of them."

Abby nodded. "So he got the truck stopped."

Jack nodded. "In the nick of time and inches from a slide-area drop-off."

After a moment of silence, she asked, "So . . . how serious are his injuries?"

"The bullet wound caused massive blood loss. The police told me that the medics decided to transport him right away, instead of stabilizing him on scene. I think he has a collapsed lung, too. They said he needed a chest tube."

"Oh, Lord. Poor Tom," said Abby. "Have you spoken with his doctors yet?"

"Yes. They're encouraging. Told me he's lucky to be alive. Barring complications in surgery, he should pull through."

Abby's mind raced. "But why was Tom the target? His whole world seemed to be that commune."

"My opinion . . . Dak Harmon may have done this," Jack said.

"Hmm," Abby said, wondering why Jack had formed that opinion, except that he'd seen first-hand Dak Harmon's violent streak. Her stomach churned as she recalled how Dak had hit her.

After a few minutes of sitting quietly, waiting for news from the doctor, Abby looked over at the elevator doors that had just opened. Kat strolled out of the elevator, walked toward them, and sank into a chair.

"We're so glad to see you, Kat. Piece this together for us, will you?" Abby said.

Kat began talking even as she removed the flip-over notebook from her shirt pocket. "Well, we're still working it ourselves. As Abby knows, we tend to be guarded about giving out a lot of information until we have a clear picture of the case ourselves, but we do try to keep the victim's family updated." Kat looked over at Jack. "There was an eyewitness driving from Boulder Bluff, on his way home. He witnessed the shooting of Tom by a tall, thin man on a motorcycle, wearing a touring helmet—full face hidden by the helmet mask—black jeans and shirt." Kat peered at the pages of her notebook, flipping through them one by one. "The witness also said he thought there was some kind of scarf sticking out of the shirt collar. He called the emergency number and stayed on scene until the medics and law enforcement arrived."

Abby stopped Kat for a second. "Wait a minute. Did you say that the eyewitness described the shooter as tall and thin?"

Kat nodded.

Abby looked at Jack. "That can't be Dak Harmon. He's stocky and heavyset. So if it wasn't Dak—and why would he want to kill Tom, anyway?—who else could it have been, and what was the motive?"

"We're looking into it," said Kat. "We believe the shooter used a forty-five-caliber automatic pistol. We found a casing on the road. We've got ballistics over at the crime lab, working on it. In the meantime, we just have to wait for input on the size caliber and also the type of firearm. A lot depends on scrutinizing the firing-pin indentations, as you know."

"When you saw Tom, was he still conscious?" Abby asked.

"No," said Kat. "He'd been hit by flying glass to the face and upper body. The gunshot pierced the left side of his upper chest, and he suffered a loss of blood and consciousness. His lips and nail beds were that cyanotic blue hue you get when you're not being properly oxygenated."

"So have you come to check on him?" asked Jack.

"I'm here to interrogate him as soon as he wakes up." Kat chewed her lip. "I'll be brief, but there are facts we need to get."

Abby nodded and put a reassuring hand on Jack's shoulder.

Kat looked at Abby. "With our resources stretched so thin, it could be a while until we get to the bottom of this. What I wouldn't give for a forensic expert all our own to help us to determine bullet distance, angle, trajectory, sequence, and a thousand other little details."

"Maybe the homicide guys helping Otto on Fiona's murder investigation," Abby said, "could look at this, too."

Her optimism was met with a shake of Kat's head. "Not likely."

"Listen, Kat, my gut tells me there's a link between Fiona's murder and the attempt on Tom's life."

"Yeah, I think so, too," Kat said. "But you know we also have to set aside our personal opinions and let the evidence lead us to the right conclusion. The DA can't prosecute a case based on a gut feeling."

"You think Tom knows who tried to kill him?" Jack asked.

"Possibly." Kat returned her notebook to her pocket and folded her hands in her lap. "I certainly think the shooting was no accident."

Jack chewed the corner of his lower lip.

Kat leaned toward him. "You met with Tom recently, didn't you?"

"Yes," he replied. "Abby and I both did."

"Well, technically, *you* met with Tom," said Abby. "I looked around the commune grounds and got this shiner to show for it," she said, pointing to her eye.

"What did you and Tom talk about?" Kat asked.

Jack sniffed and furrowed his brow, as though trying to remember. "I asked him if he had anything to do with my sister's death or if he knew who did."

"And what did he say?" asked Kat.

"He adamantly denied he had anything to do with her death."

"Do you believe him?" Kat asked, pressing on.

"Of course. Tom is no killer."

"Did he know anyone with a reason to hurt Fiona?" Kat asked.

Jack glanced at Abby. "Maybe, but he didn't name anybody," said Jack. Looking at Kat, Jack said, "My brother-in-law said that the commune was changing and that Fiona had been outspoken about it. I guess the new leaders have a life of ease, even luxury, with all the residents working at the commune or in the commune's various businesses. Premalatha, in particular, had a bad history with Fiona, according to Tom."

"Bad history? What are we talking about here?" Kat asked.

Jack straightened and leaned back into his chair. "Fiona told me that once the old leader returned to India, Hayden Marks and Premalatha Baxter were to share equally the old guy's spiritual power. They said he'd passed it on to them. Those two began implementing the changes. Hayden Marks became the 'official leader,' and Premalatha Baxter assumed the role of commune manager and banker. She recently bought a new BMW Alpina for her and Hayden Marks to share. One assumes she used the money collected from the commune folks to make the purchase. I don't even own a car, but I know this much—that particular model costs over a hundred grand."

Kat made a soft whistling sound. "That's a lot of moola."

Jack rubbed his hand across his cheek. "I don't

know if this is relevant, but during our conversation that day, Tom told me about a promise he made to Fiona."

"What promise?" Abby and Kat asked in unison.

"My sister told Tom that he had to promise he would leave the commune if anything ever happened to her. And not only that, but she made him swear to go to the police with everything he knew about the place, its dealings, and Hayden Marks and Premalatha Baxter."

"So, did Tom go to the police, like Fiona had asked?" Abby searched Jack's eyes.

Jack looked at her briefly and then turned his attention back to Kat. "No. I think he was scared. Tom said there could be severe reprisals against people who reveal what goes on inside the commune world."

"It appears that's exactly what happened to him after he talked with you," said Kat. "Did Tom reveal anything about Baxter or Marks to warrant involvement by law enforcement?"

Jack arched a brow. "Tom told me Hayden Marks hired outside help for special situations. He told me that two other people who threatened Marks ended up leaving the commune. Tom said no one knew how, when, or why they left. They just disappeared."

Kat leaned forward, with forearms on her knees, palms clasped together. "That sounds ominous. Did he mention any names?"

Jack shook his head. "No. Do you really think Tom's chat with me was the reason he got shot?"

Before Kat could answer, a call came over her two-way. She pressed her fingers to her lips, signaling the need for silence.

"Interviewing Tom Dodge can wait," Chief Bob Allen said to Kat. His voice sounded loud and clear. "We've got an address for the registered owner of the motorcycle used in the drive-by. I need you and Otto to do a knock and talk."

"On it, Chief," Kat said. She rose to leave. Turning back, she told Abby, "Text me when Tom is awake. . . . I need to ask him some questions."

Abby nodded, but before she could ask Kat to inquire of the chief the bike owner's name, Kat disappeared behind the closing elevator doors.

Tips to Ensure Success in the Making of Mead (Honey Wine)

> Mead may have been the first fermented beverage enjoyed by the ancients, brewed before wine, beer, and other alcoholic spirits were created and became popular. The ingredients list for mead is simple enough: honey, spring water, and yeast. Today other ingredients, such as rose petals, orange slices, raisins, cloves, vanilla, and chocolate, are sometimes added to impart unique flavors to the mead. There are many mead recipes on the Internet and in beverage books; however, in all the recipes, honey remains the most important flavor ingredient. When making mead, be sure to do the following:

- Always follow sanitary procedures to avoid introducing bacteria into the brew.

- Always use an organic, unadulterated honey for best results.

- Ensure that there are no bubbles in the mead and that it is clear before bottling it.

- Permit the mead to age several months to temper its sweetness.

Chapter 17

The drones' sole purpose in life is to
mate with the queen, and then they die.
Those that don't mate are useless and
are kicked out at summer's end to con-
serve the colony's resources.

—*Henny Penny Farmette Almanac*

Slumped in the hospital waiting room chair,
Abby jerked upright to reorient herself. The elevator doors banged open, and a man and a
woman stepped out, carrying a cooler, and con-
versed as they hurried past her. Rubbing the sleep
from her eyes, she looked over at Jack, who apparently had been observing her every movement.

"Sorry . . . uh . . . I . . . How long was I out for?"
she stammered.

Jack glanced at his watch. "Forty-five minutes." As
if something else was occupying his thoughts, his
brow furrowed. "What do you think was in that
cooler those two people were carrying into the OR?"

Abby yawned. "Dunno. Maybe a donated organ.
They have to keep it on ice."

"Oh, yeah. That makes sense." He shifted his position in the chair and crossed his long legs. "You know, you're kind of cute when you're sleeping." A broad grin creased his cheeks.

"That, I doubt," said Abby. She pulled the band from her hair and vigorously shook her reddish-gold mane before twisting it all back into a messy bun on top of her head. "Did you sleep?"

"No," he replied. "Couldn't. Too much going on in my noggin."

Abby plucked up the remaining errant tendrils and pushed them into the bun. "Boy, do I need a shower," she groaned and then stifled another yawn. "And my teeth feel fuzzy." Remembering that she usually kept a travel toothbrush in her daypack, she picked up the pack and unzipped the side pocket. "Has anyone from surgery come out to give you an update on Tom?"

"Once. The doctor didn't say much, except that Tom made it off the table and is recovering in the ICU," said Jack. He uncrossed his legs and shifted his position again. "A nurse showed me where it is and told me we can have five-minute visits every hour. She told me not to be surprised by all the lines they've got in him. Apparently, he's on IVs, a heart monitor, and a respirator, but they're going to take him off that as soon as he wakes up."

"That's good news," Abby said, rezipping her pack. "I'm sorry to have snoozed through all that."

"Sun's not up yet. You were tired. It's quiet here."

She rifled through her pack's inner pockets. "I guess I don't have that darn toothbrush, after all. Suppose I could get one in the gift shop, but it doesn't open until nine. So . . . what about some coffee?"

Jack nodded. "Sounds good. I smell it, but for the life of me, I can't locate the pot."

"I suppose that's by design," said Abby. She stood and touched her toes, holding the stretch for a few seconds. "They'll have a pot in the cafeteria on the first floor. Why don't we meet there in five or ten minutes?"

Jack, suddenly enthusiastic, said, "Let's go now."

"If you don't mind, I'd rather have a few minutes to wash my face," she said, reaching for her daypack. "I never look my best crawling out of bed in the morning, so I doubt my appearance is any better after sitting up all night." She only hoped she hadn't snored. With a smile and a squeeze of Jack's hand, Abby left for the ladies' room in the downstairs ER lobby.

After she'd washed up, brushed through her hair, and applied a swipe of lip gloss, she sent a text to Clay, explaining why she hadn't returned home during the night. To her surprise, her cell phone rang, with Clay calling back. Despite his mood seeming sullen, Abby did her best to sound upbeat as she shared the good news about Tom making it through the night. But from Clay's silences and one-word answers to her questions about whether he had slept well and whether Sugar had been on her best behavior, Abby knew he was mad and was not interested in hearing her excuses, no matter how good and true they might be.

In a parting shot, Clay said, "I told you long ago if we ever reached a point where we couldn't make things work, we should just keep on walking. I want you to think about that, Abby."

Abby blew air between her lips. "Look, I guess we can talk about this when I get home. I should be there by lunchtime."

"Whatever," Clay replied. He ended the call.

From the ladies' room, Abby headed to the cafeteria and bought a cup of coffee. Not seeing Jack, she paid the cashier and then located a seat nearest the cafeteria door so Jack would see her when he walked in. After a few sips of coffee, Abby dialed Kat's number.

Kat answered with a sleepy "Yeah?"

"Did I wake you?"

"Yeah. What's up?"

"Sorry. I'll be brief. Thought you'd want to know that Tom is out of surgery and is recovering in the ICU. We haven't seen him yet."

"Huh."

"And . . . I was wondering if you know any more about that motorcycle rider who shot Tom, or about the bike's registered owner."

"Do we have to have this conversation now, Abby?"

"No, of course not." Abby winced. "I'm being thoughtless. I should've known you were sleeping. Call me later, okay?"

"Wait." Kat exhaled a long sigh. "Are you obsessing about something?"

"Only about a dozen somethings. You know me too well. So, let me just ask about one thing that's really bothering me. Tom's shooter was on a motorcycle. Have you and Otto spoken with the owner of that bike yet?"

"Yes," Kat said sleepily. "The cycle belongs to Gus Morales, the mechanic who owns the mountain garage. He keeps a couple of vehicles in his shop as loaners for customers whose cars are in for servicing. One of his loaner vehicles is that older-model Harley motorcycle."

"What's his connection to Tom?"

"None we could find. He doesn't know Tom. Never done work on Tom's truck. But he's got a nephew named Billy, a marketing whiz, to hear him tell it. Billy has generated some business between the commune residents—those who still have vehicles—and his uncle, who services them."

Abby's thoughts raced ahead. "I get it. So the nephew is responsible for those flyers, too?"

"What flyers?" Kat asked sleepily.

"The ones we were given at the commune when Jack and I went to see Tom the day Dak Harmon and I had our tussle."

"Ohhh." Kat yawned.

"So no one from the LFPD has interrogated the nephew?"

"Not yet."

"But you say that older-model Harley is a loaner? So if that loaner was used by Tom's shooter, whose bike is in the shop, being repaired?"

"One of the commune members who paid for the servicing up front in cash brought in a motorcycle for Morales to fix. That fellow took the loaner bike back to the commune."

"Ah, so . . . it's likely that a resident of the commune owns the bike being fixed in the mountain garage . . . and any commune resident could have access to the loaner. Okay, Kat. Thanks. Go back to sleep, and we'll talk later."

"Huh."

Abby clicked off the call and looked up. Jack stood

in the cafeteria doorway, motioning for her to join him. "Hurry. They say we can see Tom now."

The ICU sounded like a brooder room of peeping chicks, with sounds seemingly chirping from every machine. Fully awake but looking exhausted from his ordeal, Tom rested against pillows in white cases, his hand shaking as he tried to scratch an area on one side of his whiskered cheek, beneath the green oxygen mask.

Abby assumed his skin must itch where the tape had anchored the intubation tube in his mouth to the respirator hose.

Jack said cheerfully, "Glad to see you decided to stick around, bro."

Tom managed a feeble grin.

Abby thought he looked like an elf, with his pointed ears and toffee-colored, curly hair. "Did you get a good look at who shot you?" Abby asked pointedly.

Tom shook his head.

She pressed on. "So you don't know if it was a man or a woman on that motorcycle?"

Tom stared at her. "No," he said huskily. His eyelids floated down and then sharply jerked up again. He seemed to struggle to stay awake. He licked his pale, dry lips.

Jack picked up a glass of water with a straw in it and shot a look at Abby, as if to say, "Save the interrogation for later." He helped Tom lift the oxygen mask and pinched the straw closer to Tom's lips. "You know, the landlord offered me a month-to-month lease on the cottage. You'll need a safe place to mend, and I could use help liquidating the store merchandise." His voice had the reassuring tone of an older brother counseling his young sibling. "Unless you would rather be a shopkeeper."

Tom finished his sip of water and adjusted the mask. "Fiona would've liked that," he said, his voice cracking.

The poignancy of Jack's offer suggested to Abby that he had a tender regard for this man who had married his sister. If Tom stayed around to run Ancient Wisdom Botanicals, it would be the new life Fiona had envisioned for him. But it remained to be seen which choice Tom would make. His entrenchment in the commune's cultish life suggested he'd been brainwashed. Perhaps Fiona had understood that better than anyone and had been pressuring Tom more prior to her death. Her confession of love for Tom in her journals and her desire to have a child with him had to make her untimely passing all the more difficult for Tom to bear. But maybe now Tom's life would radically change.

Suddenly, as if someone had stroked her bare arm with a feather, Abby snapped out of her reverie. Her grandmother Rose might have reminded her that unseen presences had a way of making themselves known. Abby looked at Tom, who stared across the room, as if seeing what couldn't be seen. Just then, a nurse popped in.

"How's the pain?" she asked.

"Hurts . . . bad," said Tom. Small beads of sweat had emerged across his forehead.

"The doctor has ordered something to help with that. I'll be right back."

Abby placed her hand over Tom's. "You deserve

a rich and full life. Fiona wanted that for you. Not this. Get well soon, so you can get on with it."

"My sentiments exactly," said Jack, setting the glass back on the bedside table. "There's a couch in the cottage with your name on it. I'm heading back there now, and I'll let the landlord know that we're thinking about signing that month-to-month lease. What do you say?"

Tom nodded.

Abby followed Jack into the hallway. "It's a start," she said.

"Yes, it is." Jack gazed into her eyes. "I can't thank you enough for coming. When will I see you again?"

She smiled and, with a toss of her head, said, "Soon, I hope." His expression dimmed, compelling Abby to reach out for his hand. "I hope you know I mean that, Jack."

He brightened and nodded.

Abby stopped by the post office to retrieve her business mail from the box and dropped by the feed store for a bag of scratch grains before returning to the farmette at a little past noon. She felt fully prepared for a face-off with Clay, but his truck wasn't in the driveway. Her heart's heaviness lifted with the realization that she would have some time to enjoy her sanctuary before the showdown with him.

Kneeling to hug Sugar in the backyard, she said, "I've missed you, sweetie. Did you miss me?" The dog backed up and whined, as if directly addressing Abby's question with an affirmative reply.

Abby checked on the chickens and then the bees. Inside the house, the weariness of the past twenty-four hours settled heavily on her, like a hefty woolen quilt. She longed to dive into the bed for a nap but decided to check out the master bath first. The two large windows were locked in. The tub had been set in place, along with the faucet and showerhead. The lights and switch worked, as did the fan. An old-world vanity, with its single sink set into a marble top and storage for linens behind the large doors at the bottom, lent an air of elegance to the room. But when Abby gazed out the double windows above the spa tub, her breath caught in her throat.

"Oh . . . my. I can sit in this tub with a glass of wine and feel the spa jets massaging my aching muscles . . . all the while gazing up at the ranch owned by that fine-looking Lucas Crawford. What irony. If this isn't the mother of all gifts, I don't know what is."

Around four o'clock Abby awoke from a cat nap, oddly craving chocolate mousse, but all she could do was think about it; she surely didn't have the energy to make it. Truth be told, she didn't have much energy for anything. She had to push herself to get up, do a basket of laundry, water the plants, eat a small meal, and lock the chickens in for the night. Clay still hadn't called or texted. Maybe he was nursing a wounded ego or just wanted time away from the farmette. Whatever the reason for his absence, Abby vowed to rave about the fine job he'd done with the bathroom when he returned. Around midnight, she decided to call it a day. She showered, slipped into a pair of silk pajamas, and crawled between the cool sheets. She reached out to feel Sugar's soft, warm body next to her. Sleep soon overtook them both.

A gunshot rang out. Beside her bed, the glass window shattered. Startled into wakefulness, Abby dove to the floor. Her senses went on high alert. Her pulse throbbed. Sugar yipped at a deafening pitch. Trying to gather her wits about her, Abby reached up for the knob on the bedside table drawer. Pulled the drawer open. Her fingers stretched to touch the Ruger LCP 380 semiautomatic pistol. She removed the gun and cartridge. Even in the dark, she knew how to load it.

"Shhh, sweetie. Shhh. Quiet." Abby stroked the quivering, whimpering dog. She strained to make out the sounds outside, determine the direction of the shot. "It's okay," she whispered to the dog. "All okay, sweetie. No worries."

But Abby knew it wasn't okay; she was worried. To call for help, she needed her phone. Abby's heart pounded like that of a thoroughbred entering the final stretch in a horse race. Her situation was dire. She had no backup and no partner. First rule of survival: stay calm, clearheaded, and focused. The daypack was on the bed, but she didn't know which direction the shot had come from. Could the shooter see her? Detect movement? Had she locked the house? A shiver shot up her spine. In a split second, she needed to lock the back door, find her phone, and call for help.

"Come, Sugar." She prayed the dog would follow her. "Let's go, sweetie." Cautiously, she inched over the shards and reached the hallway without cutting herself. And then . . . the kitchen. The dog sat on her haunches at the end of the hall, quiet and still. "Stay," Abby commanded as she crawled into the kitchen.

Easing up to a squat, Abby then rose and flattened her body against the wall. Like a silent shadow, she moved past the refrigerator, washer, and dryer until she reached the slider. She realized she had only partially closed the vertical blinds. Too late now. She searched for movement in the blackness beyond the door. Back by the henhouse, she saw a flash of light, like a match to a cigarette . . . and then it was gone.

Feeling for the door latch, she located the metal tab and plunged it down into the locked position. Inhaling and slowly letting the breath go, she crept along the wall to the safety of the hallway where Sugar was waiting. "Good girl."

Now to get the phone. Abby crept into the bedroom. Keeping her body below the bed frame, she stroked her hand along the top of the mattress, feeling for the daypack. When her fingers touched the rough canvas of the pack, she pinched it and pulled the pack toward her. With the pack on the floor, she remained quiet for a millisecond, listening. The stillness of the night drilled on in her ears like a high-pitched whine from electrical wires. Had the shooter finished his smoke?

Crawling back into the hallway, Abby pulled the zipper across its slide and opened the pack. She pulled out the phone. Pushed the button on the side. The green screen lit up with the time, 3:30 a.m. Abby tapped the icon for contacts and then the entry for police dispatch.

"What's your emergency?" the female dispatcher asked when the call connected.

"Attempted one-eighty-seven," Abby whispered as loud as she dared. "Two shots. Fired at me through my bedroom window."

"Is the shooter still there?"

"Think so. Yes."

"Your address?"

"Henny Penny Farmette on Farm Hill Road."

"Your name?"

"Abigail Mackenzie."

"Stay on the line with me."

Abby assumed that the dispatcher was sending the message out to all cruisers and emergency vehicles in the area.

"Are you in a safe place?" the dispatcher asked.

"Not really. The hallway."

"Can you safely get to a room with a locking door?"

"Will try."

"Police are on their way. Don't hang up."

Abby moistened her lips. "Okay. I know the drill."

With her gun in one hand and the phone in the other, Abby crawled on all fours down the hallway, with Sugar padding alongside. At the master bathroom, Abby abruptly stopped . . . listened. The patio slider lock jiggled. Her heart raced. In her head, alarm bells sounded. She had only a minute or two to hide somewhere. *But where?* She felt for the handles on the vanity double doors . . . then stopped. *Even if I fit, Sugar won't. Not an option.*

The assailant's heavy footsteps clomped beyond the exterior of the broken bedroom window. Paused.

Easy way in. Minutes . . . maybe seconds . . . all I've got, if that. Abby crawled from the master bath to the hallway's small office area. *Maybe we can hide under the desk.* She inched forward. Found the desk but was blocked by a large cardboard box. Then it dawned on her. The bathtub box. If it held the tub . . . Abby felt for the lid. Lifted it. Laid the phone inside. She hoisted up Sugar, set her inside, and then crawled in.

A loud thud at the front of the house told Abby the intruder had walked on past the broken window to check the front door. He had knocked over a metal chair on the porch. But why hadn't he used the broken window? Maybe worried about getting cut, leaving blood at the scene. Maybe this wasn't some amateur shooter?

Abby hugged Sugar in a one-arm hold. She reached up and closed the box lid. Pointing the gun straight up, she waited, ready. If the killer lifted that lid, she would shoot. Period. Sugar stopped panting long enough to lick Abby's bare forearm.

Anxiety. We're both feeling it. Abby heard the lock and the knob on the front door being twisted. Nausea swept through her. The lump in her throat couldn't be swallowed. Her pulse pounded. Holding Sugar snug, Abby hoped she could muffle any bark against her bodice. All was quiet for a moment. Then . . . glass crashed again on the bedroom floor as pieces were kicked out from the window. *So here he comes.* Panic ran riot inside her. Abby's sweaty palm quivered against the gun handle; her trigger finger trembled.

The sound of a heavy foot landing on the floor . . . then the other foot made Sugar's lean body tense. Glass crunched like ice shards crushed under a heavy roller. Sugar jerked her head at the sound.

"No . . . no barking," Abby whispered. She trained

her focus on hearing the footsteps as they walked into the master bath. She heard something else.

A faint siren sounded in the distance. Grew louder. The heavy footsteps returned to the bedroom. Crunched more glass. A man's voice cursed as he banged the wall to scramble out the window. The siren screamed, as if only yards away. Gravel crunched under tire wheels. Rubber screeched to a halt. Abby lifted the box lid. A brilliant light flashed on outside. So the cops had turned on their searchlights. Abby exhaled through pursed lips. Let the weight of the gun relax against her chest.

"Police are here," she told the dispatcher before laying aside the phone.

More sirens screamed as another emergency vehicle arrived, and pandemonium ensued. She heard multiple voices shouting. "Drop the gun. Drop the gun. Hands up. On the ground. Spread 'em."

Abby helped Sugar out of the box and then climbed out herself. She put her gun back into the drawer. Slipped a robe over her pajamas and hurried to the front entrance of her farmhouse. Abby took Sugar's panting as a level of high anxiety, but what could she do to assuage the dog while chaos was still going on? She flipped on the indoor and outside lights and saw the suspect being placed in the backseat of the cruiser at the front of her property.

"You okay?" an officer called out to Abby through the screen door she'd opened.

"I am now," she said, stepping into the pink flip-flops she kept on the front porch. "Heck of a quick response. Where were you? On a stakeout at the pancake house at the end of Farm Hill Road?" she teased.

The cop grinned. "Something like that."

"I want to see him . . . the idiot who shot out my window."

The officer led her to the cruiser and opened the door. Dak Harmon, hands cuffed behind his back, glared at her.

"Know him?" asked the officer.

Abby's stomach churned. She had the urge to throw up. She swallowed. "Yes. That's Dak Harmon. Did you find the gun he used?"

"Sure did. Did he assault you, ma'am?" The officer added, "Physically, I mean."

"Uh, no."

"That is bruising around your eye, isn't it?"

"Oh, this," Abby said, touching her eye. "Yes, well, he did do this, but not tonight. That's a whole other story."

Diverting their attention, a young rookie cop walked through Abby's side gate from the back-yard to the front driveway. "Sarge, there's an older-model Harley parked on the other side of the property, behind the chicken coop. The motorcycle engine is still warm," he said. "And there is a blood trail, indicating the suspect was heading away from her house in that direction."

Abby locked eyes with Dak, who glowered back at her. "So," Abby said, "the commune kicks out the smart people and keeps the Neanderthals." Addressing the senior officer, she said, "Take him away."

The officer slammed the cruiser door, tapped the hood, and the cruiser pulled away.

Abby walked back to the front door and waited until the sergeant had finished speaking to his rookie. Then she escorted the senior officer into the bedroom to show him the window damage. Pointing to the blood on the sill, she said, "He couldn't shoot me, so I guess he thought he'd come through the window and finish me off. Stupid lout would leave his DNA all over the place."

"We'll need your statement," said the police officer.

"And I'm ready to give it," said Abby, "but what's the chance that you might share with me the license plate of the motorcycle he was riding?"

Chocolate Mint Mousse

Ingredients:
½ cup bittersweet chocolate chips
3 tablespoons strong coffee
1 tablespoon kirsch, Kahlúa, or brandy
4 large eggs, at room temperature, separated
    (preferably organic eggs from free-range chickens*)
⅔ cup granulated sugar
¾ cup heavy cream
½ teaspoon finely minced fresh chocolate mint, plus
    4 sprigs, for garnish

Directions:
    Combine the chocolate chips, coffee, and kirsch in a double boiler or a medium saucepan and cook over low heat, stirring

continuously, until the chocolate has melted and the texture is smooth and even. Remove from the heat.

Separate the eggs, placing the yolks in a small bowl and the whites in a medium bowl.

Whisk together the egg yolks, sugar, and the minced mint and then fold the yolks into the melted chocolate mixture. Whip the cream until firm peaks are formed. Spoon the whipped cream into the chocolate and then gently fold in using a rubber spatula.

Beat the egg whites until stiff peaks form. Gently fold the beaten egg whites into the chocolate mixture. Spoon the mousse into dessert cups or ramekins and chill, covered, in the refrigerator for 4 hours or overnight until the mousse sets. Garnish each cup with a sprig of mint, fresh raspberries, or shavings of white chocolate and serve.

Serves 4

Chapter 18

A pawful of honey could mean the
wrathful sting of a thousand bees.

—*Henny Penny Farmette Almanac*

By the time the police had collected all the evidence, had removed the crime-scene tape, and had given Abby permission to clean up the broken glass littering her bedroom floor, the sun had left the eastern-facing windows. Breakfast and lunch had come and gone. The cops had pried a bullet from the wall and had bagged and tagged the shell casings. They had arrested Dak Harmon and carted him off to jail. With the gun seized as evidence and the motorcycle impounded, the case against the bodyguard strengthened.

Abby rested in her grandmother's rocker on the patio, sipping from a mug of iced coffee, glad the ordeal was over. She listened to the songbirds' cacophony and watched Sugar's tail wag where it stuck out of the lavender thicket.

"I'll bet you slept better than I did," Clay called out to her as he rounded the house to reach the patio. He looked like he had come from an all-night party and needed only a shave and a comb-through to restore his sexy good looks.

"Why do you say that?" asked Abby.

"Just that it's always so peaceful here."

Resisting the urge to detail her harrowing night, she asked a pressing question. "And where did you sleep last night?"

"In my truck at the downtown park."

"Well, that's just weird. Why did you do that?"

"Lost track of time playing darts at the Black Witch with some of the guys." He groaned. "We drank way too much whiskey. Somebody—I don't recall his name—gave me a lift back to my truck. I couldn't drive. I figured it was safer to stay put."

"Why didn't you just park in front of the bar on Main Street?"

"The downtown was packed. No space on Main, and all the action seemed to originate in that downtown park. Leastways, that's where the drinking started . . . at the booths set up to get people interested in going over to the fair. Guess the fair has almost wrapped up its run. Anyway, one of the booths promoted local wine and cheese. They hook you on the samples and urge you to go to the fair, pay the entrance fee, and buy quantities of the wine and cheese you liked."

"Uh-huh. So you had cheese and a drop of wine, and they convinced you to buy the wineglass etched with the chamber of commerce logo before you could sample more. Am I right?"

"Somethin' like that." He rubbed a sandpaper cheek and changed the subject. "Any coffee left?" he asked, then darted into the kitchen before she could even answer.

Abby had expected him to be bruising for an argument, but he seemed to be in a cheery mood. *How nice.* She sank deeper into the chair and rocked. He hadn't bothered to inquire about how she'd slept. *Oh, that's right. It's always all about you, isn't it, Clay? And you probably haven't got a clue how tired I am of dealing with your crap.*

Her gaze swept across the lawn, past the citrus trees, all the way out to where the white climbing rose scampered up the six-foot chain-link fence and spilled over with thick sprays of blooms. The perfusion of rose blooms partially blocked the view into the wooded acre behind her property. Where the rose ended, the chicken run stretched to the henhouse. It, too, obscured a section of the back fence. Past the chickens' house and run, the fence began again with a metal gate that opened between the two properties. There had never been a need to lock that gate. As she stared at it, Abby figured Dak Harmon must have checked it out and known he could easily slip onto her property from the rear. And showing up at three thirty in the morning could have been a calculation against being seen.

Her attention shifted back to Clay, who had strolled onto the patio and had taken a seat to sip his mug of coffee. "Nice to finally have some time together," he said. "What do you think of your master bath?"

"I love it." *That's what you want to hear, isn't it? When you do something for someone else, it's never out of the goodness of your heart, but for the adulation you receive. I get that now.*

"Don't worry about ever paying me back. I'll think of something. It's ready to use," Clay said, grinning. "I've been thinking about getting a piece of teak to wrap around the top edge of the tub. I can cut a track and install a glass enclosure so water spray won't hit the floor."

"Sounds lovely," Abby said, thinking that although teak and glass would add a level of elegance, it seemed so unnecessary for such a small bathroom. She knew if she said anything about his idea, he'd take offense, see it as an affront to his creativity, so she said nothing else about it.

"Teak and glass will have to wait." Clay's expression darkened. He turned to look at the rose on the back fence.

"Why?" Abby asked, wondering what had caused his whole demeanor to shift. Maybe she hadn't waxed effusive enough with her compliments.

A corner of his mouth drew up slightly, the way it always did when he found something difficult to say. "You know I'd never knowingly hurt you, Abby, right?"

She drilled him with a questioning look. "Suppose so. Why? What's going on?"

"When I came here, I thought things were going to be just like the old times. We were always good together. But you've changed. Most days, you're gone."

"But I tell you when I'm going and where. And when I come back, I tell you what I've been doing. My friend Fiona was murdered. When a victim's family is grieving and needs help, I'm not the type of person to turn my back to them."

"Yeah." He took a sip of his coffee. "I guess I was fooling myself, thinking it would be like before between us. It's true what they say. You really can't go back. It's never the same."

"Oh, come on, Clay. You know as well as I do, relationships take time and effort . . . by both parties."

"And that's my point exactly." His expression hardened. "So why do I feel like I am a party of one? You're not the way you used to be."

"Why do you say that?" Abby asked, her fingers tightening around the coffee mug.

"You really want to know?" He eyed her suspiciously. "It used to be that you were always here, working next to me on the house or in the gardens. Now you are never here. Don't make time for me. I've even had to hire a day laborer just to help get that master bath to where it is."

"I didn't ask you to build me a master bath."

"No, you didn't. I was doing it out of the kindness of my heart."

Abby tensed, swallowed her retort. *Yeah, right.*

"I thought it would be nice if we built something new together, and not just that bathroom."

Abby stared at him. If he was trying to sound hurt, it had come across like sarcasm. *How dare you pick a fight so it seems like your imminent departure is my fault?* Unable to hold her frustration inside, Abby said, "You better take a picture of the tub before you go, because I am moving it out to repair the wiring. I heard arcing in the wall when I turned on the jets. If I didn't know better, I'd swear you were trying to electrocute me."

"Oh, come on. Are you accusing me of trying to kill you?"

"The alternative is to think that in your haste to get recognition, you aren't careful. Think back, Clay, to when I first bought the place and all the neighbors came round to marvel at your work in the kitchen. Then one morning I went to make coffee and barely missed being buried under the light soffit when it fell from the kitchen ceiling. Apparently, after all the compliments, you'd forgotten to finish screwing it in place. The soffit and the tub are like our relationship—both presentations that serve some obscure purpose of yours but are never meant to be permanent. Well, Clay, hear this. In my world, I need things to function correctly. The soffit didn't. The tub isn't. And we're not."

He glared at her and set his mug down harder than necessary on the glass patio table. "Forget it. I guess we're beyond talking things through." He exhaled heavily.

Pushing a wayward strand of hair from her face and tucking it behind her ear, Abby mustered her last bit of strength to return his stare. "You know what . . . ? Just go. I don't need this."

His expression seemed grim. "Fine."

Abby looked away; she reminded herself that two couldn't argue if one left. After standing up and stilling the rocker, she started for the kitchen.

Clay reached out and clamped his hand on her forearm. "You never loved me."

"And you never loved me. Honestly, Clay, I'm tired of playing nice, of tap-dancing around your moods all the time, hoping I haven't said something that's going to set you off. I don't want to live my life that way." She looked at him coolly. "So go, already. Texas this time . . . right?"

His dark eyes registered surprise. "What makes you say that?"

"You shouldn't surf the Net, looking for your next conquest, Clay, when you've just convinced the person lying beside you that she's the one that rocks your world. She's the one you love."

His lips thinned into a tight line. . . . Eyes imparted hurt and hostility. He released his grip on her arm.

Abby summoned all the strength within her. "Just go. We're done here." She marched back to the kitchen to put her mug in the sink. Holding on to the counter with a white-knuckled grip, she struggled to remain resolute.

Through the open slider, he called out, "Fine. I can make it to Los Angeles in eight hours, two more to Phoenix. I'd like a shower before taking off . . . if that's okay with you."

"Be my guest. Clean towels are on top of the washer." Abby busied herself with rinsing the mug and then placing it on the top shelf of the dishwasher.

Clay grabbed a towel. "Why are you so mad?"

"I'm not," Abby shot back. "I'm worn out by what happened here last night, when you were doing whatever you were doing in town."

"What happened?"

"Someone tried to kill me. Did you not notice that the bedroom window has been shot out?" She turned to look at him. His expression registered shock.

After a pause, he shot back, "And yet you keep involving yourself with criminal investigations, like you are still a cop." He slammed the bathroom door.

Abby exhaled heavily. *Yeah, that's right. Make it my fault. Easier to look into the mirror then, isn't it?*

Fifteen minutes later, he reappeared in the living room, where Abby sat curled on the couch, sorting packets of seed she'd saved over the winter in labeled envelopes. He had towel dried his hair, shaved, and dressed in khakis, a narrow leather belt with a sleek silver buckle, brown lace-up oxfords, and a tomato-colored polo shirt with a Ralph Lauren label. After stashing his dirty clothes in a white plastic bag, he hoisted it under his arm and carried it, along with his suitcase and laptop bag, out the front door to his truck.

With both anger and sadness surging inside, Abby watched him leave the house. He still had the power to hurt her. And even if they couldn't be a couple, the bonds they'd formed long ago were proving stronger than she had realized. She placed the seed packets in the small cardboard box, rose, and strolled out to the front porch, with Sugar by her side. Her eyes burned, threatening tears, but she fought against them.

In the gravel driveway, Clay slammed his truck door and walked back toward her. His dark eyes locked onto hers; the scent of his soft cologne permeated the air. He stood in front of her, his expression dark and pouty. "Guess this is it." His tone sounded husky and slightly hostile.

Her chest tightened; her stomach twisted into knots. "Yes," she said. After a pause, she added, "Whatever it is you are seeking, I hope you find it. I think we know it was never me or the farmette."

He stared at the tassels on his brown oxfords. When he lifted his gaze to look at her again, his eyes shimmered. "Take care of yourself, Miss Abby Mac." He swung himself up into his truck and started the engine. A moment later, he drove away . . . out of her life.

* * *

When Kat called in mid-afternoon to see if Abby might want to come into town and meet her for coffee, Abby declined. She hadn't moved for hours after watching the dust settle in her driveway. She had not expected the deluge of tears after Clay had gone nor the conflicting feelings that had emerged after her tears dried. Feeling vulnerable and exposed, she had no desire beyond sheltering herself in solitude and the company of her chickens and bees and Sugar's unconditional love.

"Not today," Abby said.

"It's because of what happened last night, isn't it? Word of the shooting at your place is all over town. I wanted to make sure you're okay."

"I am . . . or, at least, I will be," Abby said, eyes misting up again. She sniffed.

"I heard you were there alone when Dak Harmon tried to kill you." Kat took a big breath and let it go. "Why wasn't Clay there? Of all nights, where was he?"

"He didn't want to get a DUI. He told me that he spent the night in his truck in the downtown park."

"And that would be a lie. Sorry to be so blunt."

"I know," Abby said. "He should have come up with something a little more creative. Everybody knows about that fence going up around that park when the town hosts the fair. The irony is that if he'd waited one more night, the fair would have been over, the booths in the park dismantled, and the fence taken down." Abby cleared her throat. "He probably met someone. Oh, well. It's a moot point now."

"How so?"

"He has gone. This time to Texas."

"You sad?"

"A little. But my heart gets lighter when I see that new master bath he built. Honestly, Kat, it tops any bathroom you might see in a fancy magazine."

"And I still haven't seen it. Don't know when I can get there again, though. The heat has turned up on Fiona's case now that Harmon is in the slammer. We've got ballistics going over the gun and casings."

"Anything from the motorcycle in the mountain garage that Gus Morales is repairing? I've been thinking how tidy it could be for the case if that tire tread matched the partial tire print at the scene of Fiona's burning car."

"Uh-oh," said Kat. "Hold on, Abby. The chief is calling me. I swear that man has eyes *and* ears in the back of his head."

Abby waited while Kat took the other call. When she again picked up the thread of their conversation, Kat's tone sounded urgent. "I have got to go. Chief wants me to bring Premalatha Baxter in for another interview. Get this. The gun Dak Harmon used to shoot out your window is registered to her."

"No kidding?" Abby twisted a clump of her hair around a finger as she thought about that development. "Well, you know . . . Premalatha wore a tunic when Jack and I last saw her, and it was hot enough to fry an egg on the hood of my car. Make her push those sleeves up when you get her into that interview room."

"You think that nicotine patch belonged to her,

right? They probably both smoke. Dak had a pack on him when he used you for target practice. And thanks to his stupidity, we've got his DNA on the discarded butt he dropped at your back fence."

"Saliva sample," said Abby.

"Premalatha denied being a smoker, but we'll ask her again. Now, Abby, forget about Clay. Get some rest. Sleep, chocolate, and a new man will fix what ails you."

After hanging up from the call, Abby spent the next half hour stapling screen wire to the exterior of the house, over the hole where the large window used to be. And as an extra measure against any mosquitoes and other insects entering the house, Abby also stapled sheets to the interior wall as temporary curtains. She hadn't finished pushing in the last staple before her cell phone rang. A neighbor wanted to order three jars each of Abby's apricot jam and backyard honey—the result of word getting around that both had been judged blue-ribbon winners at the county fair. And the calls didn't end with that one.

A family who lived a mile north of Dr. Danbury's place wanted fifty sample jars of farmette honey to give away as favors at their daughter's upcoming wedding. The cash deal carried a proviso—Abby would be required to deliver the sample jars directly to the home of the bride's mother. Abby's excitement mounted as she mentally tallied the income that the wedding order would generate and the potential windfall that might follow if the wedding guests became regular paying customers. But even as the thought of an improved cash flow invigorated her, a sobering thought intruded. Was there honey enough to fill the orders? Abby quickly checked the shelves above the washer and dryer. Eight small jars. Not enough. Next, she removed the lid from the white five-gallon honey bucket on the kitchen counter, but it had been drained until nearly dry.

Abby racked her brain. Who might have extra jars that she could buy back until she could open the hives to see if she might take another frame or two? Abby thought of Smooth Your Groove and Fiona's botanical shop. The former had been forcibly closed and locked by the health department. That left only Fiona's stash. And as she recalled, Fiona kept a few jars in her shop and held back the others in the storage shed near her cottage.

"By any chance are you in the cottage?" she asked after Jack answered her call.

"That I am. For the last quarter hour, I've been chatting up Paws, the landlord's long-haired, six-toed kitty. The big boy just invited himself in. Popped up the hole, he did. I've put out a tin of fish for him and a bowl of crackers for me. So, what can I do for you?"

"I'm short honey for orders I have to fill. Fiona bought two cases from me. She told me she was going to put out a few jars for sale and stash the rest in her storage shed near the cottage. Could I—"

"Buy it back? No. Come up and get it. That would be spot-on lovely."

"Could I come now?"

"I'll put out more crackers," he said with a chuckle.

"Okay if I bring Sugar?"

"Only if you promise that she doesn't remember how I previously threw the two of you out."

Abby laughed. "Don't know about that. Can't speak for Sugar."

After clicking off the call, Abby searched the laundry basket. She pulled out a folded pair of jeans and a pale green T-shirt that still held the scent of fabric softener, slipped out of her work clothes, and put the jeans and T-shirt on. From the guest bath, where she stood in front of the wall mirror, vigorously brushing her hair, she heard her cell phone alerting her to an incoming text. It was from the police chief, saying his wife wanted honey for her church—eight-ounce jars, fifteen total. Abby texted back, **I'm on it. If I have enough on hand, I'll deliver tomorrow.**

After nuking a clean, moistened washcloth in the microwave for a few seconds, Abby shook it out, tested the heat, and then draped it over her face. She dried her face with a towel and applied a light foundation, some blusher, a dab of mascara, and a couple of strokes of plum lip gloss. After grabbing a yellow paisley-patterned scarf and a heavily embroidered jeans jacket, she stuffed the pockets with treats for Sugar. She looked approvingly at herself in the armoire mirror before locking the kitchen slider and exiting the house through the front door.

The drive into the mountains before sunset had always seemed romantic to Abby, especially in late spring. She likened it to an arty Italian film with evocative cinematography—you could almost smell the earth, warm and fragrant with hedge roses, ripe grapes, and wild thyme. You could almost see a light sifting of dust floating over the patchwork hills and the medieval stone houses in villages where bell towers rang out the canonical hours. The mountains soon worked their magic on Abby. So peaceful and absorbed in thought was she that she nearly missed the big red barn turnoff, hitting the brakes just in the nick of time.

Only too eager to stretch her legs and sniff the environment, Sugar leaped from the Jeep as soon as Abby had opened the door. Jack jogged down to the mailbox and greeted her with a bear hug. Sugar yipped until Jack held out his hands, palms down, for her to smell. Her tail began to wag.

"Have I passed her sniff test, Abby? Or should I be afraid she'll take my ankle off when I stand up?"

"Oh, *please.* She weighs thirty-five pounds. How could she possibly hurt a big guy like you?"

"Yeah, well, I can think of some ways. It's the ones at the knees you have to watch out for . . . never know which spot they'll go for." He grinned and tried stroking Sugar's head, but she wouldn't back away from him.

"She'll settle down," said Abby. "Do you see that shed over there? You've got the key to it, I hope," said Abby as she advanced on the path past the mailbox.

Jack abruptly stood from where he'd squatted to pet Sugar. He reached into his long, straight-leg jeans and fished out a silver ring with several keys. "Let's find out." They walked over to the shed, with Sugar leading the way, nose to the ground.

"Gosh, why does it smell like a garbage dump?" Abby asked.

Jack wrinkled his nose. "That would be because it is. The landlord stacks his refuse bags next to that black barrel. There he incinerates them." Jack tried a key in the padlock. It released. After removing the lock and unlatching the door, he pulled the door open and waved Abby inside.

"Why let the bags just pile up like that so near the cottage?" said Abby. "You'd think there would be—"

"Rats?" Jack asked.

Sugar's shrill, high-pitched *yip-yip-yip* interrupted.

"Yes, rats," Abby replied, hurrying over to quiet Sugar. "*No*. Get outta there. Now."

Sugar pawed at the mound of plastic and paper bags of refuse. Abby tried grabbing her, but Sugar leaped from her reach, dashed to the other side of the bags.

"If she comes this way," Jack said, "I'll try to snatch her."

"It could be a rat or a mouse that's got her so excited," said Abby. "She's definitely more interested in the garbage than the treats in my pocket. If I gave her a treat now, it would just reinforce the barking behavior."

"Oh," Jack said, tapping his temple. "Now you're going all dog whisperer on me. Brilliant. So what's your strategy?"

"Beats me," said Abby. While she considered her options, Sugar plowed through the pile, knocking over bags, causing their contents to spill out. She leaped up and raced after a field mouse zigzagging toward the mailbox, up the path, and under the cottage.

"Over soon," said Abby. After a few minutes of frantic barking, Sugar abandoned the mouse to sniff around the bushes at the entrance, where the cats had undoubtedly marked their territory. "Oh, my gosh, Jack," Abby said, looking at the strewn contents of a bag near his feet. "Don't move."

Jack frowned, as if he feared the escaped mouse had a companion that was about to disappear up his pants leg. "What? That broken teacup?" He reached down.

"No. Don't . . . don't touch it," Abby demanded. "That teacup is one of Fiona's. I recognize it because it belongs to that set of china I helped you pack up."

"So it is. Good eye."

"I've got a hunch the detectives will want to check out the items in that bag—the cup, those wadded paper towels, and that disposable cup with the Smooth Your Groove logo."

"Clues?" he asked.

"I don't know. It's probably a long shot. Just the same, I'm calling it in."

Twenty minutes later, Abby and Jack stood near Dr. Danbury. Still in a stupor, the doc had stumbled outside to watch the police retrieve the plastic bag and its contents. He wore a wrinkled short-sleeve cotton shirt under farmers' overalls. His oiled silver hair lay flat; he seemed to need his cane to stand upright. By the time the two cruisers pulled away, the sun had dropped low behind the blue-green mountain ridges. Fog like fingers of smoke inched through the dark valleys below. Dr. Danbury asked Abby if she and Jack would like to come over and help him finish a bottle of a local vintner's pinot noir.

"I'll have to pass," Abby said. "Thanks anyway. But, Doc, do you mind if I ask a question?"

"Be my guest," he said, using a ropy-veined hand to smack an insect that had alighted on his hairy arm.

"Do you remember seeing Fiona on the morning she died?"

"Nope. Couldn't have," the doctor replied.

"Why is that?" Abby asked.

"I stayed overnight in Las Flores. My son's got himself a nice condo. It's right downtown. His fiancée and I took him to the country club to celebrate."

"Yeah? If I may ask, what were you celebrating?"

"His birthday. I spent the night on his couch." He cleared his throat. "Don't much like driving in the dark."

"And that's your Volvo there?" she said, pointing to his wagon. "What about that ATV in your garage? Does anyone ever take it out for a spin?"

"Nope. Got it for my boy four or five years ago. He used to tear all over the mountain. Not now. His girlfriend never went in for that sort of thing." He paused. "You interested in buying it?"

Abby smiled. "Nah. Just curious. So, to be clear, you weren't here during that twenty-four-hour period when Fiona died?"

"Nope."

"And none of your neighbors have reported seeing anyone messing around on your property?"

"Nope. That neither." He thrust his hands into his pockets. "S'pect the wine's breathed plenty long enough now," Dr. Danbury said. "You joining me or not?"

Abby shook her head. Jack had walked a few paces away to gaze at the rising full moon as the curved sliver steadily ascended to become a luminous golden disk. "Dr. Danbury wants to know if you'd like to have a drink with him, Jack."

"Oh, no. Thanks, Doc." Jack turned to face them. "Abby and I are going honey hunting."

Apparently, Jack's remark made no sense to the doctor, who spun around and walked with his cane back to his door.

When the doctor had left them, Abby said, "I kind of like the honey-hunting idea. It sounds like we're primitives going out to find hives in the wild."

"It might interest you to know that in Nepal, there is an ancient tradition of gathering honey from the hives of wild bees. Honey gatherers have two tools—rope ladders and long sticks . . . well, three, if you count smoke—to raid the hives on towering cliffs. It's risky."

"Luckily, we won't need ropes, smoke, or sticks. And we don't have to go far, just to that shed over there," Abby said with a grin. She took hold of his arm and steered him toward the shed.

"Did you know the largest honeybee in the world is the *Apis laboriosa*, and it's found in Nepal?" Jack asked.

"I did not," Abby replied as they approached the doorway of the shed. The shed's exterior was illuminated by moonlight, but the interior was as dark as a covered well. "Did you know it's next to impossible to find the honey in the dark?" She was about to add, "I'll just get my flashlight from my pack," when he pulled her into an embrace.

"Who says I can't find honey in the dark?" He tilted her face upward. His fingers trailed along her cheek.

Abby felt giddy. Her heart pounded like a thundering river. As he leaned in, Abby anticipated his kiss, but instead, he nuzzled his face against her neck, reached out into the darkness, and flipped on the light switch. Directly in her sight line, on a metal-framed utility shelf, rested the case of honey and six jars bearing her farmette label.

"Oh, you're good," she said, at once relieved at what had not happened and at the same time wishing something had. "If you'll carry the case, I'll grab these jars."

After they had loaded the honey into the Jeep, an awkward moment passed between them until the lightbulb in the shed sputtered off. They both turned to look at it. It flickered back on and then off again. A loud *pop* sounded, and the light went out.

"Jesus, Mary, and Joseph. I'd better turn off the juice. Don't want to burn down the shed," Jack said.

Abby chuckled. "No, that would never do." She reached down to stroke Sugar, who was pawing at her legs. "We'd better go," said Abby, lifting Sugar's warm, round body into the Jeep. "I've got my pooch to feed, my chickens to check on, and honey jars to fill with what little honey I have in the house."

"Well, if you must," Jack said. "I could help, if you like."

"Really? When did you last fill a honey jar?"

"Well, actually, never. But I'm a quick study. Besides, after we fill them, we can drive around delivering honey to all your customers, and I can amuse you with stories. So, what do you say?"

Abby thought about his proposition. *A sexy guy who tells the truth, is willing to help, and takes direction. What's not to like?*

"I'm game. Do you think you can find your way to Farm Hill Road? Turn right and look for the mailbox with the chicken on it. Actually, it's a rooster with tall tail feathers, but it marks my driveway. If you can get there by eight o'clock in the morning, I'll have coffee ready and some killer apricot honey bread in the oven."

Apricot-Craisin Honey Bread

Ingredients:
Vegetable oil spray, for greasing the loaf pans
1 cup diced dried apricots
½ cup Craisins
½ cup organic honey
¼ cup canola oil
⅔ cup boiling water
2 cups whole-wheat flour
2 teaspoons baking powder
¼ teaspoon baking soda
1 cup chopped unsalted pecans
½ cup evaporated milk
1 large egg

Directions:
Preheat the oven to 350°F. Lightly spray three 6-x-3-inch loaf pans with the vegetable oil spray.

Place the apricots and the Craisins in a medium bowl and add the honey, oil, and boiling water. Set aside and let cool.

Meanwhile, sift together the flour, baking powder, and baking soda in a large bowl. Add the pecans.

In a small bowl, whisk together the milk and the egg. Pour the egg mixture into the reserved apricots and Craisins and mix well.

Add the apricot-Craisin mixture to the pecan-flour mixture and stir until all the ingredients are well combined.

Pour an equal amount of batter into each of the prepared loaf pans. Allow the batter to settle. Bake for 30 to 35 minutes. Test for doneness by inserting a toothpick into the loaves. It should have no batter on it when extracted.

Cool the mini loaves and then invert them onto a clean surface. Wrap them in foil. Let the honey bread rest overnight for the best flavor.

Makes 3 loaves

Chapter 19

For a flock of appreciative clucking followers, sprinkle dried mealworms over
a dish of greens.

—*Henny Penny Farmette Almanac*

At first light, Abby ran the water in the tub of
her new master bath, but the water from the
spigot remained as cloudy and slightly greasy as
the previous time she'd cracked it on. It dawned
on her that the water had to run awhile to get rid
of the flux from the new copper pipes. It was normal with new piping. Still, she wasn't about to turn
on the jets. But as she thought about it, maybe a
bath wasn't such a good idea. Jack might arrive
early, before she had prepped everything. After
turning off the water and dashing to the guest
bathroom, she showered and did a quick blow-dry
of her hair.

Choosing a lightweight turquoise summer knit
dress with hidden pockets, a scooped neck, and a
flared skirt, Abby pulled it over her head and

stepped into a pair of black flats. She gathered her reddish-gold locks and anchored them with a black elastic band at the base of her neck. Finally, she put on her favorite turquoise, amethyst, and seed pearl earrings and then admired her image in the mirror. She hoped the look would please Jack.

After tying on a clean white pinafore apron, she began to load the dishwasher with jars and screw-top lids, rather than the ring lids she used for jam. Abby set the dishwasher running through its hottest cycle, but then she heard a ruckus from the chicken house. Dashing out the patio door and across the lawn, she saw a small fox pawing at the structure's window.

"Oh, no, you don't," she yelled, plucking two apricots from the tree and lobbing them at the fox. The fox leaped from the henhouse and scampered up the chain-link fence.

Abby stood in the chicken run until the hens had settled down. The black-and-white wyandottes resumed their alto-toned, gravelly *g-rack, g-rack, g-rack*. The white leghorns clucked in a higher pitch. Blondie, the Buff Orpington—who could be a broodzilla when she was in her broody cycle—began scratching a hole for her dirt bath. And Houdini, the rooster, let go a shrill, yet manly *cock-a-doodle-doo*. Abby knew they wanted out of the run to free-range forage, but that wasn't going to happen while there was a predator in the area. Where there was one fox, more were likely, perhaps a den of them. She could still see the fox sitting on its haunches on a hill at the rear of the wooded acre. No way was she letting her feathered friends out today. Abby checked the feeder hanging from its chain and the water dispenser. Both were half full, so Abby left the run and returned to the farmhouse.

Back inside the kitchen, she turned on the oven and set about making a batch of apricot honey bread. With the three loaf pans in the oven for the next thirty minutes, Abby carried a chair over to the washer and dryer area. From the top shelf, she took down two cardboard boxes, each holding a dozen jars of apricot jam. She set the boxes on the dining-room table.

After putting the chair back from the washer and dryer area and tucking it under the dining table, Abby then returned to the kitchen. She poured a cup of nuggets into the dog food bowl and fresh water into the canister of the water dispenser. Next, she made a pot of coffee. When it was ready, she poured herself a cup and leaned over the counter with a pencil and paper to write out the sequence of her honey and jam deliveries, starting with the chief's at the police department.

Jack arrived punctually at eight o'clock that morning, dressed in a T-shirt featuring a blue morning glory and, beneath the image, its identification, *Ipomoea tricolor*. He wore tan cargo shorts and sand-colored lace-up espadrilles. His hair lay in loose curls across his forehead, making him more boyish-looking than usual. Sugar behaved as if Jack had become her best friend; her tail wagged wildly when he strolled into the yard through the side gate. Abby didn't try to conceal her delight at seeing him, too. She gave Jack a quick hug and offered him a tour of her farmette, with Sugar bounding happily around them.

His face beamed a smile as his gaze swept over

her property. "Oh, yes, Abby. Show me this place you've created out of an old field," he said happily.

At the Black Tartarian trees, he picked a bright red cherry with a hole in its side. "Oh, well, what's a small peck out of the side of an otherwise perfectly good cherry? I don't mind sharing with the birds," he said, then popped the cherry in his mouth and promptly spit out the seed.

At the row of early bearing peaches, he gently squeezed three golden fruits until he was satisfied he'd found the ripest specimen. He offered it to Abby. When she shook her head, he peeled off the skin, ate the peach with relish, and tossed the pit to the ground. They walked a short distance farther and reached the apple trees.

He gave her a sexy look. "I feel like I'm in the Garden of Eden," he said. "But the temptress hasn't offered me the apple."

Abby laughed. "You'll have to wait."

"Oh, isn't that always the way? Eve didn't hesitate to offer one to Adam."

"She would have if they were standing by this tree."

Jack's expressive eyes danced as he regarded her quizzically.

"Well, just look at them," said Abby. "They're the size of acorns. These apples won't be ripe until autumn."

"Autumn, you say? What a pity. I might be gone by then." His eyes regarded her, as if he was gauging her response.

Abby dropped her gaze.

"Or I might just stick around."

"Would that be such a bad thing?" Abby teased.

His eyes locked onto hers with seemingly seductive intention. "No, not at all. By autumn, your apples might not be the only sweet thing I taste in your garden."

"Oh, my," said Abby, pretending to fan away her fluster with the skirt of her apron. "I think we've dallied long enough. Better have our breakfast and hit the road, or I'll be late with my deliveries."

Inside the lobby of the Las Flores Police Station, with the honey order for Chief Bob Allen's wife, Abby overheard two female dispatchers arguing. Apparently, they were both dating the same man.

"Yeah, well, he is serially monogamous," the older of the two women asserted.

"You think I don't know what that means?" said the younger dispatcher, running her fingers through her edgy bicolored black-and-platinum hairdo. She flipped her hand dismissively toward the other woman. "He dumps his current girlfriend to pursue a new one. I'm the new one."

"Don't get your hopes up, love. He hasn't dumped me yet, and I don't intend to let him." The beads braided into her mocha-colored hair gave the older woman an exotic look. "You forget, I'm from Colombia, and there we fight for our men. I'm telling you it's not over until I say it is."

The tone of the argument quickly escalated. Abby frantically pushed the buzzer on the wall, waited, and pushed it again. Nettie appeared on the other side of the glass window, her forehead creased in a frown. Alarmed and shaking her head, apparently at the argument, she told Abby through the speaker, "Be right with you."

Abby pointed to the counter and motioned for

Jack to put the case down next to the jars she'd already placed there. They waited as Nettie disappeared and returned with Chief Bob Allen. He went over to the dispatchers and called out the warring women.

"Who were they arguing over?" Abby asked Nettie as the chief took each woman aside for a talk.

Nettie rolled her eyes. "Bernie in the evidence room."

Abby burst out laughing. "You're kidding, right?"

Nettie shook her head. "Mr. I'm here for a good time, not a long time."

Abby shook her head and feigned a serious look as the chief looked over at her. The room became as quiet as a hot jar of jam before the seal popped.

"This way," the chief said after he opened the security door for her and Jack to enter. "My office is down here at the end of the hall. Officer Petrovsky and I have been interviewing a suspect in your sister's death, and I'd like to fill you in, Mr. Sullivan."

"A suspect? Any chance it's Premalatha Baxter?" asked Abby.

He nodded, leading them to the institutional chairs opposite his massive desk. "She denies any knowledge of the murder." The chief motioned for them to set the case and the jars on the desk and take a seat.

"You have proof to the contrary?" asked Jack.

"Yes, Mr. Sullivan, we do. Her fingerprint was on the broken teacup that Mackenzie's dog uncovered. We were able to match the one on the teacup with prints in the state's system because of a background check on Ms. Baxter when she applied for work in a casino. We can also tie her to the burning car crime scene through that nicotine patch that Mackenzie found in the nearby weed patch. Claims she is a closet smoker, mostly herbs through a water pipe but also tobacco. She conceals her habit and also the patch she wears to quit."

Abby felt pleased but maintained a solemn expression. "But, Chief, Fiona knew Premalatha smoked. She had to know, because Premalatha and Dak stopped by Ancient Wisdom Botanicals, asking for an herb blend for smoking, the day before Fiona died. I was there and saw the exchange. Fiona told Premalatha that the blend was out of stock."

"Yes. I read your statement. We're convinced that we've got your sister's killer, Mr. Sullivan, but we know she had to have help moving the body. We're still piecing that part of the case together."

"But you have Dak Harmon in custody," said Abby. "He's got to know what went down."

"He's not saying. We read him his rights, and he lawyered up."

"Isn't it true that the two of them were providing alibis for each other? They were at the commune that morning. They had lunch there together with the leader and everyone else."

"True," said Chief Bob Allen. "Premalatha told us that around ten thirty on the morning Fiona died, she tried to phone Fiona to apologize for their public argument at the smoothie shop. Her cell phone records indicate that she made that call."

Abby had a sudden thought. "How long was their conversation?"

"Less than two minutes."

"Okay, I'm going to suggest something," Abby

said. She then phrased her theory with flattery for the chief. "You've probably already thought of this, but here goes. What if Premalatha went to the cottage and gave Fiona poison in a cup of tea or in a smoothie she prepared in a Smooth Your Groove cup? I've been reading up on this, and Jack knows about it, too. This poisonous plant called monkshood has pretty flowers, but all parts of the plant, including the roots, are poisonous. Let's say that Premalatha makes a tincture from the plant, which they grow up on the commune land, and puts the drops in the tea or the smoothie. Then she convinces Fiona to taste a smoothie recipe she'd like Fiona to approve for the smoothie shop. Seeking Fiona's approval might have gotten the result she intended. That is, for Fiona to taste the smoothie. Maybe Fiona already had a cup of tea, and Premalatha doctored it, too, or perhaps Premalatha made her a cup of tea if Fiona complained of not feeling well after tasting the smoothie." Abby took a deep breath and exhaled.

"Go on," said the chief. His elbows rested on his desk, and his thumbs and forefingers pressed against each other.

"To create an alibi for herself, Premalatha uses her cell phone to call Fiona. Getting a message, she listens and maybe leaves one for Fiona. All the while, she's standing right there in the cottage as Fiona is dying. Then Premalatha cleans up, putting everything in that trash bag to toss onto the refuse pile where Dr. Danbury stores his trash to be incinerated. And since Dr. Danbury spent the night in Las Flores, celebrating his son's birthday, there was no one else at the estate the morning Fiona died."

"That's right," said Jack. "Tom told me he'd asked permission from Premalatha to go to Fiona's cottage that night to discuss their divorce. Also, he said he had that winery renovation job to go to early the next morning . . . the morning Fiona died."

"For your sister," Abby said, glancing over at Jack, "it was just a stroke of bad luck that no one was on the property that morning. Premalatha had already decided it would be the last time Tom would spend the night with Fiona." Abby exhaled deeply and looked back at Chief Bob Allen.

"I'm still listening." The chief leaned back in his chair and quietly tapped a finger against his desk.

"I think that Premalatha and her accomplice loaded Fiona's body in her car. They took two vehicles to Kilbride Lake. There they placed Fiona into the driver's seat but forgot to adjust the seat forward so Fiona's feet could reach the gas pedal. Premalatha is roughly five feet, nine inches. Fiona was about five-three."

"Uh-huh," said the chief. "And so . . ."

"So, Premalatha and her accomplice set the car on fire to get rid of the body and any trace evidence," Abby said. She looked over at a stone-faced Jack before continuing. "They ride back to the commune, leave their vehicle, probably a motorcycle, in the woods near the commune. That way, they can part company and slip onto the grounds unnoticed from different directions, as if they'd been present at the commune all morning."

Chief Bob Allen had been staring intently at Abby as she spoke. He sniffed deeply. "Initially, we thought Dak Harmon might have helped move the body. That partial tire print at Kilbride Lake has some similarities to the tread on the tires of the mountain garage loaner motorcycle—the one he uses when his is in the shop and the same one he rode to your house, Abby."

Abby sat a little straighter. *Thought it might.*

The chief leaned back and put his hands behind his head. "But you know as well as I do that because tires are so generic and are sold so widely, it would be difficult to tie a suspect to any one vehicle in that location. And that is true even if the print happened to be a good, usable impression. It's a little too circumstantial. Others could have easy access to that bike."

Abby nodded. "True, but who would also have motive and means and access to that bike? You said the impression appeared similar to the tread on that bike's tire."

"Wish it were a full print, but it's not. Fingerprints can get us a conviction, but a DNA match would tie up the evidence with a sweet little bow. We have it with the nicotine patch linking Premalatha to the burned car and her print on the teacup. But we all know she had help."

The chief hadn't lobbed any cheap shots at her yet, and Abby wondered if he would. Maybe since she'd brought all that honey, he was making nice, treating her like a colleague rather than a cadet. "Somebody drove the body to the lake in Fiona's car, while the accomplice followed on or in some type of vehicle. Let's say it was a motorcycle. They would have staged Fiona's body behind the steering wheel and torched the car. Was an accelerant used?"

"Yes," said the chief.

"So, where's the container? If the killer and an accomplice made their getaway on a motorcycle, they probably used lighter fluid. Easier to take the container with them than a gas can. If Dak Harmon didn't help with disposing of the body, then who did? Who else had the motive to take Fiona's life and also had access to that bike?"

Chief Bob Allen rubbed a bushy brow with four fingers of one hand while he stared at Abby, as though staring could elicit from her the answer he didn't have.

Abby thought for a moment. "Hayden Marks has a motive. Fiona threatened his hold over everyone."

The chief leaned forward. "Well, we're not ready to hold the press conference yet, but there was a second print, a thumbprint, recovered from the trash. The bag that held the broken teacup contained a print that belongs to Marks. He's an ex-felon who served time for grand theft of firearms."

"Wonder if he knows how to ride a Harley," Jack mused.

The chief nodded. "Oh, he does. Marks had a previous affiliation with a gang of outlaw bikers."

Abby smiled. "So that's it. Hayden Marks puts Fiona's body in the car. He drives it to the lake. They set the car on fire, and then Marks gives Premalatha a ride back to the commune on that motorcycle."

"There's another piece of linkage in all this," said the chief. "As part of the state's mandate to reduce prison populations, Hayden Marks was released early. He was sent to the same conservation camp, or 'fire camp,' as Dak Harmon and a few other prisoners to help fight California wildfires."

"So with Baxter and Harmon in jail, why haven't you arrested Marks?" Jack asked.

"Well, there's a problem. He's taken off," the

chief said. "We've alerted the local airports, bus terminals, and train stations. And we've put out a BOLO on him and that new car."

Abby chimed in. "Driving a hot new BMW Alpina B-seven isn't too stealthy. It won't be difficult to spot it."

"He probably didn't have a choice with his bike in the mountain shop, being repaired," said the chief, rising to lift the case of honey from his desk and to set it on the floor by the window. "Two residents saw Marks drive away from the commune. But we'll find him. And now with a plausible scenario and incriminating evidence to support it against those three, we'll soon have them all behind bars. Premeditated murder, with poison as an aggravated factor, is a capital murder charge. That means the death penalty is on the table."

Jack stood and extended his hand, his eyes shining with gratitude. "Thanks for the update, Chief. Finally closure."

"Good work, Chief," Abby said, rising from her chair.

"How much do I owe you for the honey, Mackenzie? My missus is going to—" His words stopped with the knock at the door.

Nettie popped in. "Chief, we've got a hit on the BOLO. A sheriff in Santa Cruz County is calling. Someone thought they saw the car. Do you want to take it here? Line two."

The chief pursed his lips. He nodded.

Against a desire to dally long enough to find out more about the BOLO, Abby said to the chief, "We'll settle up later with the money. Give you some privacy to take that call. Fingers crossed." She and Nettie walked back to the lobby, with Jack following.

A few minutes later, Abby pulled out of the police parking lot and steered the Jeep on a course into the mountains.

"Getting those killers behind bars is one thing. . . . Do you think the police will have enough evidence for the court trial?" Jack asked, unpeeling the wrapper from a piece of gum. He offered the gum to her.

She waved off the gum and said, "You can be sure that Chief Bob Allen and his team will do everything they can to bring a solid case to the district attorney."

"Good." Jack slipped the gum package back into the pocket of his T-shirt and settled back into his seat. He stretched out his bare, muscular legs. "There was a gorgeous moon and a clear sky last night. What's up with all this fog today?"

"Microclimates. The mountains are different from the valley." Abby tapped a button on the radio and turned to her favorite soft jazz station. As she entered the first big turn on the slick asphalt road, she gripped the steering wheel a little tighter. "Here in the Bay Area, we can have sun in the valley and fog and drizzle in the mountains. The outside temperature can change thirty degrees from one microclimate to another, like in the summer, driving from San Jose to San Francisco."

"Oh." Jack leaned back and closed his eyes, apparently enjoying the ride. "I like your taste in music," he said. "How far do we have to go now?"

"A few miles," said Abby. Her tension lessened as they drove toward the summit for the delivery to the wedding customer. A late-season storm was expected to blow through. If they were lucky enough to get any rain in the valley, it would be spotty, but the winds buffeted her Jeep now and already the mountain mist had become heavy, so rain could hit at any moment.

"Where is this Kilbride Lake?" asked Jack.

"It's not too far from where you're staying in the cottage. I could take you to see it before we make the delivery, if you like. It's a really pretty area, although today the lake water is probably choppy and reflecting the gray sky."

He spoke in a voice tinged with sadness. "It's where the killers took her and tried to burn . . . I want to see that spot."

"You got it," said Abby. She negotiated the curvy road for another half mile, cringing on the approach into the two most dangerous curves. She'd not soon forget that Timothy Kramer in his silver pickup had once forced her off the road, had taken a shot at her, and later had set that wilderness cabin on fire. For an instant, her thoughts turned to that harrowing experience. But then the Santa Cruz County Sheriff's Department had found him and arrested him. It was unlikely that local law enforcement would return to those wooded forty acres. Oh, but Hayden Marks could have.

"Oh, my gosh!" exclaimed Abby at the sudden realization. "Mind if we take a brief detour, Jack? I have a sudden urge to check that land behind Doc Danbury's estate. I think it's possible that Hayden Marks knows about that area. He could be hiding back there. And that could be why law enforcement hasn't found him."

With the two curves behind her, the road again climbed. Abby remained vigilant on the road since the cliff side had no guardrail. The rocky, tree-studded cliffs plunged eighty feet below. On the mountain side, blind curves presented another hazard to drivers. On a clear day, Abby enjoyed the drive, but when there was fog and the road was wet, like today, she hit the brakes a lot . . . and now she needed to use the wipers.

The fog concealed the drop-offs from view but did little to lessen Abby's anxiety. Despite her defensive driving, the Jeep hydroplaned after reaching the red barn. *How ironic,* Abby thought. *Hydroplaning in an area where the fog bank has thinned and visibility has improved.* Still, she navigated the series of curves before the road straightened out again. Then she spotted the NO TRESPASSING sign in white paint on the big board nailed to a tree that indicated the turnoff to the cabin in the woods. She followed the rutted road to the high hill and the stand of oaks, remembering the shot Kramer had fired at her. Shaking off the memory, she peered down toward the clearing where the cabin once stood.

"I can't make out much of anything," said Jack, leaning in to wipe the inside of the windshield with his hand.

"I was hoping the fog would be evaporating here, like it was at the barn," said Abby. She stared at the wispy sheets wafting by in front of the Jeep's headlamps.

"Ah, Abby, 'tis like we're ghosts in a netherworld," said Jack, slipping into his Irish brogue. "No one here to see. No one to bother us. It gives me ideas, it does."

Abby smiled and drilled him with a playful gaze. "Yeah? What kind of ideas?"

Jack unfastened his seat belt. His eyes conveyed desire. "This, for one," he said, leaning in.

Abby anticipated his kiss, but it never came. Instead, Jack's attention was diverted as he turned abruptly to face the source of the lights that had flicked on in the clearing. Abby stared, too. The lights appeared to be the high beams of a vehicle. Whatever kind of vehicle it was, the darn thing was headed straight for them. Abby didn't have time to debate whether or not to make a U-turn. The champagne-colored Alpina streaked past, swerving at the last minute.

"It's him . . . Hayden Marks. He almost killed us," Abby cried out.

"I see him. Go . . . go. Go after him, Abby. He's getting away."

"Too dangerous, Jack. The fog . . . can't see—"

"He's got to be stopped. Think of Fiona."

Flipping into a U-turn, Abby hit the gas. "You're right. For Fiona . . ." *And my brother.* "Call it in, Jack. The phone is on the console. We need backup."

Abby drove as fast as she dared in the deadly fog, following the Alpina's taillights. Jack alerted dispatch. At the NO TRESPASSING sign, the Alpina turned onto the asphalt road and picked up speed. Abby followed. Nearing the red barn, she saw the fog had receded over the edge of the mountain.

"Thank God. I can see." Abby breathed. "There. There he is," she said, pushing hard on the gas pedal.

"We're closing in, Abby. Closing in."

Abby hardly heard Jack. Her thoughts raced ahead to the two most dangerous curves on the mountain. The Alpina had entered one of them.

Then, in a millisecond, Abby heard the crash as the Alpina hit the granite wall. She watched the car flip into the air. Fly off the edge. Plunge down the cliff.

Abby's heart caught in her throat. Her fingers tightened into a death grip on the steering wheel. She tapped her brakes, knowing if she hit them hard, the Jeep would fishtail on the wet asphalt. She would lose control. End up just like Marks. When she got the car to a nearly full stop, she guided the Jeep into a slow roll onto the narrow turnout.

Jack jumped out. She followed. They raced to the cliff's edge to peer over. Flames from the Alpina leaped high into the air. Loud popping sounds followed, shattering the mountain's silence. Abby trembled, and Jack reached out to pull her close. He stroked her hair as they stood staring at the spectacle below.

"No one could have survived that," said Abby. She sucked in a mouthful of air and blew it out between pursed lips. "How ironic. What he tried to do to Fiona's body, he ends up doing to his own."

"It's divine justice," Jack said, drawing her closer.

Within minutes, sirens screamed in tandem on approach. The arrival of the first emergency vehicle, with its lights and siren on, shattered the quiet peace of the mountains. Cal Fire followed closely behind the deputy sheriff's cruiser. Abby slipped out of Jack's embrace when the deputy pulled in behind her Jeep. He got out and approached them. Abby recognized him from police work back in the day.

"You all right?" asked the deputy.

"Uh-huh," Abby said. "The driver is the murder suspect Hayden Marks. My friend here is Jack Sullivan. We saw Marks lose control of the Beemer, hit, flip, and fly over." She let go a sigh. "Guess Chief Bob Allen can cancel that BOLO he put out on Marks."

The deputy nodded. "We'll need your statements," he said, raising his voice to be heard over more sirens approaching.

"No problem," said Abby.

"Seeing as how it's you, Mackenzie, I don't see why we have to detain you."

"Nor do I," said Abby. "The chief knows how to reach me. So we'll let you get on with your work preserving the scene."

The deputy nodded and walked over to the fire truck.

Abby's trembling subsided once she and Jack had returned to the Jeep and she was driving back to town. Hitting the brakes to let a cruiser pass, she made a mental note to call her wedding party customer to set up another delivery date.

"Listen, Jack, I'll keep my promise to show you Kilbride Lake, but it'll have to wait for another day. The mountain's going to be shut down to through traffic. I can't make my honey delivery, and you can't go home. So, lunch at my place?"

His eyes brightened, lighting his handsome face. "You'll not have to be twisting my arm for that," he said, feigning the Irish accent.

"Lovely." Abby turned the volume up on the soft jazz and was soon bobbing to the beat of the music. "So, what about egg salad sandwiches, sweet tea, sheet cake, and lemon ice cream with fresh berries? The sun should be out down on the farmette, so we'll dine on the patio, under the umbrella, and watch the birds and the bees."

"Ohhh, Jesus, Mary, and Joseph! The birds and the bees, you say? Now you've got my attention." He turned in his seat and played with a tendril of hair behind her ear. "Oh, Abby," he said in a breathy voice. "I'd love to share with you what I know about that."

Abby smiled wickedly. "I thought you might."

Lemon Ice Cream with Strawberries

Ingredients:
1 cup superfine sugar
¼ cup fresh lemon juice
1 tablespoon lemon zest
1 cup heavy cream
1 cup whole milk
⅛ teaspoon salt
1 cup fresh sliced strawberries

Directions:
   Combine the sugar, lemon juice, and lemon zest in a large bowl.

   Slowly pour the cream, milk, and salt into the lemon-sugar mixture and stir constantly until the sugar is completely dissolved, about 2 minutes.

   Pour the lemon-cream mixture into freezable individual molds or bowls or into an ice cube tray, and then cover with foil and freeze until the ice cream is completely firm, about 3 to 5 hours, depending on the type of mold used.

Unmold the ice cream, garnish each serving with the sliced strawberries, and serve at once.

Serves 4

Acknowledgments

My heartfelt gratitude goes to Aaron Pomeroy for your encyclopedic mind and insight into law enforcement. Whenever I have a cop question, you've got the cop answer. Please know I deeply appreciate your help, and if, inadvertently, I have made any mistakes, they are all mine.

Thanks also to Heather Pomeroy for the ongoing support and enthusiasm for my Henny Penny Farmette cozy mysteries. Your paramedic background and also your experience as an evidence technician in a small-town police department have proven invaluable to me.

I also want to thank Madison and Savannah for all their questions, feedback, and ideas. There's always something new to learn from you two.

Books and magazines about beekeeping line my bookshelves, but for fast answers to my questions about bees, I know I can rely on Botros (Peter) Kemel and Wajiha (Jill) Nasrallah. You have taught me most of what I know about keeping bees and harvesting honey. Together, you have a wealth of knowledge and generously share it. Thanks to you both.

For her unwavering support of the Henny Penny Farmette, I offer my thanks to Jeanne Lederer. The element of setting in a story can serve many purposes: it can be a place of sanctuary and safety or of fear and uncertainty. Your midcentury stone house in the woods serves as a scary counterpart to the sheltered farmette of my protagonist, permitting me to generate fictional threads of rising tension from that wooded acre.

To my architect husband, Carlos J. Carvajal, who teaches me what I don't know about renovation and has patiently answered all my remodeling questions in connection with this story, I offer my heartfelt appreciation. My son Josh deserves my thanks for untold hours helping me build and maintain my Web sites. Also, Josh and Carlos, you both have earned huge hugs of appreciation for a willingness to be first-level taste testers for all my recipe creations and modifications.

For her continuing belief in me, I offer thanks, along with a huge hug and a kiss, to my agent, Paula Munier. I've been honored to have you as a lifelong friend and fellow author. Your dazzling mind and astonishing talent never cease to amaze me.

I offer my deepest appreciation to my brilliant editor Michaela Hamilton, whose insights are spot on and whose guidance is always so welcome.

Finally, I want to thank all the folks at Kensington Publishing for their knowledge, expertise, and support of my Henny Penny Farmette mysteries.

Don't miss the next delightful Henny Penny
Farmette Mystery by Meera Lester

A Hive of Homicides

Coming soon from Kensington Publishing Corp.

Keep reading to enjoy an intriguing excerpt . . .

Chapter 1

The Varroa destructor *parasite is a true*
bloodsucker, a mite that attaches itself
to a honeybee's body and feeds on the
hemolymph.

—*Henny Penny Farmette Almanac*

The steady drumming of rain had slowed to a
light sprinkle as Abigail Mackenzie navigated
her Jeep past Main Street shops decorated with
vampires, witches, goblins, and other spooky mo-
tifs. It was the week before Halloween. She hung a
left turn toward the Church of the Holy Names.
Parking behind the priest's cottage, Abby glanced
at the dash clock. Three thirty. Half of an hour remained before the start of the ceremony, but it was
well past the time for confessing the truth.

She'd had plenty of opportunities to tell Paola
Varela about how she felt. So why hadn't she summoned the courage to speak up before now? Tell
her friend the truth. But she hadn't. Not at the
Wednesday night baking classes at the Kitchen

Gadget Shop, where the two had become fast friends. Or at the Labor Day picnic in the downtown park where civic leaders held the holiday tree lighting in December and the Shakespeare festival in June. She'd even hesitated to bring up the subject at the Columbus Day parade, where they had volunteered to flip pancakes in the food tent. And what could she say, anyway? It wasn't her place to criticize Paola's decision to renew her marriage vows with her husband, Jake, even if his infidelities had become common knowledge around town. No, she'd kept silent. Now it was too late.

For Paola and Jake's wedding vow renewal ceremony, Abby had promised to lend Paola her grandmother's thin, well-worn band as something "borrowed." It seemed rather ironic, since Paola had an enviable diamond set in gold, which Jake had placed on her finger during their wedding seven years ago. But Paola had told Abby she wanted something that symbolized a long and happy marriage, in contrast to her own troubled one. Lending the ring was a way to show support for a friend Abby had come to look upon as the little sister she never had. Maybe the wrinkles in Paola and Jake's marriage would eventually smooth themselves out. Her friend deserved a bright future with the man she loved.

Glancing up into the rearview mirror before leaving the car, Abby spotted a worker cleaning up storm debris. Abby didn't recognize the man, who was bundled up against the cold, with a knit cap and upturned jacket collar, but surmised he was likely another fellow down on his luck. Father Joseph recruited helpers from halfway houses for ex-cons and recovering addicts to work on the church property. The men would do odd jobs and maintenance in exchange for a hot meal and a dollar or two in their pockets. The priest believed that anyone wanting to work deserved a job. This particular hapless man, Abby thought, looked to be in his late twenties or early thirties.

Looking more closely in the mirror, Abby flinched at the reflection of the swollen cheek beneath her left eye. Of all the stupid things she'd done since moving to the farmette, cleaning the bee fountain without donning her beekeeper's suit had to be the craziest. Even if the weather had turned cool and the bees were less active. Now, after two days, the bee sting under her left eye pooched out like a puff pastry. Donning sunglasses on a dark and rainy afternoon would look ridiculous. And bailing on her commitment to Paola was not an option.

After sliding out of the Jeep, Abby eased her raincoat's hood up and over her reddish-gold locks, which she'd braided and twisted into a bun at the nape of her neck. Cinching her coat tighter around her black silk dress, Abby thrust her hand into her coat pocket and felt for the ring that carried the vibe of a loving marriage that had lasted a lifetime. She hurried up the steps and slipped into the small chapel dedicated to Our Lady of Guadalupe, situated on the north side of the church proper. Silk-ribbon flowers adorned the chiffon that served as a backdrop for the icon. The scent of fresh roses permeated the small space. Silhouettes danced on the wall behind the flickering flames of the devotional candles as the door closed behind Abby. The chapel—with its single bench—afforded more privacy than the cavernous Holy

Names. Abby knew how her friend Paola favored that chapel when she needed spiritual solace.

Upon hearing Abby enter, Paola looked up, brightened, and stood to offer air kisses to Abby's cheeks. In her Argentine accent, Paola whispered, "Thanks to God, Abby, you have come. I could not do this without you."

"Of course you could," Abby replied. "But you don't have to."

"My nerves are a wreck," Paola said.

"I can see that." Abby clasped Paola's fretful hands in hers. "You are renewing your vows with the man you love. So what's with the nerves?"

"Can you not guess?" Paola's brown eyes darkened under heavily mascaraed lashes. A faint line creased her forehead. "In my mother's time, a man like Jake would go to jail. But now, even in Argentina, when a man cheats on his wife, she endures the pain. Or she divorces. I don't want a divorce, Abby. I want our marriage to be good again. Is this possible?"

Abby released Paola's hands and looked at the younger woman with admiration. She couldn't fathom why Jake would seek affection from other women when he had an exotic Argentine beauty by his side. After sliding her hands back into her coat pocket, Abby sought and found her grandmother's ring. The slightly misshapen band had worn thin through forty years of marriage. Yet Abby could still sense its power to ground. Perhaps Paola would feel it, too. The younger woman desired a stable, secure, and happy life, the kind Abby's grandparents had. The kind Abby wanted for herself.

"You said Jake had changed," said Abby. "That

he's promised never to betray you again. You've been through couples counseling. The worst is behind you. Surely, there are no more secrets between the two of you now." Abby hoped she sounded more enthusiastic and reassuring than she felt.

They could hear the soloist humming strains of the old hymn "O Perfect Love" from the adjoining church.

Paola looked intently at Abby. "Do you think he would have been a different husband if he'd married an American woman? An educated lady who speaks better English than I do?"

"Don't be silly," Abby said, shaking her head. She had a niggling hunch that Jake had used these excuses in the heat of arguments to intimidate the impressionable, vulnerable Paola.

"I love him, Abby. I do, but I don't understand what he wants or why he acts the way he does." Her eyes searched Abby's. "Why is that?"

"I don't know." Abby forced a smile and sought a way to lighten the mood. *No woman should have to question a husband's love on the day she's renewing her marriage vows with him.* "You are barely twenty-seven, and you're asking a woman at least ten years your senior who has yet to be a bride?"

Paola's features relaxed. "You just haven't found the right man . . . but you will."

"Maybe." Abby touched her palm to Paola's shoulder. "After all you've been through, here you are, reassuring me."

Paola murmured, "Did you bring it?"

Abby extracted the ring from her pocket. "Here you go. Let's hope it blesses your union with Jake."

Paola slipped the thin band onto the first finger

of her right hand. "Your *abuela* . . . grandmother . . . she had large fingers."

"Yes, she did." Abby chuckled. "And I have hands just like hers—all the better for kneading bread, making jam, and beekeeping," Abby said.

"I'll give it right back after the ceremony," said Paola. "I know the ring means a lot to you." She shifted her gaze from the ring to Abby. "Will you be able to read the verses with your cheek and eye so swollen?"

"Stop fretting. I'm fine. You just need to relax and be present with every beautiful moment that comes today."

"I suppose," said Paola. "God has turned Jake's heart back to me. That's what Father Joe says."

Abby leaned in and whispered, "How could your husband not adore you?"

Paola stretched out her hands and gazed upon the rings.

Abby considered the irony—the diamond-bejeweled band seemed more substantive and flashy than most, even as the marriage it symbol-ized had been withering. And the misshapen thin band that now encircled the middle finger of Paola's right hand had held Abby's grandparents' marriage together for a lifetime.

A tenor voice had joined the soprano.

"Showtime," said Abby, relieved that she didn't have to say things she might not believe—like that she was confident Jake was now fully committed. "See you inside," she said, bussing Paola's cheek.

After she'd left the chapel to cross the courtyard to the Church of the Holy Names Church, Abby encountered Jake.

"Is she ready?" he asked. His tone carried a hint

of arrogant impatience, which Abby found offensive. At five feet nine, Jake wasn't a towering figure, but he did have a commanding presence, charisma, and the looks of a model, with large dark eyes, thick brows, and a chiseled face.

"She is," Abby said, noticing his longish dark locks slicked back into a ponytail. He had grown a goatee—perhaps at the behest of Paola—and wore a gray wool suit with a crisp white oxford shirt and a striped tie.

"Good. It's past time to begin. What happened to your eye?"

"Stung by a bee," Abby replied.

"Obviously, it found your face irresistible," said Jake. "I wouldn't mind being one of your bees." Grinning, he reached out to touch her other cheek. "I know how to sting a woman without damaging her."

Abby flinched and stepped back. Brushing away his hand, she drilled him with a stare. "You wouldn't if you knew what you'd have to give up."

He tilted his head slightly, as if assessing her. "Oh, and what would that be?"

"Your life."

He grinned. "Might be worth it."

Abby's cheeks grew warm, and she looked past Jake to see if Paola could have overheard their conversation. To her dismay, Paola stood just behind Jake, her large eyes shimmering with tears. Not knowing what to do next, Abby hastened to the nearest side entrance into Holy Names. The pencil-thin heels of her shoes clicked softly against the marble floor as she entered the sanctuary. The pianist and a violinist had replaced the singers.

From the first few measures, Abby recognized Pachelbel's Canon in D.

After spotting Katerina Petrovsky, her best friend and backup—even though Abby no longer served on the police force—Abby slid into a pew beside her. "I could wring that man's neck," Abby exclaimed beneath her breath.

"What? Whose neck?" the blond, blue-eyed Kat asked.

"Who else? Jake Winston." Abby narrowed her eyes and blew air between her lips.

"Uh-oh. Trouble in paradise already?" asked Kat, smoothing her short bobbed cut, which had been moussed into waves. She turned her head to locate Jake.

"Don't look," Abby whispered. "I'll explain later." She opened her small clutch purse and removed the folded paper on which she'd copied the verses that Paola had asked her to read. She scanned the words a final time. Eventually, she looked up and gazed around the room, taking note of the many family members and friends present for the solemnizing of the Varela-Winston vows.

Abby focused on calming herself by taking several slow, deep breaths. When she felt settled, she looked toward the aisle. Jake walked past her, headed to the front, where he took his place near Father Joseph. Paola followed on the arm of her brother Emilio, who worked as the chef at Jake's family winery. Emilio was the skinniest chef Abby had ever seen. Tall too. Maybe six feet. Longish black hair framed a tan face with thick brows and large dark eyes. He had full lips and an angular chin. Emilio took his seat next to his aged father, who needed two canes to walk because of a ranching accident in their homeland, and his prim white-haired mother. Jake and Paola stood stiff and silent in front of Father Joseph, waiting for the music to end.

"So I ask you," whispered Kat, "who but Paola could stroll in from a rainstorm as fresh as an Argentine orchid?"

"Indeed." Abby trained her gaze on Paola's belted, knee-length ivory knit with three-quarter-length sleeves. The dress accentuated her petite and perfectly formed figure. Her waist-long black hair had been tied and twisted into a chignon at the nape of her neck, its only adornment a red silk hibiscus. Noticing the Stuart Weitzman bright candy-colored pumps with narrow heels Paola had chosen to wear, Abby smiled. The two of them had selected those shoes together.

Straightening her spine against the back of the pew, Abby listened to the final strains of the music and gazed at Paola's stunning ensemble. The dress's ivory hue symbolized the seven-year marriage. Abby had suggested that some colorful shoes could make a statement. The right heels, she'd told Paola, could signify to everyone that Paola was going places, putting her individual stamp on the world with her truffle business. Then they'd found the chic boho heels with splashes of red, yellow, and blue. Abby recalled how animated Paola had become as she explained why she needed the heels.

"Good fortune must be in the air," the saleswoman had remarked. She'd explained that another woman had just purchased the same heels. The woman and her husband were taking a cruise.

"A second honeymoon," the saleslady had told them. Much deserved after all the hard work they'd put in to take their Silicon Valley software company public, which had made them overnight millionaires. Paola's smile had widened, as if she had been injected with a bolus of happiness.

Jake now faced Paola, whom he'd sworn to love, honor, and cherish until death. Did he feel one iota of guilt for the come-on he'd initiated with Abby? He didn't show it. His gaze swept the room; perhaps he was checking out the females present.

The priest spoke softly, apparently guiding the couple, because Jake reached out and took Paola's hands in his. He gazed into her eyes. Father Joseph spoke again. Abby thought she caught the words "God is smiling."

Father Joseph asked the two to reaffirm before God and those assembled that they were recommitting their lives to each other. Both said yes. At the priest's prompting, Jake began to address Paola. His promises sounded sincere. When it was Paola's turn, her wan smile and questioning eyes revealed all the anxiety she must be holding inside. In a barely perceptible voice, Paola began to recite her vows.

Father Joseph said, "Love is kind. Love believes all things, endures all things, and forgives. Love is a refuge. Love is a comfort. Love never fails. "

Jake's and Paola's expressions remained somber and stoic. Father Joseph called for a short period of silent reflection and then recited a prayer. He then called for the reading.

Abby whispered to Kat, "My cue." She rose, walked to the lectern, and settled herself, paper in hand. She began with the biblical verses from the book of Ecclesiastes and the Song of Songs by Solomon.

"My lover is for me a sachet of myrrh . . . a cluster of henna from the vineyards. . . ." Abby hesitated, not so much for dramatic impact as to calm herself against the rising anger she felt at Jake's behavior. "His body is a work of ivory covered with sapphires. . . . His mouth is sweetness itself."

Abby looked up to see Jake gazing at Paola in a strange way, as if he were seeing her for the first time. Or maybe he was imagining someone else. Paola regarded him with tenderness. They were no longer holding hands but were still facing the priest. Paola now slowly twisted Abby's grandmother's ring around her finger, as if it were a touchstone for happiness.

Buoyed by the glimmer of hope she detected in the couple's faces, Abby proceeded to read the next stanza, which addressed true love's union. "I belong to my lover and for me he yearns. . . . Set me as a seal on your heart." The next verses were taken from Proverbs. Paola had confessed to Abby that she wasn't entirely sure they should be included, but in the end, she had added them. "Lying lips are an abomination to the Lord, but those who are truthful are his delight. . . . In the path of justice, there is life, but the abominable way leads to death." For some inexplicable reason, a cold shiver ran up Abby's spine as she finished reading the words. The site around the bee sting on her cheek began to itch.

As the music started up again, Abby tucked the paper of verses into her coat pocket, stepped down from the lectern platform, and walked back to her seat. She took a tissue from her purse and gently rubbed her itchy skin, eventually finding a modicum of relief. She decided to take an antihistamine as soon as the vow exchange ended, but for now she'd just have to endure the itchiness.

The priest spoke about the sanctity of marriage and Paola and Jake's renewed commitment to each other. He asked everyone to raise their hands toward the couple as he said a prayer and administered a final blessing. When it came time for the kiss, Jake took his wife into his arms, and at that moment the heavy church door creaked open.

Kat and Abby turned their heads at the same time to see who'd arrived so late. The stranger appeared to be in her early thirties. Highlighted blond tresses in a boyish cut accentuated her youthful features. She wore a dark coat dress and silver pendant earrings.

Abby searched out Eva and Luna, Paola's sisters, to see if they recognized the pretty stranger. They were occupied with shushing their rambunctious daughters, both preschoolers. Next, she sought Paola's mother and father, seated on the other side of the church. They had flown in from Argentina for the occasion. They sat beaming approvingly at their daughter and Jake. Okay, so they hadn't noticed the late arrival, either. Jake's parents were no-shows, remaining in Hawaii for their much-needed vacation after finishing the grape harvest. John Winston II, Jake's grandfather, who never ventured far from his beloved winery, sat alone in the first row, hunched over, perhaps absorbed in reading the missal. Abby stole another look at the woman, who'd slipped into a seat at the back of the church.

Kat leaned in and whispered, "You think our stranger belongs to the bride's party or the groom's?"

"My money is on Jake," Abby answered.

When the service had ended, Abby followed Kat out of her seat and down the center aisle. They fell in step behind others who followed the couple and the priest. The young woman apparently had left.

"I hope they have plenty of chilled bubbly, some great dance music, and some good-looking guys up at the winery," said Kat. "I'm ready to party. Mind if we take your Jeep?"

"Well, sure. But why not just call it like it is? You want me to be the designated driver."

"Well, of course I do," Kat replied with a sheepish grin. "Unless you can't see out of that eye," she said. "Riding with a one-eyed driver could be hazardous to my health."

"Really, Kat. Let me reassure you that I can see and drive perfectly well, thank you very much. So, let's go."

Abby walked in lockstep with Kat behind a statuesque platinum blonde with a butterfly tattoo on her neck, below her upswept do; a thin woman with chestnut-colored hair; and a twentysomething with a long yellow-blond braid. These three women fell in step behind others filing toward the church doors. Abby wondered how many of the attractive ladies present had come to see for themselves that the man they'd known as a charmer was out of the game for good. As a man and a woman argued, their voices rose above the din of friendly banter among the guests.

"Holy crap," said Abby. "Surely that's not Jake and Paola going at it already?"

Kat stretched up on her tiptoes in her suede ankle boots. "Can't see a darn thing."

Outside, on the church steps, they encountered the argument in full swing.

"You bastard. You killed her," shrieked the woman in the dark coat dress and silver earrings.

"You know better than that," bellowed Jake. "Your sister wrapped her car around a tree on Highway Nine. And let us not forget, she was twice over the limit."

"You broke her heart with your lies. You were never going to leave your wife. That ridiculous ceremony I just witnessed proves it." After turning to address Paola, the woman shrieked, "I pity you if you think it meant anything to him. He isn't going to change. And if you believe he is, you deserve each other."

"Go home, Gina," Jake told her.

"And what . . . ? Grieve?" Tears streaked Gina's face. Her eyes had a smoldering, heavy-lidded look. She lunged at Jake. He threw his arms up in defense as she smacked him with her purse. "I hate you. Hate you," she screamed.

Emilio and the other men in his family pulled Gina away from Jake. Paola's sisters walked Paola backward into the sheltering huddle of her family. Tears swam in the dark eyes of the truffle maker. Her expression bore a tortured look.

A struggling Gina blubbered, "Your family celebrates? Celebrates? While mine grieves? You're evil, Jake Winston. Evil. You will pay for what you've done." After twisting free from the men's grips, she spat at Jake and ran off into the misting rain.

"Let her go," said Father Joseph.

"Whatever!" Jake stormed down the front steps and walked toward Paola's blue Ford Escort.

A hunk of jet-black hair fell from behind Emilio Varela's ear to eclipse his cheek as he hurried to embrace Paola. After the hug from her big brother, she retreated into the church with the priest, and Emilio addressed the guests.

"Listen up. We have chilled champagne and hot hors d'oeuvres, and to follow, a sit-down dinner with fine wine. It would be a shame to waste it. So what are we waiting for?" Emilio seemed comfortable taking charge and clearly desired to get everything back on track. He trotted to the Ford Escort, where Jake had taken refuge, and tapped on the window. The two men spoke briefly, and then Jake got out and went inside the church.

Kat leaned into Abby and said, "I'm so there for the party, but I suspect our guests of honor will be delayed. I'd love to be a fly on the wall to hear what Father Joe has to say about this state of affairs."

Abby rolled her eyes. "Affairs? Seriously, Kat? No pun intended, I'm sure."

Kat replied, "Of course not."

"We should be happy for them," said Abby as she reached into her purse for the car keys.

"Well, I am," said Kat.

"As much as I want to be happy for them, I can't help feeling that this marriage is still in trouble."

On the way to her Jeep with Kat, Abby realized how tidy the parking lot looked now that the gardener/handyman had cleaned it. But she found it more than a little disturbing that as she approached her car, the man was bent over with a flashlight, peering into her Jeep. Seeing her, the man clutched the black garbage bag near the tire, carried it to a mound of other bags piled for collection at the parking lot exit, and deposited it.

"Father Joseph believes in the dignity of work and the power of a second chance for everyone. He sets a good example." Thinking about it, Abby said, "You know, I could use a helping hand around the farmette. Someone prescreened, of course, but it could be a win-win."

"Or not," said Kat. "A priest believes in the innate goodness of all people." She climbed into the Jeep's passenger seat and shut the door. "Father Joseph has that higher power thing going for him to keep those guys in line. And if something bad did happen, the church stands only blocks away from the police station. That's not true for your farmette. Who but your chickens and bees would hear you calling for help if somebody assaulted you?"

How a Honeybee Queen Mates

The honeybee queen (*Apis mellifera*) is the only fertile female in a honeybee hive. She can lay one thousand eggs a day. Unfertilized eggs become males (drones); fertilized eggs become sterile females (worker bees) or new queens. Before a swarm (the way a colony grows its population), the workers feed larvae a special food so the larvae will become new queens. Prior to the virgin queens emerging, the old queen takes flight with approximately half of the workers to find a new home. Back in the hive, the new queens emerge. One or more may leave with some workers, and those that stay behind will sting and attack each other to the death until only one queen remains. That queen will take her virgin flight through the assembled drones outside of the hive. As she flies, she releases pheromones (scents to attract the males). As many as ten drones will mate with her in flight or die trying.

Praise for Janet Dailey

"Janet Dailey's name is s

"Janet Dailey's mastery o
loyalties and searing passi
selling authors of all time
—*Lanier County News* (Georgia)

"A master storyteller of romantic tales, Dailey weaves all
the 'musts' together to create the perfect love story."
—*Leisure Magazine*

Praise for Sandra Steffen

"The charm of this tale lies in its lovely portrayal of complex family relationships."
—*Publishers Weekly* on *The Cottage*

"A charming, intense story. High drama and gentle reflection—the perfect mix."
—Stella Cameron, *New York Times'*
best-selling author on *The Cottage*

"A compelling, heartwarming tale. Sandra Steffen is a talented new author to watch."
—Kat Martin, *New York Times'*
best-selling author on *The Cottage*

Praise for Kylie Adams

"A talented and creative new voice has just joined the
romance genre. This debut novel by Kylie Adams is a funny,
sexy and slightly off-the-wall treat. Keep your eyes on Ms.
Adams!"
—*Romantic Times* on *Fly Me to the Moon*

"This side-splitting tale is so unique that it leaves you
drained, the characters so droll that they leave you speechless. Her book cover should be flame-retardant. You'll love
every moment."
—*Rendezvous* on *Fly Me to the Moon*

"An original, witty, sexy love story."
—*The Romance Journal* on *Fly Me to the Moon*

BOOK YOUR PLACE ON OUR WEBSITE AND MAKE THE READING CONNECTION!

We've created a customized website just for our very special readers, where you can get the inside scoop on everything that's going on with Zebra, Pinnacle and Kensington books.

When you come online, you'll have the exciting opportunity to:

- View covers of upcoming books
- Read sample chapters
- Learn about our future publishing schedule (listed by publication month *and author*)
- Find out when your favorite authors will be visiting a city near you
- Search for and order backlist books from our online catalog
- Check out author bios and background information
- Send e-mail to your favorite authors
- Meet the Kensington staff online
- Join us in weekly chats with authors, readers and other guests
- Get writing guidelines
- AND MUCH MORE!

Visit our website at
http://www.kensingtonbooks.com

THE ONLY THING BETTER THAN CHOCOLATE

Janet Dailey
Sandra Steffen
Kylie Adams

ZEBRA BOOKS
KENSINGTON PUBLISHING CORP.

http://www.kensingtonbooks.com

ZEBRA BOOKS are published by

Kensington Publishing Corp.
850 Third Avenue
New York, NY 10022

Copyright © 2002 by Kensington Publishing Corp.
"The Devil and Mr. Chocolate" copyright © 2002 by Janet Dailey
"I Know I Love Chocolate" copyright © 2002 by Sandra Steffen
"Sex and the Single Chocoholic" copyright © 2002 by Jon Salem

All rights reserved. No part of this book may be reproduced in
any form or by any means without the prior written consent of the
Publisher, excepting brief quotes used in reviews.

If you purchased this book without a cover you should be aware
that this book is stolen property. It was reported as "unsold and
destroyed" to the Publisher and neither the Author nor the Publisher
has received any payment for this "stripped book."

All Kensington titles, imprints and distributed lines are available
at special quantity discounts for bulk purchases for sales promotion,
premiums, fund-raising, educational or institutional use.

Special book excerpts or customized printings can also be created
to fit specific needs. For details, write or phone the office of the
Kensington Special Sales Manager: Kensington Publishing Corp.,
850 Third Avenue, New York, NY 10022. Attn. Special Sales
Department. Phone: 1-800-221-2647.

Zebra and the Z logo Reg. U.S. Pat. & TM Off.

First Printing: January 2002
10 9 8 7 6 5 4 3 2 1

Printed in the United States of America

CONTENTS

THE DEVIL AND
MR. CHOCOLATE

Janet Dailey

Chapter One

Kitty Hamilton, owner of Santa Fe's renowned Hamilton Art Gallery, lolled in the expansive tub, surrounded by mounds of scented bubbles. Her long chestnut hair was pinned atop her head, no longer contained in its customary severe bun.

Scattered about the spacious bathroom were pillar candles. Their wavering yellow flames created a certain ambience to accompany the first movement of Mozart's Serenade No. 13 playing softly in the background.

A bottle of champagne poked its neck out from the bucket of ice sitting on the tub's ledge. On the opposite side sat a plate of chocolate-dipped strawberries. Kitty selected one, took a bite, and moaned in her throat at the delicious combination of juicy sweet berry and decadently rich chocolate. A sip of champagne provided the perfect complement to the treat. She dipped the partially eaten strawberry into the champagne and took another bite.

"Perfect," she murmured with her mouth full.

Beyond the bathroom's long window, with its view of the high desert mountains, a crimson sun hung on the lip of the western horizon. The sky was a wash of magenta, rose madder, and fuchsia bleeding together. Its flattering pink light spilled into the bathroom, but Kitty took little notice of it.

Having lived in Santa Fe most of her life, she had grown used to the spectacular sunsets and sharp clear air for which the city was known and with which artists were so enamored. At the moment she was much too busy luxuriating in her sensuous bath to admire the view. It was too rare that she had the time to indulge herself this way. But tonight was a special night. Very special.

Remembering, Kitty smiled in secret delight and sank a little lower in the tubful of bubbles, convinced she had never been this happy in her life. Perhaps the world always seemed this glorious when one was in love; Kitty honestly couldn't say. But she knew she wanted to revel in this giddy contentment she felt. It was a thing to celebrate— and an evening to celebrate. Hence the strawberries and champagne, the music and candlelight. She wanted everything about this evening to be special, from beginning to end, with nothing to spoil it.

On that note, she splashed more champagne into her glass and plucked another chocolate-dipped strawberry from the plate, then alternately sipped and nibbled. She silently vowed again that, for once, she was not going to be hurried. She wanted the evening to begin with sensuous pleasures and end with sensual ones.

Suddenly the bathroom door swung open, startling Kitty. Surprise quickly gave way to annoyance when Sebastian Cole walked in, all six feet two inches of him. He was dressed in his usual T-shirt, jeans, and huaraches, but for a change he didn't reek of turpentine and oils. Judging from the wet gleam that darkened the toasted gold color of his hair, Kitty suspected he had come straight from the shower.

"Sorry. I didn't realize you were in here." He threw her an offhand smile and walked straight to the vanity table.

"Now that you do, you can leave." Irritated by the sudden sour note in her evening, Kitty set her champagne glass down and reached for the loofah sponge. Having known Sebastian for nearly twenty years she was well aware that even if he had known she was in there, he would have walked in anyway.

"First I need to borrow your razor." He began rummaging through the contents of the top drawer. "Don't you usually keep your spare ones in here?"

"It's the drawer on the other side." She rubbed the soap and sponge together and wished she was rubbing the lathered bar over his face. "With the fortune your paintings are bringing, I should think you could buy your own razors."

"But with the commission you make from selling them, you can afford to supply me with a razor now and then. Besides, I ran out." He opened the other drawer and took out a disposable razor. "Why should I go all the way to the store for one, when you live right here in my own backyard? Correction, my front yard.''

"You really need to find a larger studio, Sebastian. That one is much too small.''

"It suits me." Razor in hand, he turned to face the tub and sat down on the vanity, stretching out his long legs and giving every indication that he intended to stay awhile.

Stifling the urge to order him out, Kitty struggled to ignore him. But Sebastian Cole was much too compelling to ignore. She had never quite identified the exact cause of it. At forty, he still possessed the kind of leanly muscled physique guaranteed to draw a woman's eye. His rugged features stopped just short of Hollywood handsome. And there was something striking about the contrast of golden blond hair and dark, dark eyes. Or maybe it was all in his eyes, and that devilishly lazy way he had of looking and absorbing every minute detail of his subject, not with an artist's typical dispassion but with a caress.

And he was doing it to her now. Kitty could feel his gaze gliding along her outstretched arm, the slope of her shoulder, and the arched curve of her neck. Her nerve ends tingled with the sensation of it.

She flicked him a glance, feigning indifference, although, of all the feelings Sebastian had ever aroused in her, indifference had never been one of them. "Was there something else you wanted?''

"Thanks. Don't mind if I do," he said in response, and pushed away from the vanity table, crossed to the tub, reached across its width to lift the champagne bottle from its icy nest. Taking the water glass by the sink, he filled it with the bubbly wine, then returned the bottle to its bucket. "And strawberries drenched in chocolate, too. Perfect."

He popped one into his mouth while somehow managing to extricate the cap from it, and chewed with relish. "Mmm, good," he pronounced, and washed it down with a big swallow of wine. "The chocolate is obviously from La Maison du Chocolate. Had another batch flown in from Paris, did you?"

"Wrong," Kitty replied with some pleasure. "The chocolate is Boulanger's."

"Boulanger's?" Sebastian frowned in surprise. "That's a new one."

"It's Belgian."

"Ahh." There was a wealth of understanding in his nod. "In that case, I'll have another."

Kitty watched in disgust as he consumed another chocolate-covered strawberry in one bite. "How can you devour it like that? It's a treat that should be savored."

"My mistake. Let me try again." He picked up a third and nipped off the end, the gleam in his eyes mocking her.

"Oh, eat it and be done with it," Kitty declared with a flash of impatience. "That's what you want to do anyway."

A blond-brown eyebrow shot up. "My, but you are in a bad mood tonight."

"I was in a glorious mood until you showed up," she retorted, and switched from lathering her arms to soaping her legs.

"Of course you were," he replied dryly. "That's why you're here lazing in bubbles, surrounded by candlelight and music, sipping champagne and eating strawberries dipped in chocolate. Consolation, I imagine, for spending another lonely evening all alone. If I had known, I would have asked you to join me for dinner."

She hated that smug look he wore. "For your information, I already have a date."

"Johnny Desmond's back in town, is he?"

"I wouldn't know."

"Not Johnny, huh. Then it must be—"

Kitty broke in, "It's no one you know."

"Really?" The curve of his mouth deepened slightly. "Something tells me you've been keeping secrets from me."

"I wouldn't call it a secret," Kitty replied smoothly. "My private life is simply none of your business."

"Then, this isn't a business dinner," Sebastian concluded.

"Not at all." This time it was her smile that widened. "It's strictly pleasure. Wonderfully glorious pleasure."

He released an exaggerated sigh of despair. "Don't tell me you've fallen hopelessly in love again."

She paused, staring off into space with a dreamy look. "Not again. For the first time."

"That's what you said about Roger Montgomery and Mark Rutledge," Sebastian reminded her, naming two of her former husbands.

Doubt flickered for a fleeting second. Then Kitty mentally shook it off. "This time it's different." Lifting a leg above the mound of bubbles, she reached forward to run the loofah over it.

"You have beautiful legs," Sebastian remarked unexpectedly, studying her with an artist's eye. "It's a pity I don't have my sketch pad with me. You would make a marvelous study with the soft froth of the bubbles, the porcelain-white gleam of the tub and tiles, and the cream color of your skin. The darkness of your hair, all tumbled atop your head, and the flaming sunset behind you adds the right shock of color." His eyes narrowed slightly. "But I would need to move a couple of the candles closer."

She could see the painting in his mind and knew exactly where he wanted the candles placed. It was something she took for granted, dismissing it as the result of the two of them working so long and so closely together over the years.

"Stick to landscapes. They sell," was her response.

"So speaks Kitty Hamilton, art dealer," Sebastian replied with a bow of mock subservience.

"Well, it's true. The painting you described might be appropriate for the cover of a romance novel, but for something more artistic, it needs to be midnight-black beyond the window, creating a reflection in the glass, with a vague scattering of stars and a pale crescent moon. Now, *that* would be a great study in blacks and whites."

"Probably." Sebastian was clearly indifferent to the suggestion. "But any artist can do a black-and-white. I'm talking red-and-white."

Kitty was momentarily intrigued by the thought. "You would need a redhead for that."

"The glow of the sunset has given your hair a red cast."

"Really?" She looked up in surprise, then curiosity. "How does it look? I've been toying with the idea of having Carlos add some red highlights. It's so in right now."

"Don't." He drank down the last of the champagne in his glass, set it aside, and reached for the loofah sponge in her hand. "Here. I'll wash your back for you."

Distracted by the shortness of his answer, Kitty automatically handed it to him. "Why?"

"Why what?" He soaped the sponge into a thick lather and rubbed it over her back in slow, massaging strokes.

"Why wouldn't I look good with a few red highlights streaked through my hair?"

"I know you too well. You wouldn't be content with a few. Before it was finished, you'd be a flaming carrottop."

"Not necessarily."

"Everything is always whole-hog or die with you." His voice had a smile in it. "It can be love or business; it's always both feet. Speaking of which, who is the new love of your life?"

The hint of ridicule in his voice made Kitty loath to answer. Which was childish. After tonight, it would be public knowledge.

"Marcel Boulanger."

"Sounds French."

"Belgian."

"My mistake." The drollness of his voice was irritating, but the kneading pressure along the taut shoulder muscles near the base of her neck made it slightly easier to overlook. "Boulanger," he repeated thoughtfully. "It seems as though I've heard that name before. What does he do?"

"His family makes chocolate. In fact, many consider it to be the finest in the world."

"Ah," he murmured in a dawning voice. "The strawberries."

"Dipped in Boulanger chocolate," Kitty confirmed, and sighed at the remembered taste of it. "Even you must admit, it's absolutely exquisite chocolate. And it's no wonder, either. Marcel regularly travels to Central and South America to select only the best cocoa beans."

"I'm surprised he hasn't been kidnapped and held for ransom."

Kitty stiffened in instant alarm. "Don't say that. Don't even think it!"

"Sorry. So, when did you meet Mr. Chocolate?"

"Almost three weeks ago. He came by the gallery with the Ridgedales. He's staying with them," she added in explanation. "So of course, I saw him again that evening at the Ridgedales' preopera cocktail party."

"And you were smitten?" Sebastian guessed.

"Instantly." She almost purred the word as that deliciously exciting feeling welled up inside her again.

"Love at first bite, you might say."

"Very funny, Sebastian," she replied without humor.

"I thought it was. Obviously you're in love, since you seem to have lost your sense of humor."

"I'm very much in love," she declared with feeling.

"And how serious is Mr. Chocolate?"

"Very. He's asked me to marry him."

"And you said yes, of course."

"Naturally."

"A man who makes chocolate—how could any woman refuse?" Sebastian murmured.

But Kitty was too wrapped up in her memory of Marcel's proposal to pay any attention to Sebastian's sardonic rejoinder. Besides, she was too used to them.

"It was such a romantic setting. Dinner in the courtyard, just the two of us, crystal gleaming in the candlelight, the air scented with gardenias in bloom. There at my chair was a single red rose and a small gift. I opened it, and—do you know what I found inside?"

"An engagement ring. Not really very original."

"Oh, but it was," Kitty insisted smugly. "Maybe the ring part of it wasn't original, but the box it came in definitely was. It was made out of chocolate. Perfect in every detail, too, right down to the slot to hold the ring."

"Milk chocolate or dark?"

"Dark. It even had the Boulanger family crest embossed on top of it."

"On top of the ring?" Sebastian feigned shock.

"No, on top of the box."

"I hope the ring wasn't made of chocolate, too."

"It's one hundred percent diamond." She held up her hand, wagging her fingers, letting the stone's facets catch and reflect the light. "All three carats of it."

"That's as bright as a spotlight. Be careful. The glare from it can blind you."

"It is eye-catching, isn't it?" she murmured, admiring its fiery sparkle.

"That's one word for it," he responded dryly, and dipped the loofah in and out of the water. "Hand me the soap, will you?" She slipped the scented bar off its ridged ledge and passed it to him. "I'm not surprised you fell madly in love with him. Chocolate's a turn-on all by itself. Who needs foreplay when you have chocolate, right?"

She threw him a look of disgust. "You can be so crude sometimes, Sebastian."

"That's not crude. It's the truth. It has something to do with endorphins. Oops, I dropped the soap." He groped underwater for it, his hand sliding along the curve of her hip to her thigh.

A second later, Kitty felt the bar squirt under her leg, and his hand immediately came over the top of her thigh to search for it between her legs. He quickly became dangerously close to areas she didn't want touched by him.

She pushed at his arm. "Stop it. I'll get it myself."

"Wait. It's right here. I can feel it."

"Don't! That's not it!" As she squirmed to elude his playful fingers, she slipped in the tub. She yelped in alarm as she started to slide under the bubbles. "Stop! I don't want to get my hair wet!"

"I've got you." His muscled arm was a band across her breasts, hauling her back upright.

Suddenly everything about this scene seemed much too intimate. There she was naked in the tub with his hands all over her. And Kitty realized that at some point she had lost control of things. Worst of all, Sebastian knew it.

"You bastard. Let me go!" She tugged to free herself of his hold, but between her wet hands and his wet arm, she was hardly successful.

"I'm only trying to help," he protested.

"Help, my foot. You're copping a feel, and you know it." Abandoning the useless struggle, she located the loofah sponge and slapped at him with it.

"Hey!" He jerked back to elude contact with it, but he couldn't elude the splattering of water droplets and bits of foamy bubbles. As he reached up to wipe at his face, he accidentally bumped the plate of strawberries, knocking them into the tub.

"My strawberries," Kitty wailed.

"Let me get that plate out of there before it gets broken." He plunged both hands into the water.

"Just leave it alone," she exploded in anger, and pummeled him with her fists. "Get out of here! Out! Out! Out!"

"Will you stop it?" he yelled above her shrieks of outrage, hunching his shoulders against the raining blows.

The bathroom door burst open. Kitty squealed in dismay at the sight of the thunderous look on the face of a tall, dark man with distinctively Gaelic features—the man who was her fiancé.

"You! Get away from her," Marcel Boulanger ordered in that gorgeous accent of his.

Sebastian started to rise, then lost his footing on the wet floor and slipped halfway into the tub.

"It's all right, Marcel," Kitty rushed. "It's not what you think."

"Who is this man?" he demanded, his accent thickening noticeably.

Half in and half out of the tub, Sebastian replied. "I'm her husband. Who the hell are you?"

"Your husband?" Marcel scowled blackly at Kitty. "What is this he is saying?"

"He's my *ex*-husband." She hurried the explanation and pushed Sebastian the rest of the way out of the bathtub, while trying to hide her own self among the bubbles. "We've been divorced for years."

Whatever comfort Marcel found in that, it was small. "What is he doing here now?"

"I live here," Sebastian answered, rising to his feet.

Kitty hastened to correct that impression. "Not here, precisely. At least, not in the house. He has a studio out back. He lives there."

"A studio? This man is an artist?" He eyed Sebastian with considerable skepticism.

In all honesty, Kitty had to admit that Sebastian didn't fit the popular image of an artist. He certainly didn't possess the temperament of one. He was much too easygoing.

"This is Sebastian Cole. The Ridgedales have two of his landscapes hanging in their Santa Fe home." Conscious of the rapidly dissipating bubbles, Kitty reached for the oversize bath towel lying on the tub's tiled ledge.

The doubtful look vanished as Marcel smiled in recognition of the name. "Ah, yes, you are—"

"Please don't say the great Sebastian," Sebastian interrupted, his mouth slanting in a wry smile. "It makes me feel like a trapeze artist in a circus. Plain Sebastian will do. You must be Mr. Chocolate."

Confusion furrowed his brow. "*Mais non*, my name is Marcel Boulanger."

"He knows that . . . " Kitty gave Sebastian a dirty look as she maneuvered closer to the side of the tub. "It's just a nickname he gave you. It's his idea of a joke."

"I sampled some of your family's wares earlier," Sebastian remarked. "Kitty had a plate of strawberries dipped in your chocolate. Unfortunately I knocked it into the tub."

"That's what he was doing when you came in— looking for the plate." With one arm holding the towel high above her breasts and the other hand trying to hold the ends together behind her back, Kitty attempted to stand.

"Let me give you a hand." Sebastian moved to help her out of the tub.

"I can manage just fine." As she drew away from his outstretched hand, she stepped on a strawberry, slipped, and pitched forward with a yelp.

Sebastian caught her, swept her out of the tub and into the cradle of his arms, towel and all. Kitty was stunned to find herself in such a familiar position, and not altogether sure how she had gotten there. But the memories were much too strong of all the times their arguments had ended like this, with Sebastian sweeping her off her feet and carting her off to the nearest soft or flat surface and there making love to her. Most satisfactorily, she recalled as color flooded her cheeks.

"Put me down," she snapped.

"Whatever you say, kitten." He released her legs with an abruptness that took her by surprise.

She managed to retain her grip on the towel as she hissed an irritated, "Don't call me that. You know I hate it."

Sebastian simply smiled with infuriating ease and turned his attention to Marcel. "Since I understand congratulations are in order, you might as well know she has a temper."

"I do not!" She stamped her foot on the plush bathroom rug. The muffled sound didn't add much emphasis to her denial.

Sebastian ignored her. "I wouldn't worry about her temper, though. I'm sure you already know about her secret passion for chocolate. It doesn't matter how mad she gets, just pop a piece in her mouth and she'll melt in your arms."

"That is not true." Kitty pushed the angry words through her teeth and hurriedly wrapped the towel around her. "You're making me seem like some foolish female, or worse."

"Well, you're definitely female." His twinkling glance dipped to her cleavage.

Kitty wiggled the towel higher. "You came in here to borrow a razor. Take it and leave."

"She's a little upset about the loss of the strawberries," he explained to Marcel. "She hates to waste good chocolate."

"Go." She pointed a rigid arm at the door.

He cocked an eyebrow. "Now, you know you don't want me dripping water all through your house." He pulled at the side of his T-shirt, reminding her that half of his clothes were soaked. She hesitated fractionally, visualizing the trail of water through her beautiful home. "You still have that spare terry-cloth robe hanging in the closet, don't you?"

She hated the way Sebastian made it sound as though he knew where everything was. Of course, the truth was he did. She shot an anxious look at Marcel, worried that he might put the wrong construction on that.

"Yes, it's hanging—"

"I'll find it," Sebastian assured her, and he headed for the bedroom, a faint squelch to his woven-leather sandals.

Kitty didn't draw an easy breath until he was out of the room. Even then, she was a little surprised that he hadn't lingered to make a further nuisance of himself. Fixing the warmest smile on her face that she could muster, she crossed to her fiancé.

"I am so sorry about this. It must have looked

awful when you came in—a strange man in the tub with me. Thank God, he was fully clothed, or—'' She broke off the rush of words and allowed chagrin to tinge her smile. ''It's absolutely impossible to explain any of this. You would have to know Sebastian to understand.'' Then it hit her that she hadn't expected Marcel to arrive until much later. ''What are you doing here anyway?''

He seemed a bit taken aback by her question. ''Your maid let me into the house as she was leaving. I heard your cries and thought you were being accosted by some thief.''

''No.'' She shook her head. ''I mean—I thought you weren't going to be here until eight o'clock.''

From the bedroom closet came Sebastian's muffled shout, ''I found it!''

Deciding it was best to simply ignore him, Kitty bit back the impulse to shout back at him to put on the robe and get out. ''Pay no attention to him.'' She laid a hand on Marcel's arm, drawing his attention back to her when he half turned in the direction of Sebastian's voice.

''Yes, that is best,'' he agreed, then explained, ''I came early to your house because I received a phone call from home this afternoon. My *maman* has taken ill. Nothing too serious,'' he inserted when Kitty drew a quick breath of concern. ''But I must fly home to Brussels tomorrow. It is my desire that you come with me. I wish to have my family meet with you.''

''You mean . . . leave tomorrow?'' she said in shock, her mind exploding with hundreds of problems that would create.

''But of course. We would leave in the morning.''

''Marcel, it simply isn't possible for me to fly off

at the drop of a hat. Not with everything that's going on at the gallery. This is one of our busiest times of the year. I—"

"Surely your assistant is able to take charge while you are gone."

"Harve is very competent," she agreed. "But I have a special exhibit scheduled in two weeks—actually less than that. The shipment should be here in two or three days. And there are so many other things that must be coordinated. Honestly, it just isn't possible. I'm sorry, Marcel, but—"

A bare-shouldered Sebastian stuck his head around the bathroom door. "Sorry to interrupt, but I need a towel to wrap my wet clothes in."

Teeth gritted, Kitty snatched a towel off the bar and shoved it into his hands. "There."

"Thanks." With a smile and a nod, Sebastian was gone.

Struggling to regain her calm, she faced Marcel once again. "All things considered, I think it would truly be best if I met your family another time, especially since your mother isn't well."

"Perhaps it would be," he conceded, then reached out to grip her upper arms, his gaze burrowing into her with intensity, his eyes darkened with a passion that so thrilled her. "But it pains me to leave you even for a day."

"Me, too." The agreement came easily.

With a groan of desire, he pulled her against him and his mouth came down to claim her lips. But Kitty found it difficult to enjoy the devouring wetness of his kiss when any second they could be interrupted by Sebastian again. After a decent interval, she drew back from his kiss.

"We still have tonight, don't we?" she murmured, one hand on the lapel of his suit jacket and the other pressed against the front of the towel to keep it in place. "After all, we do have an engagement to celebrate."

"Indeed, we have much to celebrate. It may require all night."

"I certainly hope so," Kitty replied, then stepped away when he would have kissed her again. "Why don't you go fix yourself a drink while I finish up here? I promise I won't be long."

As Marcel released a sigh of regret, Sebastian rapped lightly on the door, then looked around it, this time bundled in a white terry robe. "I don't mean to keep busting in on your little tête-à-tête, but I thought I should let you know I'm leaving."

"Promise?" Kitty retorted with a touch of sarcasm.

"Cross my heart."

She didn't believe him for one minute. "Marcel, why don't you go with him and make sure he actually does leave?"

"With pleasure," Marcel declared, clearly as eager to be rid of him as Kitty was.

"Something tells me Kitty doesn't trust me." Sebastian's grin was wide with mischief.

"I wonder why," she murmured, and followed both men into the bedroom, then ushered them out the bedroom door and closed it behind them.

Alone in the bedroom, she stood there a moment and struggled to regain that gloriously happy feeling she'd felt earlier. At the moment, she was much too annoyed with Sebastian. The man had an absolute talent for getting under her skin.

Determined not to let him spoil any more of her evening, Kitty stalked to the huge walk-in closet.

The plush throw rug was damp beneath her feet, a reminder that Sebastian had been there before her. As if she needed one.

"Put him out of your mind, Kitty," she muttered to herself, needing to hear the words.

Chapter Two

Sighing, Kitty scanned the clothes in her closet. Now that Marcel had arrived early, she no longer had the luxury of dressing at her leisure. She told herself that she truly didn't mind. It was better to look on the positive side of things; this much-anticipated evening would simply begin earlier than she had expected. Now that she had finally gotten rid of Sebastian, everything was going to be as wonderful as she'd thought.

In the closet, she loosened the towel and used the drier portions of it to wipe the remaining moisture on her skin, all the while surveying her vast wardrobe, regretting that she hadn't already decided on something to wear. Until now, it was a decision that hadn't needed to be hurried.

"Too bad Picasso isn't around to do an abstract of this—Woman's Derriere Amidst a Swirl of Clothes."

At the first sound of Sebastian's familiar voice,

Kitty wheeled in fury, snatching the towel back around her. "Don't you ever knock?" she hurled angrily.

He stood in the closet doorway, clad as before in the white terry robe, a portion of his wet jeans sticking out of the rolled-up towel under his arm. "It's a bad habit I've got, I'm afraid," he replied without a smidgeon of remorse.

"It's one bad habit you need to concentrate on breaking," she retorted, then demanded, "What are you doing here again? I thought you'd left."

"I forgot the razor." His expression was much too benignly innocent to be believed.

"On purpose, I'll bet," Kitty guessed, eyes narrowing on him. Careful to keep her bottom covered, she turned back to face the racks of clothes. "Get your razor and leave. Better yet, forget the razor and grow a beard. It would fit the public image of an artist."

"You wouldn't like it," Sebastian replied easily. "I tried growing one before, and you didn't care for the way it scratched, remember?"

"That won't be a problem anymore."

He snapped his fingers as if only recalling their divorce at that moment. "That's right. You're engaged to someone else now, aren't you?"

"As if you didn't remember." She let the sarcasm through.

"Have you decided what you're wearing for the big dinner tonight?"

"That's what I'm doing now."

"I recommend the cranberry silk number."

"Good. That's one I definitely won't choose," Kitty retorted.

"You should. I have to swallow a groan every time I see you in it."

There was a part of her that was secretly pleased she could still turn him on. But only a small part.

She cast a challenging look over her shoulder. "The razor?"

"Right. That's why I came back, isn't it? I'll just get it and leave."

"That would be an original idea," Kitty muttered as he turned to leave.

Sebastian swung back. "Did you say something?"

"Not to you. Go." She waved him out of the closet.

This time when he left, Kitty wasn't convinced he was gone for good. And she was determined that he wouldn't catch her again without a stitch of clothing on. Hurriedly, she discarded the towel and donned a set of nude lingerie from the drawer. After quickly riffling through the rack of dresses, she selected a simple but elegant sheath of white lace with a plunging keyhole back. She removed it from its padded hanger and wiggled into it.

Still there was no sign of Sebastian, no sound at all to indicate he was anywhere in the vicinity. Kitty wasn't sure whether that was a good thing or a bad thing. But she couldn't help being suspicious of the silence.

Crossing to the built-in shoe caddy, Kitty considered the possibility that he might have actually left. A second later, she stiffened, panicked by the sudden thought that he was out there talking to Marcel. Heaven only knew the sort of things Sebastian might be telling him. Sometimes the man was a devil in disguise with an absolute knack for making the simplest thing sound outrageous.

She bolted out of the closet and stopped abruptly as Sebastian came out of the bathroom. "You're still here." It was almost a relief.

"As usual, you forgot to let the water out of the tub. While I was at it, I went ahead and retrieved the platter and the strawberries." He showed her the plate of sodden strawberries and partially melted chocolate.

Recovering some of her former annoyance, Kitty retorted, "When did you appoint yourself to be my maid?"

"I could have left it, I suppose. But I don't think it would have been a very pretty sight come morning. You need to tell Mr. Chocolate that the flavor combination of bathwater and his chocolate is a poor one."

"Will you stop calling him that? His name is Marcel."

"Whatever." Sebastian shrugged off the correction. "Actually the strawberries didn't fare too well in the bath either. Their flavor got pretty watered down. Here. Try one." He picked up a limp berry that dripped a mixture of brown and pink juice.

Kitty was stunned he would offer her one, even as a joke. Well, the joke was about to be on him, she vowed, and took the berry from him and squished it against his mouth.

Laughter danced in his eyes as he scraped the remains of it off his face and onto the plate. "I'll bet that felt good," he observed.

"Actually I got a great deal of satisfaction out of it."

"I thought you looked like you wanted to hit something," he observed.

"I wouldn't if you would just leave."

"Is that what you're wearing tonight?" he asked, ignoring her broad hint.

"Please tell me you don't like it. Then I'll know I have chosen the right dress."

"You look fabulous in it."

She heard the hesitation in his voice. "But what?" She was furious with herself for seeking his opinion. She blamed it on her respect for his artistic eye.

"I was just thinking—don't you think virginal white is a bit of a stretch?"

Glaring at him, Kitty demanded, "Give me that plate of strawberries so I can shove the whole thing in your face."

When she made a grab for it, Sebastian held it out of reach. "I don't think so," he said. "Something tells me you'd break it over my head. What do you say we call a truce, and I'll stop teasing you."

"I have a better idea. Why don't you go home?" Kitty suggested, then remembered, "You did get the razor."

He set the plate on a dresser top and patted the pocket of his robe. "Right here."

"Then leave, so I can get dressed in peace."

"Let me fasten that hook in back first. You know you'll never be able to reach it yourself."

To her irritation, Sebastian was right. Against her better judgment, Kitty turned her back to him, giving him access to the hook.

"I could have had Marcel fasten it for me." She could feel the light pressure of his blunt fingers against her skin as he drew the two ends together.

"I have no doubt he would have been delighted to do it."

"As long as you understand that."

"You need to wear your silver shawl with this, and those silver, strappy heels you have."

"That's probably a good choice. Silver is in this season," she recalled thoughtfully. "And I will need something later this evening to ward off the chill. What about jewelry? How about the necklace of turquoise nuggets?

"Everybody will be wearing turquoise. And it would be too chunky with the lace. Try that slender silver choker with the cabochon pendant of pink coral."

Kitty didn't need to try it. She could already visualize it in her mind and knew it would be perfect.

"Have you set a wedding date yet?"

"No. We planned to talk about it tonight." But with Marcel's mother being ill, she wasn't sure it would be an appropriate subject. "It will be sometime soon, though. It's what we both want."

"I guess that means I'll have to start looking for a new art dealer. It won't be easy. You've spoiled me."

"What are you talking about?" She twisted around, trying to see his face.

"Hold still. I almost have it fastened."

"Then explain what you meant by that." She squared around again. "Just because I'm getting married doesn't mean I can't still represent your paintings."

"True, but it might be a little difficult trying to do that from Brussels."

"Brussels?" She turned in shock, not caring that he had yet to fasten the top.

"That's right. According to Mr. Chocolate, that's

where you'll be living after you're married. I suppose you could keep the gallery here in Santa Fe and find someone to manage it for you. Although it would probably be simpler just to sell it."

"Sell the gallery? After I've worked so hard to build it to this point?"

Tilting his head, he scanned the bedroom's ceiling, exposed beams spanning its breadth. "I don't remember this room having an echo."

"Will you be serious?" Kitty demanded impatiently.

"I am serious." He brought his gaze back to her upturned face, a new gentleness darkening his eyes. "I take it you hadn't thought about where you would be living?"

Truthfully, she hadn't given any thought to it at all. The realization made her feel utterly foolish.

Once again, she turned her back to him, aware that those sharp eyes of his saw too much. "I more or less assumed we would be dividing our time between Brussels and Santa Fe. That's what is usually done when two people have separate careers."

"I suppose that could work."

Reassured, Kitty relaxed a little. "Of course it could."

"I guess that means you'll be keeping the house, too."

"Naturally. I'll need somewhere to live when I am here."

"Mr. Chocolate thought you would prefer to sell it and avoid the financial drain of maintaining two households. I told him that you didn't have to look for a buyer. I'll be happy to take it off your hands. We could even work out some sort of arrangement where you could stay here whenever you do come back.''

"That's very generous of you, but I'll keep it, thank you," she stated firmly.

"It was just a thought." The tone of his voice had an indifferent shrug to it, but Kitty wasn't fooled.

"You've had a number of thoughts. It almost makes me think that you're trying to put doubts in my mind about my engagement to Marcel."

"Would I do that?"

"In a heartbeat," she retorted.

"Honestly, I'm not trying to create doubts—"

"And just what would you call it?"

Sebastian finished fastening the hook and turned her around to face him, both hands resting lightly on the rounded curves of her shoulders. "I'm only trying to make sure that you've thought things through a little before committing yourself to this engagement. You tend to be a bit impulsive where your heart's concerned. It certainly wouldn't be the first time. You have to admit that."

"Oh, I do. And the first time was when I married you." Standing this close to him, Kitty found it difficult not to remember how madly in love with him she had been.

"As your first husband, I think I have the right to vet any future replacement."

Kitty bristled. "That is the most arrogant statement I have ever heard you make. And you have made quite a few."

"Why is that arrogant?" Sebastian countered in a perfectly reasonable tone. "You have to know that I still care about you a lot, even if we aren't married anymore. I don't want to see you get hurt again. Believe it or not, I hope Mr. Chocolate makes you very happy."

"Well, I don't," she stated flatly.

A frown of disbelief swept across his expression. "You don't want him to make you happy?"

"Of course I do," Kitty replied in exasperation. "But I don't believe that you do. And his name is Marcel."

"My mistake." He dipped his head in mild apology, a smile tugging at the corners of his mouth.

"You've made a lot of them." Kitty needed to get a dig in to negate the effects of that near smile.

"I have, but you were never one of them, kitten."

"Don't call me that. You know I hate it."

"You used to like it."

"Don't remind me, please. That was long ago. And I was very young and very foolish."

"And very beautiful. You still are." With his fingertip, he traced the curve of her jaw.

The featherlight caress made her skin tingle. "Don't start with the flattery, Sebastian. It doesn't work anymore." She did her best to ignore the rapid skittering of her pulse.

"It's not flattery. It's the truth."

"Then keep it to yourself."

"I will, on one condition."

"What's that?" she asked, instantly wary.

"You see, something tells me that I won't be invited to the wedding—"

"It's a wise little bird that's whispering in your ear."

Sebastian pretended not to hear that. "—So, this may be my only chance to kiss the bride."

"Not on your life." Kitty took an immediate step back.

"Why not?" He looked genuinely surprised.

"Because it's just another one of your tricks. You know there's a physical attraction that still exists between us. You want to use that to confuse me."

"Do you think I could do that with just one little kiss?"

"I am not going to find out," she stated.

"Don't tell me you're afraid? You, Kitty Hamilton?" His look was one of mocking skepticism.

She shook her head. "That's not going to work either. You aren't going to dare me into it, so you might as well give up."

"Now you've hurt my feelings." But his smile mocked his words.

"You'll get over it." Determined to bring this meeting to an end, Kitty stated calmly, "Thank you for hooking my dress. Now, if you don't mind, I would like to finish getting ready. And you, as I recall, were on your way back to the studio to shave—with my razor."

He started to sing, " 'You go your way. I'll go mine.' "

"Don't." Kitty covered her ears. "Singing is not one of your talents. Stick to oils."

"Kiss me and I'll go."

"Not a chance. With my luck, Marcel would walk in to see what's taking me so long. It was awkward enough when he found you in the bathroom with me."

"All right, I'll go. But it's under protest."

"Under, over, I don't care. Just go."

The minute the door closed behind him, Kitty rushed over and locked it. The sense of relief didn't last though. She had the uneasy feeling that Sebastian had given up a little too easily. She wouldn't feel safe until she and Marcel were out of the house.

As much as she would have liked to tarry, Kitty put on her makeup and fixed her hair in nearly record time for her. Taking Sebastian's advice, she wore the coral pendant and matching earrings, slipped on the strappy heels, and draped the silver crocheted shawl around her shoulders. After a satisfactory check of her reflection in the tall cheval mirror, she unlocked the door to the hall and walked swiftly to the living room.

But Marcel wasn't there.

The feeling of alarm was instant. It only intensified when Kitty heard Sebastian's voice coming from the kitchen. The high heels were the only thing that stopped her from sprinting there.

As she entered the kitchen, she saw Marcel comfortably seated at the table. Her glance ricocheted off him straight to Sebastian, leaning negligently against the tiled countertop, his hands wrapped around a toweled wine bottle, his thumbs gently easing out the cork. Marcel rose when she entered.

Her patience exhausted, Kitty snapped, "Haven't you left yet?"

"Really, Kitty," Sebastian said with a mocking *tsk-tsk*. "I credited you with having better powers of observation. Here I am, freshly shaved, wearing dry clothes, and you didn't even notice."

As he took one hand away from the wine bottle to gesture to his change in attire, the cork shot into the air with an explosive pop, caromed off a ceiling vega, sailed past Kitty's head, and bounced onto the floor. Foam bubbled out of the bottle and spilled down its side. Hurriedly Sebastian swung around to pour the effervescent wine into the tulip-shaped champagne glasses on the counter.

"Don't you know you are supposed to ease the cork out of the bottle?" Bending, Kitty retrieved the wayward cork, certain she would step on it if she didn't pick it up.

"That's what I was in the process of doing when I was so rudely interrupted," Sebastian countered smoothly.

"What are you doing back here anyway?" Kitty demanded, unable to rein in her irritation with him.

"I was just telling"—he paused, his eyes twinkling devilishly when she shot him a warning look—"your fiancé that I thought the occasion of your engagement deserved a celebratory toast. So I brought over a bottle of champagne."

Kitty's suspicion warred with her curiosity, but curiosity won. "Why do you have champagne on hand? I thought you didn't like it."

"Ever since your last divorce, I've always kept a bottle in the fridge. That way, the next time you show up at my door in the wee hours of the morning, wanting to drown your troubles in some bubbly, I won't have to go all over God's creation trying to beg, borrow, or steal one." After filling the last glass, Sebastian set down the bottle, then turned with a sudden look of regret. "Sorry. That was bad taste to mention your last divorce, wasn't it?"

Marcel turned to her in confusion. "Your last divorce? What does he mean by this?"

"Don't pay any attention to him. He's just being Sebastian." She directed a careless smile at Marcel and glared at Sebastian when she walked over to pick up two of the champagne glasses. "A name that sounds distinctly like another one," she murmured for Sebastian's ears only.

He merely smiled and picked up the remaining glass. "A toast," he began, and waited until Marcel had a drink in his hand, "to the woman who can still take my breath away, and to her future husband. Happiness always." His gaze was warm on her as he raised his glass to his lips.

Kitty did the same, a little of her own breath stolen by the unexpectedly sincere compliment. But she was careful to direct her tremulous smile at Marcel.

"I must agree with you, Mr. Cole." Marcel flicked him a glance, then smiled lovingly at her. "She is quite beautiful. And never more so than tonight."

Marcel lifted her hand and kissed the back of her fingers, a gesture that came very naturally to him. She didn't have to glance at Sebastian to know that he was observing it all with a droll little smirk.

There was no sign of it, however, when he asked, "Have you already made dinner reservations for this evening?"

"Of course." Truthfully it was an assumption on Kitty's part.

"Somewhere special, I hope." Sebastian took another sip of his champagne.

"Very special," Marcel assured him. "I have arranged for us to dine at Antoine's."

Sebastian cocked a blond eyebrow at Kitty. "Is that wise? First me, then Roger, then Mark. With a track record like that, are you sure you want to go there with him?"

If looks could kill, Kitty would have been staring at Sebastian's gravestone instead of him. "Of course I'm sure," she stated, and fervently hoped that Marcel hadn't followed any of that.

"Antoine's, it is your favorite place, is it not?" Marcel darted confused glances to first one, then the other.

"It's very definitely her favorite," Sebastian replied before she could answer.

"And why shouldn't it be?" She slipped an arm around the crook of Marcel's and snuggled a little closer to him. "The food there is superb."

"You have dined there before with these other men he has mentioned?" Marcel was clearly troubled by that. "They were special to you?"

"I think it's safe to say that," Sebastian inserted. "She married all of us. Not at the same time of course," he added for clarification, then feigned surprise. "Didn't Kitty mention that she's been married three times before?"

"She tells me she is divorced, but I did not know it was from three different men," Marcel replied stiffly, a coolness in the look he gave her.

Kitty struggled to defend the omission. "I thought you knew. It's common knowledge to nearly everyone in Santa Fe."

"That's hardly surprising," Sebastian said, coming to her rescue. "From the sounds of it, you two have had such a whirlwind courtship you haven't had a lot of time to exchange stories about any skeletons in the closet, or—in Kitty's case—ex-husbands. I guess that's the purpose of engagements. Kitty and I never had one. Two days after I proposed, we were married. With the logistics of each of you having careers in different countries, I imagine you're planning a long engagement. Have you decided where the wedding will be? Here or in Brussels?"

"In Brussels, of course," Marcel stated with a certainty that irked Kitty, considering it was something they hadn't gotten around to discussing. And it was, after all, a decision the bride was supposed to make, not the groom.

"Brussels, you say," Sebastian said and sighed. "That's a shame."

"Why do you say this?" Marcel wondered, a puzzled knit to his brow.

"I do all my traveling on the ground. I don't fly, certainly not across an ocean—not even for Kitty," Sebastian added with a smiling glance in her direction. "As much as I would like to be there to see her walk down the aisle, I won't be coming to the wedding."

"You're assuming you would even receive an invitation." Her own smile was on the saccharine side.

"You know you'd invite me, kitten," Sebastian chided. "For business reasons, if nothing else," he added, then chuckled. "I can see the wheels turning already, trying to figure out a way to arrange an exhibit of my works on the Continent. Go ahead, but don't expect me to attend."

"But you wouldn't have to fly. You could go by sea, rent a first-class cabin on some luxury liner and travel that way." Recognizing the value of having the artist in attendance, Kitty chose to work on that hurdle first.

"What if I get seasick?" he countered out of sheer perversity.

"They have a patch you can wear now to take care of that. It won't be a problem."

"And go around feeling all doped up, no thank you."

"Don't be difficult, Sebastian."

He just smiled. "You know you love a challenge. Think how dull your life will be when I'm not around."

"Where are you going?" Marcel struggled to follow their conversation.

"Me? I'm not going anywhere. It's Kitty who will be moving to the other side of the world when you two get married."

She was quick to correct him. "I'll only be there part of the time."

"Why do you say this?" Marcel drew back, again eyeing her with faint criticism. "We will be living in Brussels. It is the place of my business. It is where our home will be."

"Of course, but I do have my gallery here—"

"We will make arrangements for that." He dismissed that as a concern. "Art is better pursued in Europe. Although, after we are married, you will discover that you are much too busy to run some little shop of your own."

For an instant, his attitude made Kitty see red. But she was much too aware of Sebastian and the delighted interest he was showing in their conversation to unleash her temper. She was also aware that the blame for all of this belonged directly at his feet. Sebastian had deliberately brought up this subject to cause trouble between her and Marcel. Therefore she wasn't about to give him the satisfaction of succeeding.

Instead of objecting, Kitty smiled serenely. "It's quite possible you are right, Marcel."

"Spoken like a dutifully submissive wife," Sebastian murmured tauntingly.

Angered that he knew her much too well, Kitty resisted the urge to empty her champagne glass in his face. With an effort, she replied, "You should know."

"Believe me, I do know."

"What is this you know?" Marcel frowned. "I hear the words, but it is as if you are speaking in another language."

"I can guarantee Kitty will explain it all to you later." A smile deepened the grooves on either side of Sebastian's mouth. "I imagine there are a lot of details you two need to thrash out—without a third party listening in. So I'll be going and let you have some privacy."

"That's the nicest thing you've said today," Kitty declared. "The only thing better would be if you actually left."

"Oh, I'm going." He slid his champagne glass onto the tiled countertop, then squared back around. "But before I do—"

She sighed in annoyance. "Somehow I knew you'd come up with something."

"Since I won't be coming to the wedding, with your permission"—he inclined his head toward Marcel—"I'd like to kiss the bride-to-be. I don't know when I'll get another chance. And it's only kosher that I do it in your presence so you don't get the idea there's any hanky-panky between Kitty and me."

"I know not this hanky-panky of which you speak," Marcel admitted, then gestured to Kitty with a flourish of his hand. "*Mais oui*, you may kiss the bride."

Left without an objection to make, Kitty fumed inwardly as Sebastian stepped toward her, eyes twinkling. When his hands settled on the rounded points of her shoulders, she obligingly tilted her head up. His head bent slowly toward her as if he was deliberately prolonging the moment of contact.

At last his mouth moved onto hers with persuasive warmth. Her pulse raced, but she reasoned that it was strictly out of anger and the awkwardness of having Marcel standing so close, observing it all. She held herself rigid, refusing to kiss him back. And that was harder than she had expected it to be. Sebastian was in that familiar, slow lovemaking mode. It had been her undoing countless times in the past.

His lips clung to hers for a moistly sweet second longer, then they were gone. She immediately missed their seductive warmth. It was a vague ache inside, one that prevented her from being glad that he had kept the kiss so brief.

"I honestly want you to be happy, kitten," he murmured.

Determined to break the spell of his kiss, Kitty reached for Marcel's hand. "We will be very happy together."

There was something mocking in the smile Sebastian directed her way before he turned to shake hands with Marcel. "Congratulations."

"*Merci.*" Marcel made a slight bow in response.

"I'll be going now. Enjoy your dinner." With a farewell wave, Sebastian moved toward the back door.

"I'll show you out." Kitty moved after him. "I need to lock the door anyway after you leave."

When he opened the door, she was right behind him. The instant he stepped outside, she muttered a warning, "So help me, Sebastian, if you show up at Antoine's tonight, I swear I will take a knife to every one of your paintings."

He grinned. "Actually I plan on spending the entire evening at home. Alone, I might add. Does that make you feel better?"

"Good night," she said in answer, and closed the door, turning the lock with great satisfaction. Turning back to Marcel, she smiled with genuine pleasure. "I'm ready if you are."

Chapter Three

The Sangre de Cristo Mountains were a black silhouette that jutted into the night sky's star-crusted backdrop. But Kitty took little notice of it as the taxicab moved in and out of the glow from the streetlights that lined the road. She sat silently in the rear seat, her face devoid of all expression.

The driver slowed the vehicle as they approached the tall adobe wall that enclosed her property. Recognizing it, Kitty opened her slender evening bag and took out the fare. When he pulled up to the gated entry, she passed him the money and climbed out.

Using the key from her purse, she unlocked the wrought-iron pass-through door, stepped through, and locked it behind her. Soft landscape lighting lit the flagstone walk that led to the low adobe house. But Kitty didn't take it. Instead, she struck out on the side path that swept around the house to the studio located in the rear courtyard.

Light flooded from its windows in wide pools. She wasn't surprised. Sebastian had always been late to bed and late to rise. She paused outside his door long enough to slip off a silver shoe. With great relish, Kitty proceeded to pound the shoe against the door as hard as she could. The heel snapped off, but she kept pounding until the door was jerked open by Sebastian.

"Kitty," he began.

But she didn't give him a chance to say more. "Don't pretend to be surprised to see me. It won't work."

He glanced at the broken shoe in her hand, then reached down and picked up its missing heel. "Why didn't you simply ring the doorbell?"

"You don't get the same satisfaction out of pushing a button."

"But I liked those shoes." He examined the heel as if checking to see if it could be repaired.

"Here. Have the rest of it." She threw the rest of the shoe at him.

He ducked quickly, and it sailed over his shoulder and clattered across the floor. When he went after it, Kitty stalked into the studio a bit unelegantly wearing only one shoe. She stopped on the Saltillo tile and slipped off the other shoe.

"You like them so much, take both of them." She tossed the second shoe at him, but without the force of the first.

"I didn't expect you home so early. It's barely eleven o'clock." He retrieved the second shoe as well and set them on a side table. "Where did you leave Mr. Chocolate?"

"We had an argument, as if you didn't know." She hurled the accusation.

"Don't tell me the engagement's off? Nope, it must not be," Sebastian said, answering the question himself and gesturing to her left hand. "I see you're still wearing the headlight."

"No, it isn't off. Yet."

"I hope you don't want a glass of champagne. I opened the only bottle I had, to toast your engagement."

"I wouldn't drink any of your champagne if you had it. This is all your fault."

"My fault?" He feigned innocence. "What did I do now?"

"Don't pull that act with me," she warned. "You know exactly what you did. You set out to deliberately undermine my relationship with Marcel."

"How could I do that? I met him for the first time tonight," he reminded her in an infuriatingly reasonable voice.

"Maybe you did," Kitty conceded, then gathered back up her anger. "But you're smart and quick. You can think faster on your feet than anyone I know. And you're an absolute master of sabotage."

"You give me much more credit than I deserve. I want you to be happy. If Mr. Chocolate can do that, then great."

"But you don't think he can. That's the point," she retorted.

"It isn't important what I think. Do you think he can?"

The instant he turned the question back on her, all her high anger crumbled, making room for the doubts and questions to resurface. "I don't know, Sebastian. I honestly don't know," she replied in a hopeless murmur.

"I'll tell you what—why don't we sit on the sofa

and you can tell me all about it." His hand curved itself along her arm and steered her toward the sofa with light pressure.

Without objection, Kitty allowed him to guide her to the sofa, upholstered in a geometric fabric that echoed Zuni design. Flames curled over the logs in the corner fireplace, called a kiva. Before she sat down on the plush cushions, Sebastian slipped off her shawl and draped it over a corner of the sofa back. She sank onto the cushion and curled her stockinged legs under her.

Sebastian crossed to the kiva and added another chunk of wood to the fire, then reached for the iron poker to lever the split log atop the fire.

"Where do you want to start?" he asked, his back turned to her. "The beginning would probably be a good place."

"It began in the bathroom," she retorted with a ghost of her former anger, "when Marcel walked in and found you there. That was difficult enough to explain. Then you had to go and bring up my trio of failed marriages."

"You *are* a three-time loser." He strolled over to the sofa and sat down on the opposite end.

"I'm well aware of that. The trouble is" —she paused and sighed in discouragement—"Marcel wasn't."

"I thought you handled it rather well. It really is common knowledge here in Santa Fe. It wasn't as though you were deliberately keeping it a secret from him."

"I honestly wasn't. But . . . I think it seemed that way to him."

"Grilled you about them, did he?" Sebastian guessed.

"Naturally he asked," Kitty began, then threw up her hands in annoyance. "Why am I trying to make him sound good? Yes, he grilled me about them. And I really got the third degree over you. Quite honestly, I could understand why he did ask. I didn't like it, but I understood. If the situation was reversed, I'd probably do the same thing."

"I hear a 'but.' " Sebastian cocked his head at an inquiring angle.

She flashed him an irritated glance. "Something tells me you already know what it is. You certainly made a point of raising the issue after you so gallantly toasted us."

"What point is that?"

"About the gallery."

His head moved in a sagely nod. "I thought so."

"Marcel didn't say it in so many words, but he wants me to sell it."

"And you don't want to."

"Of course I don't. Why should I? I don't expect him to give up his work when we're married. Why should I give up mine?"

"You could always open up a gallery in Brussels," Sebastian suggested.

"According to Marcel, I'll be much too busy entertaining his friends and family, being a wife, and accompanying him on his business trips. And he believes it's definitely wrong for the mother of his children to work at anything, period. We aren't even married yet and he's already talking about children."

"I always thought you wanted a passel of little ones."

"I do, but I don't plan on becoming a baby

factory right away. I'd like to be married awhile first."

"What about that biological clock ticking away?"

"That sound you hear is a time bomb about to explode." Reacting to her own inner confusion and agitation over it, Kitty rose to her feet and walked to the corner fireplace. "I was so happy until tonight. Suddenly everything is a mess, thanks to you."

"I didn't make the mess. If I'm guilty of anything, it's of opening your eyes to it."

"As I recall, you were never to blame for anything. It was always my fault," she said with a hint of bitterness in her voice.

"I believe the official term was 'irreconcilable differences.' It covers a host of sins on both sides." His mouth twisted in a wry smile of remembrance.

Turning from the flames, Kitty frowned curiously. "Why did we break up? What went wrong?"

"We did."

"Which tells me absolutely nothing." She shook her head in disgust. "I probably got fed up with your enigmatic answers that sound so profound and say nothing."

"No, I'm serious." With unhurried ease, Sebastian stood up and wandered over to the fireplace. "I think you and I stopped trying. It's hard enough for two individuals to live together in harmony, but we also worked together. Maybe we expected too much."

"Maybe we did." She felt a sadness at the thought, and a kind of emptiness, too.

"So, how did you leave things with Mr. Chocolate?"

"Up in the air, I guess." She lifted her shoulders

in a vague shrug, then admitted, "I walked out on him."

"That was a bit on the childish side, don't you think?" His smile was lightly teasing, but his eyes were warm with gentleness.

"Probably. But it was either walk out and cool off, or throw his ring in his face."

"That bad, huh?"

"That bad." Kitty nodded in confirmation. "He never seemed to hear anything I said. If he just would have listened," Kitty murmured, her shoulders sagging in defeat. "Maybe it is inevitable that I have to sell the gallery. I realize that it will be extremely difficult to run it from a distance, and I can't count on finding someone to manage it who will care about it as much as I do. Maybe I will find married life to be as busy and fulfilling as my work. I don't know. But Marcel talks as though this all needs to be set in motion now, before we're married. Why can't it be something I ease into gradually?"

"Have you told him that?" Sebastian dipped his head to get a better look at her downturned face.

"More or less."

"Which means it was less rather than more."

"It was hard to get a word in," she said in her own defense. "He was too busy planning my life."

"Something tells me he doesn't know you very well," Sebastian murmured wryly. "So, what's the next move?"

She moved her head from side to side in a gesture of uncertainty. "I don't know. I probably should call him—to apologize for walking out like that, if nothing else. But he's staying at the Ridgedales'. You know how nosy Mavis is. I hate the thought of her listening in on even one side of our conversation."

"There's always tomorrow morning."

"Marcel's flying back to Brussels in the morning. His mother is ill."

"Oops."

"I know. My timing is lousy," Kitty admitted. "Even worse, he wanted me to go with him. That's why he came early to pick me up."

"And you refused to go, of course."

"How could I? In the first place, I can't take off at the drop of a hat. Who would open the gallery in the morning? And there's the exhibit coming up. There are a thousand things that have to be done in the next two weeks. Besides, even though he said his mother isn't seriously ill, I think it's a poor time to meet my future in-laws."

"It sort of makes you wonder if his mother took sick before or after she found out he was engaged."

Her gaze narrowed on him. "What are you saying?"

Sebastian asked instead, "How old is Mr. Chocolate?"

"Thirty-eight. Why?"

"Is this his first marriage?"

"As a matter of fact, it is. But that's not so unusual. European males tend to marry later in life. That doesn't mean he's a mama's boy."

Stepping back, Sebastian raised his hands. "I never said he was."

"No, you just hinted at it. Broadly."

"It is a possibility, though."

"You're doing it again." Kitty pressed her lips together in a grim and angry line.

"Doing what?"

"Putting doubts in my mind, making me suspicious of my mother-in-law before I've even met her. Why don't you come right out and admit you don't want me to marry Marcel?"

"All right, I don't."

Her mouth dropped open. She hadn't actually expected him to admit it, and certainly not with such aplomb. "I thought you wanted me to be happy."

"I do. Just not with Mr. Chocolate."

"Will you stop calling him that?"

"Maybe you can become a taster for the family business. Sample all the new products, or work on the quality control end."

"It is impossible to talk to you," Kitty declared angrily.

"But you love chocolate."

"As a treat, yes. But I certainly have no desire to make it my life's work." In disgust, she turned back toward the fire. "Why am I even talking to you?"

"Because you know I'll listen."

Kitty was forced to concede that was true. Sebastian didn't necessarily agree with her all the time, but he always listened. Which made it easy for her to return to the heart of the problem.

"I really do love Marcel." Yet saying the words only made her situation seem more confusing.

"As Tina would say, 'What's love got to do with it?'" Sebastian countered.

"It should have everything to do with it," Kitty stated forcefully.

"Maybe." But he was clearly unconvinced.

In some disconnected way, his reply raised another question. "Tell me something," she began, eyeing him intently. "A minute ago, you admitted you didn't want me to marry Marcel, but you never said why."

"Are you sure you want to know?"

"I wouldn't have asked otherwise."

"Okay." He nodded in acceptance. "It's very simple, really. I don't want to go through the trouble of finding another dealer to represent my paintings."

"That is the most selfish thing I have ever heard," Kitty huffed. "And you claim you want me to be happy."

"I do," Sebastian replied easily, giving no indication that he considered it to be contradictory.

"You want me to be happy so long as it isn't at your expense," she retorted in annoyance. "You certainly wouldn't have any trouble finding someone reputable to represent you. As successful as you've become, they'll be standing in line to take my place."

"But I don't want the hassle of all the meetings that go along with deciding which one to pick, not to mention the strangeness of working with someone new. We've been together too long, and I don't have any desire to change horses. Besides, you know me—I'd be just as happy selling my paintings on a street corner. That's how we met, in case you've forgotten."

"I hadn't."

The memory of that day was as vivid as if had happened yesterday. As an art major and ardent fan of works by Georgia O'Keeffe, she had come to Santa Fe during spring break to view the O'Keeffe paintings on display at a local museum. She had also planned to make a side trip to O'Keeffe's former home and studio about an hour northwest of Santa Fe.

Late one sunny morning as she walked along a street, she had spotted a half-dozen paintings propped against the side of an adobe wall, with more standing in a plastic crate. Idly curious, she had stopped to look. Mixed in with some still-life works that showed good technique but trite subject matter were a series of New Mexican landscapes and Santa Fe streetscapes that completely captivated her.

There had been, however, no sign of the artist. Each painting had a price tag attached to it, with none selling for above fifty dollars.

A hand-lettered sign with a directional arrow had instructed buyers to deposit their money in a metal cash box with a slit in its lid that was chained and padlocked to a lamppost. To her utter astonishment, Kitty had realized that this fool of an artist was selling his paintings on the honor system.

At that moment, a middle-aged couple had strolled by, paused to look at the paintings, assumed Kitty was the artist, and begun asking her questions. To this day she still couldn't say why she hadn't disabused them from that notion, but she hadn't.

Before they left, she had managed to sell them one of the Santa Fe street scenes. Buoyed by that success, Kitty had lingered. By late afternoon, she had sold a total of eight paintings, including one of the dull still lifes to a woman who bought it because the colors in it matched her living room.

Concerned that the cash box contained over four hundred dollars and curious about the artist who had signed the paintings as S. Cole, Kitty had waited, certain that S. Cole would show up sooner or later.

But she certainly hadn't expected him to be the tall, blond hunk of man who had ultimately shown up. By then she had already fallen in love with his paintings. It had been an easy step from there to fall in love with him.

"Why?"

Lost in her memory of that day, Kitty didn't follow his question. "Why what?"

"Why did you want to know my reasons for not wanting you to marry Mr. Chocolate?"

"Just curious." She shrugged, finding it hard to return to the present. "I thought it might be something personal. I should have known it would be business."

"Would it have made any difference?"

"What?"

"If my reason were personal."

"Of course not. I'll do what I want to do regardless," Kitty asserted.

"You always do."

Something in his tone made her bristle. "And what's wrong with that?"

Sebastian took a step back in mock retreat, an eyebrow shooting up. "My, we are testy. I thought you might have cooled down a little."

"I have," Kitty snapped, then caught herself. "Almost, anyway." A kind of despair swept over her again. "How do I make such a mess of things?"

"You simply have a natural talent for it, I guess." His smile took any sting from his words. "I have an idea."

"What?" Kitty was leery of any idea coming from him.

"Since I don't have any champagne to offer you, how about some hot cocoa?"

Kitty smiled in bemusement. "Hot chocolate, the ultimate comfort drink. Why not?"

She trailed along behind him as Sebastian headed for the small galley kitchen tucked in a corner of the studio. "Which kind do you want?" Sebastian asked over his shoulder. "The instant kind that comes in a packet or the real McCoy?"

"I should ask for the real thing, but I'll settle for the instant," she replied, not really caring.

"That's not like you." He opened a cupboard door and took a tin of cocoa off the shelf.

"What isn't?" She wandered over to the French doors that opened off the kitchen onto the rear courtyard.

"Settling for second best. Your motto has always been 'first class or forget it.' "

"I suppose." Beyond the door's glass panes, Kitty could see her spacious adobe home, its earth-colored walls subtly lit by strategically placed landscape lights around the courtyard. "I really should go home, just in case Marcel calls." She released a heavy and troubled sigh. "But what would I say to him?"

"I suppose it would be too much to hope that you might say 'Get lost, Mr. Chocolate,' " he said amid the rattle of the utensil drawer opening and the clank of a metal pan on the stove top.

"You'd like that, wouldn't you?" Kitty grumbled.

"More than you know," Sebastian replied. "Would you get me the jug of milk from the fridge? I need to keep stirring this."

As she stepped to the refrigerator, she noticed him standing at the stove, stirring something in a pan with a wooden spoon. "What are you doing?" She frowned curiously.

"Making cocoa—from scratch."

She stood there with the refrigerator door open, staring at him in amazement. "I didn't know you knew how."

"It can't be that hard. The directions are right on the can." He nodded to it, then glanced her way. "The milk," he said in a prompting voice.

Reminded of her task, Kitty took the plastic container of milk from the refrigerator and carried it to the small counter space next to the stove. "Bachelorhood has clearly made you domestic."

"Think so, hmm?" he murmured idly.

"I've certainly never known you to cook before."

"Making hot chocolate doesn't count as cooking. Which reminds me, did you know that chocolate was strictly a drink when it was first introduced?"

"Quite honestly, I didn't. I'm not sure I even care." Kitty watched as he stirred the bubbling syruplike mixture in the pan.

"As a connoisseur of chocolate, you should," Sebastian informed her. "Columbus was actually the first to bring it back from the New World. Nobody liked his version of it, though."

"Really," she murmured, intrigued that he should know that.

"Yes, really. It seems the Aztec were the first to grind cocoa beans and use the powder to make a drink. They mixed it with chilies, cinnamon, and cloves, and cornmeal—the four Cs, I call it."

"It doesn't sound very appetizing."

"I don't think it was. The word 'chocolate' is derived from the Aztec word *'xocolatl,'* which literally translates to 'bitter water.' "

"It sounds worse than bitter." The mere thought of the combination was enough for Kitty to make a face.

"It was drunk by the Aztec, supposedly out of golden goblets, and only by men. They considered it to be an aphrodisiac." He poured out some milk and added it to the dark syrupy mixture. "Naturally cocoa beans became highly prized and were eventually used as currency. In fact, ten beans could buy the company of a lady for the evening." Sebastian wagged his eyebrows in mock lechery.

"How do you know all this?" Kitty marveled.

"I've been boning up."

"Why?"

"To impress you, of course. You're the chocolate maven."

"Hardly." Kitty scoffed at the notion. "I simply like it."

"A lot," he added, while continuing to stir the mixture, waiting for it to heat. "For your information, Cortez was the one who added sugar and vanilla to the brew, finally making it palatable. But it was years, not until the mid-eighteen hundreds, that a solid form of chocolate was marketed—by the Cadbury company, if I'm not mistaken."

"You are an absolute mine of knowledge," Kitty teased half seriously.

"Impressed?"

"Very."

"Wait until you taste my hot cocoa." Using a wooden spoon, Sebastian let a few drops fall on the inside of his wrist, then gasped. "Ouch, that's hot."

"I think it might be ready," Kitty suggested dryly, then shouldered him out of the way. "You'd better let me pour before you accidentally burn your fingers and can't paint."

"See what I mean?" he said. "Who else would worry about me like that?"

"I'm sure you'll find someone." After transferring the two mugs to the sink, Kitty filled them with steaming chocolate from the pan. She passed one to Sebastian, then took a tentative sip from the other.

Sebastian watched her. "What do you think?"

"It's delicious, but much too hot to drink."

"While it's cooling, do you want to take a look at my latest? I finished it about an hour ago."

Kitty was quick to take him up on his offer. "I'd love to."

Sebastian was notorious for not allowing anyone to see a painting while it was in progress. It had nearly driven her crazy while they were married. Over the years, she had learned never to venture into his work space without a specific invitation, or risk his wrath. In that way, and that way only, he fit the description of a temperamental artist, complete with tantrums.

Moving into the heart of the studio, Sebastian crossed directly to an easel and turned it to show her the painting propped on it. She breathed in sharply at this first glimpse of a streetscape. At the same time she inhaled the familiar smells of oil paints and thinner.

The painting was an intriguing depiction of all that was Santa Fe: A stretch of adobe wall with its strange blend of pink and ochre tones set the scene. Placed slightly off center was an old wooden door painted a Southwestern teal green. A niche by the door was done in Spanish-influenced tiles.

Next to the front stoop was a geranium in full flower growing out of a large pot, decorated with Pueblo Indian designs. Propped against the stoop was an old skull from a cow. Most striking of all was the dappled shade on the wall.

"It's stunning," she murmured. "The sense of depth you managed to convey is amazing, simply by showing a few paloverde leaves in the upper corner and letting the intricate shadow pattern on the adobe show the rest of the tree. It's almost eerie, the three-dimensional effect you've achieved. How on earth did you do it?"

"It wasn't that difficult. I simply kept the leaves in the foreground in sharp focus and fuzzed the edges of everything else to create the illusion of depth."

"However you achieved it, it worked," Kitty declared. "But the painting itself addresses so completely the blending of cultures in Santa Fe. You have the influence of Spain in the tiles, the Mexican adobe, and the Pueblo pottery. And the cow skull is a personification of the Old West. As for the geranium, you couldn't have chosen a better flower to denote all things American—and even Old World. And I don't think there's a color more closely associated with the new Southwest than that sun-faded shade of teal green. But I like best your reference to the desert with the depiction of the paloverde tree. It's so much more original than the usual prickly pear or saguaro cactus."

"Most people won't recognize it. It'll be just another leafy tree to them." Sebastian's voice held a faint trace of irritation.

"That's their loss. There will be plenty of others who will appreciate it." If necessary, it would be a detail she would point out to them. "Have you titled it yet?"

"I've been mulling over a couple different ones—either 'A Place in the Shade', or 'In the Shade of Santa Fe.' What do you think?"

Kitty considered the choices. "Both would work, but I like the last one best, because everything in the painting shows shades of Santa Fe."

"I don't know. It almost sounds too commercial to me," Sebastian replied.

Kitty shook her head. "I don't think so. After all, it is Santa Fe you've painted. And wonderfully, too."

"I guess that means you like it." His sideways glance was warmly teasing.

"Like it?" The verb choice was much too tame for her. "I absolutely love it."

It was completely natural to slide an arm around his waist, a gesture that fell somewhere between a congratulatory hug and a shared joy in his accomplishment. His own reaction seemed equally natural when he hooked an arm around to her to rest his hand on her waist.

"Thanks." He dipped his head toward hers.

A split second later, his mouth moved onto hers with tunneling warmth. Kitty was surprised by how right it felt and how easy it was to kiss him back.

The kiss itself lasted a little longer than the span of a heartbeat before he lifted his head an inch, his moist breath mingling with hers.

"You taste of chocolate," he murmured.

"So do you," she whispered back, her pulse unexpectedly racing a little.

She wanted to blame it on her delight with the new painting. But something told her the cause was something a bit more intimate, rooted somewhere in the physical attraction that still existed between them.

Chapter Four

"I have an idea." His half-lidded gaze traveled over her face in a visual caress.

"What's that?" Kitty knew she should pull away, create some space between them, but she was strangely reluctant to end this moment.

"Let's go sit on the sofa and see how the painting looks from there."

It was an old routine they had once shared that Kitty found as easy to slip into as an old shoe, one that offered comfort and a perfect fit.

"All right."

With arms linking each other at the waist, they moved together toward the sofa. Then Sebastian pulled away with an ambiguous, "Go ahead. I'll be right there."

"Where are you going?" She frowned curiously when he circled around the sofa and headed toward the front door.

"To set the mood. There are too many lights

on." He flipped off all the switches in the main area except one to a directional lamp aimed directly at the completed canvas.

"Perfect," Kitty announced in approval, then lowered herself onto the sofa's plush cushions, careful not to spill her cocoa.

"It is, isn't it?"

Before joining her, Sebastian crossed to the kiva and added another chunk of wood to the dying fire. With the poker, he stirred it to life until the golden glow from the new flames reached the sofa.

He retrieved his mug of cocoa from the side table, took a quick drink from it, then made his way to the sofa and folded his long frame to sit down next to her, draping one arm along the sofa back behind her head.

"Better drink your cocoa," he advised. "It's just the right temperature now."

Obediently, Kitty took a sip. "Mmm, it does taste good."

"Not bad at all, even if I do say so myself," he agreed after sipping his own.

"You know, if anything, the painting actually looks better from a distance," she remarked after studying it for a minute. "It seems to increase the illusion of depth."

"It does, doesn't it?"

Some wayward impulse prompted Kitty to lift her cup in a toasting fashion. "To another stunning work by S. Cole." She clunked her mug against his and drank down a full swallow. "Good job."

"Thank you."

She settled deeper against the cushions, conscious of the brush of his thigh against hers, but oddly comfortable with the contact. "I'm glad you didn't have any champagne. Hot chocolate is much better." She idly swirled the last half inch of it in her cup. "The taste is somehow soothing."

"That's due to a chemical called theobromine that occurs naturally in cocoa. It's an antidepressant that lifts the spirits."

"More research," Kitty guessed.

"Yup. And, in addition to theobromine, chocolate also contains potassium, magnesium, and vitamin A."

"Stop," she protested with amusement. "I don't need an analysis. It's enough that I feel more content."

"Content" was the word that perfectly described her mood at the moment. And the quiet setting promoted the feeling with the lights turned down, a fire softly crackling in the corner fireplace, and a beautiful piece of art bathed in light. Background music was the only thing lacking.

"Just a minute." Sebastian leaned forward and set his empty mug on the mission-style coffee table.

"Where are you going?" For an instant, Kitty thought he had read her mind and intended to put on some music.

"Nowhere." Sebastian sat back and instructed, "Tilt your head forward a sec."

"Why?" she asked, but did as he said. She felt his fingers on her hair and the sudden loosening of its smooth French twist as he removed a securing pin.

"What are you doing?" She reached back to stop him.

"Taking your hair down. It can't be comfortable leaning against the knot it's in."

"It isn't a knot. It's a twist." Try as she might,

Kitty couldn't repair the damage as quickly as he could pluck out another pin.

"Look at it this way," Sebastian reasoned. "You'll be taking your hair down before the night's over anyway. Now you won't have to."

He didn't stop until her hair tumbled about her shoulders. "But I didn't want it down yet." It made her feel oddly vulnerable to have it falling loose.

"Too bad," he replied, and ran his fingers through her hair, combing it into a semblance of order. "You have beautiful hair." He lifted a few strands and let them slide off his fingers. "Sleek and soft, like satin against the skin."

"Thank you." But the words came out as stiff and self-conscious as she felt.

"You hardly ever wear your hair down. How come?"

"I prefer it up. It's much easier to manage that way." Kitty refused to pull away from his toying fingers. It seemed too much of an admission that she was somehow affected by his touch.

"And you like being in control."

"As a matter of fact, I do," Kitty admitted easily. "I couldn't successfully run my own business otherwise."

"You know what?"

"What?" She darted him a wary glance as he bent closer to her.

"Your hair smells like strawberries."

"It's the shampoo I use."

"Strawberries and chocolate, now there's a delicious combination."

Only inches separated them. Without warning, he closed the distance and claimed her lips in a drugging kiss. The potency of it scrambled her wits and her pulse. She couldn't think, only feel the persuasive power of it.

Her own response came much too naturally and much too eagerly. Frightened by it, she pressed a hand to his chest, intending to push him away. But the instant she felt the hard muscled wall and the hypnotic beat of his heart beneath her hand, any sense of urgency to break off the kiss faded.

He rolled his mouth around her lips, teasing them apart, then murmured against them, "A kiss like that can become addictive."

Kitty managed to pull together enough of her scattered wits to turn her face away. "That's enough, Sebastian." But her voice was all breathy and shaky, without conviction.

"Why?" Deprived of her lips, he simply began nuzzling her highly sensitive ear, igniting a storm of exquisite shudders.

"Because." She knew there was a reason; she simply couldn't think of it, not with Sebastian nibbling at her earlobe like that. It had always been her weakest point, and the surest way to turn her on.

"That's no reason," Sebastian replied, and licked at the shell of her ear with the tip of his tongue.

Swallowing back a moan of pure desire, Kitty hunched a shoulder against her neck, trying to block his sensuous invasion. "I'll . . . I'll spill my cocoa."

"That's easily handled." Seemingly all in one motion, he planted a firm kiss on her lips, took the cup from her hand, and set on the low table.

Kitty barely had time to draw a breath before he was back, once more giving her his undivided attention. Too much of it and too thoroughly. Worse, she was enjoying it.

Gathering together the scattered threads of resistance, Kitty managed to push him back and twist her head to the side, creating a small space between them.

"Will you stop trying to seduce me?" she said in quick protest.

"And here I thought I was being so subtle." He automatically switched his attention to the curve of her throat.

Kitty slid her fingers into his hair, then forgot why. "Sebastian, I'm engaged to Marcel." She managed to remember that much.

"Maybe you are and maybe you aren't. It sounded to me like it was all up in the air."

"I haven't decided that," she insisted a bit breathlessly.

"I think you have." His mouth moved around the edges of her lips, tantalizing them with the promise of his kiss.

"Well, I haven't." As if of their own volition, her lips sought contact with his.

As his mouth locked onto them, Kitty recognized the contradiction between her words and action, but she couldn't seem to do anything about it. It was difficult to care when the heat of his kiss satisfied so many of her building needs.

"Funny you should say that," he murmured, lifting his head fractionally. "That's not the message I'm getting."

"I know, but . . ."

"Sh." A second after he made the soothing sound, he began a tactile exploration along the bare ridge of her shoulder, nibbling and licking her there.

It was a full second before it hit Kitty that her shoulder shouldn't be bare. The lace dress should be covering it. Simultaneously with that thought, she felt the looseness of the material along her back and the tight constriction of the sleeves binding her arms against her sides.

"You unfastened my dress," she accused in shock.

"You didn't plan on sleeping in it, did you?" When he raised his head to look at her, the fire-light's dim glow kept most of his face in shadow. But there was sufficient light for her to see that his eyes were three-quarter lidded and dark with desire.

It was a sight that took her breath away because Kitty knew her own reflected the same thing.

"Of course I wasn't going to sleep in it."

"Then I'm saving you some time." His fingers inched the sleeves lower on her arms, making it impossible for Kitty to lift her hands high enough to push it back in place.

While she could still muster both the strength and the will, Kitty ducked away from him and scrambled off the sofa. Dangerously weak-kneed, she hurriedly tugged the lacy material higher with fingers that trembled.

"Kitty," his voice coaxed while his hand slid onto the flat of her stomach, evoking new flutters of desire.

"Stop it, Sebastian. You're not playing fair." Kitty weakly pushed at his hand.

"When has love ever been fair?" He rolled to

his feet directly beside her, his hands already moving to gather her back into his embrace.

She wedged her arms between them, needing to avoid contact with his hard male length for her own sake.

"This isn't about love. It's about sex," she insisted, half in anger. "You've always known which buttons to push."

"You pushed mine a long time ago," Sebastian murmured as he nuzzled her neck, "and ruined me for any other woman."

"Do you honestly expect me to believe that?" Kitty sputtered at the outrageous lie. "I've seen the parade of shapely bimbos that have filed past my house to this studio. What about that blonde who was draped all over you at the last showing?"

"Cecilia." He nipped at her earlobe while the pressure of his hands arched her hips closer to him.

"Yes, sexy Cecilia, that's one," Kitty recalled even as her pulse skittered in reaction to his evocative nibblings. "What about her?"

"I never said I didn't try to find someone." He lazily dragged his mouth across her cheek to the corner of her lips. "But no one did to me what you do."

"You're just saying that," she insisted, needing desperately to convince herself of that.

"Am I?" He tugged his shirt open and flattened her hand against his chest. She felt the furnacelike heat of his skin and the hard thudding of his heart somewhere beneath it, beating in the same rapid rhythm as her own. "What about the men I've watched go through your life? All those husbands of yours."

"Two. There were only two." Somehow or other, any thought of Marcel had slipped completely from her mind.

"Be honest. Did any of them make you ache like this?" His hands glided over her back and hips, their roaming caress creating more havoc with her senses.

It was becoming more and more difficult to hold on to any rational thought. "You . . . You were always good in bed," Kitty said in defense of her own weakening resistance to him.

"Good sex requires two participants. What we shared was special. Unique."

"But it's over." She needed to remind herself of that, but saying the words didn't seem to help.

"Not for me. And not for you either, or you wouldn't still be standing here."

"No." She tried to deny it, but she also knew it was true. "This is wrong, Sebastian."

"Then why does it feel so right?"

She had no answer for that as he claimed her lips in a hard and all-too-quick kiss. "Do you remember the first time we made love?" He took another moist bite of them.

"Yes." The word came out on a trembling breath.

"I'd brought you back to my apartment to look at more of my paintings." His hands, like his mouth, were never still, always moving to provoke and evoke. "It was cold that spring night. I added another log to the fire to take some of the chill off. Remember?"

Unable to find her voice, Kitty simply nodded, her memory of that night and what came next as sharp as his own.

"As I walked back to you, I took off my shirt, wadded it up, and threw it in a corner."

He stepped back from her long enough to peel off his shirt and give it a toss. But in those few seconds, when she was deprived of the warmth of his body heat and the stimulating touch of his hands, she felt horribly lost.

Then he was close again, his hand cupping the underside of her jaw, tilting her head up, his thumb stroking the high curve of her cheek.

"Do you remember what I said to you?" Sebastian asked.

The words were branded in her memory. Kitty whispered them, "I want to make love with you."

" 'Yes,' you said," he recalled, "and the word trembled from you like the aspens in a breeze." His voice was low and husky with desire, just as it had been that long-ago night. "I took you by the hand." His fingers closed around hers, their grip warm and firm but without command. "And I led you over by the fire."

He backed away from the sofa, drawing her with him as he skirted the coffee table and continued to the gray-and-black Navajo rug in front of the kiva. There he halted and kissed her with seductive languor.

When his mouth rolled off hers, his breathing was rough and uneven. "You wore a dress that night, too."

He took her lips again, devouring them with tonguing insistency. At the same time, his hands went low on her hips and glided upward, pushing the lace of her dress ahead of them until the hem was nearly to her waist.

The past and present merged into one as Kitty

automatically raised her arms, allowing him to pull the dress over her head. It flew in a white arc to the floor near a stack of blank canvases propped against the wall. Then the darkening heat of his gaze claimed her as it swept down her body.

"You're beautiful." His voice shook, thrilling her anew.

Kitty spread her hands over his naked chest, the golden glow of the firelight revealing each ripple of muscle. "So are you," she murmured.

In a mirror of the past, her hands moved to unfasten his pants while his fingers deftly unhooked her bra. Both items ended up in a pile on the floor, forgotten as his hands moved onto her breasts, feeling them swell to fill them. Then his hands slid lower to the elastic waist of her pantyhose, leaving his lips to make a more intimate exploration of the peaky nipples he had aroused.

With almost agonizing slowness, he worked her pantyhose down her stomach and hips to her thighs, then lower still to her knees and calves. His mouth followed every inch of the way until Kitty was a quivering mass of need.

First one foot slipped free from the sheer hose, then the other. Without invitation, Kitty sank to the floor, her arms reaching to gather him against her and assuage this physical ache.

They twisted together in a tangle of arms and legs and hot, greedy kisses. She cried with exquisite relief when he finally filled her. After that it was all glorious pleasure as they made love to each other, for each other, and with each other.

All loose and liquid limbed, she lay in his arms, tiny aftershocks still trembling through her, her breathing slowly returning to normal. This feeling of utter completeness was one she had forgotten somehow.

"You are still incredibly beautiful." Sebastian gently tucked a wayward strand of hair behind her ear.

She made a small sound of acknowledgment, then admitted, "I know I feel beautifully exhausted. I don't think I could move if I had to."

"And you don't have to." He folded her deeper into the circle of his arms and rubbed his cheek against the side of her head. "As far as I'm concerned, you're right where you belong."

"That's good to know, because I don't think I can move." She closed her eyes in sublime contentment, without the energy to think past this moment. For now, it was enough.

It was her last conscious thought until a harsh light probed at her closed eyelids. Kitty turned her head away from it and buried her face deeper in a dark, warm corner.

"Sorry, kitten," Sebastian's familiar voice vibrated beside her, thick with sleep. "I don't think that will work. I forgot to pull the shade down when I carried you into bed. That's the problem with this room. The window faces the east. Every morning the sun plows through it and hits you right between the eyes."

"Sun?" Groggily, Kitty lifted her head and peered through slitted eyelids toward the offending light. "You mean—it's morning?" The sun's in-reaching rays struck the stone in her engagement ring and bounced off it in a shower of sparkling colors.

Two separate things hit Kitty at the same time. She was wearing Marcel's ring and she was in bed with Sebastian.

How could she have done such a thing?

As much as she wanted to plead ignorance, Kitty remembered much too clearly that little trip down memory lane she'd taken last night—all except the being-carried-to-bed part. A little voice in her head told her that Sebastian had known all along just where that little stroll would lead.

"You dirty rotten sneak." Kitty scrambled away from him, grabbing at the top sheet to bunch it around her. "You did it an purpose, didn't you?"

"What are you talking about?" Frowning in confusion, Sebastian threw up a hand to block the glare of the sunlight. "I wouldn't have left the shade up on purpose. You know I don't like to get up early. What time is it anyway?"

"Who cares what time it is?" she declared angrily and gave the sheet a hard tug to pull it free from the foot of the bed. "I should never have come here last night," she muttered, mostly to herself. "I should have known you would pull some cheap, rotten stunt like this."

"What the hell are you talking about?"

"Don't give me that innocent look. It may have worked last night, but it won't work now." Kitty fought to wrap the loose folds of the sheet around her.

"Talk about getting up on the wrong side of the bed," Sebastian muttered, eying her with a hopeless shake of his head.

"I shouldn't even be in this bed and you know it. I'm engaged to Marcel. Remember." When she tapped her engagement ring, the sheet slipped.

"I didn't forget." His frown cleared away, its place taken by the beginnings of a smile and a knowing twinkle in his eyes.

"You knew I had argued with him. You knew it and you deliberately took advantage of it," Kitty accused.

"I don't recall hearing any objections." Sebastian's smile widened, as if he found the entire conversation amusing.

"I made plenty of objections. You simply ignored them." Kitty impatiently pushed the hair out of her eyes and looked about the room. "What did you do with my clothes?"

"They're probably still scattered around the studio."

"You loved saying that, didn't you?" The little smirk on his face was almost enough to make her want to walk over there and slap it off him. But Kitty wasn't about to get within ten feet of him again.

Intent on retrieving her clothes and getting out of there, Kitty set off toward the studio's main section.

Within two strides, she stepped on a trailing corner of the sheet and had to grab hold of the foot post to keep from falling face first on the floor.

"That robe I borrowed from you is hanging in the closet. It might be safer to put that on to get your clothes," Sebastian suggested dryly. "Otherwise you're going to break your nose, and it's much too pretty."

"Never you mind about my nose." Just the same, Kitty wadded up the length of sheet and stalked over to the closet.

After a first glance failed to locate the robe among his other clothes, Sebastian called from across the room, "It's on the hook behind the door."

Sure enough, that's where it was. Kitty snatched it off the hook, slipped her arms through the sleeves, and let the sheet fall to the floor, then stepped free of its surrounding pile. Hastily tying the ends of the terry-cloth sash around her waist, she turned back toward the door. To her irritation, Sebastian was out of bed and zipping up a pair of paint-spattered work chinos.

"I don't suppose I can talk you into putting on some coffee," he said with that infuriating smile still in place.

"Good guess," Kitty snapped, and crossed to the door with quick, angry strides.

Sebastian trailed after her at a much less hurried pace, then split away to head to the galley kitchen while Kitty began to search for her clothes. Ignoring the sounds coming from the kitchen, she retrieved her dress from the rack of blank canvases. She found her hose draped over the handle of the fireplace poker. Her shawl was still lying across the back of the sofa. After locating the obvious articles, the search began in earnest.

Sebastian wandered over to watch. "Want some juice?"

"No." Finding nothing more on top of the room's few pieces of furniture, Kitty got down on her hands and knees to look under them.

"The coffee should be done in a couple of minutes. Want me to pour you a cup?"

"No." She wanted to find her clothes and leave, but she wasn't about to ask for Sebastian's help in the search.

"Are you sure? It might improve your disposition."

"If you fell off the face of the earth, that would

improve my disposition." Spying something under the sofa, Kitty reached a hand beneath it and pulled out her nude silk panties. She tucked them in with the wadded-up dress and hose bundled in her arm.

"My, we are in a foul mood this morning."

"I wonder whose fault that is," Kitty grumbled.

"Considering that you and I are the only ones here, it must be one of us."

"I'll give you another clue," Kitty retorted. "It isn't me."

"That narrows the field considerably, doesn't it?" Sebastian replied with a smile as the aroma of freshly brewed coffee drifted from the kitchen.

"Considerably." It was awkward crawling around on the floor while holding her clothes, but Kitty wasn't about to put them down anywhere. Knowing Sebastian, she was convinced he'd probably steal them and hold them hostage. "Where is my bra?" she demanded in frustration. "I can't find it."

"It's bound to be lying around here somewhere."

"That's a lot of help." She clambered to her feet to scan the area again.

"Smells like the coffee's done. Are you sure you wouldn't like a cup?"

"Positive." Kitty circled the area again, checking behind canvases and under sofa pillows.

"Would you like some hot chocolate instead? I'll be happy to fix you a cup," Sebastian offered.

"Not on your life," she flashed. "If it wasn't for you and your hot chocolate, I wouldn't still be here this morning!"

"At least it's not my fault anymore."

"It's all your fault." Kitty looked around his work

area, first high, then low. "I should have known I couldn't trust you."

"Of course you can."

Incensed that he had the gall to make such a claim, Kitty spun around to glare at him, the missing brassiere temporarily forgotten. "No, I can't. I came to you last night as a friend. You knew I was upset over my argument with Marcel. You took advantage of me."

"If there's one person in this world least likely to be taken advantage of, it's you," Sebastian observed dryly and raised his coffee cup to take a sip from it.

"That isn't true." Pushed by the need to confront him, she crossed to the small kitchen area. "You caught me at a weak moment, when I was upset and confused. Did you try to comfort me? No, you fed me hot chocolate, spun tales about it being an aphrodisiac, kissed my neck, and lured me down memory lane."

"Sins, every one of them." He lowered his head in mock contrition, giving it a shake. "I should be ashamed of myself."

"Would you stop making a joke out of everything?" Kitty protested, furious with him. "I am trying to be serious."

"That's ninety percent of your problem, kitten. You're too serious."

"And you treat everything lightly."

"Not everything."

"Ha!" Kitty scoffed. "You don't even take your work seriously. If I hadn't come along, you'd still be selling your paintings on a street corner. You said so yourself."

"True. But that doesn't mean I'm not serious

about my painting, because I am. It's just a question of ambition. And, heaven knows, you have enough of that for both of us."

"Is there anything wrong with that?" she challenged.

"Only when it gets in the way of life and living."

"And my work doesn't," Kitty asserted. "For your information, I have a life. The proof of that is right here on my finger." She shifted the bundle of clothes to her opposite arm and displayed her engagement ring. "If I were all work and no play the way you try to make me sound, I wouldn't have had any free time to date Marcel, let alone become engaged to him."

"We're back to Mr. Chocolate, are we?"

"We've never left him."

"I beg to differ," Sebastian said. "As I recall, you did last night before you showed up at my door."

"I didn't leave him. We were arguing, and I simply walked out before I lost my temper and said something that I would regret."

"So you came here and unleashed it on me." His lazy smile revealed just how little he had been affected by it.

"You deserved it after the trouble you caused," Kitty muttered, controlling her temper with the greatest of difficulty.

"I caused it?" Sebastian drew his head back in mock innocence. "Why are you blaming me? You're the one who argued with him."

"We went over all that last night," she reminded him. "You're not going to bait me into going over it again."

"Too bad." His mouth twisted in a smile of

feigned regret. "Considering the way our conversation last night ended, it could have been a wonderful way to start the day."

Furious beyond words, Kitty growled a sound of absolute exasperation and spun away to resume her search for the missing brassiere. Before she could take a step, the doorbell chimed.

Its ring was like an alarm bell going off. Gripped by a sudden sense of panic, Kitty froze in her tracks.

Chapter Five

"Who in the world could that be?" Sebastian frowned and started toward the door.

"Wait." Kitty grabbed his arm to stop him. "What time is it?"

"I don't know."

She glanced frantically around the studio. "Don't you have a clock somewhere?" She glanced at the sunlight streaming through the French doors, but she had no idea how to tell the time of the day from the angle of the sun.

"You know how I hate them," Sebastian chided. "Why? What difference does it make?"

"Because if it's past eight-thirty, it could be Harve wondering why I haven't shown up to open the gallery this morning. If it's him, don't let him in, whatever you do." Kitty briefly toyed with the idea of making a dash for the bedroom, but if Harve happened to look in the front window, he would see her.

"Why not? He's found you here before," Sebastian reminded her.

"Not in the morning," Kitty hissed as she backed deeper into the galley kitchen, aware that its area couldn't be seen from the doorway. "And certainly not with me in a robe. You know exactly what he'll surmise from that."

"It would be true, wouldn't it?" Sebastian countered, smiling at her predicament.

"That's none of his business," she whispered angrily as the doorbell chimed again, then repeated its summons insistently. "Go. Get rid of him."

When Sebastian moved to the door, Kitty shrank into a corner, trying to make herself as small as possible. Silently she scolded herself for taking the time to gather up her clothes; she should have left Sebastian's studio the minute she got up.

The snap of the dead bolt was followed by the click of the door latch. But it wasn't Harve's voice that Kitty heard next.

"Monsieur Cole." It was Marcel who spoke, and her heart jumped into her throat and lodged there. "I am concerned for Kitty."

"Kitty?" Sebastian repeated, and she knew he was positively gloating inside.

"Is it possible that you would know whether she arrived safely home last night?" Marcel inquired.

"Had an argument with her, did you?" Sebastian asked instead. "Not over anything important, I hope."

"Mere trifling matters."

Trifling? His outrageous choice of adjective was almost enough to make Kitty charge to the door and confront Marcel. Only the thought that Sebastian would get way too much enjoyment out of such a scene prevented her from doing just that.

"Walked out on you, did she?" Sebastian said, as if he already didn't know that.

"Have you seen Kitty?" There was a note of suspicion in Marcel's question, enough to heighten the sense of panic Kitty felt.

"Isn't she at home?" Sebastian countered.

"She did not answer the door."

"What time is it? Maybe she's already left to open the gallery," Sebastian suggested.

"Not at this hour, surely," Marcel protested. "It is only half past seven o'clock."

"That early? I—"

"What is this?" Marcel demanded suddenly.

To her horror, Kitty saw Sebastian being forced to back up and open the door wider. A clear indication that Marcel had stepped inside. She flattened herself against the corner, her heart pounding like a mad thing.

"This is Kitty's shoe." Marcel's announcement bordered on an accusation, and Kitty realized that Marcel had noticed the pumps Sebastian had set on the catchall table by the door.

"Does she have a pair of heels like these?" Sebastian asked, again deftly avoiding both a confirmation and a bold-faced lie.

That's when Kitty spotted her missing bra. It dangled from the back of the sofa, a strap precariously hooked over the rounded corner of its back. It was clearly within plain sight of the door. Marcel was bound to see it; it was only a matter of when.

For now the open door blocked her from view. But if Marcel stepped past it, she could easily be seen. Kitty glanced frantically around, searching for a better hiding place. Her widely swinging gaze screeched to a stop on the French doors that opened onto the back courtyard.

Did she dare try to reach them? There was only the smallest chance she could escape detection if she remained where she was. But if she could manage to slip outside, unseen, she was home free.

"There is a lady's brassiere hanging off your sofa," Marcel declared in a tone of voice that insisted on explanation.

With fingers figuratively crossed that Marcel would be sufficiently distracted by the sight of the lacy undergarment not to notice her, Kitty tiptoed as quickly and quietly as she could across the Saltillo-tiled floor to the French doors.

"So it is," Sebastian confirmed from the front door area as Kitty fumbled ever so briefly with the dead bolt lock. The latch made the smallest *snicking* sound, but Sebastian's voice covered it. "I had company last night. She must have forgotten to take it with her."

Not a single hinge creaked to give Kitty away. She opened the French door no farther than necessary and slipped outside. Immediately she darted to the left, not bothering to close the door behind her.

Any second she expected to hear a cry of discovery from Marcel. But none came. The minute she reached the security of the exterior adobe wall, Kitty halted to lean against it and drink in a shaky gulp of air.

Now, if she could just make it to the house without being seen.

But she soon realized that was impossible. There was a taxicab sitting in the driveway. Any approach to the house would be seen either by the driver or Marcel.

She debated her next move. She could remain where she was until Marcel left, or— Kitty froze, stricken by the realization that waiting for Marcel to leave wasn't a viable option. Her evening bag was on the coffee table. Sebastian might be able to convince Marcel that two women could have the same pair of shoes. But an evening bag, too? That would be too much of a coincidence.

If Marcel noticed the evening bag, Kitty was certain he would take a closer look. When he did, he would find her driver's license and a credit card inside, along with the usual lipstick, compact, and mascara. Her escape from the studio would have been for nothing.

Kitty knew she had to do something before Marcel discovered she had been in the studio last night. She knew of only one way to accomplish that.

Hastily, she stashed her bundle of clothes under an ancient lilac bush that grew next to the corner of the building. She peeked around its branches to make sure Marcel hadn't stepped back outside. But all was clear. After double-checking the sash's knot, Kitty took a deep, galvanizing breath and dashed from behind the bush toward the studio door, choosing an angle that might convince Marcel she had come from the house.

Marcel stood just inside the doorway. Kitty had a glimpse of Sebastian's bare chest just beyond him, his body positioned in such a way to prevent Marcel from gaining further entrance to the studio.

"Marcel." She didn't have to fake the breathlessness in her cry.

He swung around with a start, a look of utter relief lighting his whole face. "Kitty!"

His arms opened to greet her. She was swept into them just outside the door. Automatically Kitty wrapped her own arms around him while he pressed kisses against her hair and murmured little endearments in French.

A guilty conscience kept her from responding to his embrace—that and the sight of Sebastian leaning a naked shoulder against the doorjamb, an amused smile edging the corners of his mouth.

"Kitty, Kitty, Kitty," Marcel murmured in a mixture of relief and joy as he drew back and framed her face in his hands. "You are all right, *non?*" He ran his gaze over her face in rapid assessment. "I had fear that you came to harm."

"I'm fine," she assured him.

"Where have you been?" The look of worry reentered his aquiline features.

"I . . . I just woke up." Kitty stalled, trying to gain enough time to come up with an explanation that might satisfy him.

With a frown, Marcel glanced past her toward the house, then brought his probing gaze back to hers. "But I rang the bell to your door many, many times, and you did not answer it."

"I should have warned you," Sebastian inserted. "Kitty sleeps very soundly. A bomb would have to go off outside her window before she'd wake up. Even then, I'm not sure she would."

There was some truth in that, but not enough for Kitty to feel comfortable fielding more questions from Marcel. The certainty of that came with his next query.

"Why did you not answer the telephone? I rang you a hundred times after you left the restaurant."

"I wasn't ready to talk to you last night." Which was the truth as far as it went. Attempting to take the offensive Kitty asked, "What are you doing here?"

"When you did not answer the door, I had worry that you suffered a mishap and did not arrive home last night. I came here to speak with Monsieur Cole in the event he was aware of your return."

Sebastian spoke up, "I was just suggesting that he might check with the hospitals or contact the police to see whether you might have been involved in some accident on your way home."

"I see," Kitty murmured hesitantly, then explained, "Actually I was wondering what you were doing here because you had told me that you were flying back to Brussels early this morning."

"Ah." Marcel nodded in new understanding. "I postponed my departure. I could not leave when I was so concerned for your well-being."

"I'm glad you didn't leave today." At least Kitty knew she should be glad. But she felt so much nervous turmoil inside that she had trouble identifying any other emotion.

"We have much that we must discuss," Marcel began.

"Indeed we do," Kitty rushed, and darted a lightning glance at Sebastian, who was unabashedly eavesdropping. "But not here." She tucked a hand under his arm. "Let's go to the house. I'll put some coffee on and we can talk."

Before she could lead Marcel away, Sebastian inquired lazily, "Did you bring your key with you?"

"My key?" She gave him a blank look.

Sebastian nodded toward the house. "I can see from here that the door is closed. It locks automatically when you shut it. Remember?"

That's when it hit her that, as always, she had locked the house when she left with Marcel last night. Without a key, she couldn't get back in. And her key ring was in her evening bag—on Sebastian's coffee table.

Thinking fast, Kitty said, "Do you still have that spare key I left with you?"

"Yes—"

"I'll get it." She pressed a detaining hand on Marcel's arm. "Wait here." She moved quickly toward the door, anxious that he wouldn't follow her inside.

"Do you remember where it is?" Sebastian shifted to the side, giving her room to pass.

"As long as you haven't moved it someplace else."

"I haven't."

"Good."

Kitty slipped inside and hurried straight to the coffee table, resisting the impulse to snatch her bra off the corner of the sofa.

Her evening bag lay exactly where she'd left it. She opened it, took out the ring of keys, and snapped it shut. With her fingers wrapped around the keys to silence their jingle, Kitty rushed back outside, straight to Marcel.

"All set," she declared with false brightness. Her smile faltered when she observed the hint of sternness in his expression. "Is something wrong?" she asked, worried that he had somehow seen through her charade.

"You do not wear slippers." His glance cut to her bare feet.

Kitty almost laughed aloud with relief, but a response such as that would have been inappropriate. "I was in such a hurry I guess I forgot to put any on. Shall we?" As subtly as possible, she urged him toward the house.

Marcel stood his ground a moment longer and nodded to Sebastian. "I regret that I troubled you needlessly."

"Oh, it was no trouble," Sebastian assured him, then let his glance slide pointedly to Kitty. "In fact, it was all pleasure."

Inwardly she did a slow burn over Sebastian's parting shot as she ushered Marcel across the courtyard to her home's rear entrance. When she stepped forward to unlock the door, Marcel took the keys from her.

"Allow me," he said with typical courtesy, then inserted the key and unlocked the door, giving it a slight inward push.

He stepped back, motioning for Kitty to precede him into the house. She had barely set foot inside when he asked, "Why does this artist have a key to your house?"

"Someone had to let the maid in to clean when I vacationed in Cancun this past winter. Since Sebastian lives on the grounds, he was an obvious choice."

Actually that was true; Kitty had left a spare house key with him on that occasion, but she'd also gotten it back when she returned from the trip. But it was another one of those half-truths that pricked her conscience.

"That is another thing I wish to discuss with you," Marcel stated.

At that instant, Kitty knew she was much too tense, and the feeling of dancing around eggshells was much too strong for her to talk to Marcel right now. She needed a respite from it, however brief.

"There is much we need to discuss," she told him. "But it can wait a few more minutes. I'm such a mess." She pushed a smoothing hand over her loose hair in emphasis. "I'd really like to freshen up and slip into some clothes first. I won't be long."

Giving Marcel no opportunity to object, Kitty hurried from the kitchen. The instant she reached the safety of her bedroom, she leaned against the closed door, tipped her head back to stare at the high-beamed ceiling and took a deep, calming breath.

A part of her wished she could stay in the room and never come out, but the rational side knew that was impossible. Pushing away from the door, she headed to the closet. Aware that dallying over a choice of clothes would accomplish little, Kitty quickly selected a pair of hunter green slacks and a cotton sweater in a coordinating apple green.

In five minutes flat, she walked out of the bedroom, fully clothed, a minimum of makeup applied and her long hair pulled back in its usual sleek bun. She decided there was some truth in the old saying that a woman's clothes were her armor. She certainly had more confidence in her ability to handle things.

Marcel had not ventured from the kitchen. He stood by the French doors in the small breakfast nook, staring in the direction of the studio. His hands were buried deep in the pockets of his trousers, his jacket pushed aside, and a heavy frown darkened his expression.

"I told you I wouldn't be long," Kitty said by way of an announcement of her return.

He dragged his gaze away from the view with a trace of reluctance that had little frissons of alarm shooting through Kitty. Had he seen something? For the life of her, she couldn't think what it might be.

Kitty hurried into her carefully rehearsed speech. "Before anything else is said, I want to apologize, Marcel, for walking out on you like that last night. It was—"

He didn't give her a chance to finish it. "It would be best for you to inform Monsieur Cole that he must move somewhere else."

Dumbfounded, Kitty stared. "I beg your pardon."

"I said, it—"

This time she cut him off. "I heard what you said." She simply couldn't believe that he'd actually said it. "But I'm afraid that what you suggest is impossible. According to the terms of our divorce settlement, I got the house and Sebastian received the studio. I can't order him to move out. I have no right."

"Then we must find a different place for you to live until we are married," Marcel stated.

He suspected something about last night. Kitty was certain of it. Some of the inner panic started to return.

"Whatever for?" She forced a smile of confusion. "This arrangement has worked for years. Sebastian lives there and I live here."

"But it is not right that you should live so closely to him."

Worried that she was back on shaky ground, Kitty attempted an amused protest. "Surely you aren't jealous of him, Marcel."

"*Mais non.*" His denial was quick and smooth, completely without question, which in itself was a bit deflating. "I simply do not wish my fiancée to associate so closely with his kind."

"His kind?" Kitty seized on the phrase, then challenged, "Exactly what do you mean by that?"

He gave her a look of mild exasperation. "It is known to all, Kitty, that such people are self-absorbed and self-indulgent, which leads them to loose ways of living."

Outraged by his blanket condemnation of an entire profession, she said furiously, "That is the most ignorant statement I have ever heard. For every artist you can show me who's into drugs and alcohol and wild parties, I can show you fifty who are honest and caring, hardworking people with families to support and a mortgage to pay."

Turning haughty, Marcel declared, "Please do not attempt to convince me that Monsieur Cole is one of these. Last night he entertained a woman in his studio. I saw with my own eyes this morning the articles of her lingerie flung about the room in wild abandon."

That nagging sense of guilt resurfaced to steal some of the heat from her indignation.

"His private life is no concern of mine," Kitty insisted in a show of indifference.

"But your life is a concern of mine, now that we are to be married. And I should think it would be a concern to you. This is what I attempted to explain to you last night, when you objected so strongly to selling your gallery. But you refused to listen to me."

"Try again," Kitty stated, her anger cooling, dropping to an icy level.

"It is quite simple, really," he began with a trace of impatience. "Even you must see that running a gallery of necessity brings you in frequent contact with such people. It would not be acceptable to continue such associations after we are married."

Kitty cocked her head to one side. "Acceptable to whom? You? Your friends? Your family?"

Sensing the hint of disdain in her words, Marcel drew himself up to his full height. "Is it wrong to value the good reputation of the Boulanger name?"

"That is the most supercilious question I have ever heard," Kitty snapped.

But before she could denounce him for being the snob that he was, the doorbell rang. For the first time in as many days, she sincerely hoped it was Sebastian. Right now, nothing would delight her more than to inform Marcel that she was the abandoned woman who had spent the night with Sebastian.

A smile of anticipated pleasure was on her lips when she opened the back door. To her eternal disappointment, the cabdriver stood outside, a heavyset man of Mexican descent.

"Por favor." He swept off his billed cap and held it in front of his barrel-round stomach. "Does the senor still wish for me to wait for him?"

"That won't be necessary. He's ready to go." Leaving the door open wide, Kitty turned back to

Marcel. "It's your taxi driver. I informed him that you'll be leaving now."

His jaw dropped. Kitty found his initial loss for words quite satisfying.

Recovering, Marcel managed to sputter, "But . . . We have still to talk."

"As far as I'm concerned, everything's been said." Kitty walked over to usher him to the door. "And you have a plane to catch. Here"—she paused to tug the diamond off her finger—"take this with you."

When she offered it to him, Marcel simply stared at her in shock. She had to actually open his hand and press the ring into his palm.

Even then he didn't appear to believe her. "You return my ring? I do not understand."

"That doesn't surprise me in the least."

"But—"

Kitty could see him frantically searching for words. "It must be obvious that I wouldn't make a suitable wife for you. And the thought of marrying a bigoted snob like you makes me sick."

In an indignant huff, he opened his mouth to object. Kitty didn't give him a chance to speak as she bodily pushed him out the door.

"Good-bye, Mr. Chocolate. Knowing you has been very enlightening and bittersweet," she added, unable to resist the analogy. "More bitter than sweet, actually, rather like your chocolate."

Marcel reacted instantly to that criticism. "Boulanger chocolate is of the finest quality."

"It's a pity the same can't be said about the family who makes it."

Across the courtyard, Kitty noticed that Sebastian was now standing outside the opened French doors to the kitchen area. As before, he was dressed in his work chinos, a cup of coffee in his hand, still without shirt or shoes.

"As much as I would enjoy trading insults with you, I really need to excuse myself." Her smile was all saccharin. "You see, I left some things at Sebastian's last night that I really need to pick up."

"Last night?" As understanding dawned, Marcel's expression turned thunderous.

"Yes, last night," Kitty repeated happily, then taunted, "I hope you don't expect me to draw you a picture. Sebastian's the artist, not me."

With that, she walked away from him, this time for good and without a single regret.

Chapter Six

The courtyard echoed with the sound of Marcel's hard-striding footsteps as he stalked to the idling taxi trailed by the slower-walking cabdriver. It was a sound that Kitty rather liked, and one that was punctuated by the creak of hinges and the metallic slam of the vehicle door.

Without so much as a backward glance, she walked directly to the gnarled lilac bush that towered by the corner of the studio. She was conscious of Sebastian watching her while she retrieved the bundle of clothes from beneath its lower branches.

"Mr. Chocolate didn't stay long," Sebastian observed when she emerged from behind the bush.

"There was no reason for him to stay." Kitty brushed a leaf off her shoulder.

"I see he took his ring with him." He used the coffee mug to gesture to her bare ring finger.

"I insisted on it," she replied, then added quickly, "But don't start thinking you had anything to do with that decision. Because you didn't. There were simply too many important issues that Marcel and I couldn't agree on." Out in the street, the taxi backfired and rumbled away. Staring after it, Kitty couldn't resist adding a parting shot, one laced with thinly veiled sarcasm. "And I wasn't about to change just to be worthy of being his wife."

"I'm not trying to start another fight by saying this," Sebastian remarked, "but he is the one who wasn't worthy of you."

Everything softened inside her at the unexpected compliment. Kitty flashed him a warm smile. "Thank you."

"For what? It's the truth."

"I know, but it's still nice to hear someone else say it."

"Even me?" Sebastian teased.

"Even you," Kitty replied, then paused thoughtfully. "You know something else? I really didn't like his chocolate all that well, either."

"I can guarantee it couldn't be as good as my hot chocolate."

She eyed him with irritation. "I should have known you wouldn't be able to resist making a reference of some sort to last night. Let's just forget about it, shall we? As far as I'm concerned, it was all a big mistake."

"I think you're a little mixed up. Getting engaged to Mr. Chocolate was the mistake."

"That was a mistake, all right. And I'm not going to compound it by getting baited into a long, fruitless discussion with you. So if you don't mind"— Kitty moved toward the open door—"I'll just get my things and leave."

"Help yourself." With a swing of the cup, Sebastian invited her inside the studio.

As she approached the French doors, she felt a sudden nervous fluttering in her stomach. Kitty hesitated briefly before crossing the threshold. When she stepped into the studio's kitchen area, her heart began to beat a little faster. She felt exactly like a criminal returning to the scene of the crime, as all her senses heightened.

Without looking, Kitty knew the minute Sebastian followed her inside, even though his bare feet made no sound at all on the tiled floor. His presence made the spacious studio seem much smaller and more intimate. Or maybe it was the sight of her silk and lace brassiere still hooked on a back corner of the sofa, combined with her own vivid recollections of last night's events.

"Would you like a cup of coffee?" Sebastian's question was accompanied by the faint sound of the glass coffee carafe scraping across its flat burner, an indication that he was refilling his own cup.

"No, thank you." Kitty snatched the bra off the sofa corner and stuffed it in with her other bundled garments.

"Are you sure? It's—"

"I'm positive." As she circled the sofa to the coffee table, Kitty was careful not to glance in the direction of the kiva and the Navajo-style rug on the floor in front of it.

"Suit yourself," Sebastian said with a shrug in his voice. "Do you know something that amazes me?"

"No, but I'm sure that you're going to tell me." Kitty was deliberately curt, inwardly aware it was a defense mechanism. It bothered her that she felt a need for it.

"It's the way you run straight here every time you break off a relationship with some guy."

"That's ridiculous." She scooped up her evening bag, the last of the items she'd left.

"Is it?" Sebastian countered. "Look at this morning. You barely gave Mr. Chocolate a chance to climb in his cab before you made a beeline over here."

"I'm here to collect my things. There's nothing strange about that," Kitty insisted, and automatically glanced around, double-checking to make certain nothing else of hers was lying about.

"What about all the other times?" he persisted.

"Actually, I've never given it any thought. And there haven't been that many 'other times,' " Kitty retorted.

"But why come here? An ex is usually the last person you would want to tell."

"We are far from being enemies, Sebastian." She threw him a look of mild exasperation.

"But we aren't exactly friends, either," he pointed out. "There's always a subtle tension running between us. Why do you suppose that is?"

"I have no idea." It wasn't something Kitty wanted to discuss, and certainly not now. She moved toward the open French door, eager to leave now that she had retrieved all her things.

Sebastian stood by the kitchen counter, one hip propped against it. "Did you tell Mr. Chocolate you were with me last night?"

"It's really none of your business whether I told him or not."

Kitty wished that she had left by the front door.

It would have been a much shorter route, and one that wouldn't have taken her past Sebastian. But she was committed to her path. If she changed directions now, Sebastian might suspect her reluctance to be anywhere close to him.

"I'm afraid it is my business," he informed her with a hint of a smile. "You know how these Europeans can be. He might decide to challenge me to a duel, and I'd like to know whether or not I should admit you were here."

"He knows. Okay?" she retorted with impatience, quickening her steps to reach the door.

"I'll bet that made him mad." Sebastian didn't move an inch as she swept past him.

"He was furious. Does that make you happy?" She threw the last over her shoulder, then opened the door, safety only two feet away.

"You're a lot more trusting than I thought you would be."

His odd statement brought her up short. On the edge of the threshold, Kitty swung back, curious but wary. "What do you mean by that?"

"I thought for sure you'd check your evening bag and make sure I didn't take anything before you left." He continued to stand there, idly leaning against the counter.

"What would you take? There's nothing in it of any value except a credit card. Why would you want that?" As illogical as it seemed, Kitty knew Sebastian had taken something. Otherwise he wouldn't be drawing her attention to it now.

"I never said I took anything."

But that knowing gleam in his eye advised that she had better look. Kitty stepped over to the small breakfast table, deposited her wadded clothing on top of it, and unhooked the clasp on the slim bag. A quick check of the contents revealed nothing was missing. But there was something sparkling at the very bottom. She reached inside and pulled out a small solitaire ring—at least, it was small compared to the multicarat engagement ring Marcel had given her.

"Find something?" Sebastian wandered over to look.

Dumbfounded, Kitty dragged her gaze from the ring to his face. Staring in confusion, she murmured, "It's . . . It's my old ring. The one you gave me."

"So it is." He nodded in a fake show of confirmation, then met her eyes, a smile tugging at one corner of his mouth. "As I recall, you had a suggestion for what I could do with it when you gave it back to me. But I thought better of it."

"But what's it doing in my bag? Why did you put it there?" That was the part she didn't understand.

"It's very simple, really." He took the ring from her unresisting fingers, then reached for her left hand. "You seem to be determined to have some man's ring on your finger. I decided it might as well be mine."

As he started to slip the ring on her finger, Kitty jerked her hand away, pain slashing through her like a knife, bringing hot tears to her eyes.

"Everything's just one big joke to you," she lashed out angrily. "I'm sure you think this is funny. But it isn't. It's cruel and heartless and mean."

"This isn't a joke," Sebastian replied. "I'm dead serious."

"And pigs fly, too," Kitty retorted, resisting when

he attempted to draw her hand from behind her back.

"I don't know about pigs. I only know about you and me," he continued in that irritatingly reasonable tone. "Since you seem so eager to marry somebody, it might as well be me again."

"That's ridiculous," she said, her voice choking up. She tried to convince herself it was strictly from the depth of her outrage.

"Why is it ridiculous?" Sebastian countered, and pushed the ring onto her finger despite her attempts to stop him. "After all, it's better the devil you know than the Mr. Chocolate you don't."

"Will you stop this, Sebastian! I am not laughing." Kitty tugged at the ring, trying to pull it off. "If this is some twisted attempt to make me feel better about breaking things off with Marcel, it isn't working."

Sebastian trapped her face in his hands and forced her to look him squarely in the eye. "Be quiet for two seconds and listen. I want to marry you again. I don't know how much plainer I can say it."

For the first time Kitty suspected that he really meant it. Suddenly her thoughts were all in a turmoil. "But . . . It wouldn't work." She said it as much to convince herself as him. "We tried it before and—"

"So? We'll try it again." A soft light warmed his eyes and his easy smile was unconcerned.

"You're crazy," Kitty declared, more tempted by the thought than she wanted him to know. "Have you forgotten the way we argued all the time?"

"Not about important things," he replied.

"That isn't true." She was stunned that he could have forgotten their many stormy scenes.

"Think back," Sebastian countered. "Ninety percent of all our arguments were about trivial things—like the proper way a tube of toothpaste should be squeezed. The only time we fought about anything major was when we let our business differences interfere with our marriage."

"Business differences?" Kitty repeated incredulously. "We don't have any business differences."

"Not anymore, now that you've finally stopped trying to promote me and settled for pushing my paintings."

"I never—" But she had. It all came back in a rush. The endless fights over his refusal to attend his own showings or to do any kind of publicity to promote his work. "It used to infuriate me the way you made fun of everything I tried to do to see that you received the recognition you deserved as an artist."

"And you took it personally," Sebastian concluded.

"Yes."

"I'm sorry for that." He pushed back a wayward strand of hair, a loving quality in his touch.

"So am I." Everything smoothed out inside her.

"So what's your answer?"

"My answer?" For a second, Kitty didn't follow him.

"Are you going to marry me or not? After last night, you can't deny the fire's just as hot as it always was."

"I think both of us are crazy," she said instead.

"Why?"

"You for asking and me for accepting."

His mouth moved onto hers even as she rose to meet it. It was a kiss full of promise and passion, a pledge one to the other. For Kitty it was exactly like coming home.

Dear Readers,

Here in Branson, we are busy gearing up for another season. And I have been busy, too, working on another novel. Once in a while a story comes along that grabs you and simply won't let you go. "Story" might not be the right word. In this case, I think I should say "family." Judging from the letters I have received from you, the Calder family has become as special for you as they have for me.

By now, you must have guessed that I have written another Calder novel. This one is called GREEN CALDER GRASS. This time the story centers around Ty and Jessy whose lives become a bit more complicated when Tara returns to Montana. Yup, she's back and causing trouble again. But Tara isn't the only one from previous Calder novels who shows up at the Triple C. I'm not going to tell you who that person is. That's my surprise. As always, GREEN CALDER GRASS is packed with action, romance, danger, and tragedy, too. But the Calder family always survives.

I know you are going to love it. Happy reading,

Janet Dailey

Please turn the page for
a first look at the newest book in the acclaimed
Calder series of contemporary romances
from national best-selling author Janet Dailey

GREEN CALDER GRASS
(A Kensington Books hardcover
available in July 2002)

The grass ocean rippled cold under a strong summer sun. A dirt track cut a straight line through the heart of it. It was a small portion of the mile-upon-mile of private roads that crisscrossed the ranching empire of the Calder Cattle Company, better known in Montana as the Triple C.

It was a land that could be bountiful or brutal, a land that bent to no man's will, a land that weeded out the weak and faint of heart, tolerating only the strong.

No one knew that better than Chase Benteen Calder, the current patriarch of the Triple C and direct descendant of the first Calder, his namesake, who had laid claim to nearly six hundred square miles of this grassland. Its size was never something Chase Calder bragged about; the way he looked at it, when you were the biggest, everybody already knew it, and if they didn't they would soon be told.

And the knowledge would carry more weight if he wasn't the one doing the telling.

To a few, the enormity of the Triple C was a thing of rancor. The events of recent weeks were proof of that. The freshness of that memory accounted for the hint of grimness in his expression as Chase drove the ranch pickup along the hard-packed road, a rooster tail of dust pluming behind it. But the past wasn't something Chase allowed his mind to dwell on. Running an operation this size required a man's full attention. Even the smallest detail had a way of getting big if ignored. This land and a long life had taught him that, if nothing else.

Which is likely why his sharp eyes spotted the sagging wire caused by a tilting fence post. Chase braked the truck to a stop, but not before the pickup clattered over a metal cattle guard. He shifted into reverse, backed up to the cattle guard, stopped, and switched off the engine.

The full force of the sun's rays beat down on him as Chase stepped out of the truck, older and heavier but still a rugged and powerfully built man.

The sixty-plus years he carried had taken some of the spring from his step, added a heavy dose of gray to his hair, and grooved deeper creases into the sun-leathered skin around his eyes and mouth, giving a crustiness to his face, but it hadn't diminished the mark of authority stamped on his raw-boned features.

Reaching back inside the truck, Chase grabbed a pair of tough leather work gloves off the seat and headed toward the section of the sagging fence six posts away from the road. Never once did it occur to Chase to drive by and send one of the ranch hands back to fix the problem. With distances being what they were on the Triple C, that was the quickest way of turning a fifteen-minute job into a two-hour one.

With each stride he took, the brittle, sun-cured grass crackled underfoot. Its stalks were short and curly, matting close to the ground—native buffalo grass, drought tolerant and highly nutritious, the kind of feed that put weight on cattle and was a mainstay of the Triple C's century of success.

The minute his gloved hands closed around the post in question, it dipped drunkenly under the pressure. The three spaced strands of tightly strung barbed wire were clearly the only thing keeping it upright at all. Chase kicked away the matted grass at the base and saw that the wood had rotted at ground level.

This was one fence repair that wouldn't be a fifteen-minute fix. Chase glanced back toward the pickup parked on the road. There was a time when he would have carried steel fence posts and a roll of wire along with other sundry items piled in the truck bed. But on this occasion, there was only a tool box.

Chase didn't waste time with regret for the lack of a spare post. Instead, he ran an inspecting glance along the rest of the fence, following its steady march over the rolling grassland until it thinned into a single line. In that one, cursory observation, he noticed three more places where the fence curved out of its straight line. If three could be spotted with the naked eye, there were undoubtedly more. It didn't surprise him. Fence-mending was one of those never-ending jobs every rancher faced.

When he turned to retrace his steps to the pickup, he caught the distant drone of another vehicle. Automatically Chase scanned the narrow road in both directions without finding a vehicle in sight. But one was approaching, of that he had no doubt.

It was the huge sweep of sky that gave the illusion of flatness to the land beneath it. In reality the terrain was riven with coulees and shallow hollows, all of them hidden from view with the same ease that an ocean conceals its swales and troughs.

By the time Chase reached his truck, another ranch pickup had roared into view, coming from the west. Chase waited by the cab door, watching as the other vehicle slowed perceptibly then rolled to a stop behind Chase's pickup. The trailing dust cloud swept forward, briefly enveloping both vehicles before settling to a low fog.

Squinting against the sting of dust particles, Chase recognized the short, squatly built man behind the wheel as Stumpy Niles, a contemporary of his and the father of Chase's daughter-in-law. Chase lifted a hand in greeting and headed toward the truck.

Stumpy promptly rolled down the driver's side window and stuck out his head. "What's the problem, Chase?"

"Have you got a spare fence post in your truck? We have a wood one that's rotted through."

"Got it handled." Stumpy scrambled out of the truck and moved toward the tailgate with short, choppy strides. "Can't say I'm surprised. Just about all them old wood posts have started rottin'. It's gonna be one long, endless job replacin' 'em."

And expensive, too, Chase thought to himself, and

pitched in to help the shorter man haul the steel post as well as a posthole jobber out of the truck's rear bed. "I don't see where we have much choice. It's got to be done."

"I know." Already sweating profusely in the hot summer sun, Stumpy paused to drag a handkerchief from his pocket and mop the perspiration from his round, red face. "It ain't gonna be an easy job. The ground's as hard as granite. It's been nearly forty years since we've had such a dry spring. I'll bet we didn't get much more than an inch of moisture in all the South Branch section."

"It wasn't much better anywhere else on the ranch." Like Stumpy, Chase was remembering the last prolonged dry spell the ranch had endured.

Stumpy was one of the cadre of ranch hands who, like Chase, had been born on the Triple C. All were descended from cowhands who had trailed that original herd of longhorn cattle north, then stayed on to work for the first Calder. That kind of deep-seated loyalty was a throwback to the old days when a cowboy rode for the brand, right or wrong, through times of plenty and times of lean. To an outsider, this born-and-bred core of riders gave an almost feudal quality to the Triple C.

Chase shortened his stride to walk alongside Stumpy as the pair tracked through the grass to the sagging post. "Headed for The Homestead, were you?" Stumpy guessed, referring to the towering, two-story structure that was the Calder family home, erected on the site of the ranch's original homestead.

Chase nodded in confirmation. "But only long enough to clean up before I head into Blue Moon.

I'm supposed to meet Ty and Jessy for supper as soon as they're through at the clinic.''

"The clinic." Stumpy stopped short. "Jessy's all right, isn't she?''

"She's fine." Smiling, Chase understood Stumpy's fatherly concern. "Ty was the one in for a checkup.''

Stumpy shook his head at himself and continued toward the rotted post. "It's them twins she's fixin' to have. It's got me as nervous as a long-tailed cat in a roomful of rockin' chairs. There's no history of twins bein' born in either side of our family. Or, at least none that Judy and me know about,'' he said, referring to his wife.

"It's a first for the Calder side, too.'' Chase looked on while Stumpy set about digging a hole with the jobber. "Although I can't speak for the O'Rourke half.''

The comment was an oblique reference to his late wife Maggie O'Rourke. Even now, so many years after her death, he rarely mentioned her by name and only among the family. This belief that grief was a private thing was one of many codes of the Old West that continued to hold sway in the modern West, especially in Triple C country.

"Twins,'' Stumpy murmured to himself, then grunted from the impact of the twin blades stabbing into the hard, dry ground. He scissored the handles together to pick up the first scoopful of soil, then reversed the procedure to dump it to one side. "Look at that,'' he complained. "The top two inches is nothin' but powder. It's dry, I tell you. Dry.'' It was a simple observation that was quickly forgotten as he reverted to his original topic. "According to that ultrasound thing the doctor did, it's gonna be boys."

That was news to Chase. "I understood the doctor was only positive about one."

"Mark my words, they'll be boys," Stumpy declared with certainty, then chuckled. "If they take after their mother, she's gonna have her hands full. They'll be a pair of hell-raisers, I'll wager— into everything the minute you turn your back. Why, from the first minute Jessy started crawlin', she was out the door and into the horse pens. She dealt her momma fits. If you ask me, it's only right that she gets back some of her own." He glanced at Chase and winked. "It's for sure you won't be complaining anymore about The Homestead bein' too quiet since Cat got married and moved out. By the way, how's the little man doin' since . . . things quieted down."

The thwarted kidnapping of his five-year-old grandson Quint was another topic to be avoided from now on. But Chase knew it had left him three times as wary of those outside the Calder circle. After all, not only had the security of his home been breached, but Calder blood had been spilled as well.

"Kids are pretty resilient. Quint's doing fine."

"Glad to hear it."

"With any luck, Ty will finally be able to throw away that sling today and start using his arm again."

The twin spades of the jobber *whacked* into the hole. Stumpy rotated the handles back and forth to carve out another chunk of hard soil. After it was removed, Stumpy took a look and decreed, "That should be deep enough." He laid the jobber aside and took the steel fence post from Chase. "I thought the doctors originally told him he'd have to have that arm in a sling for six weeks. That bullet he took totally shattered his shoulder. Them surgeons had to rebuild the joint from scratch."

"True, but Ty figures four weeks is long enough. We'll see if he manages to convince the doctor of that."

Stumpy grinned. "He's probably hopin' he'll persuade the doc to split the difference and let him take it off in another week."

"Probably."

"That reminds me." Stumpy paused in his seedling of the post. "I ran into Amy Trumbo at noon. She tells me that O'Rourke's bein' released from the hospital today. Is that true?"

"Yeah, Cat went to get him. She should have him home before dark."

Chase remembered much too vividly that moment when he realized one of the kidnappers had shot his son. He saw again, in his mind, the brilliant red of all that blood, the desperate struggle to stop the bleeding and the gut-tearing mixture of rage and fear he'd felt.

His son Ty hadn't been the only one to suffer at the hands of the kidnapping duo; Culley O'Rourke, his late wife's brother, had also been shot—in his case, multiple times.

Stumpy wagged his head in amazement. "I still don't know how in hell O'Rourke survived."

"He's got more lives than a barn cat." Chase couldn't honestly say whether he was happy about it or not. There had never been any love lost between the two men. At the same time, he knew that O'Rourke lived only for Cat, Chase's daughter and O'Rourke's niece. Maybe it was Cat's uncanny resemblance to Maggie. And maybe it was just plain love. Whatever the case, O'Rourke was devoted to her. And like it or not, Chase had O'Rourke to thank for his part in getting young Quint back, unharmed.

"I guess O'Rourke'll be staying at the Circle Six with Cat and Logan." Stumpy scooped dirt into the hole around the post with his boot and tamped it down.

"That's Cat's plan anyhow. But you know what a lone wolf O'Rourke is," Chase said. "My guess is that it'll only be a matter of days before he's back on the Shamrock."

"Is he strong enough to look after himself?"

"Probably not, but that means Cat will burn up the road, running between Circle Six and Shamrock, making sure he's all right and has plenty of food on hand." Noting that Stumpy had the job well in hand, Chase took his leave. "I'd better get moving before Ty and Jessy wonder what happened to me."

As he took a step away, Stumpy called him back. "Say, I've been meanin' to tell you, Chase. Do you remember that young bull Ty sold to Parker from Wyoming last year? The one he wanted for his kid's 4-H project?"

"What about it?"

"He walked away with the grand championship at the Denver stock show."

"Where'd you hear that?" Chase frowned.

"From Ballard. He hit the southern show circuit this past winter, hirin' out to ride in cuttin' horse competitions and doin' some jackpot ropin' on the side. That's how he happened to be in Denver. He saw a good-lookin' bull with the Triple C tag and started askin' questions." Stumpy's grin widened. "It was grand champion, imagine that. And that bull was one of our culls—a good'n, but not the quality of the ones we kept." With a wave of his hand, he added, "You need to tell Ty about it. As proud as he is of the herd of registered stock we've put together, he'll get a kick out of it."

"I'll tell him," Chase promised.

The high drone of a jet engine whined through the air, invading the stillness of wind and grass. Automatically, Chase lifted his head and scanned the tall sky. Stumpy did the same as Chase and caught the metallic flash of sunlight on a wing.

"Looks like Dyson's private jet." Stumpy almost spat the name. "Coal tonnage must be down, and he's comin' to crack some whips. You notice he's makin' his approach over pristine range and not the carnage of his strip mines."

"I noticed." But Chase carefully didn't comment further.

"That's one family I'm glad we've seen the back of."

Chase couldn't have agreed more, but he didn't say so. Ty's marriage to Dyson's daughter Tara had been relatively brief. Looking back, Chase knew he had never truly approved of that spoiled beauty becoming Ty's wife, although Maggie had. To him, there had always been a cunning quality to her intelligence, a quickness to manipulate and scheme to get what she wanted. Thankfully Tara was part of the past, another subject to be put aside, but not forgotten.

Yet any thought of Tara and that troubled time always aroused a sore point. Chase had yet to obtain title to those ten thousand acres of government land within the Triple C boundaries. The memory of that hardened the set of his jaw, a visible expression of his deepening resolve.

Without another word to Stumpy, Chase walked back to the ranch pickup, climbed in, and took off in the direction of The Homestead.

I KNOW I LOVE CHOCOLATE

Sandra Steffen

Chapter One

The sea was calm as Sam O'Connor pulled away from the minuscule island he'd named Eagle Isle. Twenty minutes later he was within shouting distance of the mainland. Other than a sailboat a local teenager was doing his best to keep moving, the only boats in the harbor were those belonging to fishermen calling it a day. The woebegone teen waved with his cell phone, the slack orange sail a bright triangle against the dark blue of the Atlantic. Sam lifted a hand in greeting even as he eased out of the path of the noisy old lobster boat coming up close behind him. Seagulls swooped nearby, as accustomed as everybody else to the comings and goings of the people who lived and worked in this small harbor town along the rocky coast of Maine.

"Any luck?" Percival Parnell called, his eyes in a perpetual squint from so many years spent making his living on the sea.

Sam whisked his baseball cap off his head and

slapped it against his thigh. "Slim pickings, Percy. How about you?"

"More of the same, boy." The old lobsterman gestured toward shore. "Looks like you've got company."

Sam nodded, but Percy had already chugged ahead, not wanting or needing, certainly not expecting an explanation regarding the man waiting for Sam on the dock. Here in Midnight Cove, a man's business was a man's business. And that suited Sam to a tee.

A long time ago, he would have at the very least grimaced at the irony of that expression. Today, he simply replaced his cap, and stood, feet apart, his legs automatically adjusting to the rocking motion as his boat rode the wake of Percy's larger vessel.

Maybe old Percy didn't wonder what the man in a hundred-dollar shirt and polished leather shoes was doing here in Midnight Cove, but Sam had a pretty good idea. Not that he could turn tail and run now. No. The time to do that had been years ago, when he'd walked into his assigned dorm room on his first day at Harvard, and a tall lanky kid had stuck out his hand and said, "Grant Isaac Zimmerman the *Thurd.*" Oh, yeah, that would have been the time to run. After all, even a still-wet-behind-the-ears, middle-class kid from Ohio knew that a guy with three names could only be trouble.

Trouble was exactly what Grant had been. A thorn in Sam's side, a pain in the—well, that hadn't changed. The fact that Grant had become Sam's best friend was beside the point.

Sam eased up on the throttle as he neared the dock, then tossed the coiled rope toward his friend.

Grant caught it easily enough. After glancing down to make sure his clothes hadn't gotten dirty, he secured the rope to the piling, then brushed the residue from his hands.

Grant always managed to come out smelling like a rose. He hadn't even gotten dirty that first week at Harvard when some older frat boys had dubbed him Giz, for his initials, and Giz, er, Grant, had taken them on, three against one. At least, that was the score before Sam had entered the fight. It turned out that Grant had a pretty good right hook. Luckily, he also had an extremely influential father, because Grant Isaac Zimmerman *the second* had been the only thing that had stood between them and expulsion their first week at school.

Every now and then Grant reminded Sam how much he owed him, and every now and then Sam told Grant what he could do with his reminder. In truth, Sam owed Grant his life, but that had come later. Today, the two men simply eyed each other, Grant on the dock, Sam in the old lobster boat he'd christened *Birdie* his first summer here.

Grant's smile was begrudging. "A hundred thousand small towns in the world, and you pick one in a rocky cove practically inaccessible to ordinary man."

Sam almost grinned in spite of himself, because in any other circumstance, Grant Zimmerman would have been the first person to insist he was no ordinary man. In his world, he was extraordinary. A renowned psychiatrist, Grant liked to say he also dabbled in parapsychology and other unexplainable phenomena.

And Bill Gates dabbled in computers.

"You look good, Sam, for a bearded recluse."

Now, Sam did grin. Grant looked okay, too. Too
well dressed to blend in in Midnight Cove, but
okay. "Ever hear of Wal-Mart, Grant?"

"I read an article about it once. You finished
feeding your pet lobsters?"

Sam cut his boat's engine. "It's called baiting
the traps."

Gesturing with a sweep of a callus-free hand,
Grant said, "What *they* do is called baiting the
traps." He spoke quietly, so his voice wouldn't carry
on the quiet evening air. "Doesn't anybody here
notice that you never bring in any lobsters?"

Sam shrugged. It was a barbaric practice. They
didn't even kill the poor creatures before they
boiled them. "If folks notice, they don't mention
it, just like they don't mention that Old Man Potter
never actually sells any of the driftwood he keeps
hauling in from the ocean, or that his wife wears
her clothes inside out. The residents of Midnight
Cove don't seem to think it's strange that Pete
Jackson hasn't slept in a bed since he came back
from his stint in Vietnam, or that you show up here
once or twice every year in—" Sam waited to finish
until after he vaulted over the side of his boat and
landed on the dock a few feet from Grant. "Tell
me that isn't a designer imprint on your pocket."

Each took a moment to size up the other. Both
were thirty-six, both on the tall side. Sam was tan
and lean and rugged. Grant was fair and citified
to the bone.

"It's good to see you, Sam."

"You, too." It was true, even though Sam was
never thrilled with the reasons for Grant's rare visits
because they usually precipitated Sam's temporary
departure from this place that asked no questions.

Going elsewhere, even for a good cause, meant risking being discovered. "Let me finish securing the boat. Have you eaten?"

Grant shook his head.

"Do you want to talk at my place? I can throw some steaks on the grill."

"That depends. Have you shoveled your place out lately?"

"It's not that bad, but fine, we'll go on up to Dulcie's for some supper. On the way you can try to talk me into whatever you're going to try to talk me into this time."

"Have you gone into town lately?" Grant asked.

Sam hunkered down, eye level with the knot he was tying. "No, why?"

"Just wondering."

That was Sam's first clue that something wasn't quite as it seemed. Grant never "just wondered" about something. He analyzed things to death, studied, planned, but he didn't "just wonder."

"What's going on, Grant?"

"I want to talk to you about something. An amnesia patient. A woman. Early to mid-thirties. She calls herself Annie Valentine, but she pulled the last name out of thin air. She was brought to my attention by one of my colleagues because her case is atypical."

Grant waited while Sam finished securing his boat. Slowly rising to his feet, Sam brushed his hands on his jeans and finally asked, "What's so unusual about this Annie?"

They walked along the dock. "It isn't her case that's so unusual. It's the woman herself. Somebody hit her on the head with a blunt object before making off with her purse down in Boothbay Harbor nearly a month ago. Witnesses say she probably wouldn't have been harmed if she hadn't fought back. She woke up in the hospital. Instead of being terrified like most amnesia patients, she was spitting mad about the inconvenience."

"You sure her amnesia's legit?"

"We're certain she isn't faking that, yes."

Both men stepped off the dock, the soles of their shoes crunching on the crushed-shell path. "What else does she remember?" Sam was looking for the reason Grant had come to him, and the reason he was being so vague about it.

"She knows tidbits about a lot of things, but not much about herself. Besides her name, she knows she loves chocolate."

Sam stopped walking. "That's it? That's all you've got? She loves chocolate? Hell, what woman doesn't?"

Grant stopped, too, and turned to face his friend. "She has vague memories of a little girl she feels is her daughter."

Now they were getting somewhere. Sam often took cases involving children or people with families they couldn't remember. His last case had involved a dying man with ESP who had some unfinished business with his estranged son. Real uplifting, his work. "I take it she's spoken to the authorities."

"She's gone through every conventional channel as well as a few unconventional means to regain her memory."

Sam was about as unconventional as they came. One day he'd been just an average, everyday world-famous golf pro. The next day a bolt of lightning decided to dance a jig on an iron sculpture a few feet in front of him. Sam didn't remember hitting the ground. When he woke up, doctors said it was a miracle he was alive. At the time, they hadn't known the half of it.

He and Grant started walking again. By the time they reached Harbor Avenue, Sam knew most of the pertinent facts about Annie Valentine, but still wasn't sure what any of it had to do with him. According to Grant, her psychiatrists were fairly certain her amnesia didn't stem from a repressed past. Her neurologist believed it was most likely due to the trauma to her head. It was possible, probable even, that her memory would return in time. Evidently, Annie Valentine wasn't the "wait and see" type.

Sam thought about the drastic measures some people were willing to take in order to regain their lives, and the drastic measures he'd taken to disappear from his. "Did you drive all the way up here to ask me to help her?"

"Not exactly."

The scent of battered shrimp, clam chowder, and strong coffee wafted from Dulcie's Diner before they entered through the screen door. The way Grant glanced around the room at the handful of diners made Sam wonder what he was looking for. "Well?" Sam prodded.

Seemingly satisfied about something, Grant said, "I'll tell you the rest over dinner. Why don't you find us a table. I'll be right back."

While Grant sauntered toward the rest room, Sam removed his hat and ambled on into the square dining room. Grant had once said the place was decorated in early squalor. Sam liked it. Besides, people didn't come here for ambience.

They came to eat. The food was good, the floors and tables clean.

The supper crowd usually thinned out early, and today was no exception. Since the middle-aged waitress was nowhere in sight, Sam chose a table in the elevated portion of the room, away from the others, where he and Grant could talk in private. Staring out the window at the quiet street, Sam wondered about Annie Valentine. If she did indeed have a young daughter, it would explain her willingness to try "anything" to speed up the process in regaining her memory. It didn't explain why the authorities could find no missing person's report on a woman fitting her description.

"Can I start you off with something to drink?"

Instead of Dulcie's sister, Trudy, Sam found himself staring into the face of a waitress he'd never seen before. Close to thirty, she wasn't pretty, exactly. Her eyes were a little too closely set, her lips a little too full, but she was a lot easier on the eyes than Trudy, who was built more like a Mack truck and had a face that looked as if she made a habit of kissing one.

"Sir?"

Oh, yes, this woman was a lot easier on the eyes than good old Trudy. "You must be new here," he said.

This woman was on the curvy side, five-four or five-five. Her dark hair had been secured on top of her head with a simple clasp and was slowly losing the battle to gravity. "This is my second day. It's tougher than it looks."

Her voice was deep and sultry, and stirred up something restless in the pit of his stomach, reminding him of how many days he spent alone and how many nights he spent putting only his boat to bed.

"Do you know what you want?" she asked.

It had been a long time since he'd given much thought to what he wanted. . . .

"Is something wrong?" she asked.

Realizing he was staring, Sam shook his head. She smiled, and that restlessness moved into more dangerous territory.

"Take your time. This is the longest I've stood still in hours. Dulcie hired me yesterday to help with the breakfast and lunch crowd. The regular waitress came down with a migraine so I'm doing a double shift. The cash register hates me and my feet are killing me like you would not believe." She looked surprised, as if she'd told him far more than she'd intended and didn't know why.

Sam knew why. People told the truth around him, whether they wanted to or not.

Out of the corner of his eye, he noticed Grant walking toward the table. "Just bring out two glasses of lemonade for now. We can order later."

"Two lemonades coming right up."

She bustled off in one direction as Grant strolled over from another. "Who was that?" he asked the instant he sat down.

"Beats me, but that's some walk, isn't it?"

"She didn't give you her name?"

If Sam hadn't been so busy watching the new waitress sashay into the kitchen, he might have thought twice about Grant's obtuse question. By the time she emerged, a heavy-looking tray held tightly in her hands, Grant was watching her, too. "You don't know her?"

"She said she's new."

Sam was pretty sure he heard Grant mutter something eloquent, like "Uh-oh."

Holding the tray in front of her, she didn't see the four-inch step elevating this portion of the floor from the other half of the room. She stumbled up it with all the grace of a person tripping on a crack in the sidewalk.

She managed to regain her footing, but there wasn't much she could do about the two desserts that went flying off the tray. One missed Grant by a fraction. The other one headed straight for Sam. He jumped to his feet, but he was too late. The bowl upended on his chest and glided down the front of him, finally clattering to the floor.

"Oh my gosh!" Flustered, she looked all around. "Oh, dear." Her hands were full, her movements jerky as she took a step in one direction, then another. "Here." She shoved the heavy tray into Grant's hands. "Hold this."

Turning to Sam, she grabbed the towel that had been tucked inside the waistband of her apron. "Look at this mess." She began dabbing at the cool, gooey mixture on the front of his shirt. "Why on earth is there a step there? How do waitresses do this?"

Since most of the blood had drained out of Sam's brain, all he could do was stand there and take her ministering like a man, which, among other things meant that his breathing hitched a little more every time her hand inched lower.

Pausing somewhere in the vicinity of his belt, she looked up at him. "Maybe you'd better take it from here." A devilish look came into her eyes, and the imp smiled. "This is a family establishment, after all."

She folded the dirty portion of the towel inside, placed it in Sam's hand, then turned back to Grant. Chatting as if waitresses told Grant Isaac Zimmerman the third to hold their trays every day, she deposited their glasses of lemonade on the table, then relieved him of the tray. Turning to Sam again, she said, "It looks like you've gotten most of it. A pity, too. It was chocolate."

Something nagged the back of Sam's mind.

One of the old fishermen sitting near the front of the diner called, "Bring that pot of coffee this-a-way, would you Annie!"

The nagging moved up, front and center. Annie?

She blew a shock of coffee-colored hair out of her eyes, then bustled away.

Slowly, Sam looked at Grant. "That's Annie?"

Grant studied him in that quiet way that saw too much. "Quite a coincidence, wouldn't you say?"

"The woman with amnesia is right here in Midnight Cove."

"Yes."

Sam looked over his shoulder. Annie was busy splashing coffee into Clem Peterson's cup and saucer. "Why didn't you tell me?"

"I didn't know she'd taken a job here," Grant said. "I was told she was working at a clothing store. Damn. Now she's seen you."

There was something in the tone of Grant's voice that set off an alarm in Sam's head. "You didn't come here to ask me to help her?"

Grant shook his head. "I wouldn't have been too late if you had a phone."

"Too late for what?"

"Perhaps you should sit down."

Sam really did not like the sound of that. He

didn't like the expression on Grant's face, either. Taking the seat he'd vacated when that pudding had gone flying, Sam said, "Don't tell me she's a wanted felon."

"Oh, for heaven's sake," Grant said. "If we knew she was a wanted felon, we would know who she is. They ran her fingerprints. As far as they can tell, she's never committed a crime, at least not a serious one. However, the psychological workups my colleague ran indicated that she . . ." Grant's voice trailed away.

Sam's eyes narrowed a little more with every passing second. "The psychological workups indicated that she what?"

"Those tests are never conclusive, of course, but it does appear as though Annie Valentine shares some strong personality traits with . . ."

Sam waited.

"With reporters, Sam."

A gong went off inside Sam's head.

"It doesn't mean she is a reporter, mind you. It just means she might be."

Sam stared at his untouched lemonade. Given a choice, he would take a wanted felon over a reporter any day. A person knew where he stood with wanted felons. Reporters were a different breed entirely. They pretended. They lied. And either they didn't know that what they did was wrong, or they didn't care. Either way, "reporter" was the dirtiest word in the English language.

Sam's newfound power had scared the living hell out of him. When news of his "abilities" had first leaked out, the press had hunted him. One day, he'd been the number-one golfer in the world. Suddenly, people blurted out the truth when in his presence. Half the world had wanted to prove he was a fake. It was the other half that had finally ruined him. Dirtbag attorneys, wives of cheating husbands, people involved in law suits, statesmen, victims of crimes, and every lowlife with a score to settle wanted to enlist his "services." They were like sharks on a feeding frenzy in a bloody ocean. He was dinner. And every reporter alive wanted the credit for serving him up on a silver platter.

His career in pro golf went down the tubes as people screamed out at him from the sidelines, searched him out wherever he went. He lost his concentration and his edge. Once, the media had been his biggest fans. Reporters had since become his worst enemies. He'd gotten no sleep and less peace. Until six years ago when he'd come here, that is. Here in Midnight Cove, he'd found peace. He had his boat, his house, the island, his anonymity. Quite by accident, he'd found that his new-found power had a quieter side. Not only did guilty people speak the truth when he was near, but an amnesia patient he'd happened to befriend had recalled things, true things, about his past. Although there was always a risk of being discovered, today Sam occasionally helped people remember. But he did so on his own terms, in his own way.

He'd read once that there were four great mysteries in America: *Who really killed JFK? Was Marilyn Monroe's death truly a suicide? Is Elvis dead?* And last but not least . . . *Where is Logan Samuel Oliver Connors?*

Sam felt for his hat and rose to his feet. Without a word, he started toward the door. He was three steps away from freedom when his progress was halted by a hand placed gently on his arm.

"Sir?"

Three measly steps and he would have been gone. How in hell the woman could trip over a step, then effortlessly get between him and the door was beyond him. "What is it?"

She removed her hand from his arm. A lot of people would have taken a giant step backward. Annie cleared her throat, looked up at him, and held her ground. "Um, that is, I was wondering . . . Was something wrong with your lemonade?"

He'd forgotten about the damn lemonade. He reached into his back pocket for his wallet.

"No, no. Don't worry about paying for it. Under the circumstances, it's only fair that I take it out of my wages. At this rate, I'll owe Dulcie money come payday."

Sam knew he was staring. He just couldn't seem to help it.

"I was wondering if you would do me a favor." She blew dark wisps of hair out of her eyes and ignored the people calling for refills and seconds.

A reporter? Sam thought. He didn't know about that, but Annie Valentine sure wasn't going to last long as a waitress.

"I know, I know," she said. "It boggles the mind that I have the nerve to ask after that little accident with the pudding, but I really am sorry about your shirt."

"What favor?" he asked.

She wet her lips and glanced toward the kitchen. "I was hoping you wouldn't mention this unfortunate little incident to Dulcie. I doubt anyone else will. This town isn't much for gossip. I've already tried and failed at three other jobs since becoming stranded up here. This is my last resort. If I lose this one, I'll be forced to apply at the fish processing plant." She gazed up at him beseechingly. "And I don't even like fish."

Something went warm inside him, and he found himself saying, "It was an accident, like you said. Don't worry. Your secret's safe with me."

"Thank you very much." Casting him a smile that made a man rethink the way he measured beauty, she turned on her heel and went back to work.

Sam didn't remember walking outside. It didn't take long for Grant to follow.

"What was that all about?" Grant asked.

Sam took his time putting on his hat and adjusting the bill. "She doesn't like fish."

Grant was quiet as he digested the relevance in that. Finally he said, "Are you considering helping her?"

Sam's first instinct was to say no. Not just no. Hell no. "It's like you said. She's already seen me. Ultimately, the damage could already be done." He rubbed at a knot in the back of his neck.

Grant glanced at his Rolex.

"What's the matter?" Sam asked. "Are you in a hurry to get back to Boston? Do you have a meeting or something?"

"I'm afraid it's more complex than that."

Sam took a closer look at his fair-headed friend. "The only thing more complex than one of your meetings is a woman."

Grant didn't reply, which was extremely telling.

"Don't tell me you're seeing someone."

Suddenly Grant was the one kneading the back of his neck. "She says I'm stuffy."

Sam fought the urge to grin. "Sounds like you're going to need your strength. You might as well grab a burger at Rocky's Tavern before you head back to Boston."

Grant made a sound only a true Boston-born-and-bred blue blood could make. "A burger at an establishment called Rocky's Tavern. How could I refuse?"

Before setting off across the street, Sam said, "You know something, Grant? You are stuffy."

An hour later Grant was digging in his pocket for antacid tablets with one hand and punching in the code to unlock his car door with the other. "What will you do about Annie Valentine?"

Sam shrugged. "I don't know yet."

"Let me know if there's anything I can do to help."

"I will."

"Good luck, Sam."

"Some people don't believe in luck."

"Some people don't believe in a lot of things."

They shared a long look and a brief smile. Sam stood back while Grant got in his Porsche and drove away.

Lost in thought, Sam stared at the street leading out of town.

An amnesia patient was right here in Midnight Cove. For once, he could help her without leaving his quiet haven. He couldn't help but wonder if this little harbor town would still be a quiet haven after Annie Valentine left.

Chapter Two

Annie hiked along an unmarked lane that ran between two side streets named after trees. By the time she came out on Main Street, which ran the entire length of the downtown district of Midnight Cove—all two blocks of it—she'd seen every last street and lane in town.

She'd set out to get lost an hour ago. It wasn't easy to get lost in a village this small. Apparently it wasn't easy to be found, either. At least, no one had found her. It pained her to think that that was because no one was looking for her. Banishing that thought, she continued walking.

It had been a rainy, dismal day. The clouds had finally moved on and the sun was shining, now that it was almost time for it to set. Like all the streets running east and west, Main Street dead-ended at Harbor Avenue. She could smell the ocean from anywhere in town, but from this end of Midnight Cove she could see it, too. Deciding that it was probably inevitable that she would end up there, she crossed the street and headed toward the harbor.

She'd read that the ocean instilled romance in the human heart. Gathering her hair in one hand, she stared out across the water, trying to remember where she'd read that. Had she seen it in a book, a magazine, at a school or college somewhere? She thought. She concentrated. She felt a headache starting. But not a single memory came. It was like cramming for an exam from a notebook full of blank pages.

Her sigh was lost in the incessant breeze, the crashing waves, and the screeching cries of the gulls. Leaving her hair to the mercy of the wind, she hooked her thumbs inside two small pockets at the waist of her long, loose-fitting skirt, and slowly wandered to the edge of a series of docks connected by narrower structures that looked like bridges. Several fishing boats were already parked, if that was what they called it, and a few others were heading in.

One thing she felt all the way to her bones: She'd never lived near the ocean. That left an awful lot of places in between.

The wind blew her hair into her face again, blinding her and making her wish she'd put it up before leaving the one-room apartment where she'd been living these past two weeks. She supposed she could have turned around and gone back to her room. And do what? Sit around feeling sorry for herself? That wasn't her style. At least she didn't think it was.

No. She knew it wasn't. She just didn't know how she knew. But she would. It had only been three and a half weeks. She recalled more every day. The important memories hadn't come back yet, but just two days ago she'd remembered that she didn't like fish. Saying that out loud in a town whose men earned a living off the sea had been a terrible faux pas that could have turned around and bitten her in the butt. Luckily, the fisherman she'd blurted it to hadn't looked offended.

He hadn't looked like a fisherman, either.

Something about his gray eyes had left her feeling strangely unsettled. It wasn't as if she'd never seen gray eyes before. She couldn't actually *remember*, but surely she'd come across other people who had gray eyes. She'd thought about those eyes for two days. In fact, she'd been thinking about them just this morning when she'd been topping off Wilhemina Jones's coffee, which was what had gotten her into her latest predicament.

"Did you come all the way out here to sigh like that?"

First of all, Annie hadn't realized she'd sighed. Secondly, she hadn't known she wasn't alone on the pier or the dock or the wharf. Oh, whatever. The gray-eyed man who'd ended up wearing chocolate pudding on his shirt two nights ago was tinkering with something on his boat. While seagulls screeched in the distance and waves slapped the boats tied nearby, she strolled closer.

He had to have looked up earlier in order to have known she was there, but she reached the edge of the dock before he looked at her again, his eyes in the shadow of the bill of a baseball cap that had seen better days.

"You have the stormiest eyes." Her hand flew to her mouth before she could stop it. "I mean gray. You have the grayest eyes." Stormy gray. She'd convinced herself it had been an optical illusion. He was watching her, his eyes as changeable as the ocean behind him. It hadn't been an illusion at all.

Shrugging as if he didn't much care what color his eyes were, he said, "You're not working the supper crowd tonight?"

She sighed again. "Or the lunch crowd, or the breakfast crowd."

"You've had the day off?"

"Guess you could say I'm between jobs again."

He wiped his hands on a stained cloth with a precision she found mesmerizing. His hair was short, the portion not covered by his hat a sandy brown. His beard and mustache were neatly trimmed, and a shade darker than his hair. His jeans were faded, his T-shirt white, his boots well worn. The man had rugged down to an art form.

"Dulcie let you go?"

"I don't think she wanted to, but Wilhemina Jones was pretty mad, and Dulcie didn't want a law suit. Everybody sues everybody these days. I guess I don't blame Dulcie. She's probably afraid of a lawsuit like that one years ago, when a man sued that fast-food restaurant because he burned himself on a cup of their coffee."

He'd finished wiping the grime from his hands and was watching her closely. Distributing his weight to one foot, he tugged his hat a little lower on his forehead. "You don't seem too upset."

Annie slanted him a smile that was surely brimming with excitement. "I just remembered that old lawsuit. I don't know if you've heard, but I have amnesia."

He continued looking at her in that quiet, thoughtful way he had. "Yeah, I heard. What happened at Dulcie's?"

She rested a hip against a post that had a rope wrapped around it. Holding her hair out of her eyes, she looked out across the water. "I was running back and forth between the kitchen and dining room, being careful, mind you, of that step that gave me trouble the other night. I mean, I may be a little uncoordinated at times, but I learn from my mistakes. Anyway, Wilhemina stopped me and insisted I top off her coffee. I should have told her I'd be back in a second, but she stuck her coffee cup out and I thought I could fill it without dropping the tray."

Annie peered at the islands dotting the horizon. There were more than three thousand islands off the coast of Maine. That was another thing she knew without knowing how she knew. If only she could remember her real last name.

"Did you drop the tray?"

"What? Oh. If only I had. The last I knew, the carafe was half empty, but I guess Dulcie filled it when I wasn't looking, and the coffee came out pretty fast and I ended up spilling some."

"She fired you for spilling coffee?"

"Not exactly. I apologized up and down. The doctor said the burns were only first degree."

"Burns?"

Annie nodded. "Wilhemina doesn't have a high tolerance for pain. Poor Dulcie hated to have to do it, but Wilhemina insisted she wouldn't frequent the diner as long as I worked there. Dulcie offered to give me severance pay. I couldn't accept, of course. I mean, I'd only worked there for three days. That would have felt like charity—or worse, it would have been like those parting gifts they give to people who lose on game shows. Ever notice how the contestants always smile and insist they're thrilled with a board game and some microwave popcorn instead of the twenty grand they almost won? I don't think I could do that, do you?"

"To tell you the truth," he said, looking at her in a manner that drove home the fact that she'd been rambling, "I've never thought about it."

"I guess a person thinks about a lot of things when she doesn't know who she is." Since there weren't a lot of ways to reply to that, she said, "As I was saying, I didn't accept charity from Dulcie. I didn't accept it from Carol Ann, either."

She watched two seabirds raising a ruckus over a dead fish. It made her really glad she wasn't a bird. Or a fish either, for that matter.

"What happened at the dress shop?"

"Pretty much the same thing."

"You spilled coffee on somebody at the dress store, too?"

She turned her head so she could see his expression. He was watching her closely. If she wasn't careful she was going to get lost in his gray eyes. Just to be on the safe side, she wrapped an arm around the post so she wouldn't topple into the ocean. "I didn't *burn* Essie Summers. Well, the truth might have scorched her ears a little, but she asked how she looked in that pantsuit."

"What did you say?"

"I told her the purple polka dots made her look as big as her house."

"Essie lives in the biggest house in Midnight Cove."

Annie nodded forlornly. "She and her husband have a lot of money, and apparently she spends a good deal of it on the clothes Carol Ann stocks, regardless of how she looks in them."

He chuckled, and vaulted off his boat, landing lightly for a man his size. "It'll be dark soon. I'll walk you back to town."

She stared up at him. "I don't know if walking with a man who wears a beard is a good idea."

"I beg your pardon?"

"Beards always make me wonder what a man's hiding."

Sam controlled his gasp, but Annie didn't. She clamped her hand over her mouth and took a backward step. If he hadn't grabbed her, she would have fallen off the dock. She appeared horrified by what she'd just said. Sam had grown accustomed to the way people blurted exactly what was on their minds when in his presence, but he understood how disconcerting it could be.

"I didn't mean that the way it sounded."

"It's all right."

"It's not all right. My mouth is going to be the death of me."

She sounded breathless. Her lips were lush, full, soft looking. She wasn't wearing lipstick. Nasty-tasting stuff, lipstick. He spent far too long wondering what her lips would taste like without it.

"I promise I'll stay in the center of the dock."

"What?"

"You can let me go now. I'll make a conscious effort not to fall in the ocean. Even if I did, I can swim." Her eyes got large again. "That's something else I didn't know I knew." She smiled. "Uh, about letting me go?"

He hadn't realized he was still holding her. At least the realization hadn't made it to his brain. Other areas were all too aware.

She eased backward, leaving him with little choice but to release her. She glanced at the water, and then finally back at him. "If your offer to walk me back to town still stands, I'd like that."

A fishing boat's engine drowned out anything else she might have added. As the boat chugged closer, Sam and Annie made their way toward safer ground. "Tell me about your amnesia."

"There isn't much to tell. I've tried hypnosis. I've been studied, analyzed, prodded. About the only thing they haven't done to me is whack me upside the head with a medium-size club. That's what put me in this situation to begin with."

"Do you remember getting hit on the head?"

"No, but evidently it happened three and a half weeks ago, while I was vacationing at a resort harbor south of here. I woke up in a hospital with a screaming headache, a lump on my head the size of Cleveland, and no memory of how I got it."

He took a moment to sort through the information. "If you'd been vacationing at a resort, why did you come here?"

They stepped off the dock and onto the crushed-shell path that led up the hill toward Harbor Avenue. "I followed my instincts. I know it's not much, but they're all I have. I'm glad I did, too. Since arriving here, I've remembered more every day. Oh, I haven't recalled the important stuff, but when you don't know anything, even the bits and pieces mean the world."

Sam understood how much the little things could mean.

Instead of going directly to the building that housed her room over the dress shop on Main Street, they turned right at Harbor Avenue and then left at Jefferson. She glanced at the street sign and for no apparent reason said, "Thomas Jefferson was born in Virginia in 1743."

"You don't say."

She shook her head and sputtered, "I don't even know where or when I was born and yet I know that."

"You don't know how old you are?"

"I suppose that could have its advantages. I wouldn't be lying if I said I was twenty-five."

"Are you?"

"Am I what? Lying or twenty-five?" Annie peered down the street at the Cape Cod–style houses sitting cozily behind their picket fences. The low drone of a lawn mower was coming from a block away. A handful of kids were tossing basketballs at a dilapidated hoop in a driveway across the street. Bikes were left on kickstands; dogs snoozed in the shade. Two old ladies in orthopedic shoes, their hose rolled down just below their knees stood talking over a low hedge.

"It's an ordinary evening in an ordinary town, or least it might be if I could figure out who I am."

She hadn't meant to say that. She didn't want pity. She glanced at her companion and found him looking at her as if he were unsure exactly how to take her. It occurred to her that a lot of people looked at her that way. Not just here in Midnight Cove, but . . . someplace else. It was as if her memory was right there on the tip of her mind, just waiting to reveal itself to her.

She slanted him another smile. "I know I'm not

a habitual liar. It was my honesty that got me fired from the dress shop, remember? And I don't think I'm twenty-five, either. I feel like I've lived more than that."

She didn't know how on earth her hand ended up on his arm, but she didn't readily remove it. It made her feel connected in a way she hadn't been since she woke up in the hospital with a bump on her head and a huge blank spot between her ears. He felt warm, solid, male. Perhaps he wasn't adverse to her touch, because he made no move to withdraw his arm. Instead, he reached over with his other hand, touching a blunt-tipped finger to one of three charms dangling from the gold bracelet on her wrist.

Again, she found it mesmerizing to watch his hands. "I was wearing this charm bracelet when I woke up in the hospital near Boothbay Harbor. Evidently, my attacker tried to steal this, too. His efforts left a bruise on my wrist. The bracelet was so sturdy the links held. I think that says something about me. Do you know anybody who's going to the fish processing plant?"

He blinked, his only indication that he was having trouble following her jump to unconnected topics. "You said you don't like fish."

Finally, someone who understood her. "I have to do something to earn a living while I wait for my memory to return."

They were back on Main Street. The sun was behind them, their shadows so long and light they glided over the sidewalk like spaceships riding a current of air. Sam slowed near a bench across the street from the building that housed Annie's tiny efficiency apartment. A few steps ahead of him, Annie stopped, too.

"Thank you for the escort, and forget I mentioned the fish processing plant. I'll find someone who's going there and wouldn't mind giving me a ride." Looking both ways, she stepped off the curb.

"Annie, wait."

She glanced over her shoulder, turning first her head and then the rest of her. Sam had noticed that she was wearing a simple green skirt and matching top the first moment he'd seen her walking toward him on the dock half an hour ago. She looked damn good in green.

"Yes?"

If he had to choose one word as his favorite it would have to be "yes," no matter what the language, especially when it was delivered in a voice deep and sultry enough to stir up that pleasing restlessness that was always laying in wait in the pit of a man's stomach. Settling his hands comfortably on his hips, he said, "There must be some other type of work you could do that doesn't involve deboning cod."

She tilted her head as she looked at him. Gesturing toward the handful of stores lining the quiet street, she shrugged. "I've already inquired everywhere I could think of. I even considered asking Wilhemina if she needed a temporary housekeeper, but I'm pretty sure I burned that bridge when I sloshed hot coffee on her sturdy wrist."

"That's not a bad idea."

For once, she was the one who appeared confused. "What's not a bad idea?"

"Working as a housekeeper of sorts."

"Do you know anyone who might hire me?"

He nodded.

She stared at him, as if waiting for him to continue. "Who?" she finally asked.

"Me."

She stayed where she was in the empty street. "You mean it?"

Sam nodded. He'd lost his mind. Any minute now he was going to care. "It isn't brain surgery, but it's honest work."

She crossed her arms, drawing her shirt tight beneath her breasts. "When do you want me to start?"

"Tomorrow morning?" he asked. Since it didn't feel right to be conducting a job interview while she stood in the middle of the street, he joined her on the pavement. With a hand placed gently at her elbow, he escorted her across. "First of all," Sam said upon reaching the other side, "you don't know me from Adam." He hoped. "You should ask for character references."

"Dulcie vouched for you."

The old-fashioned streetlight on the corner flickered as it slowly came on. That easily, it went from day to night. "What did Dulcie say?"

"She said you're not married, for one thing." She looked at him. "Why, are you?"

"No," he answered. "Are you?"

She shook her head. And then she laughed. "I'm not married. I wondered about that."

"What else did Dulcie say about me?"

"Not much. Midnight Cove, Maine, might as well be called Mind-Your-Own-Business, Maine. She did mention that you could put your boots under her bed anytime."

Sam had the uncanny feeling that Annie was

putting his face to memory. "I hate to be the one to break this to you," he said, "but Dulcie says that about every man."

"I guess I'm just going to have to trust my instincts then, won't I? Perhaps we should at least be formally introduced." She held out her hand. "I'm Annie Somebody-or-Other."

He took her hand. "And I'm Sam O'Connor. Would you like to take a look at my house before you commit?"

"It's that bad?"

"A friend of mine refuses to set foot in the place."

"The man in the Gucci shoes?"

"You're very astute."

"I am?" And then, "That's a good thing, right?"

Annie thought that if he had nodded any slower, it couldn't have passed for a nod.

"Is he your attorney?"

"Why do you say that?"

"He has that rich, useless look about him." She clamped her hand over her mouth. "Sorry. Surely I'll wear out that phrase."

"He's a friend from college. And he's not an attorney."

She wound up getting lost in the way he was looking at her. It required effort to drag her gaze away. Other than the handful of cars parked in front of the tavern on the next block, there wasn't another soul on Main Street tonight. "They'll be rolling up the sidewalks soon."

Something about the way he peered up and down the street caused Annie to wonder what he was thinking. For once, she managed to keep from blurting the question out loud. He gave her brief directions to his house. Annie reached into her pocket for her key and strolled toward the lighted alleyway that led to the stairs, only to pause. Looking back at him she said, "Sam?"

He stopped, too. "Yes?"

"What did you study?"

"When?"

"In college. You said you and the Gucci man were friends from college."

She couldn't see his eyes from here, but she could feel the intensity in his gaze as he said, "I majored in English."

"No, kidding? So did I." She knew her mouth was gaping, but she didn't have it in her to care. "I studied English in college. Well, I'll be darned. Good night, Sam O'Connor. I'll see you tomorrow."

Sam's blood pressure was on the rise. He could hear it pounding in his ears. Annie Whatever-Her-Last-Name-Was had a razor sharp mind. Astute and intuitive, she homed in on information with ease. If she wasn't already a reporter, she'd missed her calling. And he'd just invited her to work for him, to poke through his house and his life.

She was strolling away, on up the metal steps to her apartment. He reacted far more strongly than he should have to a woman wearing loose-fitting clothes and plain leather sandals. Which meant that he was reacting to the woman *in* the clothes. He should have been thinking about getting his head examined. Instead, he was thinking about seeing her again. That kind of thinking could be dangerous to a man who was going to have to keep his wits about him. Very dangerous, indeed.

* * *

Annie's efficiency apartment consisted of a square living area that contained a table and one chair, a sofa that doubled as a bed, a little refrigerator, a microwave oven, and a tiny bathroom almost too small to turn around in. Perhaps the apartment's most redeeming quality, other than the price, was the window on the wall facing the ocean. She opened it. Although there wasn't much to see in the dark, the ocean breeze was pleasant, freshening the room in no time.

She visited the tiny bathroom, washed her face, brushed her teeth and hair, and donned a nightgown she'd found on the sale rack when she'd still been working at Carol Ann's. The apartment had come furnished, right down to an old television that picked up one station. She flipped on the TV. The grainy police drama didn't hold her attention, so she turned it off again. Wandering around the one-room apartment killed another three minutes. Yawning, she gave up and went to bed.

Annie loved this time of day when she was totally relaxed and all her cares and worries were tucked away until morning. She lay in the drowsy warmth of sheets scented with an unfamiliar soap and the air scented faintly of the ocean that was slowly becoming familiar. Her body practically floated; her thoughts turned hazy.

The day had started out terribly, but had ended pleasantly. The image of gray eyes filtered across her mind. Turning onto her side, she snuggled deeper into her pillow, thinking that maybe the ocean really did instill romance in the human heart.

She was about a breath away from falling asleep when her stomach rumbled. She tried to remember how long it had been since she'd eaten. Lunch? She wished she had a candy bar. Ah, yes, milk chocolate, maybe with a little caramel and peanuts thrown in for good measure, sure would taste good right now. She tried to think of something else.

She wasn't married. And she had an English degree. She wondered where she'd acquired it. A lot of colleges taught English. Her stomach rumbled again. Mmm, chocolate.

With a groan, she flopped onto her back and stared at the ceiling. Great. Now she'd never be able to get to sleep. As much time as she spent thinking about chocolate, it was a wonder she didn't weigh eight hundred pounds. She swung her feet over the side of the bed and got up, flouncing to the drawer where she kept her emergency stash. She took her time poking through the assortment of chocolate. Breathing in the rich scent, she chose a plain milk-chocolate candy bar and slowly removed the wrapper.

The first bite was heaven, the second almost as good. She strolled to the open window and nibbled on rich chocolate in the dark. She could have been sleeping. Instead, she was eating. Having a chocolate addiction could be a real nuisance. She stared at the lights twinkling faintly from tall poles in the harbor. She sighed as she took the last bite, then returned to the bathroom to brush her teeth. A real nuisance, but such a pleasurable one.

Her craving for chocolate satisfied, she crawled into bed again. This time when she closed her eyes, her stomach didn't rumble. Her mind wandered, her body drifting a little farther toward sleep, her thoughts a jumbled mix that came and went much like the late-night breeze. It had been nice of Sam to offer her a job. Something told her that Sam O'Connor wasn't always nice. That was one of the things that made him so intriguing. That and his stormy gray eyes.

Her breathing grew shallow, and her thoughts slowed.

The directions he'd given her were to a house on the outskirts of town. She wondered how much work it would take to clean it up. Time would tell. And time was one thing she had plenty of.

The curtain billowed gently. She was so relaxed. That walk had been good for her. Hadn't the doctors told her the more she relaxed, the more she would remember?

Her memories were stacking up. She could swim. She was single. She'd gone to college. And she'd studied English. Like Sam.

Ah, Sam, with his stormy gray eyes and the confident stride and rare smiles and a lobster boat named *Birdie*. She wondered if he liked birds. Her last waking thought before drifting off to sleep was *What does a lobster fisherman do with an English degree?*

Chapter Three

Annie tucked the strap of her big plastic purse over her shoulder and started down the metal steps. Sam hadn't told her what time he wanted her to start. She distinctly remembered asking, but all she could recall him saying was something to the effect of "tomorrow morning."

Yesterday, she'd thought he had rugged down to an art form. This morning it had occurred to her that he had vague down to one, too. Since she couldn't call him, she'd decided that eight o'clock was a relatively innocuous yet universal time to start work. She didn't own a clock radio, and she'd slept like a baby. Sam's house was at least half a mile away. She glanced at the clock on the little tower at the head of Main Street. It was a quarter to eight. She didn't have time to mosey.

The only two businesses on Main Street open this early during the week were the diner and the barbershop. Now that she was gainfully employed again, she was a little relieved that she wasn't waiting tables today. Perhaps that was what put the spring in her step. She noticed the old-timers on the bench in front of the one-chair barbershop in the middle of the block. They'd been talking in earnest, but clammed up as she neared. They nodded hellos, though, as did the people driving by. She waved, but mostly she hurried. She was making good time, and had a stitch in her side to prove it.

"Hello, Mr. Potter," she called to the eighty-year-old man who was painting a new sign in front of a huge stack of driftwood. She thought that if the stack got any higher it would hide the house. Mrs. Potter came tottering outside, her house dress inside out. The old lady waved, and Annie thought the people in Midnight Cove sure were friendly. Strange, but definitely friendly.

With the exception of Main Street and Harbor Avenue, all the streets in town were named after trees or presidents. Sam's property was on a dead-end street named after the towering oaks that lined it. Winded, she paused to catch her breath just inside the gate in front of the house bearing the number he'd given her.

Yesterday, she'd thought she'd walked past every house in Midnight. She didn't recall this one. Other than a small area of grass that somebody kept mowed, the place looked . . . Words deserted her. Tangled was the best description she could come up with. The yard wasn't small, but from the looks of things, it had been overtaken a long time ago by overgrown bushes and vines and shrubs. There appeared to be no method to the madness. However, the house looked sound, what she could see of it. The roof didn't sag and the porch wasn't leaning. It had all its shutters, and the windows all contained glass. Like many of the houses in Midnight Cove, it was surrounded by a picket fence. Unlike the others, this one hadn't seen a coat of paint in years. It matched the house. There were no cars sitting on blocks, nor were there rotting benches and discarded items covered with weeds. Sam's yard wasn't messy. It just wasn't noteworthy. Maybe she had been past the house but hadn't given it a second look.

Her knock was answered quickly, as if Sam had been watching for her arrival. "Come in."

Her smile slipped a little at the way his mouth was set in a straight line. She couldn't tell if his eyes were a stormy gray this morning because he turned around before she got a good look.

The door creaked as she entered the front room. It was all she could do to control her gasp. She counted two sofas, several old stands that held lamps, old tins, books, records, radios, and other assorted junk. There was a wide assortment of old chairs, none of which could be used without first finding a place to put the items stacked on them.

Since Sam seemed to be waiting for her to say something, she said the first *nice* thing she could think of. "I wouldn't have pegged you as a man who collected antiques."

"I don't. All this junk came with the house."

Was it her imagination, or did his voice sound clipped? Following him into another room that looked a lot like the first one but had probably once been used as a dining room, she said, "How long have you lived here?"

"Six years."

She could see his face now, and his expression was definitely severe. It occurred to her that he wasn't nearly as friendly as the other people she'd seen this morning.

"Am I late?"

"I don't recall naming a specific time."

Okay. So he wasn't angry about her timing. That didn't explain the reason he clamped his mouth shut tighter than a child refusing to take medicine. All at once, Annie had a vague memory of holding a spoon of bitter-tasting liquid to the closed lips of a very stubborn, brown-haired girl. Her own smile lasted longer than the memory did. She was more certain than ever that there was a very belligerent school-age child out there somewhere, who loved her very much. Strangely, Annie didn't feel that the girl was crying her eyes out without her. Perhaps she was at summer camp and didn't even know Annie was missing. What other explanation could there be? It was all so confusing. At first it had been frustrating to recall only tidbits of memory at a time. Being frustrated only hindered the process. It required conscious effort and surely more patience than she'd been born with, but she was managing to take this slowly, one step at a time.

"Annie?"

She turned her head slowly, only to discover Sam watching her closely.

"Is something wrong?" he asked.

She shook her head. "I just had another vague memory."

Another inexplicable look of withdrawal came over him. Before she could comment, he turned his back on her and left the room. She followed him into an old-fashioned kitchen that wasn't nearly as cluttered as the other rooms had been. "That coffee smells good," she said.

"Help yourself."

Again with the clipped response. This time she knew she hadn't imagined it. Looking at him, she wondered what had changed between last night and today. "Maybe I'll take a coffee break later. Where do you want me to begin?"

"I'll leave that up to you." He headed for the back door.

She hurried after him, stopping on the top cement step, one hand still gripping the doorknob behind her. "Sam, is something wrong?"

His escape thwarted, Sam considered his answer carefully as he turned around. "Nothing's wrong," he said. And then, like an idiot, he added, "Why?"

"Oh," she said, the breeze toying with dark wisps of hair that had escaped the clear plastic clasp high on the back of her head. "I was just wondering about something."

She was staring at him so closely it required a conscious effort on his part to refrain from fidgeting. Mentally, he prepared himself for her to say that he looked vaguely familiar.

"Somebody told me there are less than three hundred people in Midnight Cove."

"Give or take a few, I guess."

"I looked for you in the phone book."

He braced himself. "I don't have a phone."

"That explains why I couldn't find your number."

"Do you need to call someone?"

She pulled a face. "Who on earth would I call?"

"Then what is it?" That had sounded impatient even to him. It didn't stop her from continuing.

"Not only are you not in the phone book, but there are no other O'Connors in the phone directory for Midnight Cove, either. You're not from here?"

Sam believed in telling as few lies as necessary. "I grew up in Ohio."

"Ah. There are probably a lot of O'Connors in Ohio, and O'Malleys and O'Learys." She took her hand off the doorknob and folded her arms in front of her. "O'Leary, now there's a good Irish name. It got a bad rep after the Chicago fire. Did you know that was a farce?"

"The fire?"

"No. The people who claimed it was started by Mrs. O'Leary's cow. I'm not saying there wasn't a Mrs. O'Leary, or that she didn't have a cow. But the Chicago fire wasn't the only fire that started that night in 1871. It wasn't even the most deadly."

Sam didn't remember retracing his footsteps, but suddenly he was standing near the bottom step, looking up at Annie, close enough to reach out and touch her. She drew him. It was that simple. She knew things without knowing how she knew. It was that complex.

She stood in the same patch of morning sunshine that was warming his shoulders. Birds twittered from their hiding places in his overgrown yard. For the first time in a long, long time, Sam didn't want to take his boat to the island. He wanted to stay here and listen to the smooth cadence in Annie's voice. That wasn't all he wanted.

She was still talking about the fire, and she was on a roll. Rather than stop her by asking questions, he simply watched the way her lips moved over the words she spoke with perfect enunciation, and listened to the excited lilt in her voice.

He could picture her in broadcast news. She had the voice for it, and the looks. Attractive without being overly so, she had the kind of face a person could relate to and would undoubtedly remember. Add to that the way she could home in on a topic, asking probing questions, finding a raw nerve with incredible ease, and she was dangerous, all right.

"Other fires broke out in Illinois that night. Some spread all the way to Michigan, but that night on October eighth, the same night as the Chicago fire, Wisconsin was struck by the worst natural disaster in its history. They called it the Great Peshtigo Forest Fire. More than twelve hundred people were killed. Only three hundred died in the Chicago fire."

Sam had never heard this. He hoisted one booted foot onto the first step, the story almost as intriguing as she was.

"Nobody knows how the fires really started. Maybe there was a meteor shower, or maybe it was just so dry that year that all it took was a spark of static electricity and a mild breeze to start a raging inferno."

He considered her theories before asking, "How do you suppose the Mrs. O'Leary's cow story got started?"

She shrugged. "A better question would be why."

"Somebody probably made it up." Probably a reporter. He scowled.

"Do you resent all women, Sam?"

His eyes narrowed.

"Or just me?"

For a long moment, he looked up at her. She was wearing loose-fitting khakis and a sleeveless plum-colored shirt. Her face was free of makeup, her gaze direct. The woman certainly called them like she saw them. Giving his head a self-deprecating shake, he said, "I don't resent all women, or you."

She studied him, as if measuring his sincerity. With a nod, she spun around and opened the door. "I'll get to work now."

"Annie?"

"Yes?" she called over her shoulder.

"Why do you think someone made up that story about Mrs. O'Leary's cow?"

Her brown eyes had a burning, faraway look in them. "Some people want an explanation for everything. Some things just happen. Others just plain are."

He couldn't have said it better himself.

Six years, he'd lived here. Alone. He could count on one hand the times in those six years he'd been lonely. After the fiasco following the lightning strike, he'd never wanted to see another crowd. He'd embraced the solitude of this place. He had four walls and a roof, running water, his boat, and the island. Oh, he'd had to deal with the occasional normal carnal desires. The need thrumming just below the surface of his skin right now was different.

"I know a lot about Wisconsin," she said.

"I noticed." He liked the way she pulled a face, the way she could laugh at herself. He liked the way she smiled and the way she didn't take what life had dished out sitting down.

"I think it's possible I'm from there."

Either that, Sam thought, or she'd done some snooping into the past. Reporters were known for their snooping. She was dangerous, all right, and getting more dangerous all the time. Putting up a stronger guard, he motioned toward his house. "I don't expect you to get everything done in one day, or hell, in one week, but any progress you make will be appreciated. Perhaps you can tackle the bathroom and the kitchen, today. I would appreciate it if you'd stay out of the two bedrooms downstairs." He thought about the door he'd locked at the end of the downstairs hall. "The cleaning products are under the sink in the kitchen. Help yourself to the food in the refrigerator. Work as many or as few hours as you want. Just keep track of them so I can pay you."

He turned then, and quickly left.

Smoothing her hand over her khaki chinos, Annie waited to return to the kitchen until after Sam strode through the gate. She noticed he didn't look back. Sometimes, she swore he seemed attracted to her. And yet he appeared to be fighting it with all the momentum of an apple cart careening down a steep hill. Surely all men didn't go from warm to cool in the blink of an eye.

She thought about that as she ran water in the kitchen sink and squirted in a little dish soap. She washed one plate, one glass, one fork, one pan. She'd met most of the residents of Midnight Cove during her first two days here, and yet she'd only met Sam a few days ago. He lived alone, worked alone, ate alone.

Did he always sleep alone, too? The thought came unbidden. Try as she might, she couldn't dislodge it from her mind. It was like trying to ignore a chocolate craving. Great. Now she wanted chocolate, too.

Once the dishes were washed and dried and the counters wiped off, she made a pass through the first floor, trying to decide what to do next. She swept the kitchen floor, but got very little dirt. Despite the state of the rest of the house, the kitchen had been cleaned recently. She strode to the bathroom next. Other than a few streaks on the mirror and some beard clippings in the sink, the room wasn't terribly dirty, either. Why would Sam clean these rooms while completely ignoring the others?

Something about his house bothered the back of her mind.

She promised herself a candy bar with a cup of coffee when she took her break later. Deciding she might as well mop the floors she'd swept, she started down the hall in search of a closet that might contain a mop. The hall was dark. Of course it was dark. One door was closed tightly and a second was open only a crack.

She took a step toward the second, only to bring herself up short. *He doesn't want you in these bedrooms,* she told herself.

Why not?

It's none of your business.

It required every ounce of willpower she possessed to do an about-face and retrace her footsteps to the kitchen. Fifteen seconds later she was back, one hand flattened against the door that was slightly ajar. It creaked as she pushed it open.

Sunshine spilled across the worn linoleum floor, causing her to blink. So this was where Sam slept. She didn't know what she'd expected, but it wasn't this. The room was comfortably furnished. The bed was big and high and neatly made.

She told herself to retrace her footsteps, close the door, and forget about Sam's bedroom. Quietly, she strolled farther into the room.

The living and dining rooms were cluttered, and that was putting it nicely. This room looked lived in, in a comfortable, masculine, pleasantly disheveled way. It was so like Sam. Something told her he'd brought this furniture with him from wherever he'd lived before. Ohio, he'd said. Two tall chests matched a simple, heavy-looking oak headboard. A television was perched on top of one of the chests of drawers, the usual loose change, gum wrappers, and matchbooks on the other. The table beside the bed held a lamp, an alarm clock, and a hardcover book. Her breath caught as she picked up the book. She hadn't known the latest L.S. Oliver suspense drama was out. She wondered what else she'd missed these past four weeks. Until that moment, she hadn't remembered that he was her favorite author.

Annie smiled. Bit by bit, pieces of her past were coming back to her. Her memories added up to very little, but meant the world to her. Still smiling, she ran a hand along the edge of a small writing desk where a variety of other books were stacked. She noticed a strange-looking battery that was plugged into some sort of charger. She'd seen that kind of rechargeable battery before, but she couldn't recall where she'd been or what it was used for. So far, she'd seen nothing in Sam's house that would require such a battery.

Sam O'Connor was no slob. There were no girlie magazines sticking out from between the mattresses, either. Why had he asked her not to come in here? What was he afraid she would find?

She strode to the open closet next. He had a lot of clothes for a lobsterman—she went down on her haunches—and a lot of shoes.

She didn't invade his privacy to the point of poking through boxes. She was no shrinking violet, and she could have used more tact, especially when she was around Sam. She was relieved to discover that she knew where to draw the line. Sam didn't want her straightening this room. Fine. She looked over her shoulder at the closed door across the hall.

Forget about it, she told herself.

She was across the hall before she'd finished the thought.

"Don't do it," she muttered under her breath even as she reached for the doorknob.

What harm could there be in peeking inside?

She pushed on the door. It didn't open as the first one had. She gripped the antique knob a little tighter and pushed a little harder. Still, the door didn't open. It was stuck. She jiggled the handle. She put her weight into it. It didn't budge. She stood back, bristling. That door wasn't stuck. It was locked.

She did an about-face and returned to the kitchen like she should have in the first place. So he kept a room locked. So what? This was his house. He had every right to lock any door he pleased.

She filled a bucket with hot water and added detergent. She located a mop hanging from a hook in a little nook near the back door, and got busy. All the while she mopped, she wondered why Sam had asked, okay, told her not to go inside that room. And why was that the only door he kept locked?

It was none of her business.

She sure wished she could get a little peek.

She wasn't here to peek. She was here to clean.

What harm could there be in just looking?

The mop slipped out of her hands as an idea washed over her. He'd asked her to stay out of the room. He hadn't said anything about peeking in from the outside. Besides, she had to be patient when it came to regaining her memory, which meant she couldn't learn more about herself. Maybe she could learn more about Sam.

She practically ran to the bathroom and looked out the window, getting her bearings. Next, she went outside and stood peering up at a high window on the back side of the house. That was the room, all right. The curtains were open a few inches. From here, all she could see was a narrow wedge of the ceiling.

Too bad she didn't have a ladder.

There was a shed out back. She had no idea if it contained a ladder. Plus, there were so many overgrown bushes and vines, she would need a machete to clear a path. She didn't have a machete. Even if she knew where one was, she shuddered to think what could happen if she attempted to use one.

She stared up at the window again. Darned high windows anyway. A chair would never be tall enough. *But a table with a chair on top of it might be.*

It took fifteen minutes to clear a path through the junk, er, furniture, in the living room so she could drag a lightweight table and sturdy wooden chair outside. Since she'd proven several times over, this week alone, that she wasn't the most graceful person in the world, she took extra care stacking old textbooks on the uneven portion of the ground under one table leg.

Satisfied that the structure was sound, she climbed on the table. From there, she went carefully up on the chair. It felt pretty solid, but her platform was still a foot too short.

This is a sign, her conscience warned her. *Better heed it. Just put this furniture back inside and forget about that locked room. If you don't, you'll be sorry.*

She'd come too far to listen to the bothersome voice of her conscience now. She made one last trip inside, only to return with a three-legged stool, which she placed on the seat of the chair. She tested it with her hand first. Steady as a rock. Well, almost.

With utmost care, she climbed up. So far so good. The stool teetered the tiniest bit as she put her weight on it, but not enough to keep her from grasping the windowsill for balance. Ever so slowly, she went up on tiptoe and peered through the window. "What the . . ."

She pressed her nose closer to the glass. The room was . . .

That solid-as-a-rock stool rocked slightly beneath her feet. The locked room was . . .

"You just couldn't resist, could you?" Startled, she looked around. Sam was striding toward her.

Uh-oh.

The stool teetered again, and then the whole thing started to crumble. Suddenly, she was airborne.

But not for long.

Chapter Four

Sam had just cleared the back corner of his house when he saw Annie perched on top of a makeshift tower constructed of a stack of books, an old table, a painted chair, and a three-legged stool. Any second now it was all going to come tumbling down, Annie right along with it. Damned fool woman couldn't even navigate the four-inch step at the diner. What on earth was she thinking trying this?

"You just couldn't resist, could you?"

Of course, she turned her head at the sound of his voice. The slight movement caused the stool to teeter and the table to rock. The chair pitched one way, the stool the other, the entire structure toppling like a house of cards.

He saw it happening, but he couldn't get there fast enough to break her fall. Twigs snapped. Cringing at the sound of her body hitting the ground, he dropped to his knees in front of her still form. "Annie, can you hear me?"

She groaned softly.

"Don't move."

Her eyes fluttered open. And of course she moved.

"Damn it, I said hold still." He ran a hand along her face, down her neck, over her shoulders and arms.

"No, you didn't," she whispered. "You said don't move."

Sam swore the woman would argue with the pope, but at least she held still.

"Sam?" she whispered.

He grunted something that meant "what," his attention on the course his hands took as he smoothed them over her, searching for broken bones. This was his fault. He'd put the sharp knives away, but he should have known she wouldn't be able to leave that locked room alone.

She moaned again. This time it sounded different. "Hmm, that feels nice. Um, Sam?" she said, a little louder than before. "Do you think you could help me out of this briar patch before feeling me up again?"

Before feeling her up . . .

He stared at her in complete astonishment. He didn't bother protesting, at least not out loud. He wasn't feeling her up, damn it. And his jeans weren't suddenly a size too small. Finally, he got his composure in check and sputtered, "I'm trying to see if anything's broken."

"Oh." A blush crept slowly up her face, turning her cheeks a vivid scarlet. She moved one leg, then the other, both arms, and her neck. "Nothing's broken." Keeping her gaze averted, she started to get up.

"Easy." He tried to be careful as he helped her. When he was certain she was steady on her feet, he said, "Are you sure you're okay?"

The clasp had come out of her hair and her arms were scratched. She looked a little shaky, but not seriously injured. Nodding, she mumbled, "Am I fired?"

What? He hadn't even thought about firing her. "No."

"You mean it?"

He felt like a heel. "Yes, I mean it. You have my word. You're not fired."

Just like that, her hands went to her hips and her chin came up. If she hadn't taken a backward step, he would have, because there wasn't a man alive who didn't recognize the sight of a woman gearing up to speak her mind.

"It's only ten o'clock. Why did you come back?" Her eyes had narrowed, part suspicion, part accusation. "I think I know. You came back on purpose, didn't you?"

He fumbled for an answer she didn't wait for.

"That room's empty. You locked an empty room."

Sam didn't know what to say. She was right. He had locked that room on purpose, not because he kept anything valuable in there, but because he knew that she would spend her day wondering what was behind that door. And if she was wondering about that, she wouldn't be wondering about him.

"It was a test, wasn't it?" she asked.

He didn't know what she was talking about.

"You *do* resent me. And you don't trust me."

He noticed she failed to mention the fact that

she'd just given him good reason not to trust her. "Look, it might seem as if I . . ."

She shook off his hand. "No, you look. On second thought, go ahead and fire me." She darted around him with an agility that was at odds with a woman who'd just taken a nasty fall and who'd been known to trip over a crack in the sidewalk and that annoying step in the diner. "You know what?" she said. "I have a better idea." She turned and walked away.

He found himself racing after her. "Where are you going?"

"Anywhere but here." She flung the words into the wind. "I think I'd prefer the smell of raw fish to this."

"What do you mean?"

"I mean," she said, turning at the gate, "you can wrap this job up, put it in your Haan loafer, and stick the entire bundle where the sun doesn't shine."

He could tell by her expression that she realized she'd just let another little faux pas slip. There was only one way she could have known he owned that particular brand of shoe. She'd snooped in his closet. If it was possible, it seemed to make her even more angry.

"That's what you can do, Sam O'Connor." She looked at him, brown eyes flashing, daring him to make something of it. "And do you know what else? You don't look Irish!"

She took a shaky breath, raised her chin another notch, and stiffly lifted the latch on the gate. Just then, the little girl with curly red hair who lived next door peddled by on a tricycle. "Anne Elizabeth Hogan come back here! Annie, I mean it!"

her frazzled-looking, freckled older brother called, hurrying after his sister.

The red-haired child didn't even slow down, but the grown woman with scratches on her arms and twigs stuck in her coffee-colored hair went perfectly still.

"Annie?" Sam said quietly.

She turned slowly, her gaze on the child nearing the end of the block. "My name isn't Annie."

She looked at the bracelet on her wrist, fingering the gold block letters, A-N-N-I-E. In a voice so soft Sam had to strain to hear, she said, "Annie is my daughter's name." She slumped against the gate. "I just remembered her face and the sound of her voice. She's twelve. Why isn't anyone looking for me, Sam?"

Sam really hated to bring this up. Keeping his voice low, he said, "Do you think it's possible your daughter is . . . gone?"

"You mean . . . gone to heaven?" She looked at him and slowly shook her head. "I don't think so. I think I would feel it if she were dead." With a sense of conviction that surely had to be part of her character, she said, "I would know."

Annie—make that *What's-Her-Name*—imposed an iron control on her emotions. The child she was slowly starting to remember was very much alive. The certainty was like a rock inside her. Now, who in the hell was *she*? This was getting terribly annoying. Stronger now, she took a calming breath and said, "Maybe nobody's looking for me because nobody likes me."

"That's impossible."

She turned her head and got lost in the heat

in Sam's eyes. "I'm outspoken. I'm clumsy. I'm a snoop."

"You're witty. You're smart. And you're very brave."

She fought to maintain her curtness. "You don't even like me."

"You're wrong about that. I like you." He was moving closer. She knew, because she'd had to grasp the top of the gate to keep from falling when she'd heard the boy call after his little sister. And she could still feel the gate beneath her hand. She hadn't moved. She couldn't.

Sam liked her. She thought about that locked room. He had funny ways of showing it. "Sam?" He was so close now she could see herself in his eyes.

"I'm listening."

"I really don't think kissing me is a very good idea."

"Know what I think?" he asked, his mouth so close she could feel his breath on the tip of her nose. "I think kissing you is the best idea I've had all day."

Her eyes fluttered closed at the first feathery touch of his lips on hers. She'd expected Sam's kiss to take her by storm, and yet this kiss was no more than a brush of air at first, a whisper meeting a sigh on a balmy summer morning. Gradually, it changed. She tilted her head slightly and parted her lips beneath his. Other than his fingers, which he threaded through her hair in order to tilt her head slightly, the only parts of their bodies touching were their mouths. He moved his lips over hers like a man who knew what he wanted, persuading her, lulling her, luring her into the haze of desire that was slowly obliterating everything except the feel of his mouth on hers and what it was doing to the pit of her stomach and the empty space behind her breastbone.

His beard was soft where it brushed her face, adding a sensual dimension that aroused her fantasies. He groaned deep in his throat, letting her know he wanted more but wasn't taking any more than she offered. It was a dreamy notion, which was strange because she wasn't normally given to dreaminess.

It had been a long time since a man had kissed her like this. She couldn't remember other men. She doubted she would ever forget Sam. The idea brought more than a rush of blood and a flutter of her heart. It brought tears to the back of her throat and warmth everywhere else.

"Annie?"

It took a moment for her to realize that the kiss had ended, and another moment for her to open her eyes, which she did, only to find Sam looking at her, his gaze steady, his eyes very, very gray.

He motioned to the sidewalk. The little girl and her brother were watching. The boy blushed; his little sister giggled before putting her feet on the pedals and scooting away toward home, her brother following after her.

What's-Her-Name watched them go. "I guess I should give myself another name."

"It's your decision, of course, but everyone here knows you by Annie Valentine. I see no reason to change it while you're waiting for your memory to return."

He didn't say *if* her memory returned. She appreciated that. "I'll think about it."

"Are you sure you're all right?" he asked.

She thought about that locked room, and how she had fallen for it hook, line, and sinker. "I guess I'm a little hurt."

He reached for her hand. "I'm taking you to Dr. Richardson."

"What? Why? No, I don't mean physically." She touched her chest with three fingertips. "I'm hurt in here."

She shook her head to clear it. What was there about this man that made her blurt out every thought at precisely the moment she had it? Recovering slightly, she put up a stronger guard and said, "I'll be fine."

She opened the gate.

"What are you doing?" he asked.

"I'm going home. I quit, remember?"

"But I thought . . ."

"You thought what? That one little kiss would change everything?" She had his undivided attention now. "I don't even know who I am, yet I speak the truth. Maybe you should try it, because no matter what you said, you don't trust me. You share next to nothing of yourself, how you feel, what you think. It's too bad, too, because I was going to ask you if I could borrow that book by L.S. Oliver I saw on your nightstand."

Oh, for heaven's sake, there she went again, reminding Sam that she'd snooped in his room. She looked at him. For a moment, she felt the way she did when a craving for chocolate came over her. She sighed. "Too bad sex is out of the question."

She heard the sharp breath he took. She struggled with her own sharp breath. Sex with Sam *was* out of the question. She had amnesia. She had a life somewhere. Besides, she'd already shared more of herself with him than he had with her. He'd locked an empty room. As far as symbolism went, it was extremely telling. She'd been open with him while he kept himself locked up tight.

"Good-bye, Sam O'Connor." She walked through the gate. This time she was the one who didn't look back.

Sam watched her go. If she'd had the decency to look, she would have seen that his eyes had darkened like thunderclouds. The woman had a lot of nerve, quitting when she was the one who'd been caught with her nose pressed to the window of a room he'd distinctly told her was off-limits. It sure as hell hadn't been the first time he'd caught somebody snooping through his things. Before he'd disappeared and changed his name, reporters had dogged his every step, camping out in hotels, posing as limousine drivers, pretending to be gardeners. They even went through his trash.

He should have been accustomed to people blurting out whatever they were thinking, and yet Annie's mention that sex was out of the question had rendered him speechless. She was outspoken, clumsy, and a snoop. She'd said so herself. So she'd quit. So what?

Good riddance.

He stomped to the backyard and carted the furniture back inside where it belonged, sputtering under his breath all the while.

He was lucky to be rid of her. Damned lucky, indeed.

No matter what she'd said, that hadn't been just a little kiss, damn it. And what the hell did she mean it was too bad sex was out of the question?

* * *

Annie was getting out of the shower when she heard the knock on her door. She wasn't expecting company. She hadn't made a lot of friends while she'd been in Midnight Cove. Actually, there was only one person she could think of who might pay her a visit this time of the evening, and she wasn't in any hurry to see him.

She took her time drying off, mindful of the sore muscles that ached and the scratches that burned when touched. The knock sounded a second time, louder than before.

She removed her shower cap, shook out her hair. She donned her long robe and took great care hanging up her towel and putting the hairbrush and shower cap away. She wasn't stalling. She was taking her sweet time.

The third knock rattled the door and anything not battened down. Cinching the sash of her robe tight at her waist, she sashayed out of the bathroom and strolled to the door. She looked through the peephole, turned the lock, and opened the door.

Sam's fist wound up knocking on thin air. He let his arm fall to his side. The streetlights were on behind him. The glow gave him a dreamy, superhero-type quality. He'd brought the purse she'd left at his house that morning. In his hand was a hardcover book and one long-stemmed rose. He'd cleaned up, probably in the shower she'd cleaned that very morning. He'd looked darned good in his work clothes. Spit and polished, he was a sight to behold.

"Yes?" she asked, as if he were selling vacuum cleaners door-to-door.

"Did I ever tell you that "yes" is my favorite word in the English language?"

There was a ghost of a smile in his gray eyes. When she failed to reply, the humor evaporated into thin air.

She'd thought about him a lot today. She'd read somewhere that good judgment came from experience, and a lot of that came from bad judgment. She was in no position to make any bad judgments.

"What are you doing here, Sam?"

Sam ran a hand down his short beard, thinking, damned if he knew. She was looking up at him, waiting for him to say something. During the ten years he'd been on the professional golf circuit, he'd made small talk with just about everybody he saw, from fellow golfers to caddies to fans and reporters. And here he was, standing before a woman he wanted to impress, as tongue-tied as a teenager in a new pair of jeans and his father's car, trying to get up the courage to talk to the prettiest girl in school.

"You said I haven't shared any part of myself with you. I came to talk."

She stared at him far longer than was considered polite. And then she stared a little more. He let her look her fill before saying, "What do you think?"

Finally, she tilted her head and said, "I really don't think that purse goes with your outfit."

He did a double take and slowly grinned, taking the fact that she was joking with him as a good sign. He doubted she could have known what the sight of her in a simple, thin yellow dressing gown was doing to his heart rate or his ability to think coherently. Before he lost every last brain cell to fantasy, he handed the bag over to her. "May I come in?"

"Would I still get to read that book if I said no?"

He handed her the book, but kept the rose to the count of ten before holding it out to her, as well.

"You're a scoundrel, do you know that?"

"Would you believe me if I told you I've been called worse?"

"Why wouldn't I believe you? Are you prone to lying?"

He supposed he couldn't blame her for baiting him. "I'm not prone to lying. I've lived alone, been alone, for a long time. I guess I'm not very good at talking anymore. I know, it boggles the mind that I could be bad at anything."

She brought the rose to her nose as she opened the door a little farther. It was all the invitation Sam needed. He stepped over the threshold and quietly walked inside.

The room was small. From the looks of things, it had come furnished. He strolled to one corner of the room; she went to another corner. A lamp was on near an overstuffed chair. As if realizing how intimate the semidark room appeared, she switched on two others. Now that the light was behind her, he could see the outline of her body through her robe.

"Why?" she asked.

He had to clear his throat to say, "Why what?"

"Why have you lived all alone, been all alone for a long, long time?"

He cleared his throat again. "At first, I wanted to be alone. I needed to be alone."

"And now?"

"Now, I find myself wanting to be with you."

Annie's heart tripped in its beat. Being wanted by Sam O'Connor was a heady sensation, but it didn't change her resolve. She couldn't let it. She didn't know why he'd given her a job if he didn't trust her. Obviously, he had issues. She had problems of her own. She examined the bracelet. At least now she understood what the Annie charm stood for. She didn't know what the quill pen symbolized, but she was pretty sure the gold charm that was shaped like a chocolate candy stood for her craving for anything chocolate.

"Are you sore tonight?"

"I ache in places I didn't know I had. I examined every square inch of my body in the shower a little while ago, and I can honestly say that although I have a few bruises and several scratches, the worst damage was to my pride and my tattoo."

"You have a tattoo?"

She dropped her face into her hands, coming dangerously close to poking herself in the eye with the rose. She had little tact and less restraint, and really, few redeeming qualities. No wonder no one was looking for her. She clamped her mouth shut and wasn't going to open it and that was that.

Sam strode toward her with a kind of animal grace and a determined expression that caused her to take a step back. "Where?" he said.

She shook her head.

"Come on, Annie. Where?"

"Never mind where."

"Okay, what is it a tattoo of?"

Her fingers shook slightly as she tucked her hair behind her ear. "My tattoo is none of your business."

Coming to a stop a few paces away, he held her gaze. Slowly, he rolled up the sleeve of his white T-shirt, then presented her with his left arm.

"Birdie," she said, reading the word beneath the bluebird gracing his upper arm. "The same as your boat."

He stood, waiting.

She swallowed tightly. "You think just because you showed me yours I'll show you mine?"

"I like the way you think."

She very nearly got lost in the way he was looking at her, only to come to her senses in the nick of time. "Forget it. I'm not showing you mine."

He rolled his shirtsleeve over his tattoo. "Then describe it to me."

"No."

He stared into her eyes.

And she whispered, "It's a kiss."

Sam heard her moan. He sympathized with anybody who tried to keep something from him, but in this instance he couldn't help using his power to his benefit. "A kiss?" His imagination was in full swing, his gaze trained on her mouth. "Do you mean like lips?"

"Not that kind of kiss. A chocolate kiss. You know. Candy. I love chocolate. Candy bars, brownies, cookies, cheese cake, sundaes. It's amazing I don't weigh half a ton."

She wasn't heavy. She wasn't even overweight. She had curves in all the right places, but he'd assumed it was genetics. Maybe he should be thanking her chocolate addiction. Somewhere on her lush body was a tattoo of a chocolate kiss, somewhere that she wouldn't show him. He pictured a few of those places in his mind. He had a very, very good imagination.

"Did you know that chocolate doesn't really come from cocoa beans?"

He gave his blood a few seconds to make its way back to his brain before attempting to make sense of the question. She was at it again, talking, spouting facts that few people could know.

"Actually, chocolate as we know it today comes from the cacao tree. Because of a mistake in its spelling, which was probably made by English importers a few hundred years ago, the beans became known as cocoa beans."

Sam stared at her, uncertain how to respond. Maybe she wasn't a reporter at all. Then what in the hell was she?

She was beautiful. She was smart. She'd probably known it once. He found himself wanting to be the one who told her, and showed her, until she believed it again.

"There I went again, going on and on about nothing."

Then and there Sam faced the fact that he knew exactly what else she was. She was a woman he wanted a great deal.

"I really hope I don't offend people with my know-it-all attitude."

"Do I look offended, Annie?"

She appeared to consider the question, and then she considered him. "You look rugged and intense and far too appealing for my peace of mind. And that's why you should go." She started toward the door. "Thank you for returning my purse. And for loaning me the book. I look forwarding to reading it." She brought the pale yellow rose to her nose again and breathed in the heady scent. "And thank you for the flower."

That made three thank-yous and one good-bye, which was one good-bye too many. Watching her smooth that rose across her cheek in a movement that was as naturally uncalculated as it was sensual, Sam's imagination took another slow dip into the erotic zone. He didn't know what the hell he was doing. He only knew he didn't want to leave. "You insinuated I was closed off."

"I did?"

"This morning. Before you left." He ran a hand through his hair. He really had lost the ability to carry on a natural, normal conversation.

She looked at him. "Yes?"

There was that word again. "I'm not that closed off."

"Pu-lease. I know nothing about you."

"What do you want to know?"

Annie considered the question. She'd been putting her application in at the marina when Sam had gotten back to the harbor that afternoon. She'd noticed the comings and goings of other fishermen. All of them carted bait and tackle and the days' catch on and off their boats. By comparison, Sam traveled pretty lightly.

"What do you do?" she asked. She held up a hand in a halting gesture. "And don't tell me you're a lobsterman." She pointed to his hands, which were strong and clean. They were rough enough to be masculine, but they weren't weathered and calloused and cracked like the hands of the men whose coffee cups she'd filled during her brief stint as a waitress. "Those aren't the hands of a fisherman."

She sensed a certain tension in his attitude, as if he was drawing away, into himself again. She told herself she hadn't expected him to tell her, therefore there was no reason to feel disappointed.

"You're right."

She swung around so fast the front of her robe opened to the middle of her thigh. Holding the edges together with one hand, she said, "I'm right about what?"

He was still looking at the material bunched in her hand as he said, "You're right about my hands. Know what I think we should do?"

"What, pray tell?"

Sam didn't blame her for being suspicious. He was getting in over his head. He knew it, yet he couldn't seem to do anything about it. He was the one with the powers. She had a few powers of her own, and in this instance hers were stronger.

"Come with me tomorrow and see for yourself."

Her mouth dropped open.

Sam didn't blame her. He was mildly surprised about the suggestion himself. Still, it felt good to be the one who wasn't speechless for a change. "You're not answering. Does that mean you have something better to do?"

She rolled her eyes.

"Or," he said, taking a purposeful step in her direction, "maybe you don't really want to know anything about me. I suppose it's possible that you're secretly afraid to put your money where your mouth is."

That did it. Her shoulders went back and her chin came up. "What time do we leave?"

"Meet me at my house at six tomorrow morning."

"Is the sun even up at six?"

So, she wasn't an early riser. "I guess you're going to find out, aren't you?"

She studied him thoughtfully, then quietly said, "I'll be there."

"I'll be waiting." He reached out, touching her face with two fingertips. Without another word, he walked out the door.

Annie stood perfectly still for a long time after he left, her hand cradling the cheek he'd touched, feeling as if she'd been kissed.

What do you want to know? Sam had asked.

Annie—she hated that she didn't even know her own name—wanted to know how a touch could feel like a kiss. While she was at it, she wouldn't have minded knowing why she was so drawn to him. He was just a man, right? He was an annoying man at that. And he had a beard. Normally, she preferred a man who was clean shaven. Another taste she'd only just recalled.

So what was there about Sam O'Connor?

And why did she have so much trouble keeping her thoughts to herself when she was with him? Perhaps that was the biggest question of all.

Chapter Five

According to the clock radio Annie had borrowed from Dulcie, the sun was up at six the following morning. It just wasn't easy to tell because of the fog.

The lights were on in Sam's house when Annie arrived, but he wasn't waiting by the door as he had been the previous day. Instead, her knock was answered from a few rooms away. "Door's open. Come on in!"

Sam didn't keep his front door locked, and yet he'd locked that empty bedroom. By the time she entered the kitchen, she was mad all over again.

Her withering stare was wasted on his back. If that wasn't bad enough, she rather liked the view. He had broad shoulders, muscular upper arms, a narrow waist. It only got better from there.

She really had no pride. "What are you doing?"

"I'm packing our lunch," he said. "Good morning to you, too."

She yawned. "It's too early to be a good morning."

Finally, he glanced over his shoulder and looked at her. "You didn't get enough sleep?"

Needing some place else to look, she meandered into the dining room. "I was up late reading. You know, Sam, a lot of this junk is probably worth some money."

"I hope you like yogurt and fruit and cheese. Do you know anything about antiques?"

"No. I don't even particularly like them. Huh. What do you know? I mean, I appreciate them, and admire the craftsmen who made them. It isn't as if they had power tools back then, right? The problem is, antiques are old, and they often smell musty. A lot of people pay a pretty penny for old, musty things."

"You think they're worth trying to sell?"

"Sure. I guess."

"Ever had a garage sale?"

She looked around her at the claw-footed chairs, flute-edged tables, trunks, pottery, and pictures. "You'd get more if you called it an antique sale."

"Then do it. We'll split the profits. Are you enjoying the book?"

She could see Sam from her position in the dining room. He was adding cans of soda and bottled water to a large cooler, the epitome of masculine ease in a gray polo shirt and faded jeans.

"I'm enjoying it very much. What kind of split are you talking about?"

"Fifty-fifty. I supply the junk. You do all the work. Even steven. How far did you get?"

She strode toward the kitchen, her mind flooded with ideas and ways to advertise Sam's antiques.

Leaning a shoulder against the trim in the doorway, she yawned again. "I got too far. I should have been sleeping. Have you read a lot of Oliver's work?"

He shrugged those massive shoulders, but said, "Yeah, have you?"

"My mother recommended his books before she died." She stopped suddenly. "My mother died four years ago."

He waited a moment before saying, "That explains why she isn't looking for you."

Her mother had been gone for four years. That was a very good reason not to be looking for her only child.

She was an only child.

"You ready?" Sam turned out the lights, closed the door.

Annie noticed he didn't lock it. Bother the man.

They set off toward the harbor, him in his tattered baseball cap and no jacket, her in turquoise-colored Capri pants and a white windbreaker. "My friend Suzette"—she had a friend named Suzette—"thinks the 'L' in L.S. Oliver stands for Laura or Lisa. I think the edge in his writing could only come from a man. Some people believe he's a priest, like that other writer, Father What's-His-Name. Another friend of mine, Rachel . . . Huh. Well, I'll be darned. Anyway, Rachel thinks he's in prison."

"Why would she think that?"

Annie tried to see Sam's expression, but she was having trouble keeping up with him. She wound up studying his shoulders again, which was not terribly conducive to keeping her wits about her. "No one's ever seen him, for one thing. Personally, I think that anybody who can get into a killer's head the way he does would have to be a little warped."

Sam stopped so quickly she nearly ran into him. He started up again, and she continued. "He probably lives in LA or New York and gets his rocks off by attending all the big parties incognito."

"Why would he do that?" There was definitely an edge in Sam's voice.

"How should I know? I have amnesia, remember? Maybe he likes hearing the praise but doesn't want to own up to criticism."

They'd reached the dock. "That's ridiculous."

A light fog hung over the water, making the air feel cooler and the voices of other fishermen preparing for a day at sea seem louder. Sam untied one rope. Following his lead, Annie untied one, too. "You asked for my opinion." She hopped onto the boat.

"I see you got yourself an apprentice there, aye Sam?" Percy Parnell called, his voice like a foghorn, his eyes in that perpetual squint. "Got enough life preservers with ya?"

Sam nodded and Annie had to force herself to smile nicely. Apparently her reputation had preceded her.

"It isn't what you're thinking," Sam said as he stepped up to the helm and started the engine. "Percy asks everyone if they have the required life preservers on board."

"Oh."

"Don't you want to know why?" he asked.

She shivered as she considered the question. Most people in Midnight Cove didn't offer explanations regarding the whys and wherefores of their daily lives. Even though she reminded herself that

Sam was only offering information about somebody else, and grudgingly at that, she softened a little. "Okay," she said. "Why?"

"One morning sixty years ago, Percy and his brother went out fishing. That night, only Percy came back." He paused for a moment, then said, "Here. You'll need these." She caught the life preserver and yellow raincoat he tossed at her.

She'd assumed the windbreaker she'd donned before leaving her apartment would be enough protection against the early morning chill. She slid her arms into the sleeves of the storm gear and then donned the life vest, and was instantly warmer. Of course, it could have had something to do with Sam's explanation. It reminded her that everyone had problems, troubles, obstacles, and the occasional brick wall to navigate. Somehow that made her feel more understood. And feeling more understood made her feel less desperate for the rest of her memory to return in the next ten minutes. Maybe brain cells healed slowly. Or maybe things like this just took time. That didn't stop her from feeling impatient at times.

She watched as the harbor grew smaller behind them. One by one, the other boats disappeared through the ribbons of fog. "Your boat is smaller than the others."

"Are you telling me size matters?"

Leave it to a man to get that connotation from a simple statement. "I'm talking about boats." She noticed Sam's beard was hiding a smile. "Where are we going?"

"You'll see."

"Now that you cleared that up . . . "

Sam studied Annie's expression. She was looking

straight ahead, her mouth shut tight. Last night, he'd considered calling Grant to request an emergency head examination. Sam didn't know who Annie Valentine was. Annie Valentine didn't even know who she was. She didn't know who he was, either, and he would just as soon keep it that way.

Then why the hell had he invited her to spend the day with him? His body knew the answer even if his brain was resisting the truth. Part of that truth was tied up in his fantasies about that tattoo she wouldn't show him.

She wanted to know what he did here. That wasn't asking so much. As long as he kept his wits about him, what harm could there be in showing her at least part of what he did and who he was? That was the clincher. This was about more than sex. He couldn't let her discover who he'd been, and yet he wanted her to know who he'd become. The truth was, he wasn't the same man he'd been six years ago, eight years ago, ten. Sam found himself wanting someone to get to know the recluse, perhaps even be glad she knew him. Not just anyone. He wanted this woman who called herself Annie to know the man he was today. And that, in a nutshell, was what made this so dangerous.

"Sam? What brought you here?"

Since she had no way of knowing he'd left his former life, or even that he'd had a former life, she couldn't have been asking about that. She only wanted to know why he'd chosen this particular place to live.

"I like the ocean."

She sank into the seat a few feet from him, seeming to ponder that for a moment. "There are other oceans."

It was disconcerting the way she could home in on the heart of an issue so effortlessly. "I considered living on the West Coast." He spoke into the wind and steered the boat around a sharp outcropping of rock. "Once, I drove through California's wine country and didn't stop until I came to the rocky Oregon coast. I could have made any one of a hundred towns my home."

"But you didn't."

He shook his head. "I spent some time on the Gulf in Florida. The weather would have been easier to live with there."

"Not everyone is looking for a temperate climate. What were you looking for?"

She'd done it again.

Sam shook his head to clear it, uncertain how to proceed. He couldn't tell her he'd been looking for anonymity, so he settled for as much of the truth as he dared reveal. "Although I didn't know it at the time, I was looking for that."

He pointed straight ahead. There in the distance, behind thin wisps of fog that were slowly dissolving beneath the yellow rays of the sun, was an island. His island.

He circled to the far side before dropping anchor. Huge flocks of birds took flight in the distance, eventually landing on the shore once again. When the anchor touched bottom and the boat was secure, Sam removed his yellow storm gear, then hauled a small barrel closer to the boat's edge.

"What's in there?"

He pried open the top. She wrinkled her nose and jumped backward. "What is that horrible stench?"

"Fish heads, mostly."

She was looking a little green around the collar.

"A colony of lobsters live down there." Using a long-handled scoop as a ladle, he began dumping the assorted fish parts over the side of the boat.

"I thought lobstermen put the bait inside traps."

"They do."

She didn't come any closer to the smelly barrel, but her color improved dramatically. "So, I was right. You're not a fisherman."

He shrugged.

"You're a conservationist."

He considered her terminology. "I wouldn't really call myself anything as political as that. I just feed them." Even that hadn't been intentional in the beginning. He'd purchased the bait because he'd been trying to look like a lobster fisherman. He'd dumped it overboard without realizing he was feeding a growing colony. A diver who worked for an agency that counted and tracked the migratory creatures discovered the unusual quantities here. Sam couldn't very well quit now.

"There's a new group emerging that is fighting for a more humane way to kill lobsters," he said, replacing the cover on the barrel. "Somebody's even invented a stun gun that puts them in a trance so they don't feel the pain of being dropped into a pot of boiling water."

Annie said, "I understand the principle, but I've never heard of an eagle being kind to the rabbit in its talons, or a mountain lion being gentle with a gazelle. Maybe since we're humans, we're supposed to be above that kind of cruelty."

She'd done it again. How could she know exactly what was at the heart of any issue he brought up?

"Tell me more about your lobsters."

"Since moving here," he said, "I've heard a lot of talk about conservation and regulation. Ninety-nine percent of the lobster fishermen in Maine know that overfishing would be catastrophic to their livelihoods. In their own way, they believe in preservation. It's become an issue of overfishing versus overregulation."

"You know what they say. With democracy comes dispute." Annie sensed Sam's smile, even if she didn't understand it. She felt a curious, swooping pull at her insides.

The first three weeks she'd had amnesia had been terribly confusing. Sam confused her in a completely different way.

She watched the disgusting fish by-products sink out of sight. "What else do you do besides feed them?"

When he didn't readily reply, she glanced up. He was looking at her, his battered baseball cap in one hand, the breeze ruffling his collar, lifting his sandy-brown hair off his forehead. As usual, his gray eyes held her spellbound.

"Once a month, at low tide," he said, "I try to count them."

"How on earth do you do that?"

He was the one who finally broke eye contact. Striding to the back of the boat, he brought up the anchor, then resumed his place at the wheel. "I would need scuba gear to count these." Pointing to the shallow waters near the island, he said, "I count those. Come on, I'll show you."

Annie felt a lurch of excitement, but remained quiet, content to watch as he steered closer to shore. This island was larger than many of the others they'd passed. The shore was rocky, but the center portion was wooded. Someone had built a dock in a secluded cove. Farther away, nearly out of sight on the jagged shoreline that formed a point, was a small stone cabin and the crumbled remains of a lighthouse that had all but washed into the sea.

High in the sky, flocks of birds glided, circling. "What are those birds doing?" she asked.

"Those are gulls. See there, at the water's edge? Those are herons, mostly. They're waiting for dinner."

"You feed the birds, too?"

"If I didn't, they'd eat the lobsters that nest in the shallow waters."

"Of course they would." All at once, she felt like a breathless girl of eighteen on the brink of discovery. The sensation brought a sudden glimpse of herself at that age. More and more of her memories were coming back to her. Any day now, the rest would return, too. She needed to know who she was, where she lived, what she did. Once she remembered, she would be leaving here to return to her life elsewhere. That brought a sense of urgency, and a yearning she didn't know what to do about.

Sam handed her a small covered bucket. Hoisting a burlap bag to his shoulder, he reached for her hand. She let him help her from the boat, and when he made no move to release her hand, she left it there. "Okay, now tell me how you go about counting lobsters."

"At low tide, when the water is shallow, you just turn rocks over and there they are. You have to have a quick finger, because they're fast. Come on.

Let's feed the birds first and then we'll try to find some young lobsters.''

He walked to a lean-to that housed what appeared to be a small dune buggy. Depositing the birdseed and the bucket in the back, he climbed in. The minute she was seated, he started off across the island, far away from the pools and eddies where the majority of lobsters lived.

She helped him scatter the seeds, but left him to the smellier job of dumping more fish by-products for the gulls and herons. They spent an hour laughing at the birds' antics before he led the way across a series of stepping stones poking above the water.

Although a little wobbly on the rocks, Annie was proud of herself for staying dry.

Reaching a particularly shallow area, he went down to his haunches.

Annie bent at the waist as he lifted a rock. And a dozen tiny lobsters scuttled for cover. "They're adorable."

"They spend the first several years of their lives growing under these rocks before migrating to deeper waters."

"Once they do, you feed them."

He didn't appear comfortable with the wonder in her voice.

"It's a good thing, Sam. What you do, I mean."

He kept his eyes averted, and she thought, *He's shy.*

She placed a hand on his cheek, his beard tickling her palm. "Why don't you tell people?"

"I don't want the attention." He took a sharp breath.

Staring at him, Annie felt on the verge of understanding something important about Sam O'Connor. He wasn't shy, as she'd thought. He was . . . something else, something as elusive as fireflies. There was something about him . . .

Something that seemed . . .

He reached for her before she knew it was happening, his arms going around her, crushing her to him. He pressed his mouth to hers, and all thoughts but one fled her mind.

Him.

Her mouth opened beneath his, his hands gliding over her from shoulders to hip, kneading her backside, drawing her up against the hard ridge of him. Shards of weak sunlight danced through her closed eyelids. Desire uncurled deep in her body, weakening her knees, turning any conscious thoughts into vapors that floated away like the fog.

Sam knew he should be ashamed of himself. A person with amnesia had been on the verge of remembering, and he'd interfered. It had been more a knee-jerk reaction than a conscious decision. Any day now, any hour, perhaps any second, she was going to recognize him. Later, he would take the time to understand his burning need to make love to her before that happened, but Sweet Mother, not now.

Chapter Six

Annie didn't know how long the kiss lasted. She'd lost track of time. No wonder. One second she'd been about to tell Sam something, and the next second she was in his arms. She became aware of the waves washing against rocks in the distance and seabirds screeching and squawking.

"Is it my imagination," she whispered, burying her face against his throat, "or am I floating?"

She felt his reluctance as he slowly lowered her feet to the ground. It wasn't until her eyes were open, the earth firmly beneath her feet, that she remembered where she was and what she'd been doing just before he'd kissed her.

"Why did you do that?"

"Only a woman would ask a question like that."

And only a man would give that kind of answer. She took a moment to straighten her clothes before studying Sam. The front of his shirt had come untucked, and he wasn't wearing his hat. She remembered knocking it askew when she'd threaded her fingers through his hair. It was lying on the ground in a shallow pool.

"Stop looking at me like that," she said.

"Like what?" he asked, all innocence.

Innocent her eye! She'd been on the verge of remembering something. Now, her mind was blank. To make matters worse, he was looking at her the way she often looked at chocolate. With open longing and waning willpower.

The strong ocean breeze fluttered her white cotton shirt, cooling skin she hadn't known was revealed until that moment. Buttoning the top two buttons, she glanced at him again as she tried to recall what it was she'd been about to remember. His brow was furrowed, his mouth set, his jaw clenched. She understood her frustration. What was Sam's problem?

"You're doing it again."

"What am I doing, Annie?"

"You're closing yourself off from me. You said you would be open with me today."

"If that kiss had gone on any longer, right now we would be in the process of being as open as two people can be with each other." His voice was a deep rumble, a slow sweep across her senses.

She didn't trust herself to have this conversation while standing on slippery stepping stones. Feeling shakier than she had getting here, she led the way across the stones to higher, dryer ground. There, she folded her arms and finally said, "I'm not talking about sex."

"I'm all ears."

"No you're not. You're all shoulders and sulk

and mystery. Why do I have the feeling that having sex with you would be a huge mistake?"

"You're the one who keeps mentioning sex."

She couldn't pull off making a face. He was right. She did keep bringing up the subject. She couldn't help it. Her body was too aware of his proximity, her mind too filled with yearnings. "My ex-husband used to say sex is a lot like air. It isn't important unless you aren't getting any." She felt her eyes widen. "I have an ex-husband."

"And I can't seem to get enough air."

This time she knew the kiss was coming. He moved toward her slowly, holding her gaze, giving her time to tell him no.

She didn't have it in her to tell him no. She lifted her face and closed her eyes.

When it was over, he drew away far enough to say, "In case you're wondering, I did that because I wanted to, because I needed to. What are you thinking?"

"Oh, no you don't. A girl has to have some pride."

He looked a little surprised by her answer. It didn't take him long to recover. "Care to know what I'm thinking?"

Warming to the subject, she took a backward step, looked into his eyes, and then slowly at the rest of him. Pride was one thing. Curiosity was another. "All right. What are you thinking?"

"I'm thinking that I'd like a quiet room, a soft bed, a gentle breeze. And you."

That sounded terribly forward and very lovely. "Do you know of such a place on this island?"

His reply was a whispered "yes" as he kissed her jaw, another one as he pressed his lips to the hollow beneath her ear, her neck, the slender ridge of her collarbone.

"Sam?" She reached a hand to his face, his beard surprisingly, sensuously soft. "I think that before the day is through, I'm going to change the way I feel about beards."

"Don't expect me to ask you if you're sure."

The deep rasp of his voice drew her gaze. He made no attempt to hide his desire for her, and yet, no matter what he insinuated, his simple statement was an attempt to do the noble thing.

She said, "You deal with your expectations and I'll deal with mine."

The shock of Annie's wit and wile ran through Sam's body, her rejoinder so spontaneous, so crammed with attitude and spunk, so much like the woman herself, he would have liked to lower her to the ground and take her there and then. He hadn't taken a woman to his bed in years. He didn't know how long it had been for her, but he knew she didn't remember the last time. He wanted to make this something she would never forget, and that required more creature comforts than the ground afforded. Reaching for her hand, he started for the cabin. They'd only taken a few steps when the need to kiss her again forced his steps to slow and his mouth to seek hers.

It was a long time before they reached the cabin.

Sam and Annie stood before the locked door, the air around them as erratic as an electrical storm. Far back in her mind, Annie wondered why Sam bothered locking this door when he didn't lock his front door back in Midnight Cove.

She practically floated inside, where she was vaguely aware of a sparsely furnished front room, wood paneling, and a stone fireplace. "Would you like something to drink?" he asked.

"No, thanks."

"Care to see the rest of the cabin?"

She knew what he was asking, and appreciated the fact that he respected her enough to ask. "I'd like that."

He led her into a narrow hallway, past a room that held a large desk, and into another room that reminded her of his bedroom on the mainland.

"Here's the quiet room you promised me." She closed the door.

"There's the soft bed."

"And the cool ocean breeze?" she asked.

He drew her with him to the window and released her hand long enough to lift the sash. Instantly, a fresh ocean breeze ruffled the heavy curtain.

"Do you sleep here often?"

He shook his head, kicked off his shoes. Annie couldn't think of a single good reason not to toe out of hers. Leaving the sandals where they fell, she strolled to the foot of the bed, where she ran a hand along the heavy wood post. The bed was covered with a simple blue quilt and four oversize pillows. It was a bed designed for comfort, where a person could laze the day away.

She could hear Sam's deeply drawn breath, could feel the heat emanating from his body, but in her mind, she heard the sound of another man's voice. "Come on, Jolie, are you going to sleep all day?"

She closed her eyes for a moment. Keith had always hated those rare occasions when she'd lazed a day away.

"Is something wrong?" Sam asked, his arms gliding around her from behind.

Her head fell back against his chest. Her memory was returning, and she was wrapped in the arms of an incredibly rugged, virile man. "Everything's wonderful. Do that again."

One hand cupped her breast. His other hand made a slow journey down her ribs, across her waist, to her belly.

She sucked in a ragged breath and moaned. Her memory was returning. That meant she would be leaving soon. Time was running out. Before it ran out completely, she turned in Sam's arms, intent upon getting him out of his shirt. He seemed just as intent to get her out of hers.

Their clothes came off tangled and inside out, with no regard for buttons or seams. When Sam had her naked and exactly where he wanted her, he stretched out on his side next to her and covered her breast with one hand. "Now," he said, his voice edged with only the barest control, "where is that tattoo?"

"That's for me to know and you to find out."

The ragged breath Sam took had as much to do with the knowing smile on her lips as it did with the brazen way she encircled him with one hand. Well, almost as much.

He kissed her mouth, her face, her neck, and breasts, checking in several places, some obvious, some not. At times he forgot what he'd been doing. It was amazing he could think at all, considering what she was doing to him with her lush body, her hands, her lips.

Drawing in a ragged breath, he said, "I'm supposed to be looking for your tattoo."

She looked up at him. "Do you want me to stop?"

He never wanted her to stop. But eventually, he resumed his search, and then it was her turn to sigh, to writhe, to need. He'd just about run out of places to look. On a whim, he rolled her over, and there it was, a work of art covering her bottom two vertebrae, a delectable tattoo, an inch and a half by an inch and a half, scratched and slightly bruised. It was a kiss, all right, far sweeter than chocolate.

"Are you going to gawk all day?"

She was one mouthy woman. "I'll show you what I plan to do all day." He rolled her underneath him, taking a moment to appreciate how perfectly they fit, her soft curves molding to the harder contours of his body. She closed her eyes when he joined them, adjusting. She didn't open them until they both returned to earth.

Other than the curtain fluttering at the window and his own deeply drawn breath, the room was quiet. It had taken a long time for Sam to catch his breath and for his heart rate to return to normal. He'd drawn the quilt over them a while ago. His arm was around her shoulder, her cheek resting on his chest.

"Are those kerosene lamps original?"

All he could see of her from this angle was the top of her head and the tip of her nose. "I thought you were sleeping."

"Close."

He knew the feeling. "I imagine the lamps are original. There's no electricity out here. I added the wood-burning stove when I first discovered the island."

"Then this place is yours?" The kiss she placed on his chest felt like a smile.

"Yes. And just so you know? You're the only person I've brought here, Annie."

"Not Annie." She kissed him again. "My name is Jolene. You can call me Jolie if you'd like."

"Jolie. It suits you."

"I know." She tilted her head slightly, and fell asleep smiling.

Sam came awake slowly and with great effort. In fact, it took a pry bar to open his eyes. Why was he sleeping in the middle of the day? And why in the hell was he as naked as a jaybird?

Annie.

He sat up.

No, her name was Jolene. Jolie.

Her side of the bed was empty and her clothes were gone. He threw off the quilt and jumped to his feet. He shoved a leg into his jeans, but had to hop around on one foot because the other pant leg was inside out.

"What's going on in there?"

Sam relaxed instantly. Not that he'd been panicked before.

He finished pulling on his jeans, then strode from the room. He found Annie, er, Jolie sitting at his desk, reading a paper he'd wadded up yesterday. Her feet were bare, her turquoise pants wrinkled, her hair looking soft where it fell over her forehead and across one cheek.

"I thought you'd gone."

She answered without looking up. "Where would I go?"

"Are you saying you're my prisoner?"

Jolene—God Almighty, it was such a joy to know her real name—finally looked at Sam. He stood in the doorway, shirtless and barefoot, his jeans slung low on his hips, the top closure open, the zipper doing little to disguise what he had on his mind.

She rose slowly to her feet, letting the crinkled paper she'd been reading fall to the floor where she'd found it. "Now I understand what you use that rechargeable battery for. I used a similar one in my laptop back home."

"And where is that?"

"I don't know yet. But I will. Soon. My name is Jolene. I was married for four years to a man named Keith. Annie is his daughter, and my step-daughter."

"You've been busy."

She took a step in his direction. "L.S. Oliver isn't a woman." She noticed a vein pulsing in his neck. She took another step. "And he sure isn't a priest." She came to a stop an arm's length away. She ran a hand down his chest, skimming lightly over sparse hair and taut muscles. "He isn't living in Los Angeles or New York."

"You don't say."

"It seems I've discovered the legendary L.S. Oliver."

He went perfectly still. "Are you impressed?"

"In case you haven't noticed, it takes a lot to impress me."

Sam didn't know what he'd expected, but it wasn't that. And yet he'd been waiting six years to hear it. She wasn't a woman who impressed easily, not by status, or bloodlines, degrees, or money, and best of all, not by fame. "What would it take for me to impress you, Jolie?" He held his breath as he waited to see if she knew the rest.

She looked up at him, her eyes wide and round and the darkest brown he'd ever seen. "Say that again."

"What would it take to—"

She shook her head. "Not that."

"Jolie?"

He could feel her melting, and tried to imagine how it must feel to go so long without knowing her name, without hearing it spoken, whispered. "Jolie. You're beautiful, Jolie. Do you know that, Jolie?"

He did away with her buttons. She arched her back. And then his mouth took over. Her clothes ended up on the floor. And they ended up back in the bed in the next room.

It was a long time before they dressed again. It was the need for nourishment that finally propelled them to go back to Sam's boat. They ate cheese and yogurt and pickles and grapes on the dock, their feet dangling over the side. The bottled water was ice-cold and tasted like heaven. It was with great reluctance that Jolie helped Sam stash their wrappers in the boat and prepare to go.

"Do you want me to untie that rope?" she asked.

"Are you in a hurry to get back?"

She looked at the glint in those dark gray eyes, the mouth she'd learned by heart, and the neatly trimmed beard that brought another level of awareness to skin already sensitized by a touch, a kiss, a caress. "If you want me to organize that antique sale before the rest of my memory returns, I'd probably better get started.''

"Jolie?"

"Yes?" She noticed his small smile, and remembered him telling her that "yes" was his favorite word.

"If you want me to take you back to the mainland, perhaps you should take your hand off my fly."

"I have a better idea." She raised her eyes and lowered his zipper.

"Have I told you how much I like your ideas?"

"I believe you have, but you can tell me again."

The dock was fashioned out of wood and extremely hard. It turned out Sam was extremely inventive. Later, they splashed in the surf, laughing like children one minute, kissing like lovers the next. Throughout the course of the idyllic afternoon, more of Jolie's memories returned. Most of the time, she whispered them to Sam. She sensed a tension in him every time, and wondered at its cause.

They finally left the island near seven o'clock. Their water supply had run out, and they'd missed supper. They hadn't gone far when Jolie reached into her pocket and drew out a candy bar. Sam watched the way she unwrapped it, inhaling its scent. "You're definitely a chocoholic."

She nodded. "I know. My mother used to tell me it was a good thing I never developed a craving for vodka."

She laughed, and Sam knew she'd just remembered that particular memory. She regained more by the minute. They hadn't discussed her insight regarding how he earned his living. Maybe she wouldn't tell anyone who he was. Maybe she would never realize who he'd been. Maybe she wasn't a reporter, or maybe she didn't watch sports. Maybe she'd never seen his picture on the cover of every glossy magazine in the free world.

Maybe she'd spent her formative years in a convent.

She took a bite of her candy bar, closing her eyes in rapture. He'd seen her do that several times today. This was the first time it was chocolate she was savoring.

She hadn't learned that in any convent.

She offered him half. He declined.

"You're awfully quiet," she said, scrunching the wrapper and tucking it back in her pocket.

"Woman, I'm damn near spent."

Jolie felt it, warmed by the look in Sam's eyes, flushed with heat, excited by something as simple as his grudging smile. She didn't need the yellow slicker anymore, and somehow she'd lost another hair clasp. Pushing her mussed hair out of her eyes and tucking it behind her ears, she said, "That's too bad, because I feel energized."

She could tell he was warming, even though his voice was gruff as he said, "That's the difference between men and women."

"Sam? I think we just about covered all the differences between men and women today."

They entered the harbor, laughing.

All but one of the other fishing boats were already in when they reached the dock. Normally, Sam beat the others back, but then, normally he didn't spend his day learning the secrets of a woman's lush body.

He'd learned so many other things today. There was a great difference between quietude and loneliness. He'd been lonely. And he hadn't even known. He wondered if it was possible to bank some of this pleasure for all the lonely years that would follow.

"Look!" she said, pointing. "A bat! Did you know bats aren't really blind?"

Jolie's memories had been returning to her like gangbusters all day. Sam had no right to dread the return of the remainder of her memory, and yet a part of him wanted more time with her.

"Betcha didn't know you were so popular, aye Sam?" Percy Parnell called from his big boat as Sam passed.

For once, Sam didn't know what Percy was talking about.

"Isn't that your friend?" Jolie asked, tipping her head toward the man standing at the end of the dock. "It is. It's the man in the Gucci shoes. My, you are popular."

Stepping out of the shadows, Grant Isaac Zimmerman lifted a hand in greeting. Jolie returned the wave. Sam kept both hands on the wheel, a sense of foreboding settling over him like bricks, for a man with three names, especially this man with three names, always spelled trouble.

Chapter Seven

Sam O'Connor was a very changeable man.

If Jolie hadn't known it before, she knew it the instant he saw the man waiting for him on the dock. His entire countenance changed. One minute he'd been relaxed, the epitome of a man who had spent a good share of his day climbing in and out of bed, and not alone. Suddenly, tension was evident in his white-knuckled grip on the steering wheel, in his squared shoulders and set jaw. A thin chill had settled over him, his gray eyes as unreadable as stone.

Jolie reasoned that it must have something to do with the man on the dock. She recognized him from the diner a few nights ago. "He's a friend of yours, right?" she asked.

The question seemed to bring Sam to his senses. He relaxed his jaw and eased up on the steering wheel. "I wasn't expecting him, that's all."

Jolie believed there was more to the sudden

severity in Sam's expression than surprise. But if he wanted her to think that was all it was, so be it.

She was quiet as she leaped to the dock and grabbed a rope as if she'd been doing it all her life. The knot she tied gave her inexperience away. Sam cut the engine, then quietly jumped onto the dock, too. "Grant, this is—"

She beat him to the introduction. "Jolie Something-or-Other."

Grant accepted her handshake. "Grant Zimmerman the Third."

"Is there a fourth?"

"Actually," Grant said with only a hint of an aristocratic lift of his eyebrows, "the woman I'm seeing says she wouldn't do that to a child."

"You're from Boston. I can tell by your accent. I grew up in Pennsylvania."

This was news to Sam. Apparently it was news to her, as well.

Recovering slightly, she said, "It's nice to meet you, Mr. Zimmerman."

"Grant."

She smiled again. "Grant." She looked from him to Sam. "I'll leave you two alone."

Sam took an involuntary step in her direction because, damn it, he hated to see her go.

It was as if she knew. "Don't look so stricken."

Who was she calling stricken?

With a wink that was all sass, she said, "You're the one who said you're spent."

Okay, now he was stricken.

She started down the dock, only to turn suddenly, catching them both watching. "I'll stop by tomorrow and start sorting out your antiques." To Grant, she said, "I know this is none of my business, but perhaps the woman you're seeing was goading you when she said she wouldn't name a child Grant Zimmerman the fourth. I get the feeling it would take a strong woman to goad a man like you."

Her gaze strayed to Sam, as if she was including him in her assessment. Without another word, she continued away from the marina. When her turquoise Capri pants were only a spot in the distance, Grant said, "How long has she known her real name?"

Sam glanced at his watch. "About seven hours."

"What else does she remember?"

Sam had a bad feeling about this. Rather than list all the things Jolie had recalled thus far, he finished tying up the boat. "Why don't you tell me what you're doing here. And when you're finished, you can tell me just how big a mistake I made today."

Grant Isaac Zimmerman the third eyed his friend. "I'd planned to begin by telling you you're screwed. Now that I've seen you, I think it would be best to rephrase that."

Sam glowered, failing to see the humor. "Just tell me what you know."

Grant ran a hand through his hair, across his face, then slowly down his hundred-dollar tie. The fact that Grant hadn't taken the time to change his clothes churned up the acid in the pit of Sam's empty stomach.

"I have some information regarding Jolene's identity."

She'd introduced herself as Jolie, not Jolene. Sam's misgivings increased by the second. "And?"

Casting a careful look around, Grant finally said,

"I left my car at the top of the hill. We can take it to your place."

Grant hated Sam's place. Before the acid in Sam's stomach ate a hole completely through his composure, he turned on his heel and led the way to Grant's car.

Except for the thud of Sam's boots as he paced from one room to the next, his house was quiet. He'd asked Grant all the pertinent questions, and Grant had answered as best he could. The personality tests Jolie's psychiatrist and doctors had run before she left the hospital had been accurate. She was a journalist, and not a two-bit one, either.

Sam stopped pacing when he came to one of the antique tables in the dining room where he'd dropped a grainy photograph and short newspaper article. The article showcased two women who were competing for a prestigious, high-profile job on one of the national morning news shows. One of the candidates had blond hair, flawless skin, straight teeth, and a nose that had surely come straight off an assembly line. The other woman's coffee-colored hair looked slightly mussed, her eyes slightly close set, her smile the sassy variety that made a person look twice and remember forever.

Grant had done a little investigating and discovered that Jolie's ex-husband was Keith Carlton, CEO of Carlton Chocolates. She'd taken back her maiden name but retained forty-nine percent of the shares in the company after the divorce. No wonder she knew so much about chocolate.

She knew a great deal about a lot of things.

According to the article, it was just like Jolie

Sullivan to slip away without telling a soul. Rumor was, she'd gone in search of the story of a lifetime that would put her over the top for the job.

A few days ago Sam had wanted to know what she had been doing in Maine to begin with. It wasn't likely that she'd been following up on an Elvis sighting at some mall.

He raked his fingers through his hair. Hadn't he known she was dangerous? Even he hadn't known just how dangerous. Her memory was returning. Any day now the final pieces would fall into place. She couldn't have planned the amnesia, but it had certainly worked to her advantage. She would take the story of a lifetime and return to New York with bells on. Even if she didn't recognize the bearded man as the legendary former golf pro, Logan Samuel Oliver Connors, she knew where L.S. Oliver, mysterious, reclusive best-selling author had been living these past six years. Knowing her, she would put the two together. Wouldn't that be the icing on the cake? In her case it would be fudge icing on a multilayered chocolate cake.

"Six years." Sam turned to Grant, who was sitting somewhat uncomfortably on an old sofa. "I was celibate for six frigging years. When I finally took a woman to bed, it couldn't have been just any woman. It was the reporter of the century! What the hell was I thinking?"

Grant rose to his feet and struck a pose psychiatrists were notorious for, weight on one foot, arms folded, chin resting on one fist. "You know what you were thinking. Look at her. That hair, those eyes, that body. Why do you think we men name our Johnsons? It's because we don't want a complete stranger making ninety-eight percent of our important decisions."

Sam shook his head. "They teach that at Harvard, Grant?"

"That came straight from the School Of Hard Knocks. What are you going to do, Sam?"

"It's a little late to do anything. Even if Jolie wouldn't have remembered my face before, she will after today."

"That good, were you?"

Sam snorted. She'd been that good. She'd been incredible, warm and pliant and strong and agile as only a woman in the throes of a strong passion could be. Heat stirred anew at the memory alone.

"There are other places to live," Grant said. "Of course, now that she knows my name and face, too, you'll be easier to track. You know I'll help in any way I can."

They were both quiet after that. Grant had said it best earlier. Sam was screwed.

Jolie waited until closer to eight o'clock to walk to Sam's house the following morning. She'd hoped he would stop in last night. He hadn't. He'd made no promises. And he'd said he was spent. She'd hoped anyway. And that really rankled.

Surprisingly, he answered her knock this morning. Her heart fluttered. That rankled even more.

Even though he wasn't wearing the customary baseball cap, she couldn't read his expression. No surprises there. He'd closed himself off from her again. She would really like to understand why. "I said I would organize your antiques today."

He held the door for her as she strode through. And she couldn't help yawning.

"You didn't sleep well, Jolie?"

It wasn't easy to regard him impassively when the sound of her name in his deep baritone weakened her knees. "I finished your book."

Sam noticed effusive praise wasn't forthcoming. He was in no mood to dig for compliments. Her hair was down this morning, long and loose around her shoulders, and still slightly damp, as if she'd recently stepped out of the shower. Her dress was black and inexpensive looking, the fabric lightweight and just loose enough to skim over her curves and delineate the smooth length of her thighs and the narrow ridge of one knee.

"Did your friend go back to Boston?" she asked.

He nodded. She must have realized he wasn't going to add more unless she did some prodding, because she finally said, "You aren't in the witness protection program, are you?"

He almost smiled at that. "No."

"The CIA?"

"Hardly."

"What does your friend do?" She motioned for him to help her move a heavy table.

"Grant is a psychiatrist."

"They must pay you a lot to write those books if you can afford a shrink who makes house calls."

"Grant isn't my shrink." They moved on to another heavy piece of furniture.

"You don't want to talk about Grant, do you, Sam?"

He shook his head.

"You don't want to talk about yourself, either."

This time he shrugged.

"A man who doesn't like to talk about himself is a real rarity."

She didn't know the half of it. Any day, she would know the rest. So what the hell was he doing drinking in the sight of her, the soft, clean flowery scent of her?

She picked up an old lamp, examined it, then put it back down. "I had fun yesterday."

She chose that moment to look his way, her gaze meeting his from the other side of the cluttered room. Quickly, she averted her eyes. It was then that he knew he was hurting her. Aw, hell.

"I had fun, too, Jolie." He raked his fingers through his hair. "I've lived alone for years. All of a sudden I've discovered that solitude and loneliness are two very different things."

He clamped his mouth shut. What the hell was happening to him? He was the one with the power, and yet he was telling her how he felt.

She smiled. And he would have said it all over again.

"It's coming back, Sam."

He'd known that. Hearing her say it out loud drove home nearly every misgiving he had. Luckily, she did most of the talking for the next hour. They lined up chairs, straightened trunks and pottery, arranged knickknacks and glass items.

"Last night I pictured my apartment in New York. It's not much bigger than mine here in Midnight. When the rest of my memory returns, I'll be returning to my life."

"Is there a particular man you'll go back to?" Sam asked before he could stop himself.

She made an unladylike sound that drew his smile out of hiding. "I don't think there are too many men out there who would risk life or limb to pull out a chair for me.''

He strode to the table and slowly dragged out a chair.

Something nudged Jolie from the inside. She was a hairbreadth away from falling in love. She doubted that was a good thing. The intensity in Sam's eyes reached inside her, spreading to a place beyond her heart, to a place she couldn't name. She had to remind herself that he'd hardly risked life or limb to hold out that chair. He was risking something else. She just didn't know what.

"Do you believe in happy endings, Sam?"

His grim expression spoke volumes.

"That's what I thought. We'd better keep moving if we want to finish. If it's any consolation, my ex-husband cured me of any romantic notions left over from childhood."

"It wasn't a pretty divorce?" he asked.

"It wasn't even a pretty marriage. The best thing about it was loving Annie."

She saw him looking at the bracelet on her wrist. She knew what two of the charms meant. One represented her stepdaughter, the other her love of chocolate. The quill pen was still a mystery. But not as big a mystery as Sam.

Her gaze was drawn to him repeatedly. Over and over, she found him looking at her. She understood what it meant when a man looked at a woman that way. And she understood what could happen when a woman understood what it meant. She rubbed her forehead, and continued to regard him. It was as if she'd seen him somewhere years ago, but couldn't place his face.

Sam knew what Jolie was doing. This time, he

didn't rush her into his arms. What was the use? He'd wandered around his house until all hours after Grant left last night. Even with the television on, the house had been too quiet. He'd thought about having a beer at Rocky's Tavern, but he knew that if he went to Main Street, Rocky's Tavern wasn't the place he would visit.

"I felt restless last night, too, Sam."

He did a double take. Could she read his mind?

She arranged several vases and milk-glass pitchers on a dresser top. "Waiting for my memory to return feels a little like, oh, I don't know. Do you remember how it felt when you were a child waiting for Christmas when you knew you'd been bad a lot that year?"

Sam hadn't planned to laugh. "Bad, as in naughty?"

She rolled her eyes.

He took a step in her direction. "Were you a naughty girl, Jolie?"

"So what if I was?"

"What about now?"

"You know how naughty I can be now."

"Care to refresh my memory?"

She looked up at him. As if propelled by a force greater than either of them, she stepped into his arms. They were in the middle of a long, passionate kiss when the doorbell rang.

"Is it ten o'clock already?" she whispered. "Oh my gosh." She pushed out of his arms. "It's after ten."

"Are you expecting someone?" he asked.

"Yes." She ran to the door.

"Who?" he asked.

A fat woman wearing a flowered dress and half

a bottle of sickeningly sweet perfume bustled in. "Hello. I'm Adaline, of Adaline's Antiques over on the highway just outside of town. Sorry I'm late."

She hurried past them, snapping pictures. "Look at all these treasures. Oh, my goodness. It's you!"

Shards of light flashed in Sam's eyes.

"I don't believe it! It's really and truly you!"

Chapter Eight

"Someone famous, right here in our neck of the woods!" The woman's voice was shrill. "This is so exciting!"

Exciting wasn't the word Sam had in mind.

"Forget the antiques," Adaline exclaimed. "Le'me get a picture of you!"

Ice spread through Sam's veins. He'd dreaded this moment for six years, and yet all he could do was stand there, frozen like a deer trapped in the glare of headlights.

"You know me?" Jolie's voice seemed to come from far away.

Understanding dawned at the exact moment Sam's vision cleared.

"Why, you're Jolie Sullivan." Adaline gushed. "You're that darling reporter up for a position on that morning news program, *Every Day.* If you ask me, somebody could have come up with a better name. Oh, never mind about that. What's in a name anyway, right, dearie?''

Sam's gaze sought Jolie's. Something intense passed between them, for he understood how important Jolie's name was to her.

"Your picture was on the news just last night," Adaline exclaimed. "They showed a picture of you and your contender. This is such a coincidence. What are you doing in Maine?''

Sam stepped in front of Jolie, shielding her from more flashbulbs. "She's recovering from amnesia, which resulted from a blow to her head. Blinding her isn't going to help, damn it.''

Adaline glanced at Sam only long enough to dismiss him as unimportant. After patting her coiffed gray hair, she darted around him and placed a chubby hand on Jolie's arm. "Amnesia? Really? You don't remember who you are?''

"Actually, my memory has been returning a little at a time." Jolie wet her lips. "Sullivan. Of course. That's my last name.''

Adaline clucked like a mother hen. "You need to sit down.''

"I'm fine, really.''

"Young man, bring that chair over here. Quick now.''

Dazedly, Jolie sat in the chair Sam placed directly behind her. Adaline barked more orders to Sam while continuing to hover over Jolie. Aside from her strong perfume, she was gentle and kind and helpful, not to mention talkative.

Unlike Sam.

Adaline barely gave him the time of day. Jolie couldn't keep her eyes off him. Her head was swimming, and yet everything she'd forgotten was right there as if it had been there all along. She could picture her friends, her stepdaughter, her rival, Selina Nelson. Jolie's mother was gone, but her father and stepmother were very much alive and well and retired in Arizona.

"Are you all right, Jolie?" Sam asked quietly.

She'd planned to smile, then changed her mind at the way his gray eyes had narrowed. She couldn't tell if he was generally resentful of Adaline's intrusion, the situation, or something else. "I'm fine, thank you."

Adaline returned with a glass of tap water she'd initially told Sam to fetch. Muttering something about men's uselessness in situations like these, she handed the glass to Jolie and waited expectantly for her to take a drink. Feeling five years old, Jolie took a sip. Adaline bustled away again.

"You're quiet," Sam said.

Something started to click far back in her mind. "Where have I seen you before?"

An inexplicable look of withdrawal came over his features. They were still staring at each other, neither speaking, when the screen door bounced closed. The woman from the antique store was back. Jolie hadn't paid enough attention to know she'd gone outside.

"Aren't cell phones wonderful?" Adaline said, beaming. "I don't know how people ever got along without 'em."

Jolie and Sam both stared at the other woman in confusion.

Adaline started straightening the room as if she owned the place. "I just called a friend of mine who works over in Sedgwick. They're on their way."

"Who's on their way?" Jolie asked.

"Why, the press of course."

"The what?" Sam's voice boomed.

"The press." Adaline's eyes darted from Sam to Jolie.

"They're coming here?" Sam glared at the older woman.

Adaline cast a furtive glance around the room, as if wondering what the fuss was about. "Actually, I told them to meet us at my store." She turned to Jolie. "You don't mind, do you? I could really use the publicity."

Jolie allowed the other woman to pull her to her feet and lead her from the room. That clicking was still going on in the back of her mind. This was what she'd been waiting for. She was thrilled with her memories, and so relieved to know who she was and where she lived and what she did.

Why wasn't Sam saying anything?

She glanced over her shoulder. He was staring back at her across the ringing silence. All at once, her feet froze to the floor. Those storm-gray eyes, that sandy-brown hair, that physique . . .

Adaline tugged on her hand, drawing her out the door.

Jolie noticed that Sam didn't try to stop her. He didn't follow her outside. He didn't even say goodbye.

Sam didn't know how long he stood in the doorway after Adaline helped Jolie into her van and drove away. Ten minutes? Half an hour? Longer? His breath had solidified in his throat and his jaw hurt from clenching his teeth.

He had to get out of there.

He was halfway down the porch steps when he realized it would do him no good to go to the island. He had no place to hide. Jolie had put it all together. He'd seen it in her eyes. She was probably meeting with the press at this very moment.

There was nothing he could do except wait for the wolf to come knocking on his door.

No one came knocking on Sam's door, not a wolf, not the press, not even Jolie. Sam knew, because he'd spent the past eight hours prowling his house like a caged tiger.

Darkness was falling, and Midnight Cove was swarming with reporters, news teams, cameras, and vans with satellites on their roofs. Jolie had been on live television. He'd watched, stretched out on his back on top of the covers, fully dressed right down to his shoes.

The camera crew did a decent job of panning the harbor, Main Street, even the driftwood piled high in the Potters' front yard. Several of the local residents were interviewed. Each and every one of them should have received a standing ovation for the way they answered the reporters' questions without answering at all, only to launch into a lengthy conversation about themselves. It was their five minutes of fame, and they weren't about to squander it. Adaline made a point to mention her many antiques. The woman who owned the dress shop modeled an outfit from her "new" summer collection. Dulcie took the cake when she looked straight into the camera and said, "That's right. Jolie worked for me in the diner. A fine waitress. 'Course, we all knew her as Annie Valentine. Loves chocolate, that gal. In fact, I had her sample some of the desserts in the collection of recipes I'm compiling. I'm calling it Ninety-Eight Ways to Sweeten Your Sex Life."

The reporter's gasp gave Sam a whole new appreciation for live television.

Something pattered the windowpane. Rain? He glanced back at the television where Jolie was being interviewed. She looked good on TV, completely comfortable and pretty. Her memory had returned, and with it the qualities that would endear her to her viewers. She smiled, she laughed, she teared up when she spoke of her stepdaughter. She had the audience eating out of her hand.

She was a pro. Sam rubbed at his sore jaw.

The noise at his window came again. It wasn't rain. It sounded suspiciously like sand or pebbles on glass. He aimed the remote at the TV and hit the mute button before moving the curtain aside and peering out. Jolie stood in the dark far below, wearing the same black dress she was wearing that very second on his television screen.

Sam opened the window. "Amazing how someone can be in two places at once."

She peered around her as if she was afraid she might have been followed. "How long have you known who I am?"

Sam had never heard a more demanding-sounding whisper.

"What difference does it make?" he said, whispering, too. "Your rival doesn't stand a chance after this."

The corner of her mouth twisted in exasperation. Without another word, she darted around the side of his house. Sam met her at the door.

With a thrust of her chin and a toss of her head, she brushed past him. "Did you know before we . . . yesterday . . . you know."

He didn't answer.

"You knew all along, didn't you?"

"Not in the beginning."

"Why should I believe you? After all, people tell the truth around you. That doesn't necessarily work in reverse, now does it?"

There was a long, brittle silence. He didn't know why the hell she was so angry. He was the one about to have his life ruined. "Annie. Jolie. I didn't know when we met, all right?"

He detected a softening around her eyes. "Then our friendship, showing me your lobsters, the island . . ." Her voice trailed away. "That at least was genuine?"

Sam ran a hand through his hair, down his face, across his beard. What difference did any of that make now? "Why are you here alone, Jolie?"

"What?"

He glanced out the window. "Where's the camera crew?"

Jolie stared at Sam longer than was considered polite. She couldn't help it. The past eight hours had been a whirlwind and an eye-opening experience. She knew her full name, her phone number, her seventh grade teacher, her alma mater. She'd spoken on the telephone with her father and stepmother, her boss, her best friend, Rachel. She'd gotten exactly what she'd wanted, what she'd hoped for, prayed for. Her memory was back, all of it.

She hadn't seen Sam in eight hours. And she'd missed him the entire time. Something intense was going on inside her, something she didn't think she'd ever felt in exactly this way. It wasn't just a simple case of her wanting a man. There was nothing simple about any of this. She didn't know what it meant, exactly, or what she was going to do about it. But she knew she didn't want to leave Midnight Cove before she found out if he felt the same way.

A car drove by, its headlights flickering across the living room wall. Sam tensed up even more. Suddenly, Jolie knew what he was afraid of. "You think a camera crew is on its way, is that it?"

"You came to Maine for a story, didn't you?"

"Maybe I did. Maybe I didn't."

She thought his derisive snort was condescending even for him.

"So that's what this is all about. The great, legendary Logan Samuel Oliver Connors doesn't like the press."

"You're a reporter. Reporters exploit. If the truth hurts, I guess you're just going to have to deal with it."

His lack of belief in her not only hurt, but really ticked her off. After everything they'd shared, done, been together. He knew all the secrets of her body. He even knew where her tattoo was, for crying out loud. "You don't trust many people, do you, Sam?"

"Not a lot of people have given me reason to trust them."

"You know, I'm getting a little sick of your attitude."

"My attitude?" His nostrils flared.

"You think I'm going to lead the press to your door?"

"Here's a news flash for you, Jolie. You are the press."

"Yeah?" *Oh, good comeback,* she thought.

They were almost nose-to-nose.

"You know something, Sam? I'm getting sick of your lack of faith in my character. And do you know what else?" She jabbed her finger into his chest. "Just because the rest of the world would be interested in a washed-up, has-been former-golf pro who's completely full of himself, doesn't mean I am!" With a lift of her chin, she spun around. "Deal with that!"

She slammed the door so hard on her way out, the windows rattled. Sam stayed where he was, a hand pressed over the muscle she'd jabbed on his chest. Deeper, he could feel his heart beating. It felt ominous, somehow.

He'd caught glimpses of her temper before, but he'd never seen her this angry. He was an idiot. He should have tried to reason with her. Hell, he should have gotten on his knees and begged her to keep his secret. Instead, he'd insulted her, irritated her, and provoked her.

He might have had a chance before. But she was sure to tell her story now. And there wasn't a single thing Sam could do except wait.

Chapter Nine

Sam leaned back in his chair. The water stain on the ceiling hadn't changed since yesterday. Or the day before. Or the day before that.

It was the end of July. The roof of his cabin had sprung a leak during the last gully washer. He should have been making arrangements to pick up the materials he would need to fix it. He lowered the front legs of his chair to the floor and looked around the room he used as an office on his island but made no move to do anything.

He'd finished his last book and should have been starting another. He came to the island every day. He sat in his chair. More often than not, he ended up staring into space. Consequently, there were no wadded-up papers on the floor.

It was all Jolie's fault.

He told himself he couldn't concentrate because he was waiting for the ax to fall. He'd listened for it on the news, scanned the newspaper headlines, checked out the covers of magazines. He'd waited an entire month. Other than a grainy photograph of the back of a man the reporter claimed was Logan Samuel Oliver Connors, taken in Australia no less, Sam's name hadn't been mentioned.

Just this morning he'd watched Jolie's rival sashay onto the set on her first day on the job. Any fool could see that Jolie was better suited to the position. Why hadn't she used her knowledge to acquire that position? What the hell was she waiting for?

He heard a deep rumble far in the distance. Thunder? He glanced at the laptop, then back up at the ceiling. He really needed to do something about that leak, about his next book, about his life.

The sound drew closer. It wasn't thunder. It was the *whomp whomp whomp* of a helicopter. Sam switched off his computer and slid the battery into his pocket. Might as well call it a day.

By the time he locked the cottage door, the helicopter was in plain view. And it was heading his way. A bead of perspiration broke out on his brow. That tiny bead turned into a river when the helicopter landed in the place he and Jolie had fed the herons and gulls a month ago.

A door opened and Jolie got out. Wearing what appeared to be a green jumpsuit, she crouched low as she ran beyond the perimeter of the whirling blades. Straightening, she strode directly toward him, like a woman on a mission, only to stop twenty-five feet away.

Sam may not have been able to control the fact that she was a sight for sore eyes, but by God he didn't have to let her know it. "I've been wondering what you've been waiting for."

Her eyes widened and her brows rose slightly.

"How did you know I was waiting for you back at your place?" Her eyes narrowed. "That isn't what you meant, is it? You still think it's just a matter of time before I take your little secret public." She folded her arms at her ribs and glared at him. "You know, Sam, you spend too much time alone."

She turned her back to him, and gestured to the man flying the helicopter. With a nod and a wave, the pilot lifted the machine off the ground.

"For your information," she yelled over the loud machine, "Rob didn't forget the big camera. He's a fire jumper, not a reporter." Her ex-husband used to ask her if she wanted cheese with that whine whenever she used that tone. If Sam mentioned it, so help her, she would clobber him.

"He sounds fascinating."

"He's also convinced he's in love with me."

"Then what are you doing here?"

She glared at him. "I guess there's no accounting for taste, is there?"

As the implication soaked through Sam's thick skull, Jolie studied him. His hair looked freshly cut, his beard freshly trimmed. He should have looked fresh. There were dark circles under his eyes, dark emotions in them. Apparently she wasn't the only one who hadn't been sleeping well.

"Why did they give the position to that other woman?" he asked.

"They had to give it to somebody after I turned it down." She held up one hand in a halting gesture. "Hold it right there. From now on, I'll be doing the talking and asking the questions."

She rather liked the way he clamped his mouth shut.

"I'm very mad at you, Sam O'Connor."

He cocked one eyebrow, but he didn't utter a sound.

"Yes, I called you Sam O'Connor. Not Logan. Not L.S Oliver. Sam. I won't tell you what I called you under my breath a thousand times this past month. But I will tell you this." She moved closer so she wouldn't have to yell. "I've been busy."

"What have you been doing, Jolie?"

She pointed her finger at him the way a teacher might at an errant student. Still, soft-touched thoughts shaped her smile. "I visited Annie. I swear she's grown three inches. And I flew to Arizona to see my dad. I sold my shares of the candy company. Oh, and I thought about you."

Jolie was pretty sure Sam hadn't moved. Therefore she must have been the one who'd strolled closer. "I watched a lot of old footage of you before you disappeared. You have a good reason to distrust the press. That doesn't mean I've forgiven you for failing to try to contact me this past month." She held up her hand again when he started to argue. "Grant told me to give you time."

"You've talked to Grant?"

"How does it feel to be kept in the dark? That's what you've done with me from the very beginning. I think I've figured out why. Care to hear what goes on in the deepest recesses of a woman's mind?"

"It'll be dark in three hours."

She stuck her tongue out at him. "Are you seeing someone?"

"Who would I see?"

"I'll interpret that as a 'no.' So I can assume the diamond ring is for me?"

"You snooped in my sock drawer?"

She shrugged. She had to do something to kill

the time waiting for him to return. "It's really a lovely ring. When did you buy it?"

"Two weeks ago."

"What were you planning to do with it?"

"I've considered several scenarios. One involved kidnapping you, another hog-tying you. Why didn't you take the job with the network, Jolie?"

"Because it wouldn't have been ethical for someone in that position to have a husband who has special powers that cause people to blurt out the truth."

Sam's first thought was, an ethical reporter? His second thought staggered him. Husband? "I thought I lost you, Jolie."

"You didn't lose me, you big idiot. You threw me away. Or at least you tried to. But it occurred to me that you didn't ask me to keep your identity a secret. That could have been because you trusted me. Or it could have been because you didn't."

Nothing about the conversation should have been lust arousing, and yet Sam's desire for this woman had never been stronger. "You never intended to tell anybody who I am, did you?"

She shook her head. "I've dropped out of the spotlight. I quit the network. I noticed you got rid of all the antiques. Before you say anything, I already know you worked out a deal with Adaline, who hauled them all off to her store."

So, Sam thought, she'd been in touch with Adaline, too. His house had seemed empty this past month. His house wasn't all.

He watched as she lowered the zipper on her jumpsuit. He wasn't certain what he expected her to do next, but he didn't expect her to reach into her pocket and draw out the little velvet box he'd last seen tucked under his socks. She placed it in his hand, then went back to that zipper.

Stilling her hand with his, he said, "I want to do this right."

Her gaze was on his mouth. Sam had the strangest urge to grin. "Not that. We always get that right."

"What then?"

He felt his Adam's apple wobble suddenly. "It seems I'm in love with a woman who loves chocolate."

She tipped her head an inch to the right. "Chocolate isn't all I love." She eased closer. "Care to hear what else I love?"

"What else do you love, Jolie?"

"Ha! As if I'd tell you."

"All right," he said, his thumb smoothing circles along her wrist. "I'll go first. I love big, round—"

She gave him an arched look.

"—Brown eyes and full, kissable lips and naughty tattoos. I love a woman who gives as good as she gets, often better." He stared into her eyes for interminable seconds. "Everyone tells the truth around me. And yet you don't. Oh, you did in the beginning, but then you stopped. How did you do that?"

She smiled knowingly. "Grant says I probably became immune. He also said you've been a real bear lately. That reminds me. How's the new book going?"

"Not good. Nothing's been good since you left."

"Poor baby."

"I can tell you're all choked up."

She grinned. Birds squawked nearby. "What's

the matter with them? Haven't you been feeding them?"

"They only look like birds. Underneath their feathers, they're hogs. They can wait. Believe me. But I can't wait another minute to do this."

He opened the velvet box. She surprised them both by sniffling. "If you go down on one knee, I'll clobber you."

"Do you want to do this?" he asked huffily.

Something went warm inside Jolie, something far deeper than her jumpsuit and skin. She'd done some investigating into Sam's background. All totaled, she must have watched a hundred hours of old tapes of his golf matches. She learned more from the tapes that came later, when former fans had taunted him, when people had made demands no human could possibly satisfy. The media had dogged his every step, leaving him no room and even less peace. No wonder he didn't trust reporters.

She looked at the ring, and then she looked into his eyes. "I love you, Sam."

"Then you'll marry me?"

She heaved a huge sigh.

"Is that a yes?"

She stepped into his arms. Going up on tiptoe, her mouth an inch from his, she whispered, "Yes. I hope I never have amnesia again. Do you know why, Sam?"

"Why, Jolie?"

"Because I would really hate to forget the next hour."

Birds squawked, waves pounded the rocks, the wind blew, and Sam thought he couldn't have put it better himself.

Dear Readers,

Several months ago, my editor invited me to participate in a novella collection. Other than word count, he gave me only one stipulation. My story had to include chocolate.

A woman? Write about chocolate? I laughed out loud, for surely this would require research I could sink my teeth into.

I'm sure you've already figured out that I love chocolate. I love men, too, which is especially nice since I have a husband and four sons! It so happens that I have a penchant for books, also, especially those about mysterious men and women. That in mind, I let my imagination soar to Maine's rocky coast. There, I discovered a lobsterman with a boatload of secrets and a woman with a bump on her head, a fledgling memory, and a craving for chocolate that rivaled my own. "I Know I Love Chocolate" was born full of mystery and fun and was meant to be enjoyed.

My debut novel with Kensington, THE COTTAGE, is also on the shelves in bookstores everywhere. This full-length novel depicts another woman of mystery, one who is a healer living in the Appalachian Mountains, a runaway boy searching for answers, and the man who followed him there.

I pour my heart and soul into every book I write, but none of them contains more of my soul than DAY BY DAY, a story set on the shores of Lake Michigan in my home state. DAY BY DAY follows the lives of a beautiful family blown apart by a horrible accident. The characters will grip you as they put their family back together, so grab a book off the shelves in July 2002, and hold on.

Indulge yourself, dear readers, with chocolate if you'd like, and with stories I think you'll love.

Sincerely,
Sandra Steffen

P.S. You may write to me via my Web site at www.sandrasteffen.com.

**Please turn the page for
an exciting sneak peek at
Sandra Steffen's newest
contemporary romance**

**DAY BY DAY
(coming in July 2002 from Zebra Books!)**

Maggie McKenzie hugged her arms close against a sudden chill. She'd been having a relatively innocent, innocuous conversation with Melissa Bradley and Hannah Lewis before Jessica Hendricks and MaryAnn Petigrue had joined them. Within seconds, the conversation had turned into a he-said-she-said gossip session, interspersed with a large dose of male bashing.

"Come on, Maggie!" Jessica declared. "Give us something low-down and dirty on Spence."

Maggie pulled a face. "I hate to disappoint you, but I'm drawing a blank."

"Are you telling me Spence doesn't do anything that annoys the hell out of you?"

Maggie ran a quick check through her mind. The truth was, she didn't have many issues with men. Spence wasn't perfect, but she didn't expect him to be. He'd grown up with three brothers, and the toilet seat had been a problem at first. She'd taken a few midnight splashes early in their marriage, but these days they both knew how to work the lid. He had a serious connection with the remote control, and he loved a clean garage but never seemed to notice when the house was a mess.

For lack of anything more serious, she shrugged and said, "Well, he's late for a lot of things."

"Not Peter," Hannah exclaimed. "He's on time for everything, and when I'm running late, he has this look, not to be confused with *a* look or *that* look. I'm talking about *the* look."

"Uh," Melissa Bradley exclaimed. "I know exactly what you're talking about. Aaron does that, too. Ever notice that when you and your husband are getting along, you like most everything about him?"

"And when you're not," MaryAnn Petigrue interrupted, "you don't even like the way he breathes."

Even Maggie smiled at that one.

The surprise party had been a success in every sense of the word. She, Yvonne, and several members of the Ladies Historical Society had planned it down to the tiniest detail, and yet Gaylord had surprised *them* with his announcement that he was making a six-figure donation to the society. It would be all over the papers tomorrow. Tonight, Maggie just wanted the party to wind down so she could go home, kick her shoes off, slip out of her dress, and unwind with Spence.

She'd been feeling strange all day. She wasn't prone to bad moods, and although she'd read about people who had premonitions, she rarely experienced them herself. Her parents, who were doing missionary work in Africa, would have blamed it on atmospheric pressure and a change in the weather pattern. Neither Joseph nor Adelle Fletcher believed in premonitions. Perhaps premonition was too strong a word. It was more like trepidation. Maggie felt antsy, uneasy. For the life of her, she couldn't say why.

She wondered where Spence was. He said he'd be here tonight, and Spencer McKenzie kept his word. She didn't know many women who'd been married nearly thirteen years and still missed their husbands simply because they hadn't seen each other all day. Sometimes, she worried that she loved him too much. How could she love him too much, when he loved her just as fiercely? She was thirty-four years old, and incredibly, undeniably happy. No one could ever accuse her of being weak. She didn't cling, and she certainly didn't define herself by her husband's success. It was just that she felt more alive when they were together.

The goose bumps that had been skittering up and down her arms trailed away. More relaxed now, she glanced at the guests scattered throughout the courtyard. Her gaze flitted over dozens of people, but it settled on one man.

Spence.

Their eyes met, held. Something unspoken and powerful passed between them. Just over six feet tall, he stood in the shadows with Edgar Millerton, looking more like a shipbuilder of bygone days than a modern-day architect.

No wonder she was no longer cold. He'd been watching her. All these years of marriage hadn't dulled or diminished the passion that had taken on a life all its own the first time they'd met, but time had honed their response to it.

She cast him a small smile, and watched the effect it had on his features. His lips parted, as if he'd suddenly taken a quick, sharp breath. The breeze lifted his dark hair off his forehead and ruffled his tie. She couldn't see the color of his eyes from here, but she knew they were a deep shade of blue, as vivid and changeable as the great lake they'd both come to love.

Spence could have lived anywhere from Alaska to Timbuktu, but Maggie, the daughter of a career army man, had known this was where she'd wanted to grow old the first time she'd visited the area some fifteen years ago. She'd lived in twenty-two towns before she'd graduated from high school, but she'd lived right here in this one small city for the past thirteen. She and Spence belonged here, the way she'd always longed to belong as a child.

Spence nodded his head at the staunch old codger he'd been talking to, but Maggie noticed he didn't take his eyes off her. Almost of its own volition, her hand went to her hair. She twirled a lock around one finger. Nobody watching could have known that the simple mannerism was her way of telling Spence that her thoughts had taken a slow, luxurious stroll to the bedroom. But he knew.

He had an angular face, and, when he chose to use it, a devastatingly attractive smile. Bidding Edgar farewell, he proved it, smiling as he strode closer. He kissed her on the cheek, an old-fashioned, gentlemanly gesture few men bothered with anymore, then said hello to Melissa, Jessica, Hannah, and MaryAnn.

The other four women moved, en masse, to the

buffet table. Maggie shifted slightly closer to Spence, so that her shoulder rested lightly against his arm. "How was the meeting?"

"All things considered, I'd say it went well. I'll tell you about it later. It looks like your party was a success, too, although everyone's more interested in talking about the surprise Gaylord had for all of you."

Maggie nodded. "Even Edgar Millerton?"

Spence ran the tips of three fingers up her arm, as if he'd waited as long as he could to touch her. Goose bumps of a different nature followed the path his fingertips took.

"You know Edgar," he said quietly.

Oh, dear. Maggie knew Edgar, all right. The man moved slowly, and spoke the same way. He took twenty minutes to order a sandwich. For excitement, he watched paint dry. Maggie herself had been known to go on and on about history, but even she had a difficult time staying focused when Edgar launched into conversation about sediment and water seepage. As tightfisted as Gaylord was generous, Edgar's idol was Jay Someone-or-Other, the United States' first Ph.D. to study groundwater. Once, Edgar had invited all the members of the Ladies Historic Society to his home, where he'd shown slides of how water drained through sand, gravel, and rock.

"Fascinating stuff, groundwater," Spence said close to Maggie's ear.

"You don't say."

"Did you know that it travels through pores in rocks one-seventieth of the speed of snails?"

Oh, dear. Maggie loved these social functions. She was perhaps the only person present who knew that they bored Spence silly. He made the best of them for her sake. It was one of the things she loved about him. There were plenty of other things.

"Biological reclamation is going well."

"Spence?"

"Evidently, it works by activating natural bacteria. It seems this natural bacteria eats most pollutants, like degreasers and solvents and septic-tank cleaners we humans have been dumping into the ground since they were invented."

She leaned lightly into him. "He must have had you cornered for a long time."

"It's hard to gage minutes when time is standing still."

She shook her head. "You were bored to death."

"I'm a big boy."

He was a big man.

"I'm surprised to see Jessica Michaels here," he said tersely. "Last I knew, she was living in the Caribbean."

Maggie shrugged. "It's Jessica Hendricks again. She took back her maiden name."

Spence gave a derisive snort. "She took John for everything he had. I'm surprised she didn't want to keep his name, too."

Maggie whispered, "I don't think I could ever do that."

"What? Keep my name?"

"No. Waste so much energy hurting someone I loved."

Sometimes, when Spence looked at her the way he was looking at her right now, she got lost in his eyes.

"I'd be a fool to give you a reason."

She smiled, because Spence was no fool.

With the barest movement of his head, he gestured toward the back steps. That was all it took, one look, and she knew he was asking how much longer she wanted to stay.

Earlier, the courtyards had been busting at the seams. There were still some forty guests milling about on this level, but the party was winding down. "We should be able to make our escape in half an hour or so. What did you have in mind?"

The sound Spence made deep in his throat was half moan, all male. Taking her hand, he led the way to a small dance floor nearby, where two other couples were dancing to music provided by a three-piece orchestra. Fitting her body close to his, he proceeded to give her a detailed outline of what he had in mind.

His words conjured up dreamy images that worked over Maggie like moonlight. Despite the heat emanating from him, she shivered again.

"Cold?" he whispered, close to her hair.

"Hmm. I don't know why, but I've been shivering all night." She closed her eyes, and for a moment, she felt as if she were looking at her life from outside herself, and something precious was about to slip away. A sense of dread washed over her. She kept her eyes wide open after that.

It didn't make sense. Her sister, Jackie, was home with the girls. Jackie loved Grace and Allison almost as much as she and Spence did. Jackie knew their favorite games, favorite foods, their latest secrets and oldest fears. She also knew the Wilsons' phone number by heart. Grace and Allison both knew how to dial 911. There had been no sirens, no weather rumblings or threats of disasters. Even the sky was clear. Why, then, did Maggie have to force herself not to hold on to Spence too tightly?

"About that getaway," she whispered.

"I'm listening."

"Think anybody would notice if we crept away right now?" she asked.

Several guests turned at the sound of the little yelp she made when he followed his smooth turn in one direction with a surprise dip.

"Nice going," she chided once she was back on her feet. "Now everybody will notice."

"I aim to please."

Yes, she thought, he did. She was overtired, that was all. Everything was fine. Perfect. Feeling more like her old self, she finished the dance in Spence's arms. Then, hand-in-hand, they mingled with the other guests, enjoying being together, anticipating being alone.

SEX AND THE
SINGLE CHOCOHOLIC

Kylie Adams

All I really need is love, but a little chocolate now and then doesn't hurt.
                                        —Lucy of the "Peanuts" gang

Acknowledgments

This romp is dedicated to the bombshells I admire from afar . . .

Helen Gurley Brown—Is there a smarter woman on the planet? I don't think so.

Madonna—Always full of surprises. And twenty years of great exercise music!

Sharon Stone—She can do no wrong in my book. Fiercely intelligent and knows how to dress for an awards show.

And to the bombshell I know personally . . .

Mary Ann Kirby—She stops traffic in both directions, makes a mint on the job, walks in a room and owns it. Little girls should follow her around at least one day a week to learn how it's done.

Chapter One

New York

"It's better than a multiple orgasm," Tatiana Fox announced.

Candace Rowley smiled. The ultimate rave review. But she held back her excitement. "Are you serious?"

Tatiana leveled a reproachful gaze. "Honey, I never joke about orgasms."

Candace felt the gooseflesh spread, watching expectantly as Tatiana continued to savor her first bite of Passion Truffle with something close to rapture. And then she could hold her patience no longer. Deep breath. "Can you taste the passion fruit?"

Tatiana closed her eyes, concentration total. "Absolutely."

Candace's aerial castles went splat. "It's too strong," she hissed miserably. "I knew it!"

Tatiana opened her eyes, if only to roll them. "Calm down. It's not overpowering." One beat. A raised eyebrow. "Do I taste guava?"

Candace could feel her own eyes shining. "Just a hint."

"Amazing. It makes me want to make out with that intern who escorted us to the green room." And then Tatiana did the unthinkable. Instead of finishing the chocolate, she returned the candy to its pink foil liner.

Candace regarded the act as a personal affront.

"I shoot a nude scene next week," Tatiana explained, skating a hand over her exposed and impossibly flat tummy. "I don't want to look bloated."

"That's *next week!*" Candace implored.

Tatiana shrugged and scarfed down the rest. "Guess I'll double up on pilates classes. By the way, nothing from Godiva could ever make me do that."

Candace beamed.

The green room door swung open. Enter Jackie, the assistant producer for *Coffee in Manhattan,* a girl who looked young enough to be on her way to a fraternity keg party. She stood there with clipboard poised, charmingly disheveled in that Bridget Jones way. "Oh, my God. I'm *so* fired. I can't believe makeup didn't come get you."

"But they did," Candace assured her. "I insisted they not do much. It's not my style."

Jackie displayed no signs of relief. "I'm still *so* fired. Wardrobe could've found you something better to wear."

"They tried, but I prefer this," Candace said. She rose to smooth down the skirt of the conservative black suit she'd snatched up for a steal at a basement sale.

"OK," Jackie said blankly. "Um . . . The woman who's supposed to be on to talk about the vaginal cream is stuck in traffic. A bike messenger got hit by a cab or something. Anyway, we're adding her four-minute segment to yours, so you have seven now."

Candace clapped with girlish excitement. "I can share my story about chocolate in ancient Mayan culture!"

Jackie's brow crinkled. "Uh, this isn't, like, the History Channel."

"Oh, but it's a fascinating tale," Candace insisted. And then she experienced a tremor of guilt. "I hope the bike messenger isn't seriously hurt."

"I heard the taxi was going sixty. He's probably dead. OK, after Didi sings "The Greatest Love of All" we go to a break, and then you're on. I'll be back in a few minutes."

"Seven minutes!" Tatiana exclaimed. "Honey, they should just call this show *Coffee with Candace.*" She reached out to take both of her friend's hands. "A little advice?"

"Of course."

"Don't forget why you're here. It's to get the Decadence Candies name out there and to sell Passion Truffles. Push, push, push. And just when you think that you've whored yourself enough, push some more. I managed to say the title of my last movie eight times in three minutes on *Good Morning, Los Angeles.*"

Candace scanned her memory. *"Lady Cop Undercover II: Massage Parlor?"*

"No, *Lady Cop Undercover III: Escort Service.*"

Candace nodded thoughtfully, even though the straight-to-video R-rated thrillers that Tatiana starred in were difficult to distinguish. "Oh, of course."

On the monitor, the show's cohost, Didi Farrell, was warbling that old Whitney Houston hit like a C-list entertainer with Branson, Missouri, dreams.

I'm on next, Candace thought, experiencing the slightest involuntary shiver. Tatiana was right. She had to push hard. So much was at stake.

On its own merits, Decadence seemed to be performing just fine. The retail shop in New York generated healthy sales, and Internet orders were higher than ever. But the candy industry was brutal, ruled by giants like Mars, Hershey, and Moore. Small companies were quick to shut down or, if lucky enough, to sell out to one of the big three. Insiders had predicted that only one hundred fifty candy companies would be left in the next ten years, down from the peak of six thousand after World War II.

Didi missed a note. *Ouch.* Candace cringed and traded a look with Tatiana.

"Is there any way we can vote her off the island?" her friend asked, inspecting a perfect nail.

Candace's mind shifted into overdrive. *Push, push, push,* she told herself. *Coffee in Manhattan* didn't pack the ratings punch of, say, *The Today Show,* but its numbers were large enough and its viewers responsive enough to jump-start serious buzz on a new product.

I need buzz, Candace reminded herself. *Buzz, buzz, buzz.* She had it all figured out. Promote Passion Truffles as the candy for couples. Her advertising agency already had the campaign pitch: "For a Perfect Night of Romance, Share a Box of Passion Truffles." Granted, it wasn't as clever/revolutionary/shoo-in for a Clio as Nike's "Just Do It," but it worked. Besides, recent surveys suggested that couples who regularly eat chocolate are three times more likely to engage in romantic activity than those who don't. That little nugget, coupled with the proven adage that sex sells, seemed like a recipe for success.

The green room door swung open again. "You're up," Jackie said. "Follow me. We'll get you miked and introduce you to Chip and Didi."

Candace turned to Tatiana.

"Remember, you're a whore," the B-movie queen/ex-*Playboy* centerfold told her. "But instead of your body, you're selling Decadence. Repeat after me. I'm a whore."

Candace tried to force the words past her lips. But for an anthropology major from Wisconsin, it was rough going. "I'm ... I'm ... I'm Britney Spears." That was all she could manage.

"Close enough," Tatiana said.

Candace trailed Jackie through the studio labyrinth and onto the *Coffee in Manhattan* set. A technician dashed over to attach a mike to her collar.

"Say something at normal voice level," he instructed.

"Testing, testing," Candace said, drying sweaty palms on her skirt.

He gave her the thumbs-up sign.

As Chip Hamilton and Didi Farrell appeared to take their places, Jackie made the necessary introductions, then disappeared.

"So you're the vaginal cream lady," Didi said.

"Hey, I feel left out," Chip piped in. "How about some penis cream!"

Chip and Didi broke up into a fit of laughter.

Candace stared back, horrified.

"That was hilarious," Didi praised the cohost, who seemed to be wearing more makeup than her. "Say it again for the cameras."

"You got it, doll face." Chip smiled, revealing teeth that were bleached a blinding, almost glow-in-the-dark white.

"Excuse me, I'm here to talk about chocolate," Candace interjected.

"Sweetheart, we have seven minutes," Didi said. "We can talk about lots of stuff." She turned to Chip. "How are my lips?"

He made an obnoxious smooching sound. "Kissable."

Didi cackled, then winked at Candace. "He's such a flirt!"

Candace leaned in to say, "I think there's been some sort of misunder—"

Chip held up a hand to cut her off. "Sorry, love. Time to make magic." And then he fixed a super smile on one of three cameras. "Welcome back!"

"Ditto!" Didi said with a laugh.

"Before we continue with the rest of the show, Didi, I just have to tell you how much your song touched my heart," Chip began earnestly. "I think everyone had a lump in their throat."

Yes, it's called gag reflex, Candace wanted to shout. But she sat quietly instead, praying their little act was just a bad joke.

"Thank you, Chip," Didi said, nodding with humility as thunderous applause broke out. "It's a song with the kind of message that we just don't hear enough of. 'The Greatest Love of All' is, after all, in us, in each and every one of us. Every morning I get up, and I go to the mirror, and I say to myself, 'Didi, I love ya, kid!' I really do!"

More applause.

"Well, guess what?" Chip put in. "I love Didi, too!" He smiled a megawatt smile for the camera. "I think we all do!"

"Enough about me!" Didi erupted, attempting to downplay the praise but clearly loving every nanosecond of it. "We have a show to do." She paused dramatically. "But thank you. I mean that. Our next guest has developed a sexual enhancer that should make every woman in the world very, very happy. Her patented Fantasy Cream is selling like gangbusters, and she's here to tell us more about it. Please give a warm welcome to Candace Rowley."

As the applause rumbled inside her chest, Candace could feel the blood siphon from her face.

Suddenly, and in the kind of lockstep twin movement found only in synchronized swimming, Chip and Didi's faces took on perplexed expressions as their right hands cupped their right ears. "Oops . . . We did it again!" they shouted in unison.

Didi turned to Chip. "What would we do without Toby, the producer?"

"I don't know about you, Didi, but I'd probably be back doing infomercials," Chip said.

"Hey, weren't you that butt firmer guy?" Didi squealed.

"Wanna see?" Chip asked, pretending to get up. The audience howled.

Candace battled hard to mask her annoyance.

"Forgive us, Manhattan," Didi said. "Candace

Rowley is here from Decadence Candies to tell us about their fabulous new Passion Truffles. Sorry, ladies. It's not a sex cream. But it's the next best thing! Good morning, Candace, and welcome to *Coffee in Manhattan.*"

"Thank you, Didi. It's great to be here."

"We'll get to your little candies in a minute. Let's talk about this Fantasy Cream. What do you make of this phenomenon?"

Candace blanched. "Frankly, I know very little about it."

"Well, I hear that it increases blood flow to the vaginal area and really ups your orgasm-to-sex ratio," Didi said. "It's about time the ladies got some magic medicine, don't you think? A lot of gals think Viagra is nothing but a nuisance drug. All these men are standing at attention—if you know what I mean—but some women just don't want to be bothered."

"Hey, I feel left out," Chip piped in. "How about some penis cream!"

The audience roared.

Candace tittered politely, her brain searching for a way to get the subject back on point. Precious minutes were fading away with talk of this ridiculous sex cream!

"Isn't he a mess?" Didi asked rhetorically. She shook her finger at Chip. "What am I going to do with you?"

"I don't know. Why don't we meet backstage with a jar of Fantasy Cream and figure it out!" Chip said.

The studio audience lost it again.

Didi slapped Chip's arm. "Oh, you! Behave yourself. We have a guest." She turned back to Candace now, tilting her head in a gesture of seriousness. "Tell us, Candace, what is *your* orgasm-to-sex ratio?"

"I beg your pardon?"

"When you make love with your partner, how often—"

"I know what you mean! I just can't believe you're asking the question!"

Stunned, Didi quickly drew back.

Chip patted his cohost's knee and leaned in toward Candace. "Didi just jumped in there a little too quick. No harm done. Let's start with the more appropriate question. Do you have a sensual lover at the present time?"

"No, I don't," Candace hissed.

Didi made a long face. "Then we're not going to press you for that orgasm-to-sex ratio." Suddenly she brightened. "Let's talk about candy! I don't know about you, but I can't turn down a watermelon Jolly Rancher to save my life!"

Chip raised his hand. "Green apple over here!"

Didi drew in an excited breath. "And what about those Junior Mints?"

Chip rubbed his stomach. "Yummy!"

Candace saw an opening and jumped at the chance to turn things around and finally get *chocolate* into the conversation. Too afraid to let go, she went on about Aztec emperor Montezuma's penchant for consuming fifty cups of chocolate a day, about cocoa beans being exchanged between bride and groom in ancient Mayan culture, and about Columbus encountering the cacao bean on his fourth and final voyage.

"Well," Didi finally cut in, "I'll never look at a Hershey's Kiss the same way again." Then she spun to face the camera. "Stay with us because when we come back, our own Chip Hamilton is going to harmonize with red-hot boy band O-Town!"

Chip mugged for the camera. "You better watch out Justin Timberlake!"

More deafening applause from the studio audience.

From out of nowhere, the technician appeared to snatch off Candace's mike. Just as suddenly, Jackie appeared to escort her back to the green room. "That was . . . interesting. But I thought you were going to talk about the Passion Truffles. We had them right there on the table for Chip and Didi to try."

Candace walked silently behind Jackie, reeling with humiliation. All she could do was play the media event as train wreck over and over again in her mind.

"Sorry about the mix-up. Chip and Didi never read schedule updates. Actually, they never read anything," Jackie said.

Tatiana stood waiting outside the green room.

Candace forced herself to look her in the eye. "Let's get out of here."

Tatiana managed an upbeat smile. "You did great."

"Nice try, but you're more convincing in the *Lady Cop Undercover* movies."

"Oh, my God!" Jackie erupted. "That's where I know you from. A guy I dated in college had one of your movie posters tacked up in his room."

Tatiana grinned knowingly. "Was he in the Greek system?"

Jackie nodded. "Yeah, Sigma Chi."

"Figures. Frat boys love me."

Stepping outside onto the people-packed Manhattan street, Candace wanted to scream.

Tatiana pulled her in for a quick side hug. "You need champagne. I believe it can solve almost anything."

Candace did a double take. "It's not even ten o'clock yet."

"We'll throw in a splash of orange juice and call it a mimosa."

They ducked into the Plaza Hotel, found a cozy spot in the lounge, and ordered up the day's medicine.

"Have you ever seen anything more pathetic?" Candace grumbled.

"Than your interview?"

Candace nodded.

"That's hard to say. I missed Chip harmonizing with O-Town. But Didi's version of 'The Greatest Love of All' was definitely worse."

Candace relaxed and laughed a little. "Let's talk about something else. How's your husband?"

"Kerr? He never wants to have sex and all he does is make noises about wanting children. That would make him my *wife*, right?"

Candace felt her eyes widen. "Kids?"

"Not this body," Tatiana shot back. *"Lady Cop Undercover V: Maternity Ward* is not in my future." She sighed. "He's looking into adoption."

Candace downed the rest of her mimosa in one greedy gulp. "I blew it."

Tatiana signaled for another round. "That you did, honey."

"I've invested so much in the development of Passion Truffles, and if the product doesn't take off, I don't stand a chance in Hollywood."

"What do you mean?"

"There's a movie called *Chocolate on Her Pillow* that's about to go into production—"

"Greg Tapper's starring in that!" Tatiana broke in.

"I know. He's also the executive producer."

"You know, we used to be in the same acting class." Tatiana moaned. "If you could ever imagine Brando from *The Wild One* and James Dean from *Rebel Without a Cause* having a baby, then it would've been Greg Tapper. He was *so* sexy." She savored the image a moment, then gave Candace a curious look. "I don't get it. What does this movie have to do with Passion Truffles?"

"Product placement," Candace said, pausing to start in on the second mimosa that had just arrived. "The chocolate that's placed on the leading lady's pillow plays a pivotal role in the movie. And this project is big budget. Most of it's being shot on location in Capri. Anyway, if Passion Truffles were to show up in the film, it could put Decadence on the map in a major way."

"Phone home," Tatiana said in a froglike voice.

Candace just stared.

"Phone home!" Tatiana repeated impatiently, thankfully in her own voice this time. "From the movie *E.T.!*"

"Oh!" Candace yelped, finally getting it. The Reece's Pieces product placement. Battle stories behind the lovable alien visitor loving Reese's Pieces instead of M&M's were legendary. Before the movie came out, Reese's Pieces sales were in serious trouble. But within two weeks of *E.T.*'s release, distributors had reordered the candy as often as ten times. In some circles it was still considered the biggest marketing coup in history.

"You know Greg Tapper," Candace said, thinking out loud. "And you've got connections in Hollywood."

"Honey, you're not looking at a girl with connections. I mean, I just signed up for *Lady Cop Undercover IV: Red Light District.* As for Greg, I knew him briefly about ten years ago. I couldn't even get my hands on a script for *Chocolate on Her Pillow.* I was begging my agent to get me a walk-on part just for the free trip to Capri."

Candace sighed, all hope fading. She needed an inside edge. All she had was an early draft of the script thanks to a winning e-Bay bid. As if the bottom of mimosa number two held the magic answer, she turned up the champagne flute.

Tatiana reached for an abandoned *New York Post* at the next table and turned directly to the gossip section. She scanned the columns for several seconds before announcing, "Speak of the devil. He's here in the city."

"Who?"

"Greg Tapper." Tatiana peered closer at the tabloid. "It says here that last night he was seen club hopping with Strider Moore. Never heard of him. But he's gorgeous." She turned the paper around for Candace's benefit.

Strider Moore! She peeked at the photo. As much as she hated to admit it, he was gorgeous. And filthy rich. And the playboy prince of the Moore Candies fortune. And obviously trying to schmooze the company's Private Selections brand into a product placement deal. Damn him! Her blood began to simmer. At this point, a third mimosa wouldn't hurt. She raised her empty glass to the waiter.

"Strider Moore is the competition," Candace said. "He's obviously vying for product placement, too."

"Maybe you'll have to pull a Julia Roberts and sleep with the enemy." Tatiana gave the candid newspaper photo a serious assessment. "I could imagine worse scenarios."

"Please," Candace scoffed. "I've heard stories about this guy. He only goes for Victoria's Secret catalog clones. And his idea of a long-term relationship is having breakfast with a girl the morning after."

Tatiana laughed. "Sounds like every actor, agent, and producer I know in Los Angeles." She studied Candace for a moment. "Think about it, though. You could play the chocolate Mata Hari. Seduce him, draw out his secrets, and then use them to your own advantage."

Round three arrived. Candace drank up immediately. The mimosas tasted so good, and she felt deliciously light-headed now. Even so, Tatiana's idea was insane! Play spy and sleep with Strider Moore? "Shut up!" Candace said, a bit too loudly.

A trio of uptight ladies turned to sneer at them.

Candace giggled. "Sorry." She started to speak in a loud whisper, "How can you sit there and suggest that I sleep with him? Look at me. Do I even remotely resemble a Wonderbra model?"

The laughter in Tatiana's eyes dimmed a little. "You could be a real stunner, Candace, only you hide behind your work and your books and your cheap clothes and your refusal to wear makeup."

Inside Candace's fuzzy mind, the accusation bounced around.

"I know girls in LA who go broke paying a colorist to get the exact shade of honey blond to their hair that you have *naturally*. And those same girls struggle with color contacts every morning for the cobalt blue eyes you were *born* with. When's the last time you exercised?"

Candace shrugged, her head buzzing. "I did a walkathon for breast cancer last summer."

"See! Girls in LA starve themselves and go through torture with personal trainers for that slender and fit look you don't have to work for." Tatiana curled her lips into a faux snarl. "Bitch. You're beautiful, and you don't even try."

Candace had not consumed *that* much champagne. She was not beautiful. Not even close. "That's the alcohol talking."

Tatiana leveled a ray-gun gaze. "Get your mother's voice out of your head, Candace. Listen to my voice. Listen to your own."

The giddy feeling faded fast. Suddenly her mother's constant refrains boomeranged in her mind. *Your eyes are too close together, Candace. It's a shame that you have your father's nose. You're going to have to develop some amazing makeup skills to do something about that mouth.*

A familiar bitterness crept up on her. For so long, Candace had considered it a personal victory to ignore all that, to not even try, to embrace the ugly duckling her mother had so often criticized. But it was really a hollow win. And Tatiana knew that. As college roommates, their friendship had been instantly sealed in the crucibles of freshmen fear,

Madonna's *True Blue* album, Ramen Noodles, and strained mother-daughter relationships.

"Did you think your mother was beautiful?" Tatiana asked.

"Of course," Candace answered matter-of-factly.

"I used to believe the same thing about my mother, but Dr. G helped me see it a different way."

Candace braced herself for the psychobabble. Tatiana spent an hour of every week in therapy.

"I never would've known how beautiful *she* was if she hadn't always been pointing out how unbeautiful *I* was."

Candace merely stared for a moment. This point really hit a nerve. It was so simple, yet so . . . *true*.

Tatiana splayed out her manicured hands. "Is this the girl you met at the University of Wisconsin in nineteen eighty-six? No way, honey. That was Mildred Walker. I changed my name, I changed my hair color, and I changed my attitude. But Dr. G says I'm still that insecure girl. That's why I jumped at the chance to do the *Playboy* layout. Plus, I wanted a house. Do you know how much money I threw away on rent? Anyway, it's also why I'm game for these movies that require me to take off my clothes. It's just one more way to shut out those things my mother told me and to prove to myself that I'm beautiful. I mean, nobody wants a homely girl to get naked. Well, maybe a homely boy. But she won't get paid for it. And they're paying *me*."

Candace felt a ripple of self-awareness, the tug of an emotional undercurrent.

"How badly do you want the product placement deal in this movie?"

Candace didn't need to contemplate her answer. *"Very."*

Tatiana nodded. "Then we need to transform you, honey. Hollywood is all about artifice. It's only big enough for one brainy chick, and Jodie Foster's got that covered."

Candace could feel the dread spread across her abdomen. For just a moment, she closed her eyes. When she opened them, Tatiana was grinning devilishly. "What?"

Tatiana mulled an obviously amusing thought. "Every covert strategy needs a code name. We're going to call this one Operation Bombshell."

Chapter Two

To take off the underwear or not to take it off?
That was the question.

"Come on!" A girl at the corner booth egged
him on. "Don't tease! Show us the package!"

Strider Moore looked down at her from his king
of the mountain position on top of the table. "Who
are you?" he shouted over a pulsating Jennifer
Lopez remix.

"I'm Ashley!"

Something about her was tickling his memory.
Somewhere in this dark mahogany-limestone
lounge were his shirt, pants, and shoes. Somehow
getting up here for this impromptu striptease had
seemed like a good idea.

"We hooked up in the Hamptons last summer!"

He remembered now. The pool party at Puff
Daddy's mansion. There were no shootings (a
major plus), but Strider had worn his bullet-proof
Speedo just in case. Ashley had introduced herself

as a model, and since she was a gorgeous heavy smoker who stayed away from the food and laughed a lot, he had no choice but to believe her. Quite naturally, they'd ended up on a chaise in a heavy make-out session, that is until a buddy tapped his shoulder to tell him that the only *modeling* Ashley had done was school picture day at Spence. She was seventeen going on twenty-five and the daughter of some billionaire media titan.

"I'm eighteen now!" Ashley screamed.

Strider's fingers were splayed out, his thumbs hooked under the waistband of his Calvins. He glanced down at his entourage, which included Greg Tapper and assorted hangers-on, Ashley among them.

The movie star laughed at him. "Get down from there," Greg said. "You don't have the balls to—"

Off went the underwear. In fact, Strider sailed it past the actor's head before he could finish the sentence.

Greg stared up in openmouthed amazement. *Size insecurity?*

Ashley blushed. *Not so worldly after all, are we?*

A gay waiter slapped twenty dollars and a phone number in his hand. *Are the Prada shoes I just threw off too queeny?*

His main point proven (never dare a well-endowed exhibitionist who works out regularly to get naked), Strider jumped down and proceeded to hunt for his clothes, fielding high fives and whistles from the cadre of party people vacuum-packed into Lotus, a three-level bar/lounge/club/restaurant/ place to be seen in the meatpacking district.

He easily tracked down everything but his shirt, an orange sherbet-colored Oxford. Then he caught sight of it—angrily gripped in a woman's hand. Seeing the Cartier panther watch curled around her wrist triggered a feeling of dread. *Please, God, no.* His gaze traveled upward for confirmation. There stood Tiko, a one-night stand in Tokyo who'd metamorphosed into an international stalking incident. *Thanks for nothing, God.*

"You lied to me!" Tiko shrieked. She took in Lotus with a circular gaze. "These people don't look hungry." She focused in on a pack of models. "Well, maybe they do. But you told me that you were helping starving children!"

Strider's brain computer went to work. Open file name OUTRAGED FORMER LOVER. Scan for LIES SHE MIGHT BUY. Search complete. "Every time I had a chance to call you in Africa it was after midnight in Japan. Then I got an urgent call from my father to take the lead on a business deal here in the States." He rubbed his temples. "It's been crazy. I don't even know what day it is. How did you know where to find me anyway?"

In Tiko's other hand was a crumpled *New York Post.* She thrust it at his bare chest. "I can read!"

Good. Then you should have no trouble understanding the restraining order. That's what he wanted to say. But all he gave voice to was, "Can I have my shirt back?"

Tiko stared daggers. *"The Full Monty* is playing on Forty-ninth Street. Why are you stripping here?"

Strider tried to take the shirt but Tiko held fast. He shrugged. "It was a dare."

"Then I dare you to marry me."

"This was a guy thing," Strider said quickly. "You had to be there."

As if against her better judgment, Tiko handed

over the shirt. "I finished new tracks in the studio today. Tonight we will make love and listen to my music."

Suddenly the waiter's offer didn't seem half bad. Tiko fancied herself a singer/songwriter, pretty easy to do if your father happens to be CEO of a worldwide recording label. With three albums and maybe twelve singles to her credit, she'd managed to churn out one minor hit, "I'm Gonna Get Your Love." The song went something like this: *I'm gonna get your love, boy/I'm gonna get your love/Don't try to run and hide, boy/Cause I'm gonna get your love.* Repeat chorus about a million times and there you have it. Obviously, she believed in her life imitating her art.

Normally, Strider wouldn't complain. After all, Tiko was an incredible Asian beauty. So much so that if Lucy Liu were her sister, the *Charlie's Angels* star would be the ugly one. And the sex was amazing. But her music. Oh, man, it was bad. Really bad. Imagine being trapped in an alternate universe where all they played was Debbie Gibson. Well, compared to listening to Tiko, that's a good place to be. But to get the Tiko sex you had to endure the Tiko music. At the end of the day, the two canceled each other out.

Slipping his shirt back on, Strider tried to think of an escape.

Suddenly Greg Tapper swaggered up beside him, hooking an elbow around his neck and pulling him in for some conspiratorial macho talk. "You're a crazy man, Strider. Can't believe you took it all off like that. Not a bad show. I've got at least a half an inch on you, though." He laughed, punctuating his delivery with a soft sucker punch to the ribs.

"What do you say we take a few of these lovely ladies back to the hotel." Greg cast a lascivious gaze on Ashley. "I've got dibs on the brunette."

Strider felt a surge of protectiveness. "She's a schoolgirl, man. Just turned eighteen."

This didn't faze Greg. "You know what they say. If she's old enough to vote, she's old enough to—"

"Could you excuse me for just a minute?" Strider cut in. He gestured to Tiko. "I've got a little situation here."

Greg nodded his understanding and headed back to the booth.

Strider locked his best come-on-baby-do-me-a-favor gaze on Tiko. "I've got to close this deal tonight." He kissed an index finger and touched the tip of her nose. "Rain check. Promise."

Tiko pouted. It was her default expression.

Strider reached into his pocket and flicked a few hundred dollar bills off his money clip. "See that young brunette over there? Her name's Ashley. She's eighteen and in over her head." He pressed the cash into Tiko's hand. "Take this and treat her to a dessert in the restaurant. Make sure she gets home safely, too."

"What about my songs?" Tiko whined.

Not a priority. It was almost past Strider's lips, but what prevailed was, "Tomorrow night."

Tiko looked suspicious. "What kind of *deal* are you working on?"

Strider pulled Tiko in close to whisper confidentially, "Greg's producer and star of a movie called *Chocolate on Her Pillow.* I'm under a lot of pressure to secure product placement for my family's Private Selections brand."

"But I want you to listen to my new song, 'Love, Love, Love.' "

No, no, no. "Listen to me. Both my father and grandfather think I'm a screwup, and if I don't make this deal happen, then my ass is going to be kicked out of the family business."

Tiko huffed a little.

Strider massaged her shoulders. "Take care of Ashley for me. I'll call you tomorrow."

"Tell me I'm beautiful."

"You're beautiful."

"Kiss me."

Not the worst job in the world. He planted one on her—deep, sensual, passionate, tongues at war. Over the steady hum of nightclub conversation and a thumping Madonna number, Strider heard the click of a paparazzo's camera. He could just imagine the headline: HOT-BLOODED HEIR TO CHOCOLATE FORTUNE GETS PHYSICAL WITH ASIAN POP TART. Dad and Grandpop will be so proud.

"Rule number one: Never pay for anything," Tatiana said. "The only cash you need is thirty-five cents for a phone call."

Candace gave her a quizzical look.

Tatiana put a hand to curvy hip. "I haven't paid for a drink since my sophomore year in college."

Candace scribbled down the instruction and underlined the word never.

"Rule number two: Always be late. But for a good reason. I mean, don't be Diana Ross. Maybe you come across a stray kitten. Or your cousin calls because her husband's fooling around, and she's trying to decide about getting breast implants. Advise against it, by the way."

Candace scratched furiously on her yellow legal pad.

"Tantrums are generally acceptable," Tatiana went on. "So is light criminal activity."

A pang of panic. This bombshell act was serious business. "I need examples."

Tatiana paused a moment. "Throwing drinks in people's faces is always a good way to show the room that you're angry. As for crime . . . light stuff like never returning jewelry to boyfriends you dump or forgetting to take back designer clothes you borrow for big events."

"I get free clothes?" Candace asked.

Tatiana nodded. "I haven't paid retail for a formal dress since my senior prom." She gave Candace a studied glance. "We need to do something about your name, too."

"What's wrong with my name?" *Candace Rowley*. She'd always kind of liked it.

"A bombshell needs a name that pops. In my case, Mildred Walker became Tatiana Fox. Did you know that Veronica Lake was once Constance Francis Ockleman?" Her eyes brightened. "I've got it. Candi Rowe. With an i. Write it down. That's your new name."

"Candi Rowe?" Candace threw back the moniker like a wrong fast-food order. "You're supposed to turn me into a bombshell not a porn star." She considered the situation. "How about Lana Rowley? My middle name *is* Lindsay. That's not too far off."

Tatiana shook her head. "Lana will always be off-limits because Lana Turner was arguably the best bombshell of all time. Besides, only drag queens steal names. Actually, though, Rowley isn't that bad. OK, you can keep the last name, but you have to drop Candace for Candi. It'll look better when you sign letters and postcards. You can do something fun like dot the i with a little heart."

It seemed reasonable, so she nodded her agreement.

Tatiana grabbed Candace's arm and sniffed the pulse point of her wrist. "What perfume is this?"

"Eternity."

Tatiana pulled a face. "Not anymore. Throw it out. Pick up Spring Flower by Creed. You'll love it."

Candace shot a glance to the top of her lingerie chest, where a brand-new bottle of Eternity perched peacefully. She grimaced.

Tatiana was in her closet now.

This will definitely be a bloodbath.

"Not as bad as I imagined," Tatiana said.

Candace perked up. "Really?"

"The shoes are a disaster, of course. We'll need three new pairs to start. That's at least a thousand dollars."

"For shoes?" Candace's stomach did a flip. "I've never paid more than—"

Tatiana raised a hand to stop her. "Don't say it out loud. The physical evidence speaks for itself."

"But—"

"The wrong shoes can be deadlier than napalm." Tatiana scanned the room. At the sight of Candace's leather purse on the bed, she raised a disapproving eyebrow. "Ditto the handbag. We hit Chanel and Gucci after we deal with shoes. Count on another thousand."

"I can't afford all this!" Candace wailed.

Tatiana didn't so much as blink. "Right," she scoffed. "Says the girl who's saved fifteen percent of every dollar earned since setting up a Kool-Aid stand at age seven."

"This is why Americans are saddled with so much debt! They think savings is there to be dipped into! It should be off-limits!"

"New rule: A bombshell should never sound like an anal-retentive accountant." Tatiana shook her head, unzipped the offensive purse, and dumped the contents onto the bed.

Candace watched her daily necessities bounce and clang into a messy pile.

"Ridiculous," Tatiana sniped. "Lose the Palm Pilot."

"My whole *life* is on that!"

"Is there a guy listed who takes you on exotic trips?"

"No."

"Is the man who gave you the best sex of your life downloaded?"

"No." Quietly this time.

"Then it's useless." Tatiana shoved the gadget aside. "Lose this, too," she added, tossing aside the cellular phone.

Candace could hardly believe it. "What am I supposed—"

"Borrow one when you need to make a call. A bombshell should be hard to reach."

A terrible sense of futility came over her. "Come on, Tatiana. Let's get serious. You can't just hide my Palm Pilot, buy me a new pair of shoes, and expect me to be some kind of sex goddess." Candace slumped down onto the bed. "This is never going to work."

"Before you give up, read this story." Tatiana fished a *New York Post* out of her shoulder bag (not sure of the brand, but it looked expensive), turned to the gossip pages (what else?), and pushed forward a photograph of Strider Moore (still gorgeous) kissing an Asian woman (also gorgeous).

HOT HEIR TO CANDY FORTUNE SEXES
UP NIGHTCLUB

Strider Moore, heir apparent of Moore Candies, engaged in some naked play at Lotus last night. Sharing a corner booth with **Greg Tapper, Ashley Beckham,** and a cluster of mere mortals, he jumped on the table for a Chippendales-inspired routine that proved this much: It's true what they say about a man with big feet—and Strider wears a size thirteen shoe! The prince of chocolate celebrated the act in a steamy lip lock with Asian pop star *Tiko.* Heading out in the wee hours, Moore and Tapper looked chummier than two summer-camp kids after a panty raid. Is there a business deal in the works, or is this just two rowdy boys having a good time?

Candace stewed in the sinister possibilities. Those damn Moores! They were going after the product placement deal with a vengeance. She thought back a few months to that unannounced visit from A.J. Moore, Strider's cousin and reportedly the family's more serious young business mind. He'd made an offer (a pretty good one, actually) to buy Decadence lock, stock, and hazelnut. Of course, she'd said no. The very idea of selling out to one of the big three that routinely gobbled up any small company that posed even the slightest threat made her sick.

Just then an ominous feeling came over her. Why *did* Moore Candies want Decadence? How could a single-shop candy company with a growing-by-the-inch Internet business be on their radar? And suddenly it hit her. *Passion Truffles!* The offer had stunned her so much that the obvious signs had escaped her. A.J. paid a visit just after Passion Truffles had been written up in *Confectioner* magazine.

"Oh, no!" Candace gasped.

"I thought the same thing," Tatiana said. "Tiko's not a pop *star*. She's had one hit, and it didn't even go top ten."

Candace slung the newspaper across the room.

Tatiana merely stared. "You're taking it worse than I did."

"It's not that. I don't care about Seiko."

"Tiko."

"Whatever. You don't understand. This is just like what happened to Victoria Mancini. She developed a new candy called Chocolate Obsession. Oh, God, it was heaven—milk chocolate, dark chocolate, white chocolate. Anyway, A.J. Moore—"

"I thought his name was Strider," Tatiana interrupted.

"A.J.'s his cousin."

"Cuter cousin?"

"Less cute cousin."

"Oh." The look on Tatiana's face conveyed considerably less interest now.

Candace's stomach tightened with anxiousness. "Please let me finish. A.J. offered to buy Victoria's company. When she refused to sell, Moore put out an almost identical candy called Chocolate Maniac. Her company's still around, but basically limping along. I heard she's willing to sell it now. There's no other choice."

"Why didn't she sue? You know, Tom Cruise's lawyers can win almost any case."

Candace shook her head. "The candy business is quirky. First, there are just so many ingredients—chocolate, caramel, nuts, peanut butter."

"You're making me hungry."

"We'll order take-out from a great little Korean place in a minute. Anyway, beyond the limited ingredients, there's the limited range of customer tastes. This is how my industry works. Companies borrow a successful product, alter it only slightly, and then resell it as their own."

Tatiana returned a knowing nod. "Honey, that's business as usual in LA. We call it Hollywood."

"I know Moore is planning to do the same thing to me. They must have a copycat to Passion Truffles in mind for *Chocolate on Her Pillow.*" Candace clenched her fists. "I *have* to get this product placement deal. I *have* to get Hollywood to notice me." For a long second, she stared lasers at Tatiana. "Show me how to dress. Tell me what to say. Make me a bombshell!"

Tatiana smiled. "Rule number three: Never sound desperate."

Chapter Three

Oh, God, Candace half thought, half prayed as she woke up. Too much champagne. But this hangover went far beyond that late-night bottle of Perrier-Jouet.

Too much Korean food. She rested a hand on an uncertain stomach. Do Hwa around the corner had delivered cold japchae glass noodles, mandu gook soup with fiery dumplings, and the bi bim bop hot pot.

Too much Shania Twain. She raised fingertips to her throbbing temples. How many times had they listened to "Man! I Feel Like a Woman" at deafening volume? At least fifty.

Too much Jayne Mansfield. She rubbed her weary eyes. It had taken hours to watch *Will Success Spoil Rock Hunter?* and *Too Hot to Handle* because Tatiana stopped the tape every five minutes to point out particular bombshell moves. Pause. *See how Jayne lingers in the entryway, breasts jutted out like torpedoes ready to fire.* Rewind. View again. Pause. *See how Jayne blows kisses with both hands.* And so on. By the end of it, Candace felt about as sexy as a fisherman's wife after cleaning the day's catch.

Going to Blockbuster had been a hoot, though. The guy checking them out (barely nineteen, still fighting acne) was over the moon to meet Tatiana in person and insisted that she autograph all the *Lady Cop Undercover* movies as well as his arm.

Too much coffee. That's what Candace needed now. She gently rose.

Heading into the tiny kitchen of her cramped West Village apartment, Candace found Tatiana slumped on the couch. On the pillow near her cheek lay a cucumber. After the last round of bubbly and before passing out, Tatiana had started to demonstrate bombshell rule number . . . one hundred thirty-seven: Be highly skilled at fellatio.

Tatiana stirred with a start. "Shit! I fell asleep with my makeup on. Where's the phone? I need to call Elizabeth Arden and see if I can get in for a deep-pore cleansing."

Candace motioned to the cordless.

Tatiana bulldozed her way in to a ten o'clock appointment, refusing to buy the booked to capacity line. The poor receptionist never had a chance.

"Coffee?"

Returning the phone to its base, Tatiana shook her head. "Bad for the skin. Drink lots of bottled water in the morning. And throughout the day, too. Hydration is key to a bombshell's luminous complexion."

Candace pushed the Colombian grounds to the far reaches of the counter. OK, maybe she had the hang of this now. If she just started doing the *oppo-*

site of what she might normally do, then chances are she would be acting the part of a bombshell.

Tatiana opened the fridge.

"You'll have to settle for tap," Candace said.

"Tap?" When it came to expressing disapproval, the B-movie queen could emote better than Meryl Streep. "Why don't you just ask me to drink out of the toilet?"

Candace shrugged. "I'm so bad. I hardly ever drink water." She paused. "But coffee's made with water. So is tea. And Tang. Maybe—"

"Stop before you start counting the cocoa bean as a vegetable." Tatiana raked her fingers through her tangled red mane, then opened the freezer and began to poke around. "Do you still keep your credit cards in a block of . . . Yes, of course you do."

"Leave—"

But before she could protest, Tatiana dumped the Visa/American Express/Discover Card ice in the sink and proceeded to run hot water over it.

Candace watched it thaw. *Fast.* She snatched the Visa. "I'm only using one of these, so you have to make me a bombshell on a budget."

"What's your credit limit?"

"Three thousand."

Tatiana considered the challenge. "Expect to reach it."

A wave of doubt crashed over Candace. "I just thought of something. Do we even have a plan? I mean, I have no idea where Strider Moore is going to show up next. Do you?"

Tatiana bit down on her lower lip. "No, but I can find out." Her tone was one of total absoluteness.

Candace shut her eyes, still mourning the loss

of coffee. "I was afraid you might say something like that."

"Let's call Enrique, my personal assistant. He's a party boy just like Strider. Men of that breed think alike. Enrique's a bit younger—early twenties—but Strider's probably still fourteen in his head, so it all balances out." She dashed for the cordless again. "Does this work on speaker?"

"Look for the blue button."

Tatiana pressed it, a dull dial tone hit the air, and she punched in a number.

"Hello?"

"Hi, it's me."

"Are you back?" The male voice—deep, melodious, instantly sexy—carried a hint of alarm.

Tatiana grinned. "I'm in a cab five minutes from the house."

There was a loud thud, followed by a girl yelling, "Ow! You pushed me off the bed. Asshole!"

Candace covered her mouth, not wanting to laugh but unable to resist.

"Why didn't you call earlier? I would've picked you up at the airport." Enrique again. Officially frantic.

"Gotcha!" Tatiana squealed in good humor. "Actually, I'm still in New York."

"Wait! Carrie! It's OK now," Enrique yelled.

"Fuck you! I should've known this wasn't your house!" Carrie this time. Officially pissed off.

Enrique groaned.

Tatiana giggled. "Wash the sheets—including the comforter—and replace the liquor. How did you get away with this? Where's Kerr?"

"He said something about a business trip."

Tatiana grimaced. "What kind of business? He's an unpublished poetry writer."

"I didn't ask. I'm your assistant, not his. What do you want?"

"Snappish, are we?"

"I really liked Carrie."

"Never lie to impress a girl. You should've learned that much from reruns of *My Three Sons.*"

"Telling a girl like Carrie that I share an apartment with two waiters and work for twelve dollars an hour as a personal assistant is not the strongest opening line at a club."

"Oh, that reminds me. Did you pick up that sunblock I like? I'm almost out."

"Done."

"OK, here's the deal, Romeo. Greg Tapper's in New York doing the town with Strider Moore. Last night they hit Lotus, and the night before that they were holed up in the Hudson Hotel bar. Any idea where they might show up tonight?"

Enrique didn't pause so much as a beat. "If I were in Manhattan tonight, I'd be at the Cutting Room. There's a private party for the release of Ben Estes's new CD."

"The disco Sinatra guy?"

"Yeah. Have you heard his new version of 'My Way'? His cool factor is off the charts. Every A-lister will be there."

"Thanks. Listen, I get in at one o'clock tomorrow. Pick me up at LAX. And no more sex romps at my house!" She clicked off the speaker phone. "We have a plan now."

"Crash a private party? I don't even know Ben Estes."

"Not a problem," Tatiana said. "Chris Noth—

he plays Mr. Big on *Sex and the City*—is part owner of the club. I played a stripper in one of his TV movies once. We had a thing on the set. This was before Kerr, of course."

"I should call Lily," Candace murmured. "It doesn't look like I'll make it into the shop today."

Tatiana stretched. "Everything's in motion. Today we shop. Tonight we vamp. Tomorrow you conquer Hollywood."

Strider was chatting up a WB actress (he couldn't remember her name or the show she starred in) when he caught sight of arguably the sexiest woman in the world. He didn't bother with a surreptitious glance. This matter required a stare of the laser-focus variety. Katie Michelle Whatever would just have to be patient.

"Surprise!"

Not the pleasant kind, Strider thought miserably as Tiko pounced into his line of vision.

"Tiko wants a kiss."

Strider tried to smile, but it died on his lips. He hated to hear people refer to themselves in the third person.

The WB girl left in a huff.

Tiko just stood there, posing expectantly.

Strider ignored them, unable to take his eyes off this mystery woman for any length of time. To simply call her amazing was the understatement of the millennium. Everywhere around him women were either trying too hard (some designer said circus-girl-on-crack was the in look this season) or not trying at all (the see-how-cool-I-am-not-to-care look of jeans, boots, and one-hundred-fifty-dollar

Helmut Lang T-shirt). Both sides of the equator bored him.

But this woman walked through the Cutting Room door and became the bar's centerpiece in a heartbeat. She wore a snug, robin's egg-blue V-neck cashmere sweater that showed enough cleavage to get a man's attention but not so much to incur the hostility of every other girl in the room. Instead of a short skirt (the predictable approach), she wore a pair of black hot pants. Her long shapely legs seemed to go on forever until they reached the impossibly sexy, gravity-defying black sling backs. The only jewelry adorning her body was a silver necklace from which dangled a modest pearl pendant. In her right hand she held a small zebra-print clutch, a smoke signal to the world that this lady had a wild side.

Pop! Strider reeled from the slap. Stunned, he stared back at Tiko.

She glared with triumph. "Now that I've got your attention . . ." And then she yanked his head down with both hands and kissed him as if the fate of civilization depended on it. He responded (he was distracted, not comatose), tried to steal a glance at this heavenly creature (Tiko closed her eyes when she canoodled), then gave in fully to the make-out assault, determined to find the girl later on, after he figured out a way to get rid of this bad pop singer/stalker.

"That was a great move to linger in the doorway for so long," Tatiana praised.

"Believe me, it was unintentional," Candace said under her breath. "Walking in these heels is murder." She stared at Strider Moore and Tiko. "Do you know where we can find a jaws of life this time of night? Otherwise I don't stand a chance of getting a word in."

"Honey, you have more than a chance. He *definitely* noticed you. Stay here and look sexy. I'm going to find Chris and thank him for putting our names on the list. Remember: Let the men come to you."

Candace watched Tatiana disappear into the smoky crowd. She tried to appear cool, but a sudden panic played over her. What if a man did approach her? She couldn't be herself. *Candace* was overly cautious, interested in school/career background first, and passed out work number only until at least the third date. *Candi* had to be confident, glamorous, thrilled by anything a man decided to talk about, clever, and always amusing.

She looked up to see Greg Tapper smiling at her. *Greg Tapper the movie star.* The one who earns twenty million a picture to run in and out of exploding buildings between love scenes with an actress at least ten years younger. Now he was approaching!

The moment of truth. Candace wanted to flee. But Candi had to stay put. She felt a bead of sweat form on her brow. Bombshell rule number forty-six: Never sweat unless you're on the treadmill or in bed with a guy. Deep breath. Desperate prayer.

"You know, I think I've met every beautiful woman in the world. How is it that I've never come across you?"

Wave of nausea. This was his opening line? Even a bombshell in training deserved better. "Maybe you have attention deficit disorder."

Greg leaned in closer. "Maybe I'm cured now."

And then he gave her the benefit of his heat-stoked gaze.

Candace was struck by the oddness of being face-to-face with a man she'd only seen on screen. He was shorter than she'd imagined and no way near as dazzling as he appeared in the movies. Makeup and lighting were good friends to this guy.

"I'm Greg Tapper," he said finally. "You might know me from my films, or maybe *People* magazine. They voted me 'Sexiest Man Alive' last year."

"Are you and Brad Pitt still on speaking terms?"

He laughed a little. "You're funny. What's your name?"

"Call me Candi."

He winked. "Sweet enough to eat, I hope."

Candace wanted to deck this creep. But Candi giggled, knowing that having the star and executive producer of *Chocolate on Her Pillow* in her corner could only help close the deal.

"If you play your cards right, Candi, tomorrow you could be on the phone bragging to your friends about how you went to bed with a movie star."

Coolly, she shifted positions to gaze at the room, not looking at him when she said, "You've got two things wrong. First, I *never* kiss and tell. Second, if we did sleep together, *you* would be the one using speed dial." And then she concentrated really hard on walking away in those damn heels without toppling over.

Tatiana appeared to intercept, grabbing on to both hands to stave off a Humpty Dumpty incident. "You just gave Greg Tapper the brush-off!" She practically jumped up and down.

Candace pulled a face. "I considered it a moral duty. He's disgusting."

Tatiana returned a knowing nod. "You could probably get better pick-up lines from a bald Amway salesman in a Holiday Inn bar. But remember, women never say no to Greg. He hasn't had to do more than crook a finger for years."

Candace couldn't stop smiling. "That felt good," she admitted.

Tatiana giggled. "Now he's not going to rest until he gets you into bed."

Candace experienced a moment's pure fear. "I'm not sleeping with him!"

"Oh, stop. Look around you. There's not a single woman in this bar—except for the rather butch girl arguing with that bartender—who wouldn't go for a tumble with Greg Tapper. It's a good story for the steam room at the gym."

"I never go into the steam room."

"Sauna?"

Candace shook her head.

"Well, talk really loud when you're on the treadmill then. A bombshell's attitude toward sex is that it's no big deal. I mean, when you think about it, why all the fuss? A man's got to do most of the work and worry about whether you've seen a bigger one or not. We can just lie there, moan a little, and if he's really successful like Greg, maybe a nice piece of jewelry shows up in a week or so."

"What's the difference between that and a prostitute?"

"Better shoes, patience, and more flexible hours."

Candace's mouth dropped open.

"I'm kidding. About everything but the shoes."

Candace pursed her lips.

"Honey, there's a big difference between being

celibate and being celibate for too long. When's the last time you hit the sheets with a guy?"

Candace didn't want to do the math. Too depressing. All she knew was this: Around the time of her last sexual experience (which clocked in at under three minutes, thank you Ronald Sykes) *Seinfeld* was still on the air in original episodes. Oh, God! If you went that long without it, were you technically a virgin again?

"I assume it wasn't in this century," Tatiana said.

"It's only 2002," Candace whined.

Suddenly Tatiana was distracted. "There's Ben Estes, the guest of honor. I want to meet him." She splayed out her fingers. "His wife owns a cosmetics company. I'm wearing her nail polish now, Jacqueline Feels Radical in Red. Sounds like an ice breaker to me." And off she went.

Candace stood there a moment and decided she wanted a drink. Something sweet with a kick. Maybe a green-apple martini. Did bombshells get their own? Wasn't a man just supposed to show up with one?

"I took a chance that you're a Midori sour kind of girl."

She spun to find Strider Moore holding out a cocktail for her benefit. "I am now." Accepting it, she took a generous sip to buy time, to build up her nerve.

Up close, he was amazing. Brown haired, brown eyed, six-foot-two, handsome to the point of distraction, athletic. His smile—dimpled, devastating—revealed a hint of rich-boy mischief, a bolt of laid-back charm. "That was quite an entrance you made," Strider said.

"You noticed?"

"Every man in the room did, including the gay ones."

"Where do you fall?"

"In the straight column. Didn't you see my floor show?"

"I've never been a fan of the circus."

He grinned.

She sipped on her drink and grinned back.

"I don't like that woman you saw me with," he said earnestly. "Really."

"Not even a little bit? You did have your tongue down her throat."

He laughed. "You're not going to make this easy, are you?"

"What?"

"Me hitting on you."

"I figure a man like you should work hard at *something.*"

"Oh, believe me, I can put the effort in." He winked.

Candace could feel a blushing heat stain her cheeks. "So where did the other half of your act go?"

"I had a friend call her cell phone to say her hotel room was on fire."

Candace nearly collapsed from laughter. It was so outrageous. She could hardly believe it. "You're not serious."

Strider bobbed his head up and down.

"What a horrible thing to do!"

"It sounds worse than it is. This woman is stalking me. I should be in court right now filing a temporary restraining order."

"So you don't want to see her anymore?"

"No."

"You could be sending her mixed signals with this habit of kissing passionately in public."

"You think?"

And then a dance beat dropped, cocooning the room in an urgent rhythm, the base throbbing, seductive, infectious. The volume went up, the lights went down, and the crowd responded. It was why they were here. To celebrate Ben Estes's disco reworking of "My Way." To be seen. To dance.

Without warning, Strider took Candace's drink, placed it along with his own on a nearby table, and pulled her toward the center of the bar, where several party people were already working up a sweat.

He was a fantastic dancer—fluid, not too showy, interactive. She'd boogied with guys who zoned out and forgot she existed, but Strider's gaze never left her. By the first chorus she forgot about the heels. Her legs felt strong and steady, her body free and limber. For the first time tonight, the clothes and shoes weren't wearing *her*. She was wearing *them!*

With both hands in the air she swayed her hips to the urgent beat, tilting her head back, closing her eyes for a spell, then opening them again to take in the scene. The sensation was glorious. Greg Tapper wanted her. The chocolate prince wanted her. Other men were checking her out. The realization became alternately frightening and arousing. Because she knew the man twirling her around would be the first in a long time. Instinctively, she knew that getting into bed with Strider Moore was inevitable. There were just a few details to negotiate. When and where.

A third point lingered ominously. How would

she deal with the fact that this monumental move for her was just another conquest for him? Unlike Tiko, she didn't have a powerful father, a pseudo career in entertainment, or anything else to get her name in boldface when the gossip columns pointed out Strider's flavor of the week. At the end of the day, she was just a plain girl. But tonight she was a bombshell, and life was a movie, and she was the name above the title. *Candi Rowley*.

So she kept on dancing.

Chapter Four

They were lost in the music, grooving to the instrumental break of tribal drum beats, when all hell broke loose. Tiko was back and looking furious enough to upgrade from stalker to killer as she pushed through a cluster of dancers to wedge herself between Candace and Strider.

"Somebody played a mean trick on Tiko!" she screamed. Then she turned on Candace accusingly. "Did you call my cell phone?"

"No."

Tiko narrowed her angry eyes to mere slits. "Why should I believe you?"

"Because I've never met you, don't know your number, and have no reason to call you." She looked at Strider, a question in her gaze. Would he fess up and put an end to this nonsense?

"It was probably just a prank," Strider told Tiko. His voice was soothing. "I heard the same thing happened to Christina Aguilera last week."

"Really?" The possibility sunk in and Tiko appeared mollified. After all, if it happened to Christina . . .

The floor was getting crowded on multiple levels. Candace hated to admit it, but she was experiencing a twinge of jealousy. One dance and she wanted Strider Moore all to herself. Not the best turn of events. A bombshell was supposed to make people jealous, not *be* jealous. Hmm. She was even thinking like one now. Tatiana would be proud. Feigning indifference, she turned to go.

"Candace Rowley. I almost didn't recognize you." It was A.J. Moore, Strider's cousin, the man who had tried to convince her to sell Decadence to their company's Private Selections division.

"I . . . I . . . I go by Candi now."

A.J. raked her up and down, his gaze settling on her chest. "You've changed more than your name, I see. Implants? Good work. Who's your doctor? My wife is thinking about—"

"It's a Wonderbra!"

Strider stepped in, pulsing with hostility. "What are you doing here, A.J.? I thought your idea of fun was swimming in shark tanks."

"Hello, *Lansing*. Actually, I do that for relaxation." He was a few inches shorter than Strider and looked up at him smugly. "Your father has been trying to get in touch. If I see you, I'm supposed to pass along this message: *Focus on the deal.* As usual, though, I see you're focusing on everything else." He gave Tiko a once-over. "I'll be sure and report back." Turning back to Candace, A.J. said, "If you change your mind about selling, please call me to discuss the particulars. Lansing here is a bit fuzzy in that area."

Strider took a menacing step forward. "You know her?"

"She owns Decadance," A.J. informed him. "The Passion Truffle is her baby."

Strider turned his gaze on Candace now. He looked dumbfounded.

A.J. relished the moment. "You should try to learn more about a girl than her room number, Lansing."

Strider's face flushed. His fists clenched. "Stop calling me that." It was so angry-little-boy-on-the-school-yard. Really cute.

A.J. clearly enjoyed the reaction. "Why? That's your real name. It's good enough for your father. It's good enough for his father. Of course, with your track record, I can understand why it's not good enough for you."

"Tiko's bored!" After this enlightening announcement, the pop star (a very minor one according to Tatiana) stomped away, turning back once to glare at Strider, daring him *not* to follow her.

Strider, cool and confident, metamorphosed into Strider, tense and uncertain. This cousin really knew how to push his buttons. "Did they send you here to check up on me?"

A.J. returned a small, triumphant smile. "Can't keep anything from you." And then he turned to Candace, gently taking her arm. "Why don't you let me give you a lift home, dear? I have a car and driver out front. Any minute now you're likely to have an attack of vertigo in those heels."

Strider's lips parted in amazement. His number-one worst-case scenario was painted all over his face: Losing a girl to A.J. He managed to steal a glance at Tiko, but he would've chosen Candace tonight. She saw the decision in his eyes. That's why she left with A.J. To drive Strider crazy. To keep him on his toes. Tatiana had taught her well.

A.J. traveled in high style. In the dark she couldn't tell whether the Mercedes was black or blue. Like a true gentleman, he opened the door and ushered her into the rear cabin. The first thing she did once she sank into the rich leather was take off her shoes. Manolo Blahniks or not, her feet were killing her. A.J. dashed around to enter the car from the other side, then called out Candace's West Village address to the driver.

She gave him a sharp look.

"Relax. Whenever we're interested in acquiring a company, we run a thorough background check."

"Pop quiz. Where did I attend college?"

"The University of Wisconsin. Majored in anthropology. Graduated with a four point."

Suddenly she felt at ease and lay back in the seat. Inside her head she could still hear the music. "My Way." The campy vocal. The insistent beat. Had Strider left with Tiko? It worried her how badly she wanted to know.

"You're a clever girl, *Candi,* but you don't need to go to all this trouble." A.J. gave her a little smirk and turned away to gaze out the window as the car cruised down Twenty-Fourth Street.

She wondered what he meant by that. She wondered if he could only speak in condescending tones. And, once more, she wondered if Strider had left with Tiko. Just then her zebra-print clutch started to ring. Snapping it open, she fished out her cell phone. Right away she knew it would be Tatiana.

"Honey, you left with the wrong man! I didn't put you through bombshell boot camp for you to go home with the creepy cousin! You could've mastered that skill in a mail-order course!"

Candace sighed. She was still curious about A.J.'s statement, *You don't need to go to all this trouble.* "I have to go. I'll meet you back at the apartment."

"Maybe," Tatiana threatened. "I'm being hit on left and right, and my husband hasn't touched me in months."

"Don't do anything you'll regret. Come home. We'll order a pizza and gossip about everyone we saw tonight."

Tatiana squealed with delight. "Just like we used to do in college! Oh, I miss being twenty. I'm looking at all these girls here with their whole lives ahead of them. It makes me feel old. I mean, I'm twenty-nine—"

"Five years ago you were twenty-nine."

"Shit, you're right! I'm starting to actually believe my Hollywood age. That's what Los Angeles will do to you. But don't tell."

"Your secret is safe with me." Candace clicked off her friend and laughed a little. She shifted in her seat to address A.J. "Sorry about that. A girlfriend in crisis. She's an actress, too, which makes everything exponentially serious."

"This would be Tatiana Fox, right?" A.J. asked. Candace nodded.

"I'd hardly call her an actress. She's more like a nude model who does occasional line readings."

His rudeness continued to stun her. It just hit

without warning, like sniper fire. "You're one of the meanest assholes I've ever met."

A.J. arched a single brow. "Promise?"

Candace fumed in her seat. Suddenly she lurched forward to address the driver. "Stop the car. I prefer to walk from here."

A.J. laughed. "In those shoes? You couldn't manage a single block before twisting an ankle."

She turned on him angrily. "Then I'll catch a cab."

"In that outfit you might catch a vice cop."

"Screw you!" Candace covered her mouth as fast as the words hit the air. She never talked like that. But this man brought out the absolute worst in people. He was pure evil.

A.J. sat there unfazed, as if she'd just offered up a nice-to-meet-you have-a-nice-day.

They rode in silence for long seconds. Finally, she cleared her throat and calmly asked, "You said something earlier about me not needing to go to all this trouble. What did you mean by that?"

A.J. opened up a beautiful Hermes attache and pulled out a thick packet of paper fastened with three brass butterfly clips. It was the script for *Chocolate on Her Pillow*.

Candace fought hard to show no reaction.

"I suppose you think your Passion Truffles are the ideal product placement for this film."

Candace stared out the window impassively. They were minutes from her building. She really could get out and walk now. Barefoot if she had to.

"Moore Candies happens to believe that our Love Truffle—that would be a new chocolate launching soon from our Private Selections line— is a more suitable choice."

The rage came so fast and furious that it sucked away her breath. The injustice smoked inside her head. She immediately thought of Victoria Mancini and her brief success with Chocolate Obsession until Moore hit the market with Chocolate Maniac and practically drove her out of business. Big, bad Moore Candies. Taking on the little companies and squashing them like bugs. Forget Bill Gates and Microsoft. The Justice Department's time would be better spent looking into these bastards!

She turned to say something, but the words stalled on her lips. There was a satisfied expression on his face. What a snake. He was enjoying this, and the offer for a lift home was just a chance to gloat. A hot, angry tear formed in the corner of her right eye. Decadence couldn't take on Goliath. It was over. "I stand corrected, Mr. Moore. You are *the* meanest asshole I've ever met. Hands down." Defiantly, she wiped the tear from her cheek.

A.J. regarded her curiously. "Do you ever take a moment and count to five, Ms. Rowley?"

She just stared at him. No wonder he was so cruel. Here he sat, short, thinning hair, a nose too large for his face, small eyes, acne scars, a double chin. And then there was Strider. The golden-boy cousin, better looks, a winning personality. In short, all the sex appeal.

"You've made a number of dangerous assumptions during this brief ride," A.J. went on.

The Mercedes slowed to a stop in front of Candace's building. She slipped back on her shoes and said, "Thank God for brevity," as she opened the door and swung one impossible heel onto the pavement.

"I want to help Decadence secure product placement in this film."

Candace froze. She eased her leg back inside, shut the door, and turned to him. "You've got forty-five seconds to tell me why."

A.J. launched in immediately. "My father was the less successful Moore brother. He drank too much, and he gambled constantly. Finally, they gave him a lump sum of cash to get lost. Dad burned through it in less than a year and was dead broke for the first time in his life. That's when he found Jesus. He runs a church in Florida now. Sometimes they run his sermons on Christian cable. I've got an M.B.A. from Harvard, and I know Moore Candies better than anyone in the company, but I'm still just the son of the black sheep brother. Strider doesn't work hard. He never has. Whatever the minimum is to get by—that's all you'll wrangle out of him. But his father and grandfather are losing patience. They've given him an ultimatum, in fact. If he doesn't land this deal with the movie, he's out. And I'm in. *That's* why I'm going to help Decadence get the placement."

Candace studied him for a moment. "That was sixty seconds. You could've skipped the bit about your dad discovering the Lord."

A.J. shrugged.

"You would deliberately sabotage your own company's chances?"

"To push Strider out of the heir-apparent seat? Definitely. Besides, *Chocolate on Her Pillow* is a love story for adults. The real product placement money is in films for children. No huge loss there."

She tried to process this odd turn of events. It seemed too good to be true. And it seemed so sinister. When people said life in the business world could get down and dirty, this is what they meant. Hardball. Cutthroat competition. A blood thirst to move in for the kill.

A.J. opened the attache again. This time he took out a large manila envelope and slid it across the seat. "A marketing proposal for Love Truffles in conjunction with the release of the movie. You should find it worthwhile."

She simply stared, as if it were forbidden reading, like the Judy Blume novel *Wifey* that she used to sneak into the closet and devour by flashlight back in middle school.

A.J. shook his head patronizingly. "A man would never hesitate."

Candace glared at him.

"Don't let a schoolgirl crush stand in the way of a lucrative business opportunity."

"How do I know I can trust you?"

A.J. gestured to the envelope. "The proof is right there."

"Those plans could be fake. I need hard evidence."

He considered this, then gave her a shrewd smile. "I underestimated you, Candace."

"It's Candi."

"So I see. I'll have the car pick you up in the morning. Say nine o'clock. We'll fly by private plane to the Love Truffles factory in Virginia. Will that be proof enough that I'm serious about helping you?"

"Yes, it will." She got out of the car, leaving the envelope on the seat.

"Aren't you forgetting something?"

"When I want to read fiction, A.J., I pick up an

Anita Loos novel. Bring the real marketing plans with you tomorrow."

He laughed, his eyes wide with genuine surprise. "How did you know?"

"Just because a girl dresses a certain way doesn't mean she's easy." And then Candace slammed the door and raced up to her apartment, first stopping at the bottom of the stairwell to take off her shoes.

Once inside, she rummaged through every closet until she found the foot spa, a gift from Aunt Janet she'd been intending to recycle. She opened it up, filled the basin with water, poured in the special salts, and let the bubbles and vibrating power work their magic. Should she order the pizza now or wait for Tatiana to get here? Hmm. The decision felt like *Sophie's Choice*. She stretched for the phone and called Professor Bombshell.

"Hey."

"Where are you?"

"In a stinky cab. I think the last passenger peed in here. How do people live in New York without their own car?"

"Try finding a parking space in the city. You'd grow to love those smelly taxis. How far away are you?"

"Hold on."

Candace heard Tatiana struggling to communicate with the driver.

"This guy doesn't speak a word of English. But he offered me a cigarette. That was nice. I've been riding for at least ten minutes. It shouldn't be much longer."

"Was Strider still at the bar when you left?"

"I didn't notice. The DJ put on Tiko's record, and I got out of there as fast as I could."

"I'm hanging up to order the pizza. See you soon." She called Patsy's Pizza on Third Avenue. They made the best thin-crust brick oven pie in the city. Her place was outside the delivery area, so she had to make a second call to a courier service to fetch the order and bring it to her door. But the extra expense was always worth it.

When Tatiana arrived, Candace filled her in on everything that happened with A.J. The retelling made her feel ashamed, larcenous, and guilty. So much for the glory of victory.

"This cousin is something else," Tatiana said. "Remind me never to marry into this family."

Candace barely cracked a smile.

"At least he's on your side."

"That's a good thing? He's a slimeball."

"You're getting the product placement. That's what you want, isn't it?"

Candace shook her head. "Not this way."

"You can't always write the script, honey. This is business. Even worse, it's Hollywood business. What I'm hearing is that A.J.'s determined to ruin Strider. If that's true, another company is going to have their candy in *Chocolate on Her Pillow*. Why shouldn't it be yours?"

"Because I'm afraid that I might not have the stomach for this."

"You're not selling Girl Scout Cookies anymore," Tatiana said. She got cozy on the couch Candace had bought secondhand, tucking her feet under her legs and stretching sideways. "This is the big leagues—money, media, ego." She made a small fist and placed it over her heart. "You've got to want this more than anything else in the world. I've been in LA for over ten years, and I've wanted to quit at least a million times." She shook her head. "What I've seen that town do to girls who want the same thing I do . . . It makes me sick, but I just keep going and try to focus on my own goals."

Candace sighed. She never imagined that something as sweet as candy could become so bitter. Tatiana was right, though. Deep down she knew that she had to take this opportunity and move on. Playing the righteous one would get her nowhere. But A.J.'s smug face continued to flash in her mind. Damn him. He was the last person on earth she wanted to align herself with.

"Of course, you realize that A.J. will come after you next, so be prepared."

Candace looked at her blankly.

"You're useful to him now, but once Strider gets the boot, you'll be a threat. He didn't mention anything about Moore Candies *not* marketing the Love Truffle, did he?"

She shook her head, getting the picture, feeling sick.

"Well, when this is over, watch out."

Candace buried her face in her hands. There were two choices. Roll over and watch Passion Truffles die. Or play ball with A.J. and pray like hell that the attention of *Chocolate on Her Pillow* strengthened her market position enough to withstand his attack later on. This was like some kind of war game! Where's General Schwarzkopf when you need him?

The pizza arrived. Candace tipped the delivery man five dollars, and they sat down to eat on the

Pier One table she'd had since college. Suddenly her appetite was pathetic. She nibbled on a single slice and barely finished half of it. Tatiana proved worse, moaning about a love scene she had to shoot next week and how the camera adds ten pounds. Any other girl would've pushed this woman into a ravine, but Candace forgave her friend's actress/model/object-of-desire neuroses and simply lobbed encouragement of this sort across the table: You look great, you're so skinny, Ashley Judd is fat, etc. It managed to impart the desired effect. They shoved the pizza in the fridge and consumed a pint of Godiva white chocolate raspberry ice cream.

After helping Tatiana pack, Candace washed her face, slathered on some expensive night cream essential to a bombshell, and crawled into bed. Tomorrow A.J. would fly her to Moore Candies' Love Truffles factory. That should've occupied her mind until sleep came. But all she could think about was Strider and whether or not he'd left the Cutting Room alone or with Tiko.

Strider played the nightclub hero and escorted a drunk Tiko back to her hotel. Now she lay asleep in her bed while he added up regret on the terrace of her suite at the Mark, a sixteen-story luxury hotel and unofficial hideaway to music-industry types.

The wind whipped and chilled Strider to the bone. He hated the way A.J. possessed this uncanny power to play voodoo with his moods. Everything had been going great tonight. Talking with the blonde, dancing with the blonde.

He couldn't believe she'd turned out to be Candace Rowley, the same girl he'd seen profiled in *Confectioner* magazine, the same girl who'd put him to sleep on whatever show those dingbats Chip and Didi hosted. She'd undergone some kind of transformation. A total Sandy from *Grease,* only without the cigarettes, home perm, and penchant for breaking into song.

From inside the room his cell phone jingled. Shit! Strider scrambled for it in record time, desperate in his attempt *not* to awaken Tiko. He didn't want her waking up and getting amorous. "Strider," he whispered, rushing back to the terrace.

"You disappeared on me." It was Greg Tapper. Strider could barely hear him over the Sugar Ray song and female laughter in the background.

"Sounds like you found your way."

"I sure did. Reeled in too many. I could use some help over here."

"I'm kind of tied up."

"With that knockout blonde I saw you dancing with?"

"Not her."

"Good. Because I'd be jealous. Then I'd do something petty like pull the plug on that deal we're trying to cut." He laughed, as if to say it was all a joke.

But Strider knew he was dead serious. "Relax," he assured him.

"She shot me down. Can you believe that? I'm Greg Fucking Tapper! Who is this woman?"

Strider hesitated. "I don't know, man. Madame X, I guess. Never caught her name."

"It's Candi something. See if you can find out her last name. You know everybody. Shouldn't be hard."

"I'll work on it," Strider promised. But he wasn't going anywhere near that, not when he was so close to wrapping up this product placement for Greg's new movie.

"You should come to the location in Capri," Greg suggested. "Meet the producer and director. That way our party won't have to stop. I keep a yacht there."

"So do I."

"How big is yours? Mine's one hundred forty feet."

Strider shook his head. This guy never stopped reminding you who he was. "It's not the size of the boat that matters. It's how you handle the water."

Greg Tapper cackled. "Whatever helps you sleep, man." And then he hung up.

Strider's mind zeroed in on the issue that was really driving him crazy tonight. The sight of Candace leaving with A.J. He really hoped she would turn down A.J.'s offer to buy Decadence. Strider hated the way his family went after these small companies. They didn't pose any real threat. Hell, there seemed to be enough chocoholics out there in the world for everyone to get a piece of the business. It was not like the Moore ledger needed another million posted to get through a day.

And then the contradiction hit him. He didn't want Candace to sell, but he didn't want her to soar, either. After all, he'd just lied to Greg to keep her as far away from this movie deal as possible. Part of him felt like a heel. The rest of him knew that he'd done it out of self-preservation.

He splashed cold water on his face and quietly slipped out. Tomorrow he left for Capri. Maybe he'd forget about Candace Rowley. Maybe Tiko would forget about him. If somebody dared him to put money on it, though, he'd bet no on both.

Chapter Five

Richmond, Virginia

To travel by private plane was heaven. Larger seats, more leg room, no doofus causing passenger gridlock as he tried to squeeze luggage that was too big into the overhead bin, etc.

As the Cessna Citation X touched down, Candace decided to add wealth beyond measure to her list of husband-material must haves. It joined the Brad Pitt gene pool requirement and other impossibilities that would likely keep her single forever.

She ignored A.J. for most of the flight. The *real* marketing plans for Love Truffles were waiting for her in her seat, so she studied them to avoid conversation. The documents were printed on special paper that couldn't be Xeroxed. This trick of Moore's was legendary. Material of this type was also routinely shredded after presentation.

Getting the inside track triggered conflicting

feelings. On one level it was exhilarating. She probably knew Strider's pitch better than he did. But on another level, what she learned was disheartening. How could she compete with Moore Candies in terms of razzle-dazzle, shelf space, and advertising muscle? They were offering the moon; Decadence could only hold out a moon rock.

In the midst of this psychic meltdown, Candace had to endure A.J.'s spirited attempts to impress her. He blathered on about his vintage car collection, how this Cessna was the world's fastest business aircraft, and other matters of no interest to her.

A white Lincoln Town Car was waiting on the tarmac to take them to the factory. That she would soon see firsthand how Moore Candies were made was all the proof Candace needed. A.J. had every intention of seeing this scheme through. Destroying marketing plans was just one of the company's 007-like tricks to ensure secrecy. They even blindfolded repair technicians when equipment went down, ushering them to the exact problem to be fixed and then out again once the work was done.

The factory looked like an old warehouse you might find anywhere in the country. A modest Moore Candies logo decorated the entrance. A.J. scanned a card and entered a secret code to gain entry.

Once inside, Candace realized that all the stories were true. The factory gleamed. *A surgeon could perform an operation here,* she thought. *It's that sterile.* Workers went about their tasks in starched white uniforms, looking more like scientists than candy makers. She watched a woman swab her area with a cloth.

"We measure work areas for bacteria several times per shift," A.J. explained. "One could argue that our floor is more sanitary than the china in any five-star restaurant."

Candace believed him. Not a single drop of chocolate scandalized the floor. It positively sparkled. Everything did, the steel all slick and polished, the entire facility dust free.

She watched warm, thick, liquid chocolate being piped from one end of the plant to the next. In another area, a latex-gloved production-line worker used calipers to measure the width of Love Truffles as machines squirted in fruit purees. The whole process seemed to take about five minutes. By the end of it a high-tech, self-loading wrapping machine had four candies packaged and ready for retail.

A.J. gave her a superior smile. "It's not too late, you know. The offer still stands. In fact, I have the papers in the car."

This bastard never stopped. He'd lured her here not just to earn her trust but to intimidate her into selling Decadence. She just stared at him.

"The price is now contingent on you winning the deal, of course, so this doesn't change the arrangement we have regarding Strider."

"Why do you hate him so much?"

"You would too if you'd grown up in this family." A.J.'s face darkened a bit, revealing the angry little boy inside. "He just skates along, doing as little as possible, yet everybody regards him with such awe. You should see how other executives stumble over themselves to win his approval. They'd probably sacrifice a limb to go out drinking with Strider. The women are worse. One conversation with him and they're blushing for a week. At least my uncle and grandfather have run out of patience. But they still take *me* for granted. I've busted my ass for years with little to no acknowledgment. Yet Strider can charm a grocery chain CEO into giving us six inches of additional shelf space, and it's cause for a parade. I'm sick of it. That's why I want him out. Maybe with him gone they'll notice what I'm doing for the company."

Candace said nothing. In a way she understood A.J.'s envy. As a child, she'd been jealous of almost everyone. The girl next door whose mother offered I love you's instead of why don't you's. The girl across the street whose father stuck around. The girl down the block who never felt alone because she had a brother and sister to play with.

A.J. reached for a Love Truffle just off the assembly line and presented it to Candace. "Care to sample the product that will ultimately eclipse your Passion Truffle?"

Any empathy she felt for this son of a bitch evaporated. "You're mean, condescending, and arrogant. What makes you believe that with Strider out of the picture, people are going to be falling at your feet? Your problems have nothing to do with him and everything to do with your terrible personality."

"How insightful," A.J. snarled.

Candace tasted the Love Truffle. Hmm. They really should call it the Like Truffle. Granted, it was good. But her Passion Truffle was better. Fantastic by comparison. Suddenly a brilliant thought struck her. She knew how to close this deal! For every bombastic marketing promise Moore Candies made, Decadence could make a subtle one.

She gobbled up the rest of the Love Truffle in one bite. Still no reaction, the taste experience hardly one to savor. The whole issue was analogous to the difference between Chanel eye cream and any cheaper variety you could find at the drugstore. Some would argue that eye cream is eye cream. But it's not. The key divider is the *purity* of ingredients. Just like her Passion Truffle. Where Moore mass-produced the Love Truffle with barnyard chocolate and standard flavorings, Candace lavished her Passion Truffle with tender loving care, using fine imported chocolate and passion fruit and guava nectar of the highest quality.

"You seem to be at a loss for words," A.J. said.

"Not exactly. 'Mediocre' comes to mind."

"No need to bring up your educational background."

Candace glowered. A.J. Moore was the worst kind of Harvard man—he never missed an opportunity to point out that he graduated from there. But she felt equally smart right now. Because she had a plan.

The script for *Chocolate on Her Pillow* was sophisticated, a sweeping love story, something like *The English Patient* only with a happier ending. Nothing got blown up. Nobody got killed. There was no deafening hard-rock soundtrack. This was a movie for adults, and in the area of product placement, it called for a grown-up chocolate. Yes! Strider Moore didn't stand a chance.

"I've seen enough," Candace suddenly announced.

A.J. ushered her out of the factory and back to the car. His body language talked upper hand, but this fool had no idea. The moment he slid into the rear cabin of the Town Car, his cell phone rang. The caller did most of the talking. When A.J. hung up, he turned to Candace. "My cousin is on his way to Capri to join Greg Tapper on the movie set."

Candace experienced a flush of nervous heat. She didn't know if it was the new development or just the mere mention of Strider. "That was him?"

"No, that was a private investigator I've retained to keep an eye on him. As incompetent as my cousin is, he could very well schmooze his way into this deal if we don't act quickly." A.J. ran his index finger across his thin lips, concentrating hard. Then he rudely sized up Candace. "Bikini or one piece?"

"What?"

"Your preference in bathing suits."

"Bikini. Why?"

"I suggest you pack one and get to Capri as soon as possible."

Instantly she thought of Tatiana, who was on her way back to Los Angeles to begin shooting *Lady Cop Undercover IV: Red Light District*, which meant Candace had no choice but to handle this mission alone. A rookie bombshell on exotic foreign soil, mixing it up with Hollywood types and playboy heirs. *Oy*. The butterflies took flight.

"Care to share your thoughts, Ms. Rowley?"

She shot A.J. a polar glare. "Yes. It's pronounced CAH-pree, not CahPREE."

Capri

Strider always stayed at the Capri Palace Hotel and Spa. It was Moroccan inspired and built high on Anacapri, the island's tallest peak at almost two thousand feet. He never worried about reservations because he partied often with the owner, Tonino Cacace.

He saw Sergio right away, a front desk clerk who knew him by name.

"Mr. Moore," Sergio said. "Welcome back. It's been too long, sir."

Strider laughed a little. "Too long? I was just here four weeks ago."

"A few days is too long. You should move to Capri. You're one of us."

Strider grinned. "Maybe I will."

"Your companion has already arrived. She's resting in your room."

Strider tilted his head as if questioning his own hearing. "Companion? I'm here alone."

Sergio looked confused. "But Tiko . . ."

Strider stood there, shocked and frozen. How in the hell did she find out where he was going *and* manage to get here first? Jesus Christ! Even Glenn Close had never been that good.

"Is there a problem, Mr. Moore?"

"Yes, Sergio, there is. But I'll handle it." He paused a moment. "On second thought, give me another room. Under the name . . . Charlie Townsend."

Sergio returned a secret smile. He obviously knew the seventies' TV show about the three beautiful female detectives.

"And please instruct the rest of the staff to keep this information from Tiko . . . my . . . ahem . . . *companion.*"

"Of course, sir."

Somewhere in the Sky

Candace had spent a full day getting ready for the trip to Capri. At times she felt like a psychotically driven efficiency expert, checking status on this, investigating that, always armed with her Palm Pilot. Thank God for Lily. She managed the Decadence shop to perfection and always volunteered to take on additional responsibilities. That helped Candace feel secure enough to steal away.

The flight seemed to go on forever. An urgent restlessness had her on edge. She made several fitful attempts to sleep but stayed wide-awake. She tried reading an Olivia Goldsmith novel but gave up after a few pages. She gave the Passion Truffle marketing proposal a go but abandoned that, too.

And then the airfone beckoned. She knew the call would cost her a fortune. She had no idea what time it was in LA. No matter, she swiped her credit card, followed the international calling instructions, and punched in Tatiana's mobile number.

"Hello?" Her friend sounded bored.

"You'll never guess where I am."

"In bed with Strider Moore?"

"No!"

"Greg Tapper?"

"No!"

Tatiana gasped in quiet horror. "Not the creepy cousin!"

"Stop!" Candace pleaded. "I'm in a plane headed for Naples."

"You're going to Capri. You bitch!"

Candace giggled. "Everything happened so fast."

"That's the life of a bombshell. You have to be

ready for travel at a moment's notice. Only grand-mothers take two weeks to get ready for a trip."

Candace gave Tatiana the lowdown on her jaunt to Virginia and her strategy to land the *Chocolate on Her Pillow* product placement.

"You are *so* smart," Tatiana said. "The Mercedes syndrome will never die. Americans are ruled by status. Take me. I'm a total snob about every-thing—shoes, handbags, beauty products. And chocolate, too. You'll never catch me with some-thing by Hershey or Moore. I'm a serious actress. I don't want chocolate that's thrown in every trick-or-treat bag from here to Delaware. Give me God-iva! Give me Decadence!" Suddenly her voice went down an octave. "Honey, give me an extra-strength Altoid. My costar had something with garlic and onions for lunch, and we're shooting a love scene."

"Yuck!" Candace couldn't imagine.

"I think he did it on purpose."

"Why?"

"We've been rolling around this bed for hours, and he's been soft as a Beanie Baby the whole time. I know with the lights and the camera and the extras and the choreographed directions it's hardly the most romantic thing in the world, but with most actors I usually feel a poke now and then. If this guy isn't gay, then I'm on the short list for the Best Actress Oscar this year."

"But why show up with bad breath for an intimate scene?"

"To torture me. Some gay men hate women. Dr. G explained it to me once, but I can't remember the fine points. I think it goes back to their mothers or something. Or is that the oedipal thing? Who cares? The point is I've got a soft man at home and a soft man at work. I should hang up and dial nine-one-one. This girl needs Russell Crowe on the double."

Candace took a deep breath.

"Honey, are you OK?"

"I'm nervous. What if I can't pull this off?"

"Oh, shut up. This deal is yours. And so is Strider Moore, if you want him."

Candace stole a glance to the passenger on her right, then inched closer to the window and cupped her hand over the phone to whisper, "Just in case, I bought some really sexy lingerie."

Tatiana let loose a long, sweet sigh. "Honey, men don't care about lingerie. They just want to get it off you. Jot that down in your little notebook. It's an important point to remember."

One of the flight attendants made an announcement about returning tray tables to their upright positions and turning off electronic devices.

"I have to go," Candace said. "Any parting words of wisdom?"

"Yes. Capri is famous for unusual romances. Don't be surprised if you leave there with a husband."

Candace steadied herself. For a moment she thought the plane had suddenly dropped altitude. But then she realized that it was just her stomach.

Chapter Six

Capri

If ever one could conjure up a true definition of breathtaking beauty, then it would be the sight of Capri when traveling by boat on the Bay of Naples. The island rises majestically out of the Mediterranean, the kind of gorgeous accident that only God can make.

Candace tried to just enjoy the view, to simply marvel at the mass of rugged limestone that made up the looming paradise. But loneliness got the best of her. This wasn't something to *ooh* and *ah* over all by yourself.

There should be a special guy here, she thought. For once, she ditched her list of must haves. He didn't need to be established and successful in his career or look like Benicio Del Toro or possess a startling intelligence and lightning-fast sense of humor. Right now, just a decent man would do. Say, for argument's sake, that Prince Charming missed his flight but Prince Doesn't Have a Criminal Record and Bathes Regularly made it. Yeah, she could go for that, as long as this guy held her hand, embraced her, and kissed like a champ.

Candace's nose tingled. She felt like she might cry at any moment. How pathetic was this? Instead of enjoying the incredible scenery, here she stood playing pity party over her single status. In defiance of her own emotions, she decided to draw up a mental ledger of the positive outcomes a girl could garner while living without love.

Hmm ... OK, there was the focus on one's career. Yes! Where would Decadence be today if she'd been distracted by a serious relationship? Probably in bankruptcy. Ooh! And then there was the ability to keep everything under strict control. Falling in love could make a girl do very stupid things. She knew someone who knew someone whose best friend followed her boyfriend's ex-girl-friend for weeks on end just to make sure he wasn't seeing her on the side. Turns out he wasn't. But then he later learned of the stalking, freaked out, and dumped her. So much for earning peace of mind.

Candace felt a little better now, but the specter of loneliness lingered. On impulse, she snatched out the cell phone she wasn't supposed to be carrying (a bombshell no-no) and called Tatiana.

"Hello?" Once again, her friend sounded bored.

"It's me. Are you still filming that love scene?"

"Honey, these things can go on for three days. They're relighting it now." Tatiana yawned. "I hope this guy I'm working with isn't a biter. I've got a tiny scar near my left areola from a scene I did with Michael Nouri once."

"The guy from *Flashdance*?"

"Yes. And FYI—he's not gay. That man was into it, if you know what I mean. Anyway, I'm glad you called. I never eat lunch on nude days, and I didn't know what to do with myself over the meal break, so I tracked down Greg Tapper. He couldn't talk long. Or so he says. Prick. I remember him when he was working at a car wash and doing bad James Dean channeling in acting class. Well, I wanted to get the dirt for you on the *real* producer of that movie. Greg's got the executive title, but that's just an ego credit. It doesn't mean shit when it comes down to the actual work. According to him, though, Leigh Crawford is tough as nails and a major budget Nazi. That's code for a very driven, stressed-out man. A bombshell is the perfect girl to relax that kind of guy. Just laugh at everything he says and tell him you think power's an aphrodisiac."

"I think I can do that," Candace said, her voice more somber than she intended.

Tatiana allowed a few seconds of silence to pass. "Honey, you sound sad."

Candace sighed. "I was just thinking."

"About what?"

"Do you realize that I've never even moved in with anyone?"

"So? That's for college kids. A bombshell insists on marriage. Don't worry. If you do this the right way, you'll probably have five husbands before you turn fifty."

"I'm not talking about being a bombshell," Candace snapped. "I'm talking about *me.*"

Tatiana gasped. "Oh, honey, I should've seen

this coming. My radar's off because I'm trying to act passionate with a gay man who doesn't brush his teeth often enough."

"Huh?"

"You're in Capri! Paradise! A place for lovers! Of course you're going to get all melancholy about being single. Listen, just go to the piazzetta. It's Capri's main square and most popular hangout. Plenty of men will hit on you there. In five minutes you'll feel like Zsa Zsa Gabor, the early years."

"I miss Jason," Candace said wistfully, naming her most significant ex.

"Oh, please," Tatiana scoffed. "You don't miss him any more than I miss wearing a retainer at night."

"But I do," she argued weakly. "I loved him."

"Honey, he criticized you just like your mother does. That wasn't love. It was only something familiar."

Now she started to laugh and cry a little at the same time. "God, why am I getting so emotional all of a sudden? It's not like I didn't get my period two weeks ago."

"Blame it on Capri, honey. It's the turquoise water, the sun, the villas. You see all that and want Steve McQueen by your side."

"Steve McQueen?"

"I know, he was manic depressive, but still sexy as hell. I would've fed him Zoloft like candy and lived happily ever after."

Candace found herself smiling. "I guess there's a point in there somewhere."

"You know, I just remembered something that Dr. G told me once. We should really be pissed at those feminists."

"What?"

"They ruined a whole generation of women. Subconsciously, we inherited all their rage. It's no wonder we're so fucked up. I married a man who refuses to have sex with me. You've come nowhere near an engagement."

"Thanks for the reminder."

"But it's true. The women's movement is so five minutes ago. I earn more than my husband. You have your own business. Face it, men are useless. Ask Jodie Foster. She's winning Oscars, having babies. She doesn't need a guy. You know, Dr. G always tells me that you have to recognize unhealthy behavior in order to change it."

Candace had never been so lost. This was a hard spiel to follow, even for Tatiana. "I'm almost afraid to ask this, but what exactly are you suggesting?"

"Honey, you need sex. Promise me you'll do it with the first hot guy you see."

"Promise me you won't hold me to that promise. I'll call you later."

Even before the boat reached port, Candace felt herself drawn in by the perfumed air of jasmine and pine. It made her spirit dance. Everywhere she looked there were people who seemed to have all the time in the world, men and women with tans as deep as their bone marrow, wearing loose-fitting cotton separates and shoes without laces or hard soles.

When she reached the Palace, the hotel's extreme splendor and high speed glamour didn't rattle her. Yes, A.J. had suggested that she stay here, if only because it was Strider's home away from home in Capri. No, she couldn't afford the three-day reservation. At these prices she should only be booked for, like, a half hour, forty-five minutes tops. Regardless, she presented her credit card to the charming man whose badge announced him as Sergio.

As he handed over her room key, Candace couldn't help but laugh to herself, Tatiana's voice echoing in her mind: *Promise me you'll do it with the first hot guy you see.* And then she turned around and came face-to-face with Strider Moore.

The man momentarily robbed her of breath. That's how handsome he was. He wore a sea island cotton shirt laundered a brilliant white, sleeves folded up to his elbows, the front unbuttoned down to his midsection, the tail hanging loose over calf-length khakis. His bare feet were dressed in pristine Gucci sneakers. He gave off strong Capri native vibrations—tall, healthy, glowing.

Strider pointed at her. "Hey, you're the girl who's dating my cousin."

Candace gave him a dumb look. "Your cousin's married."

"I know. Shame on you. We probably shouldn't dance and flirt anymore. I don't want to come between you two."

"I'm not dating him."

"Really? Sorry that didn't work out."

"I never was."

"I guess that means we can dance and flirt again."

She looked around. "So where's your stalker?"

"Upstairs in my room, I think." He paused a beat. "It's a long story. Don't worry, though. I'm working on a plan to send her back to the States."

"Maybe you should just stop sleeping with her.

I think that's called giving your stalker too much encouragement."

He leaned in closer and perked up his eyebrows. "If *you* want to start stalking me, I promise to encourage you, too."

She couldn't help but smile.

Strider smiled back. "You didn't have to come all this way to congratulate me. A nice card would've been fine."

"Congratulate you?"

"On getting the product placement deal in *Chocolate on Her Pillow.*"

"Don't alert the media quite yet," Candace said. "I came all this way to take that away from you." She brushed past him, carrying two pieces of small luggage. One good thing about being a bombshell was this: You didn't wear a lot of clothing and therefore had no choice but to pack lightly.

Strider moved to follow. "Let me get this straight. *You're* going to take it away from *me?*"

Candace continued walking. "Yes. And you can bet your trust fund on that, playboy."

He stepped in her path, grinning as if pleased with himself (more than usual, apparently), obviously loving the game, the thrill of the chase. "I've got an edge. Greg Tapper's a good friend of mine."

"That's nice. I've got a stronger edge—he wants to sleep with me."

"That's not exactly an in. Greg wants to sleep with everyone. Back in New York he hit on my cleaning lady. By the way, do you do windows?"

She maneuvered around him. "I've been known to push men out of them on occasion."

His brown eyes got big. "Remind me to move to the first floor."

She smiled, preparing to play her trump card. "Actually, I don't have time for Greg Tapper. I prefer to deal directly with the real decision makers." To build the drama, she just stared at him a moment. "That's why a no-nonsense man like Leigh Crawford is so appealing."

Strider's eyes twinkled. She thought he was about to laugh, but in the end he kept a straight face. "Is that so? Because Leigh's one of the toughest producers in the business."

"That's what I hear. My guess is that he and I share a low tolerance level for bullshit." She gave him a pointed look, then stepped into the elevator and delivered this Parthian parting shot: "Maybe we'll find *other* things in common as well."

Just as the doors closed, Strider blurted out, "More than you know!"

She took the ride up to the tenth floor, feeling a little uncertain now. Strider seemed to know something that she didn't. What had he meant by that last statement? Hmm. Candace dismissed the thought. He was merely trying to keep her off balance. A bluff game. She was sure of it.

After a quick shower and sea-salt scrub, she sat down to apply makeup using the tricks Tatiana had taught her. *Honey, I learned these from the hand of the master—Kevyn Aucoin—so consider yourself a supermodel.* Then she sifted through her clothes and decided on a baby doll cropped T-shirt with the name CANDI boldly made out in glitter and rhinestones. She squeezed into some metallic gold hot pants so daring that a little ass cheek was on display. Even Mariah Carey would blush. But when she slipped on the Dolce & Gabbana sling backs (so towering that she felt a little dizzy, but it passed), Candace knew the look was a winner.

Getting around on heels had become much easier. At least she didn't have to break out into a synchronized dance routine like the girls of Destiny's Child. All she had to do was stay erect. She gave herself a final once-over in the mirror. "OK, bombshell. It's time to detonate."

Capri was just four square miles, so it took no time to pinpoint where the movie people had set up camp. They were filming interior scenes in a famous villa on the Via Tragara. Candace made it there only to learn from a stray crew member that production had wrapped for the day.

"Head for the piazzetta," she was told. "That's where everyone goes to unwind." He turned around to display the *Chocolate on Her Pillow* title emblazoned across the back of his beige crewneck polo shirt. "We're easy to find."

Determined to get her man, Candace headed over there, stopping for a bottled water at Gelateria Scialapopolo just off the piazzetta. That's when she spotted a trio of beige polo guys clustered around a small table. She approached to ask about Leigh Crawford and rolled sevens. They pointed to the back of a pear-shaped figure about one hundred feet away.

She tottered over with no idea in her head of what she might say. But Tatiana had made clear that in an outfit like this, all a bombshell really had to do was just stand there and let things happen naturally.

When Candace got closer, she stopped, suddenly transfixed by Leigh Crawford. It was the strangest thing. The producer stood about five-foot-six, wore crudely styled ultrashort hair ... and had *breasts* ... literally. Candace was struck by the hands, too. Short fingers, square-cut nails, yet something dainty about them.

"Do you have a problem?" It was Leigh Crawford talking, in a voice very much like all the rest, of indeterminate gender.

"Uh ... No ... I was just ..." Candace stammered, stalling for time, trying to make sense of this. Tatiana had definitely said that Leigh was a man. And Strider hadn't corrected her when she referred to Leigh as one.

Yet here she was, directly in front of Leigh, and the doubts were piling up. There was no hiding the fact that the man had breasts. But some men did, Candace reasoned. Unfortunate but true. She once heard about a guy in Connecticut who was a C cup after a major weight loss.

"You were just what?" Leigh demanded.

"I was just hoping to meet the legendary Leigh Crawford," Candace gushed, then giggled, tilting forward a little to give the producer the full benefit of her cleavage.

Leigh's annoyed expression turned suspicious. "All the speaking parts are taken. If you're interested in extra work, show up tomorrow morning at five."

"Oh, I'm not an actress."

"Hooker, huh? I was trying to give you the benefit of the doubt."

"I'm not a hooker either!" Candace practically jumped up and down to drive the point home.

Leigh gave her a look and started to walk away. "Hey, that's between you and your wardrobe stylist."

The producer proceeded to lope down the cobbled street with an ambiguous gait that offered no clue to the million-dollar question. Candace felt as if she'd just stepped inside the "It's Pat!" skit from *Saturday Night Live*. Still game—and more curious than ever—she went tippy-tip after Leigh. "Wait!"

The producer stopped, spun, and sighed. "I'm not into lipstick lesbians. I prefer earthy women."

Candace got it now. Suddenly an Indigo Girls song started playing in her head. How had Tatiana missed this point? Of course, Strider had known all along. That sneaky bastard.

"I just wanted to introduce myself," Candace said, hoping to turn things around. "I'm not into lipstick lesbians, either. Well, any lesbians, if you must know. But I support the lifestyle. I saw k.d. lang in concert once. And I even practiced kissing with a girl at summer camp."

Leigh's eyes lit up with amusement. "Is that so?"

Candace nodded.

Leigh held up her right hand, thumb and index finger about an inch apart. "You're this close to being family."

"I'm Candi Rowley."

Leigh threw an obvious look to the glitter and rhinestones spelling that first name out across Candace's chest. "Apparently."

She reached into her bag and presented Leigh with a Passion Truffle.

"I've read the script for *Chocolate on Her Pillow*. This is the candy that Sam should leave on Grace's pillow."

Leigh studied her for a moment. "That script is top secret. How did you get your hands on it?"

"E-bay," Candace said. "I was the high bidder with thirty dollars."

Leigh made a face. "I knew I recognized your name. I should've set a higher reserve price."

You're TomBoy35?"

Leigh returned a guilty nod. "Don't rat me out. I swiped one of Greg Tapper's undershirts, and it went for two hundred bucks."

"Yuck. Wasn't it dirty?"

"Of course. A famous person's sweat and grime is like gold. If I could just get his underwear. Or a jockstrap. That's where the real money is." Then Leigh unwrapped the Passion Truffle and stuffed it into her mouth in one greedy gulp. "The nougat tastes weird."

Candace was horrified. She would've rathered Leigh Crawford just spit out the candy and call it elephant dung than call it "nougat." *Nougat.* As if! Decadence wasn't jockeying for space in the Whitman's sampler. Candace made her candy with a special Valrhona chocolate imported from France. She used only the purest guava and passion fruit nectars, and most noteworthy, she didn't add a single granule of sugar. Any chocolate that required extra sweetening to please the palate was inferior. Of course, all that would be lost on this woman (what a relief to finally know!) who didn't know a truffle from a Snow Cap. But Candace had to give it a go.

Leigh made a terrible sucking noise with her teeth. "Not bad. Do you have a few more of those?"

Candace offered her a handful. "I was hoping to talk with you about product placement. I have some thoughts that might—"

"Save your breath, cutie pie," Leigh cut in. "I've

got a lead actress who thinks *walking* qualifies as a stunt. She wants a double to do it, so she can stay in her villa zoned out on pills. I just had to fire an actor in one of the supporting roles. He's an Oscar winner, yeah, but he's also a drunk and can't remember his lines. Oh, and Greg Tapper took off on his yacht with some bimbo a few hours ago, so we lost half a day's shooting. And he calls himself an executive producer. Now, these are the issues I'm currently facing. Do you really think I have time to worry about what kind of candy we use in the movie?"

"But—"

Leigh held up a hand and started to leave. "Talk to Greg. I've left that monumental decision in his hands. But thanks for the chocolate."

Candace watched her walk away. "My pleasure," she murmured softly, but Leigh was out of earshot. Oh, God, what now? Swim the Mediterranean until she happened upon Greg's yacht?

"Well, you were right about one thing. You both have a low tolerance level for bullshit."

Candace turned to see Strider Moore sipping red wine nearby. In the center of his quaint table was an open bottle of expensive vintage. An empty glass sat beside it.

He gestured to the chair opposite him. "Join me."

She didn't move an inch. "What about my low tolerance level?"

"I'll check my bullshit at the door. Promise."

Candace smiled. She started toward him, feeling lucky. Those were the exact words that every single woman wanted to hear from a guy.

Chapter Seven

Strider poured as Candace sat down. "That went well. For a minute there I thought she was going to ask you back to her villa."

"Why didn't you tell me?"

"And miss the show?"

She took a generous sip and embraced the sun beaming down on her. "I deserve that, I guess. Maybe I was a little cocky back at the hotel."

Strider raised his eyebrows. "Maybe? A little? You had bigger *cajones* than a gladiator. In fact, I heard them clang when you walked."

"I was that bad?"

He winked and drank some more wine. "Not really. I like to torment."

"So . . . Greg Tapper is the last word on the product placement."

"Right you are." He refilled his glass. "Speaking of Greg, I don't know whether I should be celebrating or drowning my sorrows."

"What do you mean?"

"He left on his yacht."

"I know. Leigh's in an uproar because he didn't finish today's scenes."

"Tiko is with him."

This pleased Candace to no end. "Well, I thought you wanted her to go away."

"I did." He raised his wine in salute. "That's the part I'm celebrating. But I didn't want Greg to go away. I need him here to make a decision."

Candace shrugged. "He has to be back on the set tomorrow."

"Greg's a name above the title star, and he never lets anyone forget that. The truth is, he doesn't *have* to do anything. Besides, Tiko has a way of . . . *distracting* men. I wouldn't be surprised if they stayed gone for a few days."

"A few days?" It came out as a shriek.

Strider gave her a worried look. "Calm down. Tiko's *my* stalker. If I'm handling the absence OK . . ."

"It's not that. I can't afford to stay here much longer."

"Corporate espionage on a budget, huh? I take it you don't have any cool gadgets."

A reluctant smile pushed past Candace's lips. "Don't make fun."

"You know, I've been known to yell out anything during sex—Jesus, Buddha, first and last names of the Backstreet Boys, the secret ingredient of our Love Truffle. There's no telling. Sleeping with me won't cost you anything, but who knows, you might get lucky and learn something that'll help."

She gave him a warning look. "You promised to check your bullshit at the door."

Strider held up both hands, as if coming clean. "Everything I said is true."

She decided to test him. "OK, who's the youngest Backstreet Boy?"

He didn't pause so much as a beat. "Nick Carter."

"I can only assume you know what you're talking about because I don't know the answer."

"I'm a man who knows his teen pop."

Now came Candace's turn to give the worried look.

"I keep MTV on as background noise," Strider explained.

She laughed a little.

"But I must admit . . . I really do love 'I Want It That Way.' "

"I can't stand the Backstreet Boys, so the idea of you yelling out their names during—"

"Not so fast," Strider cut in. "That's not my whole act. Sometimes I name the Beatles, the Rolling Stones, even the Pointer Sisters once."

"That's a great trick for VH1's *Rock and Roll Jeopardy,* but it doesn't say much for your skills as a lover."

He put the wineglass to his lips, then stopped, placed it back down, and smiled. "I've got references. Testimonials from every partner except one. That would be a girl I met in Cancun on a college spring break trip. I was drunk and passed out on top of her during the act. Not my finest six and a half minutes."

Candace sat there, charmed by him, attracted to him . . . but ultimately cautious of him. She knew about Strider Moore's stripe of worm. A woman would warn you about this kind of man in the bathroom of a hot nightclub. But that same woman would end up going home with him. He was the guy who kept mental lists of how many girls he'd been with and all the weird places he'd had sex with them, the guy who made you laugh, the guy who made you come more than once. But the most important thing to remember was this: He was the guy who wouldn't call you again.

A bombshell like Tatiana could handle the Striders of the world while running a 10K and moderating a world peace summit—at the same time. But Candace, with only the emergency course, a few vampy encounters at the Cutting Room, and a disastrous interlude with a lesbian behind her, considered herself bombshell *lite.* Tangling with a man like Strider could only mean a world of hurt.

"Penny for your thoughts," Strider said.

She came back from her reverie. "It'll cost you much more than that."

He glanced down, reached for her foot, and slipped off her obscenely expensive sling back in one single, fluid movement. "Didn't your mother teach you about sensible shoes?"

"Don't get me started on my mother."

"Ah, parent issues," Strider said, grinning knowingly as he proceeded to massage her inner leg, working from her ankle to just beyond her calf. He used his thumbs first, then his palms, making firm circles, leaving no doubt that he knew how to handle a woman's body.

It felt too damn good to protest. Everything started to intoxicate her at once—the buzz of the wine, the proximity to this sexy beast, the arousal of the energy line that began at her big toe and steadily traveled up her leg to her groin. *Ooh.* She felt something where it counted. For a moment she closed her eyes.

"I have a boat here, too," Strider announced softly. "It's not as big as Greg's, but it will get us to the nearby island of Ischia. What do you say?"

Candace slipped off her shoe and kicked up her other leg. "I say you're not done yet."

He laughed and took her ankle in a firm yet sensual grip. "My real specialty's the lower back. It comes free with the boat trip. Pretty good deal."

The sensations started all over again. She thought she might moan out loud but fought hard against it. With a deep breath through her nose, she steadied herself. *Promise me you'll do it with the first hot guy you see.* Tatiana's words played inside her head.

"There is one condition, though," Strider said. "We have to call a truce before we board the *Candy Girl.*"

She smiled at the name of the boat. "That's cute."

"It was a college graduation present from my parents."

"How nice. I got a toaster oven."

He grinned. "Don't hate me because I'm rich. That's my great grandfather's fault."

It struck Candace how remarkably different the two cousins were. She couldn't detect that Strider was capable of anything but kindness. A bit caddish, yes, but harmlessly so. She imagined that all of his ex-girlfriends remembered him fondly. He probably never forgot their birthdays and always sent them a Christmas card.

"I really should get back to the hotel," Candace

heard herself say, but the words hit the Capri air with no conviction.

"Just a quick jaunt," Strider pressed. "There're still a few hours of sun left. You'll love it. Trust me." Something in his eyes smacked of a child imploring an indifferent friend to come out and play.

Candace gave in. And she imagined that it wouldn't be the first time, either.

He emptied the bottle of wine into her glass. Just an inch or so remained. "Drink up, mate." Strider's gaze zeroed in on the glitter and rhinestones spelling out her new name. "Where did this Candi business come from?"

She touched the heart symbol that dotted the i just above her breast. "A friend of mine suggested it."

"You need a new friend."

She turned up her glass and slipped her shoes back on.

"Candace is a beautiful name."

She rose quickly. Compliments unsettled her. She'd never learned how to accept them gracefully. "That's nice of you to say."

"It's not just nice. It's the truth. You're too smart to walk around with a name like Candi. By the way, that's one of the reasons I'm being so persistent here. It's refreshing to meet a girl with a sharp mind."

"Lots of us are out there. We're just not models or pop stars."

He nodded guiltily. "I know. The gossip columns have given me a certain reputation, and smart girls actually read the columns, so they never give me the time of day. Models and pop stars just scan them for their photographs or their names in bold type. If you take the time to think about it, I'm really a victim.''

"Maybe Tiko will do a benefit concert for the relief fund."

He took her arm, and they started to walk. "You're not going to give me a break, are you?"

"The odds are slim."

Strider's hand moved down to thread his fingers through hers.

Candace let it happen, heart banging inside her chest, stomach feeling like a vacuum, but once the initial surprise subsided, it seemed the most natural and comforting thing in the world.

They made it down to the Marina Grande, Capri's main harbor, where they navigated through the maze of boats big and small until they reached the *Candy Girl*, an all-white, sleek vessel with a flat sundeck that stretched for at least eight feet.

Strider started the engine. It gunned to life on the first try. Candace slipped off her shoes and held fast to the guardrails as he negotiated the busy harbor, then revved it once the *Candy Girl* had an opening. The water was smooth, a spectacular infinite blue. Suddenly the other ships in the harbor, the villas, all the details of Capri, began falling like ninepins. The island's rugged twin peaks were more pronounced now. Beneath the soles of her feet she could feel the throb of the motor.

Suddenly she forgot the whole bombshell bit and just started being herself. Breathlessly, she pointed out the icicle-shaped mineral deposits in the distance, the ones hanging from the roofs of caves. They chugged past the Blue Grotto, the famous cavernous wonder that was every serious diver's dream. She marveled at the other grottoes in the distance. It was right there that the Sirens had tempted the mythological hero Odysseus, tempting him with their sweet but treacherous song.

Candace told him about Book Twelve of Homer's *The Odyssey*, getting caught up in the story, prattling on with the whole tale. About Odysseus cutting up a wheel of wax with his sword, kneading it under the sun until it became soft, and stuffing it into the ears of all his men. How only that way could they avoid the sinister seduction. She made clear that the Sirens enchanted all men, that those who got too close met a quick death. And then she went on about how his men sailed past, oblivious to the murderous music as only Odysseus listened, having first ordered his crew to tie him up to the mast of the ship. With great enthusiasm, she relayed her favorite part of this tale, how the song tempted the hero, how he forgot his will and wanted to row toward the Sirens. But his men would not hear of it, so they tightened the ropes that bound him and drifted past the island.

Suddenly Candace stopped and covered her mouth. Oh, God. This was just like that dreadful *Coffee in Manhattan* segment with Chip and Didi. This was just like any other time that she got carried away with a favorite subject. She looked at him sheepishly.

He stared back in amusement.

"I'm sorry. You probably want to push me overboard."

"No, I enjoyed your story. In prep school I read the Cliff Notes and missed all that rich detail."

Candace studied him for a moment, gauging his

sincerity. He seemed earnest enough. She shrugged. "I love mythology."

"I can tell that you love a lot of things. You have a sense of joy about you. That's rare. It's refreshing, too."

"What do you love?"

He took off his shirt, started for the platform, and sat down. "I love the sun this time of day." His chest was flawless—smooth, sculpted, and golden, all the way down to the chiseled abs that looked as firm as a sheet of steel. "You know, it's not uncommon for women in Capri to sunbathe topless. You should try it."

Candace knew that Strider expected her to either laugh it off as a joke or to get flustered and flat-out refuse. That's why she decided to do something wild. On impulse, she peeled off her shirt and tossed it onto the deck.

His jaw dropped, the surprise on his face total.

She joined him and tilted her head back to bask in the bronzing heat of the hottest burning star. It seemed to feed a hungry part of her. In a strange way she felt a sudden awakening. Everything shined—the quiet in the aftermath of the killed engine, the turquoise water of the Mediterranean, the sexual energy between them. The sum of it all made her feel emboldened. "Your turn."

Strider began to unfasten his pants.

She giggled and pulled his hand away from the zipper. "No! I mean your turn to tell a story."

"From *The Odyssey?*"

"It doesn't have to be."

"There's actually a long-lost tale that Homer left out. You see, there was a goddess whose incredible breasts could make slaves of men. All she had to do was take off her shirt, and men would sign over their fortunes and agree to do anything she asked."

"This goddess must have traveled with a good lawyer."

"Oh, the best. He was the Marvin Mitchelson of his day."

Candace shielded her eyes from the glare to ask, "Are you *ever* serious?"

"Why ruin a good time?"

"Or make it meaningful?"

His gaze lingered on her breasts. "You have no idea how much this means to me."

"Models and pop stars might not notice when a man is glib twenty-four hours a day, but I do. Every time the conversation starts to get real, you make a joke."

"At least they're good jokes."

Candace started to see him in a different light. What if she scratched the surface and nothing was there? Men like that were legendary, especially in New York. They were rich and successful and dated a series of pretty models, actresses, and glamour job holders. This went on for years and years. Obviously, growing up was hard to do. Candace *knew* men like this. One owned the advertising firm that did creative for Decadence. Every conversation with him was the same. Maybe four strokes back and forth and then nothing left to say.

Strider seemed to wince under her silent scrutiny. "Do you really want serious, Candace? Because serious is this: If I don't make this product placement happen, I'm out of the family business." He leaned back, making a pillow for his head with both hands, and let go of a heavy sigh. "Maybe that's not such a bad thing, though. Even if I'm lucky enough to pull this deal off, there's going to be another do-or-die test down the line. My cousin will make sure of it. He wants me gone."

Candace watched as Strider's face took on an inscrutable sadness. It was the polar opposite of the malignant envy that A.J. had revealed in Virginia. "Moore Candies is a huge company with interests all over the world. Why can't the two of you coexist?"

Strider looked genuinely perplexed. "I don't know. I've tried to stay out of his way, but it's not enough. It really didn't hit me how much A.J. hates me until I was thirteen. Before that, we were inseparable." He grinned at the memory. "Thick as thieves. And whenever we got into a scrape, I took the fall. A.J.'s mom was a mess, and his dad had been branded the family loser. He seemed to live for the approval of my father, and I didn't care much whether I had it or not, so I didn't mind playing the screwup. But then we were both at Brambletye. That's an English boarding school about thirty miles outside of London. A.J. pulled a prank that went way too far. He vandalized the dressing room of the headmaster's wife and threw all her undergarments into the pool. They found a button on the floor with the Moore family crest on it, so they knew it was one of us. A.J. begged me to cover for him. He was a year younger, and I was graduating in a few months, so . . ."

Candace couldn't believe where the story was going. "You didn't."

"I did. At the time I had no idea about the vandalism. I just thought it was a few bras and girdles in the pool. After I fessed up, I found out how serious the charges were. My father came over, they expelled me, and I lost my slot at Eton. That's the senior school Prince William attended. When we came out of the headmaster's office, my father got in my face and said, 'I'm ashamed to call you my son. You disgust me.' A.J. was in the hall. I saw him crack a smile. That's when I knew. He hated me. And I actually had thought of him like a brother."

"How could you accept so much punishment for something you didn't do?"

Strider sighed again. Deeper this time. The kind of sigh that revealed years of baggage being lugged around. "I don't know. I've asked myself that question a million times. Part of me was in shock. Another part of me wanted to believe that as the shit got deeper and deeper, A.J. would stand up and do the right thing. No one really expected much from me after that. It kind of became a self-fulfilling prophecy. I didn't expect much from myself either. You know what's funny? I've been partying my ass off for twenty years, and it's been a blast. Hedonism all the way. But I'm still pissed about what happened when I was thirteen." He turned away from her, faced the sun, and blinked back a tear.

"My friend Tatiana's been in therapy for years," Candace said softly. "Her doctor once told her that we spend more years getting over our childhood than we do getting through it."

"I've never told this to anyone before. Must be the boobs."

She laughed. "Oh, God, he's *back.*"

"I do have a reputation to uphold." He rolled over and stopped mere centimeters from her mouth, his hand sweeping over to cradle her waist.

Candace took in a sharp breath.

"What's the going rate for psychotherapists these days?"

"I'm not sure. Maybe one hundred fifty dollars an hour."

"Then I better kiss you. That'll mean conflict of interest. You won't be able to send me a bill."

Candace's lips trembled on the brink of his. "You can afford it."

"I might be unemployed soon." Strider's face was so close. His appeal haunted her. It was the stuff of ancient evenings. He hovered there for the longest time, looking into her eyes, *really* looking into them.

She wondered if he could see the pools of guilt there, as she lay under him, heart hammering, telling herself a lie she didn't believe, that there was nothing to be ashamed of, that everything about this was honest. Just then an internal panic began to set in.

That's when Strider jumped off the cliff of intimacy and claimed her mouth without warning. Her lips were dry from the sun. He used his tongue to coat them with moisture and thundered on.

Candace could feel the blood speeding through her. It pulsed in her veins and pounded in her heart as the old world closed and a new world opened. A soft moan escaped her.

Strider responded, drawing her closer with his tanned and muscled arms, pushing his tongue into her mouth in a feverish attack of longing. One hand skated across her breasts, which were slick with dampness brought on from the heat.

Candace tried to push him away, her mind and body at war, but when he pressed his body against

her, advertising how eager he was, how much he
desired her, the mind lost ground and all thought
went away. She arched her neck. His mouth eased
down, to her nape, over her breasts, onto the
throbbing nipples, feasting there, distending them
to the point of overflowing lust.

Bit by bit, her body uncoiled. It had been too
long, but even before, it had never been like this.
Every part of her felt like a wet fire, slippery but
scorching hot. The cool slab of the platform lay
under her. The gorgeous chocolate prince lay on
top of her. The need for more sent her reeling
with astonishment. In one sweet second of flicking
change, she became an animal, a shuddering creature desperate to satisfy the craving that mattered
more than her next breath.

And so with trembling fingers, she reached for
his zipper. . . .

Chapter Eight

Candace wanted to call Tatiana and tell her that she'd just had sex with a man who made her come three times. But she could barely move, so she just lay there, wiping tears of sweat from her eyes.

Strider kissed his index finger, then touched her nose. "You're insatiable."

You would be too if Clinton had been in office the last time you got your freak on. That's what went through her mind. But she just smiled and released a cute sigh that spelled out SATISFACTION in all caps.

Suddenly something occurred to her. "Who is George Lazenby?" When he climaxed, Strider had yelled out the names of all the actors who played James Bond.

He grinned, obviously pleased with himself, looking like a grade-schooler who'd just won a statewide spelling bee. "Sean Connery, Roger Moore, Timothy Dalton, Pierce Brosnan—those are the easy ones to remember. It takes a true 007 fan to know

George Lazenby, *On Her Majesty's Secret Service*, 1969, featuring Diana Rigg as a Spanish contessa. Thank you. I'll be here all week."

She sighed again. "Give it a rest, Shecky."

Strider rose on one elbow. "Shecky?"

"Aren't there any number of bad comics in Las Vegas named Shecky?"

"I'm not sure, but I think I should be offended."

Candace crinkled her eyes. "Go with your instincts."

He glanced down at his crotch. "Give me about a half hour. I know how to entertain you."

She laughed—amused, delighted. This was, without a sliver of doubt, the most positive sexual experience that Candace had ever known. Almost every time before had left her wondering. Was she pleasing him? Why couldn't he please her? Even Jason, the man she thought she might marry, had been a bore in the bedroom.

With Strider, sex was so much more than a clumsy interaction between two naked people. It was a carnal roller-coaster ride—fun, thrilling, full of surprising dips, turns, and upside-down moves that triggered occasional screams. There was something more, though . . . something . . . spiritual.

His hand skated onto her stomach and started drawing imaginary circles around her belly button. "Did you see *Grease?*"

"Of course. Who hasn't?"

"Some people hate musicals."

"But everybody loves *Grease.*" She started to hum "You're the One That I Want."

"My cousin walked out after the 'Summer Nights' number."

"A.J.?"

Strider nodded.

"He's not of this earth," Candace said.

"You remind me of that movie."

She lifted her head to look him directly in the eyes. "How?"

"In the movie there's the goody-two-shoes Sandy and the tight-leather-pants Sandy."

Candace nodded.

"That's how you are. There's the good Candace who was profiled in *Confectioner* and appeared on *Coffee in Manhattan,* and then there's the bad girl Candace who showed up at the Cutting Room and here in Capri."

"And which one got your attention?"

"Both, actually. When I saw you on TV, I liked your story about Montezuma's big appetite for chocolate, but I must confess that I fell asleep when you started in about Christopher Columbus."

She covered her face and giggled nervously. "That was *so* embarrassing. They'll never have me on again."

"I thought you were cute. Really. Embarrassing was Didi's version of 'My Heart Will Go On.' "

"You mean 'The Greatest Love of All,' " Candace corrected.

"Oh, that's right. I must be thinking of another show because I know I've heard her butcher that song, too. Back to my point, though. Why the transformation?"

"Good girl Candace didn't stand a chance with the Hollywood brigade."

"But Greg Tapper is MIA with Tiko, and you struck out with Leigh Crawford."

Candace thought about it. He definitely had her there. "Well, *you* responded to the bad girl."

"Initially . . . Yes, that's true. But you really hooked me with your mind, especially that story from *The Odyssey*. That's when you let your guard down and were so real. I think I even fell in love a little bit. You don't know anything from *The Iliad*, do you?"

Candace smiled at the joke, but it didn't register. Her mind was stuck on one phrase: *I think I even fell in love a little bit*. She felt her heart lurch. Wow. What would Tatiana say about this? Probably something along the lines of, "Honey, men like Strider fall in love all the time. It's like a viral love. Usually it lasts twenty-four hours. Vegas is the best place for these illnesses because it's so easy to get married there."

Strider picked up on her inner turmoil. "Are you freaking out because I actually know about *The Iliad*?"

"Not exactly," she managed, "although that is a bit of a shock."

"See? I'm full of surprises." He stretched out flat and pulled her toward him, resting her head on his chest and stroking her hair. "If I don't get the product placement, will you hire me? I know a thing or two about chocolate."

The sun blazed—a bright orange ball bathing them in steam heat. Candace wanted the moment to stretch on forever. There was something so familiar about this, as if she were hanging out with a buddy. It felt meant to be. That's why an unstoppable urge to come clean rained down on her. "I have to tell you something."

"Oh, don't tell me you faked it. Those three orgasms are some of my best work."

"No." She laughed. "I didn't fake it." Her hand

moved down his navel, stopping just at the point where his hairs gathered thickness. "I don't want to fake anything with you."

"That's good. We can be two people who keep the Truth Channel on all the time. I'll start. First sexual fantasy. Mine was Angie Dickinson. I loved *Police Woman.* I wanted her to handcuff me. Pretty kinky for an eight-year-old. What about you?"

"Captain Kirk from *Star Trek.* I wanted to be one of the alien women that he kissed."

He pulled her closer. "That's just weird enough. *We* are made for each other."

"I have to share another truth. An ugly one." She pressed her fingers to his lips. "Don't make a joke. Please. Let me get this out. A.J. showed me the marketing plans for the Love Truffle. He also took me to the factory in Virginia and told me that you were here in Capri and where you were staying."

Strider's body tensed. "Asshole. He told Tiko I was coming here, too."

"He's hired a private investigator to keep tabs on you."

Strider's face darkened, his temples pulsed, and he shook his head incredulously.

"I didn't ask A.J. to do any of this," Candace went on. "He just offered it on the spot. At the time, I wanted this deal so bad that I couldn't resist. But now it doesn't mean anything, not if getting it means that you'll be hurt."

Strider just stared at her.

Candace had no idea how he might react. But a tremor of fear ran through her, a fear that whatever they were to each other could be over as soon as it had begun. "Go find Greg. Close the deal. I'll go back to New York."

"You deserve it more than I do. What have I done besides party with a movie star? You've actually created something."

"I don't want it this way," Candace argued.

"Neither do I. If A.J.'s willing to go through all this to get me out, then fine. I'll just leave. Maybe it's time that I struck out on my own anyway."

"Don't let him make that decision for you. That's giving him too much power." She watched him, still beautiful even in all his misery, weighing his options, considering his future, the guy with all the one-liners a million miles away. There was a depth to Strider, a capability for thought and feeling that he rarely accessed. It was at this realization that she knew, from the bottom of her uncertain heart, she knew.

Candace brushed a tendril of hair from his eyes. "I think we're both in a similar place right now. I understand the ambivalence and anger you feel toward your father. I've got the same thing with my mother. It's like we both carry around this feeling in ourselves . . . this sense that we're not good enough or that whatever we do doesn't quite measure up. We've both got fears and doubts and mistrust. Maybe we can heal each other."

Strider said nothing. He just kissed her fiercely, his lips bruising, his tongue aggressive, his hands all over. When he rolled on top of her, the intensity of his need was overwhelming. He locked his eyes onto hers and entered her quickly, making love with a passion so naked, so alternately vulnerable and ferocious, that her own pleasure seemed irrelevant. And at the moment of climax, he didn't shout out anything silly. Instead he kissed her deeply and breathed a soft moan of pleasure into her mouth. Lying there, with him still inside her, she felt complete and at peace. It was poetry.

"Pull up the anchor," Candace whispered. "Let's float away."

They were just off the coast of Ischia.

Strider sighed his longing to do exactly that. "This is a famous spot, you know. Elizabeth Taylor and Richard Burton were photographed here in a compromising position."

Candace giggled. "I'd say we look pretty compromised, too. I wonder if someone will take our picture."

Someone did take their picture. It had been wired to New York, downloaded in a nanosecond, and then splashed across the gossip columns for society gawkers to gulp down with their morning latte. Sergio delivered the faxed pages in a discreet brown envelope.

"Oh, shit." There were no better words that came to mind as Strider read the cover letter from his father. It was an angry missive that talked of irresponsibility and disappointment, ending with the news that both father and grandfather were on their way to Capri from one of the overseas plants. He was to meet them in the library of *The Chocolate Bar,* the Moore family yacht, a vessel that made the *Candy Girl* look like a toy boat for the bathtub.

Strider zeroed in on the media damage.

CHOCOLATE RIVALS MAKE LOVE, NOT WAR

Filthy rich candy hunk **Strider Moore** is playing musical beds in Capri, that Mediterranean paradise known for naughty goings-on. Moore played sensual music with international chanteuse **Tiko,** then took up with **Candace Rowley,** the Passion Truffle queen who made even Chip and Didi seem interesting during a recent (snore, snore) appearance on *Coffee in Manhattan.* But don't cry for Tiko, Japan. She sailed away with **Greg Tapper** on his yacht. In case readers are wondering, we've seen both boats, and Greg's is definitely bigger than Strider's. Wink.

The accompanying photo was carefully cropped for publication. Strider's back blocked Candace's breasts, and they were locked in a passionate kiss. He worried if racier shots would turn up elsewhere. Maybe some cheap magazine or a tacky Internet site. It infuriated him how nothing was sacred in the information age. It angered him more that this column had ridiculed Candace. He was tempted to call up Page Six's Richard Johnson and bitch him out, then decided that such a move would only aggravate matters. Tomorrow another scandal would hit, and everyone would forget about this. Everyone but his family, of course.

He tried calling Candace's room, wanting to warn her of the ambush. She'd gone there to pack, but the phone just rang and rang, finally going to voice mail. Strider dressed quickly and left his suite to go find her.

* * *

"Nasty girl!" Tatiana squealed. "Your love scene looks much hotter than the one I'm *still* filming."

Candace was genuinely perplexed. Her cellular had rung, she'd picked up on the second ring, and Tatiana had started in without preamble. "What are you talking about?"

"I'm talking about you and Strider Moore going at it like teenagers after the prom in this morning's Page Six. It looks like you're on a boat or something."

Candace froze in the middle of the piazzetta. She dropped the bag that contained the jewelry she'd just purchased from the little shop that had framed pictures of Aristotle and Jackie Onassis everywhere. She almost dropped the phone. She came close to throwing up.

"Please tell. These days Kerr falls asleep as soon as we get into bed. I haven't had real sex in weeks. Let me live vicariously."

"Tatiana, I'm in shock. I haven't seen this."

"Don't be upset. You look great, and there's a single, straight, and gorgeous guy with a trust fund all over you. Any woman who criticizes is simply jealous that it's not *her* in the picture."

Candace collected her bearings and bent down to pick up her jewelry. "What does it say?"

"Oh, something about you being boring on Chip and Didi's show, but that's old news. Besides, people will just read the headline, look at the picture, and move on to their horoscope."

Candace braced herself. "So what *is* the headline?"

"Chocolate Rivals Make Love, Not War."

Candace groaned. It was worse than she'd imagined.

"Greg Tapper must be furious," Tatiana continued with thinly veiled delight. "There's mention of him hooking up with Tiko but no photo, so Strider gets all the stud points. OK, tell me, on a scale of one to ten . . ."

"Tatiana, I need you to stop for a second and think about something. I don't live in Hollywood. I'm not an actress. Having my half-naked body splattered across a tabloid page is not good for my image profile. It's just *humiliating.*"

"I disagree on the last point," Tatiana argued. "A picture of you getting busy with the creepy cousin—*that* would be humiliating. But honey, Strider Moore is *hot.* He could make a girl push Brad Pitt out of the way. FYI, it looks like you're all the way naked, not half naked."

Sitting at a cafe table up ahead, a familiar figure captured Candace's attention. He was deep in conversation with another man, unrecognizable from this distance, but tugging at her memory just the same. She moved closer, falling into step with a small crowd to escape notice. *No, it couldn't be.*

It was A.J. Moore! Damn him. And why was he huddled with Eric O'Donnell, one of the top marketing executives at Hershey?

"Honey, are you still there?" Tatiana said.

"Yes, but I have to go."

"Don't you dare hang up this phone until you—"

"Oh, all right," Candace hissed. "It was out of this world. I came three times."

Tatiana gasped.

"I'll call you later."

"Wait! Does he have a brother?"

"No."

"How old is his father? Never mind. It doesn't matter. There's always Viagra!"

Candace hung up, shoved the cell into her purse, adjusted the brim of her Burberry hat, moved stealthily ahead of A.J. and Eric, and crisscrossed to a vacant table within earshot.

And then she listened, fury rising with every syllable she could make out.

Sergio knew nothing of Candace's whereabouts. Strider considered heading for the piazzetta, then checked his watch and decided against it. The meeting from hell was less than an hour away.

"Is there any way I can help, sir?" Sergio inquired.

"Yeah. Get me a pen and paper."

Dutifully, Sergio produced a Mont Blanc and fine stationary embossed with the Palace logo.

Strider scribbled down a note to Candace and implored Sergio to get it to her as soon as possible. Leaving the hotel, he ran into Greg Tapper and Tiko. "Back so soon? You didn't give us a chance to put your faces on a milk carton."

Tiko glared.

Greg managed a tight smile. "Strider. Just the son of a bitch I'm looking for." He turned to the one-hit wonder. "Give us a minute. I'll meet you inside."

Tiko pouted. "Tiko wants an ice-cream sundae!"

Greg placed a proprietary hand on Tiko's ass.

"Have I denied you anything since we've been together, baby? Now run along."

Tiko gave Strider a triumphant look and darted into the lobby.

"My publicist faxed me today's Page Six," Greg said coldly. "All I asked you to do was find out her last name."

"I didn't see the point, Greg. Candace deserves better than you."

Greg took a menacing step forward. "Since when is a spoiled rich kid better than a self-made man?" His nostrils flared. This fool was ready to rumble.

"Easy, action star. Are you sure you want to fight? Everybody knows you don't do your own stunts."

Greg's lips curled into a smug, superior smile. "Want some good advice, Strider? Never upstage a movie star. Hershey got the product placement deal. They made us an offer we couldn't refuse. I'll make sure you get the press release." He started to go. "Hope you and the chocolate slut live happily ever after."

Before Strider knew what was happening, his anger bomb went *tick, tick, boom!* He clobbered Greg Tapper, sending him down with one punch that landed squarely on the shit heel's cheek. It would swell, turn purple and black, hurt like hell, and delay shooting. Mission accomplished.

Strider stood over the silver-screen tough guy. "Don't bother trying to sue me, Greg. I can afford just as many lawyers as you can. And I don't think you want it widely publicized that everybody's favorite action hero got his ass kicked by a trust-fund baby."

And then Strider took off for the Marina Grande to meet his fate, massaging his aching right hand all the way. When he arrived, his father, Lansing Jr., and grandfather, Lansing Sr., were smoking cigars.

The greetings proceeded awkwardly—a few disapproving looks this way and that, stiff handshakes all around, the tension so thick in the air that it was almost hard to breathe.

His father spoke first. "I assume you've heard the news that Hershey landed the deal."

Strider nodded.

His grandfather fixed a piercing stare on him. "Maybe things would've turned out differently if you'd had your eyes on the prize and not your hands all over the girl."

Strider shrugged. "What can I say? There were forces working against me."

"Only one that I can see," his father said. "It's called immaturity."

Strider knew what was coming. But he didn't care. He wanted out. So why fight it? In the end, A.J. would get his. Life had a way of balancing out all the wrongs.

"Our position was clear as to the outcome of this matter, Strider," Lansing Sr. put in. "Your cousin A.J. is dedicated to the company in a way that you never have been."

"More than you know," Strider said.

The two Lansings exchanged annoyed looks.

His father stood up. "This isn't easy, son."

"Mr. Moore, wait, you don't have the whole story."

Three generations of Moores rubbernecked looks to the doorway.

Candace stood there, slightly out of breath, yet still beautiful. "Excuse me for interrupting. I'm—"

"Candace Rowley," his father cut in. "With clothes on, I see."

"How observant of you, sir. Your nickname should be Columbo."

Lansing Jr.'s face registered the hit.

Lansing Sr. chuckled.

Strider wanted to high-five her. *That's my girl.*

"Put out the cigars, boys. Smoke is murder on a bombshell's skin. Now someone get me a drink, and I'll tell you a little story about cousin A.J."

The three men scrambled for the bar in unison. Strider got there first. Reaching for the tongs in the ice bucket, he smiled. Nothing like a woman who knew how to work a room.

Epilogue

New York,
Six Months Later

Didi Farrell was singing "The Morning After," the love theme from *The Poseidon Adventure,* as Strider and Candace watched from the green room.

"Isn't someone supposed to have gonged her by now?" Strider asked.

Candace laughed. "I take it you don't want her new CD, *Didi's Turn.*"

"Think I'll pass."

"Well, too bad. It's in the gift basket we get for appearing on the show. There's also a copy of Chip Hamilton's new book, *Smile When You Get Up in the Morning and Other Things My Mother Taught Me.*"

"Remind me why we're torturing ourselves again."

"It's called publicity, darling. You're a boring husband now. It's harder to get media attention."

"Oh, that's right. I could cheat on you with a hot young model. That'd get some press."

"But then I'd kill you, and your death would get *too* much press. It's better this way. Trust me."

Enter Jackie, the assistant producer for *Coffee in Manhattan*. "The arrival gates are backed up at JFK. Our next guest is on a plane that's still circling the airport. He's the guy who invented the penis gel that supposedly adds an inch after fourteen days of application."

"Really?" Strider interjected. "I hope there's a sample in the gift basket."

Jackie grinned. "There isn't. Sorry."

"But Didi's singing makes my penis shrink. I need it to stay even steven."

"Here's the short of it," Jackie went on, "no pun intended—your segment is now seven minutes." She gave Candace a curious look. "Hey, didn't this happen to you last time?"

"Yes, only it was vaginal cream."

"Weird coincidence." She glanced at her clipboard. "As soon as Didi finishes her number, we'll take you to the set and get you miked up. I'll be right back."

Strider embraced Candace from behind, nuzzling her neck. "What do you suppose we'll talk about for *seven* minutes? That's almost a Barbara Walters interview."

"Don't be surprised if they ask you how big your penis is."

"You know, I've actually never measured. Don't know how. Chip might have the answer. Maybe that's one of the things his mother taught him."

Candace slapped Strider's thigh. "Please act normal. There are millions watching."

"My dad left me a voice mail. He's got a meeting, but mom's taping it, and they're going to watch it tonight before dinner."

Candace reached out to stroke his freshly shaven cheek. "That's nice."

Strider grinned sweetly. "It is nice." He paused a beat. "And I owe it all to you."

She started to protest.

"Accept the credit. If you hadn't stormed onto that yacht—"

"I didn't *storm* in. Ask the captain. I boarded the craft gracefully."

"You did something that I was just too stubborn to do, and that's tell my father the truth about A.J. I don't know. I could never get past how angry I was about the whole thing. But all my anger was directed at the wrong person."

"None of that matters now. You've got your father back. He's got his son back. Life is perfect."

"Almost perfect."

Candace stared at him.

"What about your mom?"

"One family miracle at a time please."

"It's just that—"

"I called her," Candace confessed. "We had a pleasant talk."

He looked hurt. "You didn't tell me."

"Because you would insist right away that she visit for two weeks. I'm not ready for that. Let me fix this at my own pace."

Strider pulled her in for a half embrace. "Can I take back what I said about *me* being stubborn?"

"No, that's in the official record."

"Oh." He shrugged.

"Do you think your cousin will be watching?"

"Probably not. He's too busy banging away on the organ at his father's church in Florida."

Didi warbled to a big finish with a note far beyond the range she didn't have anyway. Tone-deaf as always, the studio audience erupted with enthusiastic support. Overwhelmed, Didi pumped a fist in the air. "There *is* a morning after!" she roared.

"Not if you heard that song," Strider said.

Just then Jackie returned, and they ran the gauntlet through the studio and onto the set. Two technicians dropped in to attach microphones, then asked them to count to ten to check volume levels.

Moments later, Chip and Didi took their places, said a quick hello, and began scanning some notes.

"How did Chip manage to get on more makeup than Didi?" Strider whispered.

Candace giggled. "Hush."

Didi looked up. "So you're the chocolate lady, and you're the man with the penis."

Candace shut her eyes. *Not again.*

"I think you mean penis *gel,*" Strider said. "That's a different guest. His plane—and his enlarged penis, I presume, is circling JFK, as I understand. But for the record, I am a man with a penis."

Now Chip joined in. "If you applied the gel for a month, could you expand your penis by two inches?"

"You don't understand," Candace said. "That guest—"

Chip held up a hand to cut her off. "Time for that later, love." He fixed a blinding smile on the camera. "Welcome back!"

"Hey, no fair! I wanted to say that!" Didi screamed.

They both laughed uproariously.

"Didi," Chip started, placing a hand on her knee for emphasis, "that number from your new CD, *Didi's Turn,* was fantastic! It was so real. For a minute there I thought I was Ernest Borgnine from *The Poseidon Adventure.*" He gestured to the audience. "Am I right, people?"

They thundered their agreement with hearty applause.

"Thank you, Chip. That song is so special to me, and it really has a powerful message, because no matter what obstacles you're facing, there *is* a morning after."

"Say it, sister!" Chip said.

"It's just like in your new book, *Smile When You Get Up in the Morning and Other Things My Mother Taught Me.* I think it's chapter two where you talk about not letting life get you down."

"Mother always said, 'If you fall off your bicycle, get right back on!' "

Didi beamed. "Which is exactly what our next guest did. He had a really small penis, and one day he just said, 'Heck, I think I'll invent a gel to make it bigger!' Please welcome Strider Moore and his lovely wife Candace."

Chip leaned forward to gently ask, "Strider, how small was your penis before this miracle invention did its handiwork?"

Suddenly, Chip and Didi's brows crinkled as their right hands cupped their right ears.

"Oh, my," Didi remarked. "We goofed."

"Hey," Chip chirped. "Just like my mother says—smile when it hurts."

"As it happens, our penis gel inventor is stuck at the airport," Didi said. "Strider and Candace are here with us today from Decadence Chocolates, the upscale division of Moore Candies. Welcome to *Coffee in Manhattan*."

"Good to be here," Strider said. "I'd like to start out by saying that I have a large penis. Any number of women in New York can attest to that. This is before I got married, of course. All the sex, I mean."

Candace jabbed him with her elbow.

"But we have sex," Strider said quickly. He put his arm around his wife. "Often. And it's great. Tell everyone how big my penis is, honey."

"Your parents are taping this, darling."

Strider blanched.

"Ooh, tell us more," Didi cooed.

"My husband's penis is fine," Candace said flatly.

"Fine?" Chip pressed. "Or fine and *dandy?*"

"That would be fine and dandy, Chip. Thank you for clarifying," Candace said.

"Now there's a funny story about how the two of you met," Didi began. "I love hearing a couple's history. Strider, why don't you tell us about that? And enough about that big penis of yours. Stick to the romance, mister!"

Strider hesitated a moment. "We met at a club here in New York. The Cutting Room to be exact."

Chip and Didi howled with laughter.

"Oh, that is hilarious!" Didi squealed.

"Only in New York!" Chip put in.

"Actually, the funny part of the story is what happened later," Candace said. And then she launched into the whole tale, blathering on about the competition for the product placement, the

scandalous photo from Capri, how A.J., in his obsession to oust Strider, played double agent with Hershey to get that company the deal. But then
Chocolate on Her Pillow went through a major rewrite
and title change, became *Love on a Rooftop,* and
ultimately featured *no* candy in the final cut. And
how could she leave out the details concerning
Strider's examination of the Private Selection division's books, his discovery of its low profit margins,
and the manner in which he brilliantly proposed
that Moore shut it down and buy Decadence under
the provision that Candace run the line autono-
mously. That way Moore had a leaner investment
plus a stake in the lucrative high-priced chocolate
market. By the end of her story, Candace was
exhausted. No question is simple when you really
take the time to think about it.

"Well," Didi finally cut in, "thank you for sharing, but I believe we're coming up close on a commercial break."

"One more question before we wrap up," Chip
said. "Husband wears the big, bad corporate hat,
and you're the division head. Does that put any
stress on the marriage?"

Strider slipped his hand into hers.

Candace beamed.

"Not really," he said. "At the end of the day,
we're just two chocoholics madly in love."

Darling!

I hope you had fun with "Sex and the Single Chocoholic." It was a hoot to write, but all the talk about chocolate triggered fierce cravings that I had no choice but to satisfy. Well, thank you Godiva, M&Ms, Dove Bars, etc., for the extra five pounds! Grrr.

I'm counting on the fact that you had a blast with Tatiana Fox. Why? Because her story is coming next! I never knew what was going to come out of this character's mouth. She surprised me so many times. Can you imagine her as the mother of twins? Well, get ready! Look for Tatiana to take center stage in my upcoming book, BABY, BABY, set for release this August. In that story you'll also see more of her personal assistant, Enrique, and the egomaniacal movie star Greg Tapper. But her love match turns out to be Jack Thorpe—a hero I know you'll go banana cake over. Here's my recipe for this hunk: take one Russell Crowe, add a Pierce Brosnan, then stir until you get the best of both!

If this novella was your virgin voyage on the Kylie Adams Express, check out my first novel, FLY ME TO THE MOON. It tells the full story of Ben Estes, who was mentioned briefly here as the cool crooner who puts a disco spin on Frank Sinatra tunes.

Until the summer . . .

Air kisses,

Kylie

P.S. If you're on-line, go to my Web site at *www.kylieadams.com*. That's where the real Kylie secrets are spilled. Plus, if you join my VIP section, you'll get my monthly e-newsletter, *"Kylie Says,"* which is chockablock full of beauty tips, what's hot/what's not lists, Kylie Kontest news, and more!

Get in touch with Kylie . . . c/o Zebra Books, 850 Third Avenue, New York, NY 10022 or e-mail *www.kylieadams.com.*

Please turn the page for
an exciting sneak peek at
Kylie Adams's newest
contemporary romance

BABY, BABY
(coming from Zebra Books
in August 2002!)

"I want a man who can make love all night long, and if you're not that man, then just do me a favor and drop dead." Tatiana delivered the line with such deadly insouciance that she stunned the room.

David Walsh stared back as if she were Charlton Heston in *The Ten Commandments* and had just parted the sea.

Kip Quick looked equally mystified. He flipped his Dave Matthews Band hat to the back and regarded her strangely.

She gestured to the battered script on Kip's lap. "It's your line, unless I'm auditioning for the male lead, too."

"Oh, right," Kip blurted. He searched for his place on the page. "Is it true about your last two husbands granting you that favor?"

Tatiana stretched and spoke in a breathy voice enriched with dirty promise. "It's true that they were lousy in bed. It's true that I buried them. The rest is just gossip.''

Kip lost his train of thought again, gazing at her in awestruck wonder.

She couldn't believe that he would actually be the movie's director. After all, he looked like he needed a note from his mother to be here. In fact, he still lived with his parents. Probably had a *Penthouse* stashed under his mattress, too. Yet here he sat, after only a few videos on MTV and one Pepsi commercial, playing with the grown-ups on a big-budget film for a major studio. Only in Hollywood.

Tatiana cleared her throat.

"Does nudity make you uncomfortable?" Kip asked.

She glanced down at her pages. *Not* part of the *Sin by Sin* screenplay.

This man/child had obviously missed her series of *Lady Cop Undercover* movies. Chances are he hadn't peeked at her pictorial in the April 1998 *Playboy*, either. If he had, it would've been while under the covers with a flashlight.

"My comfort level depends on the situation," she announced matter-of-factly. "A relatively closed set is no problem. Shooting on Sunset at high noon is another matter entirely. I mean, I'm not Madonna.''

David smiled at Kip as if to say, "See, I told you so.''

And then a horrifying thought struck Tatiana. It hit like a clap of thunder. She went from confident actress auditioning for the big part to manic mother wanting to put child-safety locks on, well, *everything*. Shame rained down, *soaking* her. She was officially the *worst* parent in the world. By comparison, Joan Crawford was Carol Brady. "I can't do this right now." She started to shake. She needed a cigarette. She didn't even smoke.

David's smile faded faster than Cindy Crawford's hope of a movie career after the release of *Fair Game*.

"I just realized that I left my children with a complete stranger," Tatiana said breathlessly. "I mean, he could be a serial killer, or one of the Kennedy boys that Jackie O didn't raise, or Paula Poundstone in disguise." She placed a hand over her heart and shut her eyes for a moment. "Promise you won't tell social services. This is all new to me."

"I didn't realize you had kids," David said.

"Don't you read the tabloids? My ex-husband insisted on adopting twins and then left me. Anyway, today my nanny quit without notice, I couldn't reach my personal assistant, and the only other person available was September Moore. She's a friend and all, but I wouldn't let her watch my purse. Would you? Let her watch your wallet, I mean. Or your man purse. I hear those are big in Europe. OK, so I packed up the kids and here I am. By the way, if you smell something sour it's because Ethan threw up on me in the car." Tatiana took a deep breath. "Is this too much information?"

David and Kip stared back in slack-jawed amazement.

"This is *my* part. I *am* Nikki Alexander. But now I have to go. Don't worry. I'll work out child-care issues before shooting starts. You know what would be great? On-set day care." She paused a beat. "I'm

kidding. I don't want the kids to see me running
around with a knife or shooting people or having
simulated sex with different men. That could be
traumatic for them. And that's instinct. I didn't
have to read Dr. Spock to come up with that. Pretty
good, huh? I think I'm getting the hang of this
mommy business. OK, are we done here? Do you
need to see my boobs or anything before I leave?"

There was a long second of telepathy between
David and Kip, after which they traded a discreet
nod.

"We'll set up a screen test with Greg Tapper,"
David said.

This meant she was on the short list. Under nor-
mal circumstances she would be so excited that
cartwheels in rush-hour traffic might be in order.
But she was worried sick about Ethan and Everson.
"That sounds great," she said, somewhat absently.
"I'll wait for your call."

Unable to stand it one more second, Tatiana
dashed back to the reception area. The twins were
perched on either side of the man's hips like Anne
Geddes bookends, listening in peaceful rapture as
he read a story from the sports section of the *Los
Angeles Times.*

"Sammy Sosa hit three homers in the first round
to barely squeak into the semifinals but made the
finals by outhomering Luis Gonzalez," he was saying softly in his heavily accented voice. Could be
English, could be Australian. Tough to call. But
she wanted him to read the Yellow Pages. He
sounded *that* scrumptious.

Ethan and Everson peered up at him, little
mouths agape, as if he were Barney or something.

Tatiana was instantly suspicious. They *never* sat still like this for her. "Did you give them drugs?"

He stopped reading and just stared at her.

"I've never seen them stay in one place unless they're sleeping. Or eating. Well, Ethan does hold his position behind the sofa when he's pooping. But the rest of the time it's an insane level of activity. I can't keep up."

"I think these kids are perfect."

No, honey, you're perfect. The words were almost on her lips. She zeroed in on his firm forearms, mesmerized by the muscles flexing under his skin as he folded up the newspaper and tossed it aside. He looked sharp and mod—three-day beard, dirty-blond bed-head hair, lean body coiled into well-worn jeans and a 1999 World Cup T-shirt ripped at the left sleeve, skin basted a honey bronze.

Los Angeles was chockablock full of great-looking guys. They worked on it just as hard as the women, if not harder, slaving at the gym, sticking to the Zone diet, checking the mirror twenty times a day to ask, "Am I handsome enough?" Hot men were in such supply that Tatiana could fill a tour bus with just the ones she'd seen this week. So it said something about the one front and center that he could not only make her take a second look, but hold it—steady. Simultaneously, he gave off grit and luminosity. An unbeatable combination.

"How did your audition go?" he asked.

"They want me to do a screen test."

"Congratulations. You should ring your mum. I always ring my mum when there's good news."

She was instantly put off by this and decided to openly mock him. "Well, I'm not speaking to my *mum* at the moment. What about your audition?"

"It was horrible."

Now she felt bad. There was a slow, vague sweetness about him. "Which part were you reading for?"

"Greg Tapper's partner."

"But he dies in the opening scene after just one line."

"I tried, 'See you tomorrow, Josh' several different ways, but they just weren't feeling it."

Tatiana giggled and moved in to scoop up Everson, who started to cry immediately.

He stood up, hoisting bulky Ethan onto his hip with Mr. Strong ease, then smoothed Everson's unruly hair with his free hand, a gesture that instantly mollified her. If thirteen-month-old girls could fall in love, then Everson Janey Fox, positively swooning now, was head over heels. Tramp.

"Who are you? I should know your name since my kids think you're better than Big Bird."

"Jack Thorpe, god-awful actor, smashingly good baby-sitter."

She smiled in a way that she hadn't smiled since running into George Clooney in an elevator at the Beverly Center. "I'm Tatiana Fox."

"I know. I subscribe to *Playboy*. You were the girl who posed naked climbing on the side of a building."

"*Half* naked. I *was* wearing a thong. So how long have you been a bad actor?"

He checked his Patek Philippe watch. "About fifteen minutes. I don't think I'll stick with it. I'm actually a footballer." He pointed to his knee. "Or was. An injury put an end to my career."

"Which team?"

"Manchester United."

Tatiana's memory registered nothing. *Manchester United?* It sounded like a bank, not a football team. "Is that one of the new leagues?"

He smiled at her, revealing immaculate porcelain teeth. "I forget that you call it soccer here in the States." A sudden look of inscrutable sadness came over him, weighing down his features like old age. "I miss my mates."

Tatiana wanted to know where he came from, why he was here. This unnerved her. She usually only cared about her own problems. Meanwhile, Ethan clung to him like a koala bear. It was really adorable.

Everson started to squirm and stretch out her arms. She wanted Jack Thorpe again. The deafening cry that came next could've been picked up as far as Malibu.

Reluctantly, he stepped forward to take her.

The very second Everson's tiny hands touched him was the very second she stopped fussing.

Tatiana's humiliation was only ameliorated by the sight of him standing there, shrugging with pride, the twins climbing all over his hard body. It *defined* sexy. Any woman who melted whenever Tom Selleck showed up on cable in *Three Men and a Baby* needed to take a memo. That was then; Jack Thorpe was now.

"My name is Niall." That much he could reveal.

"Niall." She liked the name. Somehow it seemed to suit him.

"Don't shut yer heart to me, lass." The way she kept looking away was annoying. Gently grasping her by the shoulders, he turned her around. For one timeless moment they stared at each other, both wondering how just a look could be so exciting.

Without a word, Niall caught a fistful of her long fiery hair and wrapped it around his hand, drawing her closer. With the tips of his fingers he traced the line of her cheekbones, the shape of her mouth, the line of her brows.

"Give it a chance, Caitlin . . ." His face hovered only inches from her own. "Give me a chance." His appraising gaze seemed to cherish her, his words mesmerized her, and though Caitlin knew all the reasons she should pull away, she somehow did not. Then all at once it was too late.

At first he simply held her, his hands exerting a gentle pressure to draw her into the warmth of his embrace. Then before Caitlin could make a sound, his mouth claimed hers in a gentle kiss, one completely devastating to her senses. She was engulfed in a whirlpool of sensations. Breathless, her head whirling, she allowed herself to be drawn up into the mists of the spell. New sensations clamored within her. All she could think about was that her fantasies were right. A kiss could be most enjoyable.

ROMANCES BY BEST-SELLING AUTHOR COLLEEN FAULKNER!

O'BRIAN'S BRIDE   (0-8217-4895-5, $4.99)

Elizabeth Lawrence left her pampered English childhood behind to journey to the far-off Colonies . . . and marry a man she'd never met. But her dreams turned to dust when an explosion killed her new husband at his powder mill, leaving her alone to run his business . . . and face a perilous life on the untamed frontier. After a desperate engagement to her husband's brother, yet another man, strong, sensual and secretive Michael Patrick O'Brian, enters her life and it will never be the same.

CAPTIVE   (0-8217-4683-1, $4.99)

Tess Morgan had journeyed across the sea to Maryland colony in search of a better life. Instead, the brave British innocent finds a battle-torn land . . . and passion in the arms of Raven, the gentle Lenape warrior who saves her from a savage fate. But Tess is bound by another. And Raven dares not trust this woman whose touch has enslaved him, yet whose blood vow to his people has set him on a path of rage and vengeance. Now, as cruel destiny forces her to become Raven's prisoner, Tess must make a choice: to fight for her freedom . . . or for the tender captor she has come to cherish with a love that will hold her forever.

Available wherever paperbacks are sold, or order direct from the Publisher. Send cover price plus 50¢ per copy for mailing and handling to Penguin USA, P.O. Box 999, c/o Dept. 17109, Bergenfield, NJ 07621. Residents of New York and Tennessee must include sales tax. DO NOT SEND CASH.

HIGHLAND DESTINY

Kathryn Hockett

Zebra Books
Kensington Publishing Corp.

To Bob Nicholson whose honesty, determination and love for his children has inspired me. The last few years have been more precious than you know. This story is for you with love. . . .

ZEBRA BOOKS are published by

Kensington Publishing Corp.
850 Third Avenue
New York, NY 10022

Copyright © 1996 by Kathryn Hockett

All rights reserved. No part of this book may be reproduced in any form or by any means without the prior written consent of the Publisher, excepting brief quotes used in reviews.

If you purchased this book without a cover you should be aware that this book is stolen property. It was reported as "unsold and destroyed" to the Publisher and neither the Author nor the Publisher has received any payment for this "stripped book."

Zebra and the Z logo Reg. U.S. Pat. & TM Off. The Lovegram logo is a trademark of Kensington Publishing Corp.

First Printing: October, 1996
10 9 8 7 6 5 4 3 2 1

Printed in the United States of America

Author's Note

An aura of adventure and romance clings to the distinctive way of life of the Highland clans. It was said that out of the Celtic myths and mists the Irish Celts came to settle in the highlands and islands of Scotland, bringing with them a powerful perception of their racial kinship and blood ties.

Clans were first known by the badges on their bonnets and in later years by the tartans they wore. The clans lived by the sword and perished by the sword in their struggle for territory and supremacy. Loyalty to the clan chieftain was absolute. They took fierce pride in the stories of brave deeds and fateful liaisons of love that were related by the Seanachaidh around the hearth fires.

Though Christian, the Scots were a people of mystics and dreamers who believed in the second sight, a gift of prophecy by visions. The fey it was called. From their Celtic forebears came a fabric of superstition, mystery, and tradition that is as colorful as any tartan.

Such a mystery surrounds the MacLeods of Dunvegan on the Isle of Skye who trace their ancestry back to King Harald. Their most treasured heirloom is a tattered silk banner called the fairy flag, said to have been given to a MacLeod husband by his wife before she returned to fairyland after twenty years of marriage. Their parting place near Dunvegan is still known as Fairy Bridge.

There is a tradition that if the MacLeods are in desperate peril they will become invincible by unfurling the fairy flag during battle. It was used at Glendale in 1490 when they were fighting for their lives against the MacDonalds. The flag was unfurled and soon the tide of battle turned. In 1520 at Waternish, when once again the enemy was the MacDonalds, the MacLeods were victorious after the flag was unfurled. Though they were outnumbered, the MacDonalds imagined a vast army of MacLeods marching down on them.

The fairy flag is said to be the most precious treasure of the MacLeods. "Bratach Sith" is what it is known as and is now kept in the drawing room of Dunvegan Castle—a faded tan silk, carefully darned in red. Legend has it that the MacLeods are waiting until it is necessary to use the flag for the third and last time.

Highland Destiny tells the story of two lovers drawn together by the power of the fairy flag. Refusing to be parted, they find a passion far stronger than any earthly law, a love as timeless as eternity.

Prologue—1520

It was quiet, too quiet. As Colin MacLeod stood atop Dunvegan Castle's tower he squinted his eyes, trying to peer through the fog. He felt uneasy. Danger seemed to hang in the air, weaving in and out amidst the eerie Highland mist that veiled the lochs and glens like an unearthly shroud.

"Ach . . ." For just a moment he held his breath, not daring to exhale as he listened. What was the nearly imperceivable sound that he heard? Alas, it seemed but a slight stirring that all too quickly vanished into quietness again. Still, there had been something.

Leaning over the tower wall, Colin stared down at the bank. It looked down thirty feet or more to the ocean below. From either of the two towers, east or west, perched high over the cliff, the eye of anyone watching could see an enemy approaching. Unless there was fog.

"I canna see . . ." Yet for one long shuddering moment he seemed to be gifted with a second sight. "Intruders . . . !" His cry was punctuated by the drone of one note, an eerie though faraway sound that roused Colin MacLeod to action. He must warn the others.

Meanwhile, a menacing shadow moved across the land in the distance. In a raging swarm, the MacDonalds climbed the hills, moving quickly across Duirinish. A faint glint of moonlight was the only light to escape the fog, shining now on the many shields and swords of the clansmen who moved in an unrelenting tide. They had only one purpose in mind.

To engage their enemy the MacLeod, in a fierce battle for supremacy of the Isle of Skye.

Malcolm MacDonald marched at the head of the column, his dark thick unsmiling features only partially obscured by a hard leather helmet, his leather jacket, leggings, and dirt-stained boots smeared with the grime of travel. Behind him walked his armed clansmen, dour and stolid. Marching two abreast, they formed a dark ribbon over the rocky land as they moved like giant ants toward the rival castle.

The silence of the night was shattered by a droning, pounding, fiercesome sound as the din of pipes and drums announced what was to come. Warfare. Death.

"To Dunvegan!" came the cry. The MacLeod stronghold across the loch, the square-towered stone castle isolated by a deep and wide ditch on the land side, was their destination.

"Fraoch Eilean . . . !"

The castle was situated on a rock overhanging the sea. Completely surrounded by a moat, its doors were accessible only by boat, but this did not daunt the MacDonalds. They had come prepared. A fleet of small fishing boats was at their disposal which they put to good use now, sailing toward the MacLeod stronghold.

"Now. Gi' them a sound to strike fear in their hearts . . ." A bloodcurdling war cry echoed through the mists, piercing Dunvegan's walls.

From the castle battlements scrutinizing eyes stared through the fog at the threatening horde. "The MacDonalds, Colin. Ye are right, they're coming this way."

"The MacDonalds . . . !"

Cautiously the tall, lithe, red-haired man surveyed the scene. There appeared to be about fifty of them. The foe of his clan was coming in a growling, mumbling wave of ferocity that chilled him to the bone, for his own clan was outnumbered two to one.

"We canna win! The odds are against us."

The castle had been constructed with thick walls and was protected by a moat and heavy oak doors, but even so, it would not be impenetrable by so many of the MacDonalds.

"Well, they willna win this day. Our clan hae enchantment on our side. We are protected."

The MacLeods had a magical flag that, when unfurled, brought triumph and protection to the possessor. The silk banner of tattered brown silk with red embroidery was their most treasured heirloom, believed to make them invincible. It had been handed down to the MacLeods of Dunvegan since the days of the Norse King Harald Hardrada. Or so it was said.

"Fly the fairy flag!"

"Ye heard Colin. The flag, mon. The flag . . ." Immediately that treasure was snatched from its resting place to fly unencumbered from the parapet. Like a good luck charm, it emboldened the men who left the security of the castle walls to greet the enemy that dared invade the sanctity of their stronghold.

As the pale ghost moon struggled for ascendancy through the swirling fog, the two clans battled. The MacDonalds came in a noisy, floating tide, pushing across the ditch, breaking down the thick wooden doors, scaling the tower walls with rope ladders. They were met, however, by men equally determined.

Swords slashed. Axes swung. Shields clanked. Dirks struck out. Blood spilled forth in an angry carnage of destruction. Moving in a solid body, the MacLeods engaged the enemy in brutal hand-to-hand combat, meeting the challenge of the aggressors with a bravery spurred on by the belief that the enchanted flag would give them aid.

"They willna gi' up," several of the MacDonalds gasped in unison.

"They fight like demons!"

"Because o' the flag!" Malcolm spat on the ground before his flashing eyes gave a silent command. To get that cursed emblem of the MacLeods. With that thought in mind, the fighting exploded. Rival clansmen spilled inside the tower, moving toward the silk banner.

"The flag. Guard the flag!" Colin MacLeod cried.

He leaped about in a frenzy, his weapon darting this way and that as he moved up the steps of the tower in defense of the precious brown silk. His swordsmanship sent more than just a few MacDonalds crashing to the ramparts below. With a cry of victory, Colin pushed his way to the tower, looking toward the flag. The blessed flag.

"Colin!"

The child's voice, though soft, startled him. Undoubtedly the fearsome noise had instigated curiosity.

"Go to yer bed! Now, bairn! Ye canna kin the danger!"

"Colin!" The high-pitched greeting erupted into a shrill scream. A warning that came too late.

With a cry of surprise, Colin felt the tip of a MacDonald sword gouge at his flesh, striking him from behind. From *behind*. A coward's blow.

"Blessed God . . ." A hot gush of blood stained his breacon. His sword clattered to the floor, but somehow he managed to stay on his feet determined that no MacDonald hand would touch the flag or the child. "Flee, wee one!"

Colin's eyes darted to the face of his attacker, then to the small form of the child, then back again.

"Run!"

Frightened into frozen silence at first, the child at last obeyed. With relief, Colin watched as the little one ran to safety, locking the door behind her.

"Ye willna touch either o' the MacLeod's treasures," he hissed.

The battle was ferocious, but in the end the MacLeods had won. Limping away, stepping over the bodies of the dead, the MacDonalds retreated.

"The flag. The blessed flag!" There was not a man present who did not give the magical dun-colored silk its due.

But Colin MacLeod paid a tragic price for his valiantry in keeping the fairy flag from enemy hands. Crumpling at last to the floor in a heap, he lay on the cold stones in agony.

It was a time when the MacLeods should have been joyous, for they had won a stout victory over their adversaries, the MacDonalds. But instead, the leader of the clan was stooped and grieved as he looked down upon the writhing form of his son.

"Colin! Colin!" The voice was husky, a deep, rumbling thunder that gave full vent to his anger as well as his sorrow. It was an awesome man who spoke, a red-haired and bearded Scots warrior of immense strength and girth, leader of the MacLeods, whose skill in fighting was legendary. His courage and daring was the reason for the MacLeod victory, his men insisted. That and the blessed possession of the fairy flag.

"We hae won, Father." Colin MacLeod tried to hide his misery, but he knew well that he was dying.

"Aye, we won." Bending down, the man exhibited a rare gesture of gentleness as he touched his son's face. At that moment he wished he could take his son's suffering upon himself. "But at a terrible price."

"My wound is mortal. I know—"

"Nae!" He wouldn't admit the truth. "We'll send for someone skilled in healing to tend ye."

" 'Tis much too late for that." A shiver of pain convulsed his body.

"Ye talk foolishness, lad. 'Tis not too late." Ah, but as he saw the blood seeping from the wound he knew that it was. Already the face of his beloved robust son was turning as pale as any ghosts.

"It is. But we . . . we won, Father." Reaching out, Colin clutched his father's hand. "I can take heart in that. I kept them from the flag and from Cai—"

"Aye, ye guarded it admirably. 'Tis proud of ye I am. Very, very proud."

It was rumored that the first MacLeod had been given the banner as a gift from his wife before she returned to her father in the mythical land that existed in the mists. A magical flag, Ian thought now. Very valuable to the clan, but surely not worth his son's life!

"But damn the MacDonalds." They had taken his son from behind, wounding him in the back. The vile cowards. "Oh, Colin!"

"I will be avenged, Father. On my honor I so swear. I will haunt them. I swear that I will. I curse the mon who did this to me. Upon his head I will be avenged. Ye will see."

"And I will make the MacDonalds wish they had never heard the name MacLeod. That is the pledge I make to ye now." It was a vow that burned all the brighter in Ian MacLeod's breast as the life of his only son ebbed out. For a long time he stared down at the still face of the young man who had been his whole world.

"Sir? What should we do wi' the flag?" A young, beardless boy approached his chieftain shyly, hating to interrupt this moment of grief.

"What?" Ian MacLeod blinked back unmanly tears. "The flag." Oh, that it could bring life back into the body of his son, but that was not in its power. Colin MacLeod was dead and there was nothing that could return him from the dead. Nothing to keep him tied to the earth. Or was there?

From that moment on there were those who insisted they had seen the young man pacing back and forth in the tower room. That the castle was haunted was a legend that came to be believed by the villagers in the glen. Colin MacLeod was said to stalk the tower, guarding it as stealthfully in death as he had in life. Waiting for that moment when he could bring his wrath crashing down upon his murderer's head.

Part One:

A Fateful Meeting—1538
The Isle of Skye

"But to see her was to love her,
Love but her, and love forever."
—Robert Burns: *Ae Fon Kiss*

One

The early-morning sun danced down upon the land caressing the lush green heaths and fields with a brilliant warmth, stroking the rolling hills and craggy gray mountains, teasing the buds to full flower. Gently laughing brooks babbled their way to quiet pools. A breeze stirred faintly, whispering as it swept through the forest glades. In the woods, winter-skeletal trees—oak, pine, ash, and poplar— now proudly wore a thick leafy covering. Birds twittered melodious tunes as they flew from tree to tree.

The fog that often covered the land like a low-flying cloud had faded, leaving the sky clear and blue. Winter had blended into spring with a gentle fury of rain that had left the earth a dazzling shade of green. Flowers covered the highland meadows of Skye, filling the air with their fragrance.

Perched silently atop a ledge of Dunvegan Castle's tower window, Caitlin MacLeod formed a stunning silhouette as she looked down at the vast domain of her clan. This land that she could see in the distance had been inhabited by the MacLeod clan for more years than she could even contemplate.

"Like a paradise this morning," she whispered, though she knew it to be a deceptive calm that made it seem that way.

For several years the MacLeods had shared this island of Skye with two other clans. To the southwest, the MacKinnons held Strath and at times assisted the MacDonalds of Sleat in their skirmishes against the MacLeods. To the east, across Loch Snizort, were the lands of the hated MacDonalds themselves, they who marauded the countryside with their savage bands. MacLeods and MacDonalds had been at odds over land possession and other things for as long as Caitlin could remember.

"Och! The MacDonalds!" she said aloud, cursing them with upraised fist.

It had begun two hundred years ago, or so her father said, when the first chief of the clan MacLeod had challenged the supremacy of the MacDonalds on Skye. Since then, there had been a number of bloody feuds and cruelties perpetrated each on the other, represented by the stark patches of charred lands between the green fields and the desolate, blackened remains of what had once been cottages.

These incidents had been a constant source of trouble for her father, for surely it seemed the MacDonalds instigated one argument after another. As leader, ceann-cinnidh, of the MacLeods, he headed the fighting, causing Caitlin to worry lest something happen to him. To be truthful, Ian MacLeod was getting a bit too old for the great responsibility heaped upon his stooping shoulders.

Under the ancient patriarchal system the land belonged to the clan, and they worked together and fought together, giving allegiance in time of peace as well as war to the laird. Sometimes a sept, or a branch of another clan, too small to protect itself against surrounding clans, entered into a treaty with a neighboring clan for protection. And thus there was always fighting.

Warfare. Violence. Like a tireless wind, the perpetual feuding swept across the green and rocky land. There was hardly a family that hadn't lost a loved one. Hardly a clansman who hadn't shed a tear. And still the old hatreds goaded the men into turning their plowshares into swords. Would peace never come to the Highlands? Caitlin thought not, for surely men seemed stubborn in their pride and driven to fighting. Like mischievous, grumbling boys, they seemed anxious to give seed to the ballads that sprang from the misery and the grief of the turmoil.

Caitlin shivered, remembering the night that she, too, had been caught up in the tragedy of the battling. She had been just three years, frightened, huddling against the stone wall, watching as her elder brother had been struck down. A memory that still haunted her.

"Colin . . ."

He had given his life to save the beloved fairy flag from being taken by the MacDonalds. A costly price, she thought, even to protect such a treasure. But she wouldn't think about it now and stir up old sadness. It was so peaceful today. The awakening terrain was dotted with grazing sheep, goats, and cattle. Contented animals all.

If only I could feel as contented, Caitlin mused. But in truth she did not. Always before, spring had been a time that she welcomed most heartily, but this year she could only feel a wariness at its coming. Her father had adamantly insisted that this year she would be old enough to wed, an entanglement she viewed with disdain.

"I dinna want to get married," she said softly now.

Bondage, she called it. Being a young woman of strong will, an independent, resourceful lassie, she valued her freedom. Men were much too bothersome. Thinking of warfare and bickering all the time. That is, when they weren't of the mind to pinch and to pat.

A soft whispering breeze caressed her face, blowing Caitlin's flaming hair into her eyes. No, she thought stubbornly, she most definitely did not want to marry. Jamie, Adhamh, Alasdair, and Seumas were fun to tease, to pester, but it ended there. A wee bit of sparring, a battle of wits, perhaps even a kiss, but only on the cheek. She had learned to keep an arm's length away from men. When they were in their cups they too often set their hands to wandering.

As for marriage, she had a whimsical view on that. Marriage was but a settlement to impoverish the lassie's father and make of the groom a wealthy man. To give a man an unwilling partner for his nightly gropings.

Caitlin wanted to be in control of any matter. And she had been. She had been the pampered, overindulged, perhaps even spoiled daughter of the MacLeod chieftain who could come and go as she pleased. She could swim, fish, wrestle, even fight with a sword were she of a mind to. But the moment she took on a husband all that would change. She would be a cook, a bedmate, a mother for her husband's bairns. She would have to answer to someone else, someone perhaps not as manageable as her father. Her freedom would be lost.

"Nae! Not without a fight," she whispered to herself.

Unlike the other women of the MacLeod line, she would not go meekly to her bridal bed like a lamb to slaughter. If Caitlin MacLeod took a husband, it would be a man of her choice. If and when she gave her heart it would be when she was ready to so bind herself. She had no need for a man's arms, nor for a husband to share her pallet beneath the soft down quilts. Love was just a word the seanachaidh had invented. She had no need of such foolishness, she vowed, ignoring the strange stirring in the pit of her stomach whenever she pondered the matter.

"Och! Love." Someday she would give her heart perhaps, but that would not be for a long, long time. "I am not like my foolish sister, Shona," she murmured, "always floating about on a cloud, dreaming about some laddie's smile."

Shona imagined herself to be in love with Geordie Beaton, whose family seemed to possess an uncanny skill in the art of medicine. Likewise, Geordie had inherited a skill in concocting mixtures of herbs that could cure those members of the clan who were stricken down with illness. Alas, however, he had not inherited his father's skill with a sword, thereby diminishing him in Ian MacLeod's eyes.

But not in Shona's. That silly lassie thought about little else but marrying her handsome suitor. It was all she thought about, talked about, wanted. Caitlin sighed before giving voice to her wish. "Och, if only Father was not so stubborn he would let her marry first and leave me be."

Caitlin tossed her head, sending her dark red hair flying wildly about her shoulders. She wanted excitement. She wanted . . .

A chance to live!

Oh, if only she had been born a son and not a girl child, life might have been so much simpler. She would have been free to fulfill her longings for adventure. Instead, she would most likely spend the greatest part of her life sitting around with the other women, working and gossiping.

"I dinna want a husband."

Somehow she must make her father understand even if it would be a most upsetting matter. And yet it was a touchy subject. After the death of Colin, her father had tried to sire another heir, only to know disappointment at the birth of daughter after daughter, Shona, Lorna, Mairi, and Ailsa. It had been a devastating blow to her father's manly pride and goaded him into an obsessive desire to have his precious tanist.

"Ye must carry on the MacLeod line," her father insisted. "Ye must find a mon to take on our proud clan name."

"I dunna want to!" she had oft replied.

"Ye must!"

Caitlin had reasonably argued that since Shona wanted a husband it was she who should marry first, only to be thwarted in her selfish matchmaking attempt. Ian MacLeod wanted a man good at fighting, not a man who toyed with plants. He wanted a man he considered to be worthy of fathering the MacLeod heir, a man to continue the great legacy of the clan.

Caitlin had heard the story of her clans founding from her father. The clan MacLeod was descended from Leod, son of Olave the Black, who lived two centuries before. Leod's two sons, Tormod and Torquil, were founders of the two main branches of the clan. From Tormod came the MacLeods of Dunvegan, Caitlin's kin. And upon her head would come the burden of passing on the MacLeod blood.

"Och," she swore again. If only her brother hadn't died. But he had and it was said that his ghost stalked the tower, still staunchly guarding the fairy flag. "Colin's ghost . . ."

Caitlin wondered if such whisperings were true or just fantasy, for although others had attested to seeing her brother's wispy presence she had never likewise seen his long-departed spirit. Though not for want of trying. Ever since childhood she had frequented the tower late at night more times than she could even count, hoping for a conversation with her brother, but she had never seen Colin MacLeod no matter how hard she tried. Was it any wonder then that Caitlin had nearly stopped believing?

"There ye are!" Coming up behind her, Ian MacLeod was as silent as if he, too, were a ghost. "Hidin' away up here like some wee fairy, just like when ye were little more than a bairn."

Turning, Caitlin pridefully looked at this big-boned giant of a man with red hair and brown eyes the exact shade of her own. Despite his sixty-two years, he was still ruggedly handsome, with a well-defined bone structure that was striking. Her father was clean-shaven, unlike some of the others of the clan who preferred a beard. The only imperfection in his face was the once perfectly formed nose that had been slightly flattened in hand-to-hand combat.

"Aye, it's hidin' that I am," she confessed.

He winked. "Keepin' out o' sight of yer mother and the others to avoid woman's work again, I would suppose."

They laughed together.

"Aye. Weavin' and spinnin' hae ne'er been to my liking." It seemed she was rarely in a mood to join the others for the daily tasks. Weaving, spinning, sewing, washing, and cooking were tedious at best. That she found a dozen reasons for avoiding such work any time she could was no secret between father and daughter. But that wasn't the reason she was hiding today. The truth was, she was hiding from him, but she didn't tell him that.

"Ah, but how can I scold when I would be of the same mind were I in yer shoes?" He grinned as he reached out to stroke the thick, smooth threads of her hair. "I willna let yer mother know I caught ye up here."

"And in return I'll go back to the hall just in time to measure out for you the biggest portion of porridge."

"Such bribery will ensure that I keep this hiding place a secret from your mother." Ian MacLeod laughed again, but his fondness for her shone in his eyes. "Ah, ye bonny little imp, ye hae always known ye rule my heart."

Ian looked at his daughter with an appraising eye. She possessed remarkable beauty. Her finely chiseled nose, high cheekbones, and enormous dark-fringed brown eyes made her as fair of face as any kelpie. Caitlin's mouth was full and deep pink, her cheeks flushed most prettily. Her slender waist and long legs were no doubt the envy of all the women, her well-formed breasts and slim hips would inspire the songs of many a bard.

Caitlin was dressed in a forest-green arasaid now, a long garment that reached from the head or neck to the ankles, fastened at the breast with a large brooch and at the waist by a belt. Beneath this colorful length of material she wore a gown of thin beige wool which clung to her gentle curves. She made him very proud, this daughter of his. A fit mate for the boldest warrior. Nae, even a chieftain.

"Do I truly rule yer heart, Father?" His saying so calmed her fears. Surely he would not be of a mind then to see her leave his hearth just yet. She gazed upon her father's face trying to discern his thoughts.

"That ye do!" Which made the subject he felt he had to bring up now all the more difficult to express. His daughter's marriage. They had talked about the matter before and Caitlin had persuaded him to let her have her way, but this time there could be no waiting. If he was going to have an heir soon, he must insist. He wanted a grandchild.

"Then ye canna send me away." She felt triumphant.

"Caity!" Taking a deep breath, he blurted out, "It's time I must, despite my wish that I could keep ye here forever. I hae decided it's time to choose a husband."

"Nae!" At last the subject she had feared was put forth. Still, she tried to keep her poise.

"Aye! We canna wait." Ian MacLeod seemed inordinately pleased with the suggestion he put forth. "I hae decided that a MacKinnon would be a perfect choice. Ronald the chieftain's son . . ."

Caitlin sniffed her disdain as she crossed her arms stubbornly. "Not only is he bowed of leg and long of nose, but he is much too tall. I wouldna marry him."

Not to be deterred, Ian MacLeod had a second choice. "His cousin Dugald it will be then!"

Caitlin sighed, disturbed with the matter. The MacKinnons lived too far away. "He is too young, Father. A mere boy with but a hint of a beard who chatters all the time."

Ian's good humor was quickly fading. "Ronald's uncle then. Uisdean MacKinnon. He is recently widowed."

"He is much too old." Though the man was rumored to be extremely handsome, Caitlin had no liking for being a man's second wife, nor a stepmother to his many children. "And . . . and ye can tell him that."

"BiGod, lassie, ye try my patience." Only by the greatest of willpower was Ian able to control his temper. "I canna tell him such a thing."

"Then don't tell him anything at all," she shot back, determined to stand firm. "But know this and know this well. I willna marry. Not this year." *Not ever,* she thought, but did not say.

"Ye will if I say so!"

Caitlin tried to make him understand, her outburst sputtering to just a spark. "There is no reason why I shouldna be happy." Caitlin had always had her father firmly wrapped around her little finger, and thus she was certain he would eventually comply with her wishes.

"Is there not?" Ian thundered. He reached out, not to strike her but to take her by the hand, drawing her down to sit beside him on a large slab of the tower stone. "It is your duty to marry a mon who can carry on as leader of the clan when I am gone. Ye know that, lassie."

"I know." Even so, a stubborn streak deep within kept her from giving in. "And I will marry. But not this spring. Another year."

"Another year and then another and another!" Ian was tired of giving in to his daughter. Her mother was right then. He had spoiled the girl. "Nae, ye willna get yer way this time. It will be as *I* say."

"As you say," she repeated dutifully, hiding her strong feelings of rebellion, at least for the moment.

Clenching his jaw, he put forth the name of another possible suitor. "If ye dinna want to marry into the clan Mac-Kinnon I'll send ye farther away then. To Mull. A MacQuarrie it will be for yer husband. Hugh MacQuarrie, that chieftain's son."

She shook her head fiercely. "Nae. I willna leave the Island of Skye!"

"Ye willna!" Ian swallowed his angry retort, somehow maintaining his calm. "And just what makes ye think ye have a say?"

Seeing that he was dangerously close to losing his temper, Caitlin backed down a bit. "I suppose I dinna. But I thought that ye loved me."

"I do." He took her hand, trying to come to terms with the problem. He had a pensive look on his face as he paused to think. "Perhaps . . . Aye. Among our own there are several possible choices." He rattled off six names, ending with, "Seumas and Jamie." All young men who had displayed their valor.

"Seumas and Jamie?" Caitlin was horrified. Of all her clansmen they were the ones most deeply guilty of being womanizers.

"A wise choice for I hae little liking for sending you to another clan, dearie." His smile showed how pleased he was with himself. "I'll soon be rocking the next generation of MacLeods on my knee, taking them up to their beds when they fall asleep before the warm fire. Come to think of it, lass, choosing one of our own does please me."

She was aghast. For all his pretense of affection all he seemed to be thinking about now was his precious heir. She meant nothing to him at all. Having wee ones tied a woman down. Caitlin wasn't certain she was ready. "And that's all I'm to be, a breeder for your grandsons and granddaughters? I hae no say in the matter of who shares my bed?"

"Nae!"

"We'll see." Despite the precarious position she found herself in, she could not help but exhibit her own anger, tilting her chin up in the proud manner her father had always admired. Her show of defiance now, however, only added fuel to his already hostile mood.

"Ye will marry the mon that I proclaim!"

"Nae!"

"I am the MacLeod. Must you be reminded of that fact? My word is law." He bristled with the audacity of her refusal. "Were I to choose him, you would marry the very devil himself at my command."

"Would I?" Caitlin seethed with an anger to match her father's own. "I think not. I will not marry at all." Her temper had always been her greatest fault and now it poured forth full force. "Ye will hae to bring me kicking and screaming to the altar. It will be an embarrassing moment for the great MacLeod chief if ye dare push me into this. Think upon that, Father."

He could nearly imagine such a scene. "Is that so? Ye would so defy me!" His own anger was so great that for a moment he thought to strike her, but the look in her eyes stilled his hand. She was so like him that it was like looking into a mirror. With a growl, he clenched his fists.

"To keep my freedom, aye that I would." Boldly she stood up, facing him squarely.

Folding his arms across his chest, he gave proof that he would brook no defiance. "If ye dare refuse I . . . I will hae ye exiled. I mean that!"

Caitlin gasped. The clan was perhaps the most important thing in all their lives. A man's very being, his identity, was permanently bound to the clan. To be driven out, to face exile, was to lose all sense of self-worth. "Ye wouldna!"

"Ah, but I would." It was time he taught her respect.

"Nae! Nae!" Covering her face with her hands, she wept frustrated, angry tears.

Ian forced himself not to bring Caitlin any comfort. The lassie needed to be taught a lesson, needed to be tamed.

"I will, I so swear it if ye dunna change yer ways, lass." He softened a bit. "Ah, Caitlin, why must ye make it so hard, why can't ye be like most daughters?"

She lifted her face. "Because I am me."

"Aye, ye are." He thought a moment. "Ah, lass, ye canna see that I want what is best for ye, but I do. And because of that, I am agreed to give ye one more chance. I'll invite all the eligible laddies here to the hall I will, and give ye yer pick." It was an idea that made him puff out his chest with pride to be oh so clever.

Two

Flames in the vast hearth danced about illuminating the MacLeod banner, a triple-towered castle floating on an azure background. It hung proudly for all to see alongside the shields, swords, dirks, and claymores which told of the MacLeod bravery. Tables bulged with platters and bowls that were brimming with food: smoked haddock, roast grouse with sprigs of heather, roast venison, pickled herring, boiled goose eggs, beet root salad, curds, wild carrots, honey cakes, and wild raspberries. Barley broth bubbled noisily in a cauldron over the fire, its steam giving off an appetizing aroma.

The great hall rang with raucous laughter, yet the revelry had not yet reached its peak. The MacLeod and his guests had not had the chance to drink themselves into a stupor, Caitlin thought dryly. For the moment at least it was somewhat tranquil in the hall. Ah, but she doubted that it would stay that way. After dinner the men would again partake of their favorite pastime. Drinking.

She turned to her sister. "Look at them, Shona!" she said, the disdain clear in her tone. "They sound much like a herd o' bleating goats, no doubt boasting to each other about their prowess. Well, I will hae none o' them."

"None?" Shona gasped as she accidentally nicked her thumb with a knife while chopping at a turnip. "Ah, but Father has gathered them here together so that ye can choose. Ye mustna say that ye willna pick one, for ye know well what Father has threatened."

"That he will exile me if I dunna obey." Caitlin smiled impishly. "Ah, but I know him. He wouldna. He is all bluff and bluster."

Shona wasn't so certain. "Mayhap, but ye canna take a chance surely."

"Och, so ye think I should blindly do as I am told and bind myself to just any ambitious laddie?" Stubbornly she shook her head. "I willna, father or no father."

At first she had actually believed her father's threat of exile, but she knew him well. When it came right down to it, he wouldn't have the heart to hurt her in such a vile way. No, he would give in this time just as he had all the others. One more year. She would make him see that he must agree. She was determined, for she would have none of the vain men assembled in the hall.

"Let Father parade them up and down as he chooses, I mean what I say. I am determined to remain a maid."

"Och, Caity!" Shona wore a look of worry, a look her sister quickly teased into a smile.

"Dunna fash yerself. All will be fine, and then perhaps ye can marry yon laddie." Caitlin nodded her head in the direction where a grinning Geordie Beaton stood. He was a tall, lithe young man with unruly, curly dark hair that framed a face that was handsomely chiseled.

"Marry . . . ?" Following her sister's gaze, Shona blushed as her eyes met the hazel-eyed young man. Hastily she looked away, but not before she had witnessed the wink he freely gave her. "Ach, it is my fondest wish." He was the man that she wanted. She could feel it with every beat of her heart. Geordie. Geordie. Geordie. Even his very name deeply stirred her, filled her senses as deeply as a draught of her father's finest ale.

"Ye favor him, 'tis plain to see," Caitlin whispered. "By

the looks that pass between ye, it seems Father would be wise to waste no time in joining ye together."

"Caity!" Again Shona blushed, though she was not so embarrassed that she did not cast the healer another longing glance. "Do ye think he feels the same?"

Caitlin nodded. "I do." Despite her protestations about love, she felt just a wee bit of longing to have a man look at her that way, a longing she quickly brushed away as she tersely took her place beside her father. She was the only female seated on the raised dais of stone that ran the full length of the hall across from the fireplace. Though it was an honor, Caitlin had little cause to feel pleased, considering the reason.

"Smile, lass. 'Tis a happy occasion I gather these laddies together for, not a funeral." He made a sweeping gesture with his hand. "Many a fine mon there is, Daughter. Look them over."

She did, critically, deciding at once that not a one of them was for her. It was, however, an opinion she kept to herself, at least for the moment. She was hungry and wanted to appease her appetite before she set herself to quarreling. With that thought in mind, she eagerly plucked up one of the fruit-decorated bannocks that were being passed around. She nearly choked on the round, flat oatcake, however, as her father stood up and made his announcement.

"Welcome one and all to this most joyous occasion, that being the choosing of my soon-to-be son-in-law and the sire of my grandsons." Taking Caitlin's hand, he pulled her to her feet. "Before this night is over, one of ye will be most lucky, most lucky indeed if ye catch my daughter's eye."

Ian MacLeod gestured with his hand, signaling the start of a small procession. Tall, short, fat, thin, full-bearded, clean-shaven, long-haired and balding, one by one all the eligible men in the room passed by where Caitlin stood. It was the most humiliating moment of her life.

"Ach, Daughter, see how that fine mon looks at ye—"

"Like he's a rat and I a piece of cheese," Caitlin countered quickly with a toss of her head.

"Look, Donnie MacKinnon is trying to get yer eye. He's such a fine, fine strong laddie who would no doot be most capable of getting ye wi' child."

"Were I to let him in my bed, which I assure ye I would no'!" Folding her arms across her chest, Caitlin cast a scowl in that young man's direction.

"Kenneth McQuar—"

"Nae! On a battlefield his girth might be an advantage but no' wi' me."

"Dougal Mc—"

"Nae! He is much too sure of himself."

"Ewan! Ca—"

"Nae! He is too shy."

One by one her father pointed to each man with the same results. Stubbornly Caitlin either gestured scornfully with thumbs down or shook her head "no."

"Too fat. Too thin. Too short. Too tall. Nae. Nae. Nae."

"I swear to ye, Daughter, ye would try the patience of a saint. But hear me well. Before this night is over ye *will* choose!" With that determined thought in mind the MacLeod proposed a toast. "To the lucky mon, whoever that might be."

"Look no further," called out a husky voice. "Ian MacLeod, ye seek a husband for yer daughter. That mon should be me."

Looking up, Caitlin saw a tall, lithe, blond gentleman. He was an attractive man with wide blue eyes, long eyelashes, and a cleft in his chin. Instinctively she knew the man to be Rory Gordon. As vain a man as ever there was. Oh, he was good to look upon, perhaps, but not the kind of man a girl should want to marry. Quickly she started to state that opinion, but her father's hand across her lips silenced her.

"Sit down beside us," Ian MacLeod invited.

"Father!" Her protestation was useless, and thus she was forced to suffer the man's presence as they ate.

"I should hae waited until a later hour to make proper introductions, but I was of a curiosity," Rory Gordon stated. "I was anxious to see yer daughter up close." His eyes raked over Caitlin with a stare that struck her with coldness all the way to the bone. Perhaps because there was no friendliness in his eyes. Instead, it seemed that his mind was ticking away as he thought of all the advantages of being married to the MacLeod's daughter.

"As I told you, my daughter is bonny!" Ian said boastfully. "And she is always sweet of temper," he lied.

"Aye!" Rory Gordon's eyes continued their traveling, running from the curve of her neck, to her shoulders, then lower in much the same manner as if he were buying a new horse, Caitlin thought indignantly. "She is as you say, very bonny. She'll do."

His manner sorely wounded Caitlin's pride. Do? Instantly she bristled. She was the one choosing, not he.

"Aye." He patted Ian on the back. "Seek no farther. Ye hae found yer son-in-law."

"Ah, is that so . . ." Caitlin was just about to tell him just what she thought of that declaration, but, sensing her intentions, Ian MacLeod tried to rescue the moment. He maneuvered it so that Rory Gordon could sit beside his daughter. Those whom he pushed aside glowered their anger, but he ignored them as he cunningly arranged it so that Caitlin and Rory shared a trencher. Winking mischievously in her direction, he patted the Gordon on the shoulder, giving hint that Rory was his favorite.

Caitlin was grim. "Ye hae come from far away. 'Tis anxious ye must be to find a wife."

He mumbled in answer, concentrating on a piece of beef as if he were a man half starved.

"But then as cold as it is here on Skye, ye will need a warm body to lie beside ye at night."

He raised his brows. "Aye."

Caitlin smiled as she said, under her breath, "Our fine shaggy-haired cows make wonderful companions." And a cow was all he would find as a bed mate, on that point she was determined. She was just about to tell Rory Gordon so when four pipers appeared. A skirl of bagpipes announced the music as the room was cleared for dancing. Before she had time to protest Caitlin found herself swept into Robbie MacKinnon's arms.

He was tall, much more so than she, making her feel feminine and somehow fragile. His chin just touched the top of her head. At first he simply held her as the music began weaving a spell, then slowly his strength moved her across the dance floor. Despite herself, Caitlin found herself enjoying him as a dancing partner.

"So, hae ye picked yer fine laddie yet?"

Caitlin answered quickly. "Nae, nor will I, for I hae it in my mind to be alone."

"As hae I." Robbie quickly explained that he was being prodded by his father into marrying. "I hae it in my mind to keep my freedom, but were I to be looking for a wife 'tis you I would pick, Caitlin nic Ian."

Despite herself, she smiled at the compliment. Suddenly the music changed to a livelier pace. Caitlin's partner changed, too. Rory Gordon had reclaimed her and led her in a twisting and whirling display of intricate steps. Soon they were out of breath and dizzy. Taking her hands in his when the dance was over, he kissed them, letting his lips brush her fingers as lightly as the wings of a butterfly.

Startled, Caitlin pulled away. "Do ye think me so easily won? A dance and a kiss in exchange for the MacLeod name and power?"

"Aye, for of all men assembled I am best."

"The best! Ha!" Well, she would soon let him know

where his quick wooing had taken him. For that matter she
would let them all know exactly where they stood, she
thought as she noted the smug look upon all the men's
faces. It was time.

Holding up her hand, Caitlin silenced the musicians. "I
hae made my choice," she said, as all eyes turned her way.

"Ye hae chosen." Ian MacLeod raised his eyes to the
ceiling as if to give praise to God.

"Aye."

The room was silent as everyone stared. Caitlin could
even hear the sounds of breathing. For just a moment her
bravado faltered. Did she dare?

"Och, speak, Daughter. Dunna leave us in suspense." Ian
MacLeod was all smiles.

"I choose . . ." Caitlin made a sweeping gesture with her
arm, then let her arm fall to her side. Softly she said, "None
of ye!"

"What?" Ian MacLeod cocked his head, certain that he
must have heard her wrong.

Once again Caitlin's courage wavered until she forced
herself to imagine what it would be like to be tied in bondage with any of the louts assembled within the room. This
time her voice was loud and strong.

"I do not want any of these men as husband, Father. In
truth, there is nary a one that pleases me."

"By the blessed saints!"

Like a thundercloud, Ian MacLeod stormed across the
room, grabbing his daughter roughly by her arm. It was at
that moment Caitlin was forced to see the error of her ways.
Her father was angry, so much so that he was nearly blinded
by his fury. Instinctively, Caitlin pulled back.

"Father!"

"Ye hae shamed me. Before all."

Foolish girl, what had she done? No doubt her father
would lock her in her room for creating a scandal. Or would

her punishment be worse? Caitlin trembled as she remembered her father's threat of exile.

"Father . . . please . . . I didna want—"

"But ye will. Aye that ye will." Trembling with rage, Ian MacLeod made his own proclamation, a vow that tumbled from his lips before he could even think. "Ye will hae a husband all right, Daughter. The next stranger who comes to the MacLeod stronghold, be he warrior, bard or even a fishermon, 'tis he who will be yer husband."

"Ye canna mean . . ." Caitlin was stunned.

"I do!" It was a startling proposal, but by the expression on his face and the look in his eyes it was obvious that the MacLeod meant to keep his word. "Aye, the first mon who crosses the MacLeod threshold will be the one that ye shall wed." With an air of finality he stalked away, leaving her to face her punishment alone.

Three

Far to the south of the MacLeod stronghold, four miles from Armadale on a headland near Teangue in Sleat, stood another castle. Castle Camus by name, the MacDonald seat of power. There it was dark and stormy. The kind of night when ghosts, witches, and sea beasts stirred. The wind came like a roar, driving inland from the sea. Rain lashed wickedly at the shuttered windows, the wind skirled and whined through the many cracks and crevices of the castle, causing the torches in the wall sconces to flicker.

In the inner bailey it was a noisy jumble of milling men and horses as the clansmen of Castle Camus sought shelter from the storm. Even the rain, however, did not daunt the mock fight going on. The sputtering torchlights reflected upon the slashing swords and upraised shields of the two young men engaging themselves in a practice battle. And as the bold, brash clansmen thrust and parried, those of more experience took great delight in shouting out criticisms.

"Gregor, ye move as slowly as if ye were an old mon. And your thrust is from the right side all the time. Makes ye an easy target."

"Niall, vary yer aim."

"Bold move. Now ye've got him . . ."

"Good, Niall. Good. Ye dodged him just in time."

The sound of sword on sword rent the air as the two cousins fought a furious game to show who was the better man. It was just the sort of test of strength and skill both men thrived on. A grueling exhibition. Like two dancers, they moved back and forth, swaying in time to some unheard rhythm, circling one another. And all the while their swords slashed gracefully through the air, weaving dazzling patterns as the steel blades caught the light from the torch's flames.

"The finest swordsmen on all o' Skye."

"Ach! The best in the Highlands."

Both fighters were of equal height, with well-muscled bodies that bespoke of constant exercise, but that was where the similarity ended. Gregor MacDonald's hair and beard were dark brown, his eyes as black as twin coals. Niall MacDonald on the other hand, was swarthy of complexion, but as fair of hair as his cousin was dark. His thick, tawny hair had just a hint of a curl and was worn long so that it brushed his shoulders. His strong chin and jaw were visable, for he was too vain to hide his face behind a beard.

"Och! Ye fight like a bairn," Gregor was taunting now, trying to goad Niall into making a mistake.

"Fight like a bairn, do I?" With a deep, throaty laugh, he lashed out, striking his cousin with the flattened breadth of his sword to avoid drawing blood. "That is a strike!"

"Oh, it is, is it? Then here is one in answer!" This time it was Gregor who was successful, making it a point to draw blood, a thin trickle but a real wound nonetheless. "Ach, excuse me, Cousin!"

A cry of pain was his answer as Niall lunged. This time his blow was parried, as was Gregor's try at another purposeful slashing.

"I'll prove to all who are watching that *I* should be my uncle's tanist." It was a prize the dark-haired man fiercely desired. The tanist was the person next in succession to the chief, according to the Scottish laws of tanistry, or succession, by the laws of cousinry. As nephews of Malcolm, both men had an equal right to the honor. Niall's mother had been a MacKinnon, his father a MacDonald, Malcolm's brother. Gregor's claim to the tanistry was from his mother's side, for she had been Malcolm's oldest sister.

"Or ye will prove yerself a fool!" Niall's eyes were hazel, twinkling as if with suppressed merriment. He'd win this match with his dolt of a cousin or not be worthy of his clan's name. "Which will it be, Cousin?"

"Fool ye call me?" Gregor's facial contours were boldly chiseled, his mouth slanted downward so that he appeared as if he were always frowning. Certainly he never exhibited a sense of humor. "And just what are ye?"

"I'll be the village simpleton if I let such as ye win the day." Niall MacDonald was of a more jovial countenance. A man who was not afraid to laugh at himself.

The two men were a study of contrasts in temperament, as different as the night is from the day. Gregor was easily fueled to anger, Niall needed to be goaded into losing his temper. At the moment he was successful in keeping his head, while his cousin was already hopelessly provoked.

"Ye willna win!"

"I will."

"Willna."

"Will!"

Gregor was deadly with a sword, but Niall's lightning-quick agility was more than his match. Again and again Gregor lunged, his anger making him careless. Niall blocked each thrust. With a last concentrated effort he sent his cousin's sword tumbling to the ground.

"Niall wins this one!" The others in the clan gave full vent to their praise. It was apparent that of the two they favored Niall. Perhaps because he had gone out of his way to foster camaraderie. Or because he had the self-assurance of a man who was willing to take risks and likewise willing to accept the consequences of his decisions. A brave man. A canny man. The kind of man who was a born leader.

"We'll meet again at this time tomorrow, Gregor. 'Twill

be yer turn to be victor." Niall stuck out his hand amiably, but his cousin ignored the gesture. So, it was to be hard feelings again, was it?

Bending down, Niall cross-laced his curans, which had come undone in the fracas. He did not see Gregor pick up his sword, raising it up with intent to do mischief. Only a shouted warning kept Niall from serious injury.

"Gregor. Ye son of a dog!" Niall spat his cousin's name with scorn as he ducked. With a grumbled oath he lashed out with his fist, striking Gregor full on the chin. A sobering blow that seemed to quell any further attempts at retaliation.

Disdainfully he eyed the other man. His dislike of his surly, scowling cousin was intense and all for good reason. From the moment Niall had set foot in the hall, Gregor had made it obvious that he was to be an enemy. He had babbled vicious rumors, cheated whenever they sparred at mock combat so as to win at any price, and tried his best to humiliate Niall at every turn. And all the while he showed a far different face to their uncle, pretending to be Niall's advocate. Only by his wits and a measure of good luck had Niall managed to counteract such duplicity.

"Why?" It was a question that was deeply troubling, but a matter he had little time to contemplate further, for one of his younger cousins came with a summons. "Malcolm is asking to see the both of ye," he announced, pointing first at Niall, then at Gregor. "On a matter of great importance."

The two men picked up their discarded breacons, wrapping them round their waists, then draping them over their shoulders. As always, Gregor was off in a run, anxious to please the uncle who held such power. Niall's gait, however, was more leisurely. The two men approached the thick wooden door to the chamber, Gregor elbowing himself into the position of entering first.

Inside, a great fire roared, its flames dancing orange and blue light. A welcome respite from the dampness of the bailey. Malcolm MacDonald lounged drunkenly in his high-backed wooden chair by the roaring hearth, taking long gulps of his ale as he amusedly watched his two nephews. Little did they know that he purposefully stirred up the sense of competition between them. It did the young pups good to have to fight for the honor he would bestow on one of them. Whoever became his tanist would have to earn the title.

"You sent for us . . ." Niall's deep voice and Gregor's higher pitched utterance blended in unison.

"Aye. That I did." Slowly Malcolm looked from one to the other, keeping them in suspense. "The time has come to make my choice . . ."

He leaned toward Gregor in his preference because the young man was of a kindred spirit to his own. Daring. Sly. Of brute strength with little conscience to get in the way. Merciless when necessary. That one had a robustness that was almost overpowering. And yet a voice inside his head whispered that it was Niall who was the better man. Since he had first come from the MacKinnon side of the isle, after his fosterage there, he had become an integral part of the MacDonald clan. He drew men to him with a fierce show of loyalty that was seldom equaled. Certainly he was the most intelligent of the two. And his distinction on the battlefield had done the MacDonalds proud.

"My tanist will be . . ." *But why should I choose?* he thought. He would leave it to fate. A test of wit and skill between them. It would be interesting. "The tanist will be . . ." Purposefully he teased them, pausing overlong before he said, "the one who earns it."

"What?" Niall and Gregor were both stunned.

Malcolm grinned. "He who thinks of a way to prove himself to be the ablest leader."

"Proves himself?" Gregor looked questioningly at his uncle.

"Some deed of valor for the good of the clan. Something that will secure once and for all our dominance on the isle."

Gregor shrugged in confusion. "What must I do?"

Malcolm offered his nephews a wry smile. "That is but another part of the test. It is up to *you* to think of what must be done."

Niall threw the end of his breacan feille over his shoulders with a jaunty air. He knew at once just what *he* was going to do. There was but one answer really. He would boldly sneak into the MacLeod's stronghold of Dunvegan castle and steal the fairy flag. Without it the MacLeods would have lost their magic. When the MacDonalds engaged in battle a third time, *they* would be victorious. What greater act of daring, cunning, and courage could he do. His uncle would surely be so impressed that he would name him as tanist immediately thereafter.

"Tanist." The lofty honor sounded good upon his tongue. An honor he deserved. An honor his daring deed would ensure.

After the hearth fires had burned down to ash, Niall still pondered the matter, liking the scheme more and more the longer he thought about it. What's more, his friend Ogg, a tall giant of a man, liked it, too.

"Imagine. Stealing it right out from underneath the very noses of those cursed MacLeods. I canna think of a finer jest," he offered.

"Nor an act that could e'er be as stunning a blow."

The flag was rumored to have three magical properties. Flown on the battlefield it ensured a MacLeod victory, as had been seen in the past. Spread on his marriage bed it endowed the MacLeod chief with children. Ian MacLeod had not taken the promise seriously, had laughingly said he would depend on his own prowess, and he was now without a male heir. Unfurled at Dunvegan it was said to charm herring into the loch. A great loss to the MacLeods were they to find it stolen from its hiding place!

Throwing a log on the fire, Niall watched as it flared up, illuminating his face. "I hae heard that the flag is kept in the tower. The tower where Colin MacLeod was struck down. 'Tis there I will go first."

"Ooooooooooooo!" Ogg made a high-pitched, eerie sound, spreading his arms wide. "And get nabbed by the ghostie who lives there."

"Ghost. Ha!" Niall scoffed at that story. "I dunna believe in such spirits."

Ogg shivered. "I do. I hae seen them wi' me own eyes. Fearsome spectacles."

Niall laughed mockingly. "I would be more fearful o' the MacLeod's daughter. From what I hear she's a hellion who would make any ghost worth his salt cower."

"Aye, a shrew, or so it's whispered. One so bold, so willful that she has openly scorned all wi' whom her father would hae her wed." Ogg revealed the latest gossip being whispered around the hearth fires. That the MacLeod had sworn to marry his daughter to the first eligible male who entered the clan's castle.

"So Ian is trying to pawn the headstrong lassie off, is he now?" Niall clucked his tongue. "Sure and she must be as plain of face as a cow, but obviously not as docile."

"Nae. 'Tis said that she is bonny. Verrrry, verrrry bonny."

Niall did not have a reply to this, he simply stared at Ogg, his face a mask. He seemed to be deep in thought about the matter, but when he spoke it was about the MacLeod's flag and not his daughter. "I will get it, Ogg. Somehow. Some way!"

With Ogg he carefully formulated a plan. He would go by boat, traveling the waters like a fisherman. At the first wisp of dawn on the morrow he would set out on his daring mission. Within three days' time the fairy flag would be in Malcolm's possession and he would be tanist.

Four

A thick enveloping mist swirled inland like grasping fingers inland, clinging to the dewy ground of Armadale Bay. The stench of the decaying fish, discarded on the sand and rocks, drifted through the air. A reminder that the people of the nearby village made their living by fishing.

Niall MacDonald waited for the boat that would take him up the coastline to Waternish, watching as the ocean slapped the murky waves against the shore. Earlier he had had no trouble persuading one of the fishermen to loan him a tiny vessel, a small curach constructed with wicker frame and covered with hides. With a steadfast bribe he was also able to convince that same fisherman to be his guide and to keep this journey a secret so that Gregor would not hear of Niall's daring deed until Niall wanted him to.

Folding his arms across his chest, Niall contemplated his plan. Was it possible? Dunvegan Castle had a moat that surrounded it and the walls, which were said to be ten feet thick in places. Thinking it over, Niall decided that he would not be discouraged, for it seemed to him that the MacLeods were much too sure of themselves. He could outwit them. It was true that the castle was guarded against feuding and marauding armies—but against one man? Surely he could take them unaware, climb to the tower, find the flag and carry it away. And what a hero he would be upon his return. Gregor MacDonald would not stand a chance of becoming tanist then.

"A clever and resourceful mon can get past any fortifications," he said aloud, throwing back his shoulders to show pride in himself and to bolster his doubts. He would take a little boat within the boat, something hardly bigger than a man. He would use the little boat to cross the moat. As to the walls, he would scale them with hook and with rope in much the same way he had climbed his favorite mountains when he was a boy.

I can do it. I will do it. He had convinced himself that he wasn't afraid of the MacLeods. Still, the thought of the dungeon and its cruelties was the one thing that sobered his enthusiasm. He would have to be cautious lest he end up rotting there like those poor dead fish that tormented his nostrils when the breeze blew in from the sea. Above all, he must not admit to being a MacDonald or his doom would be sealed, he thought impatiently as he scanned the horizon once again.

At last he saw it, a dark shadow against the rocky shoreline. It was the small fishing boat skimming through the waters. It pulled inland when it reached the agreed-upon meeting place. The water whipped and churned around the curach as he settled himself within. The rotund, ruddy-faced fisherman greeted him with a wide smile as he introduced himself.

"Peadar is my name."

"Niall. Nephew to Malcolm," Niall announced with a tone of arrogant pride. His relation to the great clan leader, though acknowledged, did not keep him from having to help row the boat. Peadar handed him the oars, saying, "It will take both of us to make any headway."

Gripping the handles tightly, Niall pushed and pulled with all his might, all the while thinking that the sooner he got to the MacLeod stronghold the sooner he would be able to return home again. Besides, this promised to be quite an exciting adventure—at least so he thought.

As the familiar shores of Sleat vanished into the mists,

he felt an unnerving sense of wariness. Alas, when the wind began buffeting the curach, the sea voyage proved to be far from the enticing adventure he had supposed. The violently churning ocean turned his insides upside down. The waves threatened to capsize the boat. More than once or twice he was tempted to turn back and forget the whole idea.

"Dinna fash yerself. It will be a long, tedious journey but I'll get ye to Loch Dunvegan all in one piece," the fisherman said, sensing Niall's discomfort.

Peadar's words relieved some of the tension. Still, the jagged coastline seemed to extend for miles. Nonetheless, true to his word Peadar steered the tiny boat with the greatest skill past the Point of Sleat, heading for Tarskavaig Bay and beyond. Niall had heard tales of mermaids and sea people and he could not help but wonder if these creatures were waiting even now to snatch the boat as it bounced on the water.

"Hae ye ever seen a mermaid, Peadar?" he asked, staring at the churning waters.

"Once. A bonny, bonny dark-haired lassie with silver tail and fins. She blew me a kiss."

"Did she now?" Niall fully hoped that he would see one, too, and he was disappointed when he did not. He reasoned that perhaps the water was just too turbulent.

Up and down, back and forth, the boat rocked unendingly. Niall and Peadar paddled on until a dusting of powdery stars dotted the skyline, and yet they had only come halfway. While Peadar slept, Niall looked up at the familiar constellations, contenting himself by counting stars. Then it was his turn to sleep. Closing his eyes, he was lulled by the soft rhythm of Peadar's oars, soothed by the rise and dip of the blades as they slapped the waves.

A cold spray of ocean mist splashed into Niall's eyes awakening him just as the first beams of light tugged at the morning sky. He opened his eyes to see the breathtaking grandeur of Duirinish's rock formations, solidified lava from a long-extinct volcano, silhouetting the horizon, peeking up through the clouds. It was a breathtaking scene, but Niall realized that they must proceed. Taking up the oars again, Niall aided the fisherman in moving the boat through the waves.

"The Norsemen called this Skuyo Isle of Clouds," he said, "because of the mist." All his life he had heard that story, yet only now did he realize the full depth of the haunting beauty.

"It looks like fairyland . . ." Peadar responded, pausing in his rowing to gape. Then with a shrug he, too, began rowing again.

They traveled all day in a seemingly unending, up-and-down churning. Peadar kept Niall amused with stories of his fishing journeys. Niall told of battles he had won. Forced camaraderie soon blossomed into something akin to friendship in the two men as they guided the boat through the sea. At last, when Niall was beginning to think they would never reach Dunvegan, Peadar announced, "Dunvegan Head just around the curve. We're nearly there."

Both men stopped talking and quieted as they concentrated on guiding the boat toward Loch Dunvegan. In the narrowest part of the inlet Niall thought it wise to let the more experienced man row the boat to shore. Niall disembarked on the white sand-strewn beach near a fjordlike inlet to watch while the fisherman beached the skiff.

"Now, remember. Wait for me here, Peadar. It won't take long."

On the shore, shells, driftwood, logs, and seaweed littered the rock-strewn sand. Niall made his way through the tangled seaweed, carrying the man-size curach on his back like some enormous shield. The journey to Dunvegan Castle would be a long and exhausting one, he knew, complicated by the fact that he wasn't certain exactly where it was. Traveling in the fading light of dusk made visibility all the more trying.

Huffing and puffing, Niall proceeded, missing Peadar's company more and more with each step. The long hours seemed even longer without the fisherman's chatter, but he knew it had been much wiser to go alone. There was less chance of a mistake that way and, besides, he wouldn't have wanted the young fisherman to get himself into any trouble because of an association with him. The MacLeods were said to show little mercy to anyone trespassing to cause mischief.

Guided only by the fires that glowed in the dark, the smoke pouring from the crofters' cottages, he moved along. Being in another clan's territory made him extremely vulnerable. As he pushed his way through the foliage, Niall attuned his ears to any alarming sound, but paused only once when a flock of nightbirds made their presence known.

Onward he trudged, until his arms ached from the burden of the tiny boat and his legs were sore. Then, just when Niall was about to give up Dunvegan, the roughly hewn stronghold came into view. Like some multi-eyed monster, its windows glowed through the darkness.

Quickening his pace, Niall hurried toward the castle. Slipping the tiny boat into the water, he skimmed across the moat without any difficulty. Why, this was going to be as easy as taking milk from a slumbering babe, he thought, his ego stroked with his success. By the time he reached the western wall he was feeling cocky. True, it was a perilous climb, but he could manage it.

A long length of rope was tied around Niall's waist, acting as a belt, but he unwrapped it now. After tying the rope to the hook that he carried in his hand, he swung it around and around his head, flinging it upward. It struck a soft piece of the stone, the sharp points embedding in the wall. Slowly he climbed up, hand over hand. Up. Up. Up. Until his fingers were raw and bleeding. Taking a deep breath, loathing the thought of falling into the slimy and evil-smelling waters of the moat, he looked down. The drop looked awesome and he held his breath as he continued climbing.

Suddenly he lost his footing. Like a spider hanging from its fragile thread, he swung to and fro. There was a loud splash as his frantic kicking sent a rock flying into the moat. For just a moment Niall was certain that this crazy scheme would send him hurling to his death, but he somehow managed to regain his balance. Moving steadily up the rope, he reached the nearest window and climbed inside.

It was dark and quiet. Not even one taper was lit. A good omen for a man stealthfully invading another's territory, yet unnerving, too. Niall was cautious as he lowered himself down, but not careful enough. He gasped as he found himself engulfed in a powdery substance.

"By Saint Michael!" As if he were swimming, he fought to free himself. "What the . . . ?" He was in a large barrel. It was easy enough to escape from once he had made that discovery, however. Pulling himself out, he had to laugh as he struck his tinderbox and fumbled around for a candle. "A flour barrel." He had fallen unceremoniously into the castle's supply of flour. It covered him from head to toe.

Niall might have taken time to brush himself clean had it not been for a squeaking sound. Blowing out the candle, he hid behind the barrel. A paunchy man entered to gather a few supplies. Niall quickly assessed that it must be the cook! Fearing detection, he darted in and out of the shadows as he fled to the stairway, running up two whole flights, his heart racing. He had little doubt but that his life would be forfeit if he were found now. It was all too obvious that he was an intruder.

He raced recklessly through the darkness, barely seeing where he was going. Finally he found himself before a wooden door. Though he pulled frantically at the iron handle, it was locked. Swearing beneath his breath, he went on to the next door and the next. He hesitated, listening for the sound of footfalls.

Carefully ascertaining that no guards were about, he continued on his way, then hearing footsteps again, he quickly opened the door to the nearest room and stepped inside. Again he struck his tinderbox, lighting just one wall sconce. He found himself in a tower room. A room cluttered with all sorts of weapons and other relics. Cobwebs decorated the ceiling, a coat of dust layered the furniture. In curiosity he explored. Was the fairy flag within?

"We'll soon see," he whispered with bravado. Still, he couldn't help feeling more than a bit apprehensive about the whole thing. He had to be very careful lest he be caught red-handed by anyone wandering about. "Hopefully the MacLeods will all be snuggled in their beds and I will be long gone wi' the flag before they arise," he murmured hopefully. Closing his eyes for just a moment, he tried to imagine the MacLeod hall. The fires would have burned to ashes. The seanachaidh would have stopped chattering his tales. The great hall would be empty. Quiet.

"Aye, I'll be safe." With that thought in mind, Niall started rummaging through all the objects in the tower room.

Down below in the great hall, the hearth fire had burned down to ash. It was silent. The seanachaidh had ceased his stories. All the clansmen and women had sought their beds, save a few, including Caitlin who still prowled about. The argument she had had with her father was still on her mind. In but a moment, with only a few words, her whole future had been put in jeopardy because of her stubbornness and her father's great pride.

He can't mean it, she thought hopefully. *He wouldn't really force me to marry the next man who comes to the castle. It was but a threat said in anger to curb my temper and frighten me into submission.* Or was it? The possibility that her father might well have been deadly serious, that she might be forced to go far away from her homeland, played on Caitlin's mind.

Her eyes flitted about the room as if to brand a permanent image in her mind for the days ahead when she might be far away from here. Memories. So many memories. Down the center of the hall was a long hearth over which big pots from the evening's meal were still placed. How many stories of fairies, waterbeasts, witches, and ghosts had she listened to in front of the evening fire? Though her family was Christian, they knew that their lives would always be ruled by older beliefs, too, knew that other beings occupied Skye as surely as did those of flesh and blood. As a child, she had listened in awe to such stories and tales of long ago.

Before this same hearth she had blissfully enjoyed the music from fiddle, harp, and pipes, riotous songs or soothing songs of reverie that had at last lulled her to sleep. Somehow she had always awakened to find herself in her bed, thinking perhaps the fairies had bewitched her and brought her to her room. Now, she knew it had been her father who had carried her off to bed, holding her tenderly and lovingly within the strength of his arms. Now, he was pushing her into the arms of a man who might well be a stranger. A husband. How strange that sounded. Just a few days ago she had laughingly talked with one of her sisters about such a thing, had viewed her adamant opposal to any suggestion of marriage. How quickly one's fate could change.

A loom and several spindle whorls for spinning of wool stood against the farthest wall and Caitlin curled her mouth in a bittersweet smile as she recalled how often she had rebelled at joining the women for their daily chores. Cooking, weaving, and sewing bored her. Washing with the harsh lye soap seemed a thankless task. Waulking, or hand-shrinking, woolen cloth was a long and laborious process which she had no fondness for. In truth, she had scorned woman's work, finding a dozen reasons for avoiding tasks anytime she could. But now, oh, what she wouldn't give to be able to stay among these women instead of women she did not even know.

I wish that I could stay here forever, she thought, but knew it was unlikely, at least now. All she could hope was that there would be no newcomers to the castle, at least until her father had time to let his temper cool a wee bit. She would talk with him then and somehow make him understand her feelings.

"Well, well, well, the bride-to-be . . ."

Caitlin didn't even bother to turn. She knew who the voice belonged to. Jamie. "Not if I can help it."

"Lassie, 'tis whispered that ye hae no say." He threw a log onto the hearth, relighting the fire with a torch ignited by one of the wall sconces, then laughed. "The proud and haughty Caitlin MacLeod will be given to the first mon who crosses the threshold. Well, it serves ye right, lass, considering that ye could hae had me."

"Ha!" She pointed her nose toward the high, beamed ceiling.

"But ye said nae." There was disappointment in his tone. "Why?"

She answered honestly. "Because I couldna trust ye where other lassies are concerned, Jamie. I want a mon I know will be true for ever more."

A muscle tightened in his jaw, his eyes squinted. He opened his mouth to speak, but in the end couldn't say the lie. "Ye hae been reading too many fairy tales, Caitlin. Forever after just doesna happen. But I would give ye honor and respect and be true to ye in my own way."

Which means that he expects to be able to wander, albeit discreetly, she thought, feeling her cheeks grow hot at the very thought. Slowly she turned around to face him. "It isna good enough."

His face turned into a mask of anger. "Then go straight to the devil, Caitlin MacLeod." He strode quickly to the door, but turned around before he pushed it open. "And we will see just what kind of a mon ye end up wi' as yer honored husband." His tone insinuated that he hoped whoever it was turned out to be totally unsuitable, someone who would make her deeply sorry she had scorned him.

"Aye, we will see." She held his gaze steadily. In the end it was Jamie who looked away. Caitlin stared after him as he left the hall, slamming the door behind him.

Only after Jamie had left did Caitlin allow her composure to slip. Her hands were trembling. He was right. Maybe she would end up with someone who would make her regret that she had told Jamie no. Maybe she wouldn't be able to talk her father out of his decision this time. Maybe . . .

"Maybe, maybe, maybe," she breathed. Well, she wouldn't let anyone or anything get her down. Not even her father. She might be female, but she was a MacLeod through and through. Just as brave in her way as Colin. "My dearest elder brother . . ."

Without even realizing it, Caitlin's steps took her toward the tower where the air was chilly and damp. Lighting a torch, she took a step up the stairs, then another and another. If Colin's ghost really did roam about she was determined to find out tonight, for if ever she needed to engage in conversation with his restless spirit it was now.

Oh, please be there! Please materialize if only for a few moments. I need you so . . .

Closing her eyes, Caitlin said a silent prayer, then touched her fingers to the door handle. Slowly, quietly, she pulled it down, pushing it open ever so slightly, optimistic that somehow her brother would have sensed her desperate need.

"Please exist, Colin. Please . . ." Taking a deep breath, at that moment she really did believe. Even so, she was not fully prepared for the apparition that met her eyes. A ghostly white form who could be none other than *him!* "Oh!"

Niall was too entranced to hear the door open, but he heard the gasp. Turning around, he saw the most beautiful woman he had ever beheld standing there. A woman with hair the color of fire whose mouth was agape as she stared in disbelief.

"Colin!" she breathed. "Colin! Blessed Saints, it *is* you!"

Five

A lone torch flickered and sparked, casting unearthly shadows on the wall, faintly illuminating the masculine form that stood in the tower room. It was difficult to see details, but from what she could make out, Caitlin was convinced that this eerie white figure was an unearthly being. It *was* a ghost! And not just any ghost.

"Colin . . ." she said again, her eyes widening, her voice trembling just a little as she tried to still her quivering jaw.

Though she had hoped beyond hope to at last see him, a chill swept over Caitlin at the very sight. She drew her arasaid more closely about her. Spirits of the dead were frightening to behold, she thought, even if it was the spirit of her brother. Still, as the ghost returned her stare, she fought to maintain her calm. She didn't want to act cowardly or panic and frighten Colin away. And yet . . .

Caitlin's hands shook as a myriad of memories flitted through her mind. She was a child again, tiptoeing to the tower to investigate the loud noises that had awakened her from her slumber, little knowing the horror she would witness.

That man is going to hurt him! He's going to hurt my brother! Colin, watch out! Colin, beware! She remembered a sword descending with lightning speed, remembered the blood, heard once again in her mind her terrified scream.

"Oh, no! Colin." Hurriedly she closed her eyes, hoping to shut out the frightening images of warfare and death.

At the sound of the name, Niall stiffened, then when there was no reprisal, he relaxed. The lass didn't seem to pose a threat, and thus he answered, "Aye, lass, I'm here." Having prepared himself for flight or a fight if his presence was discovered, Niall was surprised at this turn of events. Pleasantly so. Hopefully this case of mistaken identity would be beneficial.

Caitlin opened her eyes, forcing the terrifying images from her mind, concentrating on the figure right before her. There were those who did not believe in ghosts, but oh how she would mock them now.

"For so many years I hae been coming here, hoping *ye* would come . . ." she said softly, clenching her hands together so tightly that the fingernails bit into her palms.

The young woman had been hoping to see him? Niall smiled for just a moment as he realized that she had mistakened him for someone else. But who? Not a MacDonald surely, for he had purposefully dressed in the plain garb of a fisherman so that his clothing would not give him away.

"Ye wished, did ye?"

"Aye, I wished and now at last ye hae appeared," Caitlin continued. "As if somehow ye sensed how much I wanted to see ye again."

Cocking his head, Niall leisurely assessed the young woman who had come upon him. "Well, lass, ye didna wish any harder than I." Whoever this young woman was, whoever she had been expecting to see, she bewitched him.

Look at that hair! Like a fire, a raging flame that whipped about her shoulders. Catching the glow of the torch, her hair blazed with magenta highlights. Niall moved closer, his gaze caressing the mounds of the woman's breasts, moving to the narrow waist which he knew he could span with his hands. The gentle swell of her hips and long legs were outlined by her gown, completing the enchanting image.

"I hae watched for ye and waited so long I had begun to think that ye didna exist." Caitlin lifted her head, staring at the presence before her. *Strange how piercing those hazel eyes are,* Caitlin thought, shivering under his stare. She had not thought a ghost's eyes would be so fiery, so filled with life, and yet they were.

"Well, I do exist!" And by all the saints so did she, a vision that completely enthralled him. Niall had known a hundred women who were by all measures beautiful, and yet when he looked into those dark-brown eyes he was lost, caught up in a fascination more potent than a witch's spell. It was totally unusual for him to feel such a sudden, compelling explosive physical attraction, and yet he did.

"Surprising how strong ye seem. Are ye as solid as ye appear?" A frown creased Caitlin's brow as she took a step toward him. She was deeply curious, and thus she blurted out, "Tell me. If I touch ye, what will it be like? Will it be like touching air? If I touch ye, will ye up and disappear?"

"Disappear?" He was taken aback by her question. For a moment he feared she might be daft. Perhaps one of those cast off from the others and left to roam the upper rooms because they were not right in the head. So thinking, he took a step back.

"No, Colin, dunna shrink from me." For a moment she felt foolish, and thus she explained. "I've never seen a ghost before, ye see."

Ghost? As the realization of what she meant swept over him, Niall was first stunned, then amused. She thought he was a ghost! She had called him Colin. No doubt she meant Colin MacLeod, the brave laddie who had been killed in this very tower protecting the very treasure he had come to steal. This lovely lassie believed him to be that long-deceased personage. And her so believing might very well save his life.

"Ah, lass, ghosts are really no different from mortals."

"No different?" Caitlin reached out.

"Except that ye canna touch me," he hastened to reply. She raised her brow. "Why?"

He explained quickly. "Yer hand will pass right through me, hinny, no matter how it might appear. Spirits such as I hae no flesh or blood."

Niall thrust out his arms, affecting what he thought to be his most "haunting" pose.

"That's why I can walk through walls as if they were no' even there. Saves me the bother of having to open doors when I am mulling about up here guarding the wee flag."

"Really? Ye can walk through doors and walls."

"Aye."

Caitlin regarded him thoughtfully, trying to imagine just what that must be like and imagined that despite the advantages it must be lonely. "Is . . . is it terrible being dead?" A blunt question.

"Sometimes yes, sometimes no." This time he couldn't resist a grin as his voice lowered to a mere whisper. "For ye see, lass, we ghosts still hae the same desires we had in the flesh." Looking at the young woman, Niall felt his blood stir. "Only we canna do anythin' about them."

"Oh . . ." Caitlin knew well that he meant more than just the longing for eating and drinking. Was it any wonder then that she blushed.

"But dunna fash yerself. Over the years I hae trained myself to be content." He winked. "But I would be far happier if I could be haunting some of those roguish Mac-Donalds instead of languishing up here."

"The MacDonalds!" Caitlin spoke the name like a curse. "I will ne'er forgi' them for killing ye, Colin dear."

"Ach, nae! Scurvy rascals though they be." Seeing a chance to use his mistaken identity as a ghost to his advantage, Niall turned the conversation to the fairy flag. "They havena a chance against us, though, lass, as long as we hae the flag. Which is why I hover here in the tower so diligently, guarding it wi' such zest."

"Aye, guarding it as loyally in death as ye did in life, Colin dear." Without realizing it, Caitlin looked toward an old wooden chest, revealing the flag's hiding place to Niall without even saying a word.

Ah, so there it is! Keeping his eye on the red-haired girl, Niall inched toward the chest, hardly daring to believe his luck. *Careful, Niall, don't be too hasty,* he instructed himself. *Move slowly. Slowly.* As he moved, he tried to keep her distracted with talk. "Such a lovely lass as yerself shouldna frown. Dunna keep anger inside ye because of what happened a long time ago."

" 'Tis not just that." She sighed. " 'Tis Father."

"Father?" Positioning himself so that the chest was behind him, he fumbled with the lid.

Caitlin was relieved to be able to come right to the point. "Father is going to gi' me away, Colin, and I do no' wish to marry." Her eyes were imploring. "What can I do?"

"Do?" Keeping his head up, his eyes level with hers, Niall slowly lifted the creaky wooden lid. "Why, tell him ye willna do it."

"I did."

"And?" Reaching inside, he cautiously felt around for the slick, cool, silken flag.

"He threatens to gi' me to the first mon who walks across the threshold."

"He does?" Niall's eyes widened in surprise. It couldn't be, could it? This lovely red-haired girl couldn't be the daughter of that sour-faced old MacLeod. Was this then the infamous Caitlin?

"And I do believe he means it."

"Nae." Niall's jaw tensed. *Of course. He should have known it to be Caitlin MacLeod. Her chin was too strong, clearly showing her to be a lass who would not be easily managed. Even the fiery hair gave proof to that.*

"Ach, but I fear he meant every word. 'Tis married I will soon be and not to a mon of my choosing."

"He doesna mean it."

"Ah, but he does and I dunna know what I can do except run away."

She looked so lovely, so forlorn, that for a moment Niall was distracted from his mission. "And go where?" He found himself thinking the most foolish thoughts.

"I dunna know, Colin. I just dunna know."

"Och, lass!" He found himself longing to reach out to her, to comfort her, but the feel of the flag touching his fingers brought him back to reality. No! Lovely or not, he must not dally here. Caitlin MacLeod meant trouble. He had best get the flag and leave this place as soon as he could. So thinking, he made a grab for the flag as soon as she lowered her head. Hastily he drew it out and stuffed it in his shirt.

"Colin?" Unfortunately his act did not go unseen. "What are ye doing?"

"Keeping the flag safe, lass. Just keeping it safe." For just a moment he turned his back on her as he moved toward the window, wondering just how quickly he could scramble down the rope. When he turned around again, he was astonished to see that she had picked up an old sword and was actually brandishing it at him. "Lass?"

"Ye are no ghost." In the act of pulling the flag from the chest, the intruder's fingers had brushed against the wood, wiping off the white substance covering them. Now, as Caitlin looked at him, she saw that his was no ghostly appendage but a hand like any other man's.

Her threatening stance, the way she held the sword gave Niall reason to fear. It was no wonder he hurried to assure her. "Ah, but I am a ghost, *sister* dearie."

"And I am a banshee." She didn't know the why or wherefore he had tried to deceive her, but whatever the reason she knew him to be a thief who now held possession of something not only she but her entire clan held precious. "A banshee whose wail will be proclaiming yer death if ye don't return that flag ye just stole to its rightful place."

"Flag?" Niall feigned innocence.

"Which ye hae hidden beneath yer shirt, *brother* dearie." She took a step toward him. "Put it back!"

For just a moment he was motionless as he thought the matter out carefully. He didn't want to put it back. He had come too far to fail now. Yet neither did he want to be skewered by some slip of a girl no matter how pretty.

"Ye heard me. Put it back!"

"Nae!"

Lashing out with her sword, she slashed his fingers, drawing blood. "Ah, ye see. Ghosts do no' bleed. At least so I hae heard." Her hostility made her eyes glow like amber. "Who are ye?"

He didn't answer.

"Cat got yer tongue?" Just to make certain he knew she was deadly serious, she exclaimed, "I'm just as skilled wi' this as any mon."

"I wouldna doubt it." Something about her seemed to foretell that she would be skilled at anything she did. Even so, he could not part with the flag, and thus, instead of backing down, Niall moved hurriedly toward the window.

Caitlin moved with all the agility of a streak of lightning and blocked his way. The very air crackled with tension. And danger. "Take one more step and ye *will* be a ghost."

"And that would be such a pity." Niall's smile was roguish. His eyes caressed her with a boldness few had dared, held her, forced her to acknowledge that there was a mutual attraction between them. "For it would mean that I could ne'er make love to ye, lassie." As he spoke, his eyes swept over her suggestively.

"Ach!" Caitlin was attracted to him, but she would have rather jumped from the tower window than admit it to herself. Perhaps that was why she was doubly hostile as she poked the point of her sword into his ribs. "Sweet talk and compliments will do ye no good. Start walking."

"Walking? Where?" For just a moment he looked bemused with the situation, then as he felt the sharp point stick him through his shirt, he slowly took a step forward. Only a fool would anger a woman, particularly one who was armed. "Where are ye taking me?"

"To my father." He wouldn't be so smug and arrogant facing the mighty Ian MacLeod. Her father had made even the bravest man cower when faced with his anger.

"To yer father." He startled her with another smile. "Good. Good."

"Good?" Of all the things he might have said, she certainly wasn't expecting this answer.

"Aye, ye see, lass, *I* am the first mon to cross the MacLeod threshold." Was he imagining it or had she gone quite pale?

"Ye canna be . . . be . . ."

"Ah, but I am."

Niall had fitfully thought of a way out of his predicament and had come up with the perfect scheme. He would concoct the story of being a fisherman come to claim the hand of the MacLeod daughter. It would buy him some time until he could think of a way to escape.

Six

The stairs leading to the lower floors of the castle were drafty, but that was not the reason that Caitlin felt chilled. It was because of the quandary she found herself in. A real "carfuffle" to be sure. She had caught a stranger in the tower, a man who had made an attempt to steal the fairy flag, for which act he should be punished. At the same time, however, that man had cunningly reminded her of her father's promise, to marry her off to the first stranger who set foot inside the castle. That man, as her captive had pointed out, was him.

"Shall we go?" Niall's voice was low, a husky rumble that seductively teased her as he spoke.

Caitlin was hesitant for just a moment as she pondered what to do. Her father was a man who always adhered to his vows, but surely under the circumstances he wouldn't even consider this tawny-haired rogue as a suitor. Or would he? Certainly the broad-shouldered, muscular man looked well able to wield a sword. And he had proven himself to be bold. And clever. And strong. All were attributes her father admired in a man.

Ah, but the flag. Her father's pride and joy. This man had blatantly tried to make off with it. Being a thief would surely spell the doom of this arrogant intruder. Moreover, he was still in possession of the flag, clear admission of his guilt. That thought gave her assurance as she pressed the sword against her captive's back, gesturing for him to walk down the stairs.

"Aye, let us go." Now it was Caitlin who grinned self-assuredly. "Ye think ye be glib of tongue, laddie, but Ian MacLeod will soon hae ye speechless with fear."

Niall didn't give her any argument. Though he walked with a swagger, he couldn't fool himself. He was apprehensive about meeting the MacLeod, ceann tigh of his enemies. Warily moving down the stairs, he could only hope that he would get out of this nightmare with a whole skin. She had called him glib of tongue but he knew it would take a seanachaidh's skill to talk his way out of this one.

He darted a quick look sideways, thinking about escape, only to find that her eyes were steadily trained upon him. Lovely brown eyes that they were, they showed not even a trace of compassion. Were he to try to escape would she stab him? He wasn't certain, but didn't want to take a chance. Caitlin nic Ian was as strong-minded a lass as he had ever crossed paths with. And she was angry. Far better to take his chances with her father, he decided, viewing each step with trepidation.

Down, down, down. The distance to the MacLeod's chamber seemed nearly as great a distance as it had been to the MacLeod castle, Niall thought sourly. Then all of a sudden the ominous destination loomed all too clearly in his path. An awesome portcullis, which at the moment was as worrisome as that behind which the devil himself waited. Worse yet were the growling russet-hued wolfhounds that guarded the door. Bristling and baring their teeth, they gave warning of what they would do if he made a wrong move.

"They dunna seem to like ye," Caitlin pointed out, taking note of the largest dog's snarl.

"That's because they dunna know me yet," Niall shot back, hoping the dogs wouldn't bite. "Easy. Easy." He moved slowly, carefully, past the two animals, hoping that they had been fed. Nervously he brushed the flour off his garments.

"Or because they *do*," Caitlin retorted with mock sweetness, raising her hand to knock loudly upon the door.

A bellowed "Who is it?" thundered from the other side. "Who disturbs a mon's sleep?"

"Caitlin, Father. I hae trapped a ghost."

"What?" The door was yanked open and Niall found himself face-to-face with his fiercest enemy. A giant of a man who now looked him up and down assessingly. "Ach, he is no ghost."

"Nae, but he masqueraded as one," Caitlin answered, giving Niall a look that warned that he would soon be in dire trouble.

"Masqueraded?" The MacLeod's eyebrows shot up warningly.

"Aye, to get his hands on this." Reaching into Niall's shirt, she withdrew the fairy flag.

"Och!" Ian MacLeod yanked it from Caitlin's hand. His brows furled in barely suppressed rage, then blistering Niall with his gaze, he asked, "Why?"

In that moment Niall could picture himself hanging in chains from the MacLeod's dungeon wall until he was little more than bones. Still, he somehow kept his poise, despite the wolfhounds' growling. "For the sake of love," he blithely answered.

"Love?" Ian MacLeod's jaw stiffened, eyes narrowed to slits, taking on a look of stark coldness. His expression warned of danger if Niall did not respond quickly.

"The love I bear yer daughter, who I hae looked upon from afar for a long, long time." Taking Caitlin's hand, he squeezed her cold fingers so hard that she winced. "I thought to daringly remove the flag from its hiding place and give it into yer hands. I wanted to prove my bravery before asking for yer daughter's hand."

"Wha . . . ?" Caitlin tried to speak but her words came

out in a strangled gasp as she pulled her hand away. The liar!

Ian swore beneath his breath, then his words exploded the silence. "To lay hands on the fairy flag is the gravest misdeed a mon can do the clan."

"If so, then I am sorry." Niall answered, bowing humbly before the man he knew had his life in his hands. "But I meant no harm."

"Meant no harm, ye say. I tell ye it doesna matter. Ye transgressed." Reaching down, Ian MacLeod scratched each dog behind the ears, then returned his attention to Niall.

Man-to-man they stared at one another, each making their judgment. Niall could tell at once that Ian MacLeod was a harsh man, a fighting man, yet at the same time a man who would exhibit fairness if he thought him deserving.

"If I did, then I beg yer mercy," he said, looking Ian MacLeod directly in the eye, remembering that Ian MacLeod had spilled an ocean of MacDonald blood. Was his to be next?

"Mercy. Ha!" Having recovered her voice, Caitlin was scathing. "Ye planned to take away the very emblem of the MacLeod's strength and soul. The gravest ill ye could do to us, as my father says."

"I didna leave the castle wi' it," Niall insisted. That at least might save him.

"Because I wouldna let ye," she challenged, standing toe-to-toe and nose-to-nose with him.

"Ah, lass, had I wanted to flee wi' the flag I would hae done it. I didna want to." His voice was impassioned. "I repeat again, I didna take it from these walls. I but wanted to prove that I was cunning, and brave. A daring, though foolish act, but one tha' I dunna regret since it gave me a chance to get close to ye, lass."

"Close? Ha!" With a toss of her head, she exhibited her scorn. "I got close enough to you to know that ye smell of fish." She wrinkled her nose.

"Because I am a fishermon," he retorted, angry at her scorn. "An honest calling that ensures that all those, living comfortably within the castle eat well." Balling his hands into fists, he fought to control his temper. The lass had a viper's tongue and a stubbornness that clearly needed taming. Too bad he wouldn't be around long enough to get the chance.

"A fishermon?" Circling Niall several times, Ian MacLeod clucked his tongue. "Ye dunna look it." For a moment he seemed to be suspicious. "Ye seem to hae a fighting mon's strength."

Niall thought quickly. "I keep my arms strong by rowing and casting out lines. And by fighting wi' staffs wi' my brothers. Any mon has to be prepared."

"Ye dinna say." Ian MacLeod looked at Niall with a measure of respect. "And would ye then think yerself strong enough to fight a battle to prove yer innocence or guilt."

Niall answered quickly. "I would." There was a long pause as he gathered up his courage. "And would ye think yerself noble enough to keep the vow ye made?" he countered.

"Vow?"

"According to yer own words yer bonny daughter should be given to me as my wife, no matter if I am the winner—or loser—of this battle ye plan." Turning to Caitlin, he smiled, thinking all the while that her old scar-faced war horse of a father wouldn't dare kill his son-in-law. "Unless I hae miscalculated, I am the first mon to enter the castle since ye made yer vow. Am I not?"

Ian MacLeod nodded grimly. "Ye are."

"Nae!" Caitlin wrestled with the dilemma of her fate, feeling a fiercesome pressure pushing at her chest as her worst fear came true. For a moment she feared she couldn't breathe. "Father, ye wouldna. He is just a fishermon."

"Ah, but I would." Ian MacLeod's eyes glittered in the torchlight. "I warned ye, Caity. I put forth mon after mon of noble heritage, but ye goaded me into this, lass. Just remember." For the moment Niall's guilt was forgotten as the MacLeod seemed intent on proving a point to his daughter.

"I dunna care. I willna marry him if he wins a hundred combats." Folding her arms across her chest, she looked like defiance personified. "A fishermon is a fishermon and ne'er the mon for me. I refuse to marry him."

"Then ye would shame me, Daughter." The MacLeod slammed his fist into the palm of his hand to vent his annoyance. "As this mon has pointed out, I made a vow."

"But—"

"Hush. The MacLeod has spoken." Taking Niall by surprise, he plucked a sword from its resting place on the wall and threw it at him. If he was stunned by Niall's quick reflex action in catching it by the handle, he didn't show it. "So, tomorrow at the first light of day, ye will hae a chance to prove yerself to me, laddie. By combat it will be proven if ye are guilty or innocent of any misdeed."

A nerve in Niall's jaw ticked angrily. "If I am proven innocent I will hae for myself a bride, but if I lose?"

"So much the worse for ye," Caitlin replied with a toss of her head. "Mayhap ye should hae stuck to yer fish and not hae dallied where ye had no business."

"Aye, and mayhap I would hae done just that had I known the MacLeod's daughter was such a foul-tempered witch. After today I find I prefer the company of mackerel to ye lass."

"Ahhhhhhh!" Caitlin looked at her father, thinking that he would come to her aid verbally, but Ian MacLeod was smiling not angry.

Niall continued, whispering angrily. "I dunna want to marry ye, Caitlin MacLeod, any more than ye be wanting marriage with me." Was there another way out? Again he asked, "What is to be my fate if I lose?"

"Either way ye are considered betrothed to my daughter so that I can keep my vow. But if ye are guilty . . ." The verdict didn't need to be spoken aloud.

Niall understood only too well. "I willna lose." He dare not!

Ian raised his brows. "Then I welcome ye to the MacLeod clan with pride."

"Father!" Caitlin wanted to rage at him, plead with him, get down on her knees if it would do any good. The stubborn jaw of her father was held so rigidly set, however, that she knew he would not go back on his word.

"And so I am to be betrothed to a simple fishermon." It was the gravest insult, not to be borne. Even so, Caitlin knew she had no say. Men. They didn't understand one wit about a woman, she thought unhappily. All they knew was fighting and war. And because women didn't fight and kill they had no voice in their own lives. No power at all. It was a sobering admission, yet the way of things.

"Aye, because I hae declared it so." Again the MacLeod had spoken.

"As ye wish." Caitlin hung her head, then quickly raised it again. She turned the full venom of her anger on Niall. "But know this, fishermon. All the while I am watching this combat my father has commanded, I will be cheering on ycr opponent, no matter who he is." That said, she turned her back and, leaving Niall in the care of her father, stalked back up the stairs.

The loud thud of the door slamming awoke Shona from a peaceful sleep. Opening her eyes, she stared into the darkness. "Caitlin?" She propped herself up on one elbow, calling out again, "Caitlin?"

"Aye, 'tis me." The tone of her voice gave the gravity of her mood away.

"What's wrong, hinny?"

"F-F-Father!" She gasped the story between sobs. "I thought he was a ghost, but then I caught him trying to steal the flag and—"

"Steal the flag? Father?"

"Nae! Nae, the fishermon."

"Fishermon? What fishermon?" Thrusting aside the covers, Shona stood up. Walking over to Caitlin, she put her arm around her. "Come, sit down on the bed and tell me, hinny. Slowly. Calmly."

Caitlin moved quickly across the room, plopping down on the thick mattress. "I came upon a stranger in the tower. I thought him to be Colin."

"Thought him to be a ghost?"

Caitlin nodded. "He was covered from head to toe with flour. It was dark and I a foolish ninny."

"Foolish? Never." Shona sat beside her.

"Aye, I was, and he a rogue if ever there be one." It angered her as she thought about it all. How he must have been laughing at her all the while as she had prattled on and on about his being a ghost. All the while he had been planning on stealing the MacLeod's greatest treasure. "But he was nae a ghost. He was a thief."

"The flag!" Shona clutched at her sister's arm.

". . . Is safe, though I fear I cannot say the same for me." She took a deep breath. "Oh, Shona, Father has given me away." In as calm a manner as she could manage, Caitlin told the whole story.

"The stubborn old goat." Shona drew her legs up on the bed, hugging them tight as she asked, "Ach, but is he handsome?"

"The fishermon?" Though she hated to admit it even to herself, Caitlin found herself telling the truth. "Aye! Extremely. But I dunna care, Shona. I hae no liking for what is going on."

"Ah, but I think it sounds grand. A mon fighting for ye, Caity. What more could any woman want?"

She answered in one word. "Love." Leaning back on the pillows, she crossed her arms behind her head and gave the matter considerable thought. "I want a mon who loves me for myself, not because I'm the MacLeod's eldest daughter." Caitlin closed her eyes. Oh, if only the stranger were not just a fisherman looking to better himself by an advantageous marriage, she might have felt so differently. As it was, his intrusion into the castle and into her life promised to cause nothing but calamity.

Seven

The combat was to be held in the same field where games were often played. It was a level stretch of hard ground covered with a dusting of wild grass and surrounded by rocks upon which the spectators sat. Caitlin's heart was in her throat as she watched the two men file onto the field. The fisherman didn't have a chance, did he?

No. I am safe. The stranger who had pretended to be a ghost, *he* didn't have a chance, for he was to have a fiercesome opponent. Angus, a brawny young man who was well known for his prowess. Looking at him, Caitlin could see that he was bigger and more ominous in his appearance than the fisherman. It was only a matter of time until he had the intruder, who only knew nets and oars, begging for mercy on his knees.

Nor was Caitlin the only one of that opinion. She heard wagering going on, men in the crowd deciding a winner and placing bets on the outcome. Few chose the fisherman.

"It will be a slaughter," one man said loudly, an opinion shared by several of the others. Still, it didn't seem to daunt the intruder to the castle.

"For ye, lass." Raising his sword, he saluted her in acknowledgment that she was his lady and he was there to fight for her. An action that she promptly snubbed.

"Ye dinna hae a chance," she taunted, wondering why he didn't seem to realize that. Sauntering onto the field, he exhibited the boldness she was certain would soon be cowered. And oh, how she relished the sight of the arrogant interloper being brought to his knees. Marry her indeed!

Voices rose in a cheer as Niall and Angus took their places, removing their plaids and throwing them to the ground. Just as the warriors in battle did, they would fight nearly naked, and Caitlin blushed at the sight of the fisherman's tall, well-muscled body. She remembered what the women had whispered around the cooking fires, that the newcomer looked to be well endowed. Now that he was devoid of his garments their chatter had proven to be true. Not that Caitlin would admit that, however.

I won't even look at him, she thought stubbornly, only to go back on her word in the blink of an eye. Though she tried to force her gaze the other way, her eyes were drawn again and again to the fisherman. His skin was golden where it had been exposed to the sun, and she could only suppose that when he was out on his boat he rode the waves without his clothes. A strange thing to do, considering that it was often cold.

"He is a fine-looking mon," a young cousin sitting next to her cooed. "Look at those shoulders. At that chest. Those legs. And his . . ." Foolishly the girl twittered, but her chatter had drawn Caitlin's attention to the part of him that marked the fisherman, a male.

"Just looking at him is strangely exciting. Stirring," another cousin said with a sigh.

"Ha!" Caitlin pretended to disagree, but the harm was already done. She felt a stirring in her blood, a languid heat that brought forth a longing that shamed her. A maiden should never think lascivious thoughts, especially about such a man.

"That golden hair. I hae ne'er seen a lion, but I hae heard aboot them and would think he would resemble such a magnificent—"

"Oh, hush!" Poking her cousin in the ribs, Caitlin gave vent to her annoyance with it all. Well, all the silly swooning would soon be over when he proved himself a coward, handsome or not.

The eerie drone of the bagpipes silenced all talk as the two adversaries advanced, swords leveled. They bent and swayed in a grotesque dance. The air rang with the sound of blade on blade. It was a brutal fight. Grueling. Dangerous. Even so, Caitlin was surprised to see that the fisherman was making a good showing for himself. Certainly he was giving as good as he was getting. Though she wouldn't have admitted it, he was slowly earning her respect.

Well, perhaps I dinna wish him to lose too miserably after all . . . But lose he must, she amended her thoughts, grimacing as he narrowly ducked out of the way of his opponent's sword. For if he didn't she would soon find herself wed. And being a wife to such a man would be terrible. Wouldn't it? Nodding her head, she gave herself reassurance that it would. And all the while the battle raging on the field grew fiercer and fiercer.

The sun beat down full force as the two men lashed out at each other again and again. Sweat ran into Niall's eyes blinding him for an instant. Caitlin could nearly feel his pain as the tip of Angus's blade tore the flesh of his arm. Covering her mouth with her hand, she stifled her cry.

"So, Caitlin. It seems ye dunna dislike him so much after all," her cousin was quick to point out.

"I just dinna want him to be killed," she responded stiffly. "A long stay in the dungeon for him is all I desire." Or so she told herself. Then why was she gripping her hands so tightly together? Why did she gasp as Angus missed the fisherman's head by little more than a finger's length?

Niall's arm blazed with pain. Despite his torment, however, he used his wits. He pressed in, driving his brawny opponent back as he tried to maneuver him onto the rough ground and over the rocks. Niall plied him on the right side, then on the left, moving with the grace of a mountain cat.

"Look at him. He moves like some ancient god," Caitlin's

cousin proclaimed. It was obvious how much she was smitten.

"Luck. Sheer luck. That is all that it is." Even so, Caitlin was impressed, but suspicious as well. How was it possible for a man who made his living with a net to be able to counter Angus's attacks so skillfully? It was a matter she was determined to find out, she thought as she watched the combat proceed.

Niall pulled himself from the ground, keeping his eyes on his adversary's sword, feeling his head grow light as the blade whistled before him. He could feel his breath hammering inside his chest and knew that he was winded. His arm felt so heavy that it took great effort to lift it.

"Ye willna escape me so easily this time." Disappointed that his weapon had not drawn blood, Niall's foe threw himself upon him. Locked together in combat, the two men rolled upon the ground as the clansmen rumbled their excitement.

"BiGod! I had no idea the mon could fight. He's a natural born swordsman." Ian's eyes held a new respect.

Freeing himself from the large man's grip, Niall stood up. This time it was he who initiated the assault, diving for Angus's legs. With a sudden burst of strength, he tore the sword from his adversary's hand and hurled it away. Was the crashing in his ears coming from the onlookers or from his heart? He fought to catch his breath, certain that his lungs were so cramped there would be no room for any air.

Angus scrambled to retrieve his weapon. The sound of sword on sword rent the air as the two men renewed their furious battle, a test of strength, courage, and fortitude. Niall's aching eyes seemed to imagine three men at one time hurtling toward him, lunging, striking. Shaking his head, he sought to clear his vision as Angus poked out with the tip of his blade. Pain pierced Niall's shoulder. The warmth of his own blood seeped from the fresh wound in his arm, mingling with the first to run in a rivulet down his arm.

Angus was trying to maneuver him to the slope of the ground to gain advantage of footing, but Niall would have none of that. Over and over again he remembered the tales of prowess and how the heroes of old had won their battles, and he mimicked their daring.

"Perhaps this willna be a rout after all," a young boy shouted out.

"Look. Angus is getting angry. And when he does he sometimes loses his head."

Caitlin looked up, dismayed to see that it was true. Angus was brawny and strong for certain, but what he had in strength he lacked in brains. It was clear to see that the fisherman was easily outthinking him, goading him into foolish moves.

"Come on. Come on," Niall taunted, baiting his combatant as one might a bear. He had to win! He would win. For the sake of the MacDonald honor. For the sake of his own.

"Hmmmph." Again and again the large man lunged, his anger at being so easily thwarted making him careless. His senses honed by danger, his sword arm swinging forward, Niall blocked each thrust until with a sudden burst of strength he knocked his enemy's sword from his hand again.

Caitlin blinked her eyes, and in just that short span of time Niall had Angus on the ground, the blade of the sword pressed against his neck. The clansmen roared their excitement.

"Nae!" She couldn't believe it. Somehow she felt betrayed. By Angus. By her father. By all the ghosts and spirits of the MacLeod who had allowed this atrocity to occur. She wanted to rebel, to shout out, but all she could do was to sit there, stunned as she listened to her father's proclamation.

"As has been promised, the fisherman is declared innocent of any evil doing concerning the fairy flag."

His announcement was met with shouts and cheers, for there was none among them who did place value on a winner.

"And . . . and . . ." Ian MacLeod cleared his throat. "He
has won himself a very dear prize. The hand of my daughter,
Caitlin." The words were spoken. Caitlin's fate was sealed.

A soft, whispering breeze caressed Caitlin's face as she
stood atop the castle battlement wall-walk. She was going
to be married. Her father had publicly made the declaration.
To the victor came the reward. Still, she couldn't quite believe it. Belonging to someone else for the rest of her life
was an unnerving thought. To be married, to a man she
hardly even knew seemed so strange. Bothersome. Odd.
And yet that was the way of things. A woman's fate was
never in her own hands, but in the hands of those she loved
and trusted.

Father, how could ye? To him it was all so simple, just
like playing a chess game. He wasn't being hardhearted
about the matter; to the contrary he had told her a hundred
times or more that he wasn't at all happy about what he
had to do. It was just that he needed a successor to take
over as clan leader when he grew old and senile. If that
made her feel a bit like a human sacrifice, like little more
than a womb to breed the future MacLeod, well, again, that
was the way of clan life.

To tell the truth, despite her irritation at the situation,
Caitlin knew she could have fared worse. There were those
women who had been forced to marry weak men, old men,
ugly men, and fools. At least her future bridegroom was
none of these.

*Will I be happy? Can I learn to be content? Will I grow
to love my husband?* She pondered the questions she posed
to herself.

Love. Did it really exist or was it just a pleasant story
warbled by the bards? Was it just a dream that women succumbed to despite its impossibility? Or was it all a lie?

Caitlin's mother was impossible to talk with on the matter. She was always bitter on the subject. Angry. It was not all kisses and embraces, she had insisted. She had said that there were things a wife had to do that were less than enjoyable, but necessary if there were to be children.

"Men lust, women love," she had said over and over again. But was it true? Caitlin blushed as she remembered the vibrant stirrings she had felt deep within her at the sight of the fisherman's body. Stirrings she had not been able to control no matter how hard she tried. Even now, remembering, she felt her body come to life with a strange, tormented longing.

Oh, but he was a man who held the eye, she had to give him that. Strange that though he wore the same saffron dyed shirt as the other men, a similarly draped breacan sported, however, with a rakish air, he looked infinitely more dashing than the others. She thought him handsome, had to grudgingly admit that he was brave. But marry him?

Caitlin drew in a deep breath of fresh air, then let it out in a sigh. Just what did she think of her bridegroom-to-be? Her emotions were hard to define and were certainly confusing. She disliked the man, thought him a strutting rooster, did she not? No. If she were totally honest with herself she would have to admit that he kindled a host of sensations she never thought she would feel. Desire?

From what Caitlin had heard the women chatter about, she knew it to be so. Some talked of their husbands with awe, some in rapture, and there were others who spoke of hating the "duties" they were called upon to enact. Men could be tender, it seemed, or brutes. What would the tall, muscular tawny-haired fisherman be like?

"Caitlin." The voice was low, a husky familiar rumble.

"So, 'tis ye," she whispered without even turning around. "Did ye come here to gloat?"

"Gloat?" He laughed softly. "No. Just to appreciate the beauty you offer, soothing and stimulating to a man's eyes. And to talk."

"Talk?" Reaching up, she brushed her flaming red hair out of her eyes. "What could we possibly hae to talk about?"

"I can think of many things." He wanted to see her smile, hear her laugh. Instead, however, he contented himself with looking at her. She reminded him of a beautiful bird and he had no wish for her to elude him. If he moved closer, would she fly away?

"Such as our wedding?" At last Caitlin turned to him.

"Aye." Slowly he moved forward, longing to gather her into his arms. Under different circumstances, Niall suspected they might really have had a chance of being happy. "Caitlin."

Her hands stretched out as if to push him away were he to come too close. "Ye want to talk. We'll talk." Her face was as expressionless as a mask.

"I only wanted to say that it wasna my intent to make ye unhappy."

"It doesna matter. *I* do no' matter. Not to you, not to the MacLeod."

"Oh, but you do." He wanted to quickly heal the rift between them. It would make things so much easier.

"Then why do ye no' leave me alone?"

"Because . . ." He slowly moved toward her.

Her eyes blazed fire. "Ach, no! I willna believe yer lies. Ye came to steal the flag, laddie, no' to marry up wi' me. I caught ye and so ye concocted yer story." She paused, then added, "At least let's hae truth between us."

"Truth. Aye, I'll tell it plainly. I find ye very, very bonny, Caitlin. On that I dunna hae to lie." His eyes were bold as he assessed what soon would belong to him, at least until he left the MacLeod stronghold. "I look forward to our marriage and—"

"I dunna want to consummate our marriage." There, she had said it.

There was a long moment of silence as Niall thought the

matter out. Then he said gently, "If, as happens with maidens such as yerself, ye are afraid of what happens between a woman and a mon, I will make it a most pleasant encounter. I—"

"I am no' afraid. I just refuse to accept any mon against my will."

"I see." Her words were a devastating blow to his pride. "I'm no ogre, lass."

"Nae, ye are not. But neither am I some prize." She spoke honestly. "A woman wants to be wooed, not won in combat."

"Wooed?" There was something enticing about her wide, sensuous mouth. For just a moment all he could think about was kissing her. Would her lips be as soft as they looked?

"Wooed." The way he was gazing at her made her shiver. Hastily she turned her head. "Besides, I dunna even know yer name."

"My name is Niall." That much he could reveal.

"Niall." She liked the name. Somehow it seemed to suit him.

"Don't shut yer heart to me, lass." The way she kept looking away was annoying. Gently grasping her by the shoulders, he turned her around. For one timeless moment they stared at each other, both wondering how just a look could be so exciting.

Without a word, Niall caught a fistful of her long fiery hair and wrapped it around his hand, drawing her closer. With the tips of his fingers he traced the line of her cheekbones, the shape of her mouth, the line of her brows.

"Give it a chance, Caitlin . . ." His face hovered only inches from her own. "Give me a chance." His appraising gaze seemed to cherish her, his words mesmerized her, and though Caitlin knew all the reasons she should pull away, she somehow did not. Then all at once it was too late.

At first he simply held her, his hands exerting a gentle pressure to draw her into the warmth of his embrace. Then before Caitlin could make a sound, his mouth claimed hers in a gentle kiss, one completely devastating to her senses. She was engulfed in a whirlpool of sensations. Breathless, her head whirling, she allowed herself to be drawn up into the mists of the spell. New sensations clamored within her. All she could think about was that her fantasies were right. A kiss could be most enjoyable.

Leaning against him, Caitlin savored the feel of his strength, dreamily she gave herself up to the fierce sweetness of his mouth, her lips opening under his as exciting new sensations flooded through her. She was aware of her body as she had never been before, relished the emotions churning within her.

Niall's lips parted the soft, yielding flesh beneath his, searching out the honey of her mouth. With a low moan, he thrust his fingers within the soft, silken waterfall of her hair, drawing her ever closer. Desire choked him, all the hungry promptings of his fantasies warring with his reason. His lips grew demanding, changing from gentleness to passion as his hands moved down her shoulders and began to roam at will with increasing familiarity. More than anything in the world he wanted to make love to this young woman. If there was to be a wedding between them, he wouldn't agree to keeping their union celibate. Only the village simpleton would strike such a bargain.

"If it's wooing that ye want, then I agree," he whispered. "And I promise to hae ye cooing like a dove in no time."

"Cooing?" Caitlin stiffened, remembering that she was the MacLeod's daughter. Not some village wench to tumble. "Let me go!" she commanded.

"Let you go?" He did, with a sudden step backward that nearly made her stumble.

Caitlin was angry, and thus she threw the first insult that she could think of at his head. "Fishermon! I wilna let ye e'er touch me!"

"Because ye think yerself so high and mighty?" Niall bit

his lip against the words he longed to say, that his lineage was every bit as good as hers, perhaps better, since he was a MacDonald. Instead, he said simply, "Well, there will come a time when ye will hae to step down from yer pedestal and walk among the common folk."

Oh, how she riled him. There were hundreds of pretty young women in the Highlands, yet somehow at this moment she was the only one he wanted. Because she was playing hard to get? Perhaps. Niall was used to women throwing themselves into his arms. Well, he would have this lass begging for his kisses, too. Soon.

"And become a fishermon's wife, weaving nets?" Caitlin affected a haughty air. "I think not."

And *I* think—"

Niall was interrupted before he was able to give her the scolding she deserved. A young man had come upon them, informing him that the MacLeod desired an audience with him.

"Dunna leave just yet." Caitlin followed after him as he descended the stairs, knowing full well what her father wanted to talk about. The wedding. She wanted to hear, wanted to know what was going to come, but knew that she would not be consulted in any way. It was as if she were invisible. Inconsequential. That did not mean she could not eavesdrop as soon as the door behind her father and her future husband was closed, however. Putting her ear to the keyhole, she listened.

"There is much I like about you. I hae need of such in my clan," she heard her father say. *"All my daughters are bonny lassies. But* women *after all. Being my son-in-law will gi' ye a measure of importance."*

Ha, Caitlin thought. Importance that will soon go to his head. Having been just a fisherman, she doubted that this Niall would be able to handle being a man of influence. Well, she would keep him in line.

"My only hope of carrying out my line is through grand-

sons, so I am hoping that ye will be quick about . . ." There
was the sound of ribald laughter.

"Father!" she breathed, blushing to the roots of her hair.
Men. They were all alike, thinking of nothing but what went
on under the covers.

*"I'll put it to ye bluntly. One of the terms of the marriage
contract is that ye gi' me grandsons right away. If ye be
unable . . ."*

*"Ye hae it on my word that I will most gladly gi' ye a
grandchild right away."*

"Ach!" Caitlin covered the gasp with her hand. How
could he? How could her father be so crude. As if what he
was negotiating was little more than the usual kind of business. He was talking about the use of her body as if talking
about the use of his lands. How could she ever forgive him?

The usual haggling followed and the cleric sent in to draw
up the contract. It specified the bride's dowry, several rich
acres of pastureland between the two strongholds. Land
made fertile with the blood of the clan in their fight against
the MacDonalds. Ian in turn asked for the use of Niall's
fleet of fishing boats, insisted on being given one out of
every five fish that were caught, and requested that Niall
lend a fighting hand whenever there was need.

"All is agreed," Caitlin heard her "bridegroom" say.

*"Then the banns will be posted on the next three successive Sundays. In the meantime there will be a celebration.
Feasting. Dancing. Drinking."*

"To celebrate my servitude," Caitlin said aloud. Well, let
them think that all was said and done. They would soon
find out that things were not always as easy as they at first
appeared.

Eight

The MacLeod clan had gone all out for the festivities that evening. The large hall was bathed in firelight and candle glow, from the planked floor to the high, lofty ceiling. Flames in the vast hearth danced about spewing tongues of red and yellow, illuminating the clan banner hanging proudly for all to see. Rushes and herbs—basil, balm, camomile, costmary, and cowslip—had been freshly strewn on the floor for the occasion. The walls of the castle were ornamented with hanging objects and artifacts—shields, swords, dirks, and clay'mors—which told of the MacLeod bravery.

Tables covered with platters and bowls were nearly sagging under the weight of the food piled high: wild duck with wine sauce, smoked haddock, roast grouse with sprigs of heather, roast venison, pickled herring, boiled goose eggs, beet root salad, curds, wild carrots, honey cakes, and wild raspberries. Barley broth bubbled noisily in a cauldron over the fire, its steam giving off an aroma that heightened appetites, as did the savory odor of roasting meat permeating the air. Platters were artfully arrayed with fruits and vegetables in great variety. Red heather and ropes of laurel hung from wall and ceiling alike and combined their fragrance with the tantalizing aromas of the betrothal feast. A celebration Ian had promised, and indeed that was the case.

A raised dais of stone ran the full length of the hall, across from the fireplace upon which many of the guests sat. Ian MacLeod sat in one of the massive chairs at a table placed across from the others. Raised at a lofty height by means of a platform, he looked awesome as he peered down at the assemblage. Extra trestle tables and several benches had been assembled to accommodate the overflow of clansmen. Niall sat to the left of the MacLeod; the vacant chair to his right was unquestionably for the bride-to-be. A bride who was still conspicuous by her absence.

Where was she? Why wasn't she here? Niall was impatient. He watched as Ian MacLeod was served the hero's portion, the first cut of meat, a gesture to show him to be the bravest of the clansmen and to assure that his status was noted by all present. As Niall drank and supped, he looked at the door from time to time, but his staring didn't bring Caitlin into the room any sooner.

She wouldn't dare be conspicuous by her absence. Or would she? The longer he sat staring at the door the more he drank, and the more he drank the more certain he became that he was about to be snubbed.

"Oh, no! I willna let her." Bolting up from his chair, he made his way to the door. He would find her. Even if he had to search the entire castle. Find her and bring her here. If he had to carry her into the hall kicking and screaming, he would make certain she obeyed.

Caitlin was at the moment taking plenty of time readying herself. And why not? She was in no hurry to go to a celebration that in her heart emphasized her doom.

Caitlin plundered her large wooden trunk and pulled several items of clothing from the pegs on the wall, determining to find just the right garments to wear tonight. Indeed, she would clothe herself with as much care as if she were going into battle. Perhaps in a way she was, she mused.

"My old threadbare undertunic," she decided aloud, and a dun-colored arasaid, the one Shona had woven for her a long time ago on the large loom in the ladies' hall. Plain garments. If her father was going to marry her to a fisherman, she would look like a fisherman's wife.

She was expert in draping the saffron-and-blue striped arasaid around her slim body, tucking it around her hips, fitting it snugly around her waist with a brown leather belt. Yards and yards of cloth fell in graceful folds just below her ankles, then looped up to cover her shoulders like a shawl. She secured it with a brooch, a handworked gold circle with intricate scrollwork.

Observing herself in a long steel mirror, she smiled as she stared back at her reflection with a certain amount of gratification. If she had decided to look like a fisherman's wife, however, she did not want to smell like one. Picking up a small packet of flowers and herbs that Shona always used in her bath, she made the decision to be frivolous on this occasion.

Since it was the third day of the week it would be the women's turn to bathe. And since everyone would be at the celebration she would have the room all to herself. In truth, perhaps she would feel much better once she had the warm cocoon of water surrounding her. It would relax her and give her time to think things out, to get used to the idea of having a husband. And with that thought she grabbed an old woolen tartan and made her way to the bath house.

Pushing open the thick wooden portal, Caitlin was grateful to see that all of the six large wooden tubs that studded the rush-strewn floor were empty. She would have the seldom granted opportunity of privacy. A well for washing or drinking water was available at the central drawing point, and thus she busied herself with procuring a plentiful supply, filling the buckets and heating the water in the large iron pots that were perched over an open fire. Struggling under the heavy burden of the large cauldrons, she nonetheless managed to carry them to one of the tubs, completing the job of filling her bath. Turning around, lifting the skirts of her undertunic up to her knees in preparation of disrobing, she heard the door creak. The sudden, unwelcome feeling that someone was staring at her crept over her. Whirling around, she was startled to find herself face-to-face with *him* again.

"So here you are," he said tonelessly, shutting the door behind him.

"Here I am indeed," she snapped, holding the tartan protectively up to her bosom to hide the outline of her breasts beneath the thin linen. "Tell me, are ye here to 'haunt' the bath house?" she asked, making reference to his masquerade as a ghost, "or to try and steal the flag again?"

The soft orange-yellow glow of flickering torchlight illuminated the room and gave her a clear view of his manly form. Hardly the body of a ghost. Her eyes took in his broad shoulders and muscled arms.

"I came looking for ye!"

"Oh?" She pretended not to know how late the hour was or that she was remiss in being absent from the hall. "Well, as ye can see I was about to take a bath."

"A bath. Now."

"Now!"

So that was the game she was playing. Well, Niall thought, two could play at the same game. "Then so will I." That said, he deliberately began to strip off his garments.

Soon he was naked to the waist, wearing only a *breacan*, revealing his manly torso and the thick wisp of dark golden hair covering his chest. Only the wounds on his arm marred his perfection.

For a long moment all Caitlin could do was stare. Then she found her voice. "It is the women's turn to bathe."

He smiled. "A moot point, particularly since we are all alone. And formally betrothed." He took a step forward. She backed away and looked toward the door.

"That doesna give ye any liberties, at least yet." The only way out was to go past him and this she did not want to do. She wanted to maintain as great a distance as possible between them.

"Nae, not yet." *But just wait a while,* his hot, burning eyes seemed to say.

"Not ever," Caitlin taunted. "I will marry ye because I must, but I am not a brood mare." She tossed her head, sending her fiery hair flying about her shoulders.

"Ye must want children, lassie." The idea of a MacLeod bearing his child made him smile. What magnificent irony. Almost as good as bringing back the fairy flag.

"Someday . . ."

In the silence that pervaded the room each one was conscious of the other, the subject of babies reminding each of them of how the seed was planted.

"I want to make love to ye, Caitlin. I want ye to want that, too."

She was aware of him in every nerve, pore, and bone in her body. "So that ye can easily fulfill the terms of the marriage contract?"

"Nae. Because ye are like a living dream. So very desirable."

He could not keep his eyes from the cleft between her breasts that showed just slightly when she bent over, nor could he keep from watching the sway of her hips as she moved. In a flickering glance he took in everything about her.

By all the saints he unnerved her most definitely, confused her with contradicting emotions. In the end it was fear that won out, however. Caitlin started to turn away, but just at that moment he reached out and captured her hand. Bending low over it, he pressed his warm mouth into the palm in a gesture he'd heard was used at the Scottish court.

She pulled her hand away with great haste. "Don't . . ." It made her feel too fluttery. Too vulnerable to the feelings he stirred within her. She found herself remembering the pressure of those warm, knowing lips against hers.

The soft material of her tunic tightened across her firm breasts. Niall fought against the urge to force her in his arms. It would only goad her resentment. Instead, he chose a more gentle kind of persuasion. "I'm a fishermon, not a bard. I know not any flowery words that will make ye fall in love with me. All I can do is speak the truth and hope yer heart will listen. Don't turn yer back on me, lass. Gi' me a chance." An impassioned plea. Then he slipped his garments back on and disappeared through the door.

Oh, but he was the canny one, she thought. Even so, the wall she had built around her heart crumbled just a little. Strange, but she hummed to herself as she quickly bathed then as soon as she was dressed, she slipped through the doorway and down the circular staircase that led to the second floor.

Boisterous laughter and mumbled voices stilled as the crowd caught sight of her. When Caitlin entered, everyone turned. The whispered gasps sounded like the rustling wind but she ignored them, making her way to the table.

"Daughter, were ye already married I would gi' yer husband my approval to beat ye," Ian grumbled beneath his breath. "Ye shame him and ye shame me by looking poverty stricken."

"And ye shame me by this mockery of a marriage," she retorted. Even so, she felt a small twinge of guilt. Perhaps the fisherman was right. Perhaps she should give him a chance, albeit a small one.

Caitlin was quiet as cups were filled to the brim with fiery whiskey. Tankards were passed among the revelers again and again. Dogs snapped at the table scraps tossed to them, fighting now and again over a tasty morsel.

The aroma of fruit-decorated bannocks, baked specially for the occasion, wafted in the air as they were passed around, but Niall had lost his appetite. He wished the evening would end, that he could take her by the hand and lead her away from this melee. There were many questions he wanted to ask, many things to be said, he to her and she to him.

"Aren't you hungry?" Caitlin's tone was gentle, showing an unusual caring as she turned to Niall.

"I've already eaten too much." The truth was that he was starved for much more than food. She was so lovely in the candlelight. He wanted to touch her again as he had in the bath house and was afforded that opportunity when she picked up a scone and handed it to him. He took her small gift, their fingers brushing in a gentle caress, one that sparked a flame deep within him.

Caitlin's sparkling eyes met his over the rim of her cup as she sipped her ale. He regarded her so intently. She wished she could read his mind. The unhappy look upon his face nearly made her feel sorry for him. Nervously she tugged at her brooch, wondering if he had changed his mind about marrying her. She had given him quite a time. And after all, at least he was handsome. She could have done worse. Glancing at him out of the corner of her eye, she began to see her betrothed in a whole different light.

Amidst the candle glow and firelight, the bard stood and began strumming the strings of his harp. He sang a droning, seemingly endless account of the MacLeod ancestry and a lavish praise of the clan, which usually held Caitlin in rapt attention but now caused her to be anxious for its end. She had other things on her mind. Like getting to know her bridegroom for one thing. It suddenly struck her that she knew nothing about him at all.

The ale she sipped relaxed her, but when she looked in her groom's direction she felt a mild anxiety. What did she really know about this man who was to become her husband? As if sensing her searching eyes, he looked again in her direction and she could tell that he was troubled, too. Was he wondering the same things she was wondering.

What will it be like to share my life with this man? Would she enjoy his lovemaking and moan with pleasure at his touch? What would she experience in the years that lay ahead? With a sigh, she turned her attention back to the bard, closing her eyes, her mind gently drifting with thoughts of what was to come. At last the song ended and the men clapped and roared their approval.

Grudgingly Niall joined in, remembering all the while that with each MacLeod victory had come a MacDonald defeat and MacDonald death. How then could he even pretend to agree to this farce of a wedding? Because the woman was beautiful and he lusted for her? Though he knew this to be partly true, he denied it to his conscious mind. It was to get his hands on the flag and only that.

"Caitlin MacLeod is a shrew. I will be well rid of her when I leave this castle," he said to himself. Yet at the same time he felt a conflicting emotion. A strange sense of loss for what might have been had they each been other than who they were.

The room became silent as Ian MacLeod stood up. "As ye know, we're gathered tonight to make celebration." He took Caitlin's hand, gently pulling her to her feet. "My daughter will gi' her hand in marriage to Niall, the fishermon. A fine and brave lad as ye hae all seen."

Caitlin looked at the tawny-haired man, expecting him to smile at her. She was met by a cold stare and could only wonder why. Was he then marrying her only for the sense of power being the MacLeod's son-in-law brought? Were his tender words in the bath house nothing but words then. Empty words? For the first time in her life her confidence slipped. Though usually sure of herself, she felt that trait no longer. Sweet Jesu, what had she gotten herself into with her stubbornness?

Goblets, tankards, and platters were cleared away. Benches were pushed back, the trestle tables folded and placed against the wall in preparation for dancing. The pipes began their keening, a familiar tune Caitlin recognized at once. First the men danced alone, a rousing dance of high, kicking feet then the women joined in, choosing partners for a spirited reel which set every foot tapping.

The great hall was a din of laughing, talking, accompanied by the drone of skirling pipes and the thumping feet of dancers. But Caitlin had no heart for the revelry. For the first time in her life she sincerely wished she could make herself invisible—flee the hall and the man who put her emotions into such violent turmoil.

Nine

Darkness was gathering under the high, lofty ceiling. Shadows hovered in the corners and behind the massive pillars of the room like eerie spirits waiting to pounce. The flames engulfing the huge logs in the hearth sputtered and burned low. One by one the smoking candles and torches that had once brightened the hall flickered, hissed, and then died out.

The hour was growing late. The women had retired with the small children, leaving the men alone with their drinking. Very few guests lingered at the trestle tables. Watching and waiting, Niall thought to himself that if he were patient, if he lingered in the hall, eventually the opportunity would arise to once again get his hands on the fairy flag.

"Just a little longer . . ." he murmured, then raising a mug of whiskey to his lips, he tried to relax as he waited it out, tried to remove Caitlin MacLeod from his mind.

One slim, haughty red-haired lass was not going to get the best of him. He'd prove to her just how little he cared. He'd avoid that often-frowning miss, pretend she was as invisible as a ghost whenever he was forced to be in her company. Aye, that he would. He'd bite his tongue before he gave her one kind word. He would be damned before he'd look her way. He'd hurry and be done with this business of the fairy flag and return to the MacDonald Hall without another thought about her.

"So, the happy bridegroom."

Niall was startled as one of the men came up behind him, a tall dark-haired youth with the look of a fighter about him. "Aye, the happy bridegroom," he answered, trying to sound enthusiastic. All the while he was envisioning his "betrothed" in his mind as if she still sat beside him, her nose at that lofty angle, her flaming hair tumbling down her back in thick waves. He had always told himself that women were as plentiful as waves in the sea. But no one was like Caitlin MacLeod. Niall leaned his elbows on the table, wanting to be alone.

Solitude was not to be his. "Jamie is my name." The young man plopped down on the chair that Caitlin had vacated.

"Niall."

"I know." There was a sparkle in Jamie's eye. "And I know just what ye are contemplating."

"Oh?" For a moment Niall was worried. There were some who were said to have the fey. Hopefully this man wasn't among them.

"Ye think to gain power on Skye by mating wi' the MacLeod's daughter. But it willna work." The expression on Jamie's face was smug.

"Ye dunna say." At that moment Niall thoroughly disliked the other man. He knew his type. A man with an inflated sense of himself. "And just why would that be?" He tried to make the question sound casual, tried to hide his aversion to the clansman.

"Ye willna be accepted. Not really." He sniffed disdainfully. "Once a fishermon, always a fishermon." Without even noticing Niall's look of anger he rattled on. "So ye see, ye hae tied yerself to that hellion for naught."

"That hellion, as ye call her, will soon be my wife." Niall's eyes glittered a warning. "I would caution ye to hold yer tongue."

"Well, I'll be . . ." Jamie threw back his head and

laughed. "Ye must be daft, laddie. Ye are taken wi' the stubborn lass."

Taken with her? Niall shook his head, denying the truth, but heaven help him it was true.

"Because she doesna want to be yours. The forbidden fruit is always sweeter."

A muscle tightened in Niall's jaw. His eyes were cold. "And the grapes a man canna claim are always sour." He took another gulp of his whiskey, suddenly putting two and two together. "She didna want ye, did she?"

The barb struck home. "Caitlin MacLeod is a fool."

"Or as wise as the Brieve who gives out the laws." Now it was Niall's turn to chuckle.

Jamie pursed his lips in anger. Raising his fist, he looked as if he might lash out, but with a smirk he merely said, "The laugh will be on ye, fishermon, for getting far, far more than ye bargained for." That said, he left in a huff.

More than I bargained for? Niall imagined for a moment Caitlin MacLeod lying naked in her bridal bed. Strange how he'd never even contemplated marrying before, had always thought marriage a curse. He must be bewitched. "Aye much more . . ." For just a moment he nearly forgot just why he had come to the MacLeod stronghold. Forgot the anger between his clan and hers. Then, all too quickly, reality pushed away his lustful fantasies.

Rising to his feet, he strode up and down the hall like a prowling wolf, waiting and watching as one by one the men departed for their chambers. Lingering behind, Niall watched stealthfully as the lights were extinguished, leaving the castle in near darkness. Brushing his long hair over his shoulder, he moved toward the door with all the furtiveness of his desperation.

He'd get himself in the tower room as quickly as possible. How he hoped that the flag had been put back in the same place. If Caitlin had hidden it somewhere else he would just have to tear the castle apart until he found it. Looking from side to side, Niall cautiously made his way up the stairs, little realizing that he was being watched.

"Just as I thought . . ." She had hoped she was wrong, but as Caitlin watched Niall's assent to the tower room, his own actions fiercely condemned him. "The villain!"

She was stung with a mixture of anger and sadness. For just a moment she had actually thought that there was hope for them in this travesty of a marriage. Now she knew she was wrong. He only wanted one thing from the MacLeod stronghold and that something wasn't her.

"He is a thief!" she gasped. And what else? What prompted him to this deceitful action? She could only wonder as she watched in outraged silence, then stealthfully followed him.

Fumbling around in the dark, Niall cursed as he anxiously searched the tower room for the flag. If he were caught he had little doubt that this time it would mean his life. A man could only talk himself out of trouble once. There would be no second battle to redeem himself. Ian MacLeod would have his hide. He would—

Niall heard a noise behind him, but not soon enough to move aside before he was jumped from behind. For just a moment he was held immobile by his assailant, then in a burst of strength he got the upper hand.

"Aha. Ye had me, but now I hae ye!"

Caitlin opened her mouth to curse him, but words would not come. She was winded. Her heart beat painfully in her breast, and she couldn't breathe. Nevertheless she struggled fiercely.

"Stop yer fighting or BiGod I will—" In that moment Niall grabbed hold of his attacker's wrists. Small wrists. Fine-boned. Though it was dark, he knew. "Caitlin."

She somehow forced herself to answer. "Aye, it's me."

"Following me like a shadow."

"Because I knew ye couldna be trusted." There was a tone of disappointment in her voice. "Oh, how could ye? And after Father gave ye a second chance."

Her criticism stung him, as did the sudden slap to his cheek as he freed her arms. Wordlessly Niall rubbed his face. "I hae my reasons, Caitlin." Oh, damn the lass. He was incensed that she had once again so thoroughly hindered his plans.

"Reasons? Well, they will be interesting to hear, do ye ken?"

He did understand. All too well. It made Caitlin MacLeod very dangerous to his well-being at the moment. All she had to do now was call out and bring the house down upon his head and he would find himself food for the gulls. But there was a way to ensure that he would be safe. All he had to do was put his hands around her throat and squeeze.

Silence her. Silence her forever. She is the only person blocking your victory and escape.

Slowly he brought his hands up, then quickly let them fall to his side. No, he couldn't kill her.

She is my enemy. A MacLeod. Her father has given orders that have sent dozens of MacDonalds to their death. And yet that didn't matter. All he knew was that he couldn't harm a hair upon her lovely head. Even so, that didn't keep him from threatening.

"I should strangle ye!"

Caitlin jumped back. "Do and my father and the others will hunt ye down like a dog."

"No doubt they would. But it wouldna bring ye back to life." He shook his head. "Ah, Caitlin lass . . ." Oh, but she smelled so good. Like spices mixed tantalizingly with flowers.

"Ye didna want to marry me." Strange how that stung her pride despite her protestations about matrimony herself. "Did ye?"

Wisely Niall didn't answer.

"Yer fine story to my father was naught but a foul lie, just as I knew all along. Well, it will soon be told to all and then ye will be punished just as ye should be."

"Nae!" Once again Niall raised his hands, the realization that he must silence her foremost on his mind. As his eyes held and locked with Caitlin's, however, he knew the futility of even contemplating the act. "Do wi' me what ye will, I canna harm ye."

For just a moment she was shaken. There had been something in his eyes when he had looked at her. A gentleness, a look of caring. Could it be? She told herself that it could not. The fisherman was nothing but an opportunist whose presence here was disruptive and dangerous. Still, she said, "It seems that ye can not." At least she could give him that. "And I will remind Father of that when he decides upon yer punishment." Which she knew well would be to languish in the oubliette, a dungeon within a dungeon where the unfortunate prisoner had just sufficient room to lie in complete darkness. A custom the Scots had learned from the French long ago. There he would slowly die of starvation with no hope of rescue. A gruesome end.

"Ah, ye will speak to yer father on my behalf. Then most sincerely I thank ye." Niall mockingly bowed, all the while masking his apprehension. Oh, but she would stir up a bee's nest down below. The entire castle would be up in arms when she sounded the alarm. Unless he silenced her. Why then was he merely standing by like a suicidal fool? Why didn't he at least tie her up. Gag her. Ensure her silence. Why didn't he—

As the door burst open any action was quickly out of his hands. "What is going on up here?" Ian MacLeod held a torch aloft in his hands. Suspiciously he looked first at Caitlin, then at Niall. Niall realized in that moment that it was possible the MacLeod had been testing his loyalty. Blindly he might have walked into a trap. "Well, Daughter?"

Tell him. Tell him that the man he so heartlessly betrothed me to is obviously a danger to the clan. Tell him that you found him with the flag. Tell him. A myriad of emotions coursed through Caitlin's body as she looked her father right in the eye. She opened her mouth to tattle, nearly choking as she said instead, "He . . . he . . ." A cry rose up in her soul and she started to condemn Niall but ended up whispering, "We were . . . were doing a bit of kissing, Father."

"Kissing?" His thick brows shot up in surprise.

"That is what those who are betrothed to be married do, isn't it?" For the life of her, Caitlin would never understand why she had lied for the fisherman, but she had. And in so doing had sealed her own fate lest she be found out to be a deceiver.

Ian was pleased. "Aye. Aye."

Wordlessly Niall played along with the charade, putting his arm around Caitlin and drawing her close.

"Ach, they say that a threesome is a bother, especially when one is the father," Ian said with a wink. Hurriedly he headed for the door, talking more to himself than to them. "I knew it would happen if ye but allowed yerself. I knew it, Caity." He was decidedly jovial as he bounded from the room.

"Why?" It was the only word that escaped from Niall's lips as the door closed behind the MacLeod. Why had she shielded him? He had been caught trying once again to steal the flag, and although he hadn't actually pilfered it, she knew. She knew. Then why? "Ye lied for me, lass. Tell me why."

"I dunna know," she whispered. And she didn't. Surely it didn't make any sense.

"Is it possible that ye care for me then, at least a little?" Niall asked, his ego bolstered by the act.

"Nae!" And just to prove it she reminded him that his fate was still in her hands. Were she to change her mind he might still find himself languishing in the dungeon. "And I will tell if you e'er try to take the flag again." She pointed toward the door. "Go, and remember I will be watching ye."

* * *

Niall lay in bed staring up at the ceiling as he mulled over a dozen things in his mind, foremost the MacLeod's daughter's last words to him. "Go, and remember I will be watching ye."

Watching! The very idea of being spied upon like a naughty boy angered him. He was one of the mighty MacDonalds, the most powerful, widespread, and ancient of all the Highland clans. The MacDonalds had ruled the Highlands as Lords of the Isles for nearly four centuries. Had the English defeated the Stewart King James III, the MacDonalds would have commanded the Kingdom of Scotland itself. How then could he allow some slip of a lassie to threaten him? And yet . . .

His annoyance at the situation quickly cooled as he remembered that she could have so easily betrayed him to her father. Just one word, one hint, and he would have found himself trussed up like a goose ripe for plucking. Instead, she had covered for him and told her father that the two of them had more amorous things in mind. Did he?

Yes. He was taken with the MacLeod woman. She was bold, beguiling, and beautiful. Unfortunately she was also a distraction to his purposes. He must ignore her, thrust her into a part of his brain where he would not be tempted. He had to be aware of his purpose here at all times and keep an arm's length away from the girl.

Alas, it was an easy vow to whisper but a difficult one to keep. The moment he closed his eyes her image danced about in his brain teasing him like an aphrodisiac. He remembered the way her breasts had felt as she had brushed against his chest, the way her fiery hair tumbled around her shoulders, the way her eyes glittered when she was angry. He remembered the way—

Niall sat up in bed with a start. What was happening to him? When had it happened. Worse yet, how was he going to control it? What exactly was he going to do? Was he going to ignore the lass or take advantage of being betrothed?

Usually Niall tried to avoid searching his soul, fearing an inward look at what drove him on. Now, however, he thought it wise to take time to think. Really think.

What are you to do about Caitlin MacLeod?

Slowly his thoughts gained coherence as he sorted out his emotions. He had come to the MacLeod stronghold with but one thought in mind, to steal the fairy flag so that he could increase his esteem and usefulness to his clan. How was he ever to suspect that such a simple mission could be so complicated by his feelings. Feelings he was not quite sure he could really identify.

Again Niall asked himself, *What am I to do about Caitlin MacLeod?*

The creaking of the door put aside that question for the moment as Niall realized he was no longer alone. Staring through the darkness, he sought a glimpse of the intruder. Who was it? Someone who posed a danger? Just in case, Niall reached for the sword he had sheathed beside the bed.

"Who is there?"

Had he expected an answer it wasn't forthcoming. Instead, he heard a rustle of cloth and the soft tread of steps as the "visitor" sped away. The escape was not hasty enough, however.

"Caitlin!" Like an enchanting ghost she had come to his room, and although Niall could only assume that she had come there to spy, her late-night visit nonetheless left him even more confused about his feelings.

Ten

Clouds and sunlight competed over the green valley. Ian MacLeod had two full days of festivities awaiting the clan as part of the betrothal ceremony. Games. Hunting. It appeared, however, that nature might not be entirely cooperative.

"Oh, who cares. Mayhap 'tis a sign."

Opening the shutter of her small bedchamber window, Caitlin peered out through the slits, gazing at the sky, thinking how the day matched the bleakness of her mood. Last night to save the fisherman's life she had lied. A sorry thing to do to her own clan no matter the reason.

"May they all forgive me!"

Her eyes touched upon her clansmen and women as they went about their morning chores. The inner courtyard rang with the sound of women's laughter and the chatter of the men as they went about the preparations for the day's events. They were happy. Content. Looking forward to the marriage that would likely bring forth the new chieftain for the clan. But how happy would they be if they knew what Caitlin knew?

"Och!"

Surely it was a calamity, one which had haunted her all through the night. She hadn't slept a wink. Acutely conscious of the fact that Niall was situated just down the hall from her own chamber she had listened to each and every sound outside in the hall, fearful that he might try to steal the flag again. At last, returning to the tower, she had taken the flag from its hiding place and brought it down to her chamber where it would be safe. Tucking it amongst her belongings, she had returned to her bed only to toss and turn. She'd made so much noise in fact that she was certain poor Shona's slumber had been disturbed.

Get a hold on yerself, lassie, she scolded silently, still caught up in her guilt. "Stop wondering what might happen." It would only bring her more frustration. The lie was told. It was over and done with. All she could do was to keep her eye on the fisherman and make certain that no further mischief would be done.

And go on with the wedding? How could a woman be married to a man she did not trust? In anger she stripped off her sleeping tunic and flung it across the room. A comb and the pillow followed. Oh, how could she have been such a fool as to lie to her father, especially for the fisherman?

"Fie, Sister, ye would hae the room in a shambles. I dinna ken what is the matter wi' ye. Canna ye not even let us hae order for just a few wee 'oors this morn?" Shona's voice matched her scolding words as she bounced from the bed to retrieve Caitlin's things. Shona was the tidier of the two and could not stand a mess.

"I'm sorry . . ."

"Och, so he's gotten under yer skin more than I realized. I should hae known." Shona clucked her tongue in sympathy.

Caitlin sighed, turning her back on her sister as she dressed in a long saffron-hued shirt and a loincloth. "I dunna ken what ye mean," she said defensively.

"Aye, ye do. I know what's wrong, Caity."

"Ye canna." Caitlin kept her eyes averted from her sister. Somehow the honey-haired girl seemed always to be able to see into her sister's heart and mind. Caitlin could not afford that now.

"I do. Ye're disappointed that he's not some noble tanist

or chieftain." Gently touching her shoulder, Shona turned Caitlin around to face her, looking deeply into her eyes. "But oh, e'en if he were, ye could not hae married a man who could equal him for looks."

"Nae, it was the mattress, that's all. It's lumpy and needs to be restuffed and I . . . I didna get a wink of sleep all night."

"I dunna imagine ye did." Playfully she tugged at Caitlin's hair in rebuke, stifling a giggle.

"Shona! Dunna think that I—that I . . ." Caitlin sighed, hurriedly nodding. "Aye, I was thinking about my betrothed all right." It was not really an untruth. Tossing her flaming red hair, she returned to the window, trying to make light of the subject. Looking at the crags and hills, she tried to focus her thoughts on other things, but the fisherman hovered in the room like a ghost.

"Has he kissed ye, Caity?" Shona's eyes sparkled with romantic-tinged curiosity.

Caitlin blushed. "Aye."

"And?"

"And what?" Why did her voice sound so shaky?

"Was it . . . was it wonderful?" Her closed eyes, the hand at her throat, made it obvious Shona was experiencing the kiss vicariously.

"We willna talk of it." Wrapping a plaid similar to the kind the men wore about her waist and shoulders, then braiding her hair, Caitlin quickly left the room, hurrying to the hall down below.

The drone of bagpipes, trill of harps, and the sound of happy chatter filled the air. A dozen or more smiling faces greeted Caitlin as she walked through the door. Though she was not in a particularly good mood everyone else was, and the gaiety was infectious, soon wiping away her frown.

It was not a feudal society here; there were no serfs to do the work. All were of the same kin, and willingly did whatever chores necessary. Even a chieftain's daughter. Eve-

ryone was busily working at some task or other, and thus
Caitlin took her place beside the women preparing the food.
Breakfast was to be simple—porridge and fruit and fish,
for the men were eager to be about the day's activities.
Filling a cauldron with water from a wooden bucket, Caitlin
was anxious for her chore to be done so that she could
hurry out to the field. Perhaps the games would take her
mind off her troubles.

She brought the water to a boil and let the oatmeal trickle
into it. From the corner of her eye she scanned the room
as the men filed in. And there he was. Fisherman or chieftain, he stood out like a bull amidst rams. The clothes he
wore were obviously borrowed. His shirt was white instead
of the more usual saffron, and he wore a colored breacan
of bright green and black plaid, striped through with yellow
and red, the MacLeod plaid. The long ends were draped
over his left shoulder and pinned in place with a brooch.
A leather sporran hanging from a belt covered his maleness.
Even in the crowded room she was aware of him and he
was equally aware of her. Over and over again she could
feel his eyes staring.

With a chill she remembered last night, thought about
the danger she had been in. He could have murdered her.
Could have stolen the flag, then silenced her accusation
forever. Why hadn't he? Stirring the pot constantly with a
spurtle—a wooden stick about a foot long—she glanced his
way, but hastily averted his gaze the moment he glanced
back.

*What is he thinking? Is he wondering if he is still in
danger? Does he fear that I will tell on him after all? Or
does he sense that I am more drawn to him than I will
admit? Does he think that I am weak for not decrying his
attempted thievery? Or does he feel smug and secure? Is
he sorry that he did not strangle me or throw me from the
tower? Or is he grateful for my silence?*

She let the porridge cook steadily for a half hour as she

mused about the matter, stirring to watch for lumps. Though she was determined not to scorch the porridge she nearly did. And all because of him. That only emphasized to her what trouble he could be and already was.

Breakfast was eaten standing. Caitlin ate her oatmeal with fresh milk and salt, choosing wild berries and curds to appease her voracious appetite. When Shona teased her about it she retorted that she needed her strength for what was planned for the day. Her brow puckered in concentration. Today there would be further celebrating. Games. Horse racing. Such competition would surely make her forget what had happened last night and help soothe her conscience. Wouldn't it? So hoping, she merged with the crowd as they left the great hall.

Banners flew, bagpipes played on, tents were placed haphazardly about. There was the same enthusiasm and joviality as when appreciating a fair. A field just outside the castle's walls was used for the popular game of shinnie, a simple game using curved sticks and a ball. It was a dangerous sport, one said to be the fastest ball game in the world. To play it a man needed extraordinary athletic abilities—a quick eye, ready hand and a strong arm, and be an excellent runner and wrestler as well. Caitlin was not one to sit idle like the other women and watch the event. She elbowed her way among the crowd to join in, just as she had done since childhood. Plucking up a stick, she aligned herself with the players.

The field had the appearance of a battle scene. That she found herself on the same side as the fisherman was the only thing that marred her exhilaration at the event. Even so, she threw herself into the fracas, pleased when at last she caught sight of a look of surprise merged with admiration on his face.

"Ye fight as furiously as the MacLeods during a battle," he said, meaning it as a compliment.

"Which should give ye warning not to trifle with me," she answered, hoping he took it to heart.

"Nor ye with me," he answered.

Niall couldn't let a woman show him up, and thus he preened his skills before the large assemblage. He was quick and strong, ran with easy grace cutting back and forth across the pasture with his stick. Fighting the others for the ball with a reckless ferocity, he strove to impress all those who scorned his supposed occupation with boats and nets.

Grudgingly Caitlin had to admire him. Though she was more than a match for Erskin, Malcolm, and even Jamie, this fisherman swung his stick as powerfully as her father wielded his sword. One more reason to make her suspect that he was not who or what he said he was. But then, who was he?

"You played a good game." Huffing and puffing, Niall tried to catch his breath, surprised that a lass of beauty could also possess skill and strength. "Nearly as good a game as ye played last night."

"Ye played a good game, too," she said with double meaning. When she might have made conversation about it, however, they were interrupted by Jamie.

"Good game, lass. Next time we'll be on the same side." With a bold familiarity he patted her on the behind, then chuckled.

"Jamie, ye . . ." Caitlin bit back her scolding. She had more important things on her mind.

"But let's see how ye measure up with a bow." Niall nodded toward a group of clansmen who were arming themselves for the hunt. "For undoubtedly ye do that as well."

It was Jamie who answered. "Aye, she does." His smile was mocking. "I told ye the lass was more than ye bargained for."

"As if I didna already know it," Niall mumbled under his breath as he chose a bow.

Caitlin took time to choose a bow for herself, running

her hands over the wood, testing the tension of the cord. Suspicion crowded into her thoughts. Why was Niall curious about her skill with arms? Was he assessing her as one might an enemy? "My father has taught all his daughters to shoot and shoot well." Again, her words held a warning. "I've been hunting since I was no higher than my father's knee."

"There isn't anything ye canna do well it seems," he answered, reaching out to touch her on the shoulder.

Caitlin shrugged off his hand. "Aye. Remember that lest ye forget." A knot squeezed in the pit of her stomach as she noted he was taking a dirk with him as well as a bow. She would have to be careful not to be alone with him lest her danger still not be over. Perhaps his interest in the hunt was because he envisioned a hunting accident.

"Forget?" His eyes stared straight into hers. "There is nothing I would ever allow myself to forget about ye, Caitlin. Nothing." After meeting her, his impression of women sitting docilely at their sewing had been shattered forever. *But she is a MacLeod,* he warned himself. *Remember that lest ye forget.*

The hunters made their way through the forest amid a tangle of horsemen, Ian MacLeod's huge russet wolfhounds leading the way, hot on the scent. Their voices mingled in an eager racket of barking which echoed through the lonely forest as they sighted their prey across a large field.

It was a predominantly oak forest. Some pine and birch. Much of the ground was high with a lot of bare rock and scrub, difficult to travel through. On such ground there was no animal better adapted than the red deer. Trees of many kinds grew well in the sheltered parts on this base-rich soil from the volcanic rock. There were green, even terraces with occasional gullies. Truly it was a beautiful landscape, Niall thought as he walked along. But MacLeod territory. He must remember that as well, he thought, breaking into a run. He was determined to catch up with Caitlin MacLeod at the top of the hill. He had to talk with her. Had to know what she planned.

"Caitlin, wait!"

Hearing the frantic shout of her name only made Caitlin run faster. Only when she had caught up with her father did she allow herself to feel safe.

"We got one, Daughter," she heard her father call out.

Bows were raised as the clan chieftain gave the signal. A whir of arrows stung the air, bringing down the quarry, a large red deer.

"He's down!" Ian MacLeod's triumphant cry was accompanied by the sound of trampling feet and a splash as the hunters forded the water. Niall, however, did not follow. He'd sighted his own target, a deer larger than this one. To his surprise he saw that Caitlin had spotted it, too, for she managed to beat him in reacting to the prize. In a flash of yellow and black she ran by him. She seemed to be intent upon filling her eyes with the beauty of the woodland, but Niall kept his eyes upon her. Wearing that short garment similar to a man's, her long, shapely legs were plainly visible beneath the hem of the plaid, drawing his stare again and again.

For the moment Caitlin had forgotten all about her fear of Niall as she took off in search of the red deer that disappeared into the forest. Stealthfully following the trail, she took note that the tracks led down a steep embankment. Following, she was careful to duck her head to avoid being struck in the face by the low-hanging branches. Pausing only for a moment by the bank of a small pool, she looked down, and it was only in that moment that she realized he was beside her.

"Dinna touch me!"

"I was merely . . ."

Run, she thought. Get away from him. Do not tempt fate! But as she turned away, he sought to stop her. He didn't want her to leave. They had to talk about last night.

"Caitlin." Having snagged and entangled his breacon in a low-hanging branch, he hurriedly took out his dirk with the intent to free himself, little realizing the panic it would inspire.

"No!" Catching sight of the weapon, Caitlin's worst fears were unleashed. So, when all was said and done he was a murderer!

"Caitlin!"

Ignoring his cry, she bolted around him, fearful of what he might say or do. She had to reach her father, had to tell him the truth before they were all ruined.

"Caitlin!"

Running so hard that she could hardly catch her breath, Caitlin looked over her shoulder. He was gaining on her. She had to move faster. She had to . . .

As familiar with this landscape as she was with her own hand, Caitlin forgot in her panic the way the terrain suddenly dropped down into nothing, descending sharply into the valley below. Taking a step forward, she stumbled. Then she was falling. Plummeting down, down, down.

"Caitlin!" Niall shouted. He screamed. His voice echoed in her ears, then she felt a fierce jolt slam through her body. She struck her head, crying out against the pain, then escaped into blessed oblivion.

Eleven

Niall ran frantically toward the edge of the hill, looking down at the crumpled figure lying on the ground. "Caitlin!" Her eyes were closed. She looked frighteningly still.

Scrambling down the hillside, he bent over her unconscious form whispering a fervent prayer. "Please let her be alive!" Seemingly his plea was answered, for as he put his head to her breast he could hear her heartbeat.

"Caitlin!"

Her breathing was even, though her face looked ashen. Apparently she'd struck her head when she had fallen. The cut on her forehead attested to that. Niall gently wiped the blood away with his fingertips. Cautiously he examined her, probing her arms and legs to determine if there were any broken bones. There did not seem to be, but still he was careful. He'd seen men suffer such tumbles in battle, knew it could be dangerous to move someone if they were hurt internally or had injured their spine. Even so, he could not just leave her here on the hard ground all alone. She needed help. She needed him.

Looking hastily about, Niall tried to get his bearings. He seemed to recall passing a small crofter's cottage a few yards back. At the time he'd only glanced at it, his thoughts intent on Caitlin and catching up with her so they could talk. Now, carefully lifting her up in his arms, cradling her head against his chest, he headed toward the cottage.

"Ye are going to be just fine, lassie. Just fine."

But was she? Looking down, mesmerized by how vulnerable she appeared, he could only hope that she wasn't more gravely injured than he suspected.

"Ah, hinny!" An all-consuming sense of protectiveness surged through him, an emotion he'd never felt for a woman before. He felt the strong desire to safeguard her, to shield her, and to love her.

He made his way back toward the cottage. He would find someone to watch after her while he went back to find her father.

His plans were thwarted when he found that the tiny dwelling of thatched wattle and daub was deserted. Kicking open the door, Niall looked all around him, taking note of the cobwebs. The walls of the cottage were cracked in several places. It had been left in a ruinous state. Broken pottery, pieces of wood, and straw littered the earthen floor. The interior was covered with a thick coating of dust which caused Niall to cough as he pushed his way inside. As he scanned the small one-room dwelling he caught sight of a straw mattress in the corner. Gently, he placed Caitlin upon it.

"Caitlin!" Oh, how he longed for her to open her eyes, to speak to him, even if her tone was scolding. "Oh, why did ye run from me, lass? Why?" What had he done to so frighten her?

Standing over her, Niall loosened her clothing to make her more comfortable, then he studied her intently. His breath was trapped somewhere in the area of his heart as he stared at the loveliness presented to him. She looked so fragile, so young, so desirable.

What would the MacLeods do if I carried her off to the MacDonald stronghold? he wondered. *Would they follow? Would they start another war? Undoubtedly.* And so, the feelings that stirred in his heart for her were hopeless. But though he tried to ignore the desire that stirred within him at the sight of her tiny waist, firm breasts, and long, perfectly shaped legs it was impossible. She was even more beautiful than he had supposed. Ach, how he wished he really was just a simple fisherman. It could have been so easy then. As it was, he had been caught in the web of his own deception.

Niall brushed her fiery hair aside to examine her head, wincing at the sight of the large lump. In empathy he crooned to her still form. "Poor lassie." It was no wonder she was still deeply asleep, he thought. He'd had experience tending the wounded, knew a cold, damp cloth would bring some relief. Tearing off a strip of his breacan, he dipped it in a rain barrel outside the door, laid it on Caitlin's forehead and sat back to wait.

"Caitlin!" Bending down beside her, he called her name over and over again, his pulse quickening as he saw her eyelids flutter. "Caitlin."

She was so lovely, he mused, from the tip of her toes to the top of her red-haired head. He let his eyes move tenderly over her in a caress, lingering on the rise and fall of her breasts. For just a moment he gave in to temptation and kissed her soft, warm mouth. A parting kiss, he thought. A sad tribute to what might have been. With a regretful sigh he moved away from her, keeping an arm's length away, to return to his vigil. She was the kind of woman he had been searching for . . . but the one woman he could never hope to obtain. Malcolm MacDonald would never welcome a MacLeod into the clan, nor would Ian MacLeod welcome him were he to find out who he really was. The longing that he felt would forever remain unfulfilled. And yet at the moment that didn't matter. All he wanted was for her to open her eyes. Niall sat unflinchingly by Caitlin's bedside, leaving only to change the cold cloth on her head. He stared at her, entranced by the way the sunlight from the tiny window played across the curves of her body beneath the coverlet, creating tantalizing shadows and reminding him of her beautiful body. The thoughts rambling through his head were dangerous and he shook his head furiously to clear such musings.

You have one purpose here and one purpose only, he reminded himself silently. *The flag. Remember.*

"Ohhhhh!"

"Caitlin?"

She was moaning, moving her head from side to side. It was the first hopeful sign she'd given of returning to consciousness. Reaching out, he touched her face, relishing the softness of her skin.

"Wake up, lass." Seeing her eyelashes flutter again, he took her hand, willing her to open her eyes.

As if subconsciously hearing him, she stirred, putting her hand to her temple. "Mmmmm. My head," she moaned. Instinctively she reached out feeling disoriented, clinging to him, needing stability. The closeness of her soft curves was nearly his undoing. The brush of their bodies wove a cocoon of warm intimacy that he relished.

Light flickered before Caitlin's eyelids as she struggled to open her eyes. Where was she? She was confused. "What happened?" she asked softly.

"You fell, lass." Pushing her fiery-hued hair aside, he examined her injury yet again. His fingers were strokes of softness as he touched her, making her feel warm and tingly inside. She nestled closer, her face buried against his chest.

"Ohhhhh."

"And hit yer head on a rock."

Suddenly recognizing *his* voice, Caitlin's eyes flew open to find him sitting on the edge of the mattress, his fingers entwined in her hair. His face illuminated by sunlight was the first thing her eyes focused on. She'd know that profile anywhere. "Niall!" She remembered now that she had dreamed that he had kissed her. Had he? Her thoughts were hazy, her head throbbed painfully as she sat up.

"Aye. 'Tis me. I brought ye here," he murmured huskily, remembering their brief embrace.

"Brought me where?"

"A crofter's cottage near the spot where you fell."

"Oh . . ."

They stared at each other, two silent, shadowy figures in the dimly lit cottage, each achingly aware of the other. The very air pulsated with expectancy. Caitlin could not help but wonder what he was going to say, what he was going to do. Sitting like a stone figure, her eyes never once left him as he moved forward.

"Ah, lassie. When I saw you fall I thought . . . I feared!" He pulled her roughly against him. "By the Saints I never realized until that moment how very special you are to me." The tone of sincerity in his voice deeply touched her.

"Special?"

"Aye, that you are."

Slowly Niall bent his head, kissing her with a fierce, single-minded passion. A kiss that sent her head spinning. Was it any wonder then that she clung to him to keep from falling?

"Ah, lass . . ." he murmured against her mouth, pulling her closer. Her lips parted in an invitation for him to drink more deeply of her mouth. He did, igniting a warmth that engulfed them both from head to toe.

His hand slid over the curve of her hip and downward to the place where her thigh was bare. Her flesh burned at the spot he touched her.

"I hae lain awake at night imagining this," he breathed, "and this." His fingers dipped inside her clothing, touching the peaks of her breasts.

Caitlin felt as if she had stepped into another realm, someplace where there were no thoughts, only feelings. Breathlessly she allowed his kisses, tingling with pleasure when he began to hungrily probe the inner warmth. Following his lead, she returned his kiss, tentatively at first, then passionately, tangling her fingers in the thick golden bristle of his hair.

"Caitlin!"

All he could think about was the pounding of his heart as he relished the warmth of her body. She'd haunted his dreams no matter how fiercely he'd tried to put her from his mind. And now she was here, his betrothed, a voice inside his head shouted out. Why not take advantage of that fact. Here and now.

Capturing her slender shoulders, he pulled her up against him as his mouth moved hungrily against hers. Her head was thrown back, the masses of her fiery hair tumbling in a thick cascade over his arm, tickling his neck. "Ah, lassie. Lassie!"

Caitlin was aware of her body as she had never been before. Her breasts tingled with a new sensation. Fighting against her own desire was more difficult than she could ever have anticipated. How could she push him away? How could she ignore the heated insistence in her blood? There was a weakening readiness at his kiss, a longing she couldn't explain but which prompted her to push closer to him, relishing the warmth of his hands as he outlined the swell of her breasts.

Caitlin didn't understand this all-consuming desire to be near him, she only knew that Niall alone aroused an urgent need within her, a longing to embrace him. She craved his kisses, his touch, and wanted to be in his arms forever. Dear God, she was helpless against this powerful tide that raised gooseflesh up and down her arms and legs.

"Niall." She moaned his name into his hair as his lips left her mouth. Soft sobs of pleasure echoed through the cottage's silence and she was surprised to find that they came from her own throat. Her senses were filled with a languid heat that made her head spin. She closed her eyes, giving herself up to the dream of his nearness.

Gently he traced a path from her jaw to her ear to the slim line of her throat until his lips found her breasts, tracing the rosy peak. Dear God, she tasted so sweet. He was mesmerized by her, by how right it felt to hold her in his arms, his hip touching her stomach, his chest cradling the softness of her breasts. The longing to make furious love to her overpowered him. Kissing was not enough to satisfy the blazing hunger that raged through him. She was too tempting, and the delicious fact that she was responding to him made him cast all caution aside. Compulsively his fingers savored the softness of her breasts as he bent his mouth to kiss her again, gently lowering her onto her back.

She stared up at him, watching as he studied her, and the look of desire she saw branded on his face alarmed her. Her woman's body craved the maleness of him, but her logical mind rebelled. Through the haze of her pleasure she suddenly remembered. She had fallen because she had been running away from him.

"Take yer hands away!" she commanded.

"What?" Reluctantly he moved away, though he didn't want to. "I said, get yer hands off me, *fisherman!*" Glaring defiantly at him, she ignored the clamor in her own body and blamed what had happened entirely on him.

He rolled away from her, coming to his feet, standing with his legs sprawled apart, his arms crossed over his chest. His breathing was deep as he struggled to get control of himself, his emotions. He swore a violent oath as he raised his hands, palms toward her.

"There, my hands are gone from ye. Are ye satisfied?"

"No!" Cautiously she looked around for the dirk, only allowing herself to relax when she realized he was not armed. Even so, she was wary. "I willna be satisfied until ye are far away." Her flashing eyes made accusations.

"Why you ungrateful . . . !" He seethed inwardly. "I should have left you lying there, Caitlin MacLeod!" A muscle in his jaw ticked warningly.

"Aye, that ye should hae, I be thinking. And ye might hae, except ye wanted to make certain of . . ."

"Of what?" Just what was she hinting. "Say it! I canna guess, I hae not the sight."

She took a deep breath, then made the accusation. "I saw ye come after me with yer knife. That's why I ran."

"Saw me . . . !" It was too ridiculous for words.

"But when ye saw me fall ye thought ye wouldna hae to do yer gruesome deed." Her breath hissed out as she continued. "Ye thought yer secret would be safe. That I was dead. But ye were wrong."

Niall exploded with rage. "If ye were not a woman I would make ye eat those words." He practically shouted at her. "If I was trying to kill ye why would I hae carried ye here, woman? Answer that if ye can!"

"Oh, I don't know . . ." She felt confused. Addled. *Oh, if only I could read yer mind and know for sure.*

Rejection and unfulfilled passion merged in a potent rage within his veins. "Well, ye can know this. I am a man of honor. I would ne'er harm a hair on yer head, no matter what ye may believe. God strike me down, I tell ye true."

Instantly she regretted her volatile temper and her cursed quick tongue. She had ranted, she had raved because she had been afraid. She had the feeling that he would long remember her careless words.

"What's going on in here?" Jamie became an unwelcome guest as he burst through the door.

"She fell!" Niall didn't even make pretense of being polite. He just wasn't in the mood.

"Fell?" Jamie's concern proved that he had some kind of feelings for his clanswoman.

"She tumbled over the hill."

"Tumbled?" Jamie's look challenged him.

"Fell." Niall's eyes blazed as he looked first at Jamie, then at Caitlin. "I give my word I didna push her."

Jamie shrugged. "I wasna thinking that ye did, only that ye should hae taken better care of her. I would hae." He pushed his way past Niall and knelt by the bed. "How are ye feeling, hinny?"

"My head hurts a bit, but that is all. I hit my . . . my head." As a reminder, her head began to pound violently and she put her hand to her temple as she sat up. "Niall came to my aid and brought me here."

"I'll bet he did." The smirk on his face made no secret of Jamie's meaning.

"I did."

"To hae a sampling before the wedding?" His hands reached out to Caitlin, but Niall, grabbing him by the wrist, pulled them away.

"Nae." Only narrowly did Niall hold his temper in check. "Unlike ye, I can keep my hands to myself."

For a moment it appeared that there might be a fight. And there might have been had Caitlin not hurried to act as mediator.

"Leave Niall be! He has done nothing to censor." She tried to get to her feet but felt dizzy so she sat back down. " 'Twas my own fault I fell. If not for yon laddie I might hae fared worse." Once again she came to his defense, though she had made far worse accusations.

"Then ye believe me?" Niall raised one eyebrow in question.

"Aye." Still, she didn't completely trust him. How could she? "For the moment I declare a truce. And ye?"

Niall didn't answer; he merely shrugged, glowering as Jamie rose to his feet and stepped in between.

"Come, Cait!" His lips curled up slightly. "The women-folk hae been busy preparing another feast while we've been gone. I'm hungry." He boasted of the number of animals killed, as if he had been the one to kill them all. "Six rabbits, four red deer, a roe buck, and several birds. The MacLeod's keisan will be filled to the brim with game. And yer father felled a buck at a hundred and seventy yards."

"For *our* betrothal feast!" Niall felt possessive and hastened to remind the dark-haired young man of his claim. "Caitlin's and *mine.*" That said, he bent down, sweeping her up in his arms.

"What are ye going to do?" She felt a strange surge of excitement, feeling his arms clamped so tightly around her.

"Carry ye all the way back to the hall if need be."

She could have told him then and there that she was strong enough to walk, yet Caitlin remained silent, enjoying the moment. There was no use denying it, she liked being in his arms.

Twelve

The great hall was warmly lit, the roaring fire inviting. Having dressed in a kirtle of plain beige wool and a brightly colored arasaid of yellow and green, Caitlin looked every bit a lady. Entering the hall with her head held high, she took the honorary seat beside her father and mother which would be hers throughout the period of preparation for her wedding.

The hall fluttered with frenzied activity as large kegs of whiskey and ale were tapped and venison was prepared for cooking. The Highlanders would boil a quarter of flesh, whether mutton, veal, goat, or deer in the paunch of the beast. The animal's skin was turned inside out, cleaned and fixed to hang on a hoop over the fire. Now the meat sizzled and gave off a tantalizing aroma. Caitlin could not deny her hunger.

"Something for your appetite, Caity." Mairi grinned as she offered her older sister an oatcake from a large wooden tray.

"My thanks."

"I made them myself just for you . . ." Mairi waited expectantly as Caitlin dipped it in honey, cherishing its sweetness. As the future bride, she was to have the honor of taking the first bite of all the delicacies tonight.

"Very tasty!"

"Cait . . ." The girl's long slim fingers grasped Caitlin's hand.

"Aye."

"It . . . it seems so strange that ye will be a bride." The blue eyes sparkled with unshed tears. "I want ye to be happy."

"I will be, Mairi." Both blinked back their tears. "I-I . . ."

"Och, this is a time for merriment, not for cryin'!" Ian's voice was gruff, but Caitlin thought she detected a mist of moisture in his own eyes. "A daughter is born to be a mother some day. And yet . . ."

"It is always hard to hand them over to another," Caitlin whispered. Indeed, Ian's youngest daughter, Ailsa, had been the first to go, fostered out to the MacKinnons to strengthen friendship between the clans when she was but five years old. In turn, the MacKinnons' small son was growing up at the MacLeod hearth.

The custom of fosterage did much to bind members of clans together, or so Ian insisted. Fosterage consisted in the mutual exchange of the infant members of families, the children of the chief being included. Since Ailsa was little more than a babe it had seemed significantly appropriate for her to be the one chosen for fosterage.

"Kindred to forty degrees, fosterage to a hundred, as they say." The custom had the advantage of enabling one half of the clan world to know the other half and how they lived.

She'd never forget how he'd cried when his youngest daughter had been bundled off by the leader of the Mac-Kinnon clan. And now in a way he was losing Caitlin, too. Handing her over to belong to another man, no more to be his little girl.

Ian let out his breath in a deep, rumbling sigh. "I'm afraid I'll be naught but a lonely old mon when my lovely chicks leave the nest."

"An old man? You? Never." Giving in to an impulse, Caitlin kissed his cheek and Shona followed.

The hall rang with raucous laughter, a babble of voices and the underlying accompaniment of music. A parade of trays and bowls passed Caitlin's way. Strangely enough, though she had thought herself to be famished, she only nibbled at the fare, trying to quiet the unusual feelings stirring in the pit of her stomach. Certainly her head ached, as if a wee brownie was inside, pounding with a hammer. Ignoring the pain that throbbed in her head, she looked in Niall's direction, fantasizing about being carried back to the castle in his arms. The look that passed between them had the potency of a kiss. Looking hastily away, Caitlin joined in the revelry that rioted in the room.

Get hold of yourself, Caitlin nic Ian! she scolded silently, but it was no use. Caitlin knew she could deny it no longer. She was drawn to the fisherman devastatingly, beyond thought, beyond reason. Indeed, she did not have to look his way to know where he stood, how he moved. She sensed it. Every time he turned his heated gaze her way the hair at the back of her neck prickled in anticipation. It was a feeling that unnerved her, she who had always had complete control over her emotions.

A vision flashed before her eyes of a man pressed close against her body beneath the quilts, lulling her to blissful sleep by the steady rhythm of his heartbeat. Closing her eyes, she allowed herself the luxury of dreaming until her father's elbow nudged her in the ribs.

"The dancing, Daughter, the dancing. It's up to you to lead it."

Ian MacLeod rose from the table and signaled for the dancing to begin. Within a matter of moments the room was transformed, tables pushed back, chairs and benches pushed against the wall. Caitlin chose her father as her first partner as the clansmen hooted their approval.

"Let's see Caitlin dance. It's her betrothal we're celebrating," cried out Jamie.

"Aye, let's see her kick her feet." Angus boldly winked.

"Everybody must dance."

Three pipers appeared, accompanied by the bard on his

lute and a small boy on a tambor. Ian MacLeod danced
with the agility of a young lad, laughing all the while.

"Ye remind me of yer mother, lassie. It's as if the years
hae been wiped away. We danced together she and I at our
own marriage feast. And now our wee bonny daughter has
grown up. Where hae all the years gone, hinny?"

"Perhaps the witches hae stole them." One of the powers
with which witches were accredited was that of the evil
eye. By merely looking at something they could destroy,
corrupt, or acquire it. That was why Caitlin always wore a
potent talisman around her neck to guard against them.

"Perhaps . . ." He reflected on that notion. "Certainly it
seems that only the dark powers could be so cruel as to
bring old age upon us so quickly."

Laughing young women chose partners, and one by one
other pairs of dancers took to the floor as Caitlin and her
father returned to their seats. Stepping gracefully, quickly,
toes pointed with precision, hands thrown upward in exuberance or warmly extended to smiling partners the revelers
frolicked. The couples met and parted, moving their feet in
spirited abandonment. Her father told her that long ago this
type of dancing was part of a magic ritual and surely there
was a primitive aura about it, she thought.

Patterns of dancers formed, then just as quickly dissolved
to form new patterns. Breacons swayed jauntily, skirts rippled as the tunes from the fiddler and bagpipes filled the
great hall.

"Let's see Caitlin dance wi' the fishermon!"

"Aye, let's see how the fishermon can dance."

"Is he as skilled at that as with a sword?"

"Let's take a wager on it."

"Come on!"

Caitlin was unable to ignore the round of shouts that echoed all around the hall, and in truth perhaps she didn't really
want to. Drawing in a deep breath, she watched as Niall
walked with lionlike grace across the wooden floor. Then

she was in his arms, surprised by how at home she felt there.

"Ye hae been ordered to dance with me."

"Aye, so ye hae . . ."

"Come," he whispered. "I want them all to know that ye belong to me."

Caitlin's breath stilled at the touch of his warm hand. Her blood quickened as his arms encircled her waist. There was a glow in his eyes, and she reveled in the knowledge that in spite of their many quarrels, he still wanted her. It was as heady a feeling as drinking too much ale.

The pipes began keening, she moved her feet dreamily as smoke from the hearth fires swirled about the hall. It was like a dream, and she was caught up in the spell. All about them her clansmen were clapping and cheering, stamping their feet in time to the music, watching as a member of a rival clan swirled her around the room.

Caitlin had never felt so passionately alive! Her whole being was filled with conflicting emotions. He was whirling her about to a jaunty tune. Her bright red hair flew about her shoulders in a fiery web as laughter bubbled from her throat. She felt immensely happy as she danced with complete abandon. Kicking up her heels, bending her slim waist, her eyes fused with his as for just a moment their faces were mere inches apart, close enough for a kiss. They were too breathless to speak, but their expressions conveyed a mutual attraction.

"Let me show you a dance we do in my village," he said at last, longing to fit her soft curves against him. He explained, hurriedly showing the others how to do the steps. It was a different kind of dance in which the women executed the intricate steps as they moved in a circle, men on the outside women on the inside.

Unlike the usual Scottish way of dancing, keeping an arm's length away, Caitlin was shocked to find that there was a great deal of touching and brushing against each other. She could not help but relive the moment they had been together in the cottage and a strange quivering took hold of her. "Ye're as graceful as a bird. Is there nothing ye can't do?" The sound of his low, husky voice teased her ears. His hard, muscular body seemed to press against her own and burn where it touched. His gaze seemed to strip her naked, and with a blush she remembered his caress.

She made no effort to pull away as he grasped her by the waist and lifted her high in the air as the pipes keened on. Indeed, she sought the firm strength of his arms. Their hearts pounded in unison. For a moment it was as if the two of them were all alone in the vast room. Och, if only he were not so handsome, and yet it was much more than that. He had revealed strength, a determination today on the field that she could not help but admire. He was in every way a most masculine man. And soon he would belong to her.

Even long after the fires dimmed, as she had settled in her bed, Caitlin's mind danced with memories of the time she'd shared with Niall in the forest and in his arms tonight. Once again she couldn't sleep, but this time it was because of happy thoughts, not recriminations.

"I hae to see him." Bolting up in bed, the necessity to be held in his arms goaded her into leaving the small chamber. Haunting the halls like a ghost, she made her way toward his room. Suddenly an arm slipped around her shoulders and she gasped. "Who . . . ?"

"Me!" Niall's voice enveloped her like a welcome cloak.

"Niall." She would never have wanted to let him know how glad she was that it was him yet her voice betrayed her. "What are ye doing here? I didna even hear ye."

"I was on my way to yer room. I-I just wanted to be close to ye." A rare confession from such a proud man. "And what about ye?"

"The same."

"Oh!" He slipped his arm around her shoulders as he

steered her around a sharp corner and down a short flight of steps. There was a crazy leap in her pulse as she felt the firm pressure of his hand. "Be careful. Watch the stairs. They're steep and slippery."

At last they came to a spot that was dark and private. Cupping her face in his hand, he tipped her chin up. "So, give me a kiss, hinny. It's what we both want."

"A kiss?" She played it coy. "And just why should I be giving one to ye?"

"Because. . . . because I canna live without it."

Caitlin felt his arms around her as he crushed her tight against him and her blood screamed with delight. Somehow it seemed that it was with him that she belonged.

"Niall . . ." She reached out to him, closing her fingers against his as he took her hand.

"Ah . . . lassie, what ye do to me." His breath was warm against her face, his voice husky. With a soft groan, he bent his head, captured her shoulders and brought her closer as he crushed his mouth against hers. So much for good intentions, he thought. His hand closed over her breast, his thumb moving back and forth over the peak as he slid his lips along her throat. Oh, why did this particular lassie stir him so?

Niall kissed her over and over, but kisses alone did not quell the blazing hunger that raged through him. His hand trembled as he pushed her away as suddenly as he had sought the embrace. She was too tempting, too soft and yielding in his arms. A moment longer and he would do something he could never forgive himself for. Take her before the wedding. So thinking, he pulled away.

"Niall?" Caitlin was totally confused. He was as unfathomable as the tide, pursuing her one moment, pushing her away the next. "What is wrong?"

"I canna kiss ye without wanting more." There, he had said it. "But we must wait."

"Wait . . . ?" At that moment she didn't want to. Her

head whirled in a dizzying awareness of him. The length of his hard, muscular body felt hot against her own. She felt desire spread languidly through her body, working its way up from her knees to the top of her head. A warm, tingling feeling. "Mayhap I dunna want to, Niall." She touched his arm.

"Oh, God. Caitlin, my Caity . . ." This time his kiss went far beyond a mere touching of lips. His tongue searched the contours of her mouth in a sensuous, exploring caress that intensified her newly found passion.

With an increasing measure of boldness, she mimicked the gentle exploration of his lips and tongue, helpless against the powerful tide that consumed her, a quivering sensation that shot through her body like a fist. Then she felt his hand slide down to cup her breast and she was lost. She wanted him here and now. Oh, but she was such a brazen hussy.

As for Niall, the heat of his body was steadily climbing. His breath was coming quickly between his parted lips. He was totally ruled by his emotions, having the devil's own time resisting the temptation she presented. Taking her hand, he pulled her slowly downward.

"I want to take off yer clothes, to touch you, learn every secret of yer body. I want to caress yer breasts, feel the warmth of yer hands touching me as I am touching ye." He pulled her up against him, showing her what male arousal felt like. He felt her shiver. "I want to be so deeply sheathed in yer softness that we are like one being. That's what I want at this moment."

"And I. . . . I want that, too." Putting her arms around him, she felt as if she were flying. Desire was like a fever, and she reveled in the sensations flooding her body.

"Caity, my sweet, sweet, Caity . . ." Dropping his head, he kissed the valley between her breasts, then caressed each soft mound with his lips and tongue, teasing the peaks until she gasped aloud.

"Ah, Niall, I love ye so. How glad I am that I am to be yer wife."

"Wife."

The word hovered in the air like a ghost, bringing him back down to earth. He swore beneath his breath softly. What he was about to take didn't belong to him. MacLeod or no, Caitlin deserved better treatment than to be tumbled like some trollop. Thus, without saying another word, he gripped her shoulders and in a seemingly determined mood propelled her up to the stairs.

"Niall, where are ye taking me?"

"Back to your chamber, lass." He pushed her ahead of him, up the narrow steps. Bad enough to steal the MacLeod's flag without stealing his daughter's virginity as well.

"Why?" She felt bereft and lonely without his arms around her.

"A matter of virtue and honor."

She scoffed. "I dunna care about them. I dunna care at all. I want . . ."

He stifled her protests with his kiss, then pulled away, walking her to her door. "I do care." Though often known to whisper words of love that he did not mean, Niall meant them now. "I love ye, Caitlin MacLeod. I do." He felt suddenly lonely and very sad. "Just remember that."

"Remember?" She laughed, cuddling up against him. "Why should I when I'll hae ye with me?"

"Just do." Kissing her lightly on the lips, he bid her a sad good night, regretting that it would soon be good-bye.

Thirteen

Caitlin shivered but not because it was cold in the room. She was nervous, mentally ticking off the time until she would be married. "So soon." Too soon. She wasn't ready. Despite her newfound feelings for the fisherman, despite the wild primitive feelings he had unleashed, she hadn't gotten used to the idea. Perhaps in truth she never would.

Soon I will no longer be a maiden. Despite her attraction for Niall, the thought brought a small stab of fear. Would he be gentle? Would she feel the same surging desire for him on her wedding night that she had last night? Closing her large brown eyes she gave herself up to dreams and visions of her coming marriage. There would be walks in the moonlight, kisses in the shadows, late nights and early mornings snuggled together beneath the quilts. She wanted so to believe in love and she might have had she not also heard some of the women complain about marriage.

Love is not all hugs and kisses. There are moments of the greatest embarrassment. Times when there is pain.

Cursing the fisherman beneath her breath for complicating her life, she rested her needlework in her lap and pulled her chair closer to the fire. Caitlin looked down at the sewing she held in her hands and tried her best to concentrate once again upon her stitches. Breathing out a sigh, she stuck her needle into the coarse cloth, gasping out in pain as she stuck her finger.

"Damn!" she swore, forgetting herself for a moment as she uttered one of Niall the fisherman's favorite oaths.

"Caitlin! Such an expression does not become you," Caitlin's mother, Fiona, frowned as she chided her daughter. "Ye are to be a married woman soon. I willna hae ye swear like some . . . some Englishmon!"

Stubbornly Caitlin refused to apologize, but she did glance at her mother out of the corner of her eye. Oh, how she wished that she and her mother had the kind of relationship other young woman had with their mothers. Caitlin's father had always taken her side, and thus a wall had arisen up between Caitlin and Fiona.

"Caitlin, did ye hear me?"

This time Caitlin nodded. Rising from her seat, she picked up a large log and threw it on the fire, basking in the warmth and glow it gave as the fires consumed it.

It was silent in the room, as all the women were engrossed in their stitchery. There was always mending to be done as well as sewing new garments. It was work Caitlin abhorred and avoided every time she could, but it was work she knew she must now get used to. As her mother had often reminded her, married women had to make themselves useful to their husbands, in more ways than one.

Useful . . . It sounded so hollow, so cold.

"Caitlin, stop daydreaming. Come, try on this gown." Caitlin felt the cool linen as her mother slipped it over her head. "I want everything to be perfect—your hair, the garments that you wear, the wedding feast. Everything. It is only right that the eldest daughter of Ian MacLeod be given the best," Fiona exclaimed.

It seemed as if the mother who had always ignored her had suddenly become obsessed with the most minute details of the wedding preparations. Fiona had spent hours sewing Caitlin's matrimonial wardrobe, had diligently taken a hand in the food preparations.

"The best . . ." Caitlin breathed, staring down at the hem of her gown.

"Are ye afraid, Caitlin?"

"Nae!" Caitlin answered too quickly but she couldn't hide the shadow that flitted across her face.

"Ye are!"

"I'm no . . . !" There was no use lying. "Perhaps a little. After all, 'tis ye who are always preaching that it is hard being married."

"Because men rarely consider a woman's feelings. They can be selfish, Caitlin, and marriage is much more than kisses."

"So I have heard." Mockingly Caitlin put her hands beneath the gown making it look like she was with child. " 'Tis a means for bringing Ian MacLeod's grandchildren into this world."

"A noble duty!" her mother admonished. She studied her daughter for a long time, then smiled. "Ah, Caitlin, you'll soon learn the ways of men. But a word of caution. Your husband-to-be doesna seem as easy a mon to wind round yer finger as yer father has been."

"Nevertheless I will tame him," Caitlin insisted, "somehow, some way." Caitlin could feel the blood rising in her cheeks.

"Or he will tame ye." For just a moment Fiona was lost in her own private world but she quickly recovered.

"Never!" Reaching up, Caitlin tugged off the gown, then, tilting her head to one side, she asked of the other woman, "Has Father tamed ye?"

"In some ways."

Caitlin couldn't keep herself from blurting out, "Do ye love Father?"

Fiona gasped at the blunt question but did not answer. Her silence bothered Caitlin, for she imagined the silence to be an answer in the negative. *Something is wrong. Something Mother has not told me.*

It was Fiona's turn to ask the question. "Do ye love the bonny young man yer father has betrothed ye to?"

"I don't think so, but I do hae certain feelings when he touches me." Caitlin hugged herself tight as she thought about it, then realizing her mother was looking at her, she put her hands back down at her sides. "Besides, he's better than Uisdean MacKinnon or any of the other fine men Father thought to gi' me to."

"Aye, his only fault is that he has spent his life keeping company with fish." Her mother sniffed her disdain. "But then at least I dunna hae to worry about my daughter going hungry."

"What's that ye say, woman?" Though he usually avoided the women's quarters, Ian MacLeod strode boldly in, like a rooster entering a hen house.

"I was just saying that I most highly approve o' yer choice for our grandchildren's father, even if he is a humble mon."

"Humble?" Ian laughed. "In truth, Wife, I would call him anything but that." Playfully he tugged at Caitlin's hair. "He'll be a good mate for my overbold lassie here. A mon wi' whom she can grow old."

"Old!" Leaning against the familiar strength of her father's chest, Caitlin tried to imagine what Niall would look like when he reached her father's age.

"Aye, he will be a boon to the MacLeod clan. I felt it the first time I saw him."

"Is that why ye didna throw him in the dungeon?" Caitlin questioned.

"It is." He looked inordinately proud of himself. "I gambled, Daughter, and I won."

She tickled him under the chin. "Oh, did ye now? We will see."

Ian MacLeod might not have made such a statement had he been able to see Niall through the stone walls. Last night he had made his decision to leave as soon as possible, and thus Niall was busy gathering together the few belongings he had brought with him and those he had been given as wedding presents. He put the smaller items in the sporran hanging from the belt at his waist; a larger satchel was to be saved for a possession he longed to be his. The flag!

I hae to go! he declared silently. *As soon as possible. I canna let this all drag out and thus hurt the lassie all the more.* And himself.

Looking toward the door, Niall shrugged his shoulders, hoping that it would be as easy to cast off his unhappiness.

"Oh, Caity!" He remembered the way her lips had felt beneath his when he had kissed her. He thought of how right she had felt in his arms. Why? Why did she have to be a MacLeod?

She's beginning to care for you, but you cannot let that keep you from what you must be doing. You came here to steal the flag, Niall MacDonald, and that's exactly what you have to do.

"The ultimate betrayal." One for which she would never be able to forgive him. Even so, it had to be done.

Fourteen

Darkness gathered under the high, vaulted roof. The flickering torches hissed and sputtered as if in warning. The smoke from the waning fire looked like a ghost. Large shadows danced on the wall, tall and menacing. It was the hour when the spirits roamed.

"The night before my wedding," Caitlin whispered, taking her place beside her father in the small, circular tower chamber.

In gaelic tradition Ian MacLeod had summoned the "seer" to look into the future and tell what was in store for his daughter and her husband-to-be. Not only did the MacLeod clan hold the distinction of having the best bagpipers in the Highlands—the skirl of their pipes would stir any Scots blood—but also they had Elspeth, the most famous seer throughout the Highlands.

She was a direct descendant of the Celtic Druid seers. Many of the neighboring clans and those of the islands used her services, but Skye was her homeland. She was a MacLeod through and through, born in Durinish on the west side of Skye. Not only did she see but also *heard* voices. No one doubted her ability, for what she foretold would eventually happen.

Elspeth was yet in her middle years. She would often see the fairy folk and a person's dopfelgager, or "other self." If this other self was seen, then the person's death was believed to be imminent.

With trepidation, Caitlin eyed the dark-haired, long-nosed woman, feeling a shiver along her spine. Elspeth had skin that was ghostly pale, an angular face, narrow lips, eyebrows that were dark and bushy. Not comely at all, yet the woman had a regal pride. She wouldn't bow to anyone. Not even the MacLeod. Was the woman secretly a witch as some had claimed? Truly, as the woman turned and stared at her with her piercing dark eyes, it seemed so.

"Ah, the lovely bride," she said in a voice that was strangely soothing despite her appearance.

"The treasure and the hope of the MacLeods," Ian declared, "as are ye, Elspeth." He had always had complete faith in her ability, but even more so since she had told of his son's coming death. Many years ago before the battle that robbed him of Colin, Elspeth had been walking the glen near the cemetery. It was a midnight that was dark and grave. Elspeth had gone into a trance in which she saw the graves open and the occupants leaving to make room for one more body, that of Colin MacLeod, the chief's son.

Though the story was told to Ian weeks before the battle that took Colin's life, he had shrugged it off as being naught but an illusion. He had tried desperately to put what she had said out of his mind but she had foreseen that there would be a violent battle in which Colin's life would end. After the MacDonald's attack on the stronghold, however, as he had cradled his dead son's body in his arms, he had remembered. Then a week after Colin had been killed, Elspeth had once again had a vision where she saw the same ghosts returning to their graves.

Some Highlanders thought Elspeth was not only a seer but a white witch, able to cure all manner of illnesses. Others thought of her only as a seer able to see future events whether for good or for evil. All knew that she had the "gift of sight," because she was famous among all the Highlanders for seeing events and objects others could not see, her dictates often passed for law. Although she was a very influential person, she charged no fee for her services.

There was no doubt that Elspeth's prophetic powers made a deep and lasting impression on the minds of all who came in contact with her. Elspeth insisted that she could seek no aid for herself from her visions which often came upon her at random and against her will. Tonight, however, she was calling upon her gift of the sight at the request of the MacLeod.

"Begin," the MacLeod said now.

Caitlin watched nervously as Elspeth spread her hands in an arch over her head, raised her chin and began chanting in an ancient tongue. If the woman had the fey, and obviously she had proven that she did, then wasn't it probable that there were things that had happened, or were going to happen that were better not to be revealed? What had happened in the tower, for instance.

Oh, if only I could take her aside, ask her all the questions I have about Niall, she lamented. As it was, Caitlin's future was to be exposed before her father's favored men who were gathered together in a circle around her. Ian MacLeod exhibited a moment of distinct pride as he watched the woman before him wrap herself in a bull hide and enter into a trancelike state. There was something eerie about her eyes as she looked toward the ceiling. It was as if she could see through the wood and the stone to the very heavens themselves.

"What does she see?" Caitlin's whisper was sternly silenced by her father's elbow in her rib.

"Aaaiiieee!" Elspeth wailed. She drew a circle, stepped into it, crossed her arms and chanted in a low voice. "Speak to me," she murmured.

"Who? Who does she want to speak?" Again, Caitlin was silenced.

It was an inopportune time to speak, for at that very moment Elspeth's eyes flew open and she stared directly into

Caitlin's eyes as if she could see into her soul. She shuddered, mumbling all the while, then seemed to be in silent conversation with someone. Her voice was deep, mesmerizing.

"I see a stranger. One who has come by water . . ."

"Niall," Caitlin breathed.

"A golden lion. From his loins will spring forth the strongest of the MacLeods. Strong sons and daughters."

"Aha. I knew it!" Now it was Ian MacLeod who spoke out. "I knew at once that he was the one for my Caity. A voice told me so."

"But beware. . ." Elspeth grabbed at her chest. "Danger. Deceit. Death. They await like thorns. Catching us unaware." Sinking to her knees, the seeress cradled her arms around herself, rocking back and forth, listening to a voice no one else could hear. Quiet filled the darkened room. Only shadows flickered against the stone walls. The floor creaked. It was so still Caitlin could hear the sound of breathing.

"Father, make her tell us what she hears . . ."

Elspeth shuddered. Her eyes narrowed, her voice grew thick. Lifting her head, she looked toward the ceiling again. "I see blood and fire. Enough to cover the glens of Skye."

"We are going to be at war?" A cold sweat broke out upon Ian's brow. "Because of Caitlin marrying a fishermon?" His tone seemed to say that if that was the way it would be he would break his vow.

"Not because of him but because of another. A dark man whose soul is as black as his hair. 'Twas he who killed yer son."

Ian bolted to his feet. "Who is he? I will run him through. I will . . ." He suddenly remembered himself. Sinking back down, he did not interrupt again, though he drummed his fingers on the arms of his chair so roughly that he practically wore holes in the arms.

"Some MacDonald or other. Death to them all," one of the clansmen threatened.

"Aye, death to any MacDonald who would dare cross our threshold," the other voices echoed. Pandemonium broke out as the men discussed amongst themselves the possibility that one of the MacDonalds might try to force his way into the wedding ceremony.

"We'll cut any MacDonald to pieces who dares come anywhere near."

"Spawns of the devil!"

"Bringers of death."

It took Ian's shout of order to get the men quiet again, but all semblance of tranquility was shattered. Suspicion reigned, and danger seemed to lurk in the darkness. There was now a stain on the future and on Caitlin's marriage.

Fifteen

Night-flying birds, ghosts, witches, and a frightening assortment of evil-looking spirits haunted Caitlin's dreams. An eerie distortion of voices and pictures disturbed her sleep. Moaning, she tossed and turned, reliving that moment when the seer had shrieked out her portent of misfortune. "Danger, deceit, death," she had warned, brought on by a dark man whose soul was as black as his hair. The man who was Colin's murderer.

"No!"

Flinging herself onto her stomach, Caitlin was besieged with terrifying visions that wove in and out of her dreams. She remembered having tiptoed to the tower, remembered bits and pieces of that moment when her beloved elder brother had been struck down. A face danced before her eyes. A frightening face.

"Colin!"

He was going to kill her brother, murder him, but there was nothing she could do. She tried to move, but it was as if her feet were stuck to the floor, she wanted to cry out, but her voice was frozen in an eternal, soundless scream. Hands were grabbing her, shaking her, so hard that she could nearly feel her teeth rattle.

"*Caity,* wake up . . ."

"No!" Caitlin's eyes flew open to see Shona standing over her. Remembering her nightmare, she covered her mouth with her hand.

"Caity, what ails ye? Ye were talking in yer sleep something fitful."

"Ails me?" Caitlin's heart was beating so wildly that it took a long moment for her to steady its tempo. "No . . . nothing ails me. Wedding nerves, that is all."

"Excitement." Shona winked. "Well, just let me be saying that I hae heard the lassies talk an' ye are the envy of more than quite a few."

Caitlin didn't really hear her sister. Bolting from the bed, she was in too much of a hurry to find a talisman. Something to guard against the evil that had been foretold.

Shrugging into her gown and arasaid, she searched for and found her cross made out of rowan wood. The rowan, called by some the mountain ash, was said to give protection from witchcraft and evil. Slipping it over her head, she felt relieved . . . until she saw a Wheatear perched outside her window. The bird was a bringer of bad luck and deeply feared in Orkney and Skye. A bad omen for a wedding day, Caitlin thought, her face paling and her hands growing cold.

"It's growing late. Ye slept over long. There are so many things to be done." A Highland wedding was an elaborate and lengthy affair with much ritual attached to it.

Gently tugging at her hand, Shona led her to the bath house where a tub of steaming water awaited. A pile of thick woolen towels were spread on an airer to warm before the fire. In a daze Caitlin stood still as several of the women stripped her of her gown.

"Oh, how I envy ye," one of the younger girls breathed, making no secret of her attraction to Caitlin's bridegroom.

"He is as bonny a mon as was ever seen on Skye."

"A mon who looks like some Viking lord of old."

Stepping into the tub, Caitlin sighed with pleasure as the pleasantly warm water surrounded her. She lay back as the women soaped her hair, but though she tried to relax it was impossible. Even the soothing cocoon of water could not slow the pounding of her heart or make her forget the coil that was forming in her stomach. Soon her life would change forever. No longer would she be a maiden but a wife. No more would she sleep all alone. Her life would be forever entwined with the life of another. A heady thought.

"Oh, the men. What devils they are." Rinsing her sister's hair, Shona related that already there was wagering going on as to how soon she would find herself with child.

"Most of the men are betting on a son. They say the fishermon looks virile," Caitlin's sister Lorna confided, handing Caitlin a towel.

"It had better be a male child or Father will hae the fishermon's head," Shona retorted.

The chatter ceased as Caitlin's mother, followed by two of the older women, arrived carrying Caitlin's dress, the pale-yellow material of which was finely woven and artfully done, decorated all over with embroidery. For a moment she could nearly imagine in her mind's eye a woman's form bent to the task, sitting before the hearth fire.

"Ah, ye will look bonny in this, my wee Caitlin," Fiona MacLeod said, handing the gown to her daughter. Affectionately she planted a kiss on her daughter's brow, instigating a truce between them. Both spirited women, it was no secret in the castle that the two women did not often get along well together. But today all that was set aside.

A white tonnag pinned with an elaborately worked brooch of gold was put around Caitlin's shoulders and a belt of leather and several pieces of brass intermixed was secured around her waist, giving the semblance of a chain and emphasized the trimness of her waist. As was the custom, she was barefoot.

" 'Twill be a sunny day, a perfect day to be wed."

"And ye have the perfect laddie."

The young women chattered and laughed with as much exuberance as if they were to be the brides. They combed and brushed her hair until it shone with a red fire. Unmarried lassies bound their hair and wore a snood, but married women left their hair to hang free. As a symbol of her newly wedded state, therefore, Caitlin's side hair was braided, her back hair left to flow freely.

"Ye look bonny, Caity!"

"Like some regal queen."

Caitlin stood before the large polished steel mirror, studying her reflection. Her father would say, "Stand tall and proud, ye are a MacLeod! A bonny one at that." Was she? Would Niall think her pretty? Though seldom conscious of her looks, she was critical now. She pinched her cheeks to make them pink, then licked her lips to make them shine. Walking down the stairs, she made her grand entrance before all.

"Ach, Daughter, ye truly are a wondrous sight." Standing beside Niall, Ian MacLeod was all smiles. Taking a large cup from the hands of a young male servant, he held it forth to Caitlin. "Drink!" he ordered.

The cup was adorned with a sprig of rosemary and ribbons. It looked like a pagan offering. As she took a sip, she could not help but wonder if some ancient Celtic tribal bride had held such an object in her hand. Handing the cup to Niall, she smiled, forgetting for the moment the trauma of the previous night. She told him that the cup had been handed down for generations, all the way from the first chieftain of the MacLeod clan.

"And I will gi' it to my son when he weds," Niall exclaimed, to be rewarded by a hearty slap on the back from Ian. With a nod of his head, Ian signaled it was time for the merry-making. Rising to his feet, he flung back his chair, leapt upon it and raised aloft the bridal cup as a whirling, high-stepping, jubilant, laughing group of revelers gave vent to their joy.

It was Highland custom for bride and groom to ride pillon on the back of a strong gelding, and thus Caitlin walked beside Niall to the stables, mounting behind him on a long-haired Highland horse for the short ride to the castle chapel on the other side of the courtyard. On the back of the horse, in a leather pouch was placed the marriage money, guarded by two strong Highlanders who walked on each side of the animal. A musical accompaniment of musicians playing harp, flute and bagpipes proceeded.

Niall's hands were gentle as he helped Caitlin dismount. "I'll be good te ye, I promise I will," he said softly. And he would. For the brief span of time they were together he would try to make her happy.

Caitlin's smile was sincere. "I know ye will!" Entering the chapel, she stood tall and proud as she took the lighted candle the priest held forth. The holy man asked the standard questions as a matter of formality; if she was of age, if she swore that she and her betrothed were not within the forbidden degree of consanguinity, if her parents consented to the marriage, if the banns had been posted, and finally and most importantly of all if she and her groom both gave free consent to the match.

"Then come forth, Daughter," he instructed, "to be joined in this holiest of vows."

Caitlin walked down the aisle, looking neither right nor left. She was fearful of the wedding night, why not admit it? She who thought nothing of wrestling and fighting with swords was afraid of being physically claimed by so obviously masculine a man. Even so, she somehow made it to that spot where the priest awaited. There she knelt at her future husband's feet in a gesture of submission.

"Rise!"

Together they faced the priest and repeated their solemn vows. The priest sprinkled her with holy water and recited an intricate mass. The ceremony unfolded so quickly that Caitlin hardly remembered what she had said. It was just babbled words in a foreign tongue. And all the while as she remembered the seer's warning, she clutched tightly to her rowan cross.

The joining of right hands concluded the transfer of a gift, Caitlin's virginity for Niall's protection and loyalty. Niall then slipped onto three of his new wife's fingers, one after another, the blessed ring that signified marriage, a blessed circle of gold that would protect her from assault by demons.

"With this ring I thee wed, with this gold I thee honor, and with this dowry I thee endow."

"A token of love and fidelity," the priest intoned.

Love and fidelity. Would he grow to love her? Would she grow to love him? Indeed, did she already?

The final phase of the ceremony was enacted. The groom was the recipient of the priest's kiss of peace, then he bent to transmit that kiss to his bride. And all the while Caitlin felt as if she were in a trance, watching all of this happen to another young woman. It was a dream. Just a dream.

Returning to the hall, bride and groom presided over the wedding feast, the food of which had been chosen by Caitlin's mother: cold mutton and fowl, haggis, stovies, and all the usual dairy produce, scones, cheese, and the oatcakes that had been Caitlin's favorite since childhood. Whiskey was drunk and the couple toasted by all.

After the feast, a riotous dance ensued, the bridal couple taking the lead in the "wedding reel." The whirling, high-stepping throng of revelers gave vent to their joy. Brightly lit torches illuminated the steps of the dark winding staircase that led to the bridal chamber. A chattering drunken throng accompanied the newly married couple up the winding stairs and to their room.

The highlight of the wedding was the blessing of the bed-chamber and the bed to dispel any curse that might have compromised the couple's fertility and to wipe away any taint of female adultery. So many times Niall had wanted to make Caitlin his. Now the moment was at hand as bride and groom took their places in bed under the watchful eyes of a circle of close relations.

"In this bed will the seed be sown that will mend my heartache," Ian MacLeod intoned; then, with as much reverence as the priest had displayed, he held forth an object.

The fairy flag, Niall thought, trying to hide his surprise. His eyes were riveted on the magical piece of cloth as Ian MacLeod waved it back and forth in a clan ritual.

"O'er the marriage bed this treasure of the MacLeods promises fertility. Thus let the future line of MacLeods come forth." He looked toward Niall expectantly, then placed it over the head of the bed, securing it carefully.

The fairy flag! So close! So tempting. It was all Niall could do to keep from looking at it longingly. But surely it was too good to be true. Ian MacLeod wouldn't just leave it here? Leave it within his reach? He felt his pulse racing at the thought.

Ian MacLeod intoned, "Hae joy of each other . . ." Once witnessed together in bed, the couple was to be left alone to consummate the marriage. The nuptial bed, which was a crucial element in marriage, symbolized what was at stake: power in and over private life. The Highland belief was that honor, marriage, and a person's very being was for the sake of the clan, and the betterment of all.

One by one the guests started to leave, to give the newly wed couple time to be alone. The festivities would continue for most of the night and for several days but for Niall and Caitlin their time would be spent in a far different manner. The very thought made her tremble, while at the same time she tingled with anticipation as she heard his husky voice.

"Bonny, bonny Caitlin . . ." His emotions were in turmoil. Dear Lord, the flag was going to be left unguarded during the consummation of the marriage. So easy to take. So very easy that it was ludicrous.

Cradling her against his chest, Niall lay silent for a long time as he savored her presence beside him while at the same time formulating his plan of action. He would wait until she was asleep, then the flag would be his.

Murmuring Caitlin's name, Niall buried his face in the silky strands of her hair, inhaling the delicate fragrance of flowers in the luxurious softness. His lips traveled slowly down the soft flesh of her throat, tasting the sweetness of her skin. Then with impatient hands he quickly loosened her garments, laughing softly as he realized how clumsy his fingers were. And no wonder.

"I am skilled at untangling fishing nets but all thumbs with lassies' garments, I fear," he exclaimed softly, his fingers parting the fabric of her gown to cup one firm, budding breast.

It seemed his hands were everywhere, touching her, setting her body afire with a pulsating flame of desire. At first frightened, Caitlin gave in to the passion he inspired, writhing beneath him, giving herself up to the glorious sensations he was igniting within her. When at last she was naked, her long, flaming hair streaming down her back, he looked at her, his face flushed with passion, his breath a deep-throated rasp. She was beautiful, more so than he could have ever dreamed.

"Bonny, so very, very bonny." His hands moved along her back sending forth shivers of pleasure, he in the touching and she in being touched. Her waist was small, her breasts perfection, her legs long and shapely. As she lay bathed in candlelight he let his eyes roam over her body.

"Am I?" Caitlin made no effort to hide her curves from his piercing gaze. As he touched her she gloried in the thought that her body pleased him, her pulse quickening at the passion that burned in his eyes. Gone was her maidenly modesty. This was her fate, her destiny, to belong to this man. She felt that in every bone, every muscle, every sinew of her body. Fee on the seer's portent of evil. It couldn't be true. Something ill could not come from something that felt suddenly so right.

"Caitlin . . ." He spoke her name softly, caressingly. Their kisses were tender at first, but the burning spark of their desire burst into flames. Desire flooded his mind, obliterating all reason. Wrapped in each other's arms, they kissed, his mouth moving upon hers, pressing her lips apart, hers responding, exploring gently to the sweet firmness of his. Shifting her weight, she rolled closer into his embrace. How could she deny what was in her heart? Deep inside her was the need to belong to him. Strange, when she had once so feared belonging to any man.

Oh, blessed Christ, Niall thought. How could he have ever realized the full effect her nearness would kindle? She fit against him so perfectly, her gentle curves melting against his own hard body. It was as though Caitlin had been made for him.

"Our bodies are filled with magic," he whispered against her mouth. He kissed the corners of her lips, tracing the outline with his tongue. He parted her lips, seeking the sweetness he knew to be there. His hands moved on her body, stroking her lightly—her throat, her breasts, her belly, her thighs. With reverence he positioned his hands to touch her breasts. Gently. Slowly. Until they swelled in his hands. He wanted to be gentle, but it took all his self-control to keep his passion in check. He wanted to make it beautiful for her, wanted to be the perfect lover.

His exploration was like a hundred feathers, everywhere upon her skin arousing a deep, aching longing. Caitlin closed her eyes to the rapture. Without even looking at him she could see his strong body, amber eyes, and tawny hair and thought again what a handsome man he was. Yet it was something far stronger that drew her, the gentleness that had merged with his strength. She touched him, one hand sliding down over the muscles of his chest, sensuously stroking the warmth of his flesh in exploration. She heard the audible intake of his breath and that gave her the courage to continue in her quest.

"Caitlin . . . !"

He held her face in his hands, kissing her eyelids, the

curve of her cheekbones, her mouth. "Caitlin. Caitlin." He repeated her name over and over again as if to taste of it on his lips.

"I am glad that I please you, for you please me, too, so very much." Her fingertips roamed over his shoulders and neck and plunged into his thick, golden hair as he kissed her once again, a fierce joining of mouths that spoke of his passion. Then after a long pleasurable moment he drew away, drawing the shirt over his head, stripping off his breacan. When he was completely naked, he rolled over on his side and drew her down again alongside him.

"I like the feel of your skin against me," he breathed.

The candlelight flickered and sparked, illuminating the smooth skin on his chest. He was a muscular man, more so than she had supposed. Although he was thin around the waist and hips, his chest was expansive. The hair upon it was soft as she reached out to him. Her hands caressed his chest, her brown eyes beckoning him, enticing him to enter the world of love she sensed was awaiting them both.

Caitlin was shattered by the all-consuming pleasure of lying naked beside him. A heat arose within her as she arched against him in sensual pleasure. Her breath became heavier, and a hunger for him that was like a pleasant pain went from her breasts down to her loins, a pulsing, tingling sensation that increased as his hand ran down the smoothness of her belly to feel the softness nestled between her thighs.

Caitlin gave way to wild abandon, moaning intimately, joyously, as her fingers likewise moved over his body. She felt a strange sensation flood over her and could not deny that before he left she wanted their spirits to be joined together. She wanted his erect manhood to fill her. His strong arms were around her, his mouth covering her own. She shivered at the feelings that swept over her.

The light of the three candles illuminated their bodies, hers as smooth as cream, his muscular form of a darker hue. He knelt down beside her and kissed her breasts, running his tongue over their tips until she shuddered with delight. Whispering words of love, he slid his hands between her thighs to explore the soft inner flesh. At his touch she felt a slow quivering deep inside that became a fierce fire as he moved his fingers against her.

Supporting himself on his forearms, he moved between her legs. Slowly he caressed his pelvis against her thigh, letting her get accustomed to the hardness of his maleness. Caitlin had no fear now that the moment had come. All thought of the doom that had been foretold was wiped away by Niall's tenderness.

"Love me, Niall," she breathed. Arching up, she was eager to drink fully of that which she had only briefly experienced.

"Aye. Oh, I will, my sweet, sweet love." Taking her mouth in a hard, deep kiss, he entered her with a slow but strong thrust, burying his length within the sheath of her softness, allowing her to adjust to his sudden invasion. She was so warm, so tight around him that he closed his eyes with agonized pleasure. No amount of schooling could have prepared him for this. He knew at that moment that love was the true meaning of life, the only thing on earth that was truly worth obtaining. Closing his eyes, he wondered how he could ever have thought that anything—Ambition—was as important as this. At the moment the only thing he wanted was to bring her pleasure, give her his devotion.

As they came together, spasms of feeling wove through Caitlin like the threads of a tapestry. She had never realized how incomplete she had felt until this moment. Joined with him she was a whole being. Feverishly she clung to him, her breasts pressed against his chest. Their hearts beat in matching rhythm even as their mouths met, their tongues entwined, their bodies embraced in the slow, sensuous dance of love. She was consumed by his warmth, his hardness,

and tightened her thighs around his waist as she arched up
to him, moving in time to his rhythm.

"Niall . . . !" It was as if he had touched the very core
of her being. There was an explosion of rapture as their
bodies blended into one. It was an ecstasy too beautiful for
words.

Languidly they came back to reality, lying together in the
aftermath of passion, their hearts gradually resuming a normal rate of rhythm. Niall gazed down upon her face, gently
brushing back the tangled red hair from her eyes.

"Sleep now," he whispered, still holding her close. With
a sigh she snuggled up against him, burying her face in the
warmth of his chest. He caressed her, tracing his fingers
along her spine until she drifted off.

Sixteen

Niall's arm lay heavy across Caitlin's stomach, the heat of his body warming hers as they lay entwined. The sound of his breathing brought a flush of color to her cheeks as she remembered the way she had moved against him. Her senses had responded to Niall the moment he had touched her. Beneath his hands and mouth her body had come alive and she had been lost in a heat of desire she had never believed possible. For a moment in time she had acted like someone wild, someone crazed. She had whispered to him the boldest things, asking him, no *begging* him to do things she would never have even thought of before.

"Ye hae bewitched me, fishermon." Surely that was what he had done. But if that was so, then the bewitchment hadn't yet ended, nor had her yearning to do everything all over again.

Whispering his name, Caitlin stroked the expanse of Niall's shoulders and chest remembering the heated passion they had shared. His skin was warm and smooth, roughened only by a thatch of hair on his chest. Against her breasts it had been more pleasurable than she might have ever have imagined.

"Caitlin?" Niall cherished the blessing of finding her cradled in his arms, her mane of bright red hair spread like a cloak over her shoulders. He felt an aching tenderness and drew her closer. "There now, lassie, that wasn't so bad was it?"

"Not too bad," she answered, too stubborn to tell him how deeply stirring their lovemaking had been. She snuggled into his arms, laying her head on his shoulder, curling into his hard, strong body. If she wasn't yet in love with her handsome husband, she was perilously close.

His hand moved lightly over her hip and down her leg as he spoke. Weeks of frustration and worry seemed to have melted away. She was his! At last he had come to know the glorious sweetness of her body. Oh, but her genuine outpouring of passion had been such a precious gift.

"I'd like to wake up every morning and find ye next to me," he confided, nibbling at her earlobe playfully. But that was not what destiny had in store for him. No matter what vows had been spoken, his union with her could not be forever, no matter how much he wished that it could be. "Caitlin . . ."

"Ye will . . ." *He was her husband. She belonged to him.* A truth that far from upsetting her now made her feel happy and content. Niall was everything a woman could wish for. The other lassies were right to be eaten up with jealousy. Determinedly she shoved aside any misgivings and clung to her optimistic feelings. At this moment she wanted with all her heart to make this union a successful one. Though her fierce pride had at first rebelled at being given in marriage to a fisherman, she knew now that there was not a better man in all of Skye.

"Caitlin, I . . ." He remembered her eyes bright with desire as he had kissed her. Eyes that would blaze anger once she realized what he had done.

I don't want to hurt you. That was never my intent. But dear God, it was inevitable. He was a MacDonald. His loyalty belonged to his clan. That loyalty meant putting the good of his clansmen above all else.

"Caitlin . . ." he whispered again, but though there were many things he wished to say, he ended up not saying a word. Instead, he reached for her, a primal growl in his throat as he kissed her hard. He caught her lips, nibbling with his teeth.

Slowly he began the caressing motions that had so deeply stirred her the first time they had made love. He touched her from the curve of her neck to the soft flesh behind her knees and up again, caressing the flat plane of her belly. Moving to her breast, he cupped the soft flesh, squeezing gently. Her breast filled his palm as his fingers stroked and fondled. Lowering his head, he buried his face between the soft mounds.

"So smooth. 'Tis said there is nothing like a woman's softness."

"Nor a man's strength." She was not content to be only the recipient of pleasure but felt a need to give pleasure as well. With that desire in mind, she moved her palms over the muscles and tight flesh of his body.

"Caitlin . . . !" A long, shuddering sigh wracked through him. "Oh, how I love your hands upon me."

Caitlin was instilled with a new-found confidence, knowing she could so deeply stir him. She continued her exploration as if to learn every inch of him. In response she felt his hard body tremble against hers.

"Ahhhh . . ." The sound came from deep in his throat.

Stretching her arms up, she entwined them around his neck, pulling his head down. Her mouth played seductively on his, proving to him how quickly she could learn such passionate skills. Then they were rolling over and over in the bed, sinking into the warmth and softness. Caitlin sighed in delight at the feel of his hard, lithe body atop hers. Her entire body quivered with the intoxicating sensations. She would never get tired of feeling Niall's hands on her skin, of tasting his kisses.

Before when they had made love, Caitlin had been a bit shy, holding a small bit of herself back from her pleasure. Now she held nothing back. Reaching out, she boldly explored Niall's body as he had done to hers—his hard-muscled chest and arms, his stomach. His flesh was warm to her touch, pulsating with the strength of his maleness. As her fingers closed around him, Niall groaned.

"Caitlin!" Desire raged like an inferno, pounding hotly in his veins. His whole body throbbed with the fierce compulsion to plunge himself into her sweet softness and yet he held himself back, caressing her once more, teasing the petals of her womanhood until he could tell that she was fully prepared for his entry.

"Oh, lassie . . ."

His tongue touched hers, gently opening her mouth to allow him entrance. His tongue thrusting into her mouth at the same moment his maleness entered the softness nestled between her thighs. She felt his hardness entering her, moving slowly inside her until she gasped with the pleasure. Her body arched up to his, searing him with the heat of her passion. Warm, damp, and inviting she welcomed him.

Writhing in pleasure, she was silken fire beneath him, rising and falling with him as he moved with the relentless rhythm of their love. They were spiraling together into the ultimate passion. Climbing together. Soaring. Sweet, hot desire fused their bodies together, yet there was an aching sweetness mingling with the fury and the fire. In the final outpouring of their desire, they spoke with their hearts and hands and bodies words they had never uttered before.

Afterward she cuddled happily in his arms, her head against his chest, her legs entwined with his. Noticing that he was tense, she gazed into his face, disconcerted to see a frown there. How could he be even remotely unhappy after what they had just shared? "Niall, what are ye thinking?"

He was thinking of the fairy flag, wondering if in truth it was really worth the price he was going to have to pay. "About nothing really. Except . . ."

"Except?"

"That there are often things beyond a mon's control.

Times when other men and circumstances control his destiny."

The fairy flag. He could not allow himself to leave without it, though leaving was the very last thing on his mind right now.

"Just as my father controlled my destiny." She lay soft and warm against him, her breasts tightly pressed to his chest. Her long hair tickled his chest as it flowed between them. "But though I rebelled against ye at first, I want ye to know that being yer wife makes me happy now, Niall."

A wave of tenderness washed over him as he reached out to stroke the soft red tresses, brushing them out of her eyes. "And being here with ye makes me the happiest of men." As if to give proof, he held her tightly against him as if he would never let her go.

It was the truth. He was happy. So happy that it made what he had to do now all the more tragic. Oh, that he really were a fisherman. At that moment were he able to trade places with Peadar he would have done so without even blinking an eye. But such things just weren't possible. He was a MacDonald, a cousin in line to be tanist. He could not allow himself to turn against his clan for the sake of his own happiness.

"Oh, Caitlin . . ." His eyes were moist as he lay gently stroking her hair.

Only after she had fallen asleep, when the soft sound of her breathing seemed to assure that she would not easily awaken did he pull away from her. The moment he had been waiting for had regrettably come.

"Good-bye, lassie," he whispered, feeling remorse clutch at his heart. "Ye'll ne'er know how much this pains me." Far more than it would her, or so it seemed, right now.

Oh, how she will hate me when she awakens and finds out what I have done. Even so, Niall didn't even hesitate. Reaching overhead, he tugged the fairy flag down with one hard yank, then without allowing himself to have any second thoughts, he picked up his garments that were lying on the floor and quickly put them on.

"Caitlin . . ." he choked.

Niall knew he should hurry away, but for just a moment in time it was as if his feet were glued to the floor. All he could do was to look down at the lovely face of the young woman who had given him such love and joy. He would remember. For the rest of his life this night would be branded in his heart, in his mind.

"Caitlin," he whispered again.

Bending down, he couldn't resist the temptation to kiss her, his lips lightly brushing her forehead, lingering. Then he was off, moving toward the door with incredible haste, yet with one backward glance, then another and another. Reaching the door, he grabbed the latch, twisted it, pushed open the door. Like the ghost he had once professed himself to be, he disappeared from the room.

Part Two:

A Woman Scorned

"Heaven has no rage like love to hatred turned,
Nor hell a fury like a woman scorned."
                    —*The Mourning Bride,* Act II, sc, 8
                    William Congreve

Seventeen

The flames from the wall sconces flickered, casting eerie shadows against the walls as Niall moved about the castle. Clinging to the shadows, alert to every sound, he stealthfully crept up the stairs. He wore the fairy flag beneath his breacan and he could only hope that it would not bode him ill. If it was good luck for the MacLeods, would it bring bad luck to a MacDonald? He would soon see.

"Careful. Careful," he cautioned to himself as he came around a corner. He paused, looking first left then right. If he were caught leaving the castle there would be no way he could account for his actions. A man just did not leave his bride alone on the night of their wedding. If he were apprehended, only by a miracle would he get off with his life. There would be no way he could talk his way out of trouble this time.

Strange. It seems much too easy. Ridiculously so. There were hardly any guards in the stairwells or corridors. No one to stop Niall or even try to block his way. This seemed much too easy.

"A trap?" Or was it just that the men were preoccupied with their ale-guzzling and were too besotted to give much of anything else a thought? He could only wonder as he made his way to the wall just outside the tower. Niall's nerves were on edge. Cautiously he took a rope from his hiding place. He had to make his way down to the ground far below, for he was unarmed, helpless were he to be set upon by any of the MacLeod's men. He would be a target for swords while he was here atop the wall, a target for arrows once he was dangling over the edge. Nevertheless, he had to take the chance or plan on staying in the MacLeod stronghold permanently. There would be no better opportunity for escape than tonight.

Securing the rope, Niall scanned the area, taking one final look at the interior of Dunvegan Castle, then he climbed over the edge of the wall. It was his misfortune that as he did, a large stone came loose to clatter loudly against the turret as it crashed downward.

"What was that?" Niall heard a voice shout out. "Who goes there?" Niall could see the top of the clansman's head as he moved toward the wall. Frantically he catapulted downward. He had to reach the ground before he was either pierced through with an arrow or the rope was cut and he crashed to his death. Already the clansman was slicing through the rope as he shouted out at the top of his lungs for help.

"God help me!" Niall breathed, fearful that he was about to meet a gruesome end. As it was, the fairy flag or God or both seemed to bring him good fortune. The rope was stronger than one might have supposed. Strong enough to allow Niall to reach a spot just a few feet above the rocks before it gave away. He fell and was winded, but as he pushed himself up he could tell there were no broken bones.

That did not mean he was safe, however. The skirl of bagpipes, the beating of drums, the blare of trumpets told him an alarm had been sounded. It would only be a short time before the entire castle was roused. Once that happened he would be the object of a relentless hunt. Well, he was determined that he wouldn't get caught.

Dodging in and out among the rocks, Niall knew that vow to be more bravado than reality. The ocean was at high tide, crashing against the rocks with a ferocity that was terrifying even to a fighting man. Even had Peadar been

waiting for him, which he knew he wouldn't be after all
this time, the sea was no way to journey tonight. He would
have to go the long and hard way over the rocky land, on
foot.

The moon was shrouded by dark clouds, his only guide
the light of the fading stars. Nevertheless he plucked up his
courage. He would get back to Sleat and be welcomed as
a hero once he handed over the fairy flag. He would be
made tanist, a worthy reward. Enough to make any man
happy.

Happy? For just an instant Caitlin's face flashed before
his eyes. But then perhaps happiness was only a dream after
all . . .

Caitlin stirred, stretching her arms and legs in slow, easy
motions as she came awake. She smiled as she remembered
her wedding night. She had never known such happiness
existed, but she had found it in the arms of a fisherman.
Marriage, at least this part of it, was infinitely pleasing.

Love. It was a wonderful word. It warmed her, made her
feel safe. In short it was a blessed emotion.

I will be a good wife, she vowed silently. Even if that
meant giving in to woman's work and the discipline marriage brought, Caitlin was willing to try. Niall made her
happy. How then could she have worried so about the outcome of what was obviously meant to be.

"Niall . . . ?" Wanting to renew the sensation of lying
in Niall's arms she turned over on her side, searching for
him with her hands and eyes. "Niall . . . ?"

He was gone.

Just like a man. No doubt he had slipped away to join
with the revelers who were celebrating their wedding. A
Highland wedding was a lengthy affair and theirs had just
begun. Well, she would soon remind him that there were
more enjoyable things that could be done in the quiet of

the night. With that thought in mind, she rose from the bed, hurriedly slipped on a tunic and went in search of him.

The stones were cold to her bare feet as Caitlin climbed up and down the stairs, seeking her groom. "Niall?"

So preoccupied was she that at first she didn't even notice the frantic cries of the sentry, but at last they penetrated through her pleasant daydreams.

"Someone has gone over the wall! Someone has left the castle in a manner that bodes no good."

Someone? The longer and harder Caitlin searched for Niall the more she came to realize just who that someone might be. Even so, she refused to listen to the voice in her head that whispered he had left her. No. No. He would never do that, not after what they had shared last night. He was simply cloistered away somewhere. He would reappear. She was certain of it.

Certain? Why then did she find herself drawn to that spot where she had watched her father put the fairy flag? Why were her fingers trembling as she fumbled about in search of it?

"Gone!"

No. Her father must have chosen another hiding place. Niall would never . . .

Ah, but he had. The heartbreaking evidence was clear. Oh, yes, he had stolen the flag in the dead of night and then disappeared.

Tears streamed down her cheeks but she dashed them away. A MacLeod must never cry. Not over a man, even if he was a husband. Despite that vow, however, the knowledge that she had been betrayed threatened to destroy her.

Eighteen

Smoke from the cooking fires stung Caitlin's eyes as she worked diligently at the loom, or at least she blamed the moisture in her eyes on the smoke. Her anger and heartache merged, threatening to choke her. How could he? How could he have done such a loathsome thing? How could he have mouthed words that would bind them together, make love to her not once but twice and then just up and go?

"Ohhhhhhh!" The very question filled her with an anger that threatened to destroy her. She had been used, then callously cast aside without even a second thought. The fisherman had wanted to get his hands on the fairy flag. Now thanks to her he had, though what purpose he had for it the clan still could not fathom, unless it was to increase the fish in the lochs where he fished.

The fairy flag had threefold magical powers that included making fighters invincible in battle, promising fertility in a marriage—and lastly, if put over the loch, it brought the herring shoals. So it seemed that Caitlin's virginity had been bartered for the sake of a school of fish.

"How could he?" This time the tears that stung her eyes flowed freely down her cheeks.

Caitlin remembered all too vividly that moment when she had awakened to find the place beside her in bed empty. Rising, she had gone in search of Niall only to be swept up in the tumult created when the alarm was sounded. The entire castle had been alerted that someone had scaled the

castle wall. That someone, she had all too soon realized,
had been her loving groom. Worse yet, she had discovered
that he had gone and not gone alone. The fairy flag was
conspicuous by its absence. It was missing, stolen. That
reality had been Caitlin's final blow.

"Fisherman, och, how I hate thee." And she did, at least
for the moment. Hated him with an intensity, a burning
rage, that nearly poisoned her. "He left me behind without
even so much as a word . . ."

Worse yet, she couldn't forget him. He filled her thoughts
by day and her dreams by night, haunting her like a ghost.
"Being here with ye makes me the happiest of men," he
had said, lying with every breath.

"Caitlin! Be careful. You're tangling the threads." Her
mother's high-pitched voice sounded a warning.

Caitlin drew in a deep breath and let it out slowly in a
sigh. "I'm sorry. I wasna paying much attention to what I
was doing." Plucking at the wool, she hastily rectified the
situation, untwisting the thread, then passing it more cautiously back and forth, interlacing the weft through the warp
threads with her shuttle.

"Ach, so we've noticed." Fiona's smile expressed her
sympathy, though she did not force her daughter to talk
about the matter. If Caitlin wanted to open up her heart to
her, she would.

Caitlin focused her attention on the loom, a simple rectangular frame made of wood, watching as the other women
rolled up an end of the finished cloth to make way for a
new length of weaving. They unwound the spindle and
measured off the vertical threads in roughly equal lengths.
The threads would be the warp of the extended length of
cloth. Setting the loom upright again, tilted against the wall,
they let the warp threads go taut, hanging down vertically
across the wooden frame.

Blessed Saint Michael, Caitlin thought, rubbing her eyes.
It somehow reminded her of the small mattress at the cot-

tage. She could imagine herself lying upon its softness, could feel Niall's strong body pressed against hers.

"Careful tipping the loom or we'll be done for it!" Shona's irritated shriek at one of the other girls startled Caitlin out of her daydreaming and she jumped. Her nerves were on edge, making her as surly as a bear.

"Ye are much too jittery, Caity." Fiona shook her tawny-haired head, then in motherly concern, she touched Caitlin's arm. "What is done is done. Ye must try and forget."

"Forget!" She looked at her mother with much the same expression she might have had if she had been slapped. "I canna forget. I was betrayed." She shuddered. "The marriage vows were consummated, Mother. Do ye hae any idea how that makes me feel? Used. Dirtied."

Fiona's look was all-knowing. "I do understand. I do." Her eyes mirrored a deep inner sadness. "But there are worse things in life, Daughter."

"Worse?" Caitlin couldn't think of what that could be.

Her mother explained it bluntly. "Ye still hae yer life and yer health."

Caitlin's cheeks colored. "Aye, I am alive," she answered tartly. "At least it seems that I am." But inside she felt as if she were dying. She couldn't eat, couldn't sleep. She kept remembering the gentle way his hands had stroked her face, belying his strength. The way he had . . .

"For which ye should be thankful." Fiona's voice was soft as she said, "Life is not so much what happens to a person but how they accept the circumstances. Ye can either see the storm clouds or the rainbows, the sunlight or the shadows."

"Be optimistic, ye mean." Caitlin looked down at her hands. "I canna be. Not now." Perhaps never again.

"Och, then it's sorry I am for ye, Daughter."

Caitlin ignored her mother's rebuke, keeping to her silence, pretending unwavering interest in the maide dalbh, the pattern sticks that served as a guide for the weaving.

She and the other women were working on a special plaid, one they hoped would be the symbol for the clan. It was a yellow-and-black plaid with just a hint of a red stripe. The dyes that were used were made from local lichens, mosses, and other plants.

It was a tedious undertaking, for the cloth was to be made from twelve ells of plaid, a long piece of cloth to be certain. They had to work carefully. Anything with more than one color increased the complexity of the weaving, necessitating more than one shuttle and a careful counting of threads to match the established pattern.

"Ha, I never thought I'd see the day when you would seek out our company for longer than a few wee minutes, Caitlin." Trying to change the subject and lighten the mood, Shona reminded Caitlin of how infrequently she kept company with the women.

It was true, Caitlin couldn't deny it. The fact was she avoided the women and their weaving every time she could. Usually one to seek the outdoor air, Caitlin had been strangely reflective these last three weeks. "I dunna want to be with the men."

Caitlin shifted in her seat and grasped her shuttle more tightly. In and out, in and out, she worked with her spindle, trying to calm her shattered nerves. The truth was, she just couldn't stand to see the way the men stared at her, as if seeing her as damaged goods. A discarded bride.

Once she had abhorred women's work. Now, however, those chores were her only escape from the thoughts and memories that taunted her. Still, she fired back a scathing answer. " 'Tis none of yer concern where I spend my time, I'd be thinking, sister dear," she exclaimed. "Lestwise I just might make it known to Father that ye hae been keeping company with a certain physician."

"Ye wouldna!"

"I would."

"Caity . . ." Her mother's tone cautioned that there would be trouble if the argument went any further.

Caitlin ignored her mother, to concentrate on her work. Ah yes, the plaid would be perfect. As soon as the cloth was finished, it would be tread on in water to fill the weave and then fluffed with dried, prickly flowers called teazels to raise the fiber. The last step to the process would be to dry the fabric and stretch it on poles to block it.

Niall would have looked grand in the new tartan. She was haunted by the memory of the way he had thrown his breacan so jauntily over his shoulder.

"No!" Caitlin gasped aloud, causing the others to stare. Quickly she covered her lips with her fingers, regretting the outburst. Why oh why couldn't she get the fisherman out of her mind? The answer screamed at her. She was trying to run away from her heart by working so diligently, but she couldn't escape her desire. She could not flee from her feelings. The sad truth was that she missed him, cared for him. More than she could allow herself to admit. Particularly when he obviously didn't care at all for her.

Where is he? Where could he have gone? She had asked herself that question many times. They had all asked that question. It was still unanswered. Though Ian MacLeod had gathered up his men, had scoured the entire countryside including the shoreline, not even a trace of the fisherman had been found.

Could he have drowned? Once again to her dismay Caitlin dropped her spindle, tangling the thread. No, she wouldn't allow herself to even think that. He couldn't be dead. Not Niall. Nor, despite her anger, would she have wished it to be so. Someday they would once again be face-to-face and when that happened she would tell him just what she thought of him.

Caitlin carefully counted the threads she was weaving, determined to put the matter out of her mind. Ten black threads. Time to change to the yellow-threaded spindle. And when the plaid was done she'd begin on another.

The din of bagpipes jarred her from her thinking. The pipes, summoning everyone to gather. The sound was unnerving. Shattering. Worse yet, it meant that something unforetold had happened.

"What is it?" Shona voiced all their fears. She could not help but wonder if another clash of shields and swords was about to ensue.

"There is only one way to know." Putting down the cloth, Caitlin was the first one to the door. The seer had foretold blood and fire. Had that moment arrived when the dark man would bring the MacLeods to the brink of destruction?

Total pandemonium greeted her as she pushed through the heavy wooden door of the large stone hall. Ominously the MacLeod clansmen were preparing themselves for the imminent danger that was to come. Brandishing their weapons, which reflected the flames ablaze in the hearth, they grumbled in anger as they waited for their chief, Ian MacLeod, to enter the hall.

Caitlin's eyes darted back and forth, searching for the familiar form of her father. Where was he? As if her anxiety conjured him up, he soon pushed through the door of the adjoining room he used as a council chamber. His face was contorted in a blaze of fury. Pulling at his beard, he strode back and forth before the fire, muttering beneath his breath.

"What is it, Father?" Only Caitlin dared ask the question that all within the room wondered.

"I've just received a message from the MacDonalds. I dinna ken what to make of it!"

"The MacDonalds?" A ripple of uneasiness swept throughout the hall.

"They hae been quiet much too long. I should hae known it wouldna last," Ian said aloud.

"Nae!" The men were unanimous in their shout.

Anger buzzed around from man to man like an enraged

bee as the clansmen savored old slights and tragedies, all at the MacDonalds' hands.

Ian MacLeod silenced the protestations by raising his hand. Though in truth he was but a few inches taller than most of the men, he seemed to tower over them as he pulled back his shoulders and held up his hand.

"They brazenly hae announced that they plan to attack the stronghold," he said curtly. "And they threaten that this time they will win."

"And we dunna hae the flag!" Caitlin's voice sounded as ominous as the seer's had that day. All the while she was struggling with her conscience. She had kept silent about the matter of having caught Niall trying to steal the flag again. Now he had accomplished that mission to the detriment of her clansmen. *With as much precision and ruthlessness as if he had been . . . had been a . . . a* MacDonald, she thought but did not say.

"Nae, we dunna hae the flag." Ian pretended not to care, though the gravity of the matter was marked on his face. "But it doesna matter. 'Twas superstition only. We can win without it."

Through the years there had been times when the MacLeods had won, times when the MacDonalds had been victors in the battles. Both clans had been losers in the toll taken on their families. Warfare between the rival clans had brought forth a torrent of heartache. Now it appeared that it was happening all over again under the worst of circumstances. Like it or not, whether the flag was really a talisman or just a measure of good luck in the minds of the clan, the lack of their flag made the MacLeods vulnerable.

Nineteen

The hall was dimly lit. Only the dying embers of the fire shed illumination on the two figures sitting side by side, intent in conversation. One was a man in the autumn of his years, the other a man in the prime of his life. Tall and lean but well muscled, he had a strength about him that was almost overpowering. Even his manner of dress proclaimed his self-esteem. He was dressed now in a breacan, wrapped round the waist and belted, a length of which was draped over his shoulder and pinned with a jeweled brooch.

"Aye, ye are a MacDonald through and through. A chip off my shoulder, lad. As dear to me as any son could e'er be."

Malcolm looked upon Niall with pride. His particular distinction was on the battlefield, and he had done the MacDonalds proud! But no physical feat could have matched the one he had just accomplished. Niall MacDonald had brought back the fairy flag. The very soul of the clan MacLeod.

"Aye, lad, I honor ye." Holding the goblet to his lips, he drank deeply of the contents, then wiped his mouth with the back of his hand. "Oh, how I wish I could see Ian MacLeod's face now. Oh that I were a spider on the wall." Throwing back his head, he roared with laughter.

Niall didn't join in the joviality. Though he had been welcomed as a hero, just as he knew he would be, his mood was somber. Leaning back in his chair, he looked southward, as if he could see through the very walls to the lands beyond.

Oh, Caitlin, why is it so very hard to put ye from my mind? Why? Closing his eyes, he could nearly see her face the way it had looked when he had kissed her good-bye. Her eyelids had been closed, she had looked so peaceful, so trusting. Trusting of the man who had so cruelly betrayed her.

"As loyal a MacDonald as ever there be. That ye are, lad," Malcolm MacDonald was saying. "Risking yer very life to bring us back the greatest boon we could hae ever received. The flag! The flag!" Again Malcolm chortled.

"Aye, I risked my life." *And lost my heart and soul,* Niall thought. He remembered vividly his escape from the MacLeod's lands, a treacherous journey that had rendered him blisters, cuts, scratches, and bruises. Most of the way had been on foot, for having told the lie of being a fisherman, he was certain the MacLeod would have lookouts posted along the coast. Climbing the curious flat-topped mountains to the southwest, known as MacLeod's Tables, he had made his way by land down the east coast, carefully dodging in and out lest the MacLeod put his wolfhounds on the trail.

It had been a mountainous and rocky terrain, rough traveling over mountains and moors shrouded by low-flying clouds. The Isle of the Clouds is what the Norsemen had dubbed Skye. Using that cloud cover to hide from any pursers, Niall had blessed the fog, all the while praying that he would make it back to Sleat alive.

Malcolm MacDonald lounged drunkenly in his carved wooden chair by the roaring hearth fire, taking long gulps of his ale, idly watching his handsome, tawny-haired nephew.

"Something is wrong with ye, lad."

He couldn't quite figure out what it was. Since coming back from the MacLeod's castle Niall was more subdued, less cocky despite the wondrous thing that he had done. He seemed deep into contemplation for long periods of time, laughed seldomly.

"Did I not know better, I'd think the MacLeod's sent back a changling in yer place, Niall. Of a sureity I would." Niall's reflective mood was troublesome.

"Perhaps they did, Uncle, for I am not the same man who left this hall. Aye, I've changed." Strange how one wee lassie could work such havoc in his life, he thought, and yet she had. Thinking about the way he had left her caused a gnawing ache in his heart that he could not remedy no matter how hard he tried.

Squinting his eyes, Malcolm tried to decipher Niall's meaning. "And I dunna like it! Cheer up. Be thankful to be back safe and sound."

"I am thankful."

"Then smile."

Niall forced his lips to curl upward, but there was no sincerity in the gesture. All he could think about was that Malcolm was planning to attack the MacLeod stronghold, bringing death and destruction to those Caitlin loved. And all because of him and what he had done.

"Why must there always be fighting here on Skye," he said softly, not to Malcolm but to himself.

Malcolm heard. "Why? Why?" His face was contorted with sudden anger. "Ask that of Ian MacLeod, why don't ye. He is the one who insists on claiming land that isna his." He took another gulp from his cup. His brows drew together in a scowl.

"And do ye never want to hae peace?"

"Hold yer tongue!" Malcolm thundered. In a show of contempt he threw his ale, cup and all, into the fire, watching as the flames sputtered. "Ye hae always been my favorite, though I hae never spoken so. I hae great ambitions for ye, laddie. There is no hill ye canna climb if ye use yer head."

And keep silent, Niall thought. Malcolm was telling him that if he behaved, did things exactly Malcolm's way, he would be tanist. The honor he had once coveted above all. Now the reward seemed but a hollow victory. Strange how life seemed so empty without the red-haired lass. Ambition could not keep a man warm at night or give him comfort.

"They hae e'er been our enemies." Seeing a fly crawling across the stone floor, he vented his anger on the hapless insect, grinding it beneath the heal of his cuaran. That was how he would crush the MacLeod!

A troubled silence ensued. Niall stared at his uncle, watching the myriad of emotions that played upon the bearded face. In most matters a reasonable man, Malcolm looked more like a snarling dog. Was that what all this fighting had brought them all to? Creatures not much better than the MacLeod's hounds? If so, then he regretted what he had done more than anything in all his life.

How many mugs of whiskey would it take to numb his mind? How much barley bree need he drink? Niall wondered before he could ease his conscience? Already his vision was blurred, his head buzzed, yet he continued to raise the mug to his lips.

"If ye drink any more of that, Niall my friend, ye will be as pickled as a herring." Coming up to sit beside him, Ogg eyed him worriedly.

"If I drink any more o' this, mayhap I can hae a little peace." Niall's heart was heavy, his temper on edge. By God, how he missed her. More so than he had ever thought it possible to miss another human being. There was something about her that he craved, like a man hankered for strong drink. She had given his life new meaning, had given him love, and how was he going to repay her? By bringing the wrath of the MacDonald down on her head.

"Peace, ye say." Though he was not bid to sit down, Ogg

plopped down on the bench beside Niall. His big frame caused the bench to quake, but Niall didn't seem to notice. "Peace from what?"

"I dunna want to talk of it." It was just too painful a subject, even to share with Ogg, at least for the moment. With a groan, Niall closed his eyes.

"Something happened at the MacLeod castle, something that has changed ye." Again Ogg wondered aloud, "What?"

Niall put his fingers to his temples, pressing hard as if by so doing he could force Caitlin MacLeod from his mind. It did no good. He could envision her now, sweeping into the room so haughty and so proud, her dark red hair flying around her shoulders like a shawl of living flame.

"Caity!"

Ogg cocked his head. "Did ye say Caity?"

Niall didn't answer; he was too disturbed by the images floating in front of his eyes. He imagined Caitlin being surrounded by a throng of Highland warriors, heard her cry out, saw her fall. It was a daydream that left him shaken and sick to his stomach.

"By the saints, Niall, ye look as sick as if ye had seen a ghost." Ogg leaned closer. "Did ye? Did ye see the ghost of Colin MacLeod? Did it possess ye?"

Niall raised his head. "Aye, possessed is what I am." And tortured by the thought of what he had done. He was a man of action, a man who went after what he wanted. *Ambitious* was the word. Now it seemed that his thirst for power had goaded him into the greatest wrong he had ever done. A wrong that could ne'er be righted.

Silence reigned, like the quiet before a devastating storm. The castle was shrouded in darkness. Everyone was abed except the two young women who sat cross-legged on the floor playing a game of wooden pegs. It was a man's game of warfare and strategy wherein the pegs were like a miniature army that could be moved around the wooden board. A game Caitlin had always enjoyed playing but which troubled her now that an armed conflict between the MacDonalds and MacLeods appeared to be imminent.

"Och, Caity, I took yer chieftain again. That's three times in a row. Ye must not be thinking, hinny." Shona clucked her tongue sympathetically, but still seemed to take great delight in having won at a game she nearly always lost. "Do ye want to play again?"

"Hmm?" The vacant look in Caitlin's eyes proved that she hadn't been listening.

"I asked if ye wanted to play again."

Pushing the game board away, Caitlin shook her head. "No. My heart just isna in it."

"Nor yer mind." Carefully picking up the carved pegs, stuffing them into a small leather pouch, Shona didn't even try to hide her concern. "Fie on ye, Caity, to let some mon destroy ye this way. Handsome he was, aye, but not worth what ye hae been going through." Gently she touched her sister's arm. "Ye are a bonny lass. There will be other laddies, all of them standing in line just for the bliss of a smile."

Caitlin took a deep breath and let it out in a deep sigh. "I dunna want a laddie. I willna marry again. Ever."

"Ever?" Shona was shocked by the finality of such a statement.

"Ever." Caitlin ran her fingers through her tangled hair. Hair she didn't even bother to comb for days on end, she who was always so proud of her fiery tresses. "I obeyed Father's command. I went willingly to the altar. He canna ask more of me than that."

"But . . ."

"Whether or no my groom chose to live with his bride, I am married, Shona. What happened canna be annulled because . . ." The marriage had been consummated, binding

Caitlin to the fisherman, at least until the Holy Church in Rome decided otherwise.

"Because he claimed his husbandly rights, the devil." In a rare show of temper, the usually gentle Shona threw the pouch with the gamepieces to the floor, scattering them all about. "Oh, how I damn a mon who could do such a thing and then vanish in the night without—"

"Hush!" Caitlin closed her eyes tightly, as if by so doing she could forget. "I dunna want to even think . . ." *Or feel.* And yet how could she shut the fisherman out of her thoughts when his image haunted her night and day.

Niall. *The fisherman.* Even now she could envision him as vividly as if he were standing right there with them in the room. She could imagine how golden his hair looked in the torchlight, how dazzling his smile appeared. She remembered his arrogant stance, the way he cocked his head, the bold way he walked as if he were the leader of some mighty clan.

"I wonder . . ."

"Wonder what, Caity?" Regretting her outburst, Shona quickly got down on hands and knees, retrieving the pegs that littered the cold stone floor.

"I wonder why and who . . . ?"

That, as much as his leaving, was deeply troubling Caitlin. It just didn't make sense. She had trouble believing that Niall was merely a fisherman. Oh, no, there was something else that lay at the root of his sudden appearance at the castle. Something she couldn't allow herself to even think. And yet . . .

The fairy flag is important to the MacLeods, but would it not also be important to the MacDonalds as well? Wouldn't Malcolm MacDonald give even his favorite sword, nae the very shirt off his back just to possess it? And were he to possess it, wouldn't that explain his sudden boldness, the cocky way he had threatened to start the fighting all over again? Aye, Caitlin answered to herself. And aye again.

Yet even having answered yes, she couldn't really allow herself to believe it. She, Caitlin nic Ian married to a Mac-Donald? Never!

Why, the very thought! After all, hadn't it been said that all MacDonalds had long noses, hair growing in their ears, big feet, and faces that could turn a lassie to stone? Of a surety that description didn't fit Niall. "And yet . . ."

"What is that?"

"What?" Caitlin looked at Shona, disconcerted to see that her face was as pale as a ghost's.

"That cry."

They both listened, their hearts quickening as they realized what it was. The cry of "hold fast." The MacLeod cry to battle. Running to the window, both young women leaned over the stone ledge, their eyes scanning the horizon.

"Look!" Two men, each carrying a pole with a cross of fire blackened wood, were visible in the moonlight. It could only mean one thing.

"The MacDonalds are coming!" The threat that they were going to attack Dunvegan Castle was no idle boast.

"Heaven help us!" Shona clutched at her chest, her fear nearly tangible. The two sisters looked at each other for a long time knowing battle was inevitable.

"We canna fight. We are helpless." Or nearly so. Still, both young women knew that their father was placed in an intolerable position. It was either fight or back down. They knew their father would choose to fight for his honor even though the MacLeods' sense of doom reverberated throughout the castle.

"To arms! To arms!" The cry was shouted out so loud that it shook the very walls. Caitlin watched as her clansmen stripped every sword, shield, targe, and dirk from the wall. Old hatreds were hard to quit and Malcolm's aggression a potent poison.

Shouts rent the air. What followed was a clashing and a slashing of swords, a bloody and violent melee.

Together the sisters watched from the window of their room in prayerful silence as the battle exploded all around them like some ghastly dance.

"Father, do ye see Father?" Caitlin was nearly frantic as he disappeared into the swarm of fighting men. Her heart skipped a beat as she saw a bearded man fall, but it wasn't him.

Shona spotted him. "He's over there. By the outer wall." Swinging his sword, he looked to be an awesome force to come up against despite his age. One by one he was felling any man foolish enough to come within reach of his claymore. His courage, stamina, and stubbornness seemed to rally the others, for suddenly it seemed the battle had turned in the MacLeod's favor. Relentlessly they were pushing the MacDonalds back.

"Back to the hellhole ye came from," the MacLeod shouted out, his voice fading to a gasp.

"What is it? What is wrong?" Shona leaned so far out the window that she nearly fell, her eyes focused southward.

"Nae!" Caitlin saw, but she didn't believe her eyes. In truth she didn't want to. "It couldna be." But it was. In an outward show of defiance and brazenness the MacDonalds were flying a banner, one all too familiar to Caitlin's eyes.

"Caity! Ye look as if ye are going to faint."

"I am." Or at least she wished she could so that she wouldn't have to look at such a travesty of fate.

At that moment Caitlin MacLeod was so devastated by what her eyes revealed she could have died. Flying high on a long pole was a piece of cloth she knew only too well. A sight that chilled her to the very bone.

"No. It canna be." But it was. There before her very eyes was proof of Niall's devastating betrayal. "The fairy flag."

Twenty

Confusion and havoc reigned. The loud clink of sword and axe rang out mingling with hostile yells and epitaphs as MacDonald and MacLeod engaged in brutal fighting. Sweat poured from Niall's brow as he parried, thrust, whirled around.

"Take care, Niall!"

Ogg's timely warning allowed him to narrowly miss the blade that cut through the air. With a mumbled oath, Niall responded in kind. Brandishing his sword, he soon vanquished his attacker.

Niall's head was throbbing as he swung his sword back and forth, pushing back anyone who threatened to get in his way. Always before he had gloried in battle; now, however, as he stumbled and nearly fell over the body of a fallen enemy he viewed it as a loathsome and destructive thing. Still, he had to do his part. He was a MacDonald, and even though he had no liking for this cruel feuding he couldn't allow harm to come to his own. Even so, he could not keep his eyes from darting upward now and again. Where was Caitlin? Was she safe? He had to think so or be consumed by guilt. Guilt that he had used her. Guilt that he had lied to her. Guilt that he had been the perpetrator of such vile betrayal.

Does she know? Has she guessed? Has she seen the flag flapping in the breeze? If so, then she would realize his identity and would know him to be who and what he was.

Her enemy! He who had been instrumental in the MacLeod's ensuing defeat.

"Ach, Niall, look at the expression on Ian MacLeod's face. He knows he willna win. They are but playing for time. They hae lost the badge o' their courage. Soon, soon the MacLeods will be forced to give up."

"Give up? Never!" Anger ruled as a MacLeod, having overheard, plunged forward. He was quickly felled.

The MacDonalds were anxious for complete victory. Egged on by Malcolm they closed around their longtime foes, wielding weapons that took a painful toll they moved. Though the MacLeods were desperate to rally, though the tide of battle briefly turned in their favor, in the end they could do little but retreat.

Bloodied, battered, and disheartened, the MacLeod clansmen limped or were carried back to the hall. Listening to the moaning and cries of pain from the wounded, Caitlin experienced the most profound sense of sadness she had ever known. It was a pathetic sight. A gruesome reminder of the carnage such violence could bring.

"How many were killed?" As Jamie passed by, she tugged at his sleeve.

"Too many!" The self-assured Jamie had been humbled, tragically so. Holding his arm to staunch the flow of blood, he retreated to the corner to see to his injuries, reminding Caitlin of an injured hound licking his wounds. He didn't want to talk about the battle that had been his greatest humiliation.

Some of the others were not as silent, however. Listening to the talk, Caitlin soon learned that it had been more costly in lives than the clansmen had first thought. Worse yet, though the MacLeods had defended the castle, the MacDonalds were laying claim to Trotternish, an area of land to the east that had been the source of contention since long before Caitlin was born.

"So, they hae stolen our flag and our land," she swore beneath her breath. What's more, she knew just who to blame. At that moment had she had the power she would have damned him to hell forever.

The sickeningly sweet odor of fresh blood assailed Caitlin's nostrils as she moved in and out among the wounded. Tearing the hems of their night gowns into strips, she and her sisters carefully tended the wounded. It was a sobering initiation for all of them into the real world.

"Very different from the glories the seanachaidh tells us of," Shona breathed, trying to ignore the screams that issued from the throat of the young man she was tending.

"Far different."

Caitlin knew this time in her life would haunt her. The eyes filled with anguish, the cries of the wounded, the moans of those who were dying all made her aware of her helplessness. There was just so much she could do. She could bathe their faces, wrap their injured limbs in bandages, try her best to make them comfortable, shower them with words to soothe their aching pride, but she could not take away their shame. Shame that they had embarrassed their very name.

"Damn the MacDonalds."

"They are little more than thieves."

"Stole the flag from under our very noses."

"Aye but how?"

Eavesdropping on the wounded men's conversation, Caitlin wanted to tell them her suspicions, but feared the reaction such a revelation might inspire. Even so, she knew. She knew! Maybe that was why she viewed the stairs with trepidation as she climbed the steps to answer the summons from her father. She knew all too well what he was going to tell her and dreaded this confrontation more than she had ever dreaded anything in her life.

Having bolstered her bravery by drinking several draughts of ale, she felt strangely dizzy and not as blissfully content as she had hoped. Perhaps then there was no potion that could take away the sting of betrayal or calm her feelings of guilt.

I should have told my father about Niall's trying to steal the flag again. If I had, all this would not have come about. Instead, she had kept silent trying to protect a man who did not deserve shielding. A thief! A liar! *And maybe even worse.*

It was a short distance to her father's room yet it seemed like a mile of plodding one foot in front of the other, up, up, up the stone stairs. Even so, once the chamber door loomed in her path, Caitlin seemed to lose all courage. How was she going to tell her father that she had kept Niall's transgression a secret? How was she going to reveal her betrayal of her own clan? Was she to brush it off as enchantment? Blindness? Foolishness? In truth, there was no way to even understand it herself. All she knew was that the ensuing circumstances had proven that she had done her father a great wrong.

Like the most awesome portcullis the door rose up before her. Raising a trembling hand to the wood, swallowing hard, she knocked hesitantly, a gesture that reflected her apprehension.

Caitlin's knock was answered by her father's shouted, "Come in!"

Her hands trembled as she opened the door. "Ye called for me, Father."

"Aye! That I did." Lighting a taper, he lowered his bulk into a wooden chair and gestured for her to do the same. Instead, Caitlin remained standing, her eyes assessing her father's well-being in but the wink of an eye. Enough time to tell that he was all right.

He came right to the point. "I hae done ye a grievous

wrong, Daughter. In my stubborn pride, my insistence that ye bend to my will I hae ruined not only ye but the clan."

She tried to speak, to tell him what she knew in her heart, but her words came out only as a strangled gasp. All she could do was stare at her father as he buried his face in his hands. Never in all her life had she seen him shed even one tear, yet he shed several now.

"Oh, lassie! Lassie! How can I bear it? How can I atone for what I hae done to ye? How can I tell ye what I know to be true? How can I reveal the shame of it? The terrible foolish stupidity."

"Father . . ." Her heart ached to know that he was suffering because of her, because he thought he had forced her into an unwelcome marriage. She had to tell him the truth, that she had secretly been more than willing, that she had lusted after her tawny-haired betrothed, so much so that she had ruined them all.

Ian MacLeod looked up slowly, his eyes meeting hers. "I learned something tonight. Something I dunna want to tell ye. Yer husband is . . . is . . ."

Caitlin's voice came out in a whisper. "I know."

Ian stiffened. "Ye ken? How?"

She tapped at her temple with her finger. "I figured it out in here. Two plus two plus two came out MacDonald. It was the only thing that could explain so many things."

He seemed relieved not to have to be the one to tell her. "Aye, the mon who pretended to be a fishermon was none other than Niall MacDonald, nephew to my greatest enemy."

"Nephew!" So, it was even worse than she had supposed. Not only a MacDonald but a member of the chieftain's family. A man her clansmen had dubbed the "MacLeod's scourge."

"The vile, deceitful bastard!" Clenching his hands into fists, the MacLeod raised them high over his head. "No fishermon at all but a MacDonald who came all the way to the castle with but one thought on his mind."

"Father . . . I . . ."

He bolted from his chair. "Oh, that I had thrown him into the dungeon that very first day. Instead, my eyes were blinded. I should hae known his foolish prattle aboot trying to prove his bravery was a falsehood. But he was such a fine-looking specimen of a mon. He seemed to be so right for ye, hinny." He hung his head. "All I could think about when he reminded me of my vow was what fine grandchildren a mon like that would sire. And so . . ."

"He fooled us both," she breathed. Moving toward Ian, she took his hand. Before she had time to make any confessions, however, he was kneeling in front of her. A homage that was unusual for such a prideful man.

"Forgive me, Caity. Please. Forgive . . ."

She could not let him take the blame. "Ye really didna force me to do anything I didna want to, Father. In truth, I found him a most desirable mon."

He drew his hand away and stood up. "Which makes it all the worse. Ye cared for him, Caity. It is written in yer eyes."

"Aye, that I did. But that does not explain nor recompense what I hae done." She could not keep from trembling at the thought of what she had to confess.

"Ye?"

She wrestled with the dilemma of her fate, at last blurting it out. "I came upon him in the tower, trying to steal the flag but I didna tell ye."

"Didna . . ." He was stunned.

Now it was Caitlin who was weeping. "I didna want any harm to come to him. I wanted to protect him."

"Protect a thieving MacDonald!" Ian MacLeod nearly choked on his rage.

"I didna know who he was. How could I? I only thought . . . that . . ."

"Och, ye didna think. That's what." His eyes glittered dangerously in the candlelight, simmering with anger. "Och, that any seed of my loins could do such a thing."

There was such a fiercesome pressure pushing at her chest that she feared she couldn't breathe. "I meant no harm." *I didn't know what the consequences would be.*

"Meant no harm!" Striking his fist on a wooden table near his chair, he startled Caitlin. "Damn it, lass, by keeping silent ye did us the greatest harm of all." He lapsed into a fiercesome tirade, lecturing her on absolute loyalty to the clan. "Instead, ye thought with yer heart like any foolish woman. Blinded by anything except strong arms, broad shoulders, and a handsome face. Ye listened to his lies and believed them like some silly ninny. When ye should hae . . . ye should hae . . ."

"Should hae told ye all." She had made a great mistake, true, but nonetheless Caitlin's pride came to her rescue. "But I am not the only one who did, I'd be saying." The way she was staring at him seemed to accuse him of sharing in her blame. "Ye admitted that ye were thinking of yer fine, strong grandsons." She held up her head. "Ye should hae let me be, Father. Ye should hae let me hae my freedom, at least for a little while longer."

Ian glowered into eyes so like his own. "Ye dare to say—"

"I do." Angrily she walked toward the door, not even bothering to say good night. There was no use bemoaning what she had done. All that was left for her now was to undo it. With that thought on her mind, she hurriedly returned to her chamber, picked up a large leather pouch and started stuffing it with some of her belongings.

"Caity, what are ye doing?" Shona opened one eye, disturbed from her sleep by the noise.

"I'm leaving."

"Leaving?" Shona bolted up from the pillows. "Going where?"

"To the MacDonald's castle!"

"What?"

"Ye heard me. I'm going to get the fairy flag back."

Shona stared at her sister incredulously. "Caity, ye must be daft! Touched in the head if ye think ye can get away wi' this. Father will hae yer head and mine as well for knowing and not telling! And it will all be for naught." Shona clutched at the folds of her nightgown, frightened for her sister and for herself. Surely Caitlin could not be serious about what she proposed, to boldly travel to Mac-Donald territory and take matters into her own hands. "Father will—"

"He will ken when he thinks about it." Remembering their confrontation made her doubly determined. It was the only way to be forgiven. Nae, to forgive herself. "I must get this matter settled, once and for all."

"But how are ye going to get there. Sleat is a long, long way . . ."

"By boat." If Niall MacDonald could do it, then so could she.

"By boat!" Shona panicked. "Ye might be taken by the cailleach uisge and I'd ne'er see ye again."

"Ach, I'm no' afraid of the water hag, and, besides, I won't be alone. I'll take someone with me. Someone I can trust."

Proving her determination, Caitlin moved about the room, gathering all the necessary items to take with her on the journey, wrapping them in a bundle. A comb, her cuarans to wear along the rocky path, a brooch, a curraichd to tie around her head if it was windy.

"Oh, Caity! Don't go! Ye'll disappear. I willna see ye again."

"I willna disappear." She tried to sound a lot braver than she felt. She had never even been in a boat before.

"Caity, what if ye are caught before ye get very far? Then a whipping will be yer only reward for being so braw!"

"I'll hae to take that chance." Her father hadn't caught Niall. Wasn't she just as canny?

"Ye canna go, Caity." Grabbing her firmly by the arm, Shona thought to stop her but Caitlin merely pushed her aside.

"I *am* going. I've made up my mind. Ye canna prevent it. Do ye ken?"

"Aye." Shona knew well that when Caitlin wanted to do something, nothing or nobody could stop her. She thought for a moment, then suddenly threw her arms around her sister. Her tears splashed Caitlin's face. "But take care, Caity. If anything were to happen to ye I'd never forgive myself."

"Nothing will happen! Ye'll see. Everything will be all right." Bold talk. The truth was, she couldn't be certain that it would be. Indeed, she could not be certain that she would ever see her sister again. Still, she knew she had to go, had to rectify the wrong she had done.

Forcing a self-confident smile, Caitlin slung the sack over her shoulder and walked toward the door. Fumbling around in the dark with her precious bundle, she said a silent prayer that she would have no regrets for her decision.

Twenty-one

Darkness had brought a cold, heavy mist. Shivering, Caitlin admitted to herself that she was fearful. As the familiar shores of Skye disappeared, she had felt an unnerving sense of wariness. Since she was a child she'd heard tales of mermaids and sea-people; water horses and water bulls that enticed unwary travelers. Nuckelavee. Glastig. Were these creatures even now lying in wait to snatch the boat as it bounced on the waves?

"I willna even think about it," she said aloud, trying to pluck up her courage. She couldn't and wouldn't go back.

"Ye look worried, lass. Everything will be all right." Donald the fisherman to whom she had given her gold brooch to take her to Sleat, hurried to assure her.

Crossing herself, Caitlin looked over her shoulder from time to time, watching the waves warily for any sign of a beastie. Fear only added to the misery she already felt. The unpleasant creatures were not her only reservation. She was instigating an act for which there might well be repercussions. Her father would be incensed if he found out what she had done. Worse, she knew naught of Malcolm. For all she knew she might well be walking straight into a lion's den. And yet she could not turn back. Her pride goaded her on.

As the boat skimmed the rough waves, however, she found herself wishing she had never had such a dangerous idea. She had been brave and fearless at home amid familiar surroundings. Now she had to fight her inner turmoil and bolster her courage.

Up and down, back and forth, the boat rocked unendingly. The violently churning ocean turned her insides upside down. But soon, soothed by the rise and dip of the blades as they slapped the waves, she drifted off into a fitful sleep.

Deep in her dreams she was conscious only of the motion of the boat and the sound of the water. Awakening for a moment, she pulled the folds of her arasaid around her body. The air was a penetrating damp cold and she hugged herself to keep from shivering, then, as complete exhaustion took control of her, she fell asleep again.

Not too long after, a cold spray of ocean mist splashed into Caitlin's face, awakening her. She stirred, stretching her arms and legs in slow, easy motions. A sea mist engulfed them, a blinding swirl of white.

"Where are we?"

"I wish I knew. Far down the coast, past MacLeod's Tables, I think." He tried to keep the tone of his voice calm, for more than the fog concerned him. The wind was starting to blow and though it would push out the fog, he didn't like it. A ferocious storm was brewing. He could read it in the churning of the sea, smell it in the air.

"Ye are worried."

"There is going to be quite a gale. We'll have to brace ourselves."

"Brace ourselves?" Caitlin gritted her teeth to keep from begging Donald to take her back home. She tried to make light of it. "I hate storms! When I was a child, my father told me that they were caused by huge sea beasties growling."

"Beasties?" He laughed, but his smile soon turned to a frown. "By Saint Michael!" He looked around him, peering out at the ocean, straining his eyes for any sight of land. "The storm! Never hae I seen one take shape so quickly."

She eyed him warily. "The water beasties are angry, I suppose."

"Angry and threatening. We're going to have to weather out the storm, lass. Whatever happens, no matter what, hold onto the side of the boat. Do ye hear me?"

"Aye!" Her heart lurched in her breast as she realized fully the danger they were in.

"If the boat flips over, swim clear of it. Do you understand?"

Caitlin nodded, hoping it wouldn't come to that. The water would be freezing. "Aye."

"Then try to swim to the curah and hold on. It's sturdy. It will float. Remember!"

Caitlin nodded again, gripping the sides as if that moment had already come. All the while she prayed that the fearful gust of wind and turbulent waves would soon abate. Oh, how she suddenly wanted to be on land again. Never would her father's castle seem so dear.

The small boat rocked from side to side as the ocean pounded viciously against the stern. Donald looked nervously over his shoulder. "Dear merciful God," he whispered. Pulling away from her, he picked up the oars that lay in the bottom of the boat.

"What is it?" Alarm rang through her, hurrying, her heart, jangling her nerves, and stretching her courage to its limit.

He confided in her, counting on her bravery. "We are off course and heading ashore."

"Ashore?" The rocks up ahead seemed to be drawing them, pulling them.

She cursed her impetuous nature which had led them into this travail. It had been her idea to sail to Sleat. She should have gone by land. Now, perhaps her daring would be the death of them both. Poor Donald. And all for the sake of a brooch. "What can I do to help?"

He pushed her back when she would have helped him row. "Just sit quiet!"

A violent wave sent her sprawling, unbalancing the boat as she hit the side. On both sides of the boat the treacherous sea flung itself in massive crests, the spray whistling into the air. The rumble of the water was so loud it caused the boat to vibrate.

"Are you all right?" Pausing in his rowing, the fisherman stared at her.

"Aye!" At least for the time being.

"We have to stay clear of the rocks!" He shouted. "Perhaps I can . . ." The roar of another wave drowned out his words.

Suddenly the boat capsized and Caitlin was hurled into the air by a giant wave. A scream tore from her throat as she felt herself hit the water. She was engulfed in icy blackness. "Blessed Saint Michael!" she cried silently. No! This could not be happening. "Please dear God," she choked between mouthfuls of seawater.

Taking a deep breath, she plunged into the water's depths, searching beneath the boat for any sign of the fisherman. There was none. A numbing fear overtook Caitlin as she realized she was alone.

"Nae! Nae!"

She was going to die. Right here, right now. She was going to drown and no one would ever know what had happened to her. That was a thought that nearly made her lose all control. In the end, however, she remembered who she was. The MacLeod's eldest daughter. A fighter. A braw lassie. If she had to die she would do it with the same bravery as the men who had fallen in battle.

"But I willna die!" she vowed. It wasn't her time yet. There were too many things that she had to do.

The watery prison seemed almost endless, yet she put one arm before the other, fighting for survival. She didn't want to believe that death was to be her fate. Oh, please!

She had so much to live for. Blessed Saint Michael! Her life was still ahead of her.

As if in answer to her prayers, the flow of the water changed direction and rose to aid her. She found herself drifting toward the shore. Caitlin knew how to swim. It was something she always enjoyed, but that was in lochs and burns, not in such threatening water. Still, she knew if only she could reserve her strength and let the sea carry her to land she might survive. Trying to control her breathing, to relax despite her fear of the icy ocean, she determined that *she* would be the victor, not the icy sea. She was strong. She was a MacLeod!

Alas, however, it seemed she was no match for the ocean. It seemed to go on forever, the round-topped mountains just a large ominous speck in the distance. The longer she struggled, the more hopeless the situation seemed. The icy water robbed her of her stamina. Her strength was wavering. She was weary. Close to giving up. Then as a rock struck her foot, she realized that all was not lost. Not yet.

Fight. Survive the waters. Don't give up.

Suddenly hands reached out for her, grabbing her, pulling her ashore. The saltwater stung her eyes so she could not see. A hazy figure loomed in front of her. With a final effort she shook her head and squinted her eyes. Though half blind she saw *him*. A giant of a man! Dear merciful Saint Michael!

Instinct told her to run. Run. Nimbly escaping the grasping hands, she sprang to her feet and sprinted across the rocks as fast as her weary legs would carry her. It was not fast enough. The giant had closed the distance and now was tugging at her hair.

Screaming in outrage, Caitlin pulled free of his grasp, fighting with all her waning strength. It was no use. With a shriek of despair she gave in to the darkness that swirled before her eyes and fell unconscious to the ground.

* * *

"Who are ye?" The huge man's deep, booming voice matched his ominous appearance.

Caitlin raised her eyes, staring at the giant with hair as red as her own. "Red Etin," she exclaimed, remembering the Scottish folk tale about the giant who kidnapped the King of Scotland's daughter. If it was not him, then by Saint Michael it was his twin.

"Red Etin," the giant repeated as if he thought that was Caitlin's name. Well, it was as good a name as any.

"What are ye doing on these shores?"

"What shores?" Caitlin really didn't know where she was. Was this MacDonald territory or was she still in her own and what of this "giant?" Looking up at him, she decided that this being was human and not the creature she had first supposed.

"Near Loch Bracadale." The giant eyed her up and down much as a fisherman would a fish he had just caught. A fish he was deciding whether to keep or throw back.

"Loch Bracadale." Caitlin sighed with relief. She was still in the territory held by her clan. That gave her courage to ask this man the same question he had asked her. "My whereabouts now being established, I'll ask ye the same question ye asked of me. Who are *ye?*"

Before he could answer, six other men stepped forward, one of them answering for him. "He is Ogg. The most fiercesome fighter the MacDonalds can claim."

"MacDonalds." Caitlin drew away. She should have recognized this group of men by the red-and-green plaid they were wearing and by the heather in their low, flat bonnets. Undoubtedly this was a band of stragglers returning to Sleat after their battle with her clansmen. The fact that their hands were tainted by MacLeod's blood made her shudder.

"Aye, MacDonalds." The name was spoken by the giant with all the pride a man could muster. "And what of ye? What clan do ye belong to, lass?"

One of the other men laughed. "MacMermaid." He looked down at her legs. "But say, where is yer tail?"

Caitlin grinned as she brushed her wet hair from her eyes. "It changes to legs on land."

"And to a tail in the water," the man answered. Taking several steps toward her, he said, "Let's throw her back in and see."

"Nae!" Ogg stepped in front of Caitlin as if to protect her. "Leave her be. She has done us no harm."

"Leave her be?" Grumbling among themselves, the others seemed to be discussing the matter, at last deciding against letting Caitlin be on her way.

"Ruaraidh and Finlay are sore wounded. They need tending."

"Aye, let's take her with us. Women always know how best to tend such things. She can conjure up a poultice for their injuries."

"Argh . . ." Ogg circled Caitlin several times, at last agreeing with the others. "She goes with us."

"With you?" Though she was wary, Caitlin didn't put up an argument. She had wanted to go to the MacDonald stronghold. If she went by sea or by land it didn't matter at all. As a matter of fact, as circumstances had proven it would certainly be safer. Alas for poor Donald that he had not been fished out of the ocean as well. Looking over her shoulder, she crossed herself, saying a prayer for his soul.

A safer journey, perhaps, but not easier as she was soon to find out, for the MacDonalds kept up a harrowing pace as they traveled the countryside. It didn't take long for Caitlin's feet to be swollen and blistered. Even so, it was a journey that proved to be pleasing to the eyes, for the land they passed was rocky, green and beautiful. Pausing for a moment to gather moss for the injured men's wounds, Caitlin feasted her eyes on the flat-topped gray mountains covered with lush emerald green. A fierce pride surged within as she realized this was MacLeod land.

She didn't have long to appreciate the view. With a loud command of "Come, lass," Ogg hurried her on her way.

It was an exhausting journey of traveling by day and sleeping at night. When at last Caitlin was certain she couldn't move another step, when all she wanted to do was to sink into a motionless heap on the ground, she heard Ogg give a welcome pronouncement.

"Castle Dunskaith, lass, is just over the hill."

"Dunskaith!" The devil's lair, or so she had always been told, and yet looking at it all she saw was a castle much like any other with a tower that stood tall against the sky. It gave proof of the MacDonald's newly acquired power and strength.

The men, with Caitlin in tow, approached the castle over a natural causeway of barren rocks that was protected from the wind by trees. Waving his arms and shouting, Ogg quickly let it be known that they were coming and that they were MacDonalds.

Torches blazed along the ramparts. The MacDonald banner was flying. Staring at it warily, Caitlin was grimly reminded that she was in enemy territory now. And yet even at that, the thought of a welcoming fire and the comfort within the castle's walls spurred her onward.

Only when she was inside the great hall did she realize that she had been duped. She had not been "invited" to come along with the men because they needed a healer but because they knew who she was. To Caitlin's mortification it was revealed that one of the men had recognized her as the MacLeod's daughter. Instead of coming freely to Malcolm's hall as she had planned, she was quickly and indignantly taken prisoner.

With her flaming hair tumbling wildly about her shoulders and falling into her eyes, she supposed she must look like some wild woman. Well, mayhap she was. Surely her fury knew no bounds.

"I willna be thanking ye fore yer hospitality, it seems,"

she said scornfully, standing toe-to-toe with Ogg, facing him as defiantly as if they were the same size. Never would her father have so treated a woman. Only enemy warriors were made prisoner.

"I'm sorry, lass." Ogg at least seemed regretful.

"Sorry?"

"Aye. I hae always been fond of braw lassies." That did not keep him from going about his duty, however. "Watch her while I get Malcolm," he ordered. Two of the others hurried to obey, hovering over her like a snared grouse.

Caitlin brushed at her gown and ran her fingers through her touseled hair. Eyeing her captors, she snorted disdainfully as she squared her shoulders. They'd soon be begging her pardon. Affecting a haughty pose, she let her eyes roam freely about the room, critically assessing it. Her father always said that a man could tell much from another man's abode. What then was Malcolm like? Did he have horns and a tail?

Certainly he seemed to have an affection for luxury. The interior of Dunskaith Castle was much grander than she had ever supposed. Just like in her father's hall, the walls were lined with benches, but they were polished and darkened, not just bare wood. The lofty hammer-beamed ceiling was hung with bright-colored banners. Even the floor was lavishly decorated with curly sheepskin rugs. Huge tapestries depicting the MacDonald bravery covered the walls, including several which very obviously spoke of victory over the MacLeods. The sight of them angered her and were a reminder of years spent in turmoil.

The wooden walls were adorned with a gaudy display of shields and weapons—massive two-handed cla'mors as well as English broadswords, axes, spears, dirks, and long tautly strung bows. Clearly the most important thing to Malcolm MacDonald was warfare, she thought with scorn. Although her father's castle also displayed some weaponry it was nothing like this! Ah, yes, she had heard about the Mac-

Donald laird's ambitions. But it was something else that quickly caught her eye. Hanging above the mantel, high on the stone wall, was the very thing she had come to fetch.

"The fairy flag." In disgust at the whole idea, she turned her gaze away. "Well, let them appreciate it while they may. I'll soon get my hands on it." Of that she was determined.

"Ogg, what is going on?" Niall's voice. "It couldn't possibly be . . ." But it was!

Niall's jaw dropped open in surprise as he entered the room and saw Caitlin standing there. For just a moment he doused his sanity. "It *is* Caitlin."

"A ghost from out of yer past I'd be thinking," she said, trying to subdue the anger that bubbled at the sight of him. "Niall MacDonald!" She spoke his name like a curse.

"Caitlin . . . I-I. . . ." Dozens of thoughts raced through Niall's mind. What could he say? How could he ever explain?

"Oh, ye be a loathsome being!" Caitlin's mind was ajumble with all the things she had dreamed of saying to him once they were face-to-face. Before she could even begin, however, a deep tumbling voice boomed through the hall.

"So . . . Ian MacLeod's spawn." Standing in the doorway was a man Caitlin took for the very devil. Huge of girth, swarthy of skin, dark of hair and beard, he looked ominous and deadly.

Thrusting himself in front of Caitlin, Niall thought only of guarding her. "Surely ye must be mistaken, Uncle . . ."

Pushing Niall aside, Malcolm growled, "Let me take a look at her."

Niall was relieved to remember that Malcolm had never seen the MacLeod's daughter. Maybe there was a chance. "I tell ye, it isna—"

"It *is*. I *am!*" Caitlin wasn't about to deny her true identity no matter what the consequences. She was proud of being the MacLeod's daughter.

Malcolm MacDonald bared his teeth in the semblance of

a smile. "Well, well, well." Crossing his arms across his ample girth, he stared brazenly at her. "Och, but she does look like her father. The very spitting image I'd be saying. Though she doesna look as dangerous."

"You'd be surprised," Niall said between clenched teeth. Oh, but this was proving to be a mind-muddling predicament. *Oh, Caitlin, you foolish lass. Ye dunna realize what ye hae done. God grant that I can save ye, now.*

"Dangerous or no I am happy that she is here." In a mock gesture of hospitality, Malcolm bowed.

"So am I," Caitlin responded sarcastically, her gaze traveling toward the flag.

Niall saw the direction of her eyes. So that was it. Silly lass. Even if she did get her hands upon the flag she wouldn't make it out of the hall alive with it. Malcolm would watch her as steadfastly as a hawk kept his eye on a soaring dove. Indeed, she might well come to the same dire fate.

Malcolm also noted her eyes dart toward the MacLeod's treasured emblem. "Och, dunna even contemplate reaching out even one finger toward it, or . . ." He made a chopping gesture with his hand.

"Touch it?" Caitlin shrugged. "That was the last thing on my mind." By the blessed Saint Michael she'd just placed herself in the hands of a demented man, as well as an enemy. Unless . . .

"I dunna believe ye. And why should I—ye are a MacLeod."

"MacLeod?" Looking toward Niall, Caitlin could see the worry on his face. So, he hadn't told his uncle everything. No doubt being married to a MacLeod wouldn't be any more tolerated in this hall than being married to a MacDonald would be in her own. And therein Caitlin suddenly knew how she was going to get her revenge. "Nae, I am not a MacLeod. I am a MacDonald."

"Caitlin . . ." If he could have, Niall would have put his hand across her mouth. "Don't."

It was too late. Malcolm had heard. "What is this? What are ye saying?"

"That *I* am a MacDonald." Walking over to Niall, looping her arms through his, Caitlin looked up at him with mock adoration. "And that yer nephew is my loving husband."

Twenty-two

Malcolm grinned, his dark eyes gleaming with merriment. "So, ye married Ian MacLeod's daughter, did ye now, Niall."

"I did!" Niall didn't even want to deny it. Let the punishment be what it may. Let Gregor have his precious reward of being tanist.

"Ye took the flag and MacLeod's daughter's maidenhead as well."

"He did!" Caitlin exclaimed glumly, though it embarrassed her to be talking about something so intimate. "And now must suffer for it, I would imagine."

"Suffer?" He was silent for along, agonizing moment, watching her intently. "Ye would like that, wouldn't ye, lass?"

She nodded.

"Well, then, I will hae to disappoint ye." Striding over to Niall, he pounded his congratulations on the back. "Well done, Nephew. Well done. I couldna thought of anything better. The MacDonalds hae two prizes now. The fairy flag *and* Ian MacLeod's daughter."

"Uncle . . ." Niall knew Malcolm well enough to discern that something sinister was being planned at this very moment.

"I willna stay here!" If he thought to in some way use her as a means to get back at her father, she would quickly put an end to that, Caitlin thought. Unless he kept her as a prisoner in the dungeon she would break free of Dunskaith.

"Ach, but ye will." A muscle ticked above Malcolm MacDonald's left eye, making it appear that he winked. "As my guest."

"Prisoner, ye mean." She tried not to panic.

"Call it what ye will!"

Caitlin made no answer. Standing in front of this vengeful Scotsman, all she could think of was that he did indeed look like the very devil.

"Ogg, I want ye to send a message to Ian MacLeod, informing him that I will consider that tattered flag of his as his daughter's dowry. Tell him that I welcome his beloved daughter to my humble home." It was obvious he meant to goad his rival, hoping the MacLeod would try to enact some kind of rescue.

"I will." Casting Caitlin a sympathetic look, Ogg left the hall.

Oh, Father, what hae I done? How could I hae compromised ye this way? She had given Malcolm MacDonald a weapon to use against her father. In trying to correct one mistake in judgment she had erred yet again. Even so, she managed bravado as she asked, "Do ye plan to shackle me in the dungeon?"

"Dungeon?" For just a moment it seemed as though he were toying with that idea.

"She is my wife, Uncle." Niall was determined to see that Caitlin was treated fairly. "And as such deserves a great measure of respect no matter what clan she comes from."

"Mmmmm." Malcolm was not agreeable to that reminder; nevertheless he saw to it that Caitlin was given a comfortable chamber on the second floor. Despite the bitter feelings between the rival clans, she was treated with deference, yet she chaffed at being anyone's prisoner. Though she was made comfortable and given food, she felt ill at ease.

Moving from the bed, putting her ear to the door, she listened anxiously. Though the voices were muffled, she could hear a heated conversation.

"I thought ye were a mon of honor, Uncle, but surely ye shame me this day."

"Shame ye? I plan to make ye tanist and that shames ye?"

"Ye know what I mean. The MacLeod's daughter. Let her go home."

"And leave the arms of her loving groom? Nae."

Malcolm's voice lowered to a whisper, and Caitlin strained her ears to hear more of what the two men were saying.

"Are you not afraid of what Ian MacLeod will say and do?"

Opening the door, Caitlin crept slowly down the stairway, hoping to hear Malcolm MacDonald's answer.

"Well, well, well!" A voice behind her startled her and she jumped. Turning around, she found herself face-to-face with a dark-haired man whose very presence behind her was menacing.

"Who are ye?"

"Gregor." He seemed surprised that any further explanation was necessary. "Nephew to Malcolm."

A prickly feeling traveled up her spine as if for just a moment she had the fey. There was something about him that seemed so familiar. Why was that?

A dark-haired man whose soul is as dark as his hair. The words of the seer whispered in her ear, reminding her of the frightening prophecy. Somehow in that moment she knew him to be a greater enemy than Malcolm could even think of being. An enemy who in some way spelled ruination for the clan.

Niall's restlessness was ill-concealed as he paced back and forth in the hall. It was all around the castle by way of gossiping tongues that there was more than just the

MacLeod's flag that had occupied his time at Dunvegan Castle.

"Fiery-haired little witch, you hae no idea of the din ye hae created with yer untimely entrance," he muttered beneath his breath. In truth, she had walked right into the lion's den, putting herself at Malcolm's mercy. "Well, she has no one to blame but herself. I dunna want to feel any guilt at what is to happen." And yet he did.

"Care for some company?" Striding across the room, Ogg ignored the negative shake of Niall's head. "Well, ye hae mine nevertheless."

"So I see!" Niall's voice was a growl.

"Och, such ill temper for a mon so newly wedded. And to a lass so very bonny." With his hands, Ogg outlined a voluptuous woman's figure in the air. "Need I say more?"

"Bonny or no, she is stubborn. I must hae been out of my mind to tie myself up wi' her."

Ogg repressed a smile, forcing his features to remain expressionless, but he did say, "No doubt I would hear the same thing from her."

"No doubt!"

Laying a hand on his friend's shoulder, Ogg seemed to sense at least some of Niall's thoughts, for he said, "It seems ye hae quite a story to tell. If so, ye can feel free to tell me."

For a moment Niall kept his silence, then after a while he began, "I was the first mon to step over the MacLeod threshold and thus I ended up with old Ian's daughter just as ye teased that I might. She caught me, ye see, and took me to her father. What else could I do but remind the MacLeod of his vow. It was either that or stay cooped up in his dungeon until I died."

Folding his arms across his chest, Niall related the story in detail, from falling into the flour and being mistaken for a ghost to his hurried departure from Dunvegan with the flag hidden on his person.

"So the lassie found a way to tame the rogue MacDonald." Ogg threw back his head and laughed. "After all the lassies ye hae loved and left, ye find yerself with a braw one that is more than yer match!"

Wanting to deny that, Niall opened his mouth to speak. The more he said no, however, the more frustrated he felt. "By Saint Michael, all right! The lass does give as good as she gets. And she is, as ye say, bonny. And braw. All the more tragic it is then that she has now put herself at Malcolm's mercy."

"An act which worries ye so because ye care!" Wiping away any trace of mockery, Ogg furled his brows. "Ye didna marry the lass just because ye were caught wi' the flag. Ye had more than a wee bit of a longing."

"Nae!" Niall's protestation sounded halfhearted.

"Then why did ye no find another way to get the flag. Like holding her for ransom, shall we say?" He clucked his tongue. "Or tying her hand and foot and dangling her from the tower."

Niall clenched his hands. "She is a woman. I didna want to soil my honor by mistreating her."

Ogg was not so easily fooled. "Devil take ye, for ye lie! There was a part of ye that wanted the lass. And why not! She is one of the prettiest lasses I hae ever seen." As if to see into his friend's heart, Ogg stared into Niall's eyes long and hard. What he read there made him gasp. "Och, dinna tell me that what ye felt for her is much more serious than that!"

Niall's silence was the answer.

"A MacLeod!" Ogg ran his fingers through his hair. "Then it is worried that I be. Malcolm will use the lass for his own gains, but he willna let ye hae any peace."

"How well I know."

"Ye will find yerself right in the middle of a tug-of-war, torn in two directions, Niall, forced to make a choice between loyalty to yer clan and loyalty to yer heart." Ogg then asked a chilling question. "Which will ye choose?"

In confusion Niall stepped back. Taking a deep breath, he answered truthfully. "I dunna ken, Ogg." God help him, he really didn't know.

Twenty-three

She was surrounded by enemies. Was it any wonder then that all that Caitlin could think about the next few days was escape? An escape that would be all the sweeter if she could take the fairy flag with her.

"Take the flag?" Alas, she might as well have wanted to reach toward the heavens and pull down a star. Not only was *she* guarded but that brown piece of silk was watched constantly as well.

Worse yet, just seeing Niall caused her pain, and there was no way to avoid him. Every morning he was in the hall for the morning meal and in the evening his presence was all too obvious as the clan gathered for their dinner feast. These were the hours of her torment, part of her consumed with anger at his betrayal, another part of her longing for his touch, his kiss, his love.

That did not mean she allowed herself to in any way show her feelings, however. She was withdrawn and cool when they met on the stairs. What conversation they exchanged was nothing more than cold, polite words of greeting. She made it obvious that she was avoiding him. Even so, no matter how sternly she rebuked herself for feelings she did not want to have, she couldn't wipe him from her heart. He was like a sweet poison for which there was no antidote except to keep so busy she didn't have time to think or to feel.

Though she might have been able to escape from the

drudgery, Caitlin took on household tasks eagerly, thankful that there was always something to be done. The work was fitted around the meal preparation, just as in her own clan, twice daily, morning and night. Here in the MacDonald castle, beef and lamb were the mainstays of the diet, eaten in some form at every meal, as were milk, cheese, and butter. Grinding and baking were daily chores, for unleavened barley bread and bannocks needed to be eaten while hot or they would soon turn hard and stale. Flour was ground from a rotary hand quern, dough kneaded in a wooden trough and baked on long-handled iron plates among the embers of an open fire. The women also hung herbs to dry and gathered wild plants to supplement the diet.

Aileen, Malcolm's wife, was a plump woman with dark-brown hair whose beauty had long ago faded. She soon made it clear that she considered Caitlin an interloper and a nuisance and reminded her to keep her place by assigning her the most unpleasant duties. Nonetheless, Caitlin finished every task without a word of complaint, so exhausted by the time she crawled into bed that she fell right to sleep.

At least I can escape Niall MacDonald at night, she thought in gratitude. *And perhaps in time I will be able to think more clearly and soothe my shattered emotions so that the next time I see him across the room it won't hurt so.* Until then, her only defense was to pretend he didn't exist.

But if she was ignoring him, the same could not be true for Niall. His piercing hazel eyes seemed to be upon her wherever she was and she knew that he watched her. The sound of his low, husky laughter teased her ears. His smile haunted her at every turn, though she did not smile back. His presence made it difficult at times for her to ignore him. In those moments when their eyes accidentally met she was filled with an aching emptiness. Oh, if only he was not so handsome.

This evening she caught him gazing at her across the width of the dais and felt the familiar lurch in her heart.

Determined to show him she really didn't care, she quickly turned her attentions to Ogg, a gentle man despite his size, who was quickly becoming her one friend in the castle.

"Was the message sent to my father?" she asked him.

"Aye, it was sent."

"Oh . . ." Looking across the table to where Malcolm sat, a place that in the MacLeod hall would have been taken by her father, she could only hope that Ian MacLeod would not so easily fall into the MacDonald's trap. He must not try to rescue her, for if he did he would put himself in dire danger.

"Red . . ." Since the moment when Caitlin had answered his question of who she was by saying "Red Etin," that was what he had called her.

"I know ye had to follow yer chieftain's orders." Caitlin touched his arm. "I know ye dunna wish my father or me any harm. It is just the way of things."

"Aye, the way of things." He seemed to notice her soulful glance at Niall, for he whispered, "But if ye can so easily understand that I must do as I hae done, why can ye not then forgive Niall?"

Instantly she stiffened. "That's different, Ogg. I trusted him," *and loved him,* "and he betrayed me."

"I know he loves ye, lass. Ye dunna ken the times he has jumped to yer defense, trying to protect ye from Malcolm's wrath. He has never done that with anyone or for anyone before."

" 'Tis his feeling of guilt," Caitlin said sourly, "I dunna want to talk more about it." Defiantly she looked toward Niall, glowering at him when he looked back. If he thought to use his friend Ogg to soften her justifiable anger it just wouldn't work.

Niall could feel the potency of her ire all the way across the room, and it irritated him in return. He was tired of the way she was acting. Tired of her refusal to even listen to his explanations of why he had done what he had done.

Well, by God, she was his wife. Perhaps it was time that
he laid aside his compassion and patience and made her
act as such, he thought, clenching his fingers tightly around
the handle of his cup. He swirled the golden whiskey about,
staring at its murky depths, remembering the blissful moments of passion they had shared.

"Yer frown is as deep as Loch Stapin." With a large wolf-
hound at his heels begging for scraps, Gregor sauntered up.
Sizing up the situation, he knew in a moment what was
wrong. His expression clearly revealed that Niall's troubles
pleased him. "For all that ye be such a great fighter and
leader of men, Cousin, it is a wee bit amusing that ye canna
seem to manage yer own wife."

"That's because that woman is not the least bit manageable." He stared Gregor right in the eyes. "Ye couldna manage her either, I'd be thinking."

"Oh, I think that I could." The tone of voice stated clearly
that Gregor was the kind of man who would subdue any
woman who crossed his path with violence. "I wouldna let
any lass so obviously scorn me."

"I willna use force. I dunna want her hate." Niall felt the
need to issue a clear warning. "Nor will I tolerate anyone
treating Caitlin unkindly."

"Unkindly?" Without being invited, Gregor took a seat
next to his cousin. "She's a spoiled, willful lassie who is
in great need of a beating to keep her in line. But if ye
prefer to allow her to publicly show ye contempt, then ye
will just hae to accept the consequences."

Niall went to Caitlin's defense. "She has reason to treat
me as she does. I lied to her and rewarded her trust with
treachery."

"To get the flag. Any mon would hae done that and
maybe worse."

Niall immediately knew what Gregor was saying. Had
Niall's cousin been the one to go to the MacLeod stronghold, Caitlin would not have escaped with her life. That

first night Gregor would have stolen the flag and then murdered her so that she could not sound the alarm. The idea made him shiver. Once again he felt the need to defend Caitlin.

"Well, no mon had better harm her while she is within these walls for any reason." One false move and he would have Gregor's head. "Do ye ken?"

"Aye." Despite what he said, however, the devilish glint in his eyes as he glanced Caitlin's way clearly spoke of danger.

The ominous look deeply troubled Niall, for he knew from experience that his cousin could be very dangerous. "Gregor, I repeat. I willna tolerate anyone harming her. Anyone." Despite his warning to his cousin, Niall knew Caitlin herself had to be warned to stay clear of the man. With that thought in mind, he sought her out as soon as the dinner table was cleared.

A shiver of pure physical awareness chased a strange sensation up and down Caitlin's spine so that she knew he was standing behind her before she heard him say, "You have been as evasive as a ghostie, lass. But ye must listen."

"Listen? To what?" Her pulse began to beat at her neck and temple, and for a moment she feared he would sense how completely bedeviled she was having him near. "Surely it is listening to ye in the first place that got me in all this trouble."

"A truth for which I am deeply sorry, Caitlin. Believe it or not, I didn't want to hurt ye." He captured her hand, his fingers gripping her slender wrist.

"But even so, ye did. Very, very deeply." She quivered at his touch, wanted to touch him back but forced herself to pull her hand away. Like a cornered deer she moved past him, bolting from the room, seeking the safety of the stairs.

Niall followed her, through the door, up the winding steps that led to a tower room. "Lassie?" He towered over her with a virility that was most unnerving to Caitlin. It reminded her too vividly of all that had happened. She stiffened and took a step backward. For a moment the only sound was the hiss of the rush light and the distant barking of the dogs, then he said, "You are trembling."

" 'Tis chilly up here, that's all." A feeble excuse.

"I'll warm you." Quickly, before she could run away, he placed his hands on either side of her body, pinning her against the wall so she could not escape. His breath was warm upon her face, his voice husky in the darkness. "Caity. Caity. I canna stand yer hatred." He wanted her to be passionate, responsive, and loving again.

"But that is all ye will be getting from me, Niall MacDonald." But though her head buzzed with anger the secret place between her legs remembered something else and she felt a wanton craving.

"Then ye are cheating both yerself as well as me." Breathing hard, he swept her body with his hands as if by so doing he could convince her.

She closed her eyes, swaying under his expert touch. She drew a deep breath, then let it out as she whispered, "Cheating ye, am I. Nae, it is ye who cheated us both by leaving me as ye did."

"For which I hae been punished each time I see ye look at me with loathing, lass." He sought her breasts, gently kneading them. Feeling the peaks harden, knowing that at least her body responded if not her heart, he smiled. "Ah, Caity. It was good between us and it can be again."

Slowly he lowered his mouth and kissed her hungrily, as if he were starving for the taste of her lips. The potent kiss sent a series of quivering tremors through her blood. His mouth held hers captive as his fingers caressed her breasts, moving to slip the arasaid aside so he could touch her bared flesh.

"Nae!" How she managed the protest she didn't know. Somehow, despite the beating of her heart, she found the strength to push against his shoulders. "Let me go!"

"Ye are my wife, Caity," he breathed. "Ye belong to me."

"Belong to ye, do I?" Her blazing eyes challenged him. She was so proud, so beautiful with her hair falling into her eyes that his love for her swept through him. "Aye, ye do."

"Nae, I do not!" Never would she belong to anyone except herself, do anything unless she wanted to.

Niall looked into her eyes and what he saw there made him loosen his hold. With a disgruntled groan, he moved away. "By the laws of the church and this land ye do, Caity love, but I am not the kind of man who would force ye. When ye come back to my bed it will be because ye want to."

Her hair flowed from side to side like a rippling wave as she tossed her head. "Never!" Yet in the saying she felt bereaved. She wanted him with just as deep an intensity as he wanted her.

"Then God help us both!"

In the stricken silence that followed, they maintained a grotesque pose, staring at each other, their eyes locked unwaveringly. Then Niall turned away. Before he descended the stairs, however, he had one more thing to say to her.

"Keep away from my cousin Gregor, Caitlin. He would seek to harm ye, and though I swear I will give ye my protection whenever I am in the castle, I canna always be near."

"Gregor?" Caitlin knew who he was only too well. The dark man. The man whose face seemed to strike a chord of recognition in her mind. The man of doom, as she thought of him now. "I will watch out for him."

"Good." He took a step and then another, hoping that she would call him back.

"Niall."

Instantly he was standing once again beside her. "Aye?"

For just a moment her hostility softened. "Thank ye for . . . for the warning."

He was disappointed that she did not say more; still, as he looked deep into her eyes he felt a sense of hope that perhaps their future together was not as bleak as he had at first supposed.

Twenty-four

Caitlin looked out the window at the rolling hills and pasturelands of the MacDonald's lands. From her window she was afforded a magnificent view. Acre after acre of grass-covered ground, blue ribbons of water winding their way in a path over the hills, trees raising their branches as if to pray.

There was a serene beauty to the countryside that reminded her of home and made her quarrelsomely homesick at times. But her longing to see her home again was as nothing compared to the pain and frustration she felt every time she caught sight of Niall. She was caught between anger and longing, heartache and the elation of knowing that he did desire her. Even so, the more she thought about his deception the more determined she was never to speak another civil word to him.

"Oh, how quickly I capitulated to his virility and charm," she said beneath her breath as she turned away from the window. Callously forgetting all that he had done to her and her clan, he had reminded her of their marriage, insisting that she belonged to him. Well, she would soon let him see that, prisoner or not, she would bend to no man's will. Not Niall's, not Gregor's, nor most assuredly Malcolm's.

Malcolm, oh how Caitlin loathed the man. He was cold-blooded, a solemn, conscienceless man who seemed to enjoy Caitlin's discomfort. The "devil's spawn" she heard him refer to her on one or two occasions. Caitlin often saw him looking at her as if he fully expected her to grow horns. Certainly Malcolm knew he was a cog in the wheel of her hopes of a daring rescue, for he watched her like a hawk.

Finishing the porridge she had brought up to her room from breakfast, Caitlin searched through the garments she had been given to wear, pondering her fate all the while. She had three enemies here. Niall, because of his legal claim to her. Malcolm, because of the danger he might pose to her father. Lastly and perhaps most dangerous of all, Gregor.

I should leave. Not tomorrow, not the next day, but now! She had made a mistake in coming here so boldly. Had she even a wee bit of common sense she would have disguised herself as a lad, an old woman—or anything but herself. Now, as it was, she had put not only herself but the whole clan in danger.

What will happen later? she worried. Aye, Malcolm had welcomed the news of Niall's marriage to the MacLeod's daughter but that was only because she could be used to lure Ian MacLeod out of his den. Would Malcolm view her as a hated enemy when her usefulness had passed?

Caitlin poured water from a pitcher into a small china basin, hurriedly washed her face, and hastened to plait her long red hair, wearing it in coils on either side of her head. Dressing quickly in a dark-green gown with a linen tonnag around her shoulders, she moved to the door. Though she had not been confined, this time when she attempted to leave her chamber she found a guard posted outside her door.

"Och, so 'tis a prisoner in the full sense of the word that I am now," she said, putting her hands on her hips. Mentally she cursed Malcolm MacDonald.

"Ye canna leave without the MacDonald's permission."

"What!" Malcolm's prisoner then in the full sense of the word. First she was stunned, then she was furious.

"I tell ye, lass, ye canna leave without *his* permission."

He nodded to where the MacDonald stood in conversation with two of his men.

Though Caitlin stormed at the man and tried to push past, her anger was to no avail. He was much too strong and brawny. "Then gi' him a message for me. Tell him that his nephew's wife wishes to be *blessed* wi' his company."

Seething with rage, Caitlin paced the room, pausing only when footsteps sounded outside. As Malcolm entered, she was immediately upon him. "Ye dare keep me in a cage."

"I do it just until tonight."

"Tonight?" She shoved at his chest.

His expression was stern. "There is to be a special celebration. I but wanted to make certain that ye dunna decide to leave before that time."

"Celebration?" She was scornful. "No doubt a celebration of my happy wedding."

"Yer wedding?" He bared his teeth as he said, "Dunna flatter yerself. I wouldna honor a MacLeod be she Niall's whore or no."

Caitlin gasped. So, it was just as she thought. Malcolm's only reason for approving of her marriage to Niall was because it offered him a chance for vengeance.

"Nor would I gi' honor to any MacDonald!"

"Ach, but ye will. This very night ye will pay homage to my successor."

Torches and tapers blazed brightly, casting a soft glow on the great hall. Smoke from the hearth fires stung everyone's eyes as the MacDonald clan gathered for the evening meal. And what a meal it was! Clearly Malcolm MacDonald had something to celebrate. Platters were piled high with mutton, beef, and all manner of fowl. There were plates of oysters, bannocks, oatcakes, barley cakes, fruit and cheese, all to be washed down with tankards of ale and mugs of the finest whiskey.

Caitlin watched as Dunskaith's servants hurried swiftly to and from the kitchen, their arms heavily laden with platters, bowls, and pitchers, thinking she would never get used to others doing the work for a few. Unlike in her father's hall there was a distinct difference between those who served and those who ruled.

"Dunna look sad. Ye are much bonnier when ye smile." Ogg was seated to her left, and as he spoke he gently touched her hand.

"I was just thinking for a moment about home . . ."

"Home?"

"Aye."

"And thinking how ye would like to be there instead of here." His blue eyes offered her sympathy and understanding.

"Perhaps ye dunna truly appreciate anything until it's far away." How many times had she longed for adventure? How many times had she bemoaned the necessity of staying by the MacLeod hearth, working with the other women? Now there wasn't anything she wouldn't give to be back there.

"And your family?"

"I miss them all very dearly. Even my mother." She hurried to explain. "Mother and I didna always get along. We were both too much the same, so we fought a great deal of the time. Funny, but I miss those arguments." Caitlin was curious about Ogg. "And what of you?"

"I didna even know my mother. I was taken from her arms shortly after my birth and fostered here with Malcolm. My clan were some of the 'broken men' from the MacRaes. My small group sought and obtained the protection of the MacDonald clan when many of our men were killed off in battle with the MacKinnons."

"So ye are a MacRae." The fact that he did not have a blood relationship with the MacDonalds pleased her. Perhaps if she was really in danger, Ogg would help her.

"I've been told my father was killed in battle, that my

mother feared his enemies would try to take my life. For my own protection I was nurtured here." Picking up a leg of mutton, he toyed with it nervously. "And for that I am grateful to Malcolm, but . . ."

But ye dunna always approve of what he does. That was important to know just in case she needed an ally. "I beg to say that the MacDonald seems to be a very harsh mon . . ."

"A bit harsh perhaps, Red. But very, very braw!" The way Ogg spoke, it was obvious that he admired his chieftain greatly.

As she listened, Caitlin couldn't help seeking out Niall with her gaze, remembering in vivid detail the passion they had shared. One brief look at him set her blood to pounding as she relived the delight of his holding her close last night. When he had pressed his hard, arousing body against hers, all thought of leaving here had vanished, dissolved in the heated torrent of their desire. What if . . . ?

Ogg caught sight of her stolen glance, the way her eyes caressed his friend. "He is a fine mon."

"I suppose that he can be."

"Nae always is. He is the bravest mon I know, and in his heart he is most kind. When the others made fun of my size Niall always took my side." He smiled. "Once he even suffered a bloodied nose given to him by Gregor and his followers because he didn't want to see my feelings hurt."

"Really?" That bit of information made her see Niall in a different light.

"Really."

Caitlin sighed, trying to concentrate on what was happening in the hall. All Highlanders were fond of music and dancing, and the MacDonalds seemed to be no different. Caitlin took great delight in listening to the pipers, knowing that the MacCrimmons, who were her clan's pipers, were much better. The harpist, however, was the best she had ever heard. Leaning back in her chair, she felt herself relaxing.

"Ye havena eaten much . . ." Ogg sounded worried. "Ye arena sick?"

"I just am not hungry."

"Eat something anyway."

She forced herself to eat a bit of the heavily seasoned food, wondering how the MacDonalds could find it palatable. She washed down the large slice of mutton with a gulp of ale.

A long time later the long trestle tables were dismantled and pushed back against the wall. Malcolm rose to his feet, putting his finger to his lips in a gesture of silence. The room quieted in an instant. Upon every face an upraised brow asked what was going to happen. That question was answered quickly as the MacDonald laird addressed the gathering.

"There has been some concern avowed as to who is to succeed me. Though I'm no' anxious to become a ghost, I've decided to address that issue now." He flashed a rare smile, enjoying the openmouthed looks of surprise. All eyes were riveted his way. "From time to time I've mentioned Gregor, other moments I've given a nod to Niall and given thought to his becoming my tanist. It is, as ye know, a most serious duty. As tanist it will be his special duty to hold the clan lands in trust for ye and yer posterity. As chieftain, my successor will be called upon to determine all differences and disputes, to protect our followers, to lead this clan in times of war. I've made my choice and tonight I will make it formal. Niall, please stand up."

Nae, Caitlin thought. Not now! She felt all hope for a future with Niall dipping away. If he was tanist, then that would eventually mean he would be the one to lead the warfare against her clansmen. As tanist he could not allow any children he might have to be another clan's successor, thereby crushing her father's dreams. All was lost! In a mood of hostile despair she watched as Niall took his stand by the sacred stone of the MacDonalds, placing one foot upon the rock as custom decreed.

Had he known last night that he would be given such an honor? Had he? And yet he had not said a word. Instead, he had initiated lovemaking and pretended he cared for her. Suspicion poisoned her mind. Tears of angry frustration stung her eyes. What had goaded him into pretending to care for her this time?

Dunna fool yerself, Caitlin dearie, she gave herself warning. Where honor and ambition were concerned a woman was naught. That was the way of men. Power was all they wanted. And now Niall had bartered her for a tanist's crown.

Caitlin watched silently as Niall was presented with a sword and a white wand while the MacDonald bard recounted all his acts of bravery. Niall mac Gilchrist was son of Gilchrist who was son of Craig and on and on and on. There was no doubt that Niall came from noble lineage, nor that he was brave in his combat with other men, and for that she admired him. But she felt a sense of hopelessness, too, for all the talk of fighting only proved that in reality there was a gulf as wide as Loch Bracadale between them.

No doubt Niall knew it, too, for not once had he even glanced at her tonight. Because of guilt? Because having secured the fairy flag had put him in Malcolm's favor? Aye. Well, now he had what he had so wanted with little care of what it had cost her clansmen.

Niall mac Gilchrist can never be mine! she thought. Suddenly the futility of her feelings for him came back to haunt her full measure. Now, when she remembered last night, she was left with only humiliation. How quickly she had succumbed to his advances, like some besotted dairy maid. He had called her his wife, had reminded her that she was naught but a possession. And that was all she was and ever would be.

I canna ever lay with him again. I canna get with child. For that babe would be a MacDonald. An enemy, though it be of her own flesh and blood. Those thoughts were tormenting, for even now the memory of the way he had caressed her and kissed her caused her body to long for the touch of his hands and mouth.

"What a fool ye were, Caitlin," she whispered to herself, watching him strut about the hall, so prideful at the honors being bestowed on him. He reminded her of a preening rooster. Warfare was all a man ever cared about. Honor. Bravery. Did she really think he would give up his role as tanist for love of her?

"Lassie, what is wrong?" Ogg put a hand on her shoulder, his eyes mirroring his concern for the tears that flooded her eyes.

"Wrong?" Caitlin dashed the tears away with the back of her hand. "Just the smoke in my eyes, that is all. Dunna fash yerself, Ogg. I'm all right."

Oh, what a lie that was. The longer she watched the ceremony, the more she realized how quickly her own unhappiness loomed ahead if she stayed here. It was glaringly apparent.

Restless and unhappy, she rose from her chair, unwilling to think another moment about it. Well, she wouldn't stay. Not for one more day. When the first light of dawn glowed on the horizon, she would be gone, taking the fairy flag with her.

"So, ye are tanist, Niall. I'd say it's about time Malcolm named ye so." Ogg pushed his way through the throng of revelers, maneuvering Niall to a far corner where they could be alone. "Congratulations!"

Niall stared hard at him, searching his face for any sign of jealousy, but the large smile that cut its way across the giant's face was not being feigned. The same could not be said for Gregor, however. Each time he looked Niall's way the anger and envy was obvious. If Gregor had not been an enemy before, he was now.

"I've admired ye all my life and never doubted for a moment that it would be ye who would be named Malcolm's successor. Ye are a fine mon, Niall. The best I've ever known. I only wish to be even half as fine a fighter as ye are."

Niall laughed. "Ye are, my humble friend. Ye are. More so."

Ogg started to grin, but that grin turned into a frown as he stared over Niall's shoulder. "Don't look now, but Gregor is staring this way, and with such an evil expression that ye had best cross yerself!"

"Gregor!" Niall spat the name with scorn. Gregor had long been his adversary, circumventing his authority at every turn. "He was so certain he was going to be named tanist that he had instructed the bard to make up a song about him."

"Ye dinna say." Ogg shook his head. "Well, he must hae suffered an unpleasant surprise then."

"A stunning shock, though not enough of one to burst his overblown pride."

"Indeed, it seems his defeat has only made him more prideful."

"And dangerous." Niall voiced aloud his greatest fear. "He has aligned himself as Caitlin's enemy."

"I know." Ogg chewed on his lower lip, deep in thought. "I hae seen him staring at her from time to time, though with a far different look upon his face than that of a foe."

"Ye mean?" The thought of Gregor even touching Caitlin with his eyes was infuriating, much less imagining any more intimate advances.

Ogg was blunt. "What better way would there be to get back at ye, Niall, then to sully that which he knows belongs to ye? A woman who is certainly most bonny."

"And my wife!"

"Gregor thinks there is no woman he canna have. Worse yet, he thinks in his canny mind that ye stole what was to be his. He won't even think twice about doing ye harm through Red."

"If he so much as comes within a foot of her, I'll kill him." As Niall looked in Gregor's direction and met his gaze, they fought a furious visual duel, as potent as with any weapon. "Ogg!" Niall put an insistent hand on his friend's shoulder.

"What is it? I'll do anything ye ask, as ye know."

"I want you to help me keep an eye on Caitlin, to keep her from that one's harm." Niall sensed danger with a warrior's instincts, and was determined to avert it at all possible cost.

"Ye dunna hae to ask."

"Ye like her."

Ogg pounded Niall on the back so hard that it rattled his teeth. "I hae right from the very first!"

Niall felt the need to pour his heart out. "When I went to Skye I had in mind to steal the flag and be gone, but I saw this lovely lassie and once I-I kissed her, I was lost."

"And ye fell in love."

"Aye. I didn't know it then, but I know it now." Niall shook his head sadly. "But alas, it seems hopeless sometimes. I did her a great wrong that I dunna think she can ever forgive."

"She can and she will."

Knowing that Ogg often sat next to Caitlin, Niall was anxious. "Has she said that?"

"No, but I can see in her eyes when she looks at ye that she cares. Nae, more than that. I think she loves, too, Niall."

Niall sighed softly. "I wish it was true."

"I would bet my breacan that it is, but what I think isna important. It's what ye believe and what ye do about it."

Ogg's meaning was very clear. "Woo her, ye mean?"

"I do." Picking up two empty goblets, he filled them up, handing one to Niall. "There isna a woman alive who doesna swoon when a mon pays court."

For just a moment Niall was solemn, then he laughed aloud as he imagined Ogg with wings and a bow and arrow. "The world's largest cupid."

"What?"

"Nothing." Niall held his goblet aloft. "Here is to women, God bless them all. And to my bonny, bonny wife." Still, there were obstacles that stood in the path of his happiness. Gregor, and the most resilient of all—Malcolm!

Twenty-five

The hearth fires had burned down to ash. One by one the smoking torches flickered, hissed, and then died. The hour was growing late. Darkness was gathering under the high ceiling. The women had long ago retired, taking the small children with them. All the women save one.

These drunken oafs will tire of their riotous celebrating and go to their beds eventually, Caitlin thought. It was her only hope, her only chance. Meanwhile, patience must be her ally. *I will find a way to get the flag. I must.*

Goaded on by the sight of the MacLeod's fairy flag which Malcolm had brazenly flaunted tonight, Caitlin was determined. Though her backside ached from her hours of sitting slumped on the bench, she refused to join the other women upstairs in their beds.

"Niall MacDonald, tanist," she scoffed, feeling the sting of his betrayal anew. He had risen to his greatest heights on the tide of her shame. How then could she feel even a shred of longing? And yet she did.

Touching her fingers to her mouth, she remembered Niall's kiss. Closing her eyes, she remembered the way his nearness had ignited a host of glorious sensations. Though she knew passion for what it was and refused to give it recognition as love, she was nonetheless caught up in the feelings that coiled within her stomach.

I willna feel this way, she ordered herself. *If I hae to succumb to the powers of a witchwoman I will tear Niall MacDonald out of my heart, my soul.*

Tears shimmered in her eyes as she stared at the dying fire. Still as stone, she reflected on a plan of escape for no one, not Malcolm, not Gregor, nor especially Niall, would get the better of her. Not now, not ever.

"Och, lassie. Such a face. It canna be that bad."

Looking up, Caitlin saw that Ogg had left Niall's side and was hovering over her. "It can be and it 'tis."

Ogg's look was sympathetic. "Niall's new honor has made ye sad."

"And why should it not? Surely then my hopes and dreams hae been scattered like leaves before the winter." She sighed. "There is no hope for happiness. No hope at all."

"Ah, but there is, lass, for it was spoken by Niall's own lips that he cares deeply for ye."

Caitlin sat straight up. "He cares for himself ye mean and his silly notion of the importance of power." She nodded with her head to where Niall sat talking to two others of his clan, stung by his seeming neglect of her. "He cares little for me."

Resting her head on her arms, Caitlin closed her eyes. Suddenly she was very tired. Tired of the constant warfare. Tired of the bickering. Tired of feeling this lonely and sad.

"Ye are wrong." Putting his hands under her arms, Ogg helped Caitlin to her feet, tending her as carefully as a child. "But come to bed. 'Tis late and the shadows rule. Tomorrow ye may think differently."

"Nae," she whispered. Still, she did not resist as Ogg picked her up in his arms and carried her up to her chamber. Setting her down on the bed, he said but one word.

"Sleep." Then, throwing another log on the fire to see to her comfort, he was gone.

Sleep. Unless she could right the great wrong done to

her and her clan, Caitlin wondered if she could or would ever sleep peacefully again.

"I curse ye, Niall MacDonald. I curse ye and all yer clan!"

Caitlin stared up at the ceiling. Beams of light danced from the fire, casting figured shadows overhead. Two entwined silhouettes conjured up memories of the embraces she and Niall MacDonald had shared, making it difficult to push him out of her mind. Thus, for several long, tormented hours she lay awake trying to exert her will over her fevered, longing body.

Ah, but no! She would not allow herself to feel this way. She wouldn't. It was a betrayal of her clan. A threat to her freedom and peace of mind. A danger to her sanity.

"Ye must leave, Caitlin nic Ian," she murmured with certainty. "You must leave and never see him again." There had to be a way.

She had to be patient. Eventually the MacDonalds would tire of their celebrating and take to their beds. Then she would return Niall MacDonald "favor" for "favor." Aye, she would get away from here and the temptation Niall MacDonald posed. She'd find another fisherman and sail back to her clan.

Fires blazed brightly in every room throughout the castle, yet even so Caitlin felt cold. The very thought of what she was about to do sent a chill traveling up her spine, wondering just what Malcolm MacDonald's punishment would be if she was caught.

"I canna allow myself to be," she promised herself. Surely she could be as sneaky a thief as Niall had been. She told herself that she could be and that she wasn't in the least bit worried, yet when the moment came and the castle was quiet, she was as nervous as a cat on a flagpole.

Moving quickly about the room, she gathered up her meager possessions. There was no time to lose. She had to hurry while the MacDonald men were immersed in their whiskey-induced slumber. There could be no turning back now.

"I can't give any more thought to leaving than Niall did when he left me," she whispered, yet, even so, the thought of never seeing him again brought an emptiness to her heart. She should never have let herself fall in love with him again. It only complicated her already turbulent emotions. So thinking, she opened the door and slipped out.

The stairway was dimly lit. Caitlin stumbled once or twice in her haste as she took the steps two at a time. Or was she clumsy because of her fear of being caught? It didn't matter. As she made her way to the kitchen, thankful that she had familiarized herself vaguely with the castle's interior, she forced herself to remain calm.

Assembling what supplies she could for the journey, Caitlin placed the larger foodstuffs in a roomy sack and the smaller in a fancily decorated sporran that she borrowed from a peg on the wall. It was just as dark in the kitchen as it had been on the stairs and she fumbled around, holding her breath once or twice when her gropings sent something falling to the floor.

"And now for the flag." She couldn't leave without it, and thus she had no choice but to tiptoe toward the hall, hoping it would be empty.

It wasn't. Lying on benches, underneath tables, and on the hard floor several of the MacDonald men slumbered. Caitlin drew back. It would be insanity to try to steal the flag when there were MacDonalds about, yet, at the same time, this might well be her only chance to get beyond the castle walls. Usually Malcolm had her watched, but tonight her "watchdogs" were among those whose loud snores disturbed the night's silence.

"I hae to do it," she swore. But oh, if only Malcolm had not placed the flag so high. It was well out of reach. Only by carefully dragging one chair and then another to the mantel, placing one on top of the other, was Caitlin able to reach it. And all the time she was tearing it down, the chairs rocked to and fro threatening to tumble.

With all the grace of an acrobat, however, Caitlin at last had the fairy flag within her possession. Tying it around her waist beneath the folds of her arasaid, she ran toward the front door, then the portculis. Tugging at the rope, she raised the iron grille just enough for her slender body to fit through, then she was running as fast as her legs could carry her.

The moon was shrouded by dark clouds, her only guide the light of the fading stars. Nevertheless, she once again plucked up her courage, looking back many times to make certain she had not been seen leaving. If only she could put as much distance as possible between herself and Niall, she would get through her heartache somehow. At least her pride would be salvaged, she thought sadly. And perhaps happiness was only a dream after all . . .

Caitlin stealthfully crept out of the castle, hiding in the shadows, conscious of every sound. That was why her ears perceived so readily the sound of footsteps behind her. Stopping in her tracks, she listened again. Her pursuer seemed to be playing a game. When she walked, he walked, when she halted, he did likewise. Trying to outsmart him, she dodged in and out amongst some barrels, but seemingly all for naught. There, looming in the semidarkness, was a hulking figure, blocking her way of escape.

"Ogg?" She was hopeful as she called out, but all too soon Caitlin recognized her follower as the clansman Niall and her own intuition had warned her about. "Gregor."

"Tired of our hospitality?" Gregor's features seemed to be carved in stone. He looked very strong and ominous as he stood there staring at her, his dark visage made darker by the night.

This time Caitlin was powerless against the storm of fear that shattered all her resolve like an eggshell. She spun around, intending to put as much distance as she could between herself and Malcolm's kinsman, but in a few strides he had caught up with her, his hand curving brutally around her arm, jerking her back to face him.

Futilely Caitlin clawed at the imprisoning hand. "It was stuffy in my room and I thought to get some air." The lie tripped off her tongue despite her trembling.

His dark eyes narrowed, but after a long moment he released his hold on her, much to her relief. "Ye were going for a walk, is that what ye would hae me believe?"

"Aye!" she said cheerily. "A walk!" Clutching tightly to her sack, she took a few tentative steps backward. "And now I'll be on my way. Back from where I came." She headed in the direction of the portcullis, intending to bluff him for a while. When he did not follow she was lulled with a false sense of security and retreated a few steps more. It was a mistake, just the move he wanted her to make, for with a snarl he was upon her, shoving her so hard that she tumbled to the ground. The impact with the hard earth jarred the sack loose and set the sack around her waist to sway, scattering objects on the ground.

Gregor gave a bitter laugh. "So, ye were just going for a stroll!" Bending down, he fingered the provisions with an oath, then stared hard at her. "And I call ye a *liar.* Ye were leaving, make no mistake about it."

"Nae! Nae." She shook her head furiously.

The hands that bruised her as they searched her person were large and brutal. Hands that could maim and kill. Hands that unfortunately went right to the flag. "Aha!" He was triumphant. His eyes were like those of a weasel, hungry and ferocious. With a chilling laugh, he moved closer. "The MacLeod flag. I wonder . . ."

"Wonder what?"

Wrapping it around her throat, he pulled it slightly. "How tight I would have to tie it to choke the life out of a MacLeod."

Caitlin couldn't breathe. She couldn't think. All she knew

was that this dark-haired, violent man was strangling her. Was that it, then? Was Gregor, obviously the man whose soul was as black as his hair, going to murder her? Would the glens of Skye then be covered with blood because of her father's revenge?

"Nae!" she cried out, coughing as the burning in her throat blocked out all air.

"Beg for mercy!" Gregor was enjoying her helplessness.

"Please . . ." Giving in to his sadistic whim, Caitlin could only hope that if she did as he said she would be spared.

"Again."

"Please."

"Please what?"

It pained her to talk, still she forced the words from her mouth. "Please don't kill me. Please let me live."

He thrust his face only a few inches from hers, and Caitlin knew suddenly that he meant to do more than just strangle her. "Niall's wife! What irony." He laughed, pinching her breast.

"Aye, I am his wife. And he will kill ye if ye dunna take me back to the castle." A place that had suddenly become a precious haven.

"Take ye back? Not yet." As if to frighten her into submission, he pulled the flag tightly around her throat again.

"Ye must be mad!" She stiffened, her mind refusing to accept what was inevitable. Taking a deep breath, Caitlin let it out in a scream. Better to die quickly than to suffer what this evil bastard had in mind.

Somehow, even from within the castle walls, Niall heard the shriek of outrage. In anguished curiosity he followed the sound. Seeing the two battling figures, he flung himself forward.

At his intrusion Gregor loosened his grasp, allowing Caitlin the luxury of pushing herself to her knees. Slowly her eyes moved to her rescuer, knowing that at that moment Niall's face was the dearest face in the whole world.

"She was tying to run away and I caught her red-handed," Gregor forced an explanation. "Ye know the orders we had from Malcolm."

"Nae! He was trying to. . . to . . ." Caitlin was too ashamed to finish.

"I know exactly what he was trying to do."

Like an enraged lion, Niall sprang, engaging his cousin in hand-to-hand combat. Grappling on the ground, the two men wrestled, Gregor the burlier of the two but Niall's lithe muscular grace giving him the edge.

"I'll kill ye. I swear that I will."

It was a melee of cursing and shouting. Fistcuffs and kicking. First Niall would falter, then Gregor would fail in his strategy. Niall's slyness and strength won out. He pummeled Gregor to near senselessness stopping only when Malcolm's guards, alerted to trouble by the noise and yells, came rushing to pull the two men apart.

"What is this all about?" Malcolm came upon the scene with all the ferocity of a thundercloud. Looking from Niall to Gregor and back again, he demanded an explanation.

"Yer tanist's wife was trying to steal the flag away. I was merely trying to hold her in check when yer nephew appeared and jumped me."

"She was trying to steal the flag?" Malcolm was as angry as Caitlin had supposed. For an instant she thought he would strike her, but he maintained control. "Ye shouldna hae done that. Ye've been dealt gently with, but from now one ye will get no such courtesy." He gesticulated to a man standing behind him. "From now on, lock her in." He smiled beneficently at her. "It is my duty as yer chieftain and kin by marriage to make certain ye dunna come to harm."

Caitlin struggled to her feet, her trembling hands automatically trying to straighten her rumpled clothing. "Make

certain that I don't leave, ye mean." Though she had been
afraid of Gregor, Caitlin found out that now she was face-
to-face with Malcolm. Now that the worst had happened,
she no longer was terrified of him.

"As ye say." Malcolm led the way back to the castle,
giving his orders to his guards as soon as they passed
through the door. This time Caitlin really was a prisoner,
and yet as she looked at Niall all she could think about was
the way he had flown to her rescue. Like some daring man
the bards told about, Niall MacDonald had fought for *her*.

Twenty-six

Niall floundered in his bed amidst the fragments of his sleep. Tossing restlessly, his mind churned as he met head-on the thoughts troubling his mind. Caitlin was in terrible danger here. Tonight there had been something sinister in the way his uncle had glared at the girl. Now she was to be locked within the castle walls for trying to escape, something any self-respecting MacDonald would have done.

What a brave lass! Little by little he was coming to fully understand just how special a woman Caitlin was. A woman who had risked her life to come to Sleat to regain possession of the MacLeod's flag. A woman who had stood up against Malcolm. A daring lass who had done something even some of the clansmen would have feared to do.

"And she might have been successful if not for Gregor."

Gregor. His cousin's name made Niall tremble with suppressed rage. There could be no denying what he had intended. To dishonor Caitlin and very likely kill her. For that he had not even been scolded, though what he had done concerned another man's wife.

But a wife that bears the name MacLeod. Thus, what Gregor had done seemed to be permissible. The truth of it enraged him, for he knew it would be a long time before he could forget the scene he had stumbled upon. And as long as Caitlin remained at Dunskaith she would be at Gregor's mercy.

But what can I do about it? he wondered. *How can I*

protect her? The truth was that he couldn't. But he could help her to escape. He could . . .

"Nae. I canna turn against my own." And yet neither could he just stand by and watch Caitlin be hurt.

Sitting up, Niall braced his legs against the cold wooden floor. Since she had been locked in her chamber, he had not had a chance to talk with her, but he knew he had to talk with her now.

Getting out of bed, Niall dressed hurriedly in a shirt and breacan and slowly opened his chamber door and made his way to Caitlin's room. Proof of Caitlin's status as prisoner was troubling. True to his word Malcolm had stationed a guard to prowl about in front of the room where Caitlin was housed. A faint gleam of torchlight glinted off the keys hung from the man's sporran, jingling as he walked back and forth. Seeing Niall, he promptly blocked his way.

"Move aside, Robert." When the guard hesitated, Niall said simply, "I hae come to see my wife. Ye canna deny a mon that."

"No, I dunna suppose that I can." Hesitantly he turned the key in the lock.

Niall opened the door and went in, pausing for a moment to gaze at the woman asleep on the bed. She lay on her side, her head resting on one outflung arm, her flaming hair tumbling across her face and spilling like a living fire onto the pillow. Huddled up as she was, she looked almost child-like to him and he was mesmerized by how truly lovely she was. The long sweep of her lashes against the curve of her cheek made her look so vulnerable, and he vowed to protect her. His eyes moved tenderly over her form, moving from her toes to the top of her head, pausing for a moment as he studied the slightly tilted nose, the generous mouth that felt so soft against his own. The sight of her lying there, the rise and fall of her breathing stirring against the thin quilt, acted like an aphrodisiac. He remembered the way her breasts felt as they stroked his chest.

"Ah, lass, how I do love ye," he whispered, "but alas, 'tis hopeless that we will ever hae any lasting happiness." Still, they could have memories to recall on long, lonely, cold nights. Breathing a heavy sigh, he bent down and touched the fiery hair where it grew near her temple in a loving gesture.

Caitlin awoke. "Who?" She jerked upright, drawing the covers tightly over her breasts as she remembered Gregor's pawing. "Ohhhh."

It was Niall who knelt beside her bed, holding a finger up to his lips to warn her to keep silent. Caitlin felt again that treacherous warmth of attraction for him.

"Niall?" She tried to adjust her vision to see him clearly in the fading firelight. "What are ye doing here?"

He looked like a man who was in need of sleep. There were hard lines around his mouth, furrows on his brow, and the flesh beneath his eyes was shadowed with blue. Truly he looked more prisoner than she. "I just came to see ye," he whispered. "I wanted to see ye. I wanted to make certain that ye were all right after . . . after . . ."

"Aye, I am, though if ye hadna come I know I wouldna be." Her eyes were soft. "Ye came to my rescue like in some heroic bard's tale."

"Did he hurt ye, Caitlin?" Caitlin had put up a valiant struggle, but nevertheless he worried that perhaps more had taken place than his eyes had seen revealed.

Caitlin knew what he meant. "I am unharmed. All that is bruised and battered is my pride." She sighed.

"Had he done what he intended I would hae had to kill him!"

Her eyes were wide as she stared into his face. His voice sounded as if he really meant it. "Would ye?"

"Aye!" He sat down on the bed. "Despite all that has happened between us, lass, ye are my wife and I care for ye."

"Really?"

"Really."

"Niall . . ." There were so many things she wanted to say.

"Hush!" His fingers were gentle as he touched her lips. "Let me talk." Niall took a long, deep breath. His fingers traced her cheekbones, then her lips. "Ye've created quite a stir, lassie, in more ways than one."

"Aye, but I almost succeeded." She felt relaxed and content being with him. There was a sudden easy relationship between them, as if those stormy earlier days had never existed.

"Malcolm is incensed with ye."

"Is he now?" Drawing her knees up to her chin, she pursed her lips. "Well, he isna the one who should be piqued, I'd be thinkin'." The corners of her mouth tugged into a smile.

Nodding his head, he caressed her with his eyes. "Caitlin . . . ye hae made me realize a great many things these last few days."

"Such as?" Her voice was soft, stroking him like a delicate hand.

"Such as what is really important in this brief blink of an eye we call life."

He felt desire stir and could not escape her web of enchantment, could not take his eyes off her. She was quite a lassie. A bundle of beauty and bravery.

"And just what is important?" Her gaze roved over him— the thick blond hair, the blue eyes with their thick lashes. The sparkling firelight shadowed the hollows beneath his high cheekbones and hard, strong jaw line. It was his perfectly chiseled mouth, however, that drew her eye again and again as she found herself remembering the taste of his kiss.

"Ye . . ." He stared grimly at the fire. "I love ye, Caitlin!" There, he had said it. Something he had never said before. But having revealed his feelings, he felt lighter of heart, as if in admitting it to her he had finally come to terms with the truth himself. He loved her.

"Love?" She hadn't expected him to say that. That he desired her perhaps, but not *love*. Oh, how she had dreamed of hearing him say those words. On impulse she reached out and took his hand, unaware of how seductive the gesture could prove, for the contact of their hands was overpowering.

Slowly he moved toward her, pulling her against him. His mouth came down on hers, engulfing Caitlin in the familiar sensations his lips always brought forth. Pressing her body closer to his, she sought the passion of his embrace. She craved his kisses with a warm, sweet desire that fused their bodies together.

"Caitlin!" He spoke her name in a breathless whisper as he drew his mouth away. Searchingly his eyes gazed into hers. A silent question.

The roaring of her blood was deafening in her ears. She gave no resistance to his embrace. *This* was what she wanted, what she had always longed for.

Niall kissed her again. There was no ignoring the flicker of arousal which spread from their joined mouths to the core of her body. Thoughts of future heartache pressed against her soul, but she pushed them far from her mind. She reached for him, as if the only safety could be in his arms. Her touch was his undoing. As their eyes suddenly met, they both knew what was to come.

How can the hands of a fighting man be so tender? she wondered. Yet they were. She didn't protest when he stretched himself the full length of the bed. The desire to run her hands over him made her tremble, though she remained perfectly still.

"Niall."

"Aye."

"I just want ye to know how very glad I am to be yer wife. I wouldn't hae wanted to marry anyone else."

"Nor I."

Niall held her chin in his hand, kissing her eyelids, the curve of her cheek. He kissed her mouth with all the pent-up hunger he had suppressed for so long, his tongue gently tracing the outline of her lips.

He felt her tremble beneath him and found himself trembling, too, with a nervousness that was unusual for him. Anticipation, he supposed. Eagerness. Desire.

Slowly, leisurely, Niall stripped Caitlin's nightgown away, like the petals of a flower. His fingers lingered as they wandered down her stomach to explore the texture of her skin. Like velvet, he thought.

"Ye are so beautiful."

She glowed under the praise of his deep, throaty whisper. "Am I?" The compliment pleased her, made her forget for the moment all the hostility and the danger of the last few days. There was now.

"Very . . ." He sought the indentation of her navel, then moved lower to tangle his fingers in the soft wisps of hair that joined at her legs. Moving back, he let his eyes enjoy what his hands had set free. "Do ye have any idea how much I want ye?" He took her hand and moving it beneath his breacan, pressed it to the firm flesh of his arousal. She felt the throbbing strength of him as her eyes gazed into his. Then he bent to kiss her again, his mouth keeping hers a willing captive for a long time.

Twining her hands around his neck, she clutched him to her, pressing her body eagerly against his chest. She could feel the heat and strength and growing desire of him with every breath. Niall, her Niall. She had spent so many nights dreaming that he would make love to her.

Caitlin tried to speak, to tell him all that was in her heart, but she could only say his name, a groan deep in her throat as his mouth and hands worked unspeakable magic.

"So much wasted time," he murmured. "But now I'll

make up for it." His head was bent low, his tongue curling around the tips of her breast, suckling gently.

Raising himself up on his elbow, he looked down at her. At that moment he knew he'd put his heart and soul in pawn. Removing his shirt and breacan, he pressed their naked chests together, shivering at the vibrantly arousing sensation.

"Caitlin . . ." Her name was like a prayer on his lips.

The warmth and heat of his mouth and the memory of her fingers touching that private part of him sent a sweet ache flaring through Caitlin's whole body. Growing bold, she allowed her hands to explore, delighting at the touch of the firm flesh that covered his ribs, the broad shoulders, the muscles of his arms, the lean length of his back. He was so perfectly formed. His masculine beauty hypnotized her. For just a moment she was content to stare, then with a soft sigh her fingers curled in the thick springy hair that furred his chest. Her fingers lightly circled in imitation of what he was doing to her.

His lips nuzzled against the side of her throat. He uttered a moan as her hands moved over the smoothly corded muscles of his shoulders. "Ah, how I love ye to touch me . . ." It seemed as if his breath was trapped somewhere between his throat and stomach. He couldn't say any more. The realization that once again she was to be his was a heady feeling that nearly made him dizzy as he brought his lips to hers. Such a potent kiss. As if he had never kissed her before.

Reaching up, she clung to him, drawing in his strength and giving hers to him in return. She could feel his heart pounding and knew that hers beat in matching rhythm.

Caressing her, kissing her, he left no part of her free from his touch and she responded with a natural passion that was kindled by his love. Her entire body quivered with the intoxicating sensations he always aroused in her. She wanted only one thing—to feel his hard warmth filling her, to join with him in that most tender of emotions.

"Niall . . ." Closing her eyes, Caitlin awaited another kiss, her mouth opening to him as he caressed her lips with all the passionate hunger they both yearned for. Caitlin loved the taste of him, the tender urgency of his mouth. Her lips opened to him for a seemingly endless passionate onslaught of kisses. It was as if they were breathing one breath, living at that moment just for each other.

Desire that had been coiling within Caitlin sparked to renewed fire and she could feel his passion likewise building, searing her with its heat. They shared a joy of touching and caressing, arms against arms, legs touching legs, fingers entwining and wandering to explore. Mutual hunger brought their lips back together time after time. She craved his kisses and returned them with trembling pleasure, exploring the inner softness of his mouth.

"Oh, my sweet, braw wife!" Desire writhed almost painfully within his loins. He had never wanted anything or anyone as much as he did her at this moment. It was like an unfulfilled dream just waiting to come true.

Niall cupped the full curve of her breast. Lightly he stroked until the peaks sprang to life under his touch, the once-soft flesh now taut and aching. His breath caught in his throat as his hazel eyes savored her.

Bending down, he worshipped her with his mouth, his lips traveling from one breast to the other in tender fascination. His tongue curled around the nubby peaks, his teeth lightly grazing until she writhed beneath him. He savored the expressions that chased across her face, the wanting and the passion for him that were so clearly revealed.

She caught fire wherever he touched her, burning with an all-consuming need. Caitlin's hands crept around Niall's neck, her fingers tangling and tousling the thick waves of his tawny hair as she breathed a husky sigh, remembering what pleasure was to come.

They lay together kissing, touching, rolling over and over on the bed. His hands were doing wondrous things to her, making her writhe and groan. Every inch of her body caught fire as passion exploded between them with a wild oblivion. He moved against her, sending waves of pleasure exploding along every nerve in her body.

"Niall . . . love me . . ." she breathed.

"In due time . . ." he promised, his hands caressing her, warming her with their heat. They took sheer delight in the texture and pressure of each other's body. Sensuously he undulated his hips between her legs. Every time their bodies caressed, each experienced a shock of raw desire that encompassed them in fiery, pulsating sensations. Then his hands were between their bodies, sliding down the velvety flesh of her belly, moving to that place between her thighs that ached for his entry.

The swollen length of him brushed across her thighs. Then he was covering her, his manhood at the entrance of her secret core. His gentle probing brought sweet fire curling deep inside her with spirals of pulsating sensations. Then his hands left her, to be replaced by the hardness she had glimpsed before, entering her just a little, then pausing. She felt his maleness creating unbearable sensations within her as he began to move within her.

Niall groaned softly, the blood pounding thickly in his head. His hold on her hips tightened as the throbbing shaft of his maleness possessed her again and again. She was so warm, so tight around him that he closed his eyes with agonized pleasure as he moved back and forth, initiating her fully into the depths of passion and love.

Instinctively Caitlin tightened her legs around him, certain she could never withstand the ecstasy that was engulfing her body. It was as if her heart shattered, bursting within her. She was melting inside, merging with him into one being. As spasms overtook her, she dug her nails into the skin of his back whispering his name.

A sweet shaft of ecstasy shot through Niall. Even when the intensity of their passion was spent, they still clung to each other, unable to let this magical moment end. They touched each other gently, wonderingly.

"Oh, what a fiery, passionate wife I hae." He nibbled playfully at her ear.

"Am I now? And are ye not pleased?"

"Aye! But not surprised." Playfully he tugged at her hair. "This gave me a warning." He nuzzled her throat. "Ye are all that I could hae asked for, all that I desire."

Cradling her against his chest, he lay silent for a long time as he savored her presence beside him. His hands fondled her gently as she molded her body to his. *If only I could keep her with me forever,* he thought, and not let the hatred between the clans destroy what they had found.

Niall realized that for the first time in his life he was truly content. Power was said to be the most important thing on earth but he knew differently. Without someone who really cared, life was hollow and made a man the emptiest of creatures. Caitlin made him feel alive!

"I will never let ye go," he uttered fervently. "I pledge my love, my very life."

This time it was Caitlin who silenced him. "Hush. Ye canna make such promises. I know and ye know that." She laid her head on his shoulder, stroking the hair on his chest. "But know this as well. Whatever happens I will always love ye."

"I canna ask more than that." And yet he would. As Niall closed his eyes, he knew at that moment he had to take control of their destiny.

Twenty-seven

Torches in the great hall burned brightly despite the late hour, their flames casting a gigantic shadow on the wall. A grotesque silhouette that looked like that of an ogre, Niall thought as he boldly strode into the room.

"I want to talk with ye, Malcolm," he announced, not even masking his frustration.

"Oh?" Sitting in his favorite chair, his feet perched on the table, Malcolm didn't even bother to look up.

"Ye canna do this, Malcolm!"

There was no answer, but Niall was not in a mood to tolerate the blatant disregard of his presence. With a mumbled oath he moved toward the table and gave it a shove hard enough to nearly send Malcolm sprawling.

"Arghhh . . . !" This time Malcolm did respond. Bounding to his feet, he looked like an angry bear.

"I said I want to talk."

The dark eyes beneath Malcolm's thick brows were slits of anger. He raised his fists. For a moment it looked as if he had been goaded into a fight, but in the end he backed down. "Then talk, ye young pup!"

"I want my wife set free. I dunna want to see her caged like some trapped animal."

"You!" Malcolm was defiant as he faced the younger man squarely. "You dunna want." His tone was scathing. Reaching out, he gripped Niall's shoulder, digging his fingers into the firm-muscled flesh with a bruising strength that proved he was still a man to be reckoned with.

Niall did not back down. Squaring his shoulders, he took a step forward. "I dunna want! Set her free."

"Nae!" Turning his back, Malcolm's manner clearly told that his answer was to be the end of it. But Niall wouldn't leave it there.

"Then ye are not an honorable mon. A mon of honor would not treat a lassie such." Without realizing it, his eyes moved upward, focusing on the fairy flag. Oh, how he regretted ever even touching it. Except for the fact that it was instrumental in his meeting Caitlin, no good had come of his mission to steal it. Had he known to what ends Malcolm would go, he would never have involved himself in the deed.

"She is not just a lassie. She is one of *them*." His lips curled up in a snarl. "And Ian MacLeod's daughter." Malcolm screwed up his face, looking angry, fierce, and formidable. "Ian MacLeod. Bah! I shall never forgi'e him. I shall be avenged. Aye, I shall!"

"By locking up his daughter?" Niall knew it would be a long time before he could forget the sight of an armed guard parading up and down in front of Caitlin's door.

"I did that for her own good." Malcolm shook his shaggy-haired head. "I wouldna want her to get lost or to come upon dishonorable men."

"Like Gregor!"

"Hold yer tongue! Gregor is yer kin. My nephew. A member of yer clan. Dunna dare criticize him to side with a MacLeod!" Malcolm clenched his jaw, only narrowly holding back his anger. "He wears the scars of MacLeod treachery."

"As they bear scars of his." Niall's eyes met those of his uncle, relating a silent condemnation of an act of cowardice that had been perpetrated many years earlier.

The reminder made Malcolm uncomfortable. He stiffened

but did not push the quarrel further. "What is done is done. Now ye are tanist, a justifiable honor I hae disposed." His upraised brow seemed to hint very strongly that Niall should show proper gratitude.

"And for that I thank ye. I will serve you well, Uncle, but as to Caitlin, ye must . . ."

"My mind is made up. Ye hae no say on the matter!" He thrust his face to within inches of Niall's. "Ye are not chieftain yet. Nor will ye ever be if ye dunna keep still."

A tight knot had formed in Niall's stomach. *Then I will do what I must do,* Niall thought but did not say. All too soon the moment he had dreaded was to become a reality.

"So be it."

Malcolm didn't speak, but by the smile that erupted across his face it was obvious he thought himself to be triumphant in the argument. More to himself than to Niall he said at last, "I hae the MacLeod's little treasure, which it willna take long for him to reclaim. So dunna fash yersel, laddie. She won't be locked in her room ere long."

"Ye will let her go once her father comes to take the bait?" Niall knew he could not wait to find out. Not after what Gregor had done tonight. He would not take the risk of Caitlin being hurt in this matter of Malcolm's desire for revenge.

Leaving the room, he took the stairs two at a time as he hurried to Caitlin's chamber. It would be a traitorous act to follow the urging of his heart, Niall thought. Even so, he knew there was no other choice. There were times when right must overpower wrong no matter what the price. True, Malcolm was Niall's chieftain, for whom he had sworn loyalty and his uncle, but kin or not, he was grievously unjust in what he was doing. So thinking, Niall pulled a sword from the wall, hoping with all his heart he would not have to use it to shed any blood, and hurried onward.

Stealthfully Niall approached the sentinel, grasping the sword, using the handle as a club, knocking the guard out cold. The man grunted, then slumped to the floor. Anxiously Niall fumbled about for the key, tearing it free and unlocking the door.

"Caitlin!" His voice was a harsh whisper of urgency.

"Mmm . . ." She came only half awake, disturbed by his hushed command, but opened her eyes wide as he shook her gently. "Something is wrong. What?"

"Nothing is wrong."

"Then . . . ?" She held out her arms, thinking him to have amorous intentions.

She was tempting, but Niall regretfully had to shake his head. "I've come to free ye, Caity, not to make love."

"Free me?"

"Aye." With gentle fingers he grasped her hand and pulled her to her feet. "Hurry and get dressed. We hae to get free of here before the goose egg I gifted the guard with is discovered. I don't know how long he'll be unconscious."

"Ye hit him?" She was worried what repercussions that might bring.

Niall ruffled her already touseled hair. "We won't speak of it now, but I think you ken. Now, no more talk!"

By the light of a candle he helped her dress, his fingers lingering overlong on the soft swell of her breast as he fastened the folds of her tonnag together with a brooch. He looked down at the fiery red tresses illuminated by the glow of the flickering light and wrapped a strand around his fingers. A yearning surged through him. He wanted her so much that it was a painful longing. If only they could go away together, give free expression to the passion that sparked between them, he knew they could be happy. But that was not to be. She had to go and he had to stay. He was willing to give up his own desires just to make certain that she was safe. Even so, he allowed himself the luxury of holding her close, just for a moment, brushing his lips against her neck. Then with a mumbled oath he pulled away.

"Come!"

More than one unwary clansman was the recipient of a painful crack to the head as Niall frantically sought Caitlin's freedom, yet slowly but surely they worked their way across the inner bailey, hiding in the shadows. Niall clasped Caitlin's hand so tightly that she winced.

Her eyes were sad. "Niall, I'm not sure I want to go."

"Ye must." Niall felt a shiver convulse her slim frame and wrapped his arms around her, shielding her from the cool air with his plaid. An unpremeditated act but one that most definitely felt right. She belonged in his arms. "Malcolm is a good chieftain on most accounts, but something is seriously amiss here. I intend to see that ye get back to yer father's hall safely before the hills and glens of Skye are stained with all our blood."

She nuzzled her cheek against his chest. "Come with me." Hope kindled anew in her heart that perhaps all would turn out as it should after all.

"Caitlin . . ." Niall's mouth hovered only inches from her own. She wanted him to give in to the moment but instead he shook his head. "I canna. Once I take ye far enough to know that ye are safe, I must come back."

"But how will ye explain . . . ?"

"I'll think of a way." He held her close for just a moment more, then pulled away. "Let us go." The dark shape of the huge outer gate loomed before them. "Push the ends of your hair inside your tonnag, lass, and keep your head down." If God was willing, they would not be discovered.

Niall tugged on the rope. The creak of the portcullis was a welcome sound, though Caitlin watched the iron grating ascend with anxiety. What would be Niall's punishment for aiding her, she wondered, knowing his betrayal of Malcolm would not be taken lightly. The realization of what Niall had risked suddenly hit her full force. How could she let him make such a sacrifice? She had thought that being tanist meant the world to him, and yet now by his actions he was throwing the honor away. She couldn't let him do it! Not and profess her love.

"Niall, let's go back. I canna let ye do this. Ye will be ruined," she breathed, her voice blending with the wind.

"I willna," he lied. "I'm a smooth-talking laddie, as ye know. I'll make up a story that Malcolm will believe." He smiled, remembering the night they had met. "Perhaps I'll just tell him that ye were a ghost and walked through the wall. Will he believe that, do ye ken?"

"Nae." Though he tugged at her hand, she wouldn't move an inch. "I willna go."

"Because ye think I will suffer. Well, I willna. I'll think of a way to make amends to Malcolm, never fear. He needs me." He kissed her lightly on the lips. "Together we can work on bringing peace to Skye, Caity. Then and only then can we ever hope to be reunited."

That was something to hope for. Still, Caitlin's face was wet with tears as she followed him through the gaping mouth of the gate running across the glen.

They formed two silhouettes on the crest of the hill, running against the wind. Caitlin felt reassured that all would be well until her eyes swept the dark-gray horizon. Were those distant dots she saw on the hill what she thought them to be? Yes! Blessed Saint Michael, they were being followed!

"Niall! Someone is coming!" she croaked, clutching his hand with fingers that trembled.

Niall looked over his shoulder, cursing loudly. Eight or ten men were running in their direction. There could be no other reason than pursuit. "They must have found Robert sooner than I supposed. Run, Caity!"

Run she did, until her legs ached, but though they had had a head start that gave them a fair to middling chance of escape, the other men were gaining on them. Looking over her shoulder, nonetheless, she cringed. "Run faster,

Niall!" Obeying her own command, she forced her feet and legs to move at a hazardous speed. They had to get away.

"Caitlin . . . !" There was a large hole up ahead, but though Niall sought to warn her, he was helpless to keep her from stumbling. All he could do was hurry back for her. Taking her by the hand, he tugged her to her feet. "Are you all right?"

She nodded, refusing to notice the pain in her ankle. Even so, the injury slowed her down. As they ran, she had to lean on Niall for support. And all the while the men pursuing them were catching up. The reality of the situation could not be denied. They could never escape now.

"Listen to me, Niall. I willna hae ye sacrificing yerself to save me. Tell them I broke free of my room and ye were chasing after me. Say it! I willna deny it."

"I willna tell such a vile lie!"

"I will! Let Malcolm think ye are a hero in capturing me. Then perhaps all willna be lost." Caitlin hushed as the clansmen swiftly encircled them. Pushing at Niall's chest, she made great show of fighting him. "Ach, ye damned MacDonald. Let me go! I willna go back."

"Aye, ye will!"

Caitlin recognized that voice at once and damned the man. Gregor. Like a cursed hound, he seemed to be always following in her tracks. "Ha! I should hae ken it would hae been ye."

"I wondered if my instincts were right. They were. I know ye set her free, Niall. I watched and waited. This time I let her get past the gate, just so there would be no mistaking yer intent." At a nod of his head four men surrounded Niall, grappling him to the ground.

Striking out blindly, Caitlin did her best to pull Gregor's henchmen from Niall. She tried to claw at them. She kicked out, baring her shapely thighs in the tussle. "Nae! Nae! He was chasing after me to bring me back to the castle!" In anger she whirled around, her eyes darting fire at Gregor.

His thin lips curled up in a snarl. "Ye are a liar, *said he*. I willna doubt my own eyes. I saw what I saw. And now he will suffer for it."

"You black-hearted bastard!" Even in his defeated position, Niall's countenance blazed defiance. "I tell you to let the lassie go!"

"Go? She'll go nowhere but back to the castle. And as for you . . ."

"I am tanist! You have no right to overrule me." Struggling against the men who held him, Niall stared his adversary down.

"Tanist? Not when it is found out what ye hae done." Malice oozed from Gregor's one eye, like a putrid wound. "Ye've brought yerself to this end. Ah, how I hae hated seeing ye get all the honors, glowing in all the glory when it's I who hae been Malcolm's right hand all these years. I've wanted to bring ye down and now I hae."

"Not yet." Even now, Niall was determined. He would talk with Malcolm, convince him somehow that what he had done was for the good of the clan.

"Aye, but I hae." Gregor was frighteningly sure of himself! Giving Niall a shove, he commanded, "Take them away!"

Twenty-eight

It was cold, damp, and dark in the prison cell. Depressing. The stale odor of straw, mildew, and rot enveloped Niall as he was shoved inside the cubicle that was little bigger than a closet.

"Yer abode, Cousin. Sweet dreams. Keep the rats company."

Niall lunged, only to be held back by two of the men who swore Gregor allegiance. "I swear, Gregor, ye will regret this! I will get my revenge," he vowed, his eyes darting back and forth for any means of escape. There was none. He was being heavily guarded, like a bird by three large cats, he thought wryly.

"By sending Ogg to wreck vengeance?" For a moment he paused, then exclaimed, "I'm not afraid of him."

"Well, ye should be, and of me when I get free." Niall lashed out, only to be kicked back down into the dark hole. The clank of the grille above his head put an end to any other threats.

"Free?" Gregor's expression was frightening as he leered down at him.

"Aye, free. Ye willna be able to keep me here." At least he hoped. And yet, what would Malcolm do when he heard Gregor's bit of "news"? As Gregor and his men left, as Niall looked around him, he could only wonder.

The cell was more cellar than prison, with a stone and iron barred trapdoor that could be locked from up above.

Niall was familiar with the dungeon. There was no way of escape, of that he was certain. Even if he could crawl up the wall there was no way he could remove the stone from the hole. He was completely at Gregor's mercy.

"I hae been thrust in here without a measure of decency. To suffer and . . ." To die? No, Niall couldn't believe that it would go that far. Or at least he didn't want to believe. And yet . . .

The sound of scurrying rats caused him to wince. Damn the rodents. How he had always loathed them. He would not be able to sleep for fear of having his flesh nibbled on. That was what Gregor meant about sweet dreams. The bastard!

"I'll get out of here and I'll slit his throat," he hissed. "I'll pierce him through. I'll . . ." Something tickled his arm. Cringing, he brushed it away. Oh, how he hated this chilling darkness. It was nearly enough to drive a man mad. But then, wasn't that the very idea? Well, he wouldn't give Gregor that satisfaction. Somehow, someway, he would get free. Hugging his knees to his chest, Niall was dedicated to that thought, for only then could he save Caitlin.

Oh, where are ye? What has Gregor done to ye. Are ye safe, lass? Putting his face in his hands, he could only worry and wonder.

Caitlin was safe, at least for the moment, though she was facing an adversary of her own. A glowering, bearded devil who made no secret of just how dangerous he was. After being pushed and dragged into his presence, she was accused by Gregor of the most hideous of crimes.

"She is a witch."

Caitlin was quick to defend herself. "I am no witch!"

"Be that as it may, under her spell poor Niall was guilty of the vilest of acts against us all."

"Niall?" Malcolm clenched his jaw. "What has he done?"

"He set her free, but I followed and reclaimed her." Gregor gave her a shove. "She is yours."

"So she is." Malcolm glared down at her.

Wincing against the pain in her injured leg, Caitlin stood proud and tall. "So what are ye going to do with me?" Was she to join Niall in the dungeon? Or did the MacDonald have other plans for her?

"Do with ye?" Malcolm pulled at his beard as if contemplating the matter. He quickly decided. "Why, nothing."

"Nothing?" It was hardly the answer she expected.

"Nothing to ye." The way he said it sounded ominous.

"And to Niall?"

"It all depends on ye. If ye try to leave here again, it will go hard on him, do ye ken? I will seek punishment on *him.*"

Caitlin had gone quite pale. "I ken!"

"But if ye conduct yerself like a good little lassie and stay here until yer father pays me a visit, then I will prove myself to be forgiving."

"Ye will set him free."

"Aye."

It was a bargain that made Caitlin have to choose between the two men she most loved in the world. She could either betray her father and watch him fall victim to his sworn enemy or betray Niall to save her father.

"Nae! Nae!" The cry that escaped from her throat was like that of a wounded animal. Sagging to the ground, she grasped his knees, hugging them with her arms as she had when she was a small girl. "Ye canna do this. Ye canna." Rocking back and forth, she sought to fight the demons that tore at her heart.

Twenty-nine

Niall seemed to lose track of time as he languished in the cell-like room. It was dismal, uncomfortable, and humiliating, a disgusting hellhole. Walls of dirt infested with all kinds of vermin. Spiders, worms, and bugs of unknown origin. Worst of all, however, it was damp and cold. He thanked God for his plaid, for it was long and thick enough to be a warm blanket to shield him from the bone-penetrating chill.

"Och, to be free again." Freedom. Something he had always taken for granted but which now was denied him.

"Caitlin!" Her eyes haunted him, her voice seemed to whisper in his ear. "Ach, I'm nearly as addled in my head as Gregor. Something sinister urged *him*. Something evil." Niall could not say what it was, but he knew there was more to the matter than at first was visible.

"Niall!"

It was Ogg's voice. A circle of light appeared above his head as a torch was held aloft. Niall stood up, blinking against the light. He put his hand up to guard him against the brightness of the flickering flames.

"The light hurts yer eyes!"

"Aye, I am slowly turning into a mole." There was a hint of bitterness in Niall's voice. "So much for the mighty tanist." Seeing Ogg, Niall thought of Caitlin. "How is she?"

"Safe, at least for the time being. But Gregor is trying to stir up feelings against her."

"Is she . . . is she caged like me?"

"Nae, though she may as well be." Ogg leaned close. "Malcolm has declared that if she even steps one foot outside the portcullis it will bode ill for ye."

"For me?"

"Aye."

"So, she is trapped just as surely as I." His voice was choked with misery.

"Because of her love for ye, she seeks to protect ye, all the while frightened of what Malcolm intends to do if her father comes to Dunskaith."

"But I don't care what Malcolm has threatened to do to me. He would not kill his own nephew." Of that at least Malcolm would not make himself guilty.

"She canna take the chance."

"Damn, Malcolm." His stubborn obstinance had created a great deal of unhappiness. "Ach, if only I could get out of here."

"Get out? I wouldna be thinking it to be very soon."

"Nor I." Niall was at the mercy of a man who had no honor, no scruples.

"Gregor has the key, and though I hae tried to get my hands on it, I havena been able."

Of course not. Gregor would guard it like a hawk. Niall could only wonder if he would ever be able to hold Caitlin in his arms again. "Ogg."

"Aye?"

"Give Caitlin a message for me."

"That ye love her." Ogg nodded, his face a mask of misery. "That I will." Bidding Niall good-bye, with a promise to come later that night, he hurried back to the hall.

Tankard clanked against tankard in drunken celebration as Malcolm MacDonald and Gregor related the story again and again to their clansmen of Caitlin's escape and capture. Each telling embellished Caitlin's duplicity and Gregor's valor. Watching from the shadows of the great hall, Caitlin wondered how many times they were going to tell the tale. It had been all they had talked about last night, this morning, and again this evening, as if her trying to escape was in some way menacing to the clan.

"I tell ye, she has the evil eye," Gregor was saying.

"The evil eye," Caitlin scoffed. As if she had the power to destroy, corrupt, or acquire an object by merely looking at it.

The clansmen in the hall had begun to believe it, however. Staring at her with frightened eyes they seemed to be waiting for her to exhibit her powers. Mumbling beneath their breath, they spoke of how she had cast such a potent spell over Niall that he had betrayed his own.

"And ye had best watch out or she will do it to you," Gregor intoned. "She is in league with the forces of evil. I witnessed with my own eyes her incantations and rituals."

"Aye. I hae seen her change herself into a cat!" Robert, the guardsman, seemed convinced of it. "That's how she escaped."

"A cat that was as red as her hair," Gregor hurried to add, knowing that he held the others in the palm of his hand. "Well, we will see that she doesna put a spell on us."

As the large stone room flickered with red and orange light, thrown by the flames of the vast hearth, Caitlin stared in fascination at the grotesque shadows cast upon the wall. What followed might have been humorous had it not been so threatening. Caitlin stood horrified as Gregor and his cronies began mumbling, supposedly to counter the effects of "the eye."

> "I make to thee the charm of Mary,
> The most perfect charm that is in the world,
> Against the small eye, against the large eye,
> Against the eye of swift voracious women,
> Against the eye of swift rapacious women,
> Against the eye of swift sluttish women."

Gregor nodded in Caitlin's direction at the last words.

"I am no witch!" she breathed. And Gregor knew that as well. But whether she was or not, the very suspicion planted in the clansmen's minds could be dangerous for her. As well Gregor knew. It made Caitlin's blood run cold that she was at the mercy of her greatest enemy.

"Pssst, Caitlin . . ." Reaching out of the shadows, Ogg took her hand, pulling her into a corner.

"Niall?" The very thought of him caused a flutter in her stomach.

"Is miserable but alive and well. He sends ye his love."

"And I send back mine." Closing her eyes, she could almost see his face, but the blare of a trumpet interrupted her reverie.

A huffing, puffing sentry bounded into the room, pointing in the direction of the north. "The MacLeods! They are here! They've come by biorlin, across the loch. They are marching this way. Listen to the bagpipes!" The ominous hum sounded like a swarm of angry bees.

"My father!" Hurrying to the window, Caitlin looked out, lamenting the boldness that had brought her here. A fear gripped her heart that far from halting the warfare her willfulness had provoked an attack.

"The MacLeods are outside the walls!" The tension in the room was taut as a bowstring. Every clansman's eye focused on the weapons hanging on the wall, poised, waiting for Malcolm's nod. Caitlin's eyes, however, were focused elsewhere.

"The flag!" Somehow when the clansmen were distracted she had to get her hands upon it. If she as a MacLeod could hold that flag aloft, it would give her clansmen heart. And at the same time she would be keeping her promise, not to step foot outside the portcullis.

Caitlin's heart turned over in her breast. Hands clasped tight, she moved to the window and leaned over the stonework balustrade in an effort to identify the clansmen beyond a doubt, having but faint hope that it was other than her clan. The red-haired, broad-shouldered man at the head of the small army left little doubt. Torchlight winked a glow from his sword, the yellow-and-black hue of the tartan beneath gnarled armor marked Ian as surely as any badge.

"Father!" Her eyes were imploring as she looked at the man who held her father's fate in his hands. "Please . . . !"

Malcolm paused for a long moment, then broke into a smile. "I hae no need to quarrel." He turned to Gregor. "By the laws of hospitality, mon, invite Ian in." He patted Caitlin on the shoulder.

Gregor followed his chieftain's bidding, opening the door to an angry MacLeod. Ignoring everyone else in the room, he jostled and shoved his way to Caitlin's side. "Are ye all right? Are ye unharmed?" Her nod assured him that she was. Only then did he unleash his chiding tirade, his face turning purple with rage. "Ye must be daft, Daughter!" Never before had he raised a hand to her, but he shook his fist now threateningly. "I should take the back of my hand to ye. Headstrong! Stubborn! Willful! All these things ye are!"

Caitlin recoiled in the face of his tongue-lashing, knowing she deserved his censor and worse. She should never have come here! If it was possible, she had aged in just the past few days. She deserved his anger. There wasn't a thing he could say to her that she had not said to herself. It was true that a selfish, naive, bold young maiden had left Dunvegan. Now she knew the painful truth, that life often held disappointments and heartache beyond human control. Sometimes the greatest show of love was in giving a loved one up. Just as Niall had been prepared to do.

"I'm . . . I'm sorry, Father."

"Yer sister told me why ye had come. Ach, I ne'er thought any seed of my manhood would go behind my back. Ye defied me!"

"I had to get back the flag." Reverently her eyes touched on it.

Ian's eyes did likewise. "Och, the flag." He reached out as if by so doing he could reclaim it.

Having watched the fiery reunion between father and daughter from a distance, Malcolm now stepped forward. There was an edge to his voice. "Which belongs to me now!"

"Oh, does it now!" Ian stood nose-to-nose with his old adversary. To Caitlin's eyes they looked much like two hounds snarling over a bone as they sidestepped each other.

"Aye, it does!"

"Doesna." Ian stood with his arms akimbo, radiating hostility from every pore.

"Does." Malcolm glowered. "Just as Fiona belonged to me until ye came in between."

Fiona? Caitlin was stunned to hear the MacDonald utter her mother's name.

"She didna want to marry ye," Ian countered. "She didna like yer ways."

"Like me or no, ye stole another mon's betrothed." Roughly he grabbed Caitlin by the arm. "And now, I hae evened the score. Fiona's daughter will stay in Dunskaith for the rest of her days."

It was dark in the tiny dungeon. Only the glow of torchlight cast a faint flicker of light through the iron grate, illuminating the dismal prison. Niall was in a foul mood as he huddled in the folds of his plaid, trying to fend off the chill. Pulling the edges of his breacan tighter, he grumbled loudly, pausing only when a soft noise disturbed his solitude. The faint moan of faraway bagpipes cut through the stillness.

Bagpipes! Niall held his breath, atuning his ears to the wail, cursing his uncle as he realized he was not imagining things. So the MacLeods had come just as he had known they would. But this time Malcolm could not place blame on anyone but himself! Were there a battle, the burden of the responsibility rested on the MacDonald chieftain and not on a MacLeod.

Rising from the ground, Niall paced back and forth across the cubicle's hard earthen floor feeling like a trapped rodent! He had to get out! He had to do *something* to divert the disaster that he knew was going to ensue.

Gripping the dirt walls, forcing a foothold, he tried to climb up the side of the hole he'd been flung into, only to slide back down each time he was within an arm's length of the top. His only reward was blistered and bleeding fingers.

Taking off the leather belt that held the sporran around his waist, he tried another approach, looping it through the bars of the iron grating. Again he failed, watching in abject frustration as the belt missed its mark again and again. It was as if the walls were closing in on him. Never had Niall felt so totally powerless in all his life. Niall had known only one fear in his life, that of being enclosed in small spaces.

"Gregor knows well the way to torture me," he muttered.

The drone of bagpipes was getting louder, taunting Niall with his own helplessness. What was happening up there? Was Malcolm going to anoint Niall's marriage with blood? Caitlin! Above all he wanted to make certain that she was safe.

A sound! Niall looked up, fearing to see the familiar hulking form of Gregor but saw instead another face looking down at him. One as dear as his own visage. "Ogg!" The giant had returned. "Get me out of here!" he implored.

"Shhh! We dunna want to stir up an alarm. At least not yet." The giant grinned.

"Did you get the key?"

"Nae. I think Malcolm has it with him. He knows ye hae many friends within the castle. I fear I'm going to hae to dig ye out, loosen the dirt around the grate, then pull with all my might."

"If anyone can do it you can." The staccato noise above his head told Niall that Ogg was doing just that. Heeding the giant's words, Niall remained silent until his curiosity got the better of him. He had to ask.

"What's happening above? Tell me, mon. Are the MacLeods going to instigate war?" Niall whispered as softly as he could. "Caitlin, is she . . ."

"With her father. Safe for the moment." His face looked troubled.

"What is it?"

"Malcolm has proclaimed to Caitlin's father that he will never let her go."

"What did ye say?"

Ogg recounted all that he had heard. "Malcolm, or so it seems, was in love with Caitlin's mother. When she scorned him to marry Ian MacLeod, it instigated a bitter rivalry."

"And this is what it was all about?" Niall thought of all those who had died. And all because of jealousy and hurt pride.

"Aye. Foolish, isn't it?" With a burst of energy, Ogg at last loosened the grille sufficiently to free his friend. Leaning over the side, he reached out, clasping Niall by the hand to drag him to the surface.

Niall breathed in the fresh air. "I owe ye a favor, Ogg. By the saints I do."

"Just be happy and have joy of Caitlin." He picked up a large leather sack. "I brought ye a few supplies we might need along the way."

"Oh?" Niall could see that Ogg had it all planned.

"I'm going to help ye rescue Caitlin." Somehow he made it all sound so easy. "We can do it if we are canny and take advantage of the turmoil raging in the hall."

"Then let's hurry!" Niall was impatient.

The shouting had started by the time they got back to

the hall. Everyone seemed to be talking at once. Accusations. Denials. Anger. Louder and louder. It seemed everyone was shouting.

Hidden in the shadows, Niall listened. "Ye whoreson! Ye vile treacherous mon!" Ian flung his epitaphs at Malcolm as everyone stared in stony silence. "Why? Why would ye do such a thing?"

"To seek reprisal, ye sneaking, backstabbing bastard!" Malcolm's eyes bulged in their sockets as he revealed his intent. "Ye took my bride, I'll take yer daughter. It's tit for tat." Baiting Ian, Malcolm boldly boasted of the deed, heartlessly goading his adversary.

"Anything that I hae done ye rightly deserved."

"Including murdering my son by stabbing him in the back?" Now it was Ian's turn to make accusations.

"Killed yer son? I didna do such a thing unless it was in battle!"

"Ye struck him from behind by treachery."

" 'Tis a lie! No MacDonald would strike down a man from behind. We are warriors, not assassins."

"I say ye are!"

Silence reigned once again, like the quiet before a devastating storm.

"To arms! To arms!" Malcolm MacDonald gave his call to war. Niall grabbed at any weapon available, settling for an old relic of a sword. Brandishing it, he looked around for Caitlin. He would allow no harm to come to her.

Ignoring the clashing and slashing of swords of the bloody and violent melee he fought his way to her, thrusting her against the wall to protect her with his body. With a growl of warning, he wielded his sword. He would allow no one to come anywhere near her. Not this time.

"Niall, ye are a traitor! Damned be ye, lad." Though occupied with the fighting, Malcolm's attention was diverted just long enough for Niall to dart by. Two MacDonalds held the doorway, but Niall was desperate to make an escape. It was the only chance he and Caitlin had. "Caitlin, we are going to make a run for it!" he announced.

"Nae!" She would not go and leave her father and the others. Stubbornly she shook her head, but her protestations were ignored. With determinedly strong hands, he pushed her toward the corridor, his weapon darting this way and that to form a path.

"Niall!" Ogg thrust himself forward, fighting savagely. "Run for it, mon!"

"I willna leave, I say." Anxiously her eyes moved toward where her father was engaged in combat with a MacDonald half his age.

"Ye canna help yer clansmen, lass. It is out of yer hands. Best that ye let me get ye out of here while I can lest Malcolm make good on his threat to keep ye his prisoner forever."

"Out of my hands?" His tone and words implied that the MacLeods had already lost.

"Come. Hurry."

She couldn't leave her father and the others behind no matter what happened. Unable to aid her clansmen, she was not so sure about that. "See to yer own safety, Niall. I hae something that needs doing," she called over her shoulder, breaking out into a run. Heading back toward the hall, she knew she had to get her hands on the flag.

"Caitlin! Come back. What are ye doing?" Putting his own well-being out of his thoughts, Niall followed her, watching as she pushed one of the wooden tables over near the wall. He knew in an instant what she intended to do. "Nae, Caity. Ye will bring about yer death."

"Then so be it. At least I'll hae died a hero's death." Her brave words were punctuated with a cry of pain as a sword pierced her soft flesh.

"Caity!" Niall hurried to her defense but was caught up in his own battle to survive. All he could do was to watch helplessly as she grabbed a sword and a shield from the wall, using them as best she could to protect herself.

"Get back! Get back, I say." Lashing out with the sword, Caitlin was amazed at the strength that suddenly possessed her. Ignoring the pain in her wounded arm, conscious only of the frantic need to come to the aid of the MacLeod fighters, she held her adversary at bay, then watched him fall.

Jumping up on the table, reaching high above her head, she touched, then grasped the cool brown silk she had risked her life for. With one persistent tug, then another and another, she soon held it in her hands. The fairy flag. Once again it was in a MacLeod's possession.

It appeared in that moment that she really did have the power of a witch, for as the others of her clan saw what she held aloft, it was as if a miracle had happened. Though the MacLeods had been struggling for their very lives, the tide of the battle turned. Now it was the MacDonalds who defended themselves against a foe that, though small, was mighty.

Thirty

The MacLeods waged a relentless battle that was brief but destructive. In the aftermath, chairs and tables were overturned, the room strewn with wounded and those who would never rise again.

"We hae won!" Sheathing his sword, the MacLeod smiled triumphantly. "I guess that will teach ye to mistreat my daughter."

"Damn ye, Ian!" Raising his fist, Malcolm MacDonald's expression was sour. "Well, this is not yet the end of it."

"Then ye will know the taste of defeat yet again." Ian hefted his sword. "We hae the fairy flag."

"Aye." Malcolm's gaze sought for and found the culprit who had put that back into the MacLeod's hands. He shook his shaggy-haired head. "Who would hae thought. A lass!"

"My daughter!" Puffing out his chest, Ian strode over to the heroine of the day only in that moment noticing that she had not been untouched by the fighting. "Caitlin . . ."

Her wound was bleeding, but though she was weak she was still standing. "It's . . . it's nothing . . ." Her face was pale as she clutched her arm.

"Nothing. Ye're bloodied, lass."

"A scratch!" She smiled grimly as she repeated what her father always said when he came back to the hall bloody and bruised.

"A scratch. Ah, 'tis much more than that. Ye're red with blood." He ran toward her, openly showing his fatherly concern. His men, some of them suffering their own injuries, followed him. Forming a circle around Caitlin, they hovered about her as Ian tore off a piece of his shirt and wrapped it around her arm.

"Ye were a wondrous sight," Jamie cried out, not even bothering to mask his admiration.

"Aye, when we saw how braw ye were, ye inspired us, lass," Angus exclaimed.

"We couldna lose," Colquhoun added.

"Ye are a MacLeod, through and through," Ian stated proudly. It was obvious that the anger he had felt when first arriving at Dunskaith had vanished. Still, as he looked over at Niall, his eyes burned with rage. "A *MacLeod!*" he shouted.

Looking across the hall, Niall was too grieved by what had happened to verbally fight back. Indeed, he greeted the outcome with mixed emotions, grateful that Caitlin had come through the battle alive, yet at the same time horrified to see his clansmen bloodied and suffering. Even as his sword arm had been thrusting and parrying, he had tried to avoid seriously harming any of his kin. Now in the aftermath as he walked among the dead and the wounded, he felt a profound sorrow. It should never have come to this.

"And I am a MacDonald," he whispered. Yet he had forgotten that a few moments ago.

Though he had spoken so softly, Caitlin heard Niall's voice and knew the anguish he must be experiencing in this the MacDonald's greatest defeat. Taking a deep breath, she started to call out to him but her father quickly stepped in her path. Sweeping her up in his arms, he was fiercely protective, cringing as he took notice of the blood that had soaked through the sleeve of her gown and was trickling over her hand.

"Come, Daughter, we must dress your wound and then be off. Our business is done in this hall." Glaring at Niall, his hand quivering just above his sword hilt, he dared him to interfere. "Ye lied to us and played us false. Know this, MacDonald, ye will never see my daughter again."

"She is my wife.' A truth which did nothing to lessen the predicament.

"She is my daughter." Ian's defiant expression dared Niall to so much as touch her. "Blood of my blood, flesh of my flesh."

"Who took the vows with me before God and all man."

"Vows!" The MacLeod spat on the floor. "By yer very lies to me I consider the vows ye spoke with her to be null and void, *fishermon!*" Hugging Caitlin close, he said, "We are going home and ye canna stop us."

"I will follow."

"And be struck down for the dog that ye are." Ian's lip curled in scorn. Angrily he pointed a finger at Niall. "Hear this an' hear this well, MacDonald. If ye set so much as a foot on MacLeod soil I will kill ye!"

The blood froze in Caitlin's veins at his words. "Father. Nae!" The very thought of life without Niall was agonizing, but the fear of his being cut down in pursuit of her was even more horrifying. "Ye canna . . ."

"Ah, but I can." Turning, he carried Caitlin toward the door, gesturing with his head for his clansmen to follow.

It was dark inside the hall. The odor of sweat and leather mixed with the smell of blood from the wounded. The silence of defeat hung in the air. Even so there was only one reality in Niall's world at the moment. She was gone. Ian MacLeod had meted out the most devastating punishment imaginable.

Niall's heart was heavy, his temper on edge. Life was unfair; fate a cruel draught. Something had been missing from his life until he had looked into Caitlin's enormous brown eyes, until he had kissed her. She had given his life new meaning. Now she was gone.

"Malcolm's fault!" *And his own.* "BiGod, already I miss her." More so than he had ever thought it possible to miss another human being. He needed her. She was a balm to his soul. There was something about her that he craved. Like some men hankered for strong drink. No, it was an ever greater yearning than that.

"Caitlin. Caitlin!"

The sound of her name to his lips brought an agonizing torment. This time their parting was for good. He would never see her again. Not in this life. Then why did he torture himself by thinking about her? He answered the question at once. He was the biggest of fools, secretly hoping that somehow by some miracle she would walk through that door, that she would come back to him.

"Caity!"

He remembered the feel of her soft body pressed against his, the sweet fragrance of her hair. BiGod, but she had so quickly gotten into his blood. He wanted her in his bed, wanted her mouth trembling and soft beneath his. He wanted her beneath him, her slender thighs entwined around his hips.

I should take a boat, sail up to Dunvegan Castle and carry her away. She is my wife! *What God has joined together no man must cast asunder.* Not even a lassie's father!

Niall smiled as the idea flitted before his eyes of throwing her over his shoulder and sweeping her from her father's hall. What would the MacLeods think of that? No doubt it would be the talk of the Highlands for quite a while.

I should do it! He should show Ian MacLeod that his threats were not as strong as a brave man's love.

His daring plotting was disturbed as the front door of the castle was thrown open. Rain blew in gusts through the open portal, swirling about the cloaked figure that pushed inside the room.

"Ogg! Did ye catch sight of her, did ye hear any word?"

"Aye. I followed Ian and the MacLeods all the way to Glen Drynoch."

"And . . . ?"

"Ye must gi' up any thought of heroics, Niall. 'Twas no idle threat. Ian MacLeod will hae yer head and display it on a spike if ye are seen anywhere near Dunvegan."

"I am no afraid."

"Then I will be afraid for ye, for if Ian MacLeod doesna hae yer head Malcolm will." Ogg shook his own head. "Gi' it up, laddie. At least for the moment."

"I canna!" His heart was totally in pawn to the fiery-haired Caitlin. Men thought they ruled the world but they were wrong. It was women. "Ah, Caity. My Caity." Over and over her name kept whirling about in his head.

"She is no' yer Caity anymore." To emphasize his words, Ogg grabbed Niall by the shoulders. "But if ye are patient, perhaps she will be again, once the dust of the battle has settled. Aye, laddie, gi' it time."

Time . . . the most precious thing of all in the wild, isolated hills, glens, and islands of the Highlands where danger ruled both day and night. Still, Niall had no other choice. He must wait and hope against all hope that he would see his wife once again.

Part Three:

Wild Wind to
the Highlands

"I arise from dreams of thee
 In the first sweet sleep of night
When the winds are breathing low,
 And the stars are shining bright."
 —*The Indian Serenade*, Stanza 1
 Percy Bysshe Shelley

Thirty-one

Large raindrops pelted through the window as Caitlin reached out to close the shutters. Brushing several strands of her damp dark-red hair from her eyes, she was startled as a pulsating ribbon of lightning shivered through the sky. A crack of thunder followed, echoing in the room like a drum. Oh, how she had always hated such storms.

One of the borrowing days, she thought, a spell of unseasonably cold weather. How bleak and lonely it made the world appear, for it eclipsed the hillocks and enshrouded the castle. The fog made it seem as if they were separate from the rest of the world. Isolated. Alone.

"Lonely," she whispered, wiping her tear-blind eyes. How well Caitlin knew the meaning of that word. Since returning to Dunvegan with her father, it was a word which fit her all too well.

Huddling by the window, hugging her knees as she sat on a large stone slab, Caitlin felt miserable. She missed Niall so much that she couldn't sleep, couldn't eat, couldn't do anything but sulk. It just didn't seem fair. She had come to the aid of the MacLeods and yet had been punished and not rewarded for it. And Niall, who had so steadfastly defended her even at the cost of his own honor had been treated with no justice. No matter how she had raged, how she had pleaded, however, Ian MacLeod had stood steadfast on the matter of Caitlin's husband. If he showed his face anywhere near the castle he was to be meted out the greatest of punishments.

"Caity . . ." Shona's voice sounded worried. "Is yer arm aching again, hinny?"

"No, my arm is just fine. The applications of seaweed boiled with lard had aided in healing her wound.

"Then is it that ye are dizzy again?" Coming to Caitlin's side, she hovered over her protectively. "Perhaps ye had better go back to bed. Or I can get ye some more—"

"I'm fine." Caitlin didn't want any more of the healer's herbal medicine. The eolas made her nauseous and gave her headaches.

"Then what is it I can do for ye?"

"Honestly?" Caitlin's eyes were wide as she looked up at her sister.

"Honestly."

The pattering raindrops had increased their frantic rhythm. Caitlin paused to listen, then sighed. "Just leave me be. I want to be alone with my thoughts just now."

Though usually acquiescent on such matters, Shona stood firm. "Leave ye alone so that ye can pine away? Nae, I willna."

"Pine away?"

With a heavy heart, Caitlin leaned against the shutters. Her sister was right, that was exactly what she was doing. And why not? Hadn't she reason? Her Father was tampering with her life again. Interfering in her happiness. Though he was the one who had forced her into marrying, he was now the one who was trying to get that marriage annulled. Even now, he was shut up with the priest as they planned out their strategy.

No more to be married to Niall! The very idea was painful. More so than any physical wound could ever be. She visualized Niall's handsome face, the look of tenderness that came into his eyes when they made love. Closing her eyes, she could nearly feel his hands upon her, stirring her blood.

"Ye loved him so much?"

Caitlin nodded. "Aye. More so than even my life!"

"Oh, Caity!" Kneeling down beside her sister, Shona cradled her in her arms. "I'm so sorry."

"I know. Ye of all people understand." Shona, too, had been made to suffer because of her emotions. She had fallen in love with her dear Geordie but was being forced to marry a MacKinnon. A man twice her age.

"Father just doesna understand."

"Because he doesna want to." Worse yet, although Caitlin's marriage had not even begun to be dissolved, her father was already going about the task of choosing another groom—a MacDonnell, a MacKenzie, a Cameron, or a Grant—one of the clans located far enough away to be ignorant of the fact that she had already been married.

"He means well." Though it was Caitlin who had always been closest to their father, it was Shona who was defending him now.

"Aye, I suppose that he does." Even so, that did not make her heartache any easier. She had known love with Niall. How then could she settle for a loveless marriage?

"Caity?" Her mother's soft voice called to her through the closed door.

Standing up, Caitlin padded on bare feet across the cold stone floor. Opening the door, she was touched to see a bowl of porridge in her mother's hands. Even so, Caitlin rebelled at the sight of food.

"I am not hungry, Mother."

Fiona's tone was authoritative as she pushed into the room. "You need some nourishment. Ye are getting much too thin. Eat."

Though usually rebellious, Caitlin took the porridge from her mother's hands.

So, my mother was the cause of Malcolm MacDonald's

anger, she thought, staring at Fiona as if somehow seeing her through different eyes. And why not? Even now it was evident that her mother had once been beautiful. But so beautiful as to inspire clan warfare?

Noticing that Caitlin was merely holding the bowl and spoon and not eating, Fiona said sternly, 'Ye need to get back yer strength, Caity. Ye canna stay cloistered up here in this room like a nun."

Caitlin bit back a sarcastic reply. To appease Fiona, Caitlin took a bite, but as soon as she swallowed she felt ill. Strangely enough, the very idea of food sometimes did that to her of late. For over a week now she had been feeling sick in the mornings. Could it be? Touching her stomach, she wondered if it was possible that Niall's child grew within her womb.

Niall's child. Oh, what a blessing that would be. A baby would make her father's plan of annulment invalid. A tiny breathing human being would be a living reminder of the love she and Niall had shared.

"Caity? What is it?"

It had to be. Twice now Caitlin had missed her monthly time but had thought it possible that it was due to the events of the last two months—the battle, her injury and the journey. Now she could only hope otherwise.

A baby! A sweet reminder of the passion she had known in Niall's arms. And yet another source of clan tension as well. If the baby was a boy it would be a MacDonald, not a MacLeod. What would her father do then?

"Pah, ye hardly eat enough to keep a mouse alive." Reaching out, Fiona gently touched Caitlin's hand, the one that held the spoon. "I even put butter and cream on it, just the way ye like it."

Caitlin took another bite, just to silence her mother's loving scolding, but as a churning began in her stomach, she quickly set the bowl down on a small table by the bed and hurried to the window. Hurriedly opening the shutters, she leaned out just in time.

"Oh . . ." She could hardy stand up, for the nausea seemed to engulf her.

"Caity." Shona and Fiona called out her name in unison.

"She has been like that, Mother. Getting sick each time she eats anything at all. Could it be her wound?" Shona hurried to stand beside her sister, holding her hand as she bent over retching through the open window.

"Hmm." Slowly Fiona walked across the floor. Putting her arm around her daughter's waist, she hugged her tightly as she brushed the hair from her face. "Have ye missed yer time?"

Caitlin nodded.

"Have ye been lightheaded?"

"Aye."

"Oh, Caity, hinny!" She laughed softly. A happy sound. "Ye are with child, lassie. I sense it. I think that ye do, too."

Turning from the window, Caitlin was surprised by her mother's elation. "And ye arena disturbed at such a thought?"

Fiona shook her head. "Why should I be. To bring forth life is the greatest of blessings." Putting her hand under her daughter's chin, she looked her in the eye. "And I can tell that ye love him."

"I do. But Father . . ." Would be furious. A force to be reckoned with.

"Will hae to realize that he has no control over such things." Taking Caitlin's hands, she led her toward the bed, pulling her to sit down beside her.

Shona sat on the floor, her expression more of surprise than anything else. "Are ye . . . are ye going to tell the MacLeod?"

Fiona shook her head. "Not yet."

"But he will hae to know!"

"I will tell him in my own time, in my own way." When

her daughters seemed uneasy, she repeated, "In my own time. Meanwhile, there are some things that need to be done." Fiona MacLeod smiled again, this time mysteriously.

The keening music of skirling bagpipes seemed to be a perfect accompaniment to Niall's tormented emotions. He had tried to push all thought of, all love for Caitlin into some obscure part of his mind but it was impossible. Not one day had gone by when he hadn't missed her, hadn't awakened imagining that she was in his arms.

"Ye haunt me like a ghost, Caity!" he couldn't help but blurt out.

Keeping to himself, haunting the castle corridors and tower, Niall was like some angry spirit. He had lost track of time, he had lost all sense of ambition. He had become a slave to his memories, his moods.

Whenever Niall was in a room, the air vibrated with tension. Unspoken recriminations reached out like long fingers. Bitter glances fell upon all those whose only misfortune was to cross his path.

Running his hand through his hair, Niall looked out at the horizon as he searched his heart and soul for the answer to his dilemma. Something had to be done. His appetite was sorely wanting. He didn't sleep the whole night through. He was so surly of late that even Ogg avoided him. Either he had to get Caitlin back or risk his sanity.

Thirty-two

A bairn, a child. Wrapping her arms around her knees, Caitlin curled up on the bed, gently touching her still-flat stomach. She was going to bear Niall's child. No matter what the future held in store she would at least have that.

"A living, breathing reminder of the love and passion that flared so fierce between us." Fierce, but alas, all in too brief a time.

She sighed, remembering. When they had been together she had truly been happy. Now she had only her memories and dreams to keep her warm at night in her lonely bed. Still, she was determined to be optimistic for the child's sake.

"Ah, dear, dear sweet bairn of mine . . ."

She tried to imagine what it would be like to have a small replica of Niall or herself running about the castle, and laughed aloud at the thought. Whether the babe had her temperament or Niall's, the child would no doubt be a handful.

"Father, 'tis possible that ye might find that with yer grandchild ye hae met yer match."

Father. As the word touched first her thoughts and then her lips she stiffened. What would be the MacLeod's reaction to the news? How would he deal with the reality of something over which he had no control? The babe would have MacDonald blood as well as MacLeod. What would he think of that?

"Ach, but I willna worry. Not now . . ." Instead, she soothed her mind by thinking about the baby that grew within her. Oh, what stories she would tell the wee one. Oh, what love she would give to the bairn. So much love that she could nearly feel her heart burst as she knew the longing to hold the child of her dear love in her arms.

Oh, Niall, if only I could tell ye, she lamented. If only ye knew so that ye could be as happy and feel as blessed as I. Truly the child was a miracle, a bond that would join them together for life, nae for eternity

"Niall!"

Closing her eyes, Caitlin smiled for the first time in a long while as she envisioned the face of the man whose soul had blended with her own to create life within her womb. For a moment she allowed herself to dream.

"Caitlin!" she heard him call out. Bending down, he wore a look of tenderness as he swept her up into his arms. "A child! A son!"

"A part of me . . . a part of you!" she whispered.

"The greatest gift anyone could hae given me," she imagined him saying. "Ah, truly, I hae never loved anyone as much as I love ye at this moment."

"Nor hae I loved anyone as much as ye." Tentatively she reached out and touched her stomach, marveling at the miracle that created life.

She had to believe that they would meet again, love again.

"Oh, Niall . . ." In a total outpouring of her emotions, she willed him to see far across the miles into her heart, into her mind. She wanted him to remember.

She would have been complimented and contented to know that he did. Lying on his back, his hands behind his head, Niall stared up at the ceiling, seeing Caitlin's image as clearly as if she were there in the flesh. So clearly that he nearly called out to her. Instead, he groaned as he remembered how her lips had felt beneath his mouth, how her breasts had felt as he had stroked them. For a moment he was consumed by his memories and by his need.

A tremor ran through him. He felt cold, he felt hot. In the silence of the room he could hear his own rasping breath mingling with the rapid beat of her heart. He squeezed his eyes so tight that they hurt, then he opened them slowly.

Dear God, how he wanted her, missed her, longed for her. More than he had ever longed for anything in all his life. And yet his longing would go unfulfilled because of the anger and bitterness of two men. Two stubborn old men who clung to the memory of an old feud.

"Malcolm, I curse ye for yer hard heart," he breathed, succumbing to a surge of anger that left him trembling. Then, as if the potency of his thoughts had conjured him up, he saw the object of his fury standing in the doorway.

"Niall . . ." Malcolm nudged a young dark-haired girl forward, boldly announcing that he had not come alone.

"Go away! Can ye no' see that I am sleeping?" If there was anyone's company that he did not welcome it was Malcolm's. "And take her with ye when ye go."

"Take her?" Malcolm laughed. "Och, Niall, dunna be so impatient. At least gi' the girl a chance to show ye what she can do."

Heeding the command, the girl came forward, her soft hands stroking his hot bare skin. He could feel her fingers, the palms of her hands, her nails. Though Niall was well prepared to resist, he was only too human.

Taking a deep, shuddering breath, he breathed, "Pretend . . ." His mind closed on that thought as the girl's hands stroked his chest, his stomach, then moved lower with a touch that could have brought a stone statue to life.

"Caitlin . . ."

He felt so much need, so much wanting that it pained him, more so as he felt her moist mouth moving slowly, sensuously on his abdomen. Moaning again, he reached for her, running his hands down the curves of her body. Soft, warm, her skin nonetheless held no delight for him. She was much too slender.

"Nae!" Even with his eyes closed he could not be fooled. Even for the sake of his aching flesh he could not touch another. By force of will he pulled away, his desire draining away as quickly as it had come. With a growl, Niall bolted up from his bed, infuriated as he saw that Malcolm was still lurking in the doorway.

"Och, such a frown. I take it then that lovely or no', she doesna please ye."

"Under different circumstances she might hae," Niall replied, nodding his head toward the door so that the girl was certain to understand. "Before I met Caity. Now I want no other woman. Not now. Not ever."

Malcolm was distracted for just a moment as he watched the young woman scurry from the room. Then he shrugged his shoulders. "Then hae ye taken up celibacy?"

"For the moment." Niall carefully veiled his emotions, yet the soul-deep loneliness was still reflected in his eyes. "Until I can be reunited wi' my wife."

"Reunited?" Malcolm's expression was sour. "I fear that will not be for a long time, if ever. In the meantime I would suggest that unless ye want to go mad, ye take what I offer ye. That is, unless ye be more interested in some crofter's wife or daughter."

"I am no' interested in anyone. No one can ever take my Caity's place."

"Nae?" Malcolm raised his thick brows. "But what of ye? Will she feel the same? Or will she bend to the will of her father? Eh, Niall? Eh?"

Niall sensed an undercurrent of meaning. "What are ye saying?"

"That although the bedsheets of his daughter hae not yet cooled from the warmth of yer body, Ian MacLeod is already looking for a mon to fill yer place."

"Fill my place?"

"Aye!" Taking his time, Malcolm strode into the room. "I hae heard from my spies that the MacLeod is openly searching for another husband."

Thirty-three

An early-morning mist hovered over the land, shrouding the hills in a thick white cloud. The bulk of the storm had passed, but a slow drizzle still fell, its moisture pervading the castle, making it damp and chilled. Pulling her chair closer to the fire, Caitlin thought how the weather matched her mood.

Looking down at the whittling knife and piece of wood in her hands, she assessed the carving of the sheep she was making for the baby and her thoughts strayed to Niall. There wasn't an hour that went by that she didn't think of him no matter where she was. What was he doing? Was he well? Was he content? For love of her he had raised his sword against his own clan. Had Malcolm been lenient with him? Most importantly of all, she wondered what he would think were he to know about their baby. Would he feel as pleased as she?

Oh, Niall, what shall we name the bairn? Pausing in her whittling, Caitlin called several names to mind. If the child was a male, names like Donald, Fergus, Fionnlagh, Geordie, Ruaraidh, and Tammas came to mind. Or perhaps Colin after her deceased brother. And if the babe was female, Alisa, Deirdre, Janet, Wilma, or even Sheena.

"But no . . ." Putting her hand on her stomach, she knew with a sudden certainty that she need not even think for a moment that it was anything but a boy child. The night in Dunskaith Castle when she had lain so blissfully with Niall she had conceived his son. "A child that could bind the MacLeods and MacDonalds together if only . . ."

The sound of her father's heavy steps outside the door disrupted any such thoughts. As he clumped inside the room, Caitlin hurried to put the carving of the lamb behind her back. Alas, she was not quick enough.

"Caitlin?" The way he scowled proved that he had noticed.

"Good morrow, Father. Despite the fact that she was peeved with him because of his decision about Niall, Caitlin smiled at him.

"Ye seem cheerful. Am I to happily take that to mean ye are completely healed, in mind as well as body?" he asked, taking a step closer, then another and another.

"I'm healed." *Except for what all this has done to my heart.*

"Then we'll be expecting ye to take yer place again with us at breakfast and dinner." Reaching out, he fondly ruffled her hair, sliding his fingers through the silky strands.

"Aye," she whispered, wondering how she was going to keep on making excuses to stay in her room.

"What do ye hae there?" Moving his hand from her head to her arm, he caught the wrist she held behind her back.

"Hae?" It was no use. Slowly Caitlin revealed her handiwork.

"A child's toy?" He looked at her with puzzlement.

"Aye." She wanted to tell him. Wanted to hurl the announcement in his face, to taunt him with it, but instead Caitlin kept to her silence. Her mother had requested that she be the one to give out the news.

"I would hae thought ye too old to crave such things, Caity." Taking it from her hand, he held it up, turning it this way and that. He looked from Caitlin to the toy, then back at Caitlin again, as if afraid of an announcement. When Caitlin didn't speak, Ian heaved a sigh. "Ah, but I do hae to admire yer talent." He laughed. "At carving wood as well as ye carved that MacDonald's hide." Once again he ruffled her hair. "Ah, Caity. Caity! Ye always were the joy of my heart."

For just a moment her fear and resentment evaporated as the warm memories of her childhood resurfaced. She thought of the laughter they had shared, the way she had always tagged after him, all the times he had carried her from the hall to tuck her into bed after the seanachaidh had finished his stories. Caitlin had admired him so much that, unlike the other girls in the castle, she had never played with dolls. She had wanted a shield and a sword. Who would ever have known that such childhood playfulness would one day save her life?

Ian took his daughter's hand, squeezing her fingers tightly. "Ah, Cait, do ye forgive me?"

"For what?"

"For forcing ye to wed with Niall MacDonald. I believed his lies, ye see, and—"

"Ye didna force me. Her voice was barely audible as she whispered, "I love him."

"Love. Bah! It doesna exist." A muscle in his cheek ticked, a sign that he was trying to hold his temper in check.

"It does." Caitlin asked a pointed question. "Did ye not love Mother?"

Ian released her fingers and started to fidget with his hands. It was several moments before he nodded. "Aye. I thought her to be the bonniest lassie I had ever set eyes on."

"And Malcolm MacDonald's future bride, or so I heard him say that day." She turned her wide brown eyes on him, searching his face. "Was he telling the truth?"

"He *was*. But it didna matter."

"Didna matter?" Caitlin was stunned. "It must hae to Malcolm MacDonald."

"He was no good for her. He was harsh. He was cruel."

"And so ye kidnapped her. Is that it?" Caitlin could

nearly see the story enfolding, saw her father sweeping her mother up and throwing her across his shoulder. It was the kind of thing the bards sang about.

Ian did not meet her eyes as he said, "I wanted to save her."

"But did she want to be saved?" The question was out before Caitlin could stop herself. Strange, that her mother had never spoken of her wedding to the MacLeod.

"I dunna want to talk about it. Those memories are private." Hurriedly he changed the subject. "I sent a message to the pope himself, asking, no *demanding*, an end to yer marriage."

"I dunna want it to end." Caitlin clutched the carved sheep so hard her knuckles turned white. "I dunna want to marry any of the men ye would pawn me off on."

"Enough," Ian reproved sharply. Trying to hold his temper in check, he began pacing, walking up and down, back and forth. At last he stopped. "I willna hae a MacDonald set foot in this castle, nor will I let ye go back to Dunskaith. If ye stay married to Niall MacDonald it will be a marriage in name only." He shook his head. "Ah, Caity, Caity, it would be such a waste. I canna allow ye to stay tied to such a mon as that young rascal. Ye are young and ye are a bonny lass. Far better be it for ye to put this mistake behind ye and begin again." Slowly he walked to the door deep in thought, but he turned before he opened the door. "Someday ye will understand and thank me for what I decided."

"Understand?" Caitlin bolted to her feet. "Nae, it is ye who dunna understand, Father. It is out of yer hands."

"Out of my hands?" His eyes narrowed to slits. "What do ye mean?"

Caitlin bit her lip. "Only that it is God who should make such decisions."

"God?" The reminder that there was a being to whom even he must answer seemed to deflate the MacLeod's fiercesome pride. He did not say another word. Instead, he merely stared at Caitlin for a long time before he left the room.

It was cold and damp. The slender tapers flickered as a breath of wind swept through the crevices of the castle. The flame's slow dance cast eerie shadows against the stone walls. Kneeling in the small chapel, Caitlin prayed aloud. "Please, God, help bring Niall back to me. Help me find a way to soften Father's heart and make him see that I canna live without my hinny." Nor did she want her child to grow up without a father or worse yet be under the control of a man of her father's choosing.

She clasped her hands so tightly together that her fingernails dug into the flesh of her fingers as she closed her eyes. Her father had gone to the pope with his adamant wishes, and thus there was nowhere else to go but seek the help of a higher power.

"Please, ye must help me for I hae nowhere else to turn . . ."

Bowing her head, she prayed as fervently as she could, so hard in fact that she did not hear the door as it opened. Not until she felt a hand on her shoulder did she realize that she was no longer alone.

"Caity . . ."

Lifting her head, Caitlin saw the silhouette of her mother's face.

"Hae ye told Father yet? Hae ye?"

Her mother's expression answered the question.

"Ye hae not!" Caitlin swallowed hard. She had counted on her mother's wisdom and courage, yet it seemed that Fiona had let her down.

"I started to so many times but . . ."

Caitlin stepped on the hem of her arasaid as she jerked to her feet. "But ye are afraid o' him."

"Afraid?" Fiona's eyes met Caitlin's. "Nae, 'tis just that I must wait until the right time."

"Right time? Sweet Jesu, when will that be." Caitlin's patience was wearing thin. "When ye put the bairn in its grandsire's arms?"

Fiona's eyes narrowed as she retorted hotly, "Hold yer sarcasm, Daughter. I repeat, I will tell yer father when *I* decide that the time is right."

Caitlin was immediately contrite, regretting her outburst. "I-I know that ye will. Oh, Mother . . ."

Reaching out, Fiona pushed aside an unruly lock of red hair that had tumbled in Caitlin's eyes. "I am no' afraid. It's just that I hae a plan of my own to follow." Her frown slowly changed into a smile. "I know just what I am doing, Caity dear."

Fiona knew it wasn't enough to confide in Ian about the impending birth. She needed an ally, one who dealt with those in high places. Moreover she had decided that something must be done to assure that Niall MacDonald would be at her daughter's side now that he was needed. With that thought in mind she had sent a very special messenger to not only give Niall the news of Caitlin's upcoming motherhood but to guide him safely to Dunvegan as well.

"Ye must trust me."

Trust. Instinctively she did.

Thirty-four

Niall stared out the window, watching as the small hunting party led by Malcolm left the castle armed with bows and arrows, swords and dirks. The winter weather was fast approaching, and thus the MacDonald and his clansmen were of necessity pressed to bring back an ample supply of meat lest everyone in the castle grow extremely tired of mutton.

"Good riddance!" Niall scoffed, relieved that the absence of Gregor and Malcolm would offer him a brief reprieve from their hostile looks and verbal badgering.

Since the battle with the MacLeods, Niall had enacted a tempestuous truce with his clansmen, but nonetheless he felt uneasy when he was in their presence. Gregor's piercing eyes seemed always to be watching him. Malcolm's fiercesome scowls, which had gotten fiercer since the episode in his room, were beginning to play on his nerves.

Though obviously suffering Malcolm's disfavor, Niall was surprised that his status of tanist had not been disturbed. His honors had not been stripped from him despite the MacDonald's ill will and Gregor's heated insistence. Nevertheless, without Caitlin beside him, Niall had lost heart.

"Ah, Caity." The words came out almost a moan. The hunting party instantly reminded him of Caitlin and that day together out in the forest.

"I've been hunting since I was no higher than my father's

knee," she had answered tartly when he had shown surprise that she intended to join the hunting party. "We'll see if ye can keep up with me." It was a challenge he had grinned at, little knowing how difficult it would be to fulfill.

"Caity, Caity, Caity," he murmured, feeling once again the restlessness he could not conceal. He paced the floor of his bedchamber in frustration. Though Malcolm had spared him the discomfort of imprisonment, he might as well have been a prisoner. Certainly in his heart he was, missing Caitlin, yet knowing it was forbidden to go to her.

The only time Niall could be happy was when he was alone in his chamber, succumbing to his dreams. Only in his fantasies did he dare give vent to his love. From the first moment his eyes were closed, he envisioned Caitlin, felt the stirring touch of her mouth, the fire of her hands on his body. His dreams were so vivid, so feverish that he awakened trembling, half expecting to find her pretty face beside his on the pillow. Instead, he always knew the disappointment of finding himself alone. Was there any hope? Ogg had insisted that there was, had advised Niall to be patient.

"Patient!" How could he be when he knew that he was besieged on both sides with enemies, both the MacLeod and the MacDonalds, who were joined in one common bond: to keep Caitlin and him apart.

Disgruntled with it all, he took one last look at the departing clansmen, hoping they would be gone a long while. In that moment he noticed a small brown-clad figure weaving in and out among the bushes in the outer bailey.

"Who have we here?" In curiosity Niall watched the skulking form, wondering what mischief was in the making. Certainly the manner in which he was darting in and out among the foliage indicated he did not want to be seen. Niall decided to have a confrontation with the "visitor" who seemed to be playing at hide-and-seek.

Taking the steps two at a time, Niall entered into the game, hiding in the shadows himself. At last the opportunity came when he could come upon the intruder from behind and grab him.

"Ah ha! Caught ye!" Niall held his quarry tight despite his struggling. "Settle down and be civilized, mon. I think ye hae some explaining to do. Such as who ye are and what ye are doing here!"

The voice was muffled, "I came to speak to the Niall of the MacDonalds!" A high voice. A frightened voice. "And I do not like being ill-treated, ye great oaf!"

"Who?" Reaching up, Niall pulled at the brown hood that covered the visitor's head. Once that head was revealed he gave a gasp of surprise at the tonsure that was clearly visible. "A priest!" In surprise he loosened his hold.

"Aye, that's what I am!" With undisguised irritation the holy man brushed at his cloak. "A priest on a very important mission. So, if ye will just take me to the young MacDonald I'll be about my business and then be on my way, forgetful of the 'hospitality' ye offered me."

It took a moment before Niall realized the priest had come to see him, but he hurriedly tried to make amends. "I'm sorry. It's just that the way ye were dodging in and out I feared ye were up to no good. These are, as ye know, troubled times."

"Very troubled." The tone of voice seemed to hold Niall partly accountable. "But if ye value yer soul ye willna interfere in what I am about." With an indignant sniff, the priest stalked off.

"Wait!" Niall hurried to catch up with him and block his way. "Ye said ye came to see Niall of the MacDonalds. I am he!"

"You?" For a moment the priest sounded distrustful.

"I wouldna lie." His gaze didn't waver as he stared the priest in the eye. "I am Niall of the MacDonald clan."

"Ye are?" The blue eyes moved from Niall's feet upward to the top of his tawny-haired head. "And obvious it is that ye be a big brute."

"Brute, nae. Tall, aye, especially in comparison to you."
Niall smiled. "But come, ye hae my undivided attention.
What was it ye wanted with me?"

The priest came right to the point. "I came to lead ye
back safely to the MacLeod Castle."

"To the MacLeods'." Niall shook his head. "Nae, I
canna. If I set one foot on MacLeod land I could start all
the old hatred boiling again. I dunna want that."

"Ye must. Caitlin needs ye."

"Caitlin?" Panicking, Niall imagined all sorts of things.
"What's wrong? Her wound. Was it more serious than—"

"Nae, her wound hae healed, at least that of the flesh.
But she pines for ye."

"Just as I pine for her." A sad truth that had come about
because of two stubborn old men. Reaching out, Niall
grabbed the priest's hand. "Is she well? Is she happy?"

"Aye, happy now that she knows."

"Knows? Knows what?" A strange shiver crept up Niall's
spine and down again.

"That she is soon to be a mother."

The unexpected news hit Niall like a thunderbolt. "A
mother?" For a long moment all he could do was to stand
thunderstruck as he mentally digested the announcement.
Then, losing all control, he was jumping up and down in
his excitement. "A baby! Mine! I'm a father!" In uncon-
trolled exuberance he picked the priest up, twirling him
around. "A son! A son! Mine!"

It was a revelation that goaded him, drove him beyond
endurance. Danger or not, he couldn't stay away from Caitlin
any longer. He had to see her. Had to let her know how happy
he was, how much he wanted them to be together.

It was suicidal to even contemplate going to Dunvegan.
Even so, Niall gathered his belongings together as quickly
as he could. No one, not even Ogg, could change his mind.

"I have to go!"

"To yer death?" Ogg was certain that Niall had lost his mind. "Ye'll walk right into a wolf's den. Caitlin wouldn't want that, ye know. She wouldn't want ye to place yerself in danger, laddie, even for her."

"I have no choice. I need to be with my wife. Circumstances hae changed, Ogg." There was going to be a child. Viewing his life in sudden clear perspective, he realized how that had opened his heart to the real meaning of the world. Life. Love. Purpose. "Everything is different."

"Different?"

"Aye . . ."

She was carrying his child! He was going to be a father! There would be living proof of the love he had shared with Caitlin MacLeod. No victory or honor could compare with the feelings that thought sparked. A father! The very thought made him want to shout out loud. He felt boastful and proud. Still, he kept his silence.

"Ye hae lost yer mind. Is that what ye mean?" Ogg snorted in derision.

"Think what ye want. I hae my reasons . . ."

Like a restless ghost, a being he had once pretended to be, Niall paced up and down, torn between the sensible decision of staying and the more frenzied desire of his heart. All the while poignant memories flooded over him shutting out any argument that Ogg might put forth.

Ogg shook his head. "I dunna ken what power that priest has over ye that he can so blind ye to danger, but I can see that ye willna listen. So . . ." Hastily he crossed himself. "I can do naught else but pray for ye, Niall."

"Aye, pray . . ." He was going to be doing a lot of that himself from now on, praying for Caitlin, for his unborn child, and lastly for himself.

"Niall, at least let me go with ye to offer ye protection." Ogg's sudden grasp of his arm was frantic and nearly brutal.

"Nae, I canna let ye come with me and put yerself in

danger." Niall had a faraway look in his eye. "Besides, I will hae all the protection that I hae need of." He nodded toward the priest, who stood in the doorway to Niall's room.

"Him?" Ogg's look was incredulous. With a mumbled oath he touched his sword.

"Aye, him. And a far more powerful being." Niall's gaze moved toward the ceiling.

"Then let us hope that God is on yer side!"

Thirty-five

It was washing day. Leaning out the window, Caitlin waved to Shona as her sister gallantly tried to balance a *skeel* on her head without spilling any of the precious water. "Careful, ye dunna even sneeze or ye will be drenched, Shona hinny."

Looking up, Shona was distracted by Caitlin's greeting just long enough to lose control of the wooden bucket. With a shriek she tried to recover her equilibrium before Caitlin's warning was fulfilled. Alas, as water sloshed every which way her attempt did her no good. Half the water was lost. "See what ye hae done, Caity! Ye wicked, wicked lass." Brushing at her water-soaked arasaid, Shona grumbled beneath her breath.

"Och, Shony, I'm sorry, but the wee brownie in me prompted such mischief."

"Ye made me spill the water I hae carried all the way from the well. But I will get even." Grabbing the *skeel* by the handle, Shona hefted it, dousing Caitlin with water in a playful act of retaliation.

The sound of laughter echoed through the castle courtyard as the two young women engaged in a water fight. Several of the others soon joined that playful combat. Soon the castle courtyard rang with the sound of merriment.

"Ah, Caity, it is so good to hear ye laugh at last." Shona beckoned her to join them as they engaged in doing the laundry, a chore Caitlin had always thoroughly enjoyed.

Linen was put into a large, low tub and trampled with the young women's bare feet as they danced up and down, singing rousing songs. The custom had started long ago when winters were long and hard. It was easier to keep blood circulating in the feet than the hands, especially when it was cold. Washing in groups, two women to a tub, the young women supported themselves with their arms thrown around each other's shoulders. Only when the laundry was ready to be wrung out would their hands touch the clothing.

Running out of the castle, tucking her long skirts up above her knees, Caitlin stepped into the huge low tub of water to join Shona. Usually the laundry was done inside in the bath house, but since it was a sunny day they had dragged the tubs outside to enjoy the last vestige of autumn.

"Are ye still feeling ill?"

Caitlin shook her head. "Nae, the fresh air is doing me some good." She concentrated on where she placed her feet, trampling the dirty garments furiously in her zest to get them clean. "Father caught me making a toy for the coming bairn. For a moment I feared he would guess." Caitlin was beginning to be impatient. "When is Mother going to tell him, do ye suppose?"

"Soon, or so she said to me."

Though Caitlin joined in to sing a rousing song, though she moved her feet and danced about just as playfully as the others, her heart was not in it now. "I dunna feel comfortable not telling him myself. He has a right to know that he is going to hae a grandchild." How was she going to continue to fool their father in the meantime?

"Aye, he does. But Mother has her reasons."

"I suppose." But what were they? Her joyful mood broken, Caitlin was silent, giving free reign to the thoughts whirling around in her brain. Was Fiona afraid that Ian would send her far away when he found out? Was that the reason for the silence? Or was there something else?

The soap from lye made with wood ash stung Caitlin's

feet, and thus she was the first from the tub. As she wrung out the garments and laid them to dry on the grass, she once again envisioned Niall in her mind, the haughty way he tilted his chin, his smile, the way he walked. Niall had a daring way of looking directly in another's eyes when talking to them. Oh that she were as bold now and could get this matter of telling her father over with. Until then, she would be overly shy in his presence. Tongue-tied. Afraid she might in some way give her secret away.

It should be joyful news, not something to hide. Her father was soon to have his longed-for successor. Why then was she keeping it hidden from him? The answer came easily. Because it was Niall's child and that complicated everything.

"Will ye love yer grandchild any the less because it has MacDonald blood?" Sadly she shook her head, hoping the hostility of the past would not taint an innocent child.

The baby that Niall and I conceived was created out of love, not hate. Love, it could be such a healing thing. Was it possible that this baby could heal the wounds of the past?

"Caity!" Turning, Caitlin saw her mother poised in the open doorway, gesturing for her to come inside.

Picking up her skirts, she hurried to join her, cautioned that it was a matter of secrecy by the finger held to Fiona's lips. "What is it?"

Though usually self-assured and calm, Fiona was visibly trembling. "It is done."

"Done!" Caitlin stiffened. "Ye told Father?"

"Nae, not yet." Her expression seemed to say it would not be an easy task. "But I will tonight. I must."

"Then what . . . ?" Her mother's nervousness was contagious. "Mother, what hae ye done?"

Fiona took a deep breath, then sighed. "I sent the priest to the MacDonalds."

"Sent the priest?" Caitlin paled as all sorts of images invaded her mind. "Why?" She had thought her mother to be on her side in all of this. "I dunna want the marriage to end. . . ."

"Nor do I. That is why I had to put an end to all this foolishness." Reaching out, Fiona grabbed her daughter's hand. "A father has a right to know about his child, Caity, to be there when it makes its first entry into this cold world."

Caitlin gasped. "Ye sent for Niall!" A truth that was frightening and yet at the same time comforting. She wanted him to know, wanted him to be with her, and yet at the same time feared what her father would do.

Fiona read her daughter's thoughts. "I couldna just stand by and watch ye waste away from the sadness of it all. No mother wants to see her daughter so unhappy. And all because of two foolish old men. It is time to bury the ghosts of the past."

"Aye, but tell that to Father." Caitlin put her arms around her mother, leaning her head on her shoulder. "Oh, Mother, do ye think it will ever end? So much sorrow, so much hatred. I dunna want my bairn to grow up feeling those emotions. I want him or her to know happiness and joy and love."

"And he will." Fiona's tone was stern. "I will see to it."

Caitlin's eyes filled with tears. "If Father harms one hair on Niall's head, I dunna think I will ever be able to forgive him. But he will! He is so obsessed with his anger that at times he is blind."

Fiona sighed. "We all are at times. But I will make him see."

Caitlin shivered. "I hope so. I love Niall, Mother. With all my heart and soul. I want us to be together. But I dunna want him harmed."

"Dunna worry. I was careful." Fiona briefly explained what she had done. Knowing that the only person who would be safe in MacLeod and MacDonald territory would be a man of the church, she had sent Father Flanigan to act as messenger. She smiled. "And he is to be joined by another man of the cloth."

"Another?"

"Yer Niall." He was going to travel to Dunvegan with Father Flanigan dressed as a priest.

Glancing about her, Caitlin viewed the untamed woodland of her hideaway as she thought about the sweet secret that she shared with her mother. Father Flanigan had been sent to accompany Niall to Dunvegan Castle. God willing, he would be here soon to learn from her own lips that he was soon to be a father. That is if he chose to come.

"Will he?"

Deep in her heart Caitlin knew that he would. Despite the danger, Niall MacDonald would not say no to Father Flanigan, nor to her mother. He *would* come. It was a thought that brought forth conflicting emotions of joy and yet a deep concern for his safety.

"Ach, but for the moment I can find tranquility here," she sighed in solitude.

Her hideaway near Dunvegan, known as Fairy Bridge, was a natural wonderland, a haven with a mossy floor hidden from view by a drapery woven of hundreds of red, yellow, and green leaves. It was an achingly lovely spot. To the south the mountains and moorlands sparkled like jewels, to the north. Each stone, each tree, every inlet of water that gourged deep into the glens was precious to her.

"Fairy Bridge . . ."

There was a story told around the hearth fires claiming that the fairy wife of a fourteenth-century chief had given her husband the fairy flag as a parting gift when she returned to fairyland after twenty years of marriage. Thereafter, their parting place, near Dunvegan, had been known as Fairy Bridge.

"So beautiful . . ."

Yet, there was a loneliness about this place, too, that touched Caitlin's heart. Today she looked at it as if viewing it for the very first time, each leaf and rock becoming precious to her.

Flocks of gulls and terns glided overhead. The wild beautiful music of the inland birds serenaded her as they flew from bough to bough, a melancholy song that fit the mood of her reverie. Staring into the azure depths of the sea, her eyes focused on the water as if somehow she might read her fate there. Would she be happy? Would her father learn to put aside his anger and hatred and let her and her husband live in peace? Closing her eyes, Caitlin prayed with all her heart that it would be so.

Thirty-six

The hills and glens seemed to stretch for acres and acres, miles and miles, yet Niall forced himself to travel at a furious pace through crofting villages, up the slopes of the Red Hills, and through a countryside that was wild and magnificent.

"I am going to be a father." That wondrous thought gave him stamina and made him forget his discomfort and the danger he was walking straight into. As he hurriedly put one foot in front of the other, the priest had a difficult time keeping up with him.

Niall and Father Flanigan had intended at first to procure a boat and go the distance by sea, but a sudden fierce storm had put an end to their plans. Now as the wind howled, all they could do was to gather their hooded cloaks about themselves in a futile effort to keep dry.

"There's a crofter's hut over there." The priest's voice was nearly swallowed by the wind. "Shall we stop?"

The thought of a warm fire was tempting, but though he might have sought shelter, might have known the warmth of a fire, Caitlin's face, hovering before his eyes, urged Niall on. "Nae. We keep going."

The sky was streaked with lightning. Rain tore at Niall's face and cut through his cloak like a knife, but stubbornly he kept on. He didn't want to stop for food, nor drink, nor to see to his own comforts. A deep fear gnawed at him. Despite the fact that Caitlin was with her own clan he worried. So many unforeseen things could happen. He was anxious to see her again. Anxious to be with her. Time was of the essence.

Father Flanigan's eyes were filled with compassion. "I understand. I, too, once had a woman I loved. But ye canna drive yerself. Ye must rest some time."

"We will. We will. As soon as we get to the other side of that hill." That was a promise Niall kept breaking as he looked northward. Just over those hills his heart was with a flaming-haired MacLeod woman who had given him her love. *Caity, what has become of you?* he agonized. *What are ye doing? Are ye well? Are ye safe?*

Niall wanted nothing more in this life so much as he wanted to gather her into his arms. But then what? He couldn't pretend to be a priest forever. Was he then going to pick Caitlin up in his arms and carry her away? Come face-to-face with the MacLeod and battle it out? Resign himself to being a prisoner in the dungeon?

Something has to be done. The baby. Aye, that had changed so many things. The feuding had to come to an end, at least where he and his wife's clan was concerned, for he refused to live apart from Caitlin and the coming child. Refused to let his son or daughter grow up without a father. Or worse yet, with another man taking his place.

Niall had been incensed when Father Flanigan had revealed to him this reason for being at the MacLeod Castle. He had come to see to the matter of having the marriage annulled so that the MacLeod could marry Caitlin off to a man he thought to be more suitable. Well, all that had changed now. Niall was determined to stand his ground, to fight for his wife and child if need be.

"I am not afraid of Ian MacLeod," he said aloud.

"Well, ye should be!" Father Flanigan hurried up beside Niall, grabbing him by the arm, forcing him to slow down. "Once ye set foot in Dunvegan, yer life will be in his hands, so be cautious, my son. The MacLeod is not at the moment a rational mon."

"Well, for that matter neither am I. Being robbed of the woman ye love is infuriating." The very thought of the MacLeod trying to end the marriage was galling. "Well, I will tell ye one thing. I will never let Caitlin go. She belongs to me! We spoke the holy vows. Til death do us part."

Father Flanigan shuddered. "I wouldna remind the MacLeod of that part of the vow, Niall."

"For fear that he might see that I hasten to my end?" Niall shook his head. "Nae, despite his threats I canna believe that Ian MacLeod would kill the father of his grandchild. It would be too big a cross to carry, too great a stain on his soul."

"Aye, but he could throw ye in the dungeon and keep ye there until ye would wish to be dead." The priest clucked his tongue. "There has to be another way. There has to be something a mon could say to make an old fool see reason. Ah, but what?"

This time it was the priest who took the lead, his vexation giving him energy. Walking ahead of Niall, he mumbled beneath his breath as he tried to think of a solution.

"So many lives at stake. What should I do? What, dear Lord?" Looking up at the sky, Father Flanigan was avidly seeking advice from a greater being. "So much unhappiness if I canna make the MacLeod see reason. But how can I make him understand?"

"Perhaps the only thing he has come to understand is the quest for vengeance." If that was so, then Niall had come prepared. Beneath his brown hooded cloak he had a sword concealed just in case he had to protect himself. And yet, how he loathed the need for bloodshed, he thought as he trudged on down the road. Experience had taught him how very costly the spilling of blood could be.

It was a long and wearisome journey, relieved only by the blessing of the sun. At last chasing away the rain, the bright, fiery orb shone down upon Niall and the priest as they passed by rolling green meadows and densely wooded forests. Sheep, goats, and small wild animals inhabited the area, roaming about freely.

"I remember passing through this very same area when I was returning to Sleat with the fairy flag tucked under my arm, Father," Niall said in recollection. "Little did I know then where my thievery would lead. I guess ye would say I got my just reward, eh, Father?"

There was no response. Looking over his shoulder, Niall could see that Father Flanigan was lagging far behind, huffing and puffing. Niall showed compassion by at last pausing along the side of the road.

"Ye look exhausted."

"I am!" Plopping down on a large rock, Father Flanigan nearly collapsed.

"I'm sorry, Father. I didna mean to cause ye to suffer so. It's just that I am in a hurry to—"

"Hush." The priest held up his hand. "Ye didna forcibly drag me. Ah, but it is such a good feeling to get off my feet." He wiped the sweat from his brow.

"It is." Only now did Niall notice his own discomfort. "Ah, Father, ye look as miserable as I feel."

"Ye must love her very, very much." Taking out a loaf of bread he carried in a leather pouch and a flask of water, Father Flanigan shared both with Niall.

"I do. More than my life!" Realizing just how hungry he was, Niall wolfed down the bread, his thoughts on Caitlin all the while.

"Love is a powerful thing. More powerful by far than hate."

"Is it?" Niall was not so sure.

"Ye must hae faith." Father Flanigan smiled. "And after all, 'twas love that brought ye all the way . . ."

"Father?" Niall turned his head, noting at once how the priest had suddenly tensed. In a moment he saw the reason why. Five MacLeod clansmen were quickly approaching them, their arms upraised in greeting. At their head was a clansman Niall recognized only too well. "Jamie." Fumbling beneath his cloak, he reached for his sword.

The priest's tone of voice was harsh, authoritative. "Ye canna."

"I must." Answering danger by fighting was a difficult habit to break. "He will recognize me and all will be lost."

Father Flanigan grasped Niall's arm. "If ye harm him ye willna hae a chance for happiness. If ye live by the sword ye will die by the sword." His voice was impassioned. "Hae faith."

Faith." Though he tried it was easier said than done, particularly when Jamie MacLeod strode over.

"So, ye hae brought a companion, Father Flanigan. Does it take two priests to dissolve a marriage?"

"Aye. Two." Agreeably the priest nodded. "This is Father Franco who has come all the way from Rome."

"Rome!"

Again Father Flanigan nodded. "Aye."

Niall kept his head down as Jamie looked his way, asking, "What do ye think of the Highlands, Father?"

"Father Franco does not understand anything but Italian and French," the priest hurried to say. Looking at Niall, he winked.

Jamie shrugged. "That willna matter. Just as long as he can sever the ties that bind Caitlin to that fool of a Mac-Donald so that I can marry her, I will welcome him." Arrogantly he grinned at Niall, not noticing how that "priest" bristled. "And to show my appreciation, I will safely escort ye to the castle."

Fool, Niall thought. It was Jamie who was the fool and not he if he thought Caitlin would ever be his bride. Hiding his resentment, however, keeping his head bent down in a gesture of humility, Niall followed after the haughty clansman as he cheerfully led them to Dunvegan.

* * *

Caitlin stared desolately out the window of the great hall. Where was Niall? When would he arrive? Rubbing her eyes against the strain of her constant staring, she was eager and at the same time apprehensive, more so than usual because she had heard her father say that the fortress was well guarded against those coming in, or those trying to find a way out. He had smugly proclaimed that if any MacDonald was fool enough to come to Dunvegan there would be no escape.

She feared for him, for surely her father's anger and hatred lately bordered on being totally irrational. He was obsessed with annulling the marriage. Indeed, it seemed to be the only thing on his mind. The only thing he talked about. Was it any wonder then that he had nearly gone berserk when he had noticed the absence of Father Flanigan in the castle? Only Fiona's explanation that the priest had gone to meet an emissary from Rome had calmed him. His rage had turned to jubilation as he had imagined that the arrival signaled the agreement of the pope to ending the marriage.

"But the laugh is on you, Father." Little did he know that the very person he thought to destroy was traveling to Dunvegan dressed in the brown cloak and robes of the church. Hopefully that disguise would keep him safe, at least until her mother had time to talk with the MacLeod and straighten this whole situation out.

Looking over her shoulder, Caitlin shivered as she thought about the conversation her mother must be having with her father right now. The time had come for the truth to be told, yet even so it made her nervous, considering her father's frame of mind. What would her mother say? How would she begin to broach the subject? And having heard the news, how would Ian MacLeod react?

Clasping her hands together tightly, looking once again out the window, she determined to keep her spirits up. She had to believe that the coming baby would make all the difference. The child would soften her father's heart. Niall *would* come. He would make peace with the MacLeods.

"All would be well."

Pacing up and down, Caitlin whispered those words, boldly at first, then with less and less conviction as the long moments passed. There was no sign of Niall. Worse yet, she could hear the sound of her father's angry shouting. It thundered through the castle. So, he had responded to the news with anger, not joy.

Caitlin placed her hands upon her stomach, wondering what the future held for the baby growing within. "Oh, Father, how could ye harden yer heart against yer own grandchild?" she lamented. And all because of his damnable pride, and a stubbornness that would not let him bury the past.

Like an all-enveloping cloak, depression engulfed her. She felt the sudden urge to go far away from Dunvegan, to hide away in a place where no one would know who she was. In some faraway glen she would raise her child. Secluded in a cottage somewhere she would protect her baby from the poison of this bitter feud. But where would she go? Looking toward the horizon, she tried to imagine. Should she head east, south, or west?

Gazing toward the winding road that led southward, Caitlin thought about making such a journey, her eyes widening as she caught sight of the small party of men whose silhouettes were darkened on the horizon.

Jamie and the others. Her heart pounded as she realized that they were not alone. Two other figures dressed in darkbrown were with them. *Niall!* She kept her eyes riveted on the two men as they came up the road. Dear God, how had they run into Jamie? *Does Jamie know who he is?*

Fearfully she watched, breathing a sigh of relief as she noticed that the two "priests" were being treated with deference. So Jamie hadn't recognized Niall, at least not yet.

"Oh, Niall. Niall. Be careful!" Closing her eyes, she whispered a silent prayer. When she opened them, she could see that the tallest of the "priests" was looking searchingly toward the castle.

Niall stared grimly at the dark, massive wall of the fortress in the distance. It rose up forebodingly. Beyond those walls somewhere was Caitlin, and though he was not short of valor or daring he had to admit that there was no way he could wrest her from her father's hands. The castle walls were impregnable *if* Ian MacLeod willed it.

His heart sank like a stone as he forced himself to face reality. He was no match for the MacLeod. Alone he could do nothing but swear and curse from a distance. The truth of the matter was that he was helpless unless he could make Ian MacLeod listen to reason. In the meantime, the one thing he treasured most in life was just beyond his grasp.

Thirty-seven

Niall kept his head down as Ian MacLeod raised his hand in greeting to the two cloaked figures who appeared at the gate. All the while Niall prayed in his heart that his disguise would not be discovered. Not now! Not when he was so close to the fulfillment of his dream of seeing Caitlin again, of holding her in his arms.

"Greetings, MacLeod." Father Flanigan quickly stepped in front of Niall in an effort to hide him from any diligent observations. The presence of five armed clansmen standing behind the Scottish chieftain spoke of trouble should the young intruder be recognized.

"Greetings." Ian MacLeod's tone spoke of barely suppressed anger and suspicion. "It's glad I am that ye decided to return, Priest, seeing as how I didna know ye planned to leave this castle in the first place."

Father Flanigan was eager to make amends. "I apologize if I gave ye reason for distress, but I was called away quite suddenly."

"Aye. To fetch yer fine brown papal sparrow." Ian MacLeod looked toward Niall with a condescending scowl, reflecting his dislike of anything that came from across the sea. Despite the fact he had needed the pope's blessing to break the ties between his daughter and her husband, there was no love in his heart for the church in Rome. Indeed, there was no resident archbishop in Scotland. The lairds held provincial councils without the presence of a church official other than a priest.

Father Flanigan touched Niall's shoulder. "May I present Father Franco."

"Franco?" Ian MacLeod squinted his eyes. "Not one of us."

"Nae. He comes from . . . from Venice."

Knowing that he was being scrutinized, Niall sought to keep at least a part of his face in shadow.

"Venice." Ian MacLeod made no attempt at friendliness. It was obvious that he resented the intrusion of anyone foreign. Folding his arms across his chest, he spat out, "Bah, I dunna hae need of him now."

"Dunna hae need?"

"That is what I said!" Again he looked at Niall with a scowl. "So ye can send him right back to where he came from." From his actions he seemed to mean right then.

Father Flanigan looked at Niall, then at the MacLeod, then back to Niall again. "If that is what ye want, then that is what I will do. But hae a heart, mon. It has been a rough journey." It was a gentle reminder of the rules of hospitality the Highlanders adhered to.

"Aye, aye. I meant not immediately." His voice grew softer as he said the next words for only Father Flanigan's ears. "But see that ye get rid of him soon. I dunna want to owe Rome any taxation for their interference. We MacLeods are fishermen, herders, and farmers and can ill afford ten percent to line the Holy Father's coffers. Besides, as I said circumstances have changed."

"Changed?"

"Och, the worst has happened!" The MacLeod took revenge on a hapless rock in his path.

Father Flanigan asked the question that was on Niall's mind. "Yer daughter. Caitlin . . . ill . . . ?"

The MacLeod shook his head. "Nae. She is fit."

"Then . . . ?"

"I am soon to be a grandfather!" Ian's voice trembled. "To . . . to . . . a . . . a—*MacDonald!*"

"A grandfather." Father Flanigan feigned surprise. "Then of course annulment is out of the question lest ye seek to make yer own grandchild bastard born."

"Which I tell ye I do not!" The MacLeod paused, allowing his answer to register before adding, "But I wouldna mind making of my daughter a widow."

Niall flinched at the vehemence in his father-in-law's voice.

"Hold yer tongue." Despite the fact that he was talking to a powerful chieftain, Father Flanigan's tone was scolding. "To say such a thing is to speak of murder. And ye must remember how such careless talk was instrumental in making of Thomas Beckett a saint."

The MacLeod was not chastised. "Nevertheless, it makes me seethe when I think of the trickery that MacDonald used to wed with my lovely young lassie. And now he has planted his seed in her belly. The final indignity." He motioned to the two priests. "But so be it. Things done can not be undone. Come inside." He strode inside the great hall with such powerful strides that it was all Father Flanigan could do to keep up with him. Niall, on the other hand, purposefully kept several paces behind.

He was inside the castle! The very thought of being so close to Caitlin made him feel lighter of heart. *Oh, Caity, how I long to look into yer eyes, to hold ye in my arms.* Still, he had to be careful. To give in to temptation now might be costly in the long run, and thus all he could do was to patiently follow Ian MacLeod and Father Flanigan as they headed toward the small chapel and adjoining rooms that were being used by the priest during his stay.

"There, just as ye left it." Opening the door, Ian MacLeod pointed to the small table that was still littered with scrolls, ink pots, and pens.

"So I see." Father Flanigan took off his cloak, hanging

it on a peg near the door, but though he assumed Ian MacLeod would now leave them, he was soon to see that he was wrong. Moreover the chieftain's presence in the room was clearly a danger.

"I need yer help, Priest!" The MacLeod plopped his large bulk into a nearby chair.

"My help!" Father Flanigan eyed the Highlander warily. "In what way?"

Ian MacLeod gripped the arms of the wooden chair, his face tightening as he thought long and hard. "Suppose. . . ." He paused, looking askance at Niall, who was now facing the wall looking at the shields and swords hanging there. Strange symbols to adorn walls adjoining a chapel, he thought.

"Dunna worry. He doesna know a word of our language."

That soothed the MacLeod's apprehension, for he quickly stated, "Suppose I didna let it be known that my daughter was expecting a bairn. Suppose we went on with the annulment anyway. Quickly. Efficiently."

"Nae!" Father Flanigan was indignant. "That would be dishonest and reprehensible!"

"But practical for my purposes were I to quickly find her another husband."

Another husband! From his place in the corner Niall seethed. He had never held a great love for Caitlin's father but he had respected him. Such a deception was beneath such a man. But having perpetrated the falsehood that he did not speak Gaelic, he could hardly give such an opinion. Nevertheless he was incensed.

"Marry her off to another with a child growing in her womb?" Father Flanigan shook his head. "Nae."

Eyes narrowing, Ian MacLeod clenched his fists, his voice a growl as he insisted, " 'Tis the only way."

"And so ye would put yer daughter at risk of her new husband's wrath when he counts the months of her confinement and realizes he has been the pawn of a terrible deception."

Ian MacLeod's mouth was seamed in a bitter, unyielding line. "I would strike a bargain with her new husband. Nor would I lie and pass the devil's spawn off as anything but what it is."

"A sweet, innocent babe who does not deserve yer scorn. A bairn who carries the blood of the MacDonalds, aye, but yer own MacLeod blood as well." Father Flanigan got down on his knees before the MacLeod, his arms upraised in supplication. "Please, I beg of ye, Ian, bury yer hatred before it brings a great ill to those of yer household. Let Caitlin hae some happiness out of all this. Let her live in peace with her husband and baby. Find a place in yer heart for forgiveness and love."

Ian MacLeod swallowed. There was a long spell of silence, a time in which a myriad of expressions chased across his face. His thick brows raised, drew together, then sagged. The glare in his eyes softened. In the end, however, his only retort was to bark out, "Yon priest . . . why does he still wear his cloak?"

Father Flanigan stiffened, exchanging a worried look with Niall. "Perhaps . . . perhaps he prepares himself for his . . . his return journey."

"Then make him understand that the MacLeod wants him to stay. Tell him to make himself comfortable."

Father Flanigan rattled off some scattered phrases in Latin that were answered by Niall's hasty garbled jibberish.

"Father Franco says thank ye, but he will leave his cloak on for now. Ye see . . . ye see he is cold."

"Cold?" Ian MacLeod's mouth curled in a snear.

Father Flanigan grinned. "Ye know the men of those warmer climates. They canna stand our damp and cold clime."

"Nae, I suppose they canna." Even so, Ian looked at Niall suspiciously as Niall toyed with a pen and ink pot. "What's more I dunna ken if they can be trusted. Something about him troubles me."

"Then, of course, let us hae a bit of privacy." Eager to avert a disaster, Father Flanigan took Niall by the arm, pushing him out the door. Once again he rattled off some Latin, then shut the door in Niall's face, explaining to the MacLeod, "I told him to seek out the kitchen. Some hot lamb stew or soup will soon warm his bones. And while he is gone we can talk about . . . about important matters."

Niall stared at the thick wooden door, feeling relief at being away from such heated scrutiny, yet at the same time perturbed to be out of earshot. He was curious as to what further plans the MacLeod was about to hatch, but though he put his ear to the door he could not understand what was being mumbled.

Well, what did it matter? All he knew was that he would never give Caitlin and his baby up to another man. If that meant he had to carry her far away, even so far as to Rome itself, well, so be it. With that determination, Niall moved through the corridors, headed for Caitlin's chamber. Opening the door, he was disappointed to see that she was not there. Her sister was, however.

"Father?" In curiosity as to why a priest had sought out her room, Shona came forward.

All kinds of thoughts swirled through Niall's mind. Foremost, he wondered if he dared trust Caitlin's sibling. Deciding he had no other choice, he pushed back his hood. "Shona, please, where is Caitlin?"

"Niall!" Her expression was exactly the same as Caitlin's had been that first time she had caught him in the tower and had assumed him to be a ghost.

"Please, Shona, dunna give me away! I came to be with my wife." His voice was impassioned. "I love her."

If he had feared Shona's betrayal, the softness in her eyes calmed that fear. "I know that ye do. And Caitlin loves ye, too. Very, very much."

"I know about the child."

"So does Father now." Shona sighed. "He is such a good mon at heart, but he is being so stubborn."

"He wants the priest to go through with the annulment and marry Caitlin to another mon. But that I canna allow!" His eyes glittered as he said it again. "I canna give my wife over to another mon."

Shona hurried to reassure him. "Nor would Caitlin ever agree."

"Then what are we to do?" For just a moment Niall felt as though the weight of the world was resting on his shoulders.

"Ye need friends to gather behind ye. Father needs to see that he canna always hae his way." Shona touched Niall's arm. "I am yer friend, Niall MacDonald."

Oh, how he had need of her friendship. It was a welcome boon. "Thank ye for that, Shona MacLeod." He grasped her hand. "It gives me hope."

"And where there is hope . . ." She smiled. "But enough of talk. Ye came all this way to see Caitlin and not me. Sit and relax. I will find her, bring her here and give ye two a bit of privacy." That said, she quickly and quietly moved to the door, giving Niall a wink before she left him all alone.

Caitlin stood as still as a statue in front of the chapel door. The chamber entrance loomed in her path like the most awesome portcullis. Raising a trembling hand to the wood, however, she knocked hesitantly, a gesture that reflected her apprehension. What was going on inside?

"Who is it?" thundered in the silence.

"Caitlin. I . . . I would like a word wi' ye, Father." She wanted a chance to look into the room to see if Niall was safe or if his disguise had been discovered. "Father . . . ?"

Furled brows showed impatience at being disturbed as

Ian MacLeod opened the door. "BiGod lass, what could be so important that ye would interrupt a mon's discussion with his priest?"

"I hae something that . . . that needs to be told." Anxiously she peered through the open doorway, but caught sight of only Father Flanigan's form. Where was Niall?

"Save yer breath, Daughter." The words exploded from his lips. "Yer mother has already told me about the bairn."

Swallowing her tears she replied, "A happening with which I can tell that ye are no' pleased."

For just a moment his face was completely blank of expression, then he grimaced. "I am and then again I am not!"

"Because it complicates all yer plotting and scheming," Caitlin blurted out, looking directly at Father Flanigan.

The MacLeod's face tightened. "That among other things . . ."

"Then because of that I am doubly glad. 'Tis time that ye didna hae yer way."

"Caity!" He held up one hand, palm out, fingers toward the ceiling. It was a gesture he always used to intimidate and silence any opposition. "I will no' hae a slip of a lassie talking to me that way. I am the chieftain of the MacLeod. My word is law!"

Though once she might have cowered, Caitlin let her rising tide of bitterness consume her. "Ye may be the MacLeod, yer word may be law on this isle, but even the mighty chief must bow to a greater power."

His face turned red, he balled his hands into fists. "Daughter!"

Caitlin's eyes glittered in the candlelight. It shouldn't be like this, she thought. The coming birth should have been a happy event. Her father should have been cradling her in his arms expressing his joy, not glowering at her with anger, as if she had erred.

"Well, even if ye dunna welcome the child, I do, Mac-

Donald or no." There was such a fiercesome pressure pushing at her chest that she feared she couldn't breathe. Then, without warning, Caitlin burst into a storm of tears. "Ye can be cruel, Father. Cruel."

The MacLeod was unnerved by her tears and regretted his outburst. Touching her shoulder, his eyes softened. "Caity, dunna cry. It's just that . . . that I canna get used to sharing a grandchild with such a loathsome old soul as Malcolm MacDonald."

Dashing the degrading moisture from her cheeks, she sniffled. "And mayhap he willna be so pleased to be sharing a great-nephew with ye."

He was visibly taken aback. "Then I dare him to come here and make a complaint!"

"Oh, how I wish that he would!" Again she squinted her eyes as she tried to catch any sight of Niall.

"And bring that bastard of a nephew wi' him!" Ian MacLeod grumbled, thereby allying his daughter's fears that he might have already been discovered.

"Niall will no' come," Caitlin hurried to say. "Thanks to ye, Father." She felt quarrelsome and might have said more had she not felt the insistent pressure of a hand on the small of her back and heard her sister's frantic voice whispering in her ear. Whirling around, she read the reason for Shona's sudden appearance in her sister's eyes.

Niall was here! Caitlin's hands trembled violently as she ran to her room and pushed open the door. Peering into the room, she expected to see him standing, waiting for her. Instead, she saw him curled up in the corner, his eyes closed, his head cradled on the crook of his arm. The soft rumble of his snoring told her how deeply he slept.

"Ye poor darling. It must hae been a terribly rough journey."

Crossing the room, kneeling down where he napped, she touched a lock of tawny hair that had fallen into his eyes. *He must hae loved me very much to come all this way and risk his life,* she concluded tenderly. As much as she loved him? She could only wonder.

"Ah, Niall, Niall."

Was there a chance for happiness for them? Surely at this moment it seemed so. Her father's blustering did little to ease her mind. Still, looking down at Niall, her love bubbled deep inside her. She loved him. There was no question in her mind as to that. Her senses were filled with wanting him.

"What happened between us was meant to be. I love ye so!" Yet, that did not keep her from feeling a bit shy as his eye lids fluttered open.

"Ye do?" Niall cherished the blessing of seeing her lovely face hovering above him, her mane of flaming hair tumbling down over her shoulders in wild disarray. He'd dreamed of her so often that for just a moment he feared her image to be merely a mirage.

"Mmm." Caitlin shrugged, suddenly tongue-tied. She did, however, stroke his neck.

"Say it again, lass." Oh, but she was the prettiest sight he had ever seen. His eyes savored the gentle swell of her breasts and hips, then touched upon her stomach. It was there his baby would sleep until it was time to come into this cold, harsh world. His baby.

"I love ye, Niall." Caitlin's voice was a hushed whisper.

"Do ye now?" He grinned like a lovestruck boy. "And I love ye, hinny. More than my very life!" Slowly his hands closed around her shoulders, pulling her to him, the passion of his kiss a testimony to the truth of his words. But suddenly he pulled away. "My child," he gasped. Tentatively he reached out and touched her stomach, marveling at the miracle that had created life inside her.

"A tiny being that is living proof of our love."

"Caity, I canna let ye go. Yer father . . ."

"Is an old fool if he thinks to bully me. Ye are and always will be my husband, Niall MacDonald. I willna ever marry anyone else!" An impassioned promise that she meant with all her heart.

"Ye willna!" This time he kissed her tenderly, shivering at the potent flicker of arousal that spread from their fused mouths to the core of his body. "Ah, Caity," he murmured against her lips.

His voice was infused with a husky plea that sent her heart into song. Her body responded to the depth of his desire. She felt alive. Soaring. "Niall!" She pressed close against him, savoring the heat of his body, the sheer, masterful strength of him.

"I love ye," he whispered in her ear. "I thank God that ye are mine. And now ye carry my bairn. I am the happiest of laddies." His hands tangled in her hair as he kissed her again, his lips drinking deeply of her very soul. The kiss was long, satisfying to them both, but not so satisfying that they did not long for more.

"Come!" Taking him by the hand, Caitlin led him to her bed. Lying down beside him, she was impatient. She tore at her garments in her hurry to remove the flimsy boundary that kept her from the tantalizing feel of his naked flesh against her own. Then she was experiencing the warmth of his fingers as he gently outlined the swell of her breasts.

"They seem fuller."

"They are. The babe."

"Ah!" The thought excited him all the more. His wife. His child. Bending down, he gently suckled the peaks.

Caitlin trembled beneath the warm wetness of his lips and tongue, aroused with a wanton urge to abandon herself fully to the glorious flood of ecstasy that consumed her. She gave herself up to his touch, straining against him, her head spinning wildly as she clung to him.

"It's glad I am that I am not truly a priest."

"And if ye were?"

"I would give up such a vow for ye, lass. Indeed, I would." That said, Niall tugged off the cloak, casting it ruthlessly aside. His hosen and tunic followed, tumbling to the floor.

Their naked bodies caressed as he lay back down. Her skin was warm against his. Feeling her body against him was highly arousing. So much so that it was all he could do to keep his own passions under control. But he did not want to be selfish. The total fulfillment of Caitlin's desires had to be equally important to the fulfillment of his own. He wanted to be a considerate lover. And yet, how difficult it was to keep his own emotions under control.

"Mmm." Trembling in an eagerness that matched his, Caitlin slid her arms about his neck, moving against him with a sensuousness that was fired by their long separation. Then they were rolling over and over on the woolen blankets, sinking into the feathered softness.

"Yer friend Jamie threatened to snatch ye out from under yer husbands nose," he growled.

"He did?"

"Aye, he did." His arms tightened around her. "But as long as I am alive he never will. Ye are mine, Caity. Ye belong to me." Once again his hands roamed over her body, asserting that claim.

"Oh, Niall!" As long as he was alive, he had said. The very thought that something might happen to threaten his existence frightened her, made her realize how precious each moment together was. "Don't . . ."

"Hush." His lips swept across her stomach in reverence to the life she carried within her. "No matter what happens I know that I will go on living because of the precious gift ye hae given me. My son."

"Or daughter."

Niall felt certain. "It is a male child."

Caitlin shrugged, not having the heart to argue. The sex of the baby didn't really matter. All that mattered was that the bairn would know its father, would grow up in the sunshine of his love. For that matter she wanted that for herself as well. She wanted to look forward to a long life with Niall. Instead, she had no way of knowing how long they had to enjoy each other's company. It was a thought that made her hug Niall all the tighter.

"Caity!" With a groan, he gently pressed himself between her thighs.

Opening to him, Caitlin gave of herself as she had never done before. For the moment her only world was Niall, bringing to her body the ultimate pleasure and to her heart the deepest love. Then it was her hands which caressed him, her lips which sought his mouth. Running her hand down his flat stomach, she stroked the bulge of his manhood, hearing his gasp of pleasure as she traced the length of him with her fingers, working magic upon that throbbing maleness that had given her so much delight.

Niall's flesh burned to the flame of her caress. His mouth was hot against her neck. He whispered words of love in a hectic frenzy as he found her secret place, then entered her. He marveled at how right it felt to be joined with her flesh to flesh. And soul to soul!

Caitlin could feel the strength of his muscled arms as they wrapped around her, his broad, lightly furred chest straining against her own. In that moment they were joined as one, offering to each other the most precious gift of all, the gift of love. Then the world seemed to quake beneath them as they moved, rising and falling like ocean waves.

Niall's face was etched in passion as an explosion of sheer pleasure flooded through them. He cried out Caitlin's name over and over as the storm washed through them both. Then in the drowsy afterglow he held her close, smiling as she snuggled against him.

"It should always be this way. Us together," he whispered, stroking her hair.

"Always."

"Oh, Caity." As if afraid she might suddenly die, Niall's hand clutched at hers, holding it tightly. Their eyes met and held, an unspoken communication of love passing between them. Then with a sigh they closed their eyes. At least for the moment they could savor their contentment.

Thirty-eight

Danger hovered in every corner. Armed men lurked in the shadows, their unfriendly eyes threatening a discovery. Even so, Caitlin and Niall braved the peril just for a chance to look at each other, to touch, to briefly hold hands or, if they were blessed with a moment of being alone, to kiss.

Each time they were together the bond between them grew stronger. Never had each passing minute been so precious. Never before had they savored every heartbeat, every whisper, the wonderful feel of skin against skin. Love. The very word seeped into the depths of their souls. In their hearts, minds, and spirits they were as one, their love personified in the child growing in Caitlin's womb.

His child meant everything to Niall. It was a miracle that overwhelmed him each time he touched Caitlin's stomach. The bairn was a living symbol and gave him all the more reason to want to live. Caitlin and the child needed him.

Never before had Niall wished so fervently to have eyes in the back of his head. He was risking his freedom, perhaps even his life, each and every time he sought Caitlin out, each time they shared an affectionate gesture or made love, and yet he could not keep away from her. His feelings for her, his desire to be with her and his child were even stronger than his fear of Ian MacLeod.

"Ye are tempting fate!" Father Flanigan always scolded, fearing that Niall's emotions would eventually give him away. "Someone is going to see ye and yer identity will be heralded throughout the halls."

"Nae, I hae been careful."

The habit Niall was wearing well disguised his appearance. From time to time he could pull the hood down lower on his forehead or the cowl collar up over part of his face.

"It doesna matter how cautious ye might be. Ye are going to take one too many chances. As it is, Ian MacLeod is questioning me why I hae not sent ye away. He is suspicious of ye, Son. I fear that there are more spies watching ye than ye could ever know."

"Ever know?" Niall held up his hands, counting on his fingers. "There are more enemies here than I could ever count. I am well aware of the danger they pose. But. . . ."

"Ye will no' use reason and go back to the MacDonald stronghold until I can make the MacLeod understand that God, and not he, is in charge now?"

"I will no' go alone!"

Oh, how he wished that he could just pick Caitlin up in his arms, hold her ever so tightly and protectively to his own trembling body and simply disappear in the Highland mists. It was his fiercest desire. He had a compulsion to flee but only if his wife went with him.

"And ye can no' go with her. It is far too dangerous at this time." Father Flanigan cast his eyes upward. "And so there is nothing that I can do but pray and ask His guidance and assistance."

"Father, when ye pray, be sure ye let Him know how very much I do love her." More than his own safety. Still, he knew that he, too, must survive in order to make a life for his wife and child.

Father Flanigan shook his head. "If ye love her, ye must protect her. And just how are ye going to do that if ye end up in the MacLeod dungeon, might I ask?"

Niall was silent for a long while. When he answered it

was in a whisper. "I will see her but one more time. I must explain . . ."

Father Flanigan sighed with relief. "Once more is one time too many." Still, Niall would have it no other way. He wanted one more chance to tell Caitlin of his love. He needed desperately to whisper his love in her ear. After that, he would follow Father Flanigan's advice and look upon her only from afar . . . that is until this matter of the marriage was at last settled and its sanctity proclaimed.

"Once more . . ." A vow that seemed nearly impossible as he caught sight of her on the stairs. Pulling at his cowl, he followed. "Caity, my Caity, where can I see ye?"

"My room. Shona will stand lookout again!"

Unable to help himself, he pulled her with him into the shadows, threading the fingers of both hands through her hair. Lowering his head, he touched her mouth with his, his lips lingering, tasting, caressing.

"Oh, Caity, Caity, you beautiful jewel, how you have enriched my life. Without you and our wee bairn—"

"Hush . . . ye willna ever be without me." In a gesture of affirmation she reached up and gently touched his cheek. "It will work out. It must." Alas, she sounded much more optimistic than she really felt. "Until then we must be content with what we hae."

"Aye."

"Och, Niall . . ." She clutched his hands, gripping them, drawing strength from him, fearful suddenly of what tomorrow held in store. Shuddering, she recalled the unhappy endings for young lovers the bards often sung about, then, as she looked into Niall's eyes, she hurriedly pushed all fear from her mind. Smiling, she whispered, "I must go now, but I will meet ye in a few moments."

"A heartbeat too long without ye," he muttered softly into the cowl collar. Their eyes met once again, then, with a groan of impatience, he descended the narrow stairway.

It seemed an eternity until they were together, but as he

pulled her close he knew that every pang of impatience had been worth it. Sweet, hot desire tempered by tenderness fused their bodies together. An aching sweetness mingled with the fury and the fire.

In the aftermath, when passion had ebbed, they lay entwined, sealing their vows with whispered words of love. Alas, it was a quietude that was much too short. With the violence of a thunderstorm their peacefulness was shattered as Ian MacLeod burst into the room. "Caitlin, I hae heard strange tattlings," he announced. "There is talk of the foreign priest . . . !"

With a terrified shriek Caitlin hastily reached for the blanket, quickly covering her nakedness and Niall's as well. "Father!"

Ian MacLeod's eyes traveled about the room, taking in every detail, including the discarded brown cloak. In that moment he knew fully the truth of the betrayal. "No priest, but a wolf in sheep's clothing. A wolf named MacDonald!" With a lunge he fell upon Niall, screaming for his clansmen at the top of his lungs.

"Leave me be! Leave us in peace. She is my wife! I hae every right."

"Right? Ye hae none." Ian MacLeod held Niall pinioned as two other MacLeods pushed into the room. "Take this 'priest' to the dungeon. Now!"

"Nae!" Like a banshee, Caitlin attacked her father, pummeling him with her fists. "If ye harm him, if ye do, I will never forgive ye. I will never, do ye hear!"

Her threat fell upon ears that were deaf with the MacLeod's anger. He gave his order again. "Take him to the dungeon."

"Nae!" This time Caitlin turned her attention to Niall, clasping her arms around his waist as if in this way she could keep him from suffering his doom. It did no good. She was callously pulled away and pushed aside. Helplessly all she could do was watch as Niall was dragged from the room.

"Consorting with the enemy! Sneaking around behind my back." Ian MacLeod's shouts vibrated throughout the chamber.

"Enemy no. He is my husband! Ye had no right. Ye had no right." Caitlin's eyes glittered as she looked him in the eye. "And if ye harm him I will hate ye forever. Do ye hear me, Father. I. . . ." Suddenly she paled. With a gasp she clutched at her stomach. "Nae. Nae."

"Caity!" The MacLeod's anger evaporated as he saw his daughter's agony.

"My babe! My bairn!" Caitlin reached out, fighting against the huge black dots that floated before her eyes. Then she saw only darkness.

The flame of the hearth fire spattered and sparked, blending its smoke with that of the burning rushes, stinging Fiona's eyes as she hovered over the pale form lying on the bed. She had joined the midwife and the physician, Mac-an-leigh, in a long vigil. With each moment that passed, her apprehension and fear grew.

"Caitlin, hinny. Please, open yer eyes!" Only a soft moan answered her as she called out her daughter's name. Though Caitlin could hear voices, could tell what was going on, she couldn't seem to answer. Instead, she merely listened.

"She is in the land of dreams. I gave her a sleeping potion." The midwife held up the glass that still held traces of the chalky white substance.

"A sleeping potion. Was that wise?"

"She needed to rest, to calm her anxieties so that her bleeding would come to an end."

"Aye, the bleeding." Fiona MacLeod winced.

"How is she?" Sheepishly Ian MacLeod entered the room to take his place beside his wife.

"Do ye really care?" Fiona MacLeod's scorn was potent. "Or is yer hatred more important than the well-being of yer daughter."

"Fie, woman. Hold yer tongue. What happened isna my fault."

Perhaps not, but realization that he was helpless to do anything to ease Caitlin's agony tore at his soul. Worse yet, the midwife had confided that it was possible for the young mother-to-be to lose her child. The spots of blood on the sheet clearly proved her right.

"Ye couldna let her be happy for even a moment. Ye had to go blustering about like a dog gone mad. Well, ye hae Niall MacDonald secluded in yer moldy dungeon. I hope that makes ye happy as ye look down and see what yer blundering has done." Fiona's eyes were filled with tears. All she could do was hold tightly to her daughter's hand and offer what comfort she could. Only the midwife with her herbs, potions, and knowing hands could help Caitlin now.

"I didna mean my own daughter harm. I didna!"

"And yer own grandchild. Yer own flesh and blood. Mac-Donald though it may be it deserves a chance at life." Fiona wiped her tears away with the sleeve of her rough woolen tunic. She had always protected Caitlin, despite their many misunderstandings. Indeed, they seemed to have grown closer lately, mainly because of the coming child, a natural time for a daughter to turn to her mother.

"Fiona . . . !" Ian MacLeod tried to comfort his wife, but it was no use. He didn't know what to say, not now, not after what had happened.

"Ye saw yer grandchild as a barrier to yer mighty plans. Tell me, husband, hae ye got Caitlin's next husband waiting outside the door?"

"Of course not!" Retreating from his wife's anger, Ian moved closer to the bed, shaken by the sight of his daughter's ashen face. Hiding his fear, he took out his anger on the nearest person. "Do something!" he swore at the midwife. "Save my grandchild, or by God I'll hae yer head."

"I can do nothing more. I gave her herbs and potions to restore her strength. The rest is up to God." The old woman's eyes spoke a truth that Ian was reluctant to admit. "I would say my prayers if I were ye, old mon."

Old mon! Strange, but in that moment the word "old" seemed definitely to apply to him.

"The bleeding." Fiona was frightened. "Has it stopped?"

This time it was the physician who answered. "Aye."

"Perhaps then it is not too late for the bairn." Fiona clutched her daughter's hand, stung by the knowledge that there was nothing she could do to take away Caitlin's suffering. If only it were *she* lying on that bed. If only . . .

"Why is it that everyone blames me for what has happened. Why does no one blame that young fool who trespassed into this castle. Why?"

"I dunna blame him because he came here in answer to my pleading." Fiona made the confession.

"Ye sent for him?" He was incredulous.

"I thought, I hoped, that once ye saw the two lovebirds together, realized how much they loved each other, ye would come to yer senses. I was wrong." She faced him squarely. "Ian MacLeod, ye can be the world's greatest and most stubborn fool at times."

He thought long and hard about that accusation. "Sometimes maybe I can be." As for now, each moan from Caitlin's lips struck a blow to his heart. For the first time he found himself regretting what he had done. He had been rash. Hasty. It was just that seeing that priest's cloak, knowing that he had been lied to again, had enraged him. "But it doesna matter now," he whispered. "All that matters is Caitlin's well-being. And . . . and that of her bairn." Silently he mouthed a prayer, though he made no promises to God. He didn't feel that the omnipotent being was asking him to do such a thing.

Fiona, however, was another story. "Ye will let Niall MacLeod out of that smelly hole this instant. Ye will fetch him and allow him the courtesy of being with his wife."

"Will I now!" The embers of the fire glowed red, casting eerie shadows upon his face. Indeed, at that moment, he looked like the very devil.

"Ye will if ye ever want to share my bed again."

"What?"

"Ye heard me!" Taking little care whether or not she fueled his anger, she continued. "And ye will put far from yer mind any thoughts of our daughter being pawned off like a tinker's wagon. She loves her husband, Ian, no matter what blood flows through his veins. Much as I love ye."

"Ye love me?" Sadly, he had never really been sure.

"I do."

"Even though I stole ye from Malcolm MacDonald so long ago."

"Even so." That much at least was settled. "Ian, there has been too much bloodshed. Give it up! Make yer truce with Malcolm and be done with it."

"A truce?" The very idea galled him. "How can I when he killed my son?"

"It was not he that killed Colin, and well ye know it!"

"Not truly he but one of his clan. For that I hold him responsible." With a grunt he considered the matter closed.

"Suppose . . . suppose I were to tell ye that Colin was not yer son." Though it was something she had long held within her heart, Fiona felt relieved to be unburdened by the confession.

"Not my son?" Ian was aghast. In two quick strides he hovered over her. "What game is this?"

Fiona shook her head. "No game but the truth at last. A truth that has haunted me every day of my life with you." She took a deep breath, then let the story out of a frightened young girl whose moonlit trysts with Malcolm MacDonald had resulted in a child, a baby who was joyfully and unknowingly claimed by the man who had abducted her from the arms of her lover.

"By God, 'tis true!" Ian MacLeod was stunned. "But why . . . ? Why tell me now?"

Fiona looked into the face of her sleeping daughter. "For her. For my sweet, sweet, Cai. I want to put the ghosts of the past to rest, even though—"

"Not my son!"

"So, ye see, Colin was in truth a MacDonald. Therefore ye hae no reason for this all-consuming hatred ye feel."

Ian MacLeod turned his back. "Woman, I will never forgive ye. Ye hae killed me."

Even so, it was Fiona MacLeod who suffered. "Turn Niall MacDonald loose. Let Caitlin be happy. Give up the feud. Make amends with Malcolm and hae done with it all. Please!"

Her supplication went unanswered as Ian MacLeod stormed to the door. Opening it roughly, he nearly pulled it from its hinges. Then he was gone.

Thirty-nine

The high-pitched shriek of the rats as they scurried about in the night made it impossible for Niall to sleep. He hated being locked up. Hated it more than anything.

"So, at last I am caged in the MacLeod's oubliette," the coffin-size prison from which there was no escape. And all the while the ghostly clang of closing gates, the rattle of keys, and heavy trod of footsteps were constant taunts of the lack of privacy he had.

"Och, how be the mighty MacDonald tanist now?" teased a guard, peering down through the grille. "Was it worth it to take away our flag, ye treacherous bastard! Was it?"

"Go away!" Niall sat up. "I dunna hae to answer to the likes of ye for what I hae done."

"Ach, then I willna gi' ye any food or water. Beasts such as are suckled by MacDonald breasts can starve and thirst for all that I care."

"I'm not hungry or thirsty. At least not for what you offer," Niall countered.

"Ye are not." The guard dangled a leg of mutton through the opening in the grille, laughing as Niall looked up.

With a snort he pulled it away. "Ye said ye were no' hungry."

"I'm not, at least for MacLeod fare." Drawing his legs up to his chest, Niall turned his back. At last the guard left, but only for a short while. All too soon he was back, this time to tease him with water.

"Thirsty?"

Niall was, desperately so. Anxiously he licked his dry lips.

"Ah, ye are, but not for MacLeod water, I would dare say." Deliberately he poured some through the grille so that it dribbled on the dirt floor. He laughed uproariously.

"Gi' yerself up to yer good humor now. Perhaps someday we will hae changed places," Niall grumbled.

"Not if the MacLeod has his way. Ye will stay down here until the day ye die."

A gruesome thought that Niall hurriedly brushed away. "He willna do such a thing to the father of his daughter's babe."

"Ach, but he will. Ye will see." Again the guard left, this time thankfully for a long while.

Time moved slowly, so slowly that at times Niall feared he might go mad. The cursed feud! The oubliette was brimming with vermin. Niall felt suddenly crawly. His own skin seemed to prick at the thought of the bugs and the rats.

Was he going to languish here forever? Was he going to die?

The dungeon was dark, and so small that Niall was unable to stand. Hunkered down, he stared into the blackness, feeling the greatest desolation he had ever known. At a time when he had everything he could ever have dreamed of, it had all been cruelly wrenched away. Was it any wonder then that he was bitter?

"And all because of two vengeful old men!" he muttered. Both of whom had shown themselves capable of great cruelty. The very thought made him shiver as he recalled Ian's threat to make Caitlin a widow. Would he dare? "Of course. He is the MacLeod. He can dare anything." But would he chance his daughter's hatred?

Caitlin's angry shouts as she had tried to come to his aid still rang in Niall's ears. But her father had coldly ignored her outraged pleas. He had brushed her away as if she were little more than a fly. Uppermost in his mind had been the desire to see Niall locked up.

Oh, if only I could get out of here, he thought, stretching out his leg in the cramped space. *I would take Caitlin by the hand and not stop running until we were somewhere untouched by the foolishness of constant squabbling. Somewhere where a feud like this would be settled by those who had begun it.*

"Malcolm MacDonald and Ian MacLeod!" In that moment he imagined the two men fighting hand-to-hand, stumbling around, rolling over and over on the ground until they were too tired to move. Too tired to cause any more trouble. Too tired to do anything but crawl on their hands and knees like the babies they were.

Suddenly Niall threw back his head and laughed. The sound engulfed him, vibrated through him, made him sound like one demented . . . but he could not stop. Had he finally gone over the edge then? For just a moment he feared as much, but the sight of Caitlin's face dancing before his eyes quickly sobered him.

"Oh, Caity! Love!" Their brief time together had been the most wonderful moment of his life, a time he would treasure for as long as he lived. However long that was to be. "Whatever is to happen I can face it bravely, having loved and been loved by ye. Caity! Caity."

Death! Dying. Despite being a warrior who faced the prospect many times in his life, he was haunted by it now. He was giving up so much. Just at a time when he truly realized what living was all about. Love. Caring deeply about another person. And now there was to be another person for him to love as well.

The child! It was possible he might never even know if it was a son or a daughter. Might never know his child's name. Or hear it call him Father.

"Oh, God!" he moaned. The walls were cold and damp, and he hugged his arms tightly around his body. Cold, hungry, and miserable, he fought against his despair. "If only . . ." What he would not give to see Caitlin once again. Just once!

Warmth. Warmth and light. Everything was soft and safe. Caitlin could sense someone was with her, but she hadn't the strength to open her eyes. Instead, she gave herself up to the sensations.

"Caity! Ah, my poor, poor daughter."

A voice was whispering in the darkness. A comforting voice, like an angel's. Fingers as gentle as a soft spring breeze were touching her.

"Caity, it will be all right. I willna let ye lose the babe."

Her body was tired. Weary. She heard faint sounds, muted, as if they were coming through deep, murky water. Gurgling. Her voice? Yes. The sound of her own breathing became louder and louder until it was a roar in her ears.

"Relax. God is wi' ye. I am wi' ye."

Relax the voice said, but how could she when she was in so much pain. "Noooooooooo!"

"Easy, darlin.' "

It was as if she were in a long, dark tunnel, groping about, fighting to come into the light. To follow. She reached out to consciousness, but it was like trying to walk through a dense fog. Darkness was upon her, and though she struggled to open her eyes she couldn't see. There were shadows. Only shadows.

"Ye must drink this. The midwife's potion will aid ye."

Drink. Caitlin tried but the wetness choked her.

"Careful. Careful. Just a wee bit."

Again she felt the liquid pass her lips, but this time she managed to swallow.

"That's a good lass."

Caitlin was lying in an awkward position, but she couldn't quite seem to shift to a more comfortable one. Dull reverberations shot through her body each time she tried to move. In panic she pushed against the mattress in an effort to sit up, only to fall back down again.

Images teased her eyes as she slowly emerged from the darkness. From somewhere far away she thought she heard the sound of a bell. Willing herself to wake up, she passed in and out of consciousness. She was dizzy. The boundaries of the room alternately advanced and receded like waves against the shore. Back and forth. Up and down.

"Niall! Niall!" she whispered.

Closing her eyes, she reached out.

"Hear that, Husband. Listen to who it is that she longs for."

"Niall . . ." Caitlin cried out again. Through the haze in her mind, she remembered. Niall was gone. Her father had taken him from her. The very thought brought moisture to her eyes.

"She is crying. It must make ye feel very, very proud."

"I tell ye that it does not! But even so, I willna let him go. Not now, not ever."

"Then it is glad that I am that it is you and not I who will hae to live with yer conscience!"

The flame of the hearth fire spattered and sparked, stinging Fiona's eyes as she hovered over the fragile figure lying on the bed. For several hours she and the midwife held a long and lonely vigil. With each moment that passed, her apprehension and fear grew.

"Caitlin!" she called softly.

Only a soft moan answered her. The realization that she was helpless to do anything to ease the agony tore at her soul. All she could do was hold tightly to her daughter's hand and offer what comfort she could.

Forty

Caitlin stirred under the mountain of quilts, stretching her arms and opening her eyes. It was going to be another boring day of inactivity, a thought that made her chafe with anxiety. Oh, how she hated being abed! She had strictly been thus confined for more than a week following the midwife's orders. Only the knowledge that it had been done to safeguard her baby ensured Caitlin's full cooperation. Above all, she wanted to do what was best for her bairn.

"Och, I feel as if I hae slept forever!" In truth, it had been a much shorter time. Nine days or so. During that time she had regained her strength but not her peace of mind. "What hour is it?" she asked her sister.

"Mid morning." Seeing Caitlin stir, Shona came quickly to her side.

"Way past breakfast."

"Aye, but not for ye." Shona handed Caitlin a hairbrush, then left the room carrying a wooden tray with a steaming bowl atop it. "How be ye today, hinny?"

"How could I be when Niall is locked in the dungeon and everyone around me seems so angry?" She sat upright with a burst of energy, drawing the covers up with her. "I might as well be among hostile strangers."

"Hush, at least until ye eat."

Caitlin quieted as Shona poured cream in the bowl, then fed her spoonfuls of porridge. Swallowing, Caitlin whispered, "All except ye and Mother." She waited for her sister to explain. When she did not, Caitlin asked, "Shona, what has happened? Father seldom comes to see me, and if he does and Mother is here, he scurries away like an angry hound."

"That's because he is." Shona shook her head sadly.

"They hae had quarrels before, but this time it is different. Tell me!" It was not a request, but rather a demand.

Shona sighed. Setting down the bowl, she clasped her hands tightly together. "It happened the day ye nearly miscarried. Mother and Father got into a discussion about what to do with yer husband and why he had come to the castle."

"Mother told him she had sent for Niall, that's why—"

"Nae. Much worse. She told Father that he should leave ye be, let ye be happy. She demanded that he make a truce with the MacDonald."

"Which of course Father refused to do." Caitlin of all people knew just how stubborn he could be.

"He did. His old anger about Colin's death and about Malcolm MacDonald's fascination for Mother all resurfaced."

Caitlin rushed to a conclusion. "And Father's jealousy fanned the flames of an argument."

"It did, though not for the reason that ye think." Shona shook her head sadly. "Ah, I still hae trouble believing it."

"Believing what?"

Shona blurted it out. "Caity, Mother threw it in Father's face that Malcolm MacDonald and not he was Colin's father."

"Nae!" Caitlin paled and threw her head back on the pillow.

"She did! But not to be hateful. I think it was in an effort to make him see reason and stop being such a blustering, vengeful fool." Hurriedly, she explained, detailing the entire story. "And though I know they deeply love each other, Father has moved out of the bedchamber they hae shared for so many years. He has called her a faithless wife, a liar, and worse!"

"So Mother's life is ruined because she sought to make mine happy." Caitlin balled her hands into fists. "And little good her sacrifice did. Niall is still in the dungeon."

"For what looks to be a long stay." Shona sounded nearly as sad about it as Caitlin felt.

"A long stay? I think not." Despite the fact she was unsteady on her feet, Caitlin got out of bed, reaching for her clothing.

"Caity!" Instantly Shona was by her side. "Get back in bed," she ordered.

"Nae. I canna stay enshrouded in my blankets while Niall wastes away in the dungeon."

"But . . . !" Looking at her sister's face, Shona knew there would be no way of reasoning with Caitlin, and thus she asked, "Where are ye going?"

"To set Niall free!"

It was a task much easier said than done, for Caitlin was slowed down by being so long abed. When she really wanted to run, all she could do was move ever so slowly down the stairs, a journey that seemed to take nearly as long as her journey to Dunskaith had taken. At last, however, her efforts were rewarded and the thick wooden door to the dungeon loomed into sight.

"And just where do ye think ye are going?" Like some unwelcome giant, Jamie loomed in her way, taking his turn at guarding the dungeon.

"To see my husband, if that is any of yer concern," Caitlin retorted.

"Then ye will hae to be disappointed. Yer father has given strict orders that he is not to be disturbed."

"Has he now." Somehow mustering together every bit of strength she possessed, Caitlin reached behind the door, pulling free a loose stone. Hefting it soundly, with a force that took Jamie by surprise, she hit him squarely on the head. Like a limp doll, he slumped to the ground.

A rattle of keys jarred Niall from his slumber. Looking

up, he squinted at the sudden light, then saw *her* face looking at him through the grille "Nae, it canna be," he said in disbelief.

Raising his head, he blinked his eyes to clear them of the vision. A dream, but so vivid as to almost make him believe that *she* was really here.

"Caity."

"Aye, 'tis me. I'm going to get you out of this place . . ." *Her* voice whispering to him.

"I'm going mad." At last it had happened.

"Nae. I tell ye that ye are not." Opening the door, Caitlin pushed her way into the tiny cell, hugging Niall close.

"Caity, my God, it really is ye! How?"

Her smile was mysterious "I hae my ways, but we will talk of it later." She moved toward him. "As for now, I want to get ye out of here."

"Out. That word is a wonder to my ears."

Winding her arms around his neck, she kissed him, a brief caressing of her lips, yet a kiss with such a tender show of emotion that he was deeply touched.

"I love ye, Caity!"

"I know. Ye wouldna hae come all this way and put yer life in danger if ye didna . . ." She rattled the keys. "But come, there is no time for passion just now. Jamie will wake up and all will be lost."

He clutched at her hand. "Then by all means . . ."

The castle was eerily quiet. Too quiet, Niall thought as he cautiously led Caitlin by the hand. Slowly they ran up the spiral stairs, expecting to meet opposition at every turn. Instead, their escape seemed to be incredibly easy. Too easy.

"Are all of yer father's clansmen under a spell?"

" 'Twould seem so."

Even so, Niall knew he had to be careful lest there be need for bloodshed. He didn't want to harm any MacLeod.

There had already been too much blood spilled between his clan and Caitlin's. He didn't want to spill any more if that was possible. All he wanted was his wife and his freedom. Was that so very much to wish for?

"Which way shall we go?" Niall asked the question as they reached the bailey and he peered over the curtain wall.

"Which way . . ." Trembling so hard that her legs could barely support her, Caitlin joined him at the wall, staring down at the foaming sea that crashed against the rocks below. "Surely, not down."

"Nae!" Obviously they could not swim the ocean, and yet the choices were limited. They could either go through the castle and Niall could fight his way through the MacLeod's clansmen, or they could slowly and carefully ease themselves down over the steep, rocky hill, move along the shoreline and find a boat. Niall chose the latter. "Come."

Caitlin started to follow, but hesitated as a wave of weakness washed over her. Could she make it? She took a step, grabbing for Niall's arm as she started to fall.

"Caity!" Looking down at her face, he suddenly realized how pale she was. "What is it?"

She hadn't wanted to tell him, didn't want him to be worried, yet now she knew she had to tell the truth. "I . . . I'm weak, that's all."

"Weak?" He knew a fear then far greater than the fear for his own safety. "Ye are ill!"

"Nae." She hurried to reassure him. "I-I hae been abed, that is all."

"Abed! Why?" He sensed the answer. "The bairn."

"Is fine! I had a bit of trouble, that is all." Trouble, she realized now, would slow them down and make escape impossible, at least for the moment.

"Ach, Caity." He gathered her into his arms. "I'll hae to carry ye. All the way if need be."

"Nae." Despite her stubbornness, Caitlin realized that if

she went with him it would only slow Niall down. "Ye will hae to go on alone."

"Alone?" He spoke the word like a curse.

"Aye. Go back to Dunskaith. I'll join ye when I regain my strength." She fought against her tears at the thought of being parted again, but said firmly, "Ye canna stay here!"

"Neither can I leave ye, Caity." His hand rested on her stomach. "Nor our bairn."

"Ye must!" A sad truth. "Come, give me a kiss and then be gone."

"A kiss." He complied gladly, his lips soft and gentle, then broke away.

"Now hurry!" She gave him a push toward the wall.

Suddenly, as if by magic, several clansmen appeared, lunging at Niall with their swords drawn. Brandishing his own sword, Ian MacLeod led the tiny army. "Get him. Dunna let him get away."

Taken by surprise, Niall paused for just a moment, then broke into a run, headed for the wall and freedom. Before he could even get one leg over, however, he was surrounded and subdued.

"Get him back to the dungeon where he belongs!" The MacLeod's command threatened that there would be punishment if Niall MacDonald was allowed to escape again.

"I willna allow it!" Caitlin's voice was shrill.

"Ye hae no choice, Daughter. Ye hae no power." Ian MacLeod knew very well when he had won. "Now, go back to yer chamber and leave men's matters to men."

Go back to her chamber! Caitlin bristled at her father's tone. Like scolding a naughty child. Well, she was finished with his cruelty. Looking first at Niall, then at her father, then at Niall again, Caitlin made up her mind. "Ah, but I do hae a choice." Taking a deep breath, she somehow gathered up her strength and courage and belted toward the wall before anyone could stop her.

"Caitlin!" Quickly Ian MacLeod moved toward his

daughter, gaping helplessly as she teetered precariously atop the wall that loomed dangerously over the ocean.

"Dunna take another step!" Her tone of voice as well as her words gave warning.

"Are ye daft, girl?" The MacLeod was horrified.

"Nae, quite the contrary. Perhaps I see the truth now. That as long as ye hold even a whisper of hatred in yer heart, there will never be peace." Slowly, fearful of losing her balance, Caitlin raised her arm and pointed toward Niall. "Let him go, Father, or by all that is holy I will jump!"

"Ye wouldna!"

Caitlin whispered a hasty prayer, hoping that her father would not call her bluff. "I would!"

"And kill yerself as well as yer child?" Ian MacLeod's voice trembled.

"Yer grandchild. A child ye dunna want, just because he carries MacDonald blood." Caitlin closed her eyes, fighting a wave of dizziness. She didn't dare look down. Didn't dare stop to think of what might happen if she swayed or lost her footing.

"Caitlin!"

"Set my husband free, Father. I willna hae my baby grow up without a father or with *his* father imprisoned by his own grandsire." When the MacLeod didn't answer, Caitlin said again, "Set him free or I *will* jump."

"Caitlin, no!" Niall fought against his captors in his attempt to forcibly change her mind, but he couldn't pull free. All he could do was to stare in horror as the woman he loved balanced atop the wall. "Ye canna . . ."

"I can! For I would rather crash to the rocks below, then let my baby grow up to be tainted by all of this senseless hatred." Once again she felt a wave of dizziness as the roar of the ocean assaulted her ears. What would it feel like to be crushed upon those rocks if she fell? What would it be like to die?

"Caitlin . . ."

There was a long moment of silence that was disturbed only by the rumble of the ocean as it slapped against the rocks. Then, in a voice that sounded strangely tired, Ian MacLeod gave the order. "Set him free!"

"On yer word of honor?"

Ian MacLeod nodded. "On my word of honor." Like a man defeated, he hung his head. "Now, come down from there, Caity, before ye fall." Holding out his hand, he moved forward, to be joined at the wall by Niall who had moved simultaneously. Together they reached out, catching Caitlin as she tottered dangerously on the edge of the wall.

"Thank God!" Niall's hand clasped Ian MacLeod's as they pulled Caitlin back. For just a moment their eyes met and held.

"Caitlin's right. It is time the feud was over." Ian MacLeod's eyes welled with tears as he clutched his daughter to his burly chest.

Caitlin stroked the leathery face of her father. "Is it truly over? No more fighting, no more anger?"

Ian MacLeod swallowed hard. " 'Tis over."

Standing up on tiptoe, she kissed his rough cheek then nodded in Niall's direction. "Then say it again. Louder, so that other ears may hear."

Ian MacLeod grimaced, finding the words hard to say. "Father . . ."

" 'Tis over. Son-in-law ye are and son-in-law ye will be. My word is good. Ye will hae no more trouble from me." Ian MacLeod kissed his daughter on the forehead, then with a grunt of resignation gave her a gentle push toward the man to whom she was wed. Above the fiery cloak of her hair, his eyes met those of the golden haired man who obviously loved her just as fiercely as he.

"Oh, Father! Father!" Caitlin wept with joy as she was

seized by Niall, then hugged so tightly she feared she could not breathe.

"Lass! Lass! I nearly died of fear I . . ."

"Hush!" Snuggling against him, Caitlin contented herself with just being in his arms.

Niall's hands stroked her body, soothingly, his breath warm against her throat. The love he felt for her was mirrored in his eyes, so much so that even Ian MacLeod was touched.

"So, it seems I should leave the two of ye alone," he said softly. "But before I do, perhaps I should give ye a welcome to Dunvegan."

"A welcome which I am grateful for," Niall said with strong feeling. "For the love of the woman and child we both hae such strong feelings for, there should be peace between us."

"Peace." Ian MacLeod smiled tightly, then clumsily gripped the hand that Niall slowly offered. Mumbling beneath his breath, the MacLeod grudgingly conceded that perhaps his daughter's marriage to a man of Niall MacDonald's mettle was not all bad. Even so, their truce was man-to-man. There was still an ocean of blood between the two clans. As Caitlin looked first at her husband and then her father, she could only wonder if the hatred and the anger was truly over.

Forty-one

Standing at the window of the castle looking out at a bright multihued rainbow, Caitlin could only hope that all the old ghosts had at last been laid to rest.

"What are ye thinking about, Caity?" Coming up behind her, Niall brushed a lock of her flaming hair from her eyes in a gesture that always stirred her.

"About everything that has happened." She turned slowly. "Do ye really think there is a chance for the feuding to be ending? Father has a terrible temper, and from what I know of Malcolm he does, too." She sighed. "Do ye really think that my Father has learned?"

"I do!" Taking her face in his hands, Niall looked for a long time into her eyes. "Seeing ye perched atop that wall must surely hae been enough to calm the fiercest heart." He shuddered. "Ah, Caity, never hae I known such fear."

"Nor I!" Quickly she pushed away the terrifying memory.

Niall paled as he asked bluntly, "Tell me, would ye . . . would ye really hae jumped?"

Caitlin shook her head emphatically. "Nae. I was playing at a bluff. I would never hae taken my life and my unborn bairn's as well, but I hoped that Father would not know that." Even so, it had been the most rash, daring thing she had ever done in her life.

In a rush of emotion he threw his arms around her, hugging her tight. "But even so, ye could hae fallen, ye could hae—"

"But I didn't and all is well, at least for the moment." Once again she sighed. "Father sent a message to Malcolm. Will he agree on a meeting? Will he?"

"He had best . . ." Niall was determined. "I willna allow two old men to ruin the life of my son or daughter. I willna!"

"Nor will—"

The din of bagpipes chillingly interrupted her contemplative conversation. The sound was unnerving. Shattering.

"What is it? What can hae happened?" Niall feared the worst. Taking her protectively by the hand, he led her in search of the sound.

The sound came from the great hall. There the MacLeod clan was quickly gathering. Brandishing their weapons, which reflected in the flames ablaze in the hearth, they grumbled in anger as they waited for the MacLeod to enter.

"So much for any thought of peace," Caitlin whispered mournfully. Looking at her clansmen, she, too, feared the worst. They were so hostile, so angry. Clutching at their weapons, they were clearly prepared for a fight. Perhaps that was why they were so disappointed by the MacLeod's declaration.

"The feuding is at an end! I hae heard from Malcolm MacDonald. He has agreed to a truce."

"Truce?" A ripple of disbelief swept throughout the hall.

"It's a trick!"

"A ploy."

"Dunna fall for it, Ian. They are up to something."

"Ye musna even think of it!" Anger buzzed around from man to man, an angry hum. The MacLeod silenced the protestations by raising his hand.

"We canna carry on the feuding forever!"

"We can!"

"We will!" Total turmoil raged. Turmoil that in the end was quenched.

"We hae the children to think about." His eyes touched

upon his daughter. "A whole new generation of MacLeods. Do we want to see them fall to the sword. Or do we want to see them build a future for themselves?"

"A future with the MacDonalds? Never!"

"We canna forget that they hae killed our fathers, sons, and brothers."

Ian held up his hand. " 'Tis so. Still, there comes a time when there must be calm. Warfare has brought nothing but a torrent of heartache." Steadfastly he declared that there would be an end to it. An ending now!

Was it really over? Was all the killing and the anger really buried? Surely seeing the two clan chieftains at last sitting down to talk in the next few days seemed like a start, but was there hope, for a lasting peace? That Malcolm had made a gesture toward a permanent truce seemed to be a good sign. There was only one thing that threatened the fragile truce, however; Colin MacLeod's fate.

"Tell me who killed my son!" Ian's gruff voice demanded a confession. But the answer had come not from Malcolm but from Caitlin herself.

"It . . . it was Gregor!" she had whispered, unaware until that moment that she had known.

"Gregor?"

There was a look of disbelief on Malcolm's face. "Nae. I dunna believe ye. Ye are just trying to cause trouble for him because of how he treated ye at Dunskaith."

"Nae, 'twas him. I was there." Caitlin felt hot, she felt cold, she trembled all over. "I saw."

"Ye were there?" Even her father scoffed.

"I was. I saw the battle. I saw . . ." Closing her eyes, Caitlin could remember that fateful moment.

It was as if a dam had burst, as if once beginning to speak she could not cease. The entire story was revealed in a flood of tears, the details of blood and killing so accurate, they could only have been recalled by one who had been a witness.

"I remember being so afraid when I saw *him* come up behind Colin. I screamed, but it did my brother no good. That dark-haired man with the evil squinting eyes stabbed him in the back."

"Ye saw him kill Colin?" Ian asked, gently so as not to add to Caitlin's grief.

"Aye!" Teardrops ran in rivulets down her cheeks. "A terrible sight that I hae locked far away in my head until now."

"Gregor killed yer son by stabbing him in the back?"

"Aye, the wound was dealt from behind."

"Och, she was just a child." Malcolm didn't want to believe in the guilt of one whose blood was so near to his own. "How could she remember?"

"The first time I laid eyes on Gregor I knew, but I wouldn't let my mind remember." But the very sight of the dark-haired man had made her blood run cold. She had thought it to be because of the prophecy of the seerer, but it had been for another reason.

"But ye remember now . . ."

Caitlin's voice rose in pitch as she relived the moment. "Colin hae care! He's drawn his sword! Ach, dear God, he's stabbed him! The blood! It's everywhere. My brother's blood pouring over the ground."

Ian was incensed. "I should kill him for what he has done!"

Caitlin sighed wearily. "It wouldna bring back the dead. It would just stain yer hands wi' blood and begin this hatred and fighting all over again. But if ye could see him brought to justice at one of the moothills." It was there in a level circle surrounded by higher ground that the Brieve and his council held their meetings to administer justice. "Would ye?" She looked right at Malcolm.

Surprisingly, Malcolm spouted no defiance, did not argue, and in fact nodded his head. Much to Caitlin's surprise, he grudgingly agreed. "If what ye say is true and yer brother was killed in such a cowardly way, aye, that I would." Perhaps it was his way of atoning for what had been done.

What would Malcolm think were he to ever find out . . .

Caitlin didn't realize that she had whispered aloud until she heard a voice beside her ask, "Find out what?" Niall slid his hand down Caitlin's arm to take her hand.

That Colin was his very own son, she thought but did not say. "Nothing . . ." It was a secret that must never be revealed, lest Malcolm take vengeance upon Ian for stealing away not only the woman he loved but his son.

Niall put his arms around her and led her out of the room. "Ah, Caity, I hae to believe in happy endings. I hae to believe that the child ye are carrying will be the answer to bringing about a lasting peace." He squeezed her hand. "The child! Ye are carrying my baby. Ah, just the very thought makes me the happiest of men. That's why I hae to believe. There will be peace!"

If Niall believed so strongly, how then could Caitlin have any doubts. "Then if ye believe, so do I." Looking out the window, the land looked so fresh and green, so peaceful. And up in the sky the rainbow could still be seen. "Look, Niall, how the rainbow arches across the clear blue sky like so many ribbons."

"A rainbow. . . ." Niall smiled. "Ye know what our cousins the Irish say about rainbows."

"That there is gold at the end."

"Aye, a treasure." Niall bent his head and kissed his wife. "And now I know it to be true, for surely I hae found mine."

The days that followed were a time for atonement. A time for explanations. A time for healing. A time for peace. A time for love.

Epilogue

Dunvegan Castle, 1539

A shrill wail echoed through the large bedchamber. Walking quickly to the wide wooden cradle that took prominence in the middle of the room, Caitlin looked down at the two tiny faces that peaked out from a brown woolen blanket.

"Ach, dunna cry so." Feeling that special tug at her heart, she repeated, "Dunna cry." Reaching down, she gently rocked their cradle.

"Ah, so we hear from our sons again." Niall's voice was filled with pride as he joined his wife by the cradle. "Such bold, lusty cries."

"That clearly say how much they hae been spoiled." Though her tone was scolding, Caitlin smiled. "And just who de ye suppose is guilty of that sin?"

Niall looked sheepish. "Surely not I!"

"Aye!" She laughed softly. "And my father and yer uncle and my mother and my sister and . . ."

"The little rogues hae learned early."

"And all too well." Reaching down, Caitlin picked up first one twin and then the other, mimicking all of Niall's pride. "Ah, but who can resist."

"Not even ye." He watched her place each tiny wrinkled face at one of her breasts. "Ah, but am I jealous. How I wish I could change places with them."

Caitlin grinned. "Have patience, Husband. Later . . ."

"Mmm." He watched as one of the baby's tiny hands latched on to the still-swollen nipple with tender possession. His big hand touched that tiny fist, feeling a surge of love course through him. His family. The greatest happiness he had ever known. "Which one is this?" Strangely enough, he could never tell, though Caitlin could.

"That's Malcolm."

"Of course, just like his namesake I fear he is a bit greedy."

"Not any more than Ian." She winced. "Ouch. The dearies are starting to get teeth." Her voice was wistful. "I will hae to wean them soon . . ."

"Then I will take their place."

"For a while." She winked.

"And just what does that mean?" He took a guess. "Another bairn?"

"Mmmmhmmmm."

"Together we hae brought forth a tanist for yer father, one for my uncle, and this one . . ."

"A little girl for me." Crooning to the infants, Caitlin sighed as she watched the amber eyes close to contented sleep. Putting them back in the cradle, she leaned against Niall as he put his arms around her. "A little girl who I hope will one day find a mon like ye to love."

"Ye are as happy then as me?"

"Aye." Her kisses showed him just how thoroughly true that statement was. Reaching up to wind her arms around his neck, Caitlin drew him closer, knowing that tomorrow awaited them with all the bright hope of their deep, eternal love.

JANELLE TAYLOR

ZEBRA'S BEST-SELLING AUTHOR

**DON'T MISS ANY OF HER
EXCEPTIONAL, EXHILARATING, EXCITING**

ECSTASY SERIES

SAVAGE ECSTASY	(0-8217-5453-X, $5.99/$6.99)
DEFIANT ECSTASY	(0-8217-5447-5, $5.99/$6.99)
FORBIDDEN ECSTASY	(0-8217-5278-2, $5.99/$6.99)
BRAZEN ECSTASY	(0-8217-5446-7, $5.99/$6.99)
TENDER ECSTASY	(0-8217-5242-1, $5.99/$6.99)
STOLEN ECSTASY	(0-8217-5455-6, $5.99/$6.99)
FOREVER ECSTASY	(0-8217-5241-3, $5.99/$6.99)

Available wherever paperbacks are sold, or order direct from the Publisher. Send cover price plus 50¢ per copy for mailing and handling to Penguin USA, P.O. Box 999, c/o Dept. 17109, Bergenfield, NJ 07621. Residents of New York and Tennessee must include sales tax. DO NOT SEND CASH.